The Books of Bergonia:

BOOK ONE

THE MAGESTICS

BY

JAMES W. BERG

This book is dedicated to my husband, whose love and support made this book possible

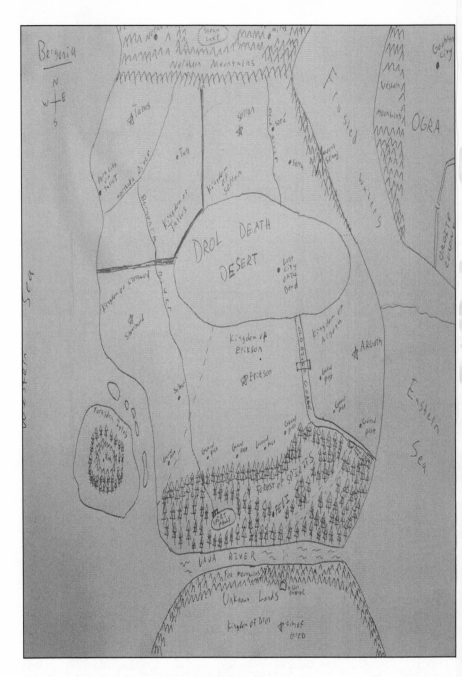

MAP OF BERGONIA

Table of Contents

Prologue:
It Begins

Thunder rumbled while the cool breeze began to pick up force. Six figures stood atop a grassy hill looking up into the sky as the wind started blowing back their hair. Lightening illuminated the quickly forming clouds. As small drops of water fell from the sky, the six friends realized they needed to find shelter. They could feel it in their bones. A bad storm was coming.

"Semaj, quit standing there and staring. We need to get out of the rain before the storm hits," Anna demanded as the rain fell harder upon them all, her long blond hair now sticking to her face.

"My dress is getting ruined," a voice chimed in from behind the two.

"Hey, don't complain to me. It was not my idea to come out here," Semaj snapped back and then stared at Anna. "You're the one that wanted to drag us all out on one of your adventures."

"No time to argue now. If we don't find shelter soon this storm will be the end of all of us," a short and plump girl said as she moved right up to the other two, tugging her damp dress from her body while she looked nervously across the darkening sky.

"Lija don't be such a chicken. A little storm never hurt anyone," teased a boy who looked like Lija in the face but was a bit taller and had a muscular body.

"Your sister's got a point, Marcus. I think the storm is going to get a lot worse than we expect. My crystal is changing colors and that's not a good thing," a real thin and shaggy blond haired boy added holding up the crystal around his neck.

"Thom! I thought you promised me you wouldn't mess with magic anymore," an average looking boy in ragged clothes yelled as he joined the other five.

"Lars, dear, I'm not using magic. It is just a crystal. An item that I wear is all," Thom explained trying not to roll his eyes.

1

"Still, you better be careful, Thom. Just saying the "M" word out loud could be enough to get you killed or exiled," Semaj said.

"Well, I hate to be the worrier again, but has anyone noticed that there's no shelter in sight?" Lija asked with fright in her voice.

The six friends looked around as the drenching rain fell with more intensity. For as far as the eye could see, there were only fields of grass. No shelters, trees or anything they could take cover under. Thunder crashed and lightening crackled as the wind began to pick up strength. Soaking wet and barely able to stand upright, the six friends began to run in the opposite direction of the approaching storm.

Marcus stops running and turns around quickly when he hears a familiar scream. Laying face first on the ground is his sister. He quickly runs back to help her up. The wind now is so strong he can barely walk against it. Just as he gets Lija to her feet, the wind and the rain instantly stop. The two siblings look around at their now calm surroundings. Lightening flashing within the huge clouds is all that remains of the fierce storm.

"You guys okay?" Anna asks as she runs back towards her friends.

"Yeah we're fine."

"Speak for yourself, Marcus." Lija glares at her brother as she tries to wipe water and mud off her dress.

"That was quite odd. One minute we're being thrashed with wind and rain, then the next the storm is gone," Semaj said as he and the others approached.

"You're telling me," Marcus adds when an unexpected boom from above them suddenly cuts him off.

The thunder in the sky roars louder as the ground beneath them shakes continuously. The force builds as they all fall to their knees. The clouds shift as a swirling cyclone forms and touches down upon the ground. From within the cyclone, a dark figure emerges, glowing red eyes penetrating their souls. The figure waves his hand and thousands of dark figures emerge and race out in all directions.

The six friends stare in shock, as in a matter of moments the land all around them bursts into flames. They can now see villages, forests, castles, people and animals burning to the ground by these dark figures. The leader of this destruction raises his arms to the sky and lets out a laugh that chills their very blood.

"Once again, this will all be mine."

"You tried once and you will be stopped again."

The group's eyes swiftly turned towards the new voice. Out of the clouds above, stepped a figure illuminated by bright colors. The figure looked to be half human, half Dragon. With every beat of his wings, a pulse of energy shot out in all directions. As the energy hit the six friends and passed through them, they could feel the very elements of the world consume them. If the dark figure was to be feared, then this new being was definitely to be awed.

"What's going on Marcus?" Lija cried as she stepped closer to his side.

"I don't know. I think we need to get out of here, like now!" Marcus shouted over the commotion.

"This has got to be the result of some kind of magic. Why aren't the alarms sounding? Where are the guards?" Semaj said glancing around.

"I don't think this is magic. It feels different. The energy coming from that man-Dragon is actually causing friction against my crystal," Thom said as he held up the object around his neck.

"I don't like this at all!" Exclaimed Lars as he stepped behind Thom, lightly squeezing his shoulders with both hands.

"Well guys, I don't think it really matters. We just got noticed," Anna proclaimed, stepping in a defensive stance in front of everyone.

The group of friends looked over to see the dark figure advancing towards them. With every step, the figure's darkness reached out and consumed the light. The shadowy head glared its red eyes right at them. Unknown words bellowed from its dark mouth as shade-like hands stretched out, palms open wide. Its eyes flared as red flames burst forth from its hands.

"All who oppose me shall die by my power," the dark figure screamed as the fire raced towards them.

The illuminated Dragon-man stepped in front of the approaching fire. He closed his eyes and held out his hands. A strong force of wind raced past them all and collided with the approaching fire, rolling it in balls. He then opened his eyes, waved his hands and smiled at them. The wind carried the balls of fire up and over their heads missing by a few feet. Without hesitation, the Dragon-man turned back at the dark being, snapping his arms forward. The force of the wind shifted, hitting the dark figure, sending it and the darkness backwards.

"Your time has come and gone Drol Greb. There is a new force in this land that will protect the world and put an end to you and your evil."

"And what, pray tell, is that force?" The dark being, named Drol Greb, laughed.

"You will find and lead the Magestics. You are the Chosen One," the Dragon-man proclaims, turning and pointing a finger at the group of friends. Before they could decide who he was pointing at, a blast of pure white energy shot from the pointing finger. They all covered their eyes as the white energy hit and engulfed them.

"No!" A figure screamed, jumping awake and rubbing a pair of sleep filled eyes.

The room was completely dark except for the moonlight coming through the window. The awakened young adult wiped away the dream sweat and sat up. Looking over at the window across from the bed, which was clearly shut, brought forth the realization that the light was coming from somewhere else. Excitement exploded when it became clear that the glowing light was radiating from the young one's own body.

Falling out of bed, with eyes now closed, the young one rubbed both head and eyes fiercely. This still had to be all part of that terrible dream. Slowly opening both eyes, a wave of calm settled in as the young one realized that the glowing was gone and that the bedroom was completely pitch black. The young one got up and opened the window, gazing out into the night.

It was all a dream, but it seemed so real. I must be getting nervous about school starting tomorrow. Speaking of, I need to get back to sleep. I have to be up early to meet everyone. It will be great to see them all, but for now, I think I will keep this dream to myself. With that thought, the young one shut the window and headed back to sleep. For tomorrow would be the start of another normal day.

****

A wave of unseen energy washed over the cavern, touching nothing except one lone person. The figure jumped awake as the energy completely absorbed into his body. The man leapt to his feet as every muscle and nerve in his body began to tingle, then started to fade as a great sensation heightened and merged all his senses into one great force. The man ran through the darkened cavern, his enhanced sight guiding him with ease. His old body rejuvenated with great energy as he burst forth from the cave's opening.

The old man stopped upon the ledge sticking out from the mouth of the cave. The ledge only extended about seven feet from the opening and was only as wide as the mouth of the cave, roughly five feet. Being this high up upon the mountain's side the wind blew with great force. The old man knew he had to act quickly before this special sensation passed.

He extended both arms in front of him, palms facing out. Reaching out with this inner sensation, he began to touch and become one with the wind. Suddenly the winds shifted, blowing completely around the mountain ledge. He quickly ran to the edge, closed his eyes and started rotating in a circle letting the heightened sensation take over completely. As quickly as it arrived, the unseen energy vanished. At that moment, the old man had stopped spinning and stood perfectly still.

He opened his eyes and stared straight ahead. Due to the height of the mountain, even with focusing his enhanced vision, he could barely make out the shape of the village area below. With the sensation gone, he still knew, as every fiber of his being told him that what he had been waiting for all these seasons would be found there.

He would have to hurry. The fact that he had been finally notified meant that the power had been awakened and that the events he had been told about and feared were unfolding. He had been waiting for this, and now everything depended upon finding the child and guiding this Chosen One to fulfill their destiny. The old man bowed his head, whispered a prayer to Venēăh and then looked up into the night sky. Against all, he hoped he would not fail.

He quickly called upon his powers causing his staff to fly from the cave and into his right hand and his travel bag into his left. He then turned and faced the direction of the village he was bound to go to. He swayed for a moment. It had been a long time since he had used his powers, but he would not let that, and his age, hinder him now. After he gained his balance, he glanced around him.

Being as where the mouth of this cave resided, there was no way physically on or off this ledge, unless you were some enhanced and skilled mountain climber. That he was not, and it was a very long way down if one were to fall. He did not have time to waste, so he called upon something different from within himself and leaped off the ledge of the mountain. As he plummeted straight down, the back of his robe began to bulge while his skin shifted. Suddenly he hit a massive wall of clouds and vanished within.

****

A young man stood gazing out his window, which over looked the city below. There was an outstretched darkened land that surrounded the city that could be seen for miles. The dry heat was not so bad at night. You could almost feel a touch of coolness in the air this high up. This late at night, you could also make out the faint red glow of the Fire Mountains on the distant northern horizon. This was not the reason why he stood at the window's edge.

He had felt it, somewhere in the distant night a great power had emerged. He was told that a day would come when he would feel it and to be ready. That night he did and without thought, he executed his training. Even at turning sixteen and becoming a man, he was still learning magic and slowly gaining strength in the skill. Even with each passing day, growing stronger, he would still have to push its limits to compliment this strange tracking ability.

Growing up he was told that he had the unique ability to sense a certain type of power, one unlike magic. Because the gift was tainted and weak in him and his castle resided so far south of Bergonia, he would only be able to pick up a very broad sense of where it emerged. At the moment he felt the power, he would have to use his magic to help narrow down the location of where it had emerged.

Beads of sweat formed on his brow as he pushed the magic with over half of his strength, while using the other portion to engulf the tingling sensation of the unseen energy. He collapsed as both the sensation and the magic left him. In front of him, he had created a parchment with a faint glowing dot on it. He gave a shout causing servants to come in to help him up while a figure in a dark black and silver streaked hooded cloak bent down, took the parchment and left.

The servants waited his command while he stood looking out his window, feeling more composed. He had gained his strength back quickly. He could never show weakness because he had a kingdom to rule and subjects to bow to him in fear. That is why he turned, took the two servants that had helped him, and threw them out the window to their deaths. No one must be allowed to think that they could defeat him. No one must stand in his way.

All his life he had been taught and trained for his destiny. He was born to help rule all lands. He was told since childhood that he would be built and given a huge fortress. The city would be his to rule and all beings and subjects throughout the city and kingdom would be instructed to bow down and follow him. He would be feared by all and lead them to great conquests. They would reclaim the land that the evil of man had taken from them, the beings of magic. There was no one to stand in his way, but one.

His only master and father, along with his personal teacher, had trained and prepped him for all this. Both of them had warned him that one being could be the end of all they planned. This one being would emerge with a power that could destroy them all. They assured him, without explanation, that he had a gift to sense this power and then he could search out and kill this being. His destiny was to kill the Chosen One and help lead their people to victory.

"Sire, the master calls for you," a servant informed, breaking him from his thoughts and gaze out the window.

"How many times have I said that no one enters without permission?"

"I beg your forgiveness but this message was of grave importance."

"Refi Llba!" He commanded as a fireball formed in the palm of his hand causing the servant to cower into the corner of the room. Bellowing a few more words, the ball of fire took flight and soared across the room, consuming the servant into its flames. After the screams stopped, he stepped out of the room instructing the other servants to go put out the fire and clean up the mess.

He quickly walked down a hallway until he came to a guarded doorway. The guards uncrossed their weapons, removed the bar and opened the door for him. He made his way down a few flights of cold stone steps until he reached another door, this time guarded by two hooded figures. They bowed and then waved their hands muttering a few words. The door shimmered and then opened. He stepped past them and entered a very dark chamber. Floating in the middle of the room was the image of his father above the four entranced witch sisters.

Since the human men of Bergonia had killed and trapped the spirit of his father in another realm, only the power of the four witch sisters could part the barriers enough to allow the image of his father's spirit to be seen and heard. One day soon, he would have the means to break down the barriers and bring his father back. Together they would be unstoppable.

"About time you got here, my son. As we have feared, the time has come. We must move quickly. We have to speed up our existing plans and take care of this Chosen One," the floating image whispered.

"Father, did you locate the exact spot?"

"No, but we were able to narrow it down some with the help of the map you created."

"Out of the Five Kingdoms Bergonia, the one we seek lies somewhere within one of these three possible kingdoms," said the black and silver streaked robed figure holding the map. His finger, flicking three different sections of the map causing a flickering glow to appear.

As the figure pulled back his hood, the dark gray skinned, pointed ears and blood red eyed face of his father's most loyal and dangerous follower could be seen. The Fire Elf did not intimidate him, for he was also his personal teacher and the closest thing he had to a physical father. He walked up to his teacher and adopted father, taking the map from his hands, and looked it over.

"Should I send my warriors to scour the lands?" He asked looking up to his father's image.

"No, we must be very careful. We don't want to draw attention to us until the time is needed. Send a band of warriors each to the Kingdoms of Sorran and Erikson. Have them search and watch but do not draw attention. When the Chosen One invokes the power again, they will then attack, capture and quickly bring this person to us."

"What about the third, the Kingdom of Argoth?"

"We don't have the warriors ready to send them there too. Have one of your loyal messengers send word to our contact there to keep a secret search and lookout for anyone in their kingdom." The Fire Elf nodded to the speaking image and left the chamber with his instructions.

"Now son, come sit, we have much to plan. It has begun."

Chapter One:
Soré, Kingdom Of Sorran

The roosters let loose their morning call as the sun peeked over the horizon. Rays of sunlight, casting away the dark, illuminated the peaceful township of Soré. Besides the capital city of Sorran, Soré was the only other somewhat prosperous village in the poor and dying Kingdom of Sorran. The fact that Soré rested right on the edge of the Dead River and was north enough along the river, the villagers were able to channel the water and make their farmlands prosperous. Not many in the Kingdom of Sorran were as lucky.

The Kingdom of Sorran was one of five kingdoms that made up the land of Bergonia. Unfortunately, the Kingdom of Sorran fell in a bad location. To the east was the Eastern Mountains, which cut the kingdom off from any means of reaching the sea for water, food, travel or trade. To the north were the Northern Mountains, which were excessively cold and forbidden for anyone to enter. Sorran's one lone river came down from those mountains, the Dead River. The reason people call it that, was that no creatures lived in it and the more south it ran, the drier it got, until it was no more by the time it reached the Drol Death Desert.

The Drol Death Desert also makes up the southern border of Sorran's kingdom. Any land near this border was completely dried out. According to legend, this desert had been created long ago in the aftermath of a deadly battle of magic. This desert was always hot and dry, even in the winter seasons. No one dares to enter, for it is far too dangerous to cross, and those who have were never seen again. There was one small path of land that safely ran between the Drol Death Desert and the Eastern Mountains. This path took you into the Kingdom of Argoth.

There had been bad blood between the two kingdoms and the King of Argoth had forbidden any to enter his land and had declined any means of negotiating trade agreements or providing help. This had resulted in the isolation of Sorran from Argoth. The same went for the kingdom to the west of Sorran, the Kingdom of Tallus, but for different reasons. The Kingdom of

Tallus had chosen to cut all ties with the other kingdoms and prosper on their own. Giant and heavily guarded walls made up the border of Tallus' kingdom to keep all out and their people in. They refused to think that anyone but them existed in the world.

For years, the Kingdom of Sorran had no one or anything to rely on except for what they had. They used what water they could from the Dead River and made the most of what grassy fertile land they had for farming. The Kingdom of Sorran and its people did what they could to keep going and depended on what little help others in Sorran could provide.

Soré was one of those places. Thanks to Soré's fertile farms, they not only provided for the people, but for King Sirus and his great city. In return for the production of food and water, they received money and supplies from the king to build and maintain a school and other necessities that most of the other villages and dwellings had to survive without. These benefits made Soré larger than most villages and becoming an actual township. It was not glamorous, but it was a great place to live and call home.

That is exactly what passed through Semaj's mind as he opened his window and gazed out upon the new day. From his window, he could see the cows grazing and the chickens stirring from the rooster's wake up call. He knew he would have a little bit of time to help with the morning chores before heading off into town for school. Even though he was now sixteen years old and attending his last year, he would still rather stay at home and attend to the farm. Due to town law, children had to attend school for eleven years. If it were not for that, and of course his five best friends, he probably would have never set foot off the farm.

With a sigh, Semaj quickly headed out to do his chores. It didn't take long until he had fed all the animals and brought in the eggs and milk from the chickens and cows. He was about to run back outside when a lone figure suddenly blocked his path. The man in his way was slightly taller and stockier than Semaj. As mean as he looked, the man had a huge heart-warming smile.

"Son, you better go and get cleaned up and ready. Your friends will be here shortly and you don't want to be late for school."

"Dad, are you sure I shouldn't stay and finish up a few more things around the farm?"

"Semaj, I can handle it. The autumn months are an easier time for your mother and I to maintain the farm. You can always help after school with what we didn't get done."

"Your father is correct, school must come first," came a very light and cheerful voice.

"Morning Lana, my love," Semaj's father said turning towards the voice.

"Morning, Boris dear." The shorter, slightly heavier woman with rosey cheeks that matched her hair, answered as she stepped out of the kitchen.

"But, mom."

"But nothing, Semaj Kucera. Now you go get ready while I set the table for breakfast," Lana playfully scolded as she kissed her husband and headed back into the kitchen while Semaj dragged himself towards his room.

By the time Semaj cleaned up, put on his shirt, pants and boots, he could hear a couple new voices coming from the kitchen. With a dash, he entered the kitchen to find Marcus and Lars sitting at the table eating. Lars sat in his ragged clothing letting Lana Kucera force tons of food in him. Lars' family lived right on the eastern edge of Soré in a very run down cottage. His family made just enough money to keep their home and put some food on the table. Lars was the youngest of six sons. By the time any clothes were passed down to him, they were pretty worn out. Lars did not care though, he believed in family and love over material possessions.

Marcus sat next to Lars, only eating a little to be polite. He had already eaten a full meal before leaving home. He and his twin sister lived in a huge house just as you entered the town. Because their father was the captain of the king's guard in Soré, and one of the best fighters, trainers and weapons masters in town, they had plenty of money and could afford a large home inside the town itself. Just like his dad, Marcus was tall and very muscular with much darker skin than most of the town's folk. His twin sister was the splitting image of him, except she was about five inches shorter and slightly plump.

Even though he was the exact opposite of Lars, the two had been best friends since birth. Their mothers had been best friends since childhood, and even now that they had grown apart in social classes, the two sons had taken over and maintained that strong bond of friendship. That is why Marcus had always walked clear to Lars' cottage and escorted him to school. Despite Lars being average and poor, no one said a word to him thanks to Marcus's friendship and protection.

That is what Semaj liked about his small group of friends. Since the day they had all met and become friends, they had accepted each other without judgment and formed an unbreakable bond. Starting with the first year of school, they had always met at Semaj's home and walked to school together. They had always vowed to stay together, but with this being the last year of school, Semaj feared what the future might hold for them all. He shook his head. He did not want to worry about that yet.

"Where are the others?" Semaj asked taking his seat at the table.

"Lija is still at home with Anna. Anna did not get in from Sorra until late last night. They are a little slow going this morning and I think Anna was still settling into the room mom prepared for her for the school year. They'll meet us right in town," Marcus informed as Semaj looked up from his plate and then glanced over at Lars

"I don't know about Thom. We stopped by his house and his mom said he had left early this morning, leaving a note that he would catch up with us on the way to town," Lars mumbled through his food-filled mouth.

Semaj glanced out the kitchen window with a nod. He was used to Thom's odd behavior. They had been best friends and neighbors all their life. Thom's parents had built their farm right next to his family's farm about the same time. Both fathers helped each other maintain adjoining fields. Even when Thom and Lars had started to become very close, they maintained their friendship. He and Thom would always be best friends.

Semaj did wonder what Thom was up to, but soon found his thoughts drifting to Anna Sparks. He had not seen her all summer. Anna's family was very poor and lived in a small

13

village down south called Sorra. Some kids, whose parents could afford it, would travel from other villages and dwellings to get an education in Soré since it was the only place with a school this side of the Dead River.

Anna's parents skimped and saved all they had to send her here for school. Anna did not mind the long journey to Soré, for she liked adventures. Once she arrived in Soré, she would stay with Marcus and Lija's family during the school year. She was Lija's best friend and got to live with her family for free. This allowed her to use what money she had to pay for her schooling. Even though she spent most of her time away from her family, she had another one here to keep her safe and warm.

"We better get going before we're late," Marcus said to Semaj, bringing his attention back, as he and Lars got up to thank the Kuceras for their hospitality.

Semaj kissed his mom and dad good-bye and followed his friends out the door. They made their way off the farm and started up the dirt road that led into town. Being so close to a river, they were blessed with not only greenery but with trees. Trees that were getting ready to change colors. Too bad the rest of the kingdom was not blessed with the abundance of trees. As they walked, Semaj took in the beauty of the land.

"Still no sign of Thom," Lars said with worry as they passed Thom's home.

"Don't worry, Lars. Knowing him, he's caught up in something and will show up shortly. You know how he is," Semaj said.

"Yeah, but he promised me he would stop that."

"Look, he's running our way now," Marcus interrupted and pointed to the west.

Running across the fields was a very thin figure, shaggy blond hair blowing against the wind. When he finally caught up with the boys, he stopped, hunched over and tried to catch his breath. They could tell he was excited about something, his deep blue eyes were radiating. Lars walked up and helped him stand on his feet, placing an arm around him for support.

"Thom, where have you been? We were all so worried," Lars asked, holding tight.

"You guys won't believe what I found," he said catching his breath.

"You can tell us as we walk. We still have to meet up with my sister and Anna," Marcus said as he urged them all to continue along the dirt road.

"Okay. Last night I had a strange dream."

"And this is different from when?"

"Semaj, let him talk."

"Calm down, Lars. As I was saying, I had this strange dream. I was sitting in the fields, only the moonlight keeping me company. Then off in the west, toward the river, a spark of light caught my eye. I found myself running in that direction until I got to the edge of the Dead River. With the water flowing, it was clear and shallow enough for me to see the bottom. I looked all over and saw nothing. I was about to shrug it off when a gleam from the moonlight pulled my gaze back to the river.

"There was definitely something at the bottom, almost submerged in the mud. I reached down into the water and pulled it out. Using the river and the sleeve of my shirt, I cleaned it off. To my surprise it was very smooth and appeared to be a clear crystal of some sort. That is when the crystal began to glow in my hands. After that, the rest of the dream was a blur and I woke with a start," Thom said as they soon found themselves within site of the town entrance.

"Let me guess, you ran out to the river to check?" Semaj laughed shaking his head.

"I had to. Everything in my gut told me that it was some sort of premonition, just like what I've read about."

"Thom! You promised you wouldn't do stuff like that. It's forbidden and dangerous."

"Don't worry, dear. I only study the art, not practice it. Even if I could actually do it, I never would for fear of setting off the alarms and being carted away."

"You know, Thom, even if you don't practice *it*, if they even found the books you could risk exile or worse."

"I agree, Marcus. I've told him over and over to burn those books he found."

"Lars is right, you should burn them."

"Semaj, you know I can't. Even though I found them buried deep within the ground, they belonged to one of my ancestral grandfathers and passed down through the generations. At some point, someone buried it in the ground for safe keeping."

"I still find it hard to believe that it was also a dream that told him and showed him where to find the books. Maybe you are weirder than we thought."

"That's not funny, Semaj. I don't know what I would do if we lost him or something happened because of this obsession of his."

"Lars, you need to relax. You can tend to get a bit overprotective."

"Well, if he is he learned it from you, Marcus."

"Point made, Thom," Marcus smiled at Lars, who started to calm down.

They were almost to the entrance into town when they saw two girls walking their way. One was the splitting image of Marcus, with her black hair and brown eyes. She wore a blue oversized dress, trying to cover her short plump body. Even with her pleasant smile and fancy dress, she could still be witty and tough like her brother. She moved a few steps slower than the girl in front of her.

Semaj smirked at the sight of the other girl. She had long blond hair, tied back in a single braid with glowing blue eyes. Unlike Lija, she did not wear dresses. Instead, she wore red leggings and a matching blouse. Her boots were similar to the ones the boys were wearing, which he knew concealed small daggers within each one. That was Anna Sparks. She loved adventures and was not afraid to get her hands dirty.

"About time you guys showed up. Thought we would have to leave without you for once," Anna teased.

"It's great to see you again, Anna," the boys all greeted her.

"What was taking you guys so long? Mom was starting to worry."

"We were getting caught up in one of Thom's dream stories," Marcus answered his sister.

"Oh? I want to hear this. I think we should stop here and let him finish before we actually enter the town," Anna said with sincere interest in her voice.

16

Making sure they were alone, the boys all waited as Thom retold the girls about his dream. "Anyway, I woke up with a start after that. All I could remember from the dream was the river and the crystal. The dream ate at the back of my mind until I finally decided to get out of bed and go check it out. I knew I had time before you all would show up so I left a note with mom and ran off towards the river."

"What happened when you got there?" Anna drew in deeper.

"I was getting to that." Taking a deep breath, he continued. "I got to the spot that I saw in my dream. I looked and looked and couldn't find anything. I wasn't going to give up though, because I know what my dream meant. I grabbed a stick and began digging around in the mud at the bottom of the river. Just when I was about to stop, a sparkle caught my eye. I pushed the mud aside and there it was. I reached in and pulled out this!" Thom exclaimed pulling a beautiful white-blue crystal out from under his shirt.

"Oh Venēäh! It's so beautiful!" Anna screamed.

"Thom, put that away. You can't let anyone see you with that," Lars panicked, looking around.

"He is right about that. We need to keep this to ourselves and you need to keep it hidden until we know what it is or what it does," Semaj said, not being able to take his eyes off the crystal Thom had found.

"I know, Semaj. That's why I attached it to a piece of chain so I can wear it around my neck and keep it hidden under my clothes."

"It can't be magic if the alarms aren't blaring," Anna added as she took one last glance before Thom slipped it back into hiding.

"You should just get rid of it along with those books."

"Lars, dear, whether this crystal is anything or not, I was meant to find it. For now, I will keep it, but I promise to be careful," Thom reassured as he squeezed Lar's hand.

"What if someone does discover it? Then what would you do?" Lija asked with added worry.

"They won't. I always carry my books in my travel bag and no one has discovered them yet," Thom said patting the bag that he used for carrying his school materials.

"We can debate this more later, we need to get going. They're already sounding the warning bell. School will be starting soon," Marcus reminded the others.

"Yeah, and we can't be late. Everyone knows that Old Lady Muerte teaches the eleventh year classes," Lija pointed out with a shudder.

"That's right. Rumor has it that a kid showed up right after final bell and she broke his arm with her teaching stick." Marcus imitated a hitting motion on his arm.

"You are crazy. She would never do such a thing. I swear you make these stories up to get your sister worked up," Semaj laughed as he led the others onward.

As they approached the entrance into town, Thom made sure the crystal was well hidden under his shirt. A guard stood at the entrance and nodded at them. As big as Soré was, it was still small enough where everyone knew each other. Since it was a friendly and prosperous little town, the people here, along with the king, wanted to keep it that way. A guard was posted at all four entrances into the town to monitor whoever came in and out.

As the group entered town, they passed Marcus and Lija's home. They looked up and waved at their mom who was shaking her finger from the window. With that motherly glare, they hurried their way and made it into the center of town. Placed right there in the middle of town was a stone statue of the town's founder, surrounded by trees with a plaque that read: *The great Soré, never to be forgotten.*

"I don't get why they make such a big deal about him," Lija remarked.

"If it wasn't for him there wouldn't be a township to call home."

"Marcus is right, Lija. It is said that Soré was a great adventurer," Anna added. "He left the city of Sorran to scout out new land for the king. The city of Sorran was still new but the king knew he had to plan for the future. With the king's blessing,

Soré set out and traveled for days with a small band of companions."

"Yeah, yeah we know the rest." Semaj interrupted. "He found a very fertile area of land by the river. After a month they had built a small village dedicated to farming. After a few years the king had sent out a search party for the missing man, only to discover the small farming and river village. When word got back to the King of Sorran, he made Soré leader of the village and they set up a trade deal between the two communities. After that, the years passed with Soré and the generations that followed him guiding and leading the village's people, and the village of Soré eventually became a great township."

"You shouldn't mock," Anna blurted and stormed off ahead of the group.

"You shouldn't do that to her," Thom told him.

"I know. I love this place and plan on farming here for years to come with a family of my own one day."

"Then why do you treat her like that?"

"I don't know. Maybe I like to see her riled up," Semaj laughed.

He did not know why he got like that with her at times. He knew they could never be anything more than friends. They were two very different people. She liked to look for wild adventures while he preferred to settle down and live a quiet life on the farm. He could not picture her working the fields, the same way he could never see himself running off on some grand adventure. He shrugged the thoughts off, as he knew there was no point in dwelling on any of it.

"I think someone has a crush."

"I do not, Marcus!" Semaj said blushing.

"Hey, no reason to get snappy, I was just teasing."

"You guys better hurry up."

"We're coming, sis. Don't worry. We'll make it."

They finally reached the section of town that was setup for schooling. Kids of all ages, whether in groups or escorted by parents, scrambled everywhere. The first day of classes always looked busier than a town festival. The six of them made their way through the crowds of people until they reached the section of school they were supposed to be at. The school was not large but every class had their own area. They made their way to the top of a hill behind the school. This is where the eleventh-year classes were taught. Semaj turned and looked back down the hill.

At the bottom of the hill, just behind the school was a field that was used for recreational activities, playtime, and classes that required physical training or competitions and games. Years one through ten held all their classes directly inside the school building. Since they were in their last year of school, they were placed apart from the others up here in the open air. It was hard for Semaj to believe that once they had been down there and now they were up here for their final year of school. He took a deep breath as they all turned and headed to join their class.

There were plenty of trees to shade the class area. A cool breeze touched each student as they took their seats. Semaj and his friends took the seats in the very back. They barely sat down when the final bell rang. All the students faced forward as a short stocky older woman now stood before them. Her large velvet dress swaying in the wind while her long graying hair held firm in a tight bun upon her head. There was complete silence as she captured everyone's attention.

"Welcome everyone. I am Miss Muerte and I will be guiding you in your last year of school. Your teaching sessions are done. You'll spend the first half of the school year deciding what you want to do with your life. Then after winter break, you will be set up with apprenticeships.

"You will get hands on experience with the different skills and trades you need. These will all prepare you for what you choose to do after you leave school. Whether it is nothing, starting a trade right away or going off to study more advanced skills or study a higher level of teaching. No matter what happens, keep in mind that I will be guiding you and grading you. I expect you all in attendance everyday no matter what your plans are after school is over," She lectured.

Semaj looked over and already saw Lars and Anna dozing off. Thom was clearly daydreaming while Marcus and his sister paid attention with sincerity. He could care less. He knew what he wanted to do with his life and he didn't need any teaching or guidance. His parents had taught him everything he needed to know. This was all pointless to him. His mind began to wonder as he watched his other friends drifting off as well. Soon his eyes closed as the last thing he heard was Lars snoring.

With a sudden pop in the air, Lars stood up from his seat. He looked around and noticed that the teacher and the rest of the class were gone. *Where did everyone go?* He thought to himself when he suddenly jumped as a hand touched his shoulder. He turned around to see it was Thom and right behind him stood Anna and Semaj. They too were looking all around with confused expressions on their faces.

"Where did everyone go?" Lars asked his friends.

"I don't know. One minute I'm daydreaming and then the next I feel a strange warm heat and then there was a pop in the air and everyone's gone but us," Thom said rubbing his chest were the crystal laid hidden.

"Same here. I was dozing off then a loud pop woke me. Hey, where are Marcus and Lija?" Anna asked as she began searching around the hilltop.

"They're not here. This is very strange. Maybe your crystal did something to all of us that were falling asleep," Semaj said, half joking.

"That would explain the pain on my chest and why we are the only ones here," Thom said as he pulled the crystal out from under his shirt.

"I knew it. Did I not tell you that you should have gotten rid of that thing? The guards will arrest us all and we'll be prosecuted for messing with *magic*," Lars screamed then whispering his last word.

"Get a hold of yourself. For all I know, I could be the only one dreaming thinking you all are here with me. Trust me, I have had stranger dreams than this before. Either way, this is more exciting than listening to Old Lady Muerte," Anna said flicking her boot shoe, flinging a dagger up and into her hand and scouting around the hill.

"Anna may be right. This does feel like a dream, almost familiar, but I have this other weird feeling. Like this energy is pulling at me from all around this hilltop. Almost as if a strange force is trying to draw me to something," Semaj said as he walked a little off balance towards Anna, glancing at Thom's crystal and Lars overreacting.

"I kind of feel it too," Anna and Thom whispered together.

"I don't feel anything but danger. How can this be a dream if we are all here? I think Thom's crystal is affecting us in some way. Thom, I think you better use that crystal and put things back. I swear it will be the death of us," Lars said with tears forming.

"Calm down, dear. My gut tells me that there is more to this than my crystal," Thom said taking Lars in his arms for comfort.

"You might be right. Look over there on the distant southern horizon," Anna said pointing with her dagger.

"What is it?" Thom and Lars asked coming up behind her.

"It almost looks like the figure of a person or something."

"I agree, Semaj. It's too far away to tell what it is or what it's doing."

"Anna, whatever it is, I can feel it watching us," Semaj said with a shiver as the others all nodded in agreement.

"I don't know about the rest of you but I think it is starting to get a little warm," Lars said as he wiped the sweat from his brow.

They all took their attention from the distant figure and looked back upon each other. Beads of sweat were forming upon all their foreheads as they realized the air around them was dry and that it was definitely getting hotter by the minute. Anna looked down and saw that the grass under her feet was wilting and turning brown. Suddenly the hilltop burst into flames creating a circle surrounding them.

"How?" Semaj started to ask as the fire grew higher with intensity.

"What should we do? The flames are too high to run through or jump over," Lars panicked.

"This way!" Anna yelled as they all followed her to the center of the hill. The flames now covered the whole hilltop and were slowly moving towards the center where they all stood, temporarily safe from the fire but not the heat.

"What now? It won't take long for the fire to spread and reach us here," Thom said as he tried to remain calm for Lars.

"Thom, is there any way you can make that crystal magically get rid of the fire?" Semaj asked, wishing more than anything that if this was a dream that he would wake up.

"If there is, I don't know how. I don't even know if it is truely magical."

The four friends stood back to back as the ring of fire drew closer. There was nowhere to run. Thom held Lars tight as Semaj found his hand reaching out for Anna's hand. Anna's hand moved, but instead of taking hold she pushed him backwards. Anna stepped in front of them all and stood her ground before the fire. Anna did not scream as the flames consumed her and then the rest of them.

"No!" screamed a voice full of terror.

Everyone jumped and turned around towards the back of the room. Miss Muerte shot up and moved quickly past all her students until she reached the back of the class. She pointed and glared. "That will be enough of that. How dare you fall asleep and then disturb my class. If this is any indication of your ambitions I might as well fail you all right now."

"Miss Muerte."

"No excuses!" She screamed cutting off Lars. "I guess some people are just destined to be failures and not do anything with their lives. You four will remain after class."

Marcus glanced over at his friends as their teacher headed back to the front of the class, lecturing about what will happen to anyone else who chooses not to pay attention during her lectures. He noticed all four of them were sweating and looked a little flushed. He leaned forward and shook his head as he could have sworn he saw a white-blue light fade from under Thom's shirt.

Before he could get a closer look, something else caught his eye. There was something, or someone, standing behind a tree at the bottom of the hill. He squinted his eyes and realized it was a figure of an old man who seemed to be staring right up at him. Marcus rubbed his eyes and looked again. The figure was gone. Had he been seeing things? He was not sure.

"I take it you want to stay after too, Mr. Masters?"

"No ma'am.'

"I thought not. I am sure your father would not take too kindly to that."

"No ma'am." Marcus stuttered as he turned his attention back to the front of the class. *So much for a good start on the first day of school.*

23

****

While their four friends served time after school, Marcus and Lija walked over to their mom's clothing shop to tell her about Anna and the others. Marcus' mom ran a very profitable business. A few women in town sew and make various types of clothing and then sell them to his mom, Adryann Masters. Adryann then turns around and sells the items at a slightly higher price in her shop to those who stop in or the visitors and traders passing through town. People come to her shop because she only buys and sells the very best. One of the women who made clothes for Adryann was Thom's mom, and she made some of the best clothing, which tended to sell more than any of the other women's clothes.

That day, Tasha Raven had been in the shop dropping off her latest creations. Marcus and Lija went running in and plowed her over. Adryann gasped in fright and flew out in front of the counter to help Tasha up while, with one of her looks, made her children start picking up the dropped clothing as fast as they could move.

"What is the meaning of this? I did not raise my children to act in such a manner. Apologize to Mrs. Raven," Adryann scolded.

"Sorry, Mrs. Raven," they both apologized.

"That is quite alright. Where's my son?" She asked looking around.

"That is why we came running in here. We wanted to tell my mom what happened to Anna and the others."

"Marcus, what is it?"

"Did something happen to my son?"

"Yes, but nothing too bad," he said at the two worried mothers.

"They all got caught sleeping in class and Miss Muerte held them after," Lija blurted out.

"What a relief. I thought something bad might have actually happened," Tasha said with a laugh.

"I don't think this is something to let slide so lightly. I know Anna is not my child but she will follow rules in our house. I will discuss this with your father and we will talk with Anna tonight."

"Oh, Adryann, don't be too hard on the girl. You can't tell me you never fell asleep in class."

"Never, I always paid attention. I didn't get the life I have now from daydreams and slacking off."

"Well, I better get going before this gets too heated," Tasha laughed taking her money for the clothes she had brought. "I will let Semaj's parents know that he'll be arriving late." She waved to the three and headed out the door avoiding Adryann's unapproving glare.

"I have to close up early here anyway to go over to the market and get some food and supplies. I will have your father send someone out to the Lehbors' cottage so they don't worry about Lars. I'm so glad you two had the sense to pay attention."

"Mom, the teacher did yell at Marcus too for not paying attention, but she let him off with a warning," Lija said sticking her tongue out at her brother.

"Marcus!"

"Wait, mom."

"That's enough. We will all talk about this later. Why I let you hang out with those boys is beyond me. I'll make a lady out of that Anna yet."

"Mom, they didn't do anything wrong."

"That is enough, Marcus. We will discuss this when you get home. You all are at that age where it is time to grow up and become proper men and women. You two wait for Anna and Lars and come straight home. One of your father's men will see him home tonight," Adryann commanded as she locked up her shop and headed off to find her husband.

"Why did you get me in trouble?"

"I'm tired of you thinking your better than everyone else and that you can always get away with things just because you're the son of the Captain of the Guard."

"I do not act that way."

"You do to."

"Fine, think what you want. At least I'm not a spoiled little girl whose only ambition in life is to marry a rich man and never have to lift a finger."

"I am not spoiled!"

Marcus and Lija walked the rest of the way back to school without saying a word to each other. Marcus grumbled to himself while Lija pouted. As mad as they were, they knew it would not last long. They were very close and their twin bond was too strong to stay mad after an argument. Once they got to the school, they sat under a big shady tree. Marcus sat on the grass while Lija sat upon a large rock, after dusting it off, both in complete silence.

"About time you guys got done," Marcus shouted after what seemed like an eternal wait.

"Did Old Lady Muerte break your arms?"

"No Lija, she didn't break our arms," Anna said as she and the others came towards them.

"We just had to sit there and listen to her yell at us. It was a real waste of time if you ask me. My parents are not going to be too thrilled at me coming home late."

"Don't worry, Semaj, we can come up with some kind of story."

"I wouldn't count on that, Thom. Your mom was in my mom's shop today and we had no choice but to tell her."

"She said she was going to tell Semaj's mom and have our dad send someone out to let Lar's mom know he would be late tonight," Lija finished.

"Great, more lectures," Semaj sighed.

"Don't worry. We can't get into too much trouble. I mean we are basically adults now. They cannot control us forever. It's time for us to go off and be on our own."

"Anna, this is not some big adventure. We all have things we are expected to achieve. We just can't go running off on some fool's quest," Marcus grumbled as they all began heading home.

"What happened while you were sleeping? It must have been some dreams you all had to make you all scream out like that in unison. I about had a heart attack," Lija said as she stared at her friends, noticing a light red tint to their faces. She did not think they had been in the direct sunlight that long today.

"I just had a strange dream. Nothing major," Semaj said glancing at Anna.

"It must be the last year of school nerves or something. I had a weird dream too, but it seemed so real," Anna said making eye contact.

"Okay guys let's admit it. We all had the same weird dream about being burned alive by fire all because of Thom's stupid crystal," Lars said with growing worry.

Marcus and Lija stopped walking and turned around when they realized no one else was following them. Lars stood facing Thom, Anna and Semaj whose face were now pale white. No one said a word as Marcus and his sister rejoined the group.

"What's going on guys?" Marcus asked as he had never seen his friends look like this before. He could tell something was definitely wrong.

"There is no way that could have happened," Semaj whispered.

"It's just a big coincidence."

"No, it is not, Anna. That crystal of Thom's did it. He needs to get rid of it."

"Lars, quit over reacting. There's no way the crystal could have done it. Wouldn't the alarms have sounded if it had?" Thom asked looking around as if he excepted the alarms to go off at any moment.

"Your probably right, Thom, but I could have sworn I saw it glowing when you guys woke up," Marcus responded as he too looked around making sure they were safe from outside eyes or ears.

"Well, what ever happened, it was really weird and felt real. I don't think it's anything to panic over though."

"Anna's right. Let's just call this one of those weird occurrences and leave it at that," Thom said as he calmed Lars while gently touching the crystal under his shirt, worrying about losing both.

"Oh, speaking of weird, did any of you guys see that strange old man?"

"What old man?" Semaj asked as the others stared at Marcus.

"There was this old man hiding behind the trees at the bottom of the hill. One minute he was there watching us, then the next he was gone. Before I could get a better look, Muerte busted me."

"Did he have long brown hair with a lot of white streaks in it and weird white eyes?"

"Lija, you saw him too?"

"Yes, I did."

"Why didn't you say something earlier at school?"

"Well I didn't see him there."

"Then where did you see him?"

"I noticed him following us all the way home from school. I didn't think anything of it until you said something. He's right back there," Lija said pointing behind the others.

They all turned around but no one was there. Anna flicked her daggers into her hands as she searched their surroundings. The others glanced around but found no one in site.

"Are you sure about that, Lija? There's no one following us."

"I swear it, Anna. He was right there only moments ago."

"That is strange. Even if someone was following us there is nowhere for him to have hid so fast," Thom added.

"I think we are getting ourselves spooked out here."

"I agree with Semaj. Let's wait and talk about this tomorrow. I think we all just had a stressful first day of school," Thom said trying to convince himself of his words.

"I thought your mother said to go straight home!" A loud dominating voice shouted causing them all to jump.

They all turned around as Anna quickly hid her daggers back into her boots. Coming up the path was a very tall, muscular man. He looked like a bigger and older version of Marcus. Behind him were eight of his guardsmen. They all inched behind Marcus, placing him directly in front of his father's path.

"We are dad. We were just talking."

"Marcus, no excuses, I want you and the girls to head straight home. Two of my guards will escort you. Lars, I will have another two men escort you while another two take Semaj and Thom home. Marcus, tell your mother I will be home late tonight."

"What's going on?"

"There have been reports of strange men outside the boundaries of town. I have even heard of a few sightings of an odd man lurking around town. Until me and my men have secured the parameters I don't want anyone out alone at night. Now go before it gets any darker."

Marcus and the others said goodbye as Broc and his remaining men raced back into town. Thom gave Lars a quick kiss as he was thrown up on a horse and was taken away. Thom and Semaj waved as they were put up on horses and taken home. Marcus and the two girls walked in silence as their escort took them home.

Marcus was not sure what was going on, but he could not help but wonder if it had anything to do with the dream the others had and that mysterious old man he and his sister had seen. Whether or not they were all related, only time would tell. He would just have to worry about it tomorrow.

Chapter Two:
Essej & The Drogans

Semaj was up before the rooster. Even though his parents were not too hard on him he still felt guilty for getting in trouble at school and not getting home in time to help his dad in the fields. He figured he could make up for lost time by getting up early and starting on the morning chores. His dad knew where his heart was so did not press the school issue. His mom, on the other hand lectured him about school and the importance of making a future for himself. No matter what, he knew what the future held for him, a nice little family on the farm. Nothing was ever going to change that.

Just as he was about to step out the back door he heard a twig snap. Something was out there and it was not the animals. Semaj debated whether he should go wake his dad or not. Ever since yesterday, he had been a little on edge. Them all having the same dream was too freaky. Something in his gut told him that there was more to it than Thom's crystal.

"Who's out there?" Semaj called softly as he grabbed the wood axe.

When no one answered, he raised the axe and slowly walked towards where he had heard the noise. Suddenly a white glare caught his eye. It had come from behind the barn. *Maybe it's that old man Lija and Marcus had seen,* Semaj thought as he got closer to the barn. He did not hear anything, but he knew something was behind the barn.

Once he got to the side of the barn, he slowly inched his way to the back, axe raised high. His heart was beating through his chest. He did not like things like this. He was a simple farm boy, nothing more. Why couldn't this be happening to Anna or Marcus? They lived for this kind of action. Just as he neared the corner, he paused and took a deep breath. *This is it, now or never,* Semaj exhaled.

"Surrender or die!" Semaj screamed as he leapt around the corner axe high in the air.

Semaj suddenly stopped and looked around. There was no one there. He started laughing at himself. He was such a fool. He turned around just as a foot kicked the axe out of his hand and two hands pushed him back against the barn. He was about to scream when a hand covered his mouth. Eyes wide, he began to struggle.

"Semaj, calm down, it's me, Thom!"

"Léhl, Thom, I could have taken your head off," Semaj swore.

"Semaj, that's why I circled around and kicked the axe out of your hand when I realized you were approaching. Honestly, even with the axe you're not much of a threat," Thom said laughing as he dodged a flying fist.

"Not funny. What are you doing out here so early?"

"After yesterday's events I wanted to go somewhere secluded to see if I could find any answers in these magic books in conjunction with this crystal. With the guards keeping watch now, I have to be more careful so I thought getting up earlier than normal I could sneak off into your barn and study in private."

"You don't think anyone would find candle light from inside a barn at this hour as strange?"

"I guess I didn't think of that. You know how I get when it comes to this stuff. I was drawn to these things and I feel a strange connection to something greater here."

"What do the books tell you?" Semaj asked, not wanting to encourage his friend but his curiosity was getting the best of him.

"That's what's so frustrating. I know I was meant for this but I can't get anywhere."

"What are you talking about, Thom? You ramble about those books all the time."

"You're my best friend and I have to tell you something. I don't understand those books as much as I tell you guys I do."

"What do you mean?"

"Well these two books are clearly different I know that much. One looks like a journal describing almost all things and beings of magic and seems very ancient in its writing. Harder to completely understand but I am getting better with it. The other I think is a book on magic. I cannot translate it but I have this feeling. The more I study it the more I try to understand and memorize the types of words. At times, I hear the words swirl in my mind. I would attempt to speak what I think it says but I am afraid to try so I don't do something and trigger the alarms."

"Really, I always got the impression that they belonged to your great grandfather and were passed down to you. That you were mastering the art destined to follow in his footsteps," Semaj said with a little playfulness.

"I really don't know if they belonged to him and I really don't understand them at all. My parents never talk about my ancestors and forbid any talk about them or magic. I did have the dream that accidentally led me to them but I made up the part about how it was my grandfather who came to me."

"What are you talking about?"

"Wait, let me finish. I have always been considered average and never had high expectations placed on me. I have always dreamed that I was destined to be something more than I am. When I found the books I just told everyone they were magic books passed down from my mysterious grandfather so I could look important."

"You know you don't have to pretend with us. We are all friends. For Venéăh's sake! I've known you my whole life and accept you for you no matter what."

"I know that."

"Even if the books are nothing, you now have that crystal you found."

"Yeah about that, there was no dream. I could not sleep and so I went out by the river to study the books like I always do. I did see a glimmer, dug into the river, and found it. I had never seen anything like it so I put it around my neck and made up the story." Thom began to cry as he held the crystal in the palm of his hand.

"Wow, you had us all fooled. Maybe you should be a performer," Semaj joked putting his arm around Thom. "Seriously, you are important to all of us."

"Yeah I know. I did such a good job that I even have Lars all stressed about it and you know I hate lying to him. It's just that you guys view me as this potential, living on the edge, descendant of powerful magic. As great as that feels it also shames me to lie to you all and I hate it. This crystal is probably nothing more than a shinny rock."

"I don't understand why you think you have to."

"Don't you see? You all know what you want and have important roles to take. You want to settle down and are happy with being a farmer. Since that is not my desire, I have secretly heard talks between our parents that when you take a wife that our land will be sold to you and your family, while mine moves to the great capital city of Sorran. I know it's your plan to run and create a great land of farming and production, but I,"

"But, Thom."

"Let me finish. You have that while Anna is known as the adventurer. We all know she plans to go out to travel and explore the lands of Bergonia for fame and glory. Marcus and Lija are part of the upper class. Marcus will become a great warrior like his dad while Lija dreams of becoming a princess and court high society.

"Even Lars has it all planned out for himself. He is known as the sensitive and caring one. Despite his background, he has been offered the chance to go study at the University in Sorran," Thom said as he wiped the tears.

"Really? I did not know that."

"Yeah, it's supposed to be a secret so don't say anything. Lars is very smart and his teachers have gotten word to the professors and the king in Sorran. If he successfully completes this last year of school and does well with his apprenticeship, the teachers are going to help pay and work a deal with his parents to send him to Sorran. There he can study to become a great teacher and help others and even help bring his family out of the poverty they live in."

"That is great!"

"Yeah but where does that leave me? I have no directions and would probably follow him and fade into the background. I just wanted to be known for my own thing and look like I was heading for greatness too. This way none of you would see the truth that everyone else knows, including me. I am and never will be anything special and will fade away as you all step into your roles."

"Oh, Thom, don't think that way. You'll always be special. I bet you'll find something great to do. I mean come on, a farmer isn't all that grand."

"Yeah, but as simple of a life as you claim it to be, everyone knows it will still amount to something for you and your family. You all have your set roles while I don't. Then after what happened yesterday, I thought just maybe there was something magical about the crystal. I thought maybe it would actually make my dreams come true, but alas, I sit here looking at both the books and the crystal and get nothing," Thom finished with a gentle sob.

"Hey, don't be too hard on yourself. Everything will work out the way it's supposed to. No matter what happens, we'll all be there for each other. Crystal or not, you'll always play the role of my best friend," Semaj laughed shaking Thom playfully.

"Thanks, and one other thing."

"Don't worry, I won't tell the others. It's our secret," Semaj interrupted.

"I appreciate that. So, what do you think really happened?"

"Happened to what?" A voice asked from around the barn.

Both of them jumped up as Semaj's father came around the corner. They were so deep in conversation that they had not noticed the sun starting to rise and the rooster calling out for all to wake up. Semaj quickly stepped in front of Thom blocking him from his dad's immediate view.

"Nothing, dad, just wondering about the extra guard patrol is all."

"That is why you shouldn't be out here alone so early in the dark. Why are you out here? Is that Thom?"

"Yes sir," Thom said as he quickly slid the books into his bag and the crystal under his shirt.

"I felt guilty about being held after class so I got up early to do extra chores."

"And I was out doing the same for my dad and saw a light near the barn and just ran up here to check it out."

"Then Thom and I just got to talking and lost track of time."

Boris just laughed at the two and their stories. As grown up as they were becoming they were still boys. He knew they were up to something but decided not to press. The two had been up to no good since they were toddlers. Might as well let them have their fun while they still can.

"Mom has breakfast going. Why don't you two help me get the milk and bring in the eggs? Then we can have a bite to eat before the guardsmen arrive to escort you to school," Boris said clapping a hand on the boy's backs guiding them away from the barn. "Just promise me you boys won't go off in the dark again until they have declared it safe again."

"We promise, dad. I just wonder what the commotion is all about."

"I don't know, but with all the reports, they have to check it out. It has been a long time since this town has seen any excitement. Will probably do us all some good," Boris laughed as he and the boys got to work.

****

"Anna, you should try wearing a dress sometime. It would make you look more like a lady."

"I don't need to dress like you, Lija. I'm happy with what I'm wearing."

"How are you ever going to find a husband?"

"I don't need a man to make me happy. I'll do fine just by myself."

"Not me. I'll capture the heart of a great prince who will give me everything I could ever hope for," Lija sang as she twirled.

Anna laughed to herself as she watched Lija in front of the mirror. Lija had on a pretty purple dress that came down to her ankles. Lija smoothed out the wrinkles in her dress as she rubbed her hands up and down her plump body. Anna always admired how she never let her weight stop her from being beautiful. She was bound and determined to snag herself a rich man and live her life as a princess.

Not Anna though. She did not need a man. She would make herself happy and rich all on her own. She would never let herself fall for some guy. She just could not see herself settling down and raising a family. Her heart was meant for the great unknown. She smiled at herself as she put on her boots. Who cared if she wasn't lady like? She didn't.

"Captain! Captain!" Came a loud commotion from outside.

35

Anna ran quickly out of the room. She collided with a fast-approaching figure. Anna looked to see whom she had knocked down. It was Marcus. He quickly jumped up and ran for the door that led outside. Anna followed quickly after him. As they reached the door, they saw Lars walking in with Adryann Masters while Broc Masters stood outside talking to his guardsmen.

"Now you kids stay right here and leave your father to his business. Last thing he needs is you in his way. I'm going to finish getting breakfast ready."

Marcus and Anna walked towards Lars as Adryann vanished into the kitchen. Lars looked out of sorts and flushed with excitement. Marcus and Anna quickly helped him to a chair. They waited for Lars to catch his breath before they urged him with what happened.

"What is going on?" Lija asked as she came gracefully down the stairs.

"We don't know yet. Lars was just about to tell us," Marcus said as his sister joined them.

"What is that all about?" Anna pressed.

"Sorry, I just have to catch my breath. We rode so hard all the way here."

"What happened?" They all asked in unison.

"Well, some of your dad's men showed up to escort me here. Just as we were halfway to town, we saw something off in the distance near a grove of trees. A couple of the guards dashed out towards them to investigate."

"What was it?" Anna asked.

"I was getting to that," Lars exclaimed as he drew in a breath and began his tale.

****

"Lars, you better get going. The guardsmen will be here any moment to take you into Soré."

"Yes, mother, I'm coming," Lars answered back at the screeching voice.

Lars got up and out of bed. It was not the world's most comfortable bed but it was a place to sleep. At least he no longer had to sleep on a pile of straw covered by a blanket. There were only two big beds in this room for six brothers. Now that his oldest brother Paul had married and moved out and his brother above him had ran away a few years ago, it opened up a spot for him on a bed. They did not have a lot of wealth but they made do.

His mother had met his father when they were in school. His father was an only child whose parents had nothing but a rundown three-room cottage while his mother came from wealth. During their last year in school, his father's parents were killed in an accident leaving him with the cottage and the land it sat upon. His father had decided to continue his father's trade as a craftsman and take over the family home.

Against her family's wishes, Lars' mother gave everything up to be with the one she loved. Even though his mother began to drift away and lose her friends and family, they both remained completely happy and in love. His mother did not mind tending to the cottage and the small garden while his father carved and built things to take and sell to the surrounding villages and townships. They lived a poor but comfortable life.

Soon after, his eldest brother Paul was born. Even though it was an extra mouth to feed, they still lived comfortably. It was not until a few years later life got a little tougher. His mother had given birth to three more sons at the same time. This was a rare event, so they took it as a gift from Venēāh and made adjustments. They combined the family room with the kitchen and made the third room into a bedroom for the four boys.

Then in the next year another son was born followed by Lars the year after that. Suddenly his parents had found themselves with six boys to care for. It was rough going for the next few years with money and food being very small. Paul senior knew that in time his sons would be old enough to help with the craftsmen trade and help support the family. As long as they had each other, they could endure anything. And they did.

As the six boys got older, they quickly learned and mastered their father's trade. Working together they made just enough to keep the family going. Everyone made sacrifices and was dedicated to each other, their family home and their father's trade. This was the way it would always be, and the four eldest boys had sworn to it. The only problem came from the two youngest boys. They started to see things differently.

They both felt the same way but for different reasons. As Lorin got older, he got a taste for adventure. He began listening to and making up stories of olden days. He no longer wanted to be tied to this rundown land. He wanted to go out and become famous or discover great adventure. For years he argued with his parents about where he belonged.

Paul Sr. told him he would finish school and then take up the family trade just like all his older brothers. Lorin dreamed of ditching school, grabbing a sword and heading out into the wild unknown. His father and his older brothers had made it clear how things would be under the family roof. With that in mind, the rebel he was at barely the age of fifteen, Lorin grabbed his travel pack and disappeared with nothing but a note left behind.

Lori wanted to go after him but Paul Sr. would not have it. He said that if that was his decision than he would no longer be their concern. That is why Lars was afraid to tell his parents he kind of agreed with Lorin. His was a different agenda from his brother though. He wanted to excel and further his schooling and learning. He wanted to help support his family by going out and achieving a great paying job rather than the hard labor his family did.

Maybe because he was the baby of the family or maybe his mom had softened, but he did tell her and she supported him. She said to study hard and she would help him, but they would have to keep his dream secret from his father until the day came for him to choose his apprenticeship. On that day, they would tell him together. That is what Lars did for the next few years. He studied his heart out.

In a few months I will have to tell dad, Lars thought to himself as his mother's screaming snapped him back to the present. He grabbed his bag of schoolbooks, ran out of his room and kissed his mother.

"About time you got out here. I was afraid you wouldn't have time for breakfast."

"Sorry, mom. Where is everyone?" Lars asked as he but a small piece of bread in his mouth.

"Your father and Paul have already headed out. The township to the north is having a big festival and they wanted to get there and try to sell some of their work. The triplets are out back working."

"Lehbors, your escort has arrived," someone suddenly shouted while pounding upon the door.

Lars kissed his mom goodbye and went out the door. Lars froze as he almost ran into a tall and very muscular guardsman. Standing behind the guardsman was five other guards. Each of them sat atop a great steed. Lars was amazed that so many guards were escorting him. The guardsman quickly lifted Lars up with ease and placed him upon a sixth horse. The man then leapt up and straddled the horse, placing himself right in front of Lars.

"Hold on tight," he shouted back at Lars as he gave the command for his men to move out.

Lars closed his eyes and held onto the man with all his might. He never realized that a horse could move so fast. Just as he began to gain control of his senses, the horse came to a sudden stop. He had no idea what was going on until he looked over to his left and saw what the guards were pointing at. There was a mass of figures surrounding something down at the end of the grassy field, near the edge of a patch of woods.

The guard he was riding with shouted orders and three of the guardsmen drew their swords and raced towards the gathering. As the three riders approached, the figures all stepped back and faced them. Suddenly one of the figures reached down and picked up what they had been huddled around. A half-shredded cow was thrown into the riding guardsmen by what appeared to be a group of men who were fleeing into the woods.

Lars' heart raced as he was lifted from his horse and placed upon the back of another one. He tried not to panic as he kept his eyes on the scene down by the woods. The guardsmen had evaded the flying cow and were in pursuit of the men who had dashed into the woods.

"You two take him to town immediately. Inform Captain Masters what we saw and hurry!" Lars' ex-riding partner shouted as he dashed off after the other three guardsmen.

"So, we rode like crazy till we got here," Lars finished his tale as they all listened with amazement.

"Why would a bunch of men be tearing up a cow?" Anna asked out loud.

"Yuck, that is just gross," Lija shivered as she held her stomach.

"To be honest, I don't think they were men at all."

"Why would you say that, Lars?" Marcus asked placing a hand on his friend's shoulder.

"I know I'm not crazy but I know what I saw. That group of men ran into the forest but I saw something else leave."

"What did you see?"

"Well, as we were riding away I took a quick glance back and I swear that off in the distance, towards the end of the wooded area, figures with wings were disappearing off into the sky."

"Are you sure they weren't just birds?"

"No, Lija, they were not birds. Even though they were far off I could tell they were human-like with wings."

"Maybe they were creatures of magic," Anna said with excitement.

"Don't be silly, Anna. If they were, the alarms would have sounded."

"My sister is right. According to my dad, creatures of magic no longer exist. They are just fantasy stories," Marcus said.

"No, Anna may be right. As much as I hate the idea of magic, Thom says they still exist. According to legend they were all driven into exile and they all live in the Forest of Spirits."

"Even if that was true, Lars, there's no way they could make it clear from Southern Bergonia all the way up here."

"Well, if they had wings like Lars said, it could be possible."

"Maybe so, Anna, but why would they come up here? I don't see how they could have made it out of the forest and pass over the southern kingdoms without being spotted or setting off the alarms," Marcus argued.

Before any of them could continue the conversation, Marcus' dad came through the door. He had a very concerned look on his face. "Adryann!" Broc shouted as he dashed into the kitchen. Moments later he rushed past them and was gone out the door. Adryann followed with a very worried look on her face.

"What's going on mom?" Marcus asked with concern.

"Nothing you kids need to worry about. Your father and his men are heading out to investigate the surrounding boundaries. I suppose he'll be very late getting in tonight," she sighed deeply, "he told me that Thom and Semaj just arrived and that an escort will walk you to school."

Adryann rushed the four out the door as they greeted their other two friends. They had two guards in front of them and two behind them so they had to walk quickly to keep up with their pace. They all noticed that there were more guards patrolling the area than usual. This had to have been the most excitement this town has seen in ages. All six of them could hardly contain themselves but they knew to be cautious in front of the guards.

As they walked, Lars filled Thom and Semaj in on what happened to him on the way in from his home. Semaj laughed but Thom was completely drawn into the magical creature theory. They did not talk a whole lot and kept their voices to a bare whisper in fear of the guards hearing their conversation. Once they reached the school, the guards left and they could speak more freely.

"Guys, I really have a feeling something is going on. First I find this crystal and then we have that weird dream and now the mysterious creatures shredding that cow."

"Thom, don't forget about that strange old man that Marcus and I saw."

"Lija, I don't think that really counts as strange. The more I think of it, we probably were making something out of nothing."

"You both were probably seeing things so you didn't feel left out," Semaj joked.

"I don't think they were. I think he exists."

"Why do you say that, Thom?" Marcus asked and then froze as he saw where Thom was pointing.

"That's him!" Marcus and Lija gasped in unison.

They all stood there staring at their class area, eyes as wide as could be. At the front of the class, behind the teacher's desk, stood someone other than Old Lady Muerte. It was an older man with long brown hair accented by the white streaks that ran all through it. His face was clean-shaven and smooth with just a small touch of wrinkles showing. Even though his long hair covered his ears, you could still see his white-like colored eyes. They almost blew a chill into your heart.

The six shivered in unison from an unseen chilly wind that seemed to come from him. The man walked out from behind the desk, using a small walking stick to limp towards them. Even with the limp, he managed to stand almost six feet tall. He wore all white from his boots, pants and shirt to his cloak that draped over the teacher's chair. He raised his hand and began to motion at all of them.

"Come sit down. Class is about to begin," he instructed with a voice that not only felt chilling but comforting at the same time.

"Who are you and what happened to Miss Muerte?" Marcus asked as they all took their seats quickly looking at each other with panic on their faces.

"Now that everyone is here I will introduce myself. My name is Jesse Niwel, but you may call me Jesse. No need to be formal." Jesse then moved to the center of his desk and sat leaning on the edge balancing on his walking stick that he had placed directly in front of him.

"Miss Muerte has fallen ill. I'm here from the University in Sorran visiting. The head of the school has asked me to fill in for her until she is feeling better. Now let me get to know the rest of you." As he took roll, the six of them watched him carefully.

"This guy gives me the creeps," whispered Lija.

"I know what you're saying. Something about his eyes and his voice gives me the feeling that he's no mere teacher," Anna replied back.

"You guys are being silly," Semaj told them even though he did find it odd how Mr. Niwel was acting so interested in who they all were if he was only filling in for a short time.

"And you are?" Mr. Niwel's question came silencing them all.

"Oh, my name is Semaj. Semaj Kucera," he stuttered as he felt those eyes pierce and drill into his soul looking for answers to something.

"Interesting name you have there. I don't recognize the last name but your first name is unique. Where did your parents come up with that? Do you know the story behind your name?"

"Nothing special to tell," Semaj said trying to look away, "My mother told me that they named me after Mount Semaj." He saw Mr. Niwel's eyes grow bright at the mention of that name of reference. "My father says that Mount Semaj is the tallest mountain in Bergonia. It stands tall, strong and looks over all the land as if protecting it. So that is why I'm named Semaj."

"Does anyone else here know how Mount Semaj got its name?"

"No one knows. It has always been called that. Legend says it is named after a famous warrior from long ago, but no one really knows for sure," Thom chimed in as his classmates agreed in unison. Jesse Niwel calmed them down and leaned back against his desk.

"You are correct, it is named after a great warrior. Possibly the greatest warrior Bergonia has ever seen. However, that will have to be a story for another time. Now, back to our introductions," Jesse said as he stared back and forth from Semaj to Thom, who felt like the old man was looking at his chest, making him graze the spot where his crystal hid with his fingers.

After answering what seemed like a ton of unnecessary questions about his background, family and dreams, Mr. Niwel finally moved on to Anna. Semaj breathed a sigh of relief as he listened to him question his other friends. He did not know if it was just his nervous perception, but it seemed like he was spending more time on the six of them in comparison to the rest of the students. It was as if he was looking for something. He did not know what that would be but he figured that if they could just make it through the rest of the day all would be fine.

The lunch bell rang and the six friends quickly walked away from class and down the other side of the hill. They decided to sit under a bunch of trees to eat their lunches. It gave them some privacy to talk. Lija stood so she would not stain her dress as everyone else sat on the ground. As they ate their lunches, everyone could not help glancing up at where their odd teacher stood, almost staring at them as his gaze swept the area around them.

"Man is that guy weird or what?" Marcus said as he sat down next to his friends.

43

"You're telling me. I don't think he's a teacher at all. I think he did something to Miss Muerte and is after something or someone," Anna agreed, hand instinctively wanting to grab her daggers she kept hidden in her boots.

"Anna, you're always looking for excitement of some kind." Semaj then looked down at his food and added, "I do have to admit though, his eyes were weird. It felt like he was searching for something, especially from one of us." Semaj's eyes went to Thom's chest.

"I know what it is!" Shouted Lars as he moved from Thom's side and leaned over to stare directly at Semaj.

"What?" Everyone asked as they all looked over at him.

"He is undercover for the guards or the king. They know about the books or maybe the crystal and they are looking for them and the person using them. Thom, I told you messing with magic was wrong. You need to get rid of them before they catch you."

"You're over reacting, Lars. No one knows that I have these but you guys. If I had actually managed to use magic, the alarms would have gone off. That old man is just a teacher and you're being a tad paranoid."

"Thom is right. There's nothing to worry about. When school is over today I'll ask my dad and he can check him out for us."

"I think that is a good idea, Marcus, but be careful just in case they are searching for what Thom is hiding," Lars said as he rested back down next to Thom.

As everyone began to finish their lunches and talk about other things, Anna moved over next to Semaj. She had noticed his odd expression and reaction from the conversation they were having about Mr. Niwel. She suddenly felt drawn to him.

"Are you okay?"

"I'm fine, Anna. That guy just gave me a weird feeling and I would just as soon forget about it."

"You know, Semaj, it's okay to let your mind explore the unknown. There's more to life than sitting on a farm."

"Anna, would you please stop?" Semaj began to plead as they both found their hands reaching for the others.

44

Their hearts began to race. They did not know where this feeling from within was coming from but they were being drawn closer. As their hands touched, a surge of energy stung them and caused their hands to jerk back away from each other. They both looked at each other in shock as they felt their hands and then bodies tingle all over inside.

"What just happened?" Semaj whispered to Anna without taking his eyes of his own hand.

"Semaj, Anna, something's happening!" Marcus yelled interrupting them.

"You saw it too?" Anna asked as they realized Marcus and the others were now right next to them.

"How can we not? There are dozens of them," Thom answered.

Semaj and Anna jumped to their feet realizing that their friends were not talking about them. On top of the hill, they heard screaming and saw a bunch of figures running around waving swords as classmates fled. Mr. Niwel was nowhere to be seen.

"Those look like the men I saw this morning."

"Are you sure, Lars?" Thom asked squeezing his hand in fright.

"Marcus, I'm scared. I want to go home," Lija began to cry.

"I think we're in trouble," Anna said as her hidden daggers appeared in her hands with a flick of each boot.

As the group of friends looked in front of them, they saw six of those men moving towards them. They were tall and looked very muscular. They wore all black with a dark blood-red breastplate for armor. They wore no helmets revealing their bald heads and red eyes. They each carried one sword that was made up of a black handle and a red blade that did not look like typical steel. They raised their swords with the intent to attack.

Anna, on instinct, threw her blades at the approaching men as she pulled two more daggers out of her boots. Panic gripped their souls as they saw one of the daggers bounce off the red armor and the second dagger approached one of the strange men. He swung his sword at it, the red blade hitting the dagger and sending it back landing a few feet in front of Anna. They all looked down to see the dagger's blade dented inward from the impact of the other sword.

"What do we do now? They'll be upon us in no time," Lars said as he desperately looked for an escape route while holding on to Thom.

"We can't fight them. Anna's the only one with weapons and we saw how effective those were," Marcus said wishing he had his own sword with him.

"Don't worry my young friends. Hope is not yet lost." They all gasped as they suddenly noticed Mr. Niwel standing between them and the approaching men.

"Oh great, what is he going to do, question them to death?" Thom laughed nervously.

The older man glanced at the six of them. His eyes and skin were shifting to a white-like color. He held out his arms and turned back to face the approaching men. They could all feel the wind beginning to pick up. The men screamed with anger and Marcus blinked as he thought he saw them starting to change their appearances. Before he could be sure, strong gusts of wind came from all directions and hit the approaching men lifting them up and blowing them back and out of site.

Suddenly they heard a massive roar come from the top of the hill. All the men that were up there had suddenly stopped and were looking straight down at them. Mr. Niwel turned and quickly pointed his hands towards the top of the hill. The wind shifted direction and blasted the men over the hill and out of site. He then lowered his arms and fell to one knee.

"Mr. Niwel!" Marcus shouted as he went to his side.

"I'm okay, my boy. It has been ages since I have used such force of power."

"How did you use such magic without raising the alarms?" Thom asked, his heart pounding.

"Like those creatures, my power has nothing to do with magic."

"You're not really a school teacher are you, Mr. Niwel?" Anna said eyeing him closely.

"No, I am not. My true name is Essej."

"What's going on? Who are those men?" Semaj chimed in.

"Those are no ordinary men. Those creatures are called Drogans. There will be enough time for explanations later. I have bought us some time but we need to get out of here quickly. Those things will not rest till they have the one of you they are searching for."

"They are after one of us? Why?" Lars began to panic, looking at Thom.

"No time for that now. We have to get out of here."

"Where are we going?" Marcus asked.

"I have a place we can hide once we get out of town. Quickly now!" He shouted as Marcus helped him up and move onwards.

Not sure of what was really happening to them, they all followed Marcus and Essej. It was better to find a place of safety and hear this old man out than it was to risk facing those men he called Drogans. Marcus knew the town well and managed to help them make it out without being spotted. They were almost near the path that led into a patch of woods when two of the Drogans appeared blocking their escape route.

"Surrender the man children to us," hissed one of the men.

"Never, they are now under my protection."

Marcus steadied Essej as he raised his arms, skin and eyes turning the whitish color again. This time a small boom sounded as a vacuum of air was sucked completely away from the area around the Drogans causing them to gasp and fall to the ground unconscious. Still weak from his last performance, Essej dropped to the ground, barely able to stay conscious himself. He knew until he got used to using his gifts again, he would be more of a hindrance than help.

"We need to get to safety fast," Essej whispered as Marcus and Semaj helped him to his feet.

"There is no escape for you. We will have what we came for. Grab the man children and kill that old fool!"

They all turned to see four more of the Dogran's behind them. This time they were in for a surprise. The Drogans began shifting form right before their eyes. One minute they were men and the next they were something else. They grew taller and broader. Their skin went from flesh to a more scale-like substance that was the color of red. Their hands became claws, as their faces looked more like snouts baring sharp teeth. Medium Dragon-like wings the color of fire sprang from their backs.

They all stood there in shock and began to panic at the sight of these Dragon-like men standing in front of them. One of the Drogans opened its mouth and a ball of fire erupted from it. Moving at an alarming speed, the ball of fire raced directly at Thom. Essej was too weak to act against the fire attack. Everyone began to scream as Lars instinctively shoved Thom out of the way and was consumed by the blast of fire.

"No!" Screamed Thom as the others began to scream out in tears at the sight before them.

Essej used what strength he had left to take control of a pocket of air to cause the fire consuming the screaming Lars to snuff out. Lars's body dropped to the ground in silence. Thom crawled to Lars and cradled his charred body in his arms. He could hear the creatures laughing as he cried. Lars' eyes opened and looked up at him.

"I will always love you," Lars whispered, trying to reach for Thom's face but failed as the life faded from his body.

Thom let out a huge scream as he laid Lars' body on the ground and stood up. Grief and anger seemed to be powering his body now. Everyone, including the Drogans kept their eyes on him as the crystal under his shirt began to radiate a bright white-blue light. The crystal lifted up and over his shirt exposing itself for all to see. Out of nowhere, images began to form in Thom's mind, as he looked directly at the Drogans letting his mind form words to his lips.

"Werpo Llba Fo Gicma!" Thom commanded, pointing his finger at the Drogans.

Suddenly a small ball of white energy appeared at the tip of Thom's finger. With great speed, it shot out towards the Drogans growing larger with each second as it approached them. Before the murderous creatures could leap out of the way, the ball of energy hit them causing a huge explosion. Flames and millions of Drogan pieces laid everywhere. Thom then dropped to the ground unconscious.

"What did he just do? The alarms are not sounding. Did he use the same power you have?" Anna started asking Essej while still wiping away her tears. Like her friends, the shock of what just happened to Lars and with Thom not setting in.

"No, that was definitely magic. As to why it was shielded, that is a mystery," Essej nodded as he looked over at the crystal that slowly dimmed out.

"I want my mom. I want my mom," Lija cried repeatedly as Anna held her best friend in her arms. Lija was now going into hysterics.

"Is Thom?" Semaj asked as he saw Marcus lifting him up in his arms.

"No, he is alive, thank Venēăh, but poor Lars," Marcus cried at the sight of his best friend, lying there, burned and lifeless.

"What do we do?" Semaj kneeled down by Lars' body.

"I know he was a friend of yours but there is nothing you can do. We have to go while we still can."

"Essej, are you crazy? We just can't leave him here," Semaj cried.

"Semaj, you must understand. Already heading this way will be dozens of Drogans. Not only will that explosion bring them but the guardsmen will be here too. If we don't get to safety now, you will all surely die. I don't have enough strength to take on either of them. Don't let your young friend's sacrifice be for not."

"I hate to say this, but Essej is right. Lars was my best friend but staying here and dying would dishonor what he did for Thom. We have to get my sister and the others out of danger. Once we do that, Essej will have a lot of explaining to do. We will come back for him, I promise."

Everyone quickly paid their respects to Lars and followed after Essej. Semaj helped support the mysterious stranger's weight as he led them all into the woods. Marcus carried the unconscious Thom as Anna held and pushed Lija onward. No one said anything. It all seemed so unreal. They moved on as this unbelievable nightmare forced them into hiding, consumed with grief and fear, while leaving a great friend behind.

Chapter Three:
Lucian & The Unknown Lands

Once again, the night had taken over the land and the glow of the Fire Mountains could be seen lighting up the northern horizon. The dry heat and warm air caused by the mountains cooled ever so slightly with the coming of dark. Lucian Darkheart did not mind the hot climate for he found the glow from the mountains to be breathtaking and well worth the burden of the day's heat. With a sigh, Lucian walked away from his window and stepped in front of a blackened mirror. Not everything could be viewed as beauty.

"Lectref," Lucian whispered with a wave of his hand as the blackened mirror shimmered and became reflective glass. Lucian winced at what he saw looking back at him. Peering back was the image of a young man almost six feet tall with an average build, black shoulder length hair, emerald green eyes, and a nicely trimmed goatee. Lucian frowned as he stared at his shirtless body, the mirror revealing his deformity that covered every inch of skin on his body with purple blotches that looked rough and callused but very smooth to the touch.

As much as he loved beautiful things, he hated that he would never have beauty himself. He knew he was repulsive to look at so he wore long black-dyed hair and bore facial hair to help mask his purplish face. As for the rest of his body he always wore clothing, including gloves that never exposed an inch of skin. Those that got close enough to reveal shock at his scared face usually did not live to tell the tale. It made him feel lonely and ugly at times. He was always wishing he could be with someone who would gaze at him with love and wanted to be with him for him. Not because they wanted something or because of *who* he was. Especially not these subjects and servants who come to him, trying to pretend that he wasn't grotesque because of fear of his position as their lord and prince.

It wasn't so much his deformity but the memories and stories behind it that made him wince and then fill with anger. Anger that helped drive him into becoming the young man he was today with the ambition and desire to inflict revenge upon the non-magic humans while crushing and taking over the Five Kingdoms of Bergonia. They had done this to him and destroyed his family. They were the ones who were responsible for this life he lived.

The mirror became black again with his command as he stepped away and stared back out into the night's sky. His father, along with his father's most trusted friend and Lucian's teacher, the Fire Elf Docanesto, had revealed the truth to him when he had been old enough to understand it all. That truth of what had happened to him, his father, his family and why they lived in the Unknown Lands cut off from the rest of Bergonia is what motivated every one of his actions and right now, occupied his thoughts.

His parents had lived in a small village in the southernmost part of the Fifth Kingdom, otherwise known as the Kingdom of Argoth. The village had rested between the Eastern Sea and the southern tip of the Old River Gorge that separated the Kingdom of Argoth from the Forest of Spirits. His father had been the village leader and everyone loved him and his wife. The village even held a celebration when word got out that his parents were going to have a baby. They were the center of attention and worshiped by all until they had discovered his father's little secret.

At night, his father would take a raft and sneak down the coast until he reached the bank of the Forest of Spirits. There he was safe from prying eyes and the magic alarms of the Five Kingdoms. There he would meet his best childhood friend, Docanesto, and they would practice magic. Even though magic was forbidden and outlawed, his father would meet his friend every night to study and try and develop a way to use magic for good. They had done this for years until the night of Lucian's birth.

Lucian's father had been heading home from his nightly meeting unaware that the village people had a spy watching him the last few days. That night, the village spy had seen him practice magic in the forest with an Elf and had then rushed off to tell the village people. They all gathered and then marched toward his parent's home just as Lucian's father had stepped through the door to see the midwife helping with the birth of his son.

After a few moments the midwife was wrapping a beautiful screaming baby boy into a blanket. The midwife placed the baby in his mother's arms as they all smiled with joy. His father had stepped closer as his mother, pulled back the blanket and revealed Lucian to his father. His father took a short pause when he noticed a dark birthmark oh his child's stomach in what appeared to be the shape of a heart. Of course, he was the only one to think nothing of it.

"Look upon the spawn of evil. It bares the father's evil mark of magic!" Lucian's father turned toward the voice to see a man waving a torch outside the bedroom window. Behind the man was a mob of village people waving torches and different forms of weaponry. They had all begun to shout and demand he turn himself over, along with his demon child.

"You all are crazy. Go home now before I call the guards," his father had warned.

"The guards are here with us. I saw you doing magic in the forest. Turn yourself in."

"I don't know what you are talking about," his father had shouted with fear but was cut off as a torch crashed through the window setting the bed on fire. "Go for cover" he shouted as his wife, who held on tight to the child and leapt from the flaming bed. The midwife grabbed water to toss over the fire. Shouts of storming the house drew his attention away from his family.

Anger, fear and panic had taken over his father as he suddenly reached out his hands and began reciting words he had been taught by his best friend. Suddenly a huge flaming ball of fire appeared and then flew out through the broken window and into the crowd of village people. Those that jumped clear watched in fright as those who had been consumed by the fire began to scream loud enough to match the belting of the magic alarms.

Before his father could contemplate what he had just done, a mob of people broke through the front door. They grabbed his father and drug him outside as he fought with all his might. As they beat him with their hands and weapons he had tried with all his might to summon the magic to protect his family. Suddenly the mob stopped as another group of villagers caused the small home to explode in flames. They all had watched and cheered as his mom's dying screams pierced the night, almost muffling the sound of the magic alarms.

With all the strength he could gather within, his father stood up and began to summon every ounce of magic and power he had left. His body draining as he shouted odd words and forcing his wish and desires to take shape. The village people turned towards the emotional husband and father in awe as he began to glow and a huge portal opened right above his head. A great vacuum started to pull the village people towards the opened portal. His father had laughed as he commanded the portal to send them all to Léhl for what they had done to his family.

He stopped laughing when he felt a strange tingle. He looked down to see a dagger sticking into his leg. One of the men had managed to throw the dagger at him before being sucked into the portal. Before he could react, another man lunged at him and managed to thrust a pitchfork into his chest before the portal grabbed and sucked the villager inside it. Lucian's father swayed as the glow vanished and the portal began to close.

"No … you must … all pay," his father had whispered spitting out blood and attempting to gain control of the magic again. As the portal closed the power of the vacuum had ceased, releasing its hold on the remaining murderers. Two men quickly ran forward, grabbed him and hoisted him up and into the portal. Lucian's father screamed his final breath as he vanished along with the portal. The villagers, satisfied with having killed the magic user and his family, headed back into the village to carry on with their lives.

In their celebration they had overlooked two things. Little Lucian still crying softly and a strange man running up to the burning home. Docanesto had heard the magic alarms go off and made haste for he only knew of one person who could have set them off and that he must be in danger. He had arrived too late to help his best friend and gasped in horror at what he just witnessed. He watched his best friend murdered, thrown into a vanishing portal, and the burning house collapsing inward in a blaze of fire as the mob of people walked away.

Wiping away a tear, Docanesto ran to the house ruins. He knew that no one could still be alive in what was left of the burning home. He was going to leave when he heard Lucian's small whimper. Heart racing, Docanesto found a section that he could peer into. Burning pieces of the home lay atop two charred and lifeless bodies. He soon noticed a small moving hand under one of the dead women.

Taking advantage of his Elven eyes and ears, he could tell that the baby was still alive but barely. The mother's body was acting as a shield from the fire for her baby. Knowing the magic alarms would take a few more minutes to shut off, he acted quickly. Using his magic, he put a protective shield around his body and dove into the burning home. Using his strength and magic, he had made it out and away from the doomed house with the small baby.

When he was far enough from the wreckage, he placed the baby on the ground. He could tell the baby was badly burned and barely breathing. Placing his hands on the newborn, he called forth what magic he had left to try to heal the little one. When the glow faded, Docanesto sighed, his energy severely spent. He smiled as he looked down upon a laughing baby boy. Even though he was able to give life back to this child, his magic was unable to remove the scares from the fire. The baby's skin, from head to toe, was forever marked by this night.

"I too, find myself thinking back to the day of your birth, Lucian, and I smile."

Lucian turned around quickly grabbing a shirt and putting it on. Normally he would punish an intruder for coming into his room unannounced, but the person in front of him caused him to stop and calm down. The figure pushed back the dark hood of his black & silver streaked cloak to reveal the face of Lucian's mentor and adoptive father Docanesto.

"Why? It was the day the normals took away my family and you lost yours."

"I smile because it was the day I gained a son."

"Which caused your people to disown you and send you off into exile."

"That is true, but if I had not chosen you over my Elven kin we would have never come into the Unknown Lands and met the witch sisters." Docanesto crossed the room and looked up into Lucian's eyes. "Thanks to them and their magic, we were reunited with the spirit of your real father and my best friend."

Lucian was touched by his mentor's words, but anger still filled his heart. He had been reunited with his father, but because of the normals, it was only a spirit, which was barely held into this world by the mercy of the four witch sisters. He had to find a way to bring his father back before the witches lost their hold on him, losing him forever. Until then, he had to focus on their revenge.

As he had grown into young adulthood, we watched as Docanesto and his father's spirit worked towards being able to wage war against the normals of the Five Kingdoms, conquering and allowing them to rule a land of magic once again. His fathers worked on building a large empire in the Unknown Lands, along with creating an army of great force, and training Lucian to become a powerful figure to lead them all to victory.

Over the years, they had drilled Lucian with lessons as he quickly mastered his education and skills in combat and weaponry as well as the art of magic, which was propelled by his desire for revenge. They were shaping Lucian into the fearless warrior and leader they would need. During this same time, they were able to convince the creatures and beings of the Unknown Lands as well as any others that came there, to unify and swear allegiance to Lucian and his father.

The Unknown Lands quickly became an empire as Castle Darkheart was built in the center of what Lucian's father now called the City of Greb. Preaching the great cause to reclaim the Five Kingdoms from the normals and help from magical experiments, a great army was quickly forming. Everything was almost ready for Lucian. They would soon take back what had been taken from them. No one could stop them, except for one.

"Have we received word from the Drogans?" Lucian asked as he walked away from his mentor changing the conversation and mood to the concerns of the present.

"Yes, the Chosen One has been found."

"Where?" Lucian's adrenaline levels began to rise as he turned back towards the Fire Elf. "Have they managed to capture the evil that plans to stand in our way?"

"They spotted the Chosen One in the township of Soré, which is located in the Kingdom of Sorran," Docanesto quickly informed the young prince. "They have not yet captured the evil human who has, for now, managed to slip into hiding. Word has been sent out to the other search parties to move quickly to Soré and help with the search and capture."

"Good, we need to be careful though. Send General Vex. I want that town completely taken over. No one leaves the city. Those that approach are immediately taken prisoner. This way we can rip the town apart to search and capture our prey without alerting King Sirus."

"I'll send him immediately." Docanesto bit his tongue. He may be the prince, but he only allowed the young boy to think he was in charge because his father had asked Docanesto to do so to help with his training and confidence. The minute he failed or lacked the ability to lead, Docanesto would do what needed to be done, son or not.

"One more thing," Lucian caught his mentor before he stepped out of his bedroom. "Make it clear that they are not to needlessly kill anyone unless there is no other choice. We can use the townspeople and the town for a secret base of operations within the Kingdom of Sorran. It could prove useful for another stage of our plans later on."

With that, Docanesto disappeared from Lucian's sight. They were so close he could taste it. He refused to push the rest of their plans forward until he had a handle on this Chosen One. According to his father's spirit, it was prophesized that a being would be born with a power that could stop his army from prevailing over the evil normals of the Five Kingdoms of Bergonia.

Lucian did not believe in those superstitious stories, but he did not want to take any chances, so he made a point to be cautious and patient. He only began to worry about this prophesized Chosen One after he had felt the first surge of this unknown power. This proved what his fathers had told him and about his ability to sense it. After this, he decided to take his father seriously and sent the Drogans out. After this and the strange dream he had the day before, he was convinced that this Chosen One was out there and could pose a threat to him.

He had thought about telling his father or even Docanesto about the previous day's dream but decided against it. A part of him kept telling him to wait and hold his tongue. There was more he wanted to explore before he brought it to his father's attention. Saying anything right now might panic his father and cause delay in their plans for conquest. He had been taught that patience was a virtue and he would bide his time.

For now, he would focus on what they had to do next. They had already secured a hold on one of the Five Kingdoms. When the time came, that kingdom would bow down and hand over complete control and allegiance to him. *Whether the king knows it or not,* Lucian smiled to himself. Even though they had a plan in the works for taking the Kingdom of Sorran, this sudden presence in Soré could turn out to be a helpful backup. As long as nothing went wrong that would tip off King Sirus or any of the other kingdoms of Lucian and his father's plans, they should be victorious. However, there was always that chance, a small chance they could fail.

That chance was the Chosen One turning up. That wild card could prove troublesome and had to be squashed quickly and quietly. With a little luck, hopefully both goals could be achieved without one affecting the other and not delay or prevent their takeover of the Five Kingdoms. Once they had two of the five they could then move in on the other three kingdoms. This should not be too hard to do, except for the Kingdom of Erikson.

The Kingdom of Erikson was the home of very skilled and powerfully trained warriors. They were trained to battle and prevail over all adversaries, magical or not, but specifically the creatures of magic. Out of all the Kingdoms of Bergonia, Erikson's hatred and intolerance for magic was the strongest. That is why they had declared themselves the guardians against the Forest of Spirits that lay on their southern border.

Even though many felt the Forest of Spirits being a home for the last remaining creatures of magic was a myth, they still never entered it. They had a superstition that the forest was haunted and that anyone who entered would never return. So, they trained and placed their guards to watch the borders to make sure nothing ever came out of it, and if something ever did, they could and would kill it.

They would be the hardest to conquer, but he had a plan and the army to do it. Once Erikson fell, then there would be no others to stand in his way. He would have three kingdoms in his power and the remaining kingdoms would not stand a chance since one did not believe in fighting and the other was isolated from and oblivious to the world around them. Lucian's eyes began to grow heavy as he dreamed of revenge and of new beginnings.

Lucian suddenly jumped as his body has hit by a sharp surge of power. He immediately opened his eyes and stood up. He looked around and realized he was no longer in his room. He was standing on a cliff somewhere in the Unknown Lands. He could almost feel the heat from the Fire Mountains but yet he was untouched. At that moment he knew what was going on.

"The dreams are happening again," he whispered to himself, "I can feel it. The Chosen One is using the power again. Last time this happened I was able to faintly see them and I think they saw me."

Lucian walked to the edge of the cliff and closed his eyes. He let the power signature overwhelm him and he began to concentrate. He could feel a pull and a connection within the source to the person causing it. He then opened his eyes and could now see beyond the Fire Mountains towards the location of the Chosen One.

He knew that it was coming from far away. Even though he could see images, they were still blurry and hard to totally make out. He knew that if he were closer he would probably see things a lot clearer. For now, he would have to do his best to make it all out and see what he needed to know. There was a message in all this.

He had come to realize that his connections to the dreams were more than just a way to locate the Chosen One. At first, he had used it and his magic to find a location. Then he realized that if he didn't focus so much on location and surrendered himself to the dreams he could learn a lot more. For some reason the dreams were pulling him, and the Chosen One, he assumed to something.

Last time, he faintly made out a giant hill covered in flames with people standing on it. When he woke, he sent a message to his Drogans. As it turned out, they found that the township of Soré had a large hill. Soon after the power was used again and right there the Chosen One had been discovered proving his vision right. He had to do it again. This way he could keep one step ahead of them and have a surprise waiting for them when they got there.

Lucian looked closely and all he could make out were giant mountain ranges. He swore to himself, he just could not see past the Fire Mountains. Just as he was about to turn away he realized he had made an error. He looked again and saw he had been wrong. Those were not the Fire Mountains he was looking at. These mountains did not glow red. Instead, they were covered in white.

He looked at every detail he could make out at this distance. It appeared to be a whole series of large mountains covered with a substance called snow. He had never seen or touched something so cold but he had learned about it in his teachings. He was about to turn away when something else began to happen.

The mountains had begun to shake fiercely. He could not feel them but he sensed tremors of great force. Something was happening to the ground causing the mountains to shake. He could not make out much more then what might look like figures dodging falling rocks and eruptions of earth from the ground. Then, like last time, he felt like he made eye contact with one of the figures.

A force of energy came his way forcing him back. At the moment of impact Lucian jumped awake at his desk. He wiped the sweat away from his brow as he looked around. He was back in his room. It had been a dream. He quickly jumped up and ran to the map he had pinned to the wall.

"Servant, fetch me Docanesto at once," Lucian shouted as he looked over the vague map of Bergonia. He had to find what he had seen in his dream.

There were only five mountain ranges that he was aware of. He could easily rule out three of them; The Fire Mountains of the Unknown Lands, the cluster of mountains on The Forbidden Isles, and the Western Mountains on Ogra because they were not located actually on the land of Bergonia. That left only two ranges of mountains.

The Northern Mountains and the Eastern Mountains, that ran down the coast of the Kingdom of Sorran, were the remaining choices and both were also near Soré. Lucian had to think. It had to be the very snow covered Northern Mountains. In his dream the mountain range was also very large and the Eastern Mountains were just a small strip running down a coastline.

"You called for me?" Lucian jumped at the sound of the Fire Elf's voice.

"I hate it when you do that, Docanesto."

"Sorry, Lucian, but you need to remember to be more aware of your surroundings."

"I have no time for lectures. I know where the Chosen One is escaping to."

"How do you know this?"

"I had..." Lucian began and then remembered he was not quite ready to divulge everything yet, "felt another one of those power surges. That is why I was studying the map so closely. My magic points to a certain spot on the map. This evil creature plans to escape into the Northern Mountains."

"I will send a message to General Vex to have the Drogans head into the Northern Mountains."

"No, Docanesto, I don't want them to go. I need them to focus on Soré. We need that area secure and need them searching just in case I'm wrong about this," Lucian said as he turned and walked over to look out his window. "Plus, I can't risk those idiots causing a stir with the Dwarves. We don't know what has become of them up there and there is no need to draw them out of their isolation from the world just yet."

"I agree. Involving the Dwarves could be an added wild card in our plans. I will go then."

"No, you are needed here. I want this done quickly and quietly. I want to send Natureza."

"That is out of the question. Natureza is too free and not completely sworn to our cause. Perhaps we should speak with your father and see what he thinks a good course of action would be."

"No, that is not necessary. Natureza is loyal to me and that should be enough," Lucian interrupted as his voice grew loud and harsh, "My father has too much going on to be worried about this. He put trust in me to find and capture this Chosen One. My father would also agree that you couldn't go to the Northern Mountains. You'll be needed on another important mission."

"What you speak is true, but it is important that we succeed. Sometimes your youth blinds you."

"Docanesto, my father may be coming back to the world but until then I am the lord and master." Lucian quickly stepped directly in front of his mentor. "This is my decision."

"Yes, master," Docanesto whispered between gritted teeth.

"Natureza has my full trust as a follower and as a converted Fire Elf," Lucian said as he backed away towards his window. "I think the Wild Elf heritage that still dominates from within along with Natureza's unique Elven talent is what we need to sneak into the Dwarven territory and bring our prey back without any trouble."

"I'll inform Natureza immediately."

Lucian sighed as he watched his mentor and teacher disappear to carry out his orders. He hated treating him like that but he had to. If Docanesto or his father got to the Chosen One first he would not get the answers to some questions he needed answered. Using Natureza, he could trust receiving the Chosen One first before being handed over to his father. For now, his dreams and the questions they brought had to be his alone for now to answer.

****

Docanesto walked into the dark chamber hidden below Castle Darkheart. This was a very secluded chamber that was well-hidden and protected. If someone had managed to get past the first two guards on the first level and then defeated the two Fire Elves outside the chamber door, they would still have to get through the actual door itself. Only the right magic would allow it to open. Even if that was possible, there were a few other secret traps, but for Docanesto, he could enter with ease.

The chamber was very dark with only a faint glow coming from the center of the room. Even though he could see well enough in the dark with his Elven eyes, Docanesto felt the need for a little light. "Rchto Ghtli," Docanesto said with a wave of his hand calling forth his will into the magical words and gesture that caused the nearby torches on the walls to ignite in flame. Now he could see the chamber more clearly.

Docanesto looked around the very damp and chilled room. The room was almost completely barren with only two doors. The one he came in from and the door on the far-left wall that served as a secret entrance into the castle's dungeon. Besides the torches, the only other items kept in the room were the belongings, special objects and ingredients needed by the four witch sisters. Docanesto glanced to his left and saw the Fire Elf by the dungeon entrance. He was the only other being that stayed in this room along with the four sisters.

Docanesto walked toward the center of the room where the four sisters laid on the cold stone floor sleeping soundly. It did not bother him that they slept for they were not as defenseless as they appeared. If any object, life form or magic energy got within a certain distance of them a special barrier would form and wake them immediately. Without moving any farther, he glanced at what the sister slept around.

Right there, in the dead center of the chamber was what had given off the faint glow when he had entered the room. It was a large magical symbol that he and the four witch sisters had carved into the stone floor, about a few inches in depth and empowered with magic. The outer outline was a large diamond shape that came to four points, north, south, east and west. At each point was a large circular dot large enough for one person to stand in. Each dot had a straight line that ran directly inward of the diamond and stopped after a couple feet when they connected with a giant carved circle. Within the circle were a series of holes that formed the shape of a star-like pentagram.

It had taken many years, but eventually with the help of the witch sisters, they had created the design. This design, along with the help of the four witch sister's magic, they were able to open a portal that allowed their master to appear before them. The magic was not powerful enough, nor have they the knowledge or ability, to bring him fully back to this world. It was enough to allow his spirit to pass through and still cling on to the world he was forced to once leave until they found a way to bring him back completely.

"Witches, wake up!"

Docanesto grew angry when they did not respond to his command. They were either in one of their deep healing and energizing sleeps or they were ignoring him. Even though the chamber was magically created to imprison them here, its magic also bonded with the sisters to prolong and sustain their lives. He knew the chamber's magic was not enough and that they needed their healing sleep too, but he urgently needed them.

Docanesto shouted a few words and series of balls made of pure light flew from his fingers and headed right for the witches. Just before they reached their targets, a barrier of energy appeared around the sisters, absorbing the balls of light as they impacted with it. A surge of energy from the barrier hit each sister forcing them awake and on their knees. As they stared at the intruder they each stood up as the barrier was sent away.

"How dare you wake us from our sleep," one of the sisters snarled.

"I need to speak with Drol Greb immediately."

"Is there danger?" Chimed one sister.

"Something seriously wrong?" Asked another.

"No, but there is something that has come up and I need to speak to him."

"We are too weak."

"If there is no danger, there is no need to call our master."

Docanesto stared at each of them with intense anger. He took deep breaths as his eyes went from one sister to the other. It was very uncommon and rare for a mother to give birth to three children at once let alone four. All four of these sisters were born healthy and identical, but that was not the case anymore. No one knew just how old these sisters were but time had caused them to hunch over, turn their hair straggly white and leaving their skin old and wrinkly along with raspy voices.

All four sisters wore filthy faded black robes and walked with the help of canes. The only way to tell them apart was that Thea had her right eye sealed shut, Thia had only her pinky fingers and thumbs on each hand, Tia had no left arm and Tea wore a cloth around her head covering her eyes since they had been both burned away. Never the less, Docanesto knew that despite how they looked they were still very powerful together.

"Dingbin Oseno," Docanesto shouted the fail-safe magic words his master had created that defied the barrier and formed tight rings around the sister's necks.

"Please we can't breathe."

"Then you will summon the master now."

"Yes, we'll do it. But we'll need a special sacrifice to do this," Thea gasped for breath as the rings vanished from around their necks.

"You are in luck," Docanesto said as he turned toward the guard, "bring me the Elven spy."

The door shimmered and the guard was gone. After a few minutes he arrived with a small Elven boy whose gray painted body was fading back to a normal flesh tone. Docanesto motioned to the Fire Elf as the guard dragged the screaming Elf to the center of the magic symbol. The four witch sisters then whispered a few words in unison causing the Elf's hands, legs and neck to bind to the design of the star. Docanesto smiled as he watched the coming ritual.

Each sister stepped onto one of the spots located on the four tips of the diamond. One of the sisters waved her hand and spikes came up through the holes that made up the star design piercing the screaming Elf's body. The Elf's screams began to die as the blood and life drained from his body. The blood quickly filled in the carved circle surrounding him. As the blood over filled and ran down the four straight lines leading to each sister it took on a small glow.

"Odblo Ot Rgyene Llfi Su Pu," all four sisters chanted in unison over and over as the blood hit their feet.

As each drop of blood touched the sister's spot it turned from liquid to energy, engulfing each of the sisters from head to toe. After a few minutes the sisters stopped their chanting. Each of them glowed brightly with energy as all traces of blood were gone and the body of the lifeless Elf dissolved into mist. Each sister then stretched their arms or stub straight out running parallel to the carved lines of the diamond that connected each of the four sister's dots.

The sisters began chanting things Docanesto could not make out. Suddenly energy shot out from the sister's arms causing the diamond lines to glow bright. With the same force, energy shot out from each sister heading down the front lines hitting the circle they surrounded. Blue energy swirled around the circle creating a cylinder looking barrier. After a few more chants, the sisters went silent and dropped to their knees, heads down as the energy continued on.

"My master," Docanesto whispered as he went to one knee as the image of a large face appeared within the glowing barrier.

"Rise my old friend. Why do you summon me?"

"I do not wish to go against Lucian's wishes but I felt I must tell you of his recent actions," the Fire Elf explained as he rose and then recited all of what Lucian had done and instructed him to do without word to his father.

"I am glad you came to me. Despite what we want Lucian to believe, your loyalties will always lie with me first and foremost," the sound of the glowing head's voice responded.

"What shall I do?"

"I think there is no harm in this and we should let it be. I doubt that he'll find what he's looking for in the Northern Mountains. There is no way the Chosen One made it past the Drogans. If we deny Lucian his orders it may stir things up and we're not ready for the truth to come out yet."

"I shall fulfill his orders immediately."

"Wait, before you go. Is your daughter still trying to find ways of gaining your complete attention and approval?'

"Yes, but you know Lucian will always come first to me."

"Don't worry. Maybe we can use this to our advantage. Have her follow Natureza. Under no circumstances is she to reveal herself. She will be our secret eyes and ears for what Lucian is having Natureza carry out."

"You are always so wise and cunning, my Lord. All will be done."

Docanesto exited the chamber with haste to locate his daughter and Natureza. The glowing head vanished along with all the glowing energy surrounding the symbol and the four witches. Each of the sisters then collapsed with exhaustion as the chamber went completely dark.

Chapter Four:
Essej's Tale & The Quest Begins

Semaj woke up to the sound of birds singing wildly outside the window above him. He rubbed his temples to ease the pain in his head. It seemed like such a terrible dream. None of it could have been real. As he sat up and looked around the small room, he got one good look at his friends and realized that his fears were true. In this strange and very small room, Thom sat staring at the wall in a trance as Anna rocked a sobbing Lija in her arms while Marcus stood over him peeking out the window. They were all here except for poor Lars and...

"Where is the old guy?" Semaj asked as he quickly sat up from the hard floor, wiping the freshly started tears from his eyes.

"He left a few moments ago," Marcus answered as he knelt down near his friend. "He was ranting about one of us using *the power* again and he had to make sure we wouldn't be discovered."

"This seems so strange. I can't believe this is happening. I can't believe Lars is gone."

"I know what you mean. Lars was my best friend and I swore I would always protect him and I have failed."

"Don't think that way. He died saving Thom. What he did was very brave."

"I know, and poor Thom, how he must feel."

"How's he doing?"

"Well, when he woke up he began calling out for Lars. After I told him where we were and explained all that has happened he just turned towards the wall and has been staring at it ever since."

"I'll go over and see if I can talk to him. How are the girls holding up?"

"Anna is tough, she'll be fine, but my sister I think has been traumatized by the whole event. Anna is taking care of her for me."

"What do we do now? I mean we can't go home. Not with those creatures hunting for us." Semaj stood up. Stretching out his stiff back, he walked over to Thom.

"I don't know what's going on, but what I do know is that a certain old man is going to be answering a lot of questions. I don't think his presence at our school was a coincidence and I'm holding him responsible for what happened to Lars." Marcus pounded his fist against the wall as he went back to gazing out the window.

"Thom, how're you doing?"

Semaj sat down next to his best friend. No reply came for his question. Thom continued to stare at the wall, tears running down his cheeks from red puffy eyes. Semaj put his arm around his friend wishing he could do something to make things better.

"Thom, it'll be okay, I promise."

With that, Thom leaned into Semaj's arms and began to cry. Semaj just held him, letting his best friend mourn the loss of the one he loved. Semaj did not know what they were going to do next. They would just have to wait till the old man returned and see what happens. All Semaj knew was he wished he was back with his parents tending to the farm.

"We're safe for now, but we better not stay here much longer," boomed a voice as everyone jumped at the sudden return. "Those creatures haven't figured out that we are this far from the town. That won't last, especially if *the power* is used again. We better get moving."

"We're not going anywhere with you," Marcus shouted grabbing the old man's arm, "not until you start explaining what's going on here."

"We don't have time. Trust me, I mean you no harm. We just need to get to a safer place," Essej replied shaking his arm free as he faced the angry young man.

"Marcus is right. If you don't tell us what's going on, I swear I'll do to you what I did to those murdering creatures," Thom shouted as he snapped back to life, pushing Semaj aside and heading for the old man. Semaj jumped up quickly and came to his side to hold him back.

"Calm down, Thom, there will be no more killing. As for you, it's time to start talking."

Essej looked at the girl named Anna as she spoke. Even though she was calm he could see the fire in her eyes. Everything had happened so fast and did not go the way he had hoped it would. As much as he would like to push them onward, he knew that if he expected them to follow and trust him, he would have to provide answers. He sat down upon the floor and motioned for the others to do the same.

"You are correct. It has been a long time since I have conversed with people and tend to forget myself."

"Who are you? What are those creatures? What does this all have to do with us?" The five of them started shouting out questions as they took to the floor in front of the old man.

"Gather close and I will try and answer all your questions. Be warned I may not know all the answers but I will tell you what I know. My name is Essej Lewin and I am here to honor a promise I made to a very dear companion of mine."

"What was this promise and who did you make it to?" Marcus asked trying to calm his anger for his sister, who had finally calmed down and was sitting next to him.

"His name was Semaj Lightheart, and he died during the final battle with the evil Drol Greb."

"Wait a minute. Are you lying to us? According to myth, that final battle ended the Magic Wars, which in turn lead to the banishment of all magic," Thom exclaimed as he filled with passion on the topic of all things magical.

"That's no myth my son, it's all true."

"I've studied this. If you really knew Semaj Lightheart, then you were alive during the Magic Wars, making you over four hundred years old and that's not possible."

"Actually, I am one thousand, four hundred and ten of your years old and it is possible," Essej smiled as he pushed back his long brown white-streaked hair to reveal two pointed ears.

"I can't believe it! You're an Elf?" Thom shouted in surprise, his sadness temporarily suppressed.

"He can't be. Mom says that Elves are just make-believe."

"I assure you Lija, Elves are just as real as all of you but I am only part Elf. My mother was half Elf and half human."

"That explains your powers you used. It was Elven magic."

"Not quite," Essej smiled at Thom's statement.

"If Elves are real, then where are they? Where's your family?" Anna asked as she began to take great interest in this half-Elf's story.

"My mother is long dead and I never knew my father. As for my Elven kin, I imagine they are alive and hidden well from human sight." Sadness showed behind his eyes.

"You imagine? Don't you know?" Semaj asked as he was drawn into the tale of this man who knew Semaj Lightheart.

His mother said he was named after the greatest mountain in all of Bergonia, which represented that he would grow up big and strong. He liked that story, but according to Thom and his myths, Mt. Semaj was actually named after Semaj Lightheart in honor of his sacrifice to save the world from great evil. Thom insisted that he was named after the hero and not the mountain. Semaj never paid much attention, until today. With the possibility of there really being a Semaj Lightheart, a small hidden twinge of curiosity grew within him.

All five of them were now captivated by the man in front of them. Here stood a creature that was supposed to be an element of a child's story and a myth rarely spoken about by adults. Anna the adventurer and Thom the dreamer of magic took to the man's words like a hungry man to food. They all sat, waiting to hear more of his story.

"Like I said, it has been a very long time since I have had contact with anyone, human or Elf. Now, if you will all sit back and listen to my tale, you will come to see why I am here and how important it is that you trust and follow me." Essej took in a deep breath and began.

"I was born about one thousand B.M., Before Magic Wars, in the great Elven City of Essejro. By this time, the Dragon Wars had been long over and the Dragons of the world no longer existed. The Age of Races had begun sparking the re-colonization of the world by the different races. My grandfather and king of the Elves, Essejro had established a great Elven city naming it after himself; and there I was raised."

"Dragon Wars, I can't believe that Dragons exist too." Thom glowed with excitement.

"Actually, Thom, Dragons are well believed to be extinct."

"What about those creatures?"

70

"Anna, those creatures are not true Dragons. They are Drogans, humans magically spawned from Dragons. I also believed them to be extinct, until now."

"Why are they here and what do they want with us?"

"Let's not jump ahead here. We don't have much time. Let me finish my tale, back where I was born, Essejro."

"Speaking of your home, you said your mom was half human, so you weren't raised with them?" Lija asked quietly.

"No, I was not. My grandmother, Leah was a human who had fallen in love with an Elf. They had a love affair that they both knew could not last. My grandfather, Essejro had been named king and their love would never be accepted by each other's people. With that, they had gone their separate ways never to see each other again.

"My mother was born almost a year later. Her Elf heritage was kept hidden and never spoken of. Then, on the day she turned one hundred, she decided to go in search of her father and Elven heritage. By this time most of her family and friends had long passed. The year I was born, my mother had finally found her father's city, exhausted and ready to give birth to her child.

"All that she said was that she had been attacked by an unknown human and nothing more was ever said about my father. Essejro and the Elves took my mother in and nothing more was ever said again, until my mother's passing. With her dying breath, she whispered a single word to me, which I never shared with no one but my dear Semaj.

"At this time, I was about five hundred years old, no longer a child and almost an adult. My grandfather soon passed and his son became king. With bad blood between the new king and myself, I decided it was time to leave my Elven home and set out into the world on a journey of self-discovery and in hopes of learning the identity of my father.

"For the next five hundred years I traveled the lands of Bergonia with no success. In that time, I did meet a lot of interesting people and creatures and learned a lot about myself. Now keep in mind, that at this time in history, Bergonia was not divided into five human kingdoms but a land of many races and creatures.

"About twenty years before the Magic Wars would begin, I came across a large mountain range. Something within the mountain seemed to call to me. I used my unique talents and followed the call straight up to the very top of the mountain where I discovered a small ledge. I landed on it and took in the wonders of being so high above the world. That is when I saw an opening that led me into the mountainside.

"The cave was dark. It was not very large and did not go that deep into the mountain. It was the right size for a single person to dwell in. That is if you didn't mind the darkness and the cold temperature. My gift did help keep most of the cold wind out. I lay down to sleep and figured I would head back down to the earth below in the morning. That is when my path took an unexpected turn.

"What happened next, I swore was real, but I was sure I was still dreaming. The cave took on a small glow that gave sight to my eyes. I didn't know where it was coming from since the outside sky was still dark as night. Suddenly it seemed like the cave no longer ended but went on forever. Even with my enhanced vision, I could barely make out a glowing figure deep within that never-ending passage.

"Just as I was gaining the courage to explore what my eyes were showing me, a gentle wind blew my way carrying a voice upon it. All around me the wind whispered softly in my ear, *find the one...bring him to me...the one named Lightheart...without him... evil... will destroy the world...*then a gust of wind burned an image into my eyes and a scent to my nose. I woke up both frightened and compelled. I immediately left the cave in the mountain and headed back to the world below.

"My heart was racing. I didn't know what had just happened. All I knew was that when I closed my eyes I could still see the image and when I breathed in deeply I could smell his faint scent. Whether I had imagined it all or not, I now had found my purpose in life. I had to search for this man named Lightheart and if he existed, bring him back to the mountain.

"It wasn't easy but I didn't let anything or anyone get in my way. I had to find him and no matter how tired or frustrated I got I pushed on with my quest. I searched all of Bergonia for almost twenty years and was ready to give up till one day I entered a small village and there he was. Our eyes locked and I knew instantly he was the one I had been searching for all these years. Semaj Lightheart.

"A lot of things had begun to happen in the world while we got to know each other. It was near the end of the final year before the Magic Wars. Thus, the calendar would end, as the Magic Wars would begin. A devastating war that would last about ten years, more depending on who you talked to since most lost track of time during this war.

"A great and evil man named Drol Greb had made his move that would pit good against evil. Drol was very strong and gifted with *magic* and the world shook as he began his conquest of Bergonia. At this moment it was clear this man had to be stopped. Semaj now believed that my quest to find him and take him to the mountain was connected to having to stop Drol Greb.

"We had both connected and pledged ourselves to each other and to the quest of defeating Drol. Through great dangers and many obstacles, I led him back to the mountain. Semaj immediately expressed a strange bond and vibe from the mountain. He urged me with haste as I used my gifts to take us both to the cave opening at the top. Semaj bolted into the opening as it began to glow. I quickly followed.

"To my surprise, when I had entered the cave the light was gone and darkness remained. I called out and then realized Semaj was no longer with me. I screamed and used my power to search within the cave for my dear companion with no success. I was all in tears when I felt a presence on the wind telling me to calm and to wait. And that is what I did.

"I laid there for years waiting for the return of my dear Lightheart, wondering and worrying where he might be and if he would ever come back to me. I went through many emotions and even blamed myself for partaking in this quest when two years before the Magic Wars would come to an end I awoke to Semaj standing before me.

"I had asked him where he had been and what happened. He said that he had discovered a great and ancient power that would help save Bergonia from Drol. He said that the reason he was gone so long was because he was being trained. He wouldn't go into any more details about who trained him or what happened. He just gave me a brief description but that was it. You see, I loved him dearly and followed him with no questions. Plus, we had a world to save.

"When we left the cave in the sky, my Semaj was not the only one that had changed. Drol Greb and his evil forces were winning and the whole world was at war. Many groups of people were fighting different battles, it was hard to keep track of all that was going on. Our mission was to find Drol Greb and stop him, which we did in the final year of the war.

"By this time, we had located Drol Greb's fortress and had recruited a band of twelve others. From the time we left the cave till the time we were on the border of Drol Greb's land we had met and bonded with twelve brave beings. After all these years their names almost elude me but I still clearly remember this diverse group of defenders. Along with Semaj and myself we had a stubborn Dwarf, an angry Minotaur, an uncertain knight, a passionate woman, a brave human warrior, an outcast from the water folk, a powerful cleric, an uncontrollable Were-Beast, a loving Orgite, a good-natured Goblin, a Wild Elf and a non-violent Centaur. We were an odd group but we had a common goal.

"It was a hard fight, but in the end, we had reached Drol Greb himself. That final battle was something else. Power like no other erupted from Semaj as he battled Drol Greb one-on-one. By this time, five of our group had been killed while four others were seriously injured. Drol was winning; Semaj was near death and all seamed lost until that final moment.

"Suddenly, thirteen colors glowed brightly and I found a gem in my hand baring all colors. I heard my Semaj in my head telling me to go. I didn't want to leave him but with great tears the remaining eight of us escaped and got far away. Soon, a giant explosion that not only rocked the world but created the Frosted Waters on one side and turning Drol's land and surrounding area into what is now known as the Drol Death Desert. This was all created when Semaj sacrificed his life and Drol Greb was banished from this world.

"We had won, but at a great loss. As the others left to become heroes, I vanished from the world. Before Semaj had died, he sent a message into my mind, telling me that he loved

me and not to mourn. He also gave me instructions of what I
needed to do next.

"I had to go back to the cave in the sky and shatter the gem,
which I did causing thirteen colors to fly off into the night.
Semaj had fused his new powers into the gem so they would not
be lost to the world. Each descendent of the twelve defenders
would be granted one of the twelve powers. As for the thirteenth,
my job was to wait and watch and if ever a great evil were to
arise again, Semaj's descendent would awaken and I would have
to find this person and then return to the cave in the sky.

"That is what I did, for four hundred years I lived in that
cave waiting until now. The power has been invoked meaning
Drol Greb or something similar to him, has made its move and
Semaj's descendent has awakened and is needed to battle this
evil.

"Those creatures that are after you, the Drogans, it seems
they can sense when that power is used and that is how they can
track us. They will either kill you or take you back to their
master. That is why it is important I get you all to the cave atop
Mount Semaj. As my Semaj instructed me, all would be revealed
and the battle to save Bergonia will begin."

They all stared at Essej with opened mouths when he
concluded his tale. It was all so hard to believe, except for Thom,
he took it all in. If it hadn't been for the Drogans and other
strange things that had happened to them, they would never have
believed the story at all. They all needed time to think but they
knew that was a luxury they did not have.

"Do you see why I have to get you all to Mount Semaj?"

"We all can't go. Someone has to warn King Sirus of what
is going on. My father and the town needs help," Marcus
pleaded.

As they all debated back and forth about all that has
happened so far, Semaj noticed Anna had gone quiet. Beads of
sweat were forming on her brow. He quickly went to her side
and touched her hand, which he pulled back immediately from a
small shock.

"Anna, are you okay? Your skin feels like it is burning up."

"I don't know, all this has got me worked up. I feel like I
am burning up and my head feels weird."

"Anna, tell me what you're feeling," Essej shouted as he rushed to her side silencing everyone immediately.

"I don't know. It feels like I'm on fire. I feel very warm, like I am absorbing all the heat around me."

"Marcus, open that window. Anna, look out that window and focus all your thoughts on that tree stump. Think nothing but the stump, wishing all this heat would be there instead of in you. Do it now, there isn't much time."

Anna did as Essej instructed. As she concentrated on the tree stump, she could feel the heat leaving her. She felt a wave of coolness as the heat rushed out of her and towards the tree stump. She snapped awake when the screams of her friends revealed that the tree stump was now on fire. Essej used his gift to quickly extinguish the fire with a vacuum of air around it.

"Anna, are you okay?"

"Yes, Semaj, I feel better. I no longer feel hot."

"Good, it has passed. I know who I must take to the cave now."

"What just happened? How did you do that?" Thom asked

"I thought I saw her skin turn red," Lija told her brother.

"That was probably from her feeling hot. Is she the one they are after? Did she cause that fire?"

"We don't have time for any more explanations. It is important we leave now as they will have felt the power," Essej said as he helped Anna to her feet.

"I'm okay. I may be a little shaken up, but I agree with Essej. We must hurry. I'll go with you to Mount Semaj. This is the adventure I have been waiting for all my life."

"Anna, you can't go alone. I will go too," Thom said as he thought of Lars and vowed not to lose another one dear to him.

"That is wise of you, Thom," Essej said looking at his crystal, "I would have insisted you come along anyway."

Semaj looked at his best friend and Anna. As much as he wanted to go home and have no part in this, he knew he had to go with them. "I will go too."

"I would like to go too and help you guys, but someone has to warn the king and my sister needs to be taken to a safer place."

"Marcus, you and your sister are not needed to come along. You two will be safe for they are not after either of you. Take your sister to King Sirus and tell him what is going on. Being the son of the captain of the King's Guard, he'll take your words seriously. If all is decided, we must hurry before we are discovered. I have horses out back and rations for each of us."

They all said their good-byes as Marcus and Lija mounted a single horse and headed west to Sorran to alert the king. Anna felt better that Lija was being taken out of danger. She still felt weird about what had happened to her but she now felt excited and very important. She did not know what to expect next, but as the four of them each mounted a horse and raced out, she knew her journey was just beginning.

Chapter Five:
To Find A Mountain & A Castle

They had been riding their horses hard for almost a full day. Essej had led them off the roads and across the plains and kept within what tree coverage they could to avoid being spotted or followed. He knew it would be a long journey, but by pushing them they would make it to Mount Semaj in about two days. They were making good time with only a few stops here and there to rest the horses and to eat. The sunlight had nearly faded away and darkness was fast approaching.

"I think it will be safe to stop here for the night," Essej said as he brought their horses to a stop.

"Do you think we were followed?" Semaj asked as he looked over his shoulder. Sighing as he feared he would never see his home or his parents again.

"It's hard to say, but I'm hoping those creatures aren't smart enough to find us," Essej said as he helped Semaj tie up the horses to a nearby tree.

Semaj looked around at their wooded cover. This was the farthest he had ever been from home in his whole life. Only being a day's ride from home, the land did not look much different, except that there seemed to be fewer trees and plant life. From what he had heard, he knew other lands were richer but he was happy for what they had. The tree cover, as small as it was, he hoped would be enough for them to hide within.

Semaj looked over at Anna and Thom and then thought of his other two friends traveling the other direction. Would any of them be the same again? Could things ever go back the way they were? Semaj just did not know and that scared him. Strange creatures had attacked Soré and he just prayed that Marcus and his sister would make it to the king in time to save their home and loved ones.

He wished that he could be there with his parents, seeing that they were safe with his own eyes. He had no choice. Racing home would only get him captured by those creatures or worse, killed like poor Lars. Semaj wiped a forming tear and nodded to himself. That is why he had to help Thom and Anna now. These creatures were hunting them and the only way to protect them was to follow this odd old man.

This man, Elf, or whatever he was, believed that one of them was some kind of Chosen One and that they had to get to Mount Semaj if they wished to survive. Normally Semaj would have laughed at the guy, if not for those creatures killing Lars, Thom somehow working magic and Anna having that fire episode back at the cabin. Even though he was glad that he was not special, he feared for his friends and would do what he could to help them.

"Wake up, Semaj. Don't fade out on us now," Anna shouted breaking his deep thoughts.

"Sorry, was just thinking of the others and my parents," Semaj said as he walked over to the group. Anna smiled at him as Essej began forming a small circle with stones.

"I'm sure Marcus and Lija will be fine. He's tough like his dad and will reach the king in no time."

"I know, Anna, but I just hope mom and dad are okay."

"Don't worry, Semaj. Marcus's dad and the rest of the guard will keep everyone safe until more help arrives."

"I still don't think making a fire is wise. It will blow our cover, even in these trees," Thom said as he approached them with the branches and sticks he had gathered for Essej.

"That won't be a problem. I'll use my power to make the wind carry the smell and smoke low and far away from us. By the time it moves far enough from my power's control, it will have faded. We will need the warmth if we are to sleep out here tonight," Essej said as he sat down in front of the stone circle.

"That's fine and all, but how are we even going to get it started?" Thom asked as he placed what he had gathered into the center of the stone circle.

"That's what we have Anna for," Essej smiled as he motioned for her to sit next to him.

"There you go, Anna. Better start rubbing those sticks together," Semaj laughed for the first time as he took a seat around the stone circle with the others.

"Anna, you will make the fire but not with sticks. I may not have all the answers but I am familiar enough with your power to start giving you your basic training."

"What are you talking about?" Anna looked at the old man in surprise.

"Just like you did back at the cabin, I'm going to show you how to use that power to create the fire,"

"I can't, you saw what happened last time,"

"Yes, but that was unexpected. The sooner you start to familiarize yourself with and gain control of your gift the more confident you will become," Essej reassured her as he moved so he was sitting behind her. "Are you ready?"

"I guess," Anna said with both fear and excitement in her voice. Thom stared at her in silence and fascinating awe while Semaj paced a little.

"Won't using her powers attract those Drogans?" Semaj asked glancing around the area.

"Not with this kind of power. I believe the Drogans can only track a specific use of the Chosen One's power. Same way I can sense it when it's being used. What I do and what I will be showing Anna is different and not trackable by those creatures," Essej tried to explain to the group, hoping he was not wrong as these creatures did seem diferent than the Drogans of his past.

"I still don't understand it all but I'm ready," Anna said wanting to get back to the lesson.

"Now, Anna, no matter what, you must concentrate and do exactly what I tell you to do without interrupting." Anna nodded and then looked forward as she felt Essej place his hands on her shoulders.

"Close your eyes and clear your mind. In time, this will all come easier and faster but for now just relax and breathe deeply. Now, as you relax, I want you to reach out with your senses and feel the heat all around you. In the air, the trees, the earth and all living things, reach out and touch the warmth with your senses," Essej's soothing voice instructed her.

Anna, eyes closed, felt foolish at first. Just as she was about to open her eyes and laugh she suddenly felt a prickle of heat. She soon found herself doing as he instructed. She couldn't explain it but suddenly she could feel heat from all around her. It's like her senses could touch and recognize the heat in everything as it opened up to her and surrendered its control to her will.

"You can feel it can't you. It is now yours to manipulate and instruct but you must always remember to use it wisely and with care. Now I want you to evenly pull the heat towards you and become one with it. Once you are in complete equilibrium I want you to open your eyes and stare directly at the branches in the stone circle without breaking concentration," Essej whispered to his pupil.

Anna nodded slightly as Semaj and Thom sat waiting for something to happen. To them it didn't seem like she was doing anything but they could tell she was going through something. As they watched, Anna could feel the heat joining with her and then as Essej had instructed she opened her eyes and stared straight at the sticks as beads of sweat formed on her brow.

"You're doing great, Anna. Now I want you to focus only on the heat around and within the sticks. I want you to become one with and only feel that heat. Now will it to intensify while pulling outside energy, adding that heat to it, willing it to grow and become hotter and hotter."

Anna was in a state of panic and intense exhilaration. She could actually feel and *see* the heat around the sticks. She had never felt such power and control. She could feel it becoming hotter and hotter and it was because of her. Even though her friends couldn't see anything she knew they could feel the heat since they had moved back from the warming pit.

"Now this is the tricky part. With strong will, I want you to take the heat to the next level. Quickly force the surrounding heat into the stick's heat and demand it to expand and explode and will it to burst into fiery flames. Once that is done, shut off all ties and feelings with any heat except that of the sticks. For that one split second, let it only be you, the fiery sticks and the heat on the sticks, then cut yourself off and release the power."

Anna bit her lip as she did as she was told. Only thing that was part of her world at this moment was Anna, the sticks and the power. With great pain and force she commanded the sticks to erupt. At that moment, to everyone's surprise, the stick burst into flame and they had a campfire. She quickly tried to cut off from everything like Essej has said, but there was one problem.

"Anna, the fire is starting to grow too high. Shut off the power!" Essej yelled as he jumped to his feet.

"I can't. I can't let go of the fire," Anna said with fear.

Essej quickly used his powers to cause the air to grow thin around Anna as she felt feint, breaking loose from the power. "Don't worry dear, practice makes perfect and we do have a nice fire," he said catching her and nodding towards their small campfire.

"Anna, that was amazing!" Thom shouted. "What did it feel like?"

"Like nothing I have ever known," She said gaining her footing but still feeling a bit dizzy.

"How did she do that?" Semaj asked. "Can Thom do that?"

"I only know what I picked up from my Semaj in comparison to my powers. As for anything else, all will be answered once we reach our destination," Essej said as he went to his horse's saddlebag, "and for Thom, I don't doubt he could but his abilities still puzzle me for now."

Essej soon prepared their supper as he let the three friends talk about what had just happened. She had done great for her first lesson, a real natural. Hopefully all would fall into place and they would all be prepared for what he feared was to come. After they ate, Essej had pushed them all to sleep while he sat staring at the fire using his powers to hide the smell and smoke. He felt calm and didn't need to sleep yet. He would rest once they made it to the mountain. He hoped all would be well and that nothing would go wrong.

****

Marcus and his sister sat before a nice fire he had made while they ate their supper. Despite her crying, whining and complaints about the dirt and her wrinkled dress, Lija was holding up well. It was all he could do to keep from losing it over the loss of his best friend Lars. He knew Lars died bravely and that the only way to honor that act would be to keep his sister safe and bring help to Soré.

The main road from Soré had been deserted. They had not run across anyone or anything thus far. They had been traveling for about a day now and nothing had gotten in their way. Marcus had decided to camp for the night and had moved them off the road and into the protection of the trees. He had to be on watch for others now that they were less than a day's journey to the great city of Sorran.

He couldn't wait to see the mighty castle. He and his sister had been there once, when they were very little. His dad had been awarded the title of Captain of the Guard for Soré and they had gone to Sorran for the ceremony. Ever since then, Marcus had wanted to be like his dad and Lija had fallen in love with the castle and decided she was going to be a princess.

"How much longer till we get there?" Lija whined.

"It shouldn't be much longer. Less than a day," Marcus said as he consistently watched the area around them.

"I can't wait. First thing I need is a bath. I am just filthy. I have dirt under my nails and on my dress and my hair is just a mess."

"Now is not the time to be worrying about how you look."

"Marcus, we'll be in the presence of royalty and I need to look my best."

"What am I going to do with you?" Marcus rolled his eyes as he got up and began to make their sleeping area for the night.

"I can't wait till I can sleep in a real bed again. I am so tired of lying on the ground like some animal."

Marcus tuned out his sister while he thought of the others. He hoped that they had made it to their destination without being caught by those monsters. He was sure that they would be okay. He just had to concentrate on getting to the king and getting help. He didn't worry about his family because his dad was the best and he would protect his mom and the town with ease.

He was soon startled back to reality when he heard a faint noise off in the distance. Instinct and his dad's training kicked in as he quickly doused the fire and moved the horse farther back into the woods. He then ran up to his sister and dragged her down behind a bunch of bushes.

"What are you doing?"

"Lija, quiet, something's coming up the road. Until we know what it is we need to get out of sight. It might be those creatures," Marcus told her as she thought of Lars and then covered her mouth in terrifying silence.

A few minutes later, two men clad in dark black armor galloped by on their large black steeds. Marcus didn't recognize the men or armor so he made sure his sister kept hidden and quiet. They both released a breath of relief as the men on horseback disappeared down the road heading towards Sorran. Lija started to get back up until Marcus caught something moving out of the corner of his eye. He quickly yanked his sister back down and told her to be quiet. Something else was coming up the road.

Marcus realized that the two men on horseback were front guards. Now a giant horse drawn carriage was passing in front of them. The design of the carriage was hard to make out in the dark of night but they could see that a man sat in front pulling the reigns of four horses. Two guards on horseback rode on each side of the carriage. Marcus could also see that two more guards rode slightly behind the carriage.

Marcus could make out candle lit shadows of what seemed like five or six people inside the carriage windows. As the carriage moved past them, he saw a giant golden *A* on the back. Marcus wasn't sure who was in there but it must be someone very important heading towards Sorran. After what seemed like ages the caravan was gone and out of sight.

"Who was that?" Lija asked.

"I don't know. By the emblem on the back of the carriage, I might guess they were from the Kingdom of Argoth. If I'm correct, why would they be this far into our kingdom?" Marcus pondered.

"Those men looked pretty scary with their black armor and horses," Lija said as she dusted off her dress and stood up next to her brother.

"I don't know much about them, but according to dad the people of Argoth are not too pleasant or friendly."

"You think they're heading to see the king too?"

"That would be my guess," Marcus pondered as he led his sister over to the camp they had setup.

Lija sat there complaining as usual as Marcus went and brought the horse back closer to camp. When enough time had passed to assure that the caravan would not notice them and be long gone down the road, Marcus got the fire going again. Soon after, Lija was asleep and Marcus was alone staring into the fire. He was glad Lija had finally drifted off. She needed to rest, as did his ears. He needed to sleep too but he was too protective and worried to find sleep so easily. Thoughts kept creeping into his mind. What if the king would not believe them or send help? Or what if they arrived back home and found that they were too late?

Marcus shook his head. He had to put such thoughts out of his mind. He knew all would work out. He would get his sister safely to Sorran and he would ride with the king's men back to Soré and rescue everyone from those evil creatures. With those thoughts, Marcus finally found himself fast asleep.

Marcus woke just as the sun began to rise and the birds sang their songs. Marcus used his boot to nudge his sister up. Their fire was still hot enough that he warmed them up a little food for breakfast. They didn't have much left but it wouldn't be long before they would reach Sorran. With breakfast down, Marcus put out the remaining embers and mounted his whining sister upon their horse. He then leapt up, joining her and they were off at a hard gallop, against his sister wishes and complaints.

They raced all day, only stopping for a quick lunch and the occasional pit stop. Before they knew it, the day was almost over and the sun would be setting soon. Lija screamed with joy as Marcus noticed that off in the distance you could see the top of the great castle in Sorran. They were almost there and Lija didn't have to worry about the pace. Mentally, she was already there.

Just as the night began to take over they came to a dead stop. Just up the road they could see the great entrance into the City of Sorran. Guards could be seen on either side of the gate as well as the guards in the watchtowers that stood high above the gates and spread along the perimeter of the city walls.

Even at this distance they could hear the busy noise of the people and life of the great city inside. It was very overwhelming, but what took their breath away was the magnificent sight of the castle. Even though the castle sat in the center of a city surrounded by walls, you could still see the top of the castle and its towers. The castle was made of your basic stone but it was still pretty to look at.

"It's better than I remember," Lija whispered in awe.

"I know and I'm glad we finally made it safe and sound," Marcus said as he neared his sister and touched her hand.

"One day I'll have a castle of my own."

"I'm sure you will, but for now, let's keep moving. We need to get into the gates before dark and request an urgent audience with the king," Marcus said as he and his sister moved towards the gates and the grand castle behind them.

****

Semaj jerked awake as he felt the ground tremble beneath him. He had heard of earthquakes, but he didn't think they happened around here. He jumped up and noticed that he was standing on top of a mountain. As he managed to keep his footing, he saw that large mountains surround him from every side. Before he could ponder how he got here two familiar faces were stumbling toward him.

"Semaj, I think we are in one of those weird dreams again," Thom said holding up his glowing crystal.

"Were not alone, look," Anna said pointing at what looked like a very short plump figure.

"What is that?" Thom asked.

"I don't know. Whatever it is, it's too far away to make out clearly," Semaj answered.

"It looks like a Dwarf," Thom said smiling.

"How would you know? Dwarves are stories of myth," Anna said as the earth tremors began to grow stronger.

"I read about them in one of my books. It is said that over three hundred years ago the Dwarves had vanished into the Northern Mountains isolating themselves from the growing evil affairs of humans," Thom informed them as he lost his footing and fell to the ground.

"You have too big an imagination, Thom," Semaj said as he helped his friend up.

"Look, some kind of weird opening is forming over there in the distance," Anna said pointing off towards the very far south.

"That's the least of our worries, the tremors are causing the mountain to crumble," Semaj said as he saw chunks of mountainside beginning to fall down on them.

"Thom, use your crystal and get us out of here quick!" Anna shouted above the roar of the falling rocks.

They all screamed as they looked up and saw a giant boulder falling straight down on them with nowhere to run. Thom grabbed his crystal and screamed along with the others and held it up. Before the boulder could crush them or the strange portal could actually open all the way up in the south, Thom's crystal engulfed them in a bright white-blue flash.

"No," Anna shouted as she jumped awake. She quickly stood up and looked around her realizing it was all a dream.

With a sigh of relief, she walked over to her horse and took out her flask of water. As she took a swig she saw that Thom and Semaj were still asleep. Either they were not a part of her dream or they were that tired to wake from that. She glanced over and saw that the fire was out and Essej was fast asleep himself.

The sun would not be up yet for a while, but Anna could not go back to sleep. Instead, she went and sat back down staring at the skyline of mountains. Essej had told them that it wouldn't be too long and they would be at the base of Mount Semaj. From there, they would see the great mountain in all its beauty.

This had been a great adventure so far, considering everything. She just wandered what would happen next once they reached the mountain. How would their lives change after that, despite the fact she had this weird power in her? Could she really be some Chosen One? It all scared her but yet fulfilled her thirst for adventure.

Just as she was about to try and lay back down she thought she heard rustling coming from her left. She looked over as her daggers appeared in her hands. Out of the dark came four Drogans, stopping to stare at the girl who stood between them and three sleeping figures.

"There they are," shouted one of them as he gave the order for all four of them to release a blast of fire from their mouths.

Anna was paralyzed with fear. There was no way she would wake her friends in time to avoid the fire. She began to feel funny as she reached out with fear and panic and grabbed hold of something familiar, trying to remember her training sessions. She thrust her arms out in front of her right at the approaching fire. She could feel the heat but didn't' know what to do, so she kept drawing it inside of her.

Just as the fire neared her and her friends she screamed at the top of her lungs as the fire snuffed out and she could now feel the heat and fire all inside her, burning her alive. She felt her power tug and then in pure panic of being burned alive, she pushed out causing the heat to leave her body and catching the trees to her left and right on fire. Anna swayed and fell into someone's arms.

"What's going on?" Semaj shouted, catching Anna, as he and the others were at her side the instant her scream woke them.

"That *power* was used again and they found us. I felt it being used but I must have been too tired to realize it and wake up. This fire will draw others," Essej said as he used his powers to snuff the two fires out immediately.

"Surrender to us or die," one of the Drogans shouted, its wings flapping while fire began to build within its mouth.

"Not today you fowl creatures," Essej said calling upon his powers again.

"Essej!" Anna screamed as the old human-Elf dropped to the ground, grunting in pain.

A small dagger was embedded in his shoulder. He had not been quick enough in his summing, which allowed an opening for one of the Drogans to throw a dagger. He did not remember these creatures to be that smart in the use of daggers, but thankfully they had bad aim, as the dagger had hit is shoulder and not his heart.

"Anna, Essej is wounded, do something."

"I can't, Semaj. What I did with the fire was pure accidental luck," Anna cried as she tried to feel for her power while reaching for her knife.

"Maybe I can," Thom said as he stepped in front of them all, his crystal glowing bright, "for Lars."

Thom could not explain it. After the Drogans had injured Essej, he began to think about what they had done to Lars. He felt a strange pull as his crystal began to glow. He sensed a strange energy from within as words began to form in his mind.

He did not know where they came from or how he knew them but they were there.

"Omebec Onest!" Thom shouted as he felt the energy leave his body along with the words.

The white-blue energy engulfed the Drogans as they tried to scramble out of the way. When the light faded all four creatures were encased in stone. Thom dropped to one knee, out of breath, as his crystal's glow dimmed to nothing. Anna ran over and helped him to his feet.

"How did you do that?" She asked in amazement.

"I don't know. It just began to glow and then there were words in my head. I don't know what they mean but I knew I just had to say them," Thom shrugged still looking at the creatures made of stone.

"I should have handled them. I am not as strong and fast as I once was in my youth. I hoped it would come back to me faster," Essej said as he yanked the dagger from his shoulder.

"That looks bad," Anna said as she cut the old man's sleeve with her knife and using it to tie around the wound to act as a bandage.

"I'll be fine. It looks worse than it is. Luckily, they don't know how to effectively use a dagger. Normally they stick to their swords and fire breath," Essej said as he let the boys help him to his feet.

"I see the suns coming up, I better get breakfast ready," Anna said at the chance of practicing her powers again.

"Actually, I think we should forget breakfast and make haste. I want to put some distance from here in case there are more Drogans on the way," Essej said as walked toward the horses.

"You're right, I don't think we are ready to deal with any more of those creatures," Anna said with a hint of disappointment at not getting to create a fire.

They mounted their horses and quickly rode off. They pushed the horses as fast as they could go. Anna noticed Essej grunting from the pressure of the ride on his wound but he kept saying he was fine. She could not wait until they reached the mountains. She thought she was getting better at her power, but it seemed that under pressure she had trouble using it. If she was to be the Chosen One and had to save the world then she needed to be harder on herself.

The sun was now high in the sky as they reached mid-day. Essej signaled them to a halt as they had finally reached the mountains. Essej guided them to a path that led between two mountain sides and passed by a small stream. It was a nice area tucked within the base of the mountains.

"Tie the horses here. They will be safely hidden and able to drink freely while we are busy," Essej said as he tied up his horse and knelt down to refill his flask with water and then drink from it.

"Which one of these mountains is Mount Semaj?" Semaj asked looking upwards.

"This one here," Essej said pointing to the mountain base to their left.

Everyone looked up and saw that the mountain went straight up, higher than any other mountain. They couldn't even see the top. It just vanished high up within the clouds. It was a sight to be seen and so magnificent. They had always heard about the mountains but neither of them had ever seen one in person. Even Semaj, who liked his farm, enjoyed this thrilling sight.

"A beauty isn't it?" Essej smiled as he joined the three staring up at the mountains.

"Yes, it is. I never thought I would ever see anything like this," Thom barely whispered.

"Essej, where's the cave opening that you spoke of?" Anan asked.

"The cave is near the very top of Mount Semaj," Essej said pointing straight up.

"How are we supposed to reach that?" Semaj asked.

"I was wondering that myself. I can't help but notice that there are no paths leading up the mountain," Anna added.

"Don't worry, I will get us up there," Essej said, "but first let's eat and rest up."

They all agreed, even though they had no idea how they would reach the top of such a tall mountain. Anna, getting a little better, was eventually able to create a fire. While Essej managed the flames and dinner, the three stripped down to their under garments and washed themselves and their clothes in the stream.

Thom, at first, did not want to get into the cold mountain stream but Anna took care of that. Anna stepped into the stream and used her powers to heat the water around her. It took a lot of concentration to keep the ever-flowing water constantly warm around them but Anna had managed to make it last long enough for them to get in and clean up.

"You are getting better at this, Anna. I just wish I could learn to use my powers like you, but they only seem to work when the crystal wants it to work," Thom said stepping out of the stream with the others.

"You'll get there," Anna encouraged her friend as she began to shiver.

"It was nice to clean up, but now we're all cold and wet and it will take a while for our clothes to dry by the fire," Semaj shivered.

"I think I can handle this too," Anna smiled as she reached out with her powers.

She touched the heat all around them and drew it in making each of them feel warmer. In a matter of moments, they were all dry and comfortable. She then reached out and moved the heat around their hanging clothes. Making the air warmer the water evaporated and their clothes began to dry.

"I am impressed by how good you are getting," Essej said as Anna got dressed with the others.

"I have the heating things up part down but I wish I could still get more control over the creating fire," Anna said as they joined Essej around the fire.

"Don't worry my child, that and more will come in time," Essej encouraged as he handed each of them a plate of food.

By the time they were done and had things put away the daylight had begun to fade away. They were all finally feeling good and rested since their long journey from Soré to Mount Semaj. Essej now stood on one side of the fire facing his three young companions.

"I think we should head up to the cave now. I really don't want to risk sleeping down here tonight now that we are so close to our goal," Essej told them.

"I still don't think it will be an easy trip up the mountain," Thom said looking up.

"Don't worry, it will be easier than you guys think," Essej smiled.

"No matter how we go, I think we should wash your wound in the stream and redress it before we start our hike," Anna said glancing at the old human-Elf's wrapped shoulder.

"Don't worry, my shoulder is," Essej started to say when the cloth came loose and fell off revealing his bare shoulder.

"Your wound, it's gone," Anna gasped.

"How can that be?" Semaj asked as he stared at the unmarked shoulder.

"I know Elves have healing capabilities but I didn't think you could heal a wound that fast and complete," Thom added.

"Actually, there is something I haven't told you guys, but now it's time," Essej said as he threw off his cloak.

"What are you talking about?" Anna asked.

"You see, the reason I heal fast is the same reason that is going to get us up the mountain."

Essej expanded his arms out and up. The three friends stared in shock as Essej's skin began to shift to a scaly white color and texture. The wind blew back his hair reveling his pointed ears and white eyes. Suddenly, large radiantly white Dragon wings erupted from his back, expanding outwards. Essej stared at them all as his wings flapped softy in the air.

"You see, I'm not just half human half Elf. I'm,"

"A Drogan!" All three of them yelled realizing the trap they had been led into.

Chapter Six:
The City Of Sorran

Marcus and his sister sat inside the guard's post waiting impatiently. Marcus knew they did not have time to waste. Every second could mean grave danger for his parents and his town. He also knew that if he lost his temper and didn't wait like they had been commanded, they would never get to see the king. He was lucky that the guards sent word to begin with.

When Marcus and his sister had reached the gates, the guard had commanded them to halt and state their business. It must have been an odd sight to see two young adults on horseback this late at night. Marcus had quickly told them who they were, whom his father was and that monsters where invading Soré. He didn't go into any grave detail about all that had occurred. He would save that for the king himself.

The guard began to laugh at such a story but had sent another guard to the castle to inform the king. If it had been any other person, they would have been turned away as nothing but a bunch of kids telling stories. The fact that he knew his father, Broc as the great captain of Soré's guards and that his children would never be this far away alone at night meant something was amiss. Out of respect for his dad, the guard sent word to the king and would let him decide what to do.

After what seemed like days, the guardsman of the gate entered and motioned at the two of them to come outside. They looked up to see that the messenger had returned with an answer. "The king has agreed to see you two, only because of your father. I hope for your sake you are not wasting his majesty's time and beseech your father's good name."

Marcus did not say a word but only glared at the guardsman as he helped his sister up on her horse. He then quickly mounted and they followed the messenger guard towards the castle. They rode in silence at a slow steady trot while Marcus and his sister looked at their surroundings. Even though time was precious, they realized so was the sight of the city they were in.

Sorran was not the world's grandest city but it was still large in size and very clean and well managed. It had a plain kind of beauty. Just as you entered the gates you could see houses built everywhere. They were simple dwellings but still seemed nicer than most of the houses built in Soré. All of the peasants and most common folks lived in homes surrounding the outskirts of the city.

Most of them did not mind. Even though they could not afford to live directly in the city they were still protected by the guarded walls and gates of Sorran. Because of that and the peace and quiet, very few complained. No matter your social status, Sorran was a great place to live. Marcus was impressed with what he saw and by the look of his sister's face, he knew she was already planning her move.

It did not take long before they reached the city. Marcus could not believe his eyes. It was nothing like what they had in Soré. Shops, merchant stands, Inns, dwellings and more made up this city for as far as the eyes could see. This late at night there was not that much activity but he could just imagine the commotion of people, wagons and animals moving in every direction when the day's sun gave life to the city.

"I bring the children to see the king. Send word at once," their escort shouted bringing Marcus and his sister's attention upward to guard standing on the wall that surrounded the castle and the land it sat upon. The gate doors soon moved towards them granting them access.

They had finally reached the castle. It was a beautiful site even in the moonlight. The castle was very impressive in size. It was nothing fancy, just simple and beautiful like the rest of the city. Candlelight could be seen through some of the window openings. Flags flapped in the winds atop the five castle towers. Marcus could faintly make out the guardsmen standing watch atop the towers.

A large gravel road led up to the castle doors, only grassland and a few trees could be seen on either side of the road. When they reached the castle doors the guard had them all dismount as the doors parted allowing them to enter. A strange looking man appeared and led their horse off to the king's stable. As they entered the castle, another guard of medium build and an older lady dressed in servant's attire holding a lighted candle approached them.

"Greetings, son of Broc and my lady," the guard bowed kissing Lija's hand making her blush, "I have not seen you two since you were babies."

"You know us?" Lija asked still smitten by the man.

"Yes, I am Bruce Peters. I went to school with your father," the man said as he removed his helmet revealing his short sandy blond hair and shaven face, "but we lost touch after he was assigned to Soré and I became a guard here at the castle."

"Nice to meet you sir," Marcus nodded at the man.

"Likewise, my boy, now if you will follow Lynda here she will show you to your quarters."

"What about the king? We need to see him right away," Marcus pressed.

"Not tonight. It is late and his majesty is still entertaining his guests, the royal family from Argoth."

"King Allen of Argoth is here? That was his carriage we saw," Lija remarked to her brother.

"Soré and my father are in danger. I must speak with him now. There are monsters attacking and," Marcus shouted dismissing his sister before being cut off himself.

"Marcus, I am sure it is very important but as per the king's orders you will retire for the night and he will see you in the morning after you have been bathed and properly dressed."

"Properly dressed?" Lija's eyes lit up.

"Yes, my lady, we will make sure you are fitted into a new dress. The king has invited you to join him and his daughter for breakfast. That is when he will hear your tale," Bruce said giving a final glance at Marcus.

"Fine," Marcus grunted as Lynda led him and his sister up a flight of stairs.

They walked down a long hallway that was illuminated by candles hanging along the walls. When they reached a door half way down the hall, Lynda stopped and unlocked it.

"Here is where you and your sister will sleep for the night. I will fetch you at dawn's light to prepare you for your audience with his majesty." She motioned them into the room, lighted a couple candlesticks on a table near the door and smiled, "Please sleep well." She then closed and locked the door behind them.

"Guess they don't want us roaming the castle at night," Marcus huffed as they each picked up a candle and surveyed the room.

It was a very small room with a single window, which was closed by two small wooden doors. Marcus took note that the only items in the room were two beds, a small table between them and a larger table along the wall near them. On the table where they had grabbed the candlesticks was a small container of water, two cups and a small tray of rolls.

"These are quite good," Lija mumbled shoving the rolls in her plump mouth.

"I really wish we could see the king now, but I guess we have no choice but to wait."

"You think mom and dad will be okay?"

"Don't worry, I am sure they'll be just fine," he said as he squeezed his sister's shoulder in reassurance, "we will see the king first thing in the morning and he'll send help immediately." Marcus then walked towards the beds as he whispered a prayer up to Venéäh that he was right.

"This is such lovely material and the beds are so soft," Lija said now enthralled by where she was, "I could really get used to living in a castle."

Marcus rolled his eyes. "We need to get to sleep. I'm sure tomorrow will be a very busy day," Marcus told his sister as he placed the candle on the small table and stripped down to his under garments.

"Yes, and we get to eat with royalty," Lija smiled as she did the same and then slipped into bed.

Marcus wished his sister a pleasant night and then blew out both candles.

****

Marcus jumped up quickly at the sound of someone pounding on the door and calling out. He leapt out of bed and pulled on his pants as the door unlocked and Lynda walked in with a few other servants.

"Is it morning already?" Lija whined as she sat up wiping the sleep from her eyes.

"Yes, barely, but we need to get you two ready so you are not late for your audience with the king," Lynda said as she motioned to the servants.

Before Marcus could say a word, Lija excitedly jumped out of bed putting on her old dress and followed the servants out of the room to be pampered. Lynda then motioned to Marcus as he pulled on his shirt and reached for the sword he had taken from Essej's place.

"You can leave that there. Weapons are not permitted at the king's breakfast table. It'll be safe here and you can retrieve it when you leave. I will now take you to where you can bathe," Lynda said as she headed out the door.

Marcus set his sword down and hurried out after the older lady. They quickly came to another small room and she opened the door for him.

"Inside you will be able to clean up. When you are finished you will find that a nice new outfit has been laid out for you, as a gift from the king. Your old clothes can be tossed aside and we will have those filthy things burned."

"Thank you, ma'am," Marcus bowed as he stepped into the room.

"Do try to hurry. You don't want to be late or keep the king waiting," Lynda said as she shut the door behind her.

The room was slightly smaller than the room they had slept in. He imagined that this must be the servant's bath and that the finer baths were reserved for the king and his more important friends and guests. Either way he did not care, he just could not wait to finally clean up and put on some fresh clothes. He quickly tossed his old clothes aside and got in the tub that sat in the middle of the room.

Washed and feeling much better and refreshed, Marcus dried off with a towel and stepped over to a table under a mirror. On the table were some new undergarments and a nice new pair of pants and a shirt. He liked the material, which was very soft and durable, but he did not care for the color. Blues were not his style but clothes were clothes, especially if they came from the king as a gift.

After making sure he looked presentable in the mirror he sat down and pulled on his new boots, also a shade of blue but very comfortable. He then walked out the door where Lynda stood waiting for him.

"Well done. Now follow me," She said as they headed down the hallway.

"Where is my sister?"

"She will meet us there."

They came to a flight of stairs and soon found themselves at a set of huge wooden doors with a guard on each side. Lynda explained that they would wait for his sister and enter together. Marcus was so anxious to get inside to see the king that his stomach began to turn. His parents and friends were counting on him and he needed to bring back help immediately.

"Marcus?" He turned at the sound of his sister's voice.

He was speechless. Her hair was combed back with a purple flower placed within it. Her smile lit up the room as she spun around showing off her new fancy dress. It was a pretty shade of lavender with white lace around the collar and hem of the sleeves and bottom that touched the floor. A nice ribbon was tied around her waist and into a bow at the small of her back.

"Don't I look like a princess?" She glowed, beaming from ear to ear.

"You look beautiful," he said, glad to see her smiling after all they had been through.

"Breakfast is waiting, you two may enter now," Lynda said as the guards parted opening the doors for them.

Marcus took his sister's arm and they stepped inside. They found themselves in a great banquette hall. All along the walls were candles, paintings and other fancy decorations. The room was very eloquent. In the middle of the room was a giant table, draped with a white cloth and covered with silver dinnerware and tons of food. Their smiles vanished and they froze when they realized that there were people already sitting at the table.

Lynda stepped forward and bowed, "Your majesty, may I present Marcus and Lija Masters of Soré. Son and daughter of Broc Masters, captain of the guard in Soré."

Marcus and Lija quickly bowed as the man at the head of the table stood up and smiled, "Greetings, young ones. How you have grown into such fine young adults. I can't believe how long it has been since I have seen you. Your father doesn't bring you to visit like I tell him he should."

Lija blushed as Marcus stood there staring at the king. King Sirus was slightly shorter than him with an average build. He had wavy shoulder length hair and a slightly graying brown beard. His royal robes were the same shade of blue that he wore. Marcus also noticed that he bore a very warm and inviting smile that soon relaxed his nerves.

"Thank you, your majesty," they both said and bowed again.

"King Sirus, we thank you for seeing us. We have come a long way with dire news and in need of your help," Marcus pleaded as he moved forward with urgency.

"Yes, yes. That is what I've heard, but first let's eat. I'm sure we are all hungry and can do more on a full stomach," King Sirus motioned as two servants lead them to two empty chairs on the right side of the table.

Marcus wanted to protest his urgency but knew better than to go against the king and embarrass his father's name. They sat in silence as King Sirus took his seat and then addressed them once again.

"I would like you to meet my daughter, Sera," Sirus said pointing at a young girl with beautiful curly brown hair seated across from the king.

The girl just smiled and went back to her food. Marcus could tell she was very shy and quiet and had to only be a few years younger than him and his sister. The king then directed their attention to the four people sitting across from them. Marcus assumed that the older two where the king and queen from Argoth and the other two had to be their sons.

"I would like you to meet King Allen and Queen Illyria of Argoth. This is their eldest son Prince Aradan and their youngest son Prince Arron who is the same age as you two," Sirus introduced as they bowed slightly. The younger prince was the only one to smile and greet back until his mother's stare silenced him.

The two siblings took in the king and queen. Just by looking at them you would never guess that they were the same age. While the king appeared older and rough looking with dark bags under his eyes, the queen was very pretty and had a younger look about her. She had short dark black hair and deep green eyes. Like her husband she wore fancy black and red royal attire but with shinier jewelry and was better groomed.

Marcus could tell from the look she had given her son that a very strong and powerful woman rested within the king's bride. As for her children, Prince Aradan and Arron both had short black hair and green eyes like their mother. The only difference between the two was that Aradan wore a beard and gave off a serious aura while Arron was very slender and had a kindness to his eyes.

Marcus noticed Prince Arron staring at Lija. The thought of someone taking an interest in his sister made him feel uneasy and overprotective. He glanced at his sister and realized she was paying no attention to the young prince but to the queen's right hand.

"You like my ring?" Queen Illyria asked tapping the medium sized stone.

"Yes, your majesty. It's very pretty," Lija commented in awe, "it reminds me of the crystal my..."

"It is very nice to meet you, your majesties and thank you for the meal and allowing us to speak with you, your highness," Marcus interrupted as he bowed to the King and Queen of Argoth and then turning to King Sirus. The last thing he wanted was his sister to reveal that their friend had a magic crystal and get them thrown in jail for questioning.

"Now, Allen back to what we were discussing before these two joined us," King Sirus smiled as he turned to the other king.

"Your majesty, I hate to sound rude but I really must speak to you, it is of grave importance," Marcus blurted out realizing that time was of the essence.

"Marcus, out of respect for your father I have invited you here, but we will talk later."

"But sir, winged monsters are attacking our home and we need your help," Lija cried out in support of her brother.

"Winged monsters?" Queen Illyria asked glaring at the two siblings with interest.

"That is enough!" King Sirus shouted as he stood. "I will not have you show disrespect in my court with such tales. Lynda, take these two to my waiting chamber. I will deal with them after my business with the king and queen here is finished."

The king turned away from the two of them as Lynda and a few guards quickly escorted them out of the banquet hall and to a small chamber. The room was small and was decorated with just a few candles and paintings on the wall. A few chairs facing a throne against the far wall were the only other items in this room.

"The king will be here shortly. I suggest you behave yourself till then," Lynda said as she and the guards left the room closing the door behind them.

"I can't believe he threw us out," Marcus spat as he kicked a chair.

"What are we going to do? What about mom and dad?" Lija began to cry.

Before Marcus could answer a knock came from the door as it opened allowing a slender figure to step through. Marcus noted the black and red royal outfit right away and bowed politely.

"Prince Arron, your majesty," Lija said giving a slight curtsy.

"You don't have to call me that. Arron will be just fine. I am not one for all that royal business. I leave that all up to my brother."

"What are you doing here?" Marcus asked. "Has the king sent for us?"

"No, I was dismissed by my mom. King Sirus said I could come sit here with you while they finished."

"What are they talking about? Why are you here visiting our kingdom?" Lija said as they all sat down.

"My mom doesn't tell me much. They're all about my brother. You see, in order to improve relations and trade between our two kingdoms, my dad is asking for King Sirus to allow my brother to marry his daughter."

"No offence but your brother is so much older than Princess Sera," Lija said as she quickly apologized for being so blunt.

"That's okay. I agree, I think two people should marry out of love not politics."

"What do you mean Prince...I mean Arron?" Marcus asked growing more curious.

"My mother says that your kingdom is falling apart and growing too poor. If King Sirus forces his daughter to marry my brother and let him move here as the new prince of Sorran then my dad will open up the trade barriers between our kingdoms."

"Well, we could really use the help. From what my dad says we have been trying to get trade relations with your kingdom for years," Marcus nodded at the young prince.

"What does Princess Sera say?" Lija asked thinking of the little girl.

"She's oblivious to the whole thing I think. She's infatuated by my older brother and will do anything her father tells her to do. I just hate that my brother is willing to use a girl just to gain power."

"I can't see King Sirus allowing this to happen even if it would mean helping his kingdom," Marcus added.

"My mother says he doesn't have a choice. After the queen died giving birth to the princess, King Sirus swore never to remarry. If he doesn't force Sera to marry my brother then he also risks the chance of never having an heir to take his place. A kingdom without a king would spell disaster for everyone."

They all agreed how terrible that would be but also felt bad for Princess Sera. Marcus now understood why King Sirus was acting the way he did. Marcus also knew that Soré was also at risk. He had to see the king right away. His thoughts were soon interrupted by the chamber door opening.

"The king has sent me to tell you that he has retired to his personal chamber and will summon you later," Lynda informed them

"I need to speak with the king right away!" Marcus shouted at the woman, losing his patience.

"The king needs some time alone. You have two choices, wait here till he calls for you or you can leave the castle grounds immediately," Lynda said with a stern voice. When no one spoke, she nodded and turned to Prince Arron, "your parents are preparing to leave. They said you may wait here and they will send for you when they are ready to depart for Argoth."

Arron turned to face Marcus and Lija as Lynda left closing the door behind her. "Why is it so important to see the king?"

"We come from a small township east of here called Soré," Marcus said to the prince as he told Arron everything that had happened to them leaving out only the part about Thom's crystal and his magic using. That was a secret he could not trust anyone with in fear of being arrested for violating the no magic law.

"I can't believe that, monsters, magic and an old Elf. It sounds so exciting, even though I'm sorry about the loss of your friend. Nothing like that ever happens to me. My mom keeps me isolated in the castle away from everything and everyone while my brother is spoiled and gets to go everywhere."

"Are you serious?" Lija said feeling sorry for the prince.

"Yes, coming here is the first time I have ever left the castle."

"Well, I fear if I don't get to the king soon everyone we know could end up killed by those creatures," Marcus said pulling them back to the crisis at hand.

"Marcus, is what you say the truth? You swear on Venēăh?"

They all jumped realizing that they were not alone in the small chamber room. Standing off in the corner was a guard. Marcus assumed that the man had been placed there in secret to keep an eye on them. As the man stepped closer and into the candlelight they recognized him from last night.

"Sir Peters, we didn't know you were there. You startled us," Lija said catching her breath.

"Marcus, I beg of you, is what you say true? Are there monsters attacking? Is your father and Soré in danger?" He asked raising his voice in concern.

"Yes, sir, that's why I need to see the king and ask for his help," Marcus pleaded with the older man.

"Your father was a great man and if he is in danger I will do what I can to help him," Bruce told the children as he walked towards the chamber door.

"Then you will take us straight to the king?" Lija clapped.

"In a minute, you wait right here, I'll be right back," Bruce Peters said as he quickly left the room.

"Do you really think he'll help us?" Lija asked as she smoothed out the wrinkles in her dress.

"I think so, since he was an old friend of dads," Marcus said as he watched the door tapping his foot with anticipation of Bruce's return.

"Okay you two let's go," came Bruce's voice from behind them.

"Where did you come from?" Arron asked jumping with surprise at the guard.

"There's a secret passage in the wall." Bruce stepped to the side to reveal a small door leading into a dark passageway. "Lynda is busy right now and the two guards out front think I went to get food for you three. We have some time before we're noticed missing."

"Why not just go directly out the door? I am sure they wouldn't question you," Marcus asked as Bruce urged them towards the passageway door.

"I'm not a high ranked guard. I'm just a grounds guard. I have no authority to take you anywhere and would be quickly questioned. This passage will lead us directly to the king and once he hears your plight, he will forgive us all."

"We better hurry then," Marcus said stepping into the passageway.

"Gross, my dress is going to get all dirty," Lija whined as she stuck her head in.

"We do not have time, Lija," Bruce said taking her hand and helping her into the passageway.

"I'm coming with you," Arron said but was soon blocked by Bruce.

"I can't allow that. You need to stay here and wait for your parents."

"I will not. I never get to do anything exciting. If you don't let me come with you I'll yell for the guards," Arron said with a smile as they let him win and he dashed into the dark passageway.

Bruce Peters stepped in and closed the stone doorway as they became hidden in the dark passageway. Bruce picked up his burning candle and led them down the narrow passageway. After a few minutes they came to what looked like two small holes in the wall. Bruce informed them that they were spy holes that allowed a person to see into the room through a painting on the other side.

"I want to look, I hear voices," Arron whispered.

"No, we don't have time for this," Bruce said but then sighed as Arron, Marcus and Lija leaned near the holes. The room was dark and they couldn't see anything or make out whom the voices belonged to.

"I want those kids taken care of. The king must not learn of the Drogans and their attack on Soré." Lija gasped and covered her mouth at what they had just heard.

"The children are missing. The guards don't know where they have gone. It won't be long before the kings are alerted," came a new voice into the darken room.

"Find them before the king's men do and dispose of them."

"I don't believe this. There are traitors among the king's castle," Bruce swore under his breath.

"We have to get to the king before they find us," Marcus said lowering his voice.

"I need to alert my parents!" Arron shouted as his voice filled with fear and excitement.

"What was that?" A voice asked from the other side of the wall.

"Marcus!" Lija screamed as a rat ran past her foot.

"It's them, they're behind the wall. Move, now!" Screamed a voice causing them all to panic.

"Quickly, follow me," Bruce commanded as he ran forward with the other three not far behind him.

"Marcus, I can't run in this dress," Lija panted trying to keep up with her brother.

"Lija, you have to keep moving I can hear them coming behind us."

"They must have discovered the passage," Bruce said looking back at Marcus and his sister.

"Look! I see a faint light up ahead," Arron shouted.

"We're trapped," Lija began to cry.

"No were not," Bruce said as he moved something on the wall beside them. "This way," Bruce pointed as he jumped through the hole that had just appeared in the wall.

"Looks like some kind of chute," Arron said looking in, "I wonder where it goes?"

"No time to ponder," Marcus said as he urged Arron down the hole.

"My dress!" Lija screamed as Marcus grabbed his sister and forced her down the chute and then dived in after her.

They slid down in darkness for what seemed like forever. Suddenly Marcus grunted as he landed on top of a pile straw. He got up and looked around and found that they were all standing in a small dungeon-like room. From the torchlight, he could see Arron grinning with joy as he threw his dirty robe to the side and his sister whining and trying to dust off her dress.

"What is this place?" Marcus asked stepping near his sister.

"Back when this castle was built, in the event of an attack, they built escape chutes throughout the castle. Right now, we are under the castle and if we follow this tunnel it will lead us past the castle grounds and we'll come out above ground, just outside Sorran."

Marcus could not believe this was happening. Was it possible that they were tracked here to Sorran and now they and the king were in danger? Whatever the reason they had to get out and get to the king. Lives depended upon it.

"Hurry, this way," Bruce shouted as he led them down the tunnel.

The tunnel went on for miles. They were all growing tired from the running but they knew that whoever was chasing them would not be far behind them. They soon came to a dead end with a ladder leading upwards.

"This will take us above ground, I will go first to make sure it is clear," Bruce said taking flight up the ladder with Arron, Lija and Marcus following right behind.

Bruce called it clear and they all made it out of the hole in the ground. As they all caught their breaths Bruce placed the cover back on the hole leading down. Marcus saw that they had come out in a small patch of woods about a few miles south of Sorran.

"We need to get back to the city and send word to the king," Bruce said as he pulled off his helmet and tossed it aside.

"Over here! Look, were saved. I think those are two of my parent's guards," Arron shouted waving at the approaching men in armor.

"Arron stop, I don't think those are guards. Those are…"

"Drogans!" Lija screamed finishing for her brother.

Bruce drew his sword as the two men began to shift in size, claws and wings growing forth. Bruce swung at the first Drogan and missed by a few inches. Losing his balance from the over swing, the Drogan batted him away sending him hard to the ground.

"No use running. The king has declared you kidnappers of the prince. There is now a price on each of your heads. Doesn't really matter, like you, Sorran will soon be ours," the creature laughed as he opened his mouth.

Marcus knew what would come next. He quickly lunged and hit the second Drogan with force sending him between Bruce and his attacker, the flame from the first Drogan engulfed the second in a blaze of fire. Marcus then grabbed the creature's fallen sword and swung at the second Drogan. He was shocked at how easy the red blade sliced through the creature's scaly skin sending its head a few feet from the lifeless body.

"Their skin appears to help protect them from fire, but it still hurts and slows them down," Marcus said as he used the red bladed sword to finish off the burning creature.

"Thanks for the save. I must be winded from the flight," Bruce said with shame. His lack of skill with a sword was one of the reasons he never made a higher rank.

"What are those things?" Prince Arron gasped at the two dead creatures.

"Those are the creatures we were telling you about that attacked our home. They are half human, half Dragon and dangerous. We lucked out," Marcus said helping Bruce to his feet.

"What do we do now?" Lija began to cry.

"We can't go barging into town if what he says about the price on our heads is true, especially with traitors inside the walls orchestrating our demise. I can already see guards lining up on the walls from here, we can't risk how they will greet us," Bruce said as he took another look at the dead creatures that were shifting back to human form.

"Now we look like murderers," Aaron added, taking note that it was hard to tell moments ago these had been winged creatures.

"We can't go west, the Kingdom of Tallus has their borders walled and won't grant entrance to no one," Bruce said as Marcus walked over and comforted his sister.

"I don't think we can go east."

"Why is that, Arron?" Lija sniffed.

"Because of those." They all turned to see a bunch of winged creatures flying low to the ground off in the distance.

"We need to move or they will be on us in no time. Arron, you head back and say you got away. No point in you going with us and being in danger."

"No, I want to come. Why should my brother have all the fun," Arron said as he glanced at Lija with a wink making her blush.

"He might be safer with us," Marcus said hoping he would not regret his words as he saw the way the prince looked at his sister.

"Very well, then. You ever use a sword?" Bruce asked the young prince.

"No sir."

"Here, you can have mine. It is light and easy to handle," Bruce said tossing the young prince his sword and picking up the other creature's sword, "I think this will come in handy."

"Thanks," Arron said still feeling the excitement of his first adventure.

"We head south," Bruce said as he urged them to get moving.

"We can't go south. There's nothing there but the Drol Death Desert," Marcus said, knowing there was no way anyone could survive that place.

"We are going to die for sure," Lija cried hugging her brother.

"No, we won't. If we get running now we will have a good lead on those creatures. Not too far from here, an old friend of mine owns a small farm. If we hurry, we should make it there in a few hours."

"Then what? We can't hide out there forever, if those creatures don't find us, eventually an angry King Sirus or Allen will," Marcus said taking notice of the Drogans off in the distance getting closer.

"I say we do more running and less talking," Prince Arron suggested, glancing to the east and taking off at a dead run south with Bruce following and Marcus, taking up the rear helping his sister along, who seemed more scared of ruining her new dress than the creatures that were after them.

After a few miles of running Bruce spoke up again. "I think we will be safe from those creatures. They don't seem to be moving as fast and staying as close to the ground near the castle grounds. I imagine they don't take full flight in fear of being spotted by the people of Sorran."

"I just hope that they don't take Sorran like they did Soré," Marcus huffed.

"Marcus, I can't run any longer. My feet are tired and I just want to go home."

"I know, but we can't stop now."

"Don't worry, we should be reaching my friend's place soon. There we can eat and rest for a bit. After that I will see if he can't give us a few horses and supplies."

"Then where do we go?"

"You won't be going anywhere, young prince. Those creatures are after us not you, so I will have my friend get you safely back to your parents while the rest of us ride southwest towards the Drol Death Desert. You can then tell your parents and the king of what has truly transpired. With horses, we should be able to track through the northern edge of the desert going southwest along the border, passing through quickly and safely reaching the northeast border of the Kingdom of Silversword," Bruce said, as even he tried to believe that traveling on the edge of the desert was safe.

"But, no one entering the Desert ever comes back," Lija cried in a whisper, panting for breath while trying to keep up.

"Don't worry, I'll protect you," Prince Arron said dropping back next to the girl holding up his new sword with no intentions of ever going back to his old boring life.

"You think King Thadius of Silversword will help us? Don't you think we should stay closer to Sorran until Arron clears our names?" Marcus asked as he found it harder to keep his sister moving while keeping an eye on the *inexperienced* prince.

"I hope so, from what I have heard they are a very noble people," Bruce said glancing back occasionally at the trio of young adults. He did not answer the last question as he feared they may not be able to return to Sorran, or at least himself after this.

"How much farther?" Lija asked bursting with tears.

"There it is now," Bruce said as their pace slowed to a fast walk.

They looked up and saw a small farmhouse with a stable and small farming land around it. Just as they neared the front of the house Bruce gave a shout, "Patches! We need some help!"

At the sound of the cry, an old man with long gray hair and matching beard sporting a brown patch over his right eye, came out in time to see four figures collapse in his yard.

Chapter Seven:
Mount Semaj & The Magesti

"Stop! I'm not a Drogan," Essej shouted as he called forth his powers to blow the three attackers backwards and onto the ground.

Anna, Semaj and Thom stared at the man who now had white Dragon wings flapping behind him and a scaly white skin tone. They still were trying to get over the fact that what they had been running from was the same thing that had been leading them.

"Then what are you?" Anna shouted as she stood back up, dagger in one hand and reaching out for her power with the other hand. Thom and Semaj took a stance on each side of her.

"It doesn't matter, he lied to us," Thom said as he tried to will his crystal to life.

"I didn't lie to you. I told you that I was part human and part Elf. Which is true, but I am also half Dragon. My mother was half human and Elf while my father was, as my mom whispered it in my ear, a Dragon," Essej said, taking a deep breath and locked eyes with the three of them.

Anna's anger began to soften as she felt the truth in his words. "Then what are you if you're not a Drogan?" Anna lowered her dagger and withdrew her grasp on her powers.

"I am a Huelgon. My species is very rare, rarer than Drogans." Essej knew he should have been more open from the beginning but he was afraid that if he had revealed his true self they would never have come and his promise to his Semaj would never have been kept.

"I really don't see a difference. I think we should head home. We were fools to follow him. Now our families will be lost because of him," Semaj said as tears began to swell in his eyes. All he could think about was his parents and how much he craved to be home safe with them and not out here in the middle of nowhere.

"There's a big difference my young friend," Essej's wings folded back nicely against his back. He stepped closer to the three, "A Drogan, being only part human and part Dragon and usually created by unnatural means, is limited to their power and are not very intelligent. While a Huelgon, being also part Elf is much smarter and free of mind and has more control over their powers. Believe me when I tell you that everything I've told you is true and I'm good of heart. Please believe me, the fate of the world rests upon the Chosen One being brought to the top of this mountain."

"There is no mention of Huelgon in my books, or Drogans for that matter. The fact they don't set off magic alarms makes me think they are not truly beings of magic," Thom said as he studied the creature in front of him while rubbing his crystal while Essej said nothing more.

"I say we leave."

"No, Semaj. In my heart I know we can trust him."

"Anna is right. Usually when I'm in danger my crystal aids me and this time it didn't. Not so much as a spark at him."

The three sat there in silence for few minutes as they watched the winged Dragon- man-Elf. They could see the plea for urgency and help in his eyes. Looking in his glowing eyes they could see a man of true kindness and goodness. Anna was the first to step forward.

"I say we try and trust him. The people back home are depending on us. How are we supposed to all get to the top?"

"That will be a little tricky. In my younger days I might have been able to carry all three of you but I am afraid I will need to take you up one at a time."

Anna agreed to go first, dagger in hand just in case. Essej stepped behind her and put his arms around her. As his wings expanded and began to flap he reached out with his powers causing a strong force of wind and air to hit them from underneath. Essej used his wings to take them up as the wind he controlled gave him added strength and upward force. Anna was in awe as the ground vanished and she soon found herself high up in the sky.

After a few minutes she felt solid ground under her feet. They were now standing on a small ledge that extended out from a passageway into the mountain itself. She turned to Essej only to discover that he had already headed back down. She wanted to look around but was afraid to move so that the stronger winds up here wouldn't blow her off the edge.

"It's cold up here." She turned to see Semaj standing near her.

"Yes, it is." Anna found herself beginning to shiver.

"Maybe you could use your powers to keep us warm till the other two come back?"

Anna could have slapped herself. She kept forgetting about them. Having powers was something she still had to get used to. She reached out with her powers and found that it was getting easier to do. In no time she had pulled heat all around them and they were no longer shivering.

"It still freaks me out but I could get used to this," Anna smiled.

"This all seems like a dream. The Drogans, Essej, you having powers and everything that has happened to all of us."

Anna felt the same way, but before she could reach out to him she realized Essej had returned with Thom. "That was amazing. I wonder if my crystal can make me fly."

"Let's get out of this wind and into safer quarters," Essej urged them into the mountain's cave as his wings vanished and his skin took on a more human look again.

They paused as they stepped into the dark cave. It was pitch black and they could not see a thing. Essej, having sight of a Dragon and Elf had great night vision, forgot that the humans would need some light. He reached down and picked up a stick and pointed it toward Anna. "Anna, I want you to use your powers and focus them around the top of the stick." Essej then quickly instructed her on what she needed to do.

Anna was amazed at how easy it was to perform the task. In a matter of moments, she had felt and pulled the heat around the tip of the stick and then willed it hotter and hotter until it ignited into flame. She found, with greater ease, she was able to pull back and cut off her connection with the power. She smiled with accomplishment as they all could now see inside the cave thanks to the flaming torch.

The cave wasn't very big. It was cozy enough for them all to stand in but they noticed that they could jump up and touch the ceiling and that a few feet in front of them they reached a dead end. The cave went no further into the mountain. Besides the four of them, there was absolutely nothing else in this cave.

"Okay, now what?" Anna asked turning on Essej, wondering if they had made the right decision to let the Huelgon bring them op here.

"We wait."

"What do you mean wait? What is it you're supposed to show us?" Semaj asked as his patience was beginning to wear thin.

"I do not know what will happen now. All I know is I am supposed to bring the Chosen One here."

"You don't know? What do you mean you don't know?" This time Thom was growing angry.

"Just have patience. When my Semaj came here he just vanished. I do not know what to expect, just that I was to bring you here." Essej could feel tears forming. Being here was starting to bring back old memories and feelings. He prayed to his dear love that something would happen, anything.

As the three of them started to grow impatient and shout at him, Essej could feel doubt rising in his soul. Had he held on to a false dream? Was everything that he believed in just a fantasy of a lost love? As he gently began to lower his head he realized that silence had overcome the cave and that the cave was illuminated by something other than the torch, which appeared to have gone out.

"What is going on?" Anna said as she gripped her dagger tight in one hand and reached for Thom and Semaj with the other.

"Where's that light coming from?" Thom whispered as his eyes darted all around the cave. The light was not coming from one source. It was as if the light was projected from all around them and from everything.

"I don't believe my eyes." This time it was Essej who sounded in awe.

As they looked around frantically, they realized that they were no longer looking at the back of the cave's wall. The wall was now behind them and they were staring into a large room that was lit by the same mysterious light as before. The room was so large that they could not see where any of the other three walls were or the ceiling above them.

"Greetings to you all," said a voice out of nowhere. It was as if the wind itself carried it to their ears.

"Did you hear that?" Anna asked as she quickly armed herself with her other dagger. Now both ready to protect her and her friends.

"I've been awaiting and dreading this moment for ages. It brings me great joy and yet great fear."

"Essej, who's that speaking?" Thom asked holding his crystal up as he and Anna stood in a protective stance around a weaponless Semaj.

"I'm not sure but I feel a great kinship within it. Put your weapons away, we have nothing to fear here. This is what we have been searching for," Essej said as he quivered and fell to one knee.

They couldn't figure out what the old man was doing until they realized they were not alone. Essej was kneeling to something that was materializing out of thin air before them. They all gasped in fear as they saw a giant, translucent white Dragon looking down at them. The creature sat on all fours. Its tail wrapped around its body as giant wings could be seen resting against its sides. The Dragon's head was low enough for them to see its chilly eyes and large maw with sharp teeth.

"A Dragon!" Screamed Anna as a dagger flew from her hand, passing completely through the creature and landing somewhere unknown behind it.

"Relax, I mean you no harm. Dragon is what I used to be, now I am all but a spirit of what was," the wind carried voice told them.

They could see now that the Dragon was not solid but what appeared to be a ghost of sorts. They all stood there shaking in fear except for Essej who stood back up and approached the Dragon. The creature peered down at the old man and a hint of sadness could almost be seen in its eyes. *"Essej, you have finally returned with a wielder of the Magesti."*

"The what?" Semaj asked to his two friends.

"*I see you found the Chosen One, which means the evil he must fight has moved back upon this world,*" the Dragon spirit said as he nodded down at Semaj.

"Why are you looking at me? Anna is the Chosen One," Semaj said glancing at Anna for help who just shrugged.

"*No, descendant of Semaj Lightheart, you are the Chosen One. Your friend here is just one of the great Magestics,*" the Dragon spirit smiled with a small bow to Semaj.

"Wait a minute. Essej, you said Anna was the Chosen One and had to come to the mountain."

"At first, I didn't know which one of you was until Anna used the fire. At that moment I knew she was a wielder of the power but you were the one I have been watching for all these years," Essej said as he still kept his eyes on the Dragon spirit. He couldn't help but feel a strange connection to this spirit. That there was something more than just Dragon attributes between them.

"What about Thom?" Anna asked tapping his crystal.

"*What your friend there has is an artifact of great magic. It has nothing to do with the Chosen One or the power of the Magesti. It seems to be a source of connection between Thom and magic. I am afraid there is nothing more I know or can tell you.*"

"If it's a source of magic than why don't the alarms sound?" Thom asked, excitement in his voice at the confirmation that he held something of magic.

"*Something greater shields it from detection, but like I said, that is all I know.*"

"This is all too much. I don't understand. My parents never said anything to me about being related to Semaj Lightheart. I am no Chosen One, I'm just a simple farmer like my parents," Semaj said as he held his head trying to shake away the tears of confusion.

"*For whatever reasons, your parents kept this from you. I assure you that you share more than the first name of Master Lightheart. You are the one to lead the Magestics to save all of Bergonia from evil.*"

"What is a Magestic and just who are you?" Anna looked up at the creature while putting an arm around Semaj.

"Please, sit, all of you. I have much to explain and little time to do it in. Evil has already made its move and it's important that I instruct you in what you need to know and do to fight it," the Dragon spirit said as the four of them reluctantly sat upon the ground. They had no choice and nowhere to run.

"Why would my parents keep this from me? I'm no leader." Semaj continued to become flustered.

"I know this seems like a lot but we've come this far. We might as well hear the Dragon out," Thom told his two friends, still reeling from the artifact of magic around his neck. If this was magic, then his books had to be truly connected to magic as well.

"We can decide what to do after we hear what the Dragon has to say," Anna added in agreement.

The three friends now turned and stared right at the large, scary but awe-inspiring Dragon spirit. Essej remained frozen, staring up at the great Dragon, speechless with lots of questions. He knew that everything was about to become clear and nothing was going to be the same again, for any of them.

"My given name, when I was alive was Dwin. I was one of twelve great Dragon Kings. But I will get more to that in a bit. It seems like the best place to start is at the beginning. In order to understand the power you hold, you must know where it came from and how it has shaped this world. Especially since you humans choose to ignore and pretend that none of this ever existed. What I am about to tell you are a mix of personal knowledge, a rough history and lore passed down to me.

"In the beginning, the world was dominated by Dragons. As time passed, primitive humans and other creatures evolved as Dragons grew more intelligent and colonized the world. The first ruler of the Dragons was named Bergonia, which the land was named after. All Dragons lived in peace and harmony with the other creatures of the world. This was known as the Age of Dragons.

"It is unclear how it happened but it is said in Dragon lore that about forty-four thousand seasons before the Dragon Wars, or to you humans forty-nine thousand years before the Magic Wars, a group of Dragons stumbled upon a mysterious power

source and unleashed it on the world. The power now known as the Magesti.

"It is said that the Magesti bonded with the Dragons changing them, altering their appearance and extending their average life span by thousands of seasons. After about nine thousand seasons, Dragons began to be born with colors and fewer non-colored Dragons were being born. By about one thousand seasons before Dragon Wars or six thousand years before Magic Wars to you humans, all Dragons were born with one of fifteen colors.

"At this time, each of the thirteen colors: brown, white, red, blue, yellow, black, gray, gold, orange, pink, purple, green and silver, found that they could tap into a specific element of the Magesti power while the other two colors: bright rainbow and dark rainbow could not use any power. Even though they all got along, each color colonized their own regions in the world.

"At this point, the world of Bergonia had greatly changed too. There were now forests, seas, mountains and other land formations and areas due to the effect of the Magesti being unleashed and used. Humans and other human-like creatures had developed intelligence while the influence of the Magesti helped create races such as Dwarves, Ogres, Minotaurs, Goblins and many others.

"With all this happening, the Dragons still dominated all species and made themselves like gods. No race challenged them. They feared and respected the mighty Dragons. About one thousand seasons before Dragon Wars, thirteen Dragons were born at the exact same time. Each one from one of the thirteen single colors but with two differences than any other Dragon – their scale color was very bright and they were the first Magestics, beings with the ability to tap into the Magesti at will and wield and control it with great unlimited power and force.

"As they grew older all the Dragons realized what they were and what they could do. All thirteen of them grew to become the great Dragon Kings and ruled all Dragons. Because of our power and status, we took on names that represented our element of power in our ancient tongue. Ethar the Brown, Ifre the Red, T'ligh the Yellow, Thead the Grey, Bydo the Orange, Losu the Purple, Awret the Blue, K'dra the Black, D'min the

Gold, Terah the Pink, Feli the Green, Menteles Lal the Great
Silver and myself Dwin the White.

"By five hundred seasons before Dragon Wars, all thirteen
of us kings had absolute power and ruled their own color and
territory. Bonds and friendships between the colors started to
break as the powerless bright rainbow and dark rainbow
Dragons were pushed to the side. Even the now colonized races
began to fear the coming storm. The world was about to change
again.

"In the time you humans call five thousand years before
Magic Wars, the Dragon Wars began. K'dra the Black decided
that she was more godlike than any of the other Dragon Kings
and felt she should be ruler of all Dragons and all of Bergonia.
Of course, many of us opposed her, but with promises of more
power the Kings and Dragons of brown, gray, orange, red and
the dark rainbows used as slaves, joined her cause for world
domination.

"Menteles Lal the Silver declared that all should rule
equally and live in peace and felt that the world needed to be
protected from the Dragons of Dark. So, us Kings and Dragons
of gold, yellow, white, blue and the bright rainbow Dragons,
which we used wrongfully as slaves too, joined the silvers as the
Dragons of Light to battle K'dra.

"The Dragons of pink, green and purple chose to remain
neutral while all other races knew they would be caught in the
crossfire prepared for survival. While Dragons were taking sides
and preparing for war, a set of rainbow twins were born in my
region, Wrinboa who had bright stripes and Boawrin who had
dark stripes. I was the only one that thought this was a sign but
was immediately disregarded.

"The memory of what was to come still plagues me today.
The Dragon Wars lasted about three thousand seasons. To us
Dragons who now had a much longer life spans, it didn't seem
that long, but to the other races and the world time took its toll
and lasted for what seemed like forever. Both sides created
damage and bloodshed and I regret it to this day. This entire
power struggle came at a great cost.

"By about four thousand seasons before Magic Wars, the
Dragon's powers and the Dragon King's control over the

Magesti started to weaken due to the abuse of the power and the destruction to the land of Bergonia. I've always had a theory that the Magesti and the elements of its power were greatly tied into the world around us. That a balance must always be kept. Either way, the land was changed due to our war – forests were burned away, mountains were destroyed and what you call the Fire Mountains and the Forbidden Isles were created.

    "During this time, the rainbow twins were grown and they had disappeared. They wouldn't be seen for another thousand seasons. What they had done is unknown to us but when they returned it would be too late for the rest of us to care," Dwin sighed as Essej came to life and spoke up.

    "If I may interject, from what I studied in the Elven history books about Elven creation, I might be able to fill in that gap. It is said that two twin rainbow Dragon gods had discovered a force called *magic*. With this newfound power they began teaching other rainbow Dragons how to use it and during that time of practicing and learning they created and enhanced other races– the Elves, clerics, wizards and other magical creatures were born. Even though we honor the twin Dragon gods for giving our race life, we were still taught that Dragons are evil. That is why, even to my people, it is important to hide any Dragon heritage."

    "Essej, what you say validates what happened later. As sad as it is that you refer to us Dragons as evil, we deserved it. After what we all did, good and bad Dragons alike, we deserve to be called evil for how corrupted we all became and the damage we caused to the world and her creatures. That is what happens when good battles evil in a struggle for power.

    "Now, where was I, oh yes, after another thousand seasons of war pass, the power to call upon the Magesti had weakened even more. Even us great Dragon Kings were having trouble controlling it. The cost of war was too high and many Dragons and other races had too many casualties. We even lost five of the great Dragon Kings- two from the Dragons of Light and three from the Dragons of Dark. The Dragons of Light finally won but it was a very sad time. We had all been friends once.

    "K'dra, greatly wounded took her forces and retreated to what you call the Unknown Lands in the south, except for Ethar

and the browns. He decided to take his fellow Dragons into the Northern Mountains. Those that didn't want to follow either of them just went into their own isolation. With them gone, and the neutral Dragons still hiding, Menteles Lal, Awret and I rallied the remaining Dragons of Light to begin rebuilding the land. We were glad that the Dragon Wars were over, or so we thought.

"That following season is when the rainbow twins resurfaced and made their move. At this point, we could no longer rely on the power of the Magesti. We had abused it and drained its power immensely. The Magestics were no more and we no longer cared. We were powerless to what happened next.

"The twins waged war on all remaining Magesti based Dragons and Dragon Kings. All non-powered rainbow Dragons, both bright and dark that had been slaves to us rose up and attacked us. Almost all of them, including the twins were wielding this force called magic. *We didn't know where or how they discovered and learned it but they knew how to use it. With our powers weakened, we were just not prepared to defend against this force called* magic.

"To make matters worse, the magical creatures, Elves, wizards and clerics had rallied all the other races to rise up and help attack the Magesti Dragons. Even the Dragons of Dark were found and hunted down. Now that war was being waged on us and we had become the hunted, the neutral Dragons had no choice but to come out of hiding and make a stand with the rest of us.

"The next five hundred seasons were the worst for us. There is a great difference between fighting a war for power and fighting a war for survival. Our downfall was upon us and whether we wanted to admit it or not, we had brought it upon ourselves. The twins and their forces had won and what was left of us, scattered into hiding.

"All the Dragon Kings had appeared to have been killed except for Menteles Lal and myself. The great silver had created a gem that held the remaining power of the Magesti and wanted to find a safe place to hide it and urged me to vanish myself. Which I did. I found a way to make myself look human and I blended away, staying hidden and watching as the races of the world began to regroup and colonize again.

"Now the Dragon Wars were coming to an end. There were now two Dragon rulers-Wrinboa who wanted all to live as one in peace and rule over the races and Boawrin who wanted to continue the Dragon Wars and completely hunt down any remaining Magesti Dragons, rule the whole world making the other races their food and slaves. Within the next season, it found twin versus twin in the final stage of the Dragon Wars.

"Boawrin and his forces waged war on Wrinboa, his forces and the remaining Magesti Dragons. Now, disguised as a human they couldn't find me but I was able to learn other things. All the non-Dragon races had decided to secretly plot to rid the world of all Dragons and thus ridding the world of evil and war. They made an agreement to side with Boawrin who had the stronger force to help rid the world of Wrinboa and the Magesti Dragons.

"After about another five hundred seasons the Dragon Wars finally came to an end. To my knowledge all Magesti Dragons had been hunted down and killed. I wasn't even sure if Menteles Lal had sucedded hiding his gem. I was the only one remaining of my kind, which meant I had to stay hidden. I kept moving from place to place so that people wouldn't wonder why a human could live so long. The power of the Magesti had faded away and the world was now dominated by magic.

"Boawrin had been slain and Wrinboa tried to pick up the pieces and bring what was left of the Dragons back together. While they were trying to bring peace back to the Dragons, it left them unprepared for the war the non-Dragon races had been plotting. With great unity, force, weapons and magic, the non-Dragon races struck from nowhere and hunted down all remaining Dragons. After thousands of seasons of battling each other the remaining Dragons had left themselves weakened and unready to fight a group they had always thought was weak and beneath them.

"During this time, I thought it would be best if I headed out and found a new life for myself, away from all the fighting. As seasons passed and Dragons became fewer and fewer I had made a home for myself in a small village. I did feel guilty for not joining up with my fellow Dragons, but I was tired of the fighting and didn't care what became of the world. I wanted to be alone, or so I thought.

"I believe it was about one thousand and one years before Magic Wars, in human time, when I met her, the love of my life. Even though I knew it was forbidden to even think of a Dragon loving a non-Dragon, I was living as human now and felt it didn't matter. I had been walking in a wooded area when I bumped into her. She was beautiful and come to find out she was half human and half Elf.

"She had been traveling away from the Elves in search of her human father. We talked and talked and instantly fell in love. I even told her about my true self. She didn't care. We spent many nights together knowing that it was forbidden for us to be together for so many reasons, but that didn't stop our love from growing. I once again had feelings and cared about life. On what would be our last night together, I told her I had to head near the mountains to hunt for food for the winter.

"We agreed to meet back at my place the following night where we would plan to run off and be married. With joy in my heart I headed out hunting. That is when tragedy struck. As I was hunting near the mountains I found something shining in the ground. I picked it up and discovered the gem the Great Silver had created.

"As soon as I touched it I felt the power of the Magesti within it and a final message from Menteles Lal. The gem was to be used to one day bring the power of the Magesti back into Bergonia as a force of good to protect against evil. That he had learned where the Dragons had went wrong and how it could be used as a better source of good. It wanted me to take up that mission.

"I couldn't, I had a life now and a bride to be. As much as the gem called I swore it away and shattered it on the mountainside. Without warning, power erupted from the shattered gem and engulfed me in a powerful light of many colors. I was ripped back into my Dragon form and then that power took me and crushed me into the mountainside in a huge explosion.

"When I woke, I had found that the gem and its powers had merged me with the mountain. It had created the great Mount Semaj, as you call it now, with my spirit forever trapped within with no choice but to wait for the time when I would be needed to

pass on the power of the Magesti. I knew I was destined to help a greater good, but it pained me to know I would never see my true love again."

"I knew it! I felt it!" Essej began to scream up at the Dragon spirit. "Your love's name was Leajra, who was also my mother. Which makes you my father," Essej said as his voice began to shake.

The three kids were taken back by this revelation. It shocked them more than what they had already heard from Dwin. They felt compelled to go near Essej but knew it was better to let this play out between the two of them.

"Yes, Essej, I am your father. Oh, how I longed to tell you."

"What? You knew this whole time and never told me? All my life I had been searching for the Dragon that had abandoned my mother with child and left her heart broken so I could make him pay and now I find…" Essej's voice faded as he looked up with tears and anger.

"Don't be angry with me. I never abandoned your mother and you. I truly loved her and as you can see I was taken from her without choice. It pains me to have never been able to be with her but it tears me apart to know that she died thinking I abandoned her. I really wanted to tell you, my son."

"Why didn't you? When I was here with Semaj or all those years sleeping in this cave you could have come to me. Why didn't you?" Essej asked as pain made his voice grow louder and harsher.

"I couldn't tell you, as much as I wanted to. I feared that if I told you any time before now, that it might risk causing you not to help Semaj Lightheart battle the evil or take up the mission to bring back the next Chosen One to me now. As you can see, I had to once again sacrifice my heart for the greater good. You have to believe that I truly wanted to be a part of your life," Dwin pleaded as his head shifted down closer to look into Essej's eyes.

"I can feel the truth in your words but I still wish you had told me sooner."

"Please let me finish the tale," Dwin interrupted his son. *"Now that I was trapped within the mountain I could do nothing but wait. That next season you were born, and I had felt it*

though the connection of our power and bond through the Magesti. That broke what was left of my heart to know I had not only lost my bride but a son too. As I went into a waiting sleep, I sensed that same season my son was born, was also the season Dragons were declared extinct and the Age of Races had begun.

"Another thousand seasons passed when suddenly I was pulled awake from my sleep. I could feel that great magic and evil had broken loose and that the Magesti was calling for a Chosen One to rise up and save the world. I sat here waiting wondering what would happen. Then, after a few seasons I felt two beings enter my cave. One was the Chosen One and the other I knew was my son.

"I wanted to reveal myself then but knew I couldn't. I had to make sure Semaj Lightheart fulfilled his destiny and that you, Essej had to help him do it. I pulled in Semaj and left you outside alone so not to risk you finding me out. Semaj told me how the Magic Wars had begun and that an evil man named Drol Greb was trying to take over Bergonia.

"I knew what I had to do, but in order to find freedom I made a fatal mistake that not only cost the life of a great man but also my freedom to be with my son. I thought if I trained Semaj in the ways of the Magesti and gave all the power to just him he would defeat the evil faster and then I would be released from my prison.

"It didn't work out that way. When Semaj sacrificed his life, the power of the Magesti and his mind touched me and I knew that he had discovered what needed to be done and what I should have done in the first place. The power of the Magesti isn't meant for one person to wield or one race. Semaj realized that.

"So, he had cast the power into a gem too and then gave instructions of what needed to be done. This time the power was sent directly into the descendants of the twelve brave souls who risked their lives to save the world, as well as his descendant. Next time when evil rose and the power of the Magesti is needed, Semaj's descendant would awaken with the power and Essej would bring him here so I could instruct him. He would then gather the other twelve and together they would defeat the evil.

125

*"I knew this had to happen right or I would never be free.
You had to be focused on finding and bringing the Chosen One
here. Now that you are here and I have told you what needs to be
told, Semaj, like your ancestor, you must take up the cause and
bring together the Magestics. Only this way can the power of the
Magesti, being used by the thirteen different beings of good
coming together as one, can truly defeat evil and be in harmony
with the world once more. Only then can I be free."*

"What if I don't want to do this?" Semaj said starting to feel
faint.

*"You have to. So much is depending upon you and the
Magestics. We Dragons misused the power and allowed it to
fade away as that force of magic took over. Now there is no
power in the world and the way the world sits now, there is no
way it can protect itself from the coming evil. You all are needed.
It is now the Age of the Magesti. You will accomplish what needs
to be done to save Bergonia."*

"It just seems like so much to handle."

"Semaj, we have to do it. It is the only way to save our
families. Don't worry we will all be here to help you," Thom
said as the excitement of it all exploded in his voice.

"He's right, Semaj. This is more than just an adventure.
This is a legacy of something great passed down from our
ancestors. If anything, do it for your parents and friends," Anna
said as she stepped near him. Wondering with pride, about her
ancestor who had fought and passed this power down to her.

"She's right. If you refuse, then all I have done, my life,
what my Semaj sacrificed will have all been in vain. It's the only
way to save the world and give my father back to me," Essej said
as he looked up at his father's spirit giving reassurance that there
was hope for the both of them.

"As much as I don't want to, I can't do nothing and just
watch my friends and family die. So what kind of powers do I
have and how do I find the other Magestics?" Semaj asked
causing everyone to smile and silently applaud him.

*"You actually don't have any powers, like Anna has. You
are not so much a Magestic, but the Chosen One with the ability
to bring them together and lead them."*

"I don't understand?"

"You have the ability to sense the Magestics and the power they wield. You can ignite that power from within them and guide them. We Dragons believed that the Magesti is a power source that flows though all things and is made up of twelve elements- Earth, Wind, Fire, Water, Light, Dark, Soul, Body, Mind, Heart, Death and Life. The Magestics are the beings that can actually tap into that power to use and control."

"Wait a minute," Semaj said finally realizing something. He quickly recounted to Dwin everything that has happened to them including all the dreams he had been having.

"Why didn't you say anything about your dream? It's like you predicted everything, me with my crystal, Drol coming and Essej here," Thom said looking at his best friend while touching his crystal and thinking of Lars.

"I don't know. I just thought it was a dream and kind of forgot about it or wanted to forget about it," Semaj felt his gut turn as he peered into his friend's eyes. "Now with all that has happened and the continued dreams, I have to accept that it all means something now. The dreams are real and having meaning, right?" They all looked to the Dragon spirit.

"Yes, your dreams were a way for the Magesti to communicate, guide and show you where you needed to go to find the Magestics. That first dream was the awakening, the beginning of what was to come. The dream with Anna and the fire represented her being a Magestic and that she controls the element of fire. Then when you touched her, that spark was you boosting the power within her."

"He can only track them when he's asleep? So, all of us being in the dream had nothing to do with me?" Thom asked feeling disappointed.

"Actually, the dream is one way to get in touch and communicate with the Magestics. I will show you how to use that tracking power while awake. Right now, the dreams were a way to access your power while your subconscious was more open to the Magesti. As for your crystal, Thom, it is a powerful artifact of magic.. It did somehow unite with Semaj's abilities and it gave a more reality to the dream while pulling you all in together."

"Then the last dream we were in with the mountains, what did that mean?" Anna asked.

"It would appear that where you need to go next is the Northern Mountains. That is where the next Magestic can be found. As for what the event in the dream meant appears that the Magestic there welds the element of earth," the former Dragon King said as his gaze looked out past them all.

"Whom we seek must be a Dwarf," Essej said agreeing with his newly found father.

"Are you sure? I thought I saw a man," Thom said scratching his head as he looked up at Dwin.

"Yeah, I saw him too," Anna and Semaj both replied as they then told Dwin about the figure that appeared in all the dreams.

"Is he a Magestic too?" Semaj asked.

"I fear not," Dwin roared as his face took on a sterner look. *"I sensed this but wanted to brush it aside as nothing but from what you have told me, I know the danger is real."*

"What are you talking about?" Essej stood up becoming more serious.

"The force of evil is somehow connected to a being that also has abilities similar to Semaj. The ability to track the Magestics,"

"How is that possible?" Essej paced in panic.

"I don't know, but luckily it isn't as strong as Semaj's ability, which means we must move fast. I assume you won't be the only ones searching for the Magestics, but unlike you their intentions will not be about saving the world, which you all have experienced by the attack of the Drogans."

"It seems things are different than the time with my Semaj. Even the Drogans are different."

"What do you mean, my son?"

"Drogans of the past were fueled by magic, but these now, I could feel a connection. They are somehow connected to the Magesti, like me, and can also sense when Semaj connects to the power."

"Are you sure they are using the Magesti?"

"Yes, I can feel it when they summon the fire. Plus, it doesn't set off the magic alarms. These new Drogans are far more intelligent and have better speech than their ancestral creations. I just don't know how they got the ability to use the

Magesti, like me. Now, I know mine is from my natural bloodline with you, father, but..."

"It seems something, or someone is able to fuse them with the Magesti, which makes your mission even more dire."

"What do we do now?" Anna asked ready for the adventure to begin.

"First, I need to give you further training and instructions that you will need to continue your journey. After that, I have an idea using Thom and his crystal that will allow us to connect with the other Magestics more quickly," Dwin said as he urged them to follow him deeper into the endless room.

James W. Berg

Chapter Eight:
Deserts & Dreams

Marcus woke to the scent of fresh tea. The soothing smell almost made him think he was back home with his parents. As he sat up he realized he was anywhere but home. He looked around and saw that he was in a small room, barely illuminated by the sun's light. He assumed the room must be a guestroom of sorts with a table, a couple chairs and two beds, one of which he was sitting on. He exhaled with relief when he saw his sister fast asleep on the other bed. He hated that she was being put through so much danger, but he would do everything he could to keep her out of harm's way.

He got up and looked out the window to see the sun beginning to set. It would be dark soon. He had not realized how long he had been sleeping. After a few minutes, he stepped away from the window. There were no signs of those dreadful creatures, but for how long? He headed towards the door where he could hear voices coming from the other side.

He opened the door and stepped out into a small hallway and closed the door quietly as to not wake his sister. He followed the voices down the hall till he reached a small living room. The room was beautifully decorated with flowers, woodcarvings and other various handmade items. In the middle of the room was a small couch where Prince Arron laid fast asleep.

"Well hello, sweetie. Did you sleep okay?" Marcus turned at the voice to see a plump old woman with a huge smile standing in the entryway of a small kitchen. Behind her, sitting at a small wooden table was his dad's old friend Bruce Peters visiting with an older man, who wore a patch over his right eye.

"Yes, thank you ma'am."

"Oh, dear, you can call me Elle. Please come sit, I've made some fresh hot tea." Elle smiled as she placed a cup of tea at the table.

"What's going on?" Marcus asked as he sat and sipped the tea. "This is very good, thank you." Elle smiled at the boy and then began to hum to herself as she tended to whatever she was cooking on the stove.

"Marcus, I would like you to meet my dear friend Patches and his lovely wife Elle. He used to be a weapons trainer for the king."

"It's nice to meet you. Is that how you lost your eye?" Marcus asked, his curiosity getting the best of him.

"Nah, I was born without it. Been wearing the eye patch since birth," the old man said tapping his covered eye.

"Even so, you won't find a better marksman with a bow anywhere in Sorran," Bruce bragged about his friend.

"That was a long time ago. Ever since the king thought me and my ideas were getting too old, the little lady and I have retired to the farm full time. Nice and peaceful out here," Patches laughed as he sipped his tea.

"You know you miss the excitement," Elle sang and then went back to her humming.

"I have filled him in on what has happened with you and your friends as well as our encounter with the Drogans and the chase from Castle Sorran."

"I find it hard to believe. There hasn't been trouble in Sorran for hundreds of years." Patches' wife paused and turned to the table. "You all are welcomed to stay the night, even if Bruce here thinks that if you guys don't leave soon that we might be in danger," Elle said before turning back to the pot on the stove. "Supper should be ready shortly."

"You never mind, woman. I've been telling you for years that I've been feeling something brewing in the world. I can feel it in my bones," the old man snapped at his wife.

"We appreciate your help, Patches." Turning to Marcus, he added, "Patches is going to let us take a couple horses and Elle has already made a bundle of rations for us. As soon as we eat, I'll take you and your sister and we'll head to Silversword."

"What about Prince Arron?" Marcus asked, glancing over at the prince, who was starting to sit up, rubbing his eyes.

"Once you three are gone and it looks safe enough, Elle and I will take him back to the castle."

"You think it would be a good idea to leave my sister here?"

"Not a good idea. Those creatures are looking for you and your sister. She'll be much safer with us."

"I agree with Bruce, especially if there's a traitor within the castle grounds," Patches remarked looking at the boy. "You look just like your father."

"You knew my father?"

"Yes, he was in my class till he advanced up. He was a good man, but I never got to know him like I did Bruce here."

Bruce looked down. He still got a little jealous of how Broc had moved up and that he was never able to advance any farther than he had. Even though he wished that he would have become more than just a grounds guard, he would never regret the friendship and closeness he had forged with his teacher. "Well, we better be..." Bruce started to say when he was silenced quickly by a loud explosion.

The force of the blast had flipped the table sending Marcus and the other two men rolling into the living room. Marcus jumped up to see a huge hole in the wall as the screaming voice of Elle confirmed that she and her kitchen were set afire. Marcus stood in shock while Bruce ran to the burning hole as Patches doused his wife with a basin of water putting her out.

"What was that?" Arron jumped up off the coach yelling as Lija came running into the living room bumping into him.

"You two stay back!" Marcus yelled as he moved near the old couple on the floor.

"They found us. As far as I can see there are only three of them out there. Their combined fire blasts must have caused the explosion." Bruce then glanced down at his friend, "Elle! Is she okay? This is our fault. We should never have come here."

"Calm down, Peters." Patches looked down at his wife as he held her. Most of her hair was singed and her face and arms were badly burned. "Elle, are you still with me?"

"You can't get rid of me that easily, you old fool," Elle coughed as she tried to reach and wipe the tear from her husband's eye.

"Save your strength, my love. Arron, come hold her! Lija, in that cabinet is a jar of salve. Take it and rub it all over her arms and face. It will help sooth and heal the burns," Patches barked the orders as he left Elle in Arron's arms and grabbed a crossbow.

"I don't know how much help an arrow will be against the creature's tough skin," Marcus said as he watched the old man's sudden speed.

"Those creatures are approaching the house pretty fast," Bruce reported and then pointed fiercely, "wait, one of them is stopping. I think it's getting ready to blast another ball of fire."

"Well let's see how they fare against my arrow." Marcus watched in awe as the man jumped in front of the kitchen's new opening and held up the crossbow. Closing his good eye, Patches aimed and fired. The arrow hit with amazing speed and accuracy as it entered the creatures opened mouth and then exploded, taking off the creature's head.

"I see you still have a few of your inventions around," Bruce said as he drew his sword.

"That was for hurting my wife," Patches shouted out at the creature and then grabbed two round items from a nearby pouch and quickly threw the balls at the last two creatures. The balls exploded upon contact, sending the creatures to the ground. "That's for ruining my supper."

"Nice shot, but it looks like their hide is pretty tough. They are still in one piece and starting to get back up," Bruce said as he saw his friend move back over to his wife.

"Wait! Look!" Marcus shouted as he had made his way to look out the hole in the wall. The creatures had almost made it up when they suddenly went still and fell back to the ground.

"A little gadget I had worked up. The liquid and fumes in those things causes its victims to become paralyzed for a while," Patches shouted over his shoulder as he helped the shaking Lija put the salve on his wife's burns.

"Is she going to die?" Lija cried as she began to think back to what had happened to Lars.

"Not if I can help it, honey. We need to get out of here and to Silversword quickly," Patches said as he took over for Lija. Lija got up and quickly ran into her brother's arms.

"You can't go with us. It's too dangerous and she won't survive the journey," Bruce pleaded to his old friend as he finished dousing the remaining flames in the kitchen with water.

"It's too dangerous to stay here. She's tougher than you think. She has a better chance if we come with you and get her to a doctor in Silversword. If we stay here or try to get to Sorran those creatures will surly find and kill us." Patches laid his wife down and began packing things. "We need to move out now. It won't be long before this place is crawling with more of those creatures."

Marcus and Bruce ran about helping Patches as Arron sat near Elle comforting both her and Lija. He knew he should be scared or sad but this was the most excitement he has ever experienced in his life. This meant that he did not have to go back home and that he could continue on this adventure. He knew his parents would be mad but he did not care since this time it was about him and not his brother.

"How are we going to carry her?" Arron asked as Patches stopped by again to check on his wife.

"I have a small covered wagon that we can use. The wheels I built for the thing are steady enough to track through the desert sand."

In a matter of moments, Patches and Bruce had the small covered wagon attached to two horses. The wagon was big enough to carry all their supplies, Patches' weapons and gadgets and blankets for Elle to lay upon with Lija sitting by her side. In front of the wagon was a seat where Patches would ride with Prince Arron next to him. Marcus and Bruce would ride upon their own horses.

Darkness had completely covered the land and the day was well over by the time they had reached the border between the Kingdom of Sorran and the Drol Death Desert. Marcus had always heard tales about the desert but never thought he would ever see it in person. Due to whatever its nature was, a haze rose up from the border that made it completely impossible to see into the desert.

"How is Elle?" Bruce asked Patches as he moved his horse next to the stopped wagon.

"Elle seems to be stable for now and Lija is sleeping soundly. She has been doing a great job looking after my wife," he said never taking his eyes off the wall of haze that separated them from the desert.

"I think it's giving her something to focus on and take her mind off of what is happening," Marcus added as he moved his horse to the other side of the wagon.

"Yes, at this age you are becoming adults but a shame you have to deal with all of this so young," Patches sighed as he then glanced down at the sleeping prince next to him.

"I don't like the idea of us *kidnapping* the Prince of Argoth like this," Bruce said glancing down too.

"We don't have a choice. He would be in danger if we left him behind or tried to get him back to the castle. Our safest bet is to head into the desert and away from those creatures," Patches said as he reached back and then handed each of them some dried meat. "You've been awfully quiet, my boy. What's on your mind?"

Marcus reached for the meat. "I was just thinking about my other friends, wondering if they made it to the mountain without any trouble, if my parents are okay, a lot of things I guess."

"You know if I hadn't seen this all with my own eyes I would never have believed your story. I just hope the king and the entire kingdom will be able to protect themselves and be safe until help can be found."

"As do I, Bruce, but if what Marcus here has said so far about that strange Elf is true, I think these Drogans are just the beginning. I fear evil is once again stirring in Bergonia and things will never be the same." Patches took a swig of water from his flask and then added, "I think we better get moving."

"Head into the desert now? Maybe we should camp here for the night and head out at first light," Marcus said as his nerves started to get to him at the thought of entering the dreaded Drol Death Desert.

"Not a good idea. I'm not sure what to expect in there but I think it will be safer and much cooler to travel the desert during the concealment of the night sky. Then during the day, we can all squeeze into the shade of the wagon's safe cover."

"If all goes well we should only have to sleep one day in the desert before reaching the border of Silversword," Bruce added as he finished his dried meat and looked back behind them for any signs of Drogans.

"As long as we don't get lost," Marcus remarked as he wondered how they would actually make it through the desert.

"Don't worry. The Desert's haze will conceal us from our enemy. We will travel close along the border's edge and I have my handy compass that I made. It will help guide us in the direction we need to go," Patches smiled as he reached into his pocket and held up a small round object. "Shall we?"

"At least we can move back out to safety if needed," Marcus mumbled more to himself.

"Well, until we reach the section walled up on the borders of the Kingdom of Tallus. At that point it will be a no turning back dash to Silversword," Bruce said as he got his horse moving.

Marcus swallowed hard as both horses and wagon moved slowly towards the desert. He could feel the change the minute they passed through the hazy border. The air went from cool to warm instantly. As he looked around, all he could see by the moon's light was desert, desert hills, sand and more sand. They had clearly entered the wasteland known as the Drol Death Desert.

As a child his dad had told him how the desert was so vast and unknown that anyone who entered never returned. When asked, his dad would say that it was easy to get lost and die of heat and dehydration, and if that did not kill you then the creatures of the sand would. The thought made him shudder and worry, even if they were stories told by parents to keep the kids away.

"With daylight gone do you really think it would be safer not to camp for the night?" Marcus asked looking up at Patches.

"Are you afraid of the dark, Marcus or maybe that the desert monsters will get us?" Prince Arron teased as he sat next to the one-eyed man controlling the horses pulling the covered wagon through the sand.

"That's nothing to make light of, my young prince," Patches glared over, removing the smile from Arron's face.

"Stop teasing the boys, Patches," Bruce chuckled as he brought his horse around near Marcus and the covered wagon.

"My dad used to tell us stories, but those were just tended to scare us and keep us from venturing into the desert," Marcus said as he continued to glance around at the quiet dark desert.

"Take note, stories or not, there are dangers in this desert." Patches grinned as all three men drew into his words. "It isn't named Drol Death Desert for nothing."

Patches had never been the insane fool that everyone thought he had become. Not only did he secretly keep knowledge of the world's history and tinker with gadgets, he also studied and researched the world they lived in. Not only did he view that as smart, but also kept him attune to survival. Patches looked at his audience and when no one breathed a word he continued on.

"The Desert is named after the great evil known as Drol Greb. As you all may or may not know, little over four hundred years ago, the Magic Wars ended with the defeat of Drol Greb. His demise was followed by a great magical explosion that not only created this desert wasteland but also altered the people and creatures magically into something horrid."

"Like what?" Prince Arron asked barely above a whisper.

"Not much is known, just theories and speculations, but there are dangers out here."

"What makes you think we're any safer at night rather than traveling in the morning when we can see the dangers?" Marcus asked as he pushed his horse forward to keep pace with the others.

"I don't." Patches then began to laugh. "We'll just stay cooler."

As the group pushed on not much more was said. They wanted to make it as far as possible and reach a good distance to Silversword before sunrise. Eventually they reached the walled edge of Tallus & found themselves up against a small sandstorm that had blown up making it hard to see clear. They pushed onwards relying on Patches' compass. Even though he kept reassuring them they were still on track, they all felt like they were lost. Marcus tried hard not to worry, but he could not see the Tallus wall and doubted it was the effect of the desert haze or sandstorm.

"The storm is picking up. I think we need to find or setup some kind of shelter before the sand becomes too overwhelming for us and the horses," Bruce yelled over to Patches, spitting out the taste of sand.

"You're right, but honestly I don't know where we'll find it," Patches said as he tossed them all pairs of goggles and masks he had made to help protect their eyes & mouths from the sand.

"Guys, look over there," Marcus yelled, pointing off in the distance.

Bruce brought his horse around to their left. Through the blowing sand they could see a figure running and then collapse. It was hard to make out exactly what the figure was but it appeared to be a man in need of help.

"What do you think he's doing out here?" Bruce asked aloud.

"I don't know. Probably not too common for someone to wonder into a desert and get lost," Patches said as he jumped down off the wagon and peered inside. "How is she?"

"I keep applying the salve like you said but she still hasn't woken up," Lija said as new tears ran over dried ones.

Patches heart sank. He wished there were more he could do for his dear love, but for now all he could do was make her comfortable until they reached Silversword. He would have to let her be as someone else needed his help and if she had been awake, she would have insited he help that man.

"Arron, hand me those two bags there," Patches said as Arron did as he asked. "There's a man off in the distance, we are going to go see to him. Arron, I am counting on you to watch over these two."

"I can take care of myself," Lija glared at Arron, but smiling at the thought of a prince protecting her.

Patches nodded and then leapt onto the back of Bruce's horse. It was better to see if their approaching guest was friend or foe away from the wagon. They took off at a gallop, going as fast as the sand would allow the horses to go. They soon made it to the man, who was still face down in the desert sand. Marcus held the horses still as Bruce and Patches dropped to their knees.

"I can't find a pulse, and his skin feels so cold," Patches remarked turning the man over.

"No, he's alive," Bruce said as the man began to cough up sand. With the sand, goggles and the night sky, it was hard to make out the appearance of the sand-covered man. His skin was covered and filthy, as was his dark black hair. He was bare foot and bore no shirt and his pants were torn up to the knees.

"Mister, are you okay? What are you doing out here?" Patches asked helping the man sit up.

"Escaping," the man said weakly, barely opening his mouth or his eyes.

"From what?"

"Them," the man pointed as they both looked up toward the direction he had come from to see about a dozen figures approaching them very quickly. Bruce was about to ask what they were but the man whispered one last word before passing back out. "Vampires."

Both men were on their feet as Marcus jumped off his horse to join them. Bruce and Marcus drew their swords as Patches loosened the ties on the bags on his hips reaching a hand into each of them.

"What's a Vampire?" Marcus asked as the creatures were almost upon them.

"They are creatures of the undead. In addition to their heightened senses, strength and agility, they have very sharp claws and fangs. They can't fly, but they can leap and glide a good distance. Normal weapons will not kill them, and a bite from them could turn you into one of them," Patches said impressing Marcus with his knowledge.

"How can we defeat them?" Bruce asked, his nerves beginning to get to him.

"Sunlight kills them, as will fire. Other than a wooden stake through the heart, your weapons will only be of use by beheading them."

"Is this for real?" Marcus asked in wonderment. First there was the Drogans, and now these Vampire creatures.

"I once thought them to be stories of myth until I encountered a man who had come out of the desert and told me all about these creatures. I didn't think we would see any this close to the border, but this is why I wanted to travel at night. Can't fight the creatures of the night if we're sleeping," Patches said and then whipped out his hands from the pouches and flinging two objects into the air.

The Vampires had reached them at an alarming speed. Two of the Vampires had leapt into the air right at them as the other ten circled around to trap them from all sides. Thanks to the creature's pale white skin and glowing yellow eyes they were fairly easy to make out through the blowing sand and night sky. The objects Patches had thrown each hit the leaping Vampires, exploding in a blast of fire. The creatures howled in pain as the fire quickly consumed them and leaving nothing but smoke and ashes in their places.

"You have killed our brethren. We will take great pleasure in returning the favor," one of the creatures hissed baring its fangs.

The horses began to cry and leap up and down as Marcus tried to calm them. They could see that they were completely surrounded with no escape. Patches shouted for him to leave the horses as the creatures attacked. Marcus took his stance, back to back with his comrades facing the creatures, protecting the man in the middle of them.

Marcus felt his blood rushing throughout his body as he eagerly faced his attacker. He swung his sword with all his might. He was amazed, as this Drogan blade hit the first Vampire. It shimmered red and sliced the creature easily in two causing it to burst in flame and become ash. He was glad to have such a weapon in his hand, making him feel more confident. He turned at the sound of another creature and swung his blade separating the head from its body. As the creature vanished into ashes, Marcus, not sure what the blade was made of, thanked whoever made it.

As Marcus's training and desire to be a great warrior like his dad kicked him into battle mode, Patches stood his ground, flinging bottle after bottle at the Vampires. If they didn't take them out, it at least served the purpose of keeping them at bay with their bursting fire. He knew his age was catching up to him, but he still fought on, he was feeling alive again. He threw two more bottles and was able to take out two more Vampires. He cheered when he saw that there were no more Vampires around him.

Marcus shouted and Patched turned to see two Vampires standing over Bruce. He was on his back with his sword far from him. One Vampire laughed as the other sat on him ready to bite into their friend's neck. Marcus was too far to help and Patches found that he only had one vile left. He threw it quickly at the creature on top of Bruce causing it to erupt into flame.

Bruce pushed it off, burning his hand as it turned to ashes. Bruce tried to get up but the second Vampire backhanded him sending him back down. The creature's fangs glimmered in the moonlight as it began to laugh. Patches didn't have much time. He reached into his inner pocket and pulled out his wooden pipe. He hacked off the end with his knife leaving a sharp end and flung it.

The pipe hit and stuck into the Vampire's chest where its heart should be. The creature looked down and then laughed. Even though it had stuck, the throw hadn't been strong enough to actually go through and pierce the heart.

"You're as weak as your friend here," the creature laughed as it prepared to leap at Patches.

Bruce, hating that he had once again been the weakest link, kicked his boot out hard, hitting the pipe with force. The creature's undead laugh stopped as it exploded into a pile of dust. Bruce sat up slowly as he saw Patches come towards him.

"Did we get them all?"

"All but one. I assume it headed back where it had come from." Patches gave Bruce a hand and helped him to his feet. Bruce was a little bruised but would be okay. Marcus walked up to them, not even a scratch on him as he smiled from ear to ear.

"What a rush. My dad was right, I'm a born warrior."

"You did your dad proud," Patches said and then saw the sadness behind his eyes. "Don't worry, son. We'll get help and your dad will be just fine. He can take care of himself."

Marcus had to believe that and just smiled. He was still high from the battle. After this he knew he could take on anything. He looked around and then knelt down next to the stranger and his two comrades. "The horses are gone."

"No time to look for them. They are long lost. We need to take cover quickly. This storm is getting much worse," Patches said as he and Bruce helped the man to his feet.

"Thank you for your help," the stranger finally began to speak in a small whisper, "I can take you somewhere safe. There is an underground shelter not far from here. I was staying there until I was discovered. It will keep us safe from the sand storm."

"Marcus, run back to the wagon and bring it quickly here. We'll head to safety once you're back," Patches said as Marcus nodded and ran off.

"How are you feeling?" Bruce asked the man.

"I have been better, but my strength is returning. I'm Korvan Salee."

"You can call me Patches, and this is my comrade Bruce Peters."

"Glad to meet the two of you. If not for you those creatures would have had me."

"What are you doing in the desert and why were they after you?" Bruce asked as they tried to bare the increasing sand winds.

"I wondered into the desert to seek adventure. I soon found myself captured by a group of Vampires and taken to what is called the Lost City of the Dead. That is where the Vampires and creatures of the dead live, safe from the sunlight. Their leader, Lord Suras wanted to make me one of them. He failed and I managed to escape. I have been on the run ever since," Korvan told them his tale of escape.

"You're lucky we got to you when we did. I'm just amazed to find Vampires this close to the border," Patches said as he looked and saw the wagon approaching.

"Border, which border are you referring to?"

"We are near the borders of Sorran and Tallus. If my compass is correct, we should reach the Kingdom of Silversword in about a day's journey."

"I'm sorry to tell you my new-found friends, but you are not where you think you are. The desert winds can easily confuse a person. The Lost City of the Dead lies toward the center of the Drol Death Desert, directly north of the Erikson-Argoth border."

They both looked at Korvan questioningly as he continued on, "I have been running directly west for two days."

"Which means?" Bruce began to answer Patches' fears.

"I calculate that if you head straight west you will actually reach Silversword in about two days travel by your horses."

"I don't believe it. We have been heading southeast all this time instead of west, southwest along the borders," Patches swore fiercely.

Marcus finally arrived and Patches explained the situation to him as Bruce helped the man onto the wagon. Bruce and Marcus squeezed into the back with the others while Korvan sat with Patches in front so he could lead them back to the shelter. It didn't take long for them to reach safety, just in time as the wind began to pick up strength.

It was a handy little shelter with a stone covering that protected the door in the ground from being buried by blowing sand. Korvan opened the hatch as Bruce and Marcus carefully carried Elle down into the underground shelter. Arron and Lija followed after while Korvan helped Patches place the wagon close enough under the shelter to survive the storm.

"What about the horses?" Patches asked.

"You can lead them down. It is an easy slanted tunnel and the horses will fit. There is plenty of room underground. I don't know who created this shelter but they must have planned for it to be a permanent home of sorts," Korvan said as he helped untie the two horses from the wagon and lead them to the hatch's opening.

"You think we should head out right after the storm and keep moving?" Patches asked as Marcus and Bruce returned to take the horses down.

"No, you all are very tired. We have time before the Vampire reaches Lord Suras and they head back after us. We're fine to spend the day sleeping and resting out of the day's heat. Right before sunset we will head out and move quickly. By the time night falls and they get here again, we should be close enough to Silversword and safely far from them," Korvan said as he glanced out into the sandstorm.

"Sounds like a good plan," Patches paused and looked back, "You coming?"

"I thought I saw your other horses. You head down and I will run out and take a quick look."

"Let me come with you."

"No, the storm is starting to pick up. I won't take long."
With that Korvan ran out into the storm and out of sight quickly.

Patches walked down the tunnel and came to another door.
He opened it and found himself in a very large room. The room
was the size of his house. Marcus and Bruce had already lit a
bunch of candles and lanterns to make it visible. He saw that off
to one side the horses were tied and resting calmly. Off to the
other side was an area with four beds, one that his wife laid
upon. They agreed to let Lija and the prince to take the other
two. Marcus would sleep next to his sister while Bruce insisted
on sleeping on the sandy ground so that their host could have the
fourth bed.

"It looks like there isn't much of anything else in here. It
must have been ransacked over the years. Besides the beds,
everything else is petty destroyed," Marcus told Patches as the
man sat at Elle's bedside.

"Must have happened when the Vampires attacked
Korvan," Bruce added as he looked around, wondering a little at
their new-found friend's great navigation and survival skills in
the desert, as well as his quick recovery.

"He must be one lucky guy to escape them. Good thing we
showed up when we did or his luck would have finally run out,"
Marcus said as he exchanged glances with Bruce, nodded and
headed back to the wagon to grab the supplies they needed for
the day and to check on their missing host.

"Oh, my dear Elle, you must hang in there," Patches
whispered as he kissed her hand. She had been burnt and injured
in the explosion worse than she had initially led on.

"She'll be okay won't she, mister Patches?" Lija asked.

"I hope so, my dear, I hope so."

"What do we do now?" Prince Arron asked.

"We'll sleep soon. Close to sunset, we'll head out and
travel quickly by night again. If we push hard and have no more
delays we should reach Silversword in a day or so," Patches said
still swearing at his bad navigation of the Desert.

There was a sudden commotion that made them all turn
towards the door that lead out into the tunnel. Bruce and Marcus
came through carrying the supplies followed by Korvan leading
a single horse.

"I was only able to find the one. The storm is unbearable. I'm afraid the other horse is lost."

"That's okay, you found the one and that is better than having lost both."

"The sun is beginning to rise," Marcus added as he and Bruce placed the supplies on a large table they had found in the room.

"We should all sleep. It has been a long night and we'll need our rest," Patches said as he lay down next to Elle.

Marcus and Lija were soon asleep, as were Arron and Bruce. Korvan insisted on Bruce taking the bed as he said he preferred the floor. Once everyone was fast asleep Korvan put out all the lights and they all disappeared into the darkness.

****

Marcus woke with a start as he hit the floor and felt something heavy on top of him. There was a dim light that allowed him to see a little bit. He realized that he was on the floor and Korvan was on top of him. He quickly shoved him off.

"What's going on?" Marcus shouted as he got to his feet.

"I don't know. I heard this weird noise and as I tried to find my way in the dark a pulsing white-blue light startled me and I tripped. I didn't mean to fall and knock us both to the floor," Korvan apologized as Marcus helped him up.

"It's okay. You startled me is all," Marcus began and then stopped as he realized that they were no longer standing in the underground shelter.

"What the?" Korvan added as he also noticed that they now stood in a small cavern that was mysteriously lit with an unknown light source.

Marcus looked around and saw that they were alone in this cavern. He was on the verge of panic when a strange familiarity hit him. It almost felt like Semaj and the others were near. Maybe this was one of their shared dreams he heard them talk about and they were trying to communicate with him using Thom's crystal. Korvan had just happened to be near him to get pulled in with him. That had to be it.

"Don't worry. I think some friends of mine are trying to reach us through a magic crystal induced dream. It's hard to explain," Marcus began to say when he saw a strange look in Korvan's eyes.

"I feel like I'm being pulled forward. Like something or someone is summoning me," Korvan interrupted and started to walk forward down the tunnel. Marcus followed quickly behind.

They came to a large opening and found themselves on a small balcony overlooking a large dark chasm. The room was circular and Marcus counted, including the one they were standing on, twelve balconies all around the large chasm. The chamber was lit, but not bright enough to make out the figures that each stood on a balcony. He then glanced down at the source of the light and gasped.

"Is that what I think it is?" Korvan asked peering down and then quickly stepping back, away from the balcony ledge.

In the center of the chasm, surrounded by the balconies was the image of a large, glowing white Dragon. Its paws were held up and he could see a figure standing in each of them. Marcus then noticed an older man standing on the very top of the Dragon's head. He instantly recognized him as that crazy old man that had started this whole mess they were in. At that thought he glanced back down and realized that the two figures were Semaj and Thom. If they were here then that means…

"Marcus, you're here?" He turned to see Anna standing on the balcony to his right.

"Anna, what is going on?"

"It's a long story, but we met the spirit of a Dragon. It turns out that Semaj is the Chosen One, that I'm actually a Magestic and Essej is part Dragon. Anyway, the Dragon spirit we met is using Semaj and Thom's crystal to summon all Magestics here in this dream world to tell about the coming evil we must face."

"Magestic? What?" Marcus was confused and still in shock.

"The Dragon will explain soon, but if you're here than that must mean you're…" Anna started to say and then saw another figure step past Marcus.

"This is too strange," Korvan interrupted as he stepped back onto the balcony.

"Finally, we're all here. Let's begin," the Dragon's voice echoed through the whole room.

Marcus turned looking at Korvan and realizing it was not he that pulled Korvan here, but the other way around. He quickly stepped back to be out of the way but still able to see and hear what was about to happen.

"I am Dwin, spirit of one of the once great Dragon Kings of Bergonia. I have summoned you all here because a great evil has risen and the power of the Magesti is needed," Dwin said and then began to tell them his tale and all about Semaj, the Magesti power of the Magestics, their ancestors and the battle of Drol Greb.

Marcus heard the Dragon say something about why they summoned them in this dream. That evil was on the move and that everyone needed to be made aware, for if they waited for Semaj to find them each individually, it may be too late. Marcus still could not believe what was going on. He slowly looked around the room not paying too close attention to what the Dragon was saying.

The Dragon was glowing brighter and he could finally see each figure clearly on each balcony. He also noticed a tunnel behind each of them. You could almost see where they came from, like it was a portal of some kind. Marcus quickly looked behind him and saw images of the Drol Death Desert. This was getting to be too much. It had to be a major dream. Suddenly he noticed it had gone deathly quiet.

"That's the man from the other visions!" Anna screamed as he and everyone else turned to look to where she was pointing.

Down at the bottom of the chasm were a small fire-like portal and a dark figure standing within it. The man was looking around and had started to laugh. "What do we have here?"

He stopped laughing as his eyes locked with Essej's eyes. Before anyone else could speak, Essej and Dwin both shouted and waved their hands in unison and a strong blast of wind hit the dark figure forcing him back into the portal. In an instant the man and portal were gone.

"We're all in danger. The evil we face now knows us. We don't have long. He'll try and come back. We'll never be able to meet like this again. I never intended to do what I'm about to do

next but you all can't wait for Semaj to invoke them. You will need access to all your powers now."

Marcus stared wide as energy could be seen erupting within the body of the Dragon spirit. That same energy then flowed through its arms and hit both Semaj and Thom. Thom was engulfed in his crystal's light as Semaj was engulfed in weird silver light. Power shot out and up from each of them and merged into one powerful beam that hit Essej straight in his chest.

Essej then pointed his staff at each balcony, shouted a word, channeling power from Semaj, blasted each figure upon it causing them and their balcony to glow a specific color. The first figure looked like a very short, plump woman standing in front of a portal of the Northern Mountains. As Essej shouted *Earth,* a blast hit her causing her to glow brown. Essej was moving quite fast.

He looked over when he heard *Fire* and Anna screamed as she was hit with a blast making her glow red. Before he could react, Essej shouted *Soul* and he jumped back as Korvan was hit turning Purple. Marcus stood up against the wall, still amazed by what he was seeing. Korvan looked just as shocked. Marcus glanced to see Essej blasting the last balcony, a creature that looked almost like a smaller version of an Ogre, tuning it gray.

"You must go now and prepare. Semaj will find and guide you. Go!" Marcus heard the Dragon say as a blast swept him and Korvan back into the portal behind them. Marcus sat up and found himself in bed back at the underground shelter. He was drenched in sweat. The room was empty, besides Korvan sitting on the floor near him with his eyes open in shock.

"About time you two woke up. The sun will be setting and we're ready to move out. Patches told me to come down now and wake you. We have to get moving before the Vampires return," Lija said as she headed back up the tunnel.

Marcus got up and reached for his sword and belongings when Korvan slowly stood up, staring at him. They both exchanged glances and knew things were about to get a little more interesting.

Chapter Nine:
The Northern Mountains

"Are you well?"

Lucian Darkheart looked up to see Docanesto standing over him. He must have passed out. It was the first time he had been forced into a dream. One minute he was sitting there discussing plans with his father's head and the next he was looking at a chasm filled with beings surrounding a giant white Dragon. He didn't get much of what they were saying before being spotted.

He did hear something about them being the descendants of the Magestics and before being blown away he did get a look at some of them on their balconies. He had also been in the presence of the Chosen One. He knew in his blood that one of them was the one he sought. He had felt something, but what it was and with whom he could not fathom, yet.

"What happened, my son?" His father's glowing head asked.

"How long was I out for?"

"Lucian, you have been unconscious for several hours." Docanesto helped Lucian to his feet and snapped orders having a servant bring him some water. Lucian drank down the water as fast as it took Docanesto to dispose of the servant that had witnessed the weak moment of the prince.

Lucian wasn't sure what had happened. One minute he was standing there and the next he felt an odd pull, passing out and waking up in a strange cavern. He knew that this time it was more than just a dream giving him visions, this was something much more but what he could not be certain. He knew that he had to say something to his father, but he did not have to reveal anything about his other dreams. Not until he got the answers he needed from the Chosen One first.

"It was something to do with the Chosen One and my power to sense him," Lucian said trying to clear his head.

"He used his powers again and you were able to sense him and his location?" Docanesto asked as he eyed Lucian carefully.

"Not really. This was different in a way." Lucian looked over at his father and began to tell him about the cavern, giant

Dragon and the three figures as well as the twelve balconies and their owners and portals. At his father's command, he described the Dragon and the figure standing upon its head.

"I know one of the two figures in the Dragon's paws was the Chosen One but I couldn't tell which nor could I get a good look at either of them from the angle I was standing at," Lucian said speaking the truth. What he did not say was that he felt a strange connection but he didn't know what it was.

"I don't know who the Dragon was, but the creature upon its head was none other than Essej himself. I would know his description anywhere," Docanesto told them through gritted teeth.

"Who is this Essej?"

"He is an uncle of sorts to me. Let's say he helped in my exile and has a hatred for your father."

"Is he a major threat?" Lucian asked remembering how old the man had appeared.

"Don't let his appearance fool you. He is what you call a very rare crossbreed. He's a Huelgon. Unlike a Drogan that turns more Dragon-like, has limited power and intelligence, Essej's Elven heritage allows him to maintain intelligence, a more human-Elf appearance and can actually wield a far greater power," Docanesto spat.

"Can't we create our own like the Drogans?"

"No, Lucian. Even though it takes great power to create the Drogans, magic can't create the Huelgon. We have tried and failed drastically. It has something to do with the Elven make-up. Even in the rare instances where a child was naturally born of all three it never survived long after the birthing process," Lucian's father said.

"Essej is one of those rare ones that survived and seems to be still roaming the land of Bergonia causing evil," Docanesto added.

"The fact that he's with the Chosen One means that once again he is on the move rallying his forces against me," Lucian's father snarled.

"Is that what those other beings were, the descendants of this Mejesti power?" Lucian asked looking at his father and his teacher, thinking of what he had heard in the dream.

"The power of the Mejesti is what Essej and Semaj Lightheart used to try and take over Bergonia during the Magic Wars, but it proved too much and ended up being destroyed along with Lightheart," Lucian's father said. "Or, so I thought."

"I'm still not understanding the true meaning of all this," Lucian said as he gave questioning looks to his fathers. He always felt there was something being kept from him.

"You see, the Mejesti is an ancient power source of great evil that had been thought destroyed long before the time of the Magic Wars, until Semaj and Essej showed up to take over the world.

"It was too much for Semaj to control himself and it resulted in his end. Now in the time of your father's rebirth and the retaking of the land that was taken by the forces of evil, prophecies have risen," Docanesto said looking at his student and adoptive son.

"You refer to that of the Chosen One?" Lucian asked already knowing the answer.

"Yes, my son. This Chosen One, the direct descendant of Semaj Lightheart is said to be able to harness this evil power of the Mejesti and then use it to kill me and all that follow me. To keep us from defeating the normals and setting the beings of magic free," the glowing head answered.

"He must be stopped. Where are we with our plans?" Lucian asked turning to Docanesto.

"Soré has been taken and become an outpost for General Vex and the Drogan army. The group of kids had split up and the Chosen One escaped the Drogans and made it to Mount Semaj, where they defeated another group and then vanished while the other two made it to Sorran to try and warn the king. Our inside allies managed to mark them as kidnappers and sent them on the run into the Desert leaving our plans to take over Sorran on track," Docanesto reported.

"Those two are as good as dead in the Drol Death Desert and we now know from Mount Semaj that the Chosen One will be heading into the Northern Mountains next. I will make sure he is intercepted there," Lucian said glancing at his trainer knowing Natureza should be there already or real close.

"With recent developments, we will now have to move up our time line as well as hunting down the next generation of Magestics before they can gather together. Son, I need you to try and remember and describe any of the fowl creatures that were on those balconies," Lucian's father said, surprising Lucian for not questioning him on who was being sent to the Northern Mountains. Either his father was distracted and trusted him or Docanesto told him and has made other arrangements. Whatever the case, he just hoped Natureza got to the Chosen One first.

****

"Are you guys doing okay?" Semaj asked as he appeared before his two friends, walking them to the exit of the cavern giving Essej a little time with his father, the Dragon spirit.

"Us? What about you, Mr. Chosen One?" Anna asked with a smile.

"You were gone for a long time. What kind of training did you get? Do you have powers like Anna?" Thom asked as he touched his crystal, wishing he could have gotten more answers.

"I don't remember much of the training. It was like a big wind going through my mind. Dwin said I will know what to do when I need to do it. I don't have any powers just that I can help those with the power of the Mejesti to better control their gifts," Semaj said as he wished more than anything he could be back home on his farm.

"I get it. When you are near me I seem to have better control of my gifts and they are stronger. You're like a natural booster and sedater," Anna said as when she stepped near Semaj she could fill the power in her pulse.

"That's nice and all but what good is having powers if you don't know how to use your gifts?" Thom asked, not sure if he meant Anna or himself as he rubbed his crystal between his fingers.

"That's where I come in," Essej said walking up to the trio. "Your job is to find them while I will help in their training, especially since their powers have now been fully unlocked."

"*The more reason you need to get moving since the evil forces working against you will be looking for them as well,*" the voice of Dwin carried to them upon the wind flowing from the cavern.

"What about Marcus? You said you saw him with another Magestic?" Semaj asked Anna as he now grew concered for his friends and if they would be safe on their journey to see the King of Sorran.

"The dream is still foggy. I thought he was a Magestic too till I saw him with another man who stepped up and was identified as the Magesti of Soul," Anna answered.

"What was he doing with a Magestic? Did they make it to King Sirus?" Semaj asked.

Anna looked at Thom and then back to Semaj. "I didn't get a chance to ask him. He looked perfectly fine. Before I could ask him anything more, the story from Dwin started and then I woke up back here. Before I was hit with the blast to come back here, I noticed a desert in the background of his portal."

"I could be wrong, but it seems he and that Magestic might be in the Drol Death Desert," Thom added with a little worry.

"You think Lija is with him? Why would he be in the Desert?" Semaj asked now worried.

"I don't know." Anna wish she had the answers.

"Maybe we should head there next to find him and that Magestic with him," Thom suggested.

"What does your gift tell you?" Essej asked.

"I feel a pull towards the Northern Mountains," Semaj said in a whisper as he whished it not to be true.

"Then that is where we must go," Essej said with a firm nod.

"*I agree with my son. I sensed no danger from any of the Magestics at that time. You must head to the Northern Mountains if that is where the Magesti wants you to go,*" Dwin's voice on the winds said.

"Ok," Semaj said as he received a confirmation nod from Anna, telling him they had to go for the Dwarf first and trust Marcus and his sister were safe.

"Now that we are all in agreement, it is time to go," Essej said as he moved toward the edge of the cliff.

"We can't travel at night through the mountains," Thom said thinking of the cold.

"It'll take us days," Semaj added feeling no joy about hiking in the mountains.

"We can do it and I can keep us warm, but it is a long journey to the Northern Mountains," Anna said excited but deep down had concerns too about the cold.

"Don't worry, with the help of my father, our ride should be here any second," Essej said as he cherished the moment he had binding his gifts with his father's to send a message out upon the winds. Not only did this bring him closer to his long lost father but it rejuvenated and refueled his powers.

"What is that?" Anna asked suddenly as her daggers were instantly in her hands.

Everyone turned to look out past the cliff and into the night sky. A shape off in the distance had appeared and was quickly getting larger as it got closer. Now, a few feet from the ledge, the group of friends could make out the creature. It looked to be the size of a small Dragon but had no legs, arms, head or face. The creature had three sets of wings on its very long wide body and a strange mouth with hundreds of large sharp teeth. The creature was as white as snow. It looked like a large worm with wings.

"That is a Snowpede. They are a distant cousin of the Dragons. There are not many left in the world and they like to burrow deep below the ground in the snowy lands of the Northern Mountains," said Dwin's voice.

"With the help of my powers, she should be able to carry us quickly and safely to the Northern Mountains and the home of the Dwarves. If we hurry we should be there by dawn," Essej said as he made his way to the large creature.

"There's no turning back now," Thom said as he clasped a hand on each of his friend's shoulders.

"I know I must do this, I can *feel* it, but I can't help but think of our parents and friends," Semaj said glancing over at Thom and Anna.

"Hey, if I know Marcus, he's already got the king's forces saving the day and making mincemeat of those Drogans," Anna said with encouragement, trying not to worry why he was in the Desert and focus on the excitement for their adventure to meet the Dwarves. If he was in danger, she was sure he would have said so in the dream.

"Be careful out there and safe journeys, my son," Dwin said upon the wind and then vanished.

"Don't worry, father. I will return," Essej said quietly to himself and then made his way to the Snowpede. "Everyone aboard."

The four travelers mounted the creature. Semaj was worried how they were going to keep from falling off without a saddle of any kind until the strange skin of the Snowpede started to move and thousands of small, thin, sticky hair-like strands grew out and fastened themselves to their legs and bottoms. They all were surprised at how firm and strong their hold was. Essej chuckled and with a command the Snowpede took flight as he called upon his powers to help add flight, speed and support to the large creature transporting them to their new destination.

****

"We're almost there," Essej shouted over his shoulder as the first rays of dawn began to appear. "I think our best bet will be with the Dwarven City of Mirax. They secretly trade with humans and are not as isolated and stubborn as the Dwarves of Norax." Thankful of what information his father was able to give him about the currant affairs of the Dwarves.

"Even you have to admit this is nothing like the farm," Anna shouted behind her as Semaj finished wiping the sleep from his eyes and stared out to the side.

Thanks to Essej diverting the wind some and Anna generating a little heat the flight through the night had been tolerable. As Semaj looked at the brightening sky, he was all but speechless. The beautiful snowcapped mountains were quite the site. They seemed to go on forever in every direction and glistened as the sun's rays touched upon their snow coverings. He could see the tops of some mountains but others still went high above them as they appeared to be flying a lot lower than when they had started out.

"I always wanted to believe Dwarves were real, but dealing with humans. How can that be?" Thom shouted as he couldn't get enough of looking from side to side at the Northern Mountains.

"What I know about the Dwarves since they vanished into the mountains so long ago, was that there are two feuding clans. One led by King Norax, who moved their city into isolation and refused to ever have dealings with the outside world again and King Mirax, who believes to survive you have to connect with the world again.

"King Mirax allows Dwarves to trade with humans, but only in disguise as to not alert those humans that would hunt and fear them that they still exist. This trading with humans is what has helped fuel the war between the Dwarven clans," Essej said as he too was a bit nervous as he had not really been in contact with the Dwarves since the battle against Drol Greb so long ago. He was pretty sure that the Dwarf they were looking for would be among the Dwarves of Norax, but they would survive and have a better chance if their first contact was with the Dwarves of Mirax.

"What," Anna began to say when the Snowpede suddenly made a high piercing squeal as something caused it to twitch violently and descend quickly to the ground below.

"Hold on!" Essej screamed as they started moving faster and faster towards the earth. The strands were still holding them but were slowly losing grip as whatever had hit the creature caused it to panic and lose control.

Essej tried to use his powers to slow the descent but even he wasn't strong enough to keep them all afloat on his own as the creature had now passed out. He strained to look ahead, as he realized they were about to hit head first into a frozen lake. Luckily it was not quite the winter season yet so the once beautiful lake was slowly freezing over and the iced top should not be very thick. Using what strength he had left, Essej called upon his powers and sent a strong blast of wind a head of them at the frozen lake causing it to shatter and break making it easier on them as they suddenly plunged deep into the lake's chilly waters.

At the moment of impact, the Snowpede came to life and shot straight up into the air, breaking free from the icy water, causing its four riders to fall loose and back into the cold lake. Essej sunk with despair as he watched the creature launch itself in the air, across the lake and land headfirst into the snowy ground, quickly burrowing itself deep below the ground and out of sight leaving them in the dead center of the lake. Essej knew he was too weak to save them all. He turned to see the same fear in the three young one's eyes as they started to sink back below the frozen waters.

Thom was moments from blacking out when he felt a strange heat from his chest. He looked down and saw his crystal was glowing. With the bright light, he also began to hear voices in his head, words forming. He opened his mouth and was surprised when, instead of water rushing in, a mouth full of commands came out. Thom felt energy pulling from within his body as power was released from either him, the crystal or both. They all gasped for air as a large hand made of water and highlighted with white-blue light lifted them up and threw them across the lake and onto the snow banked edge.

"Thom, how?" Semaj tried to ask though chattering teeth.

"I..." was all Thom got out before he fell unconscious.

"Anna, quickly, you must use your powers or you will all freeze to death," Essej said as he knew the young humans would not live long out in the snow, soaked and wet.

Anna's body shivered and she tried to concentrate. She found it so hard to focus on the heat when she was so cold. She felt a burst of energy as she looked down to see Semaj place a hand on her arm. With a look into his eyes and his chattered smile, she felt the power and confidence rise in her. Taking on his energy and Essej's instructions she soon found and pulled the heat source around them closer to all their bodies. The snow under them began to melt as they all started to feel warmer and their clothes dried.

"Now hold that heat right there. You don't want us bursting into flame," Essej said with a hint of a smile.

"You're doing just fine," Semaj said as his hand lingered and then he pulled it back with a blush.

"Thanks," Anna said and then let the moment pass as she quickly turned to Essej while Semaj turned his attention to Thom. "What happened?"

"I'm not sure. Something hit the Snowpede stunning it," Essej said as he got to his feet and was impressed with how quickly he had dried off.

"Were they aiming for us?" Anna asked.

"I don't know, but we might want to get moving," Essej said as he carefully looked around to see if they were alone.

"Are we dead?" Thom asked as he slowly began to wake.

"No, you saved us. I still can't believe it," Semaj said hugging his best friend.

"Me either. One minute I thought I was going to drown and next the crystal was glowing while something was whispering in my head and, magic, we are saved," Thom chuckled as he touched the crystal around his neck trying to cover how nervous and scared he actually was.

"It comes in handy, but from the way you passed out you might want to be careful till we get some answers," Semaj said as he looked to Anna and Essej.

"Where are we?" Thom asked as he got to his feet.

"We have arrived at Steam Lake. It lies directly between the two Dwarven cities, dividing them," Essej said as he tried to get his bearings and sense of directions from the wind. "We go that way, east to the City of Mirax," he said as he started walking.

"But, something is pulling me this way," Semaj said as he looked off to the west causing their guide to come to a dead stop.

"Then who we are searching for is in the City of Norax," Essej said confirming his suspicions and uneasiness of dealing with those Dwarves.

"Then we go that way," Anna said as she marched to the west as her two friends followed before Essej could protest. Essej followed, hoping for the best.

Since it was not yet winter, the snow fall was lighter and the chill in the air was not as cold. This was good since Anna could not heat them and trek through the snow at the same time. Also, Essej did not have the strength to continuously divert the wind. They had let Essej take lead as he was better to guide them in the direction of Norax. They did not know how long it would take them, but they hoped it would be soon.

It was nearing midday when they found a small cave and took shelter from the cold. Anna created a fire as they prepared some food. Most of their rations had been ruined or lost in their crash landing in the lake. They had just enough for another day and then they would have to hunt for food. Essej was pretty sure they could reach the city of the Dwarves before then, but Semaj feared they would not give them food or worse, the city no longer existed. They ate in quiet when a strange roar came from somewhere in the mountains.

"I don't even want to know what that was," Thom said as he instinctively cuffed his crystal.

"You never did tell us what else is out here in the Northern Mountains," Anna said as she glanced at Essej.

"Most common animals in these parts are basic small animals, snowbirds, mountain goats and a few other unique creatures like the Snowpede," Essej said as he listened to the sound as it multiplied to determine what it might be.

"Like, what other creatures?" Semaj asked as he looked out of the cave, getting more worried with each roar.

"Well, there are Frostites, but they tend to be more friendly than vicious, usually. They are about the size of small bear and look on the weak side, but are strong, quick and agile. They have white fur and sharp claws. Their faces are flat with circular blue eyes kind of on the sides that allow them to see from all directions. They have great senses and very intelligent. For defenses they have a tail with icicle-like spikes all over the end and they spit a frost like substance from their mouth that can stun or freeze its attacker," Essej described the creatures with a concerned look on his face.

"I'm guessing that's not what is making those sounds out there," Anna said as she stepped up next to Essej who was now standing outside the cave.

"No, my child, I'm afraid it's something much worse," Essej said as they all saw a handful of shapes moving down the mountains and towards their direction.

It didn't take long before they had a clear view of what was charging towards them. Semaj had never seen anything like these monsters before. There were five of them in total, all about nine feet tall, big and muscular. They were bald with white eyes, small deformed ears and pale white skin. Their fingers had a claw-like appearance that looked sharp and strong. They did not look intelligent, but they looked mean and dangerous.

"I've read about those in my books. They're Snogres. Almost like Ogres but live in the snow," Thom said with awe and fear at the same time.

"Yes, and they usually travel in packs of five, to explore and hunt. One will usually hold back to assess the situation before leaving to report victory or bring reinforcements," Essej said knowing they would have trouble dealing with five let alone a whole heard of Snogres.

"Then we need to make sure we take out all five?" Anna asked with a smile as she had her daggers in her hands.

"There's no way we can take on those things. We should make a run for the Dwarven city," Semaj suggested as he hated feeling helpless.

"We wouldn't make it. Snogres are pretty quick and would be upon us before we even reached Norax," Essej said as he doubted they would even help them if they did make it to the city in time.

"It's now or never," Anna said as she charged at the first monster that reached the area of their cave.

"Die, fleshling," the Snogre grumbled as it used its clawed hands to scoop up a large snowball and hurl it at the girl.

Anna dodged just in time as the ball of snow hit behind her. She leapt up and over onto the monster's back and slammed her daggers deep inside. The creature roared as it tossed her to the side. Anna tucked and rolled with the fall and got back on her feet. All her time training and learning to fight with Marcus was paying off. The creature stopped and growled as it tried to reach the daggers implanted in his back. Anna used this moment to grab a large rock, leap up and slam it down upon the Snogre's head. As the creature fell unconscious, Anna quickly retrieved her daggers, ready for the next one.

"Smell Elf," a Snogre said licking his lips as he and another approached Essej.

Essej quickly tapped into his powers and called upon the winds. With a wave of his staff, he then pointed at the creatures for emphasis. A huge gale of wind slammed into one of the Snogres causing it to collide with the one next to him and fall to the ground. Essej then mumbled a few words and slammed his staff to the ground causing a cyclone of air to pull snow from the ground and then dump it upon the two creatures burying them. He knew that would not hold them for long but it would buy them some time.

Semaj watched as his friends went into battle. Anna was engaging one while two more approached Essej. He saw Thom holding his crystal and moving towards a Snogre that was holding back a ways as if it was trying to decide to attack or flee. Semaj did a quick count and realized one of the creatures was missing. Where had it gone? Then the thought hit him, maybe it had already headed back for reinforcements. Semaj stepped out of the cave to alert the others when he slammed into something big, knocking him back.

"Meat," the Snogre said as it swiped the side of the cave entrance with its claws digging out a chunk and lifting it high to bring down for a lethal blow.

Semaj closed his eyes to await the blow when he heard a whistling in the air followed by a hard thunk. He opened his eyes to see an arrow sticking out of the monsters left eye. The creature roared and stumbled before a second arrow took out its other eye. The Snogre screamed as it dropped its weapon and reached for the arrows. Semaj scrambled out of the way when he saw a woman leap over him, land on the creature's shoulders and wrapping her legs around its neck. She then took each of her fists and hit both sides of the Snogre's head, which upon impact, two blades extracted out stabbing and killing the monster. The blades retracted as she leapt backwards off her victim landing upon the ground as the Snogre fell forward.

"Looks like we got a runner," Thom said as he moved after the Snogre that had stood back and now turned to run.

Thom had hold of his crystal and willed it to do something to help him. The crystal stayed dark as Thom swore at it while the Snogre got further away. Thom wished he could figure out how to get the blasted thing to work. He was about to give up when he gave one final push with his will and the crystal blared to life. With all his might he tried to sort the words in his mind and shouted, "Ezefre Het Turecrea!"

Thom could feel the power building within his body as the crystal grew brighter. He suddenly felt the air suck right out of him as if the crystal itself was ripping the magic right from his body. He staggered as a powerful blast shot from him and the crystal and hit the snow. Thom watched as the blast seemed to gather snow from the ground and got larger and larger as it

neared the fleeing Snogre until a massive snowball was almost
upon it. The creature stopped and turned just in time to be
consumed by the giant snowball. Thom smiled as he saw the
large ball of snow sitting still upon the mountain side just before
he blacked out.

"Thom's down," Essej said as he turned to see the magic
snowball followed by Thom going face first into the snow.

"His gifts would be more helpful if he didn't pass out each
time he used that thing," Anna said as she moved to help Thom
before a loud roar brought her attention back.

The two Snogres that had been buried in the snow by Essej
had exploded upwards breaking free from their snow prison.
Essej moved his staff and prepared to use his gifts when one of
the Snogres back handed him sending him flying up through the
air and landing hard on a snowbank. Anna had both daggers in
her hands but didn't know how well she could handle two of
these creatures. She ran at one and tried to do the same trick as
before but she felt something grab her leg and fling her back
down upon the ground.

Anna lay there, in pain and out of breath from the shock of
the impact upon the ground. One of the Snogres headed toward
Essej as the other one stood over her, grunting and drooling. All
she could do was look at those long claw-like fingers and
wonder how soon she would be skewered. The Snogre roared as
it drew its clawed hand up ready to strike when a few snowballs
hit it in the face. The creature wiped its face and turned to see
what had hit him. Anna was both thankful and worried to see
Semaj standing there, hurling snowballs at the Snogre.

"How do you like that?" Semaj asked trying to hide his
nerves as he attempted to walk backwards and lure the Snogre
away from his friend.

The large creature stared intently at Semaj. Its strange white
eyes sent shivers up and down his spine. Semaj kept throwing
snow balls and sighed with relief when he saw Anna slowly
crawl in the opposite direction of them. The Snogre raised its
arms in anger and prepared to charge. Semaj swallowed hard and
hoped his new friend would hurry up because he did not have
much else to defend himself against a rampaging monster. He
had almost given up hope when he heard several howls.

Before the Snogre could register what was happening, three creatures the size of small bears leapt upon the monster and began clawing and biting it. From the description Essej gave earlier, Semaj knew these were Frostites. It didn't take long for the three attackers to get the Snogre to fall onto its back. Seconds after, the ground shook from impact, the three Frostites moved away as a fourth Frostite, a little bigger and had a blue scar across its right eye, leapt upon the Snogre's chest, opened its mouth and blew out a strange mist. The Snogre's face frosted over as it suddenly remained still.

"Thanks" Semaj said, not sure if the creatures that saved him could really understand him.

The four Frostites turned and looked up as a figure leapt past them all and moved at a quick speed toward the Snogre that was charging Essej. Semaj, for a split second, thought she had abandoned them but was glad to see he was wrong. The woman moved with ease over the snow as she got closer to her prey. Without missing a step, she released three arrows, one after another, each hitting the Snogre, one in the head and two in its back. The Snogre stopped in mid charge and turned in time to see a figure jump, hit him dead in the chest with her feet causing him to fall backwards as she propelled back in the air, summersaulting and landing upon the ground releasing one last arrow that hit it dead between the eyes.

"Now that was amazing!" Thom exclaimed as he sat up just in time to see the Snogre go down.

"I've never seen anything like that. She saved my life too," Semaj said missing the glare from Anna as they all moved closer to the woman.

"Well, unfortunately your friend's trick didn't stop the Snogre before he passed out. It'll alert others before we can catch up to it," the woman said as she glanced toward the direction the Snogre had fled and then back to the group staring at her.

Semaj and Thom could not take their eyes off her. She was about five and half feet tall with a very slender and toned body. She wore boots, leggings and a sleeveless top that were a bluish grey color that matched her hooded cloak. She wore her outfit well but almost looked as if she was uncomfortable in them. A bow and quill of arrows rested on her back as she had some kind of wrist bands that went part way up her arm that concealed her blades. Her skin was a tannish color and she had green eyes and long brown hair that rested part way down her back and flowed down in front over her shoulders.

"Thanks for the assistance, my child, but what is a Wild Elf doing so far north?" Essej asked as he walked up to the group.

"I don't," the woman began to protest when the old man moved his fingers causing a gust of wind to blow her hair back revealing pointed ears.

"You're an Elf!" Thom exclaimed as he saw another creature he had only read and dreamed about.

"Yes, from the Forest of Spirits. My name is Natureza, but you can call me Nat," the Wild Elf said as she kept her eyes on Essej, studying him as much as he was her.

"I am Essej. This is Semaj, Anna and Thom," Essej introduced his group but said no more.

"What is a half-Elf doing with a bunch of humans?" Nat asked as she sensed there was something more to the old man but was not sure what it was.

"We are just on our way to visit the Dwarves, kind of a peace keeping mission of sorts. You still didn't answer why you're out here all alone," Essej said not real sure if he trusted her.

"Adventure, plain and simple. I got tired of being isolated in the forest and decided to travel the world. I was nearby when I heard the commotion and came to check it out," Nat said slowly taking her eyes from the old half-Elf.

"Good thing or I would have been done for," Semaj said telling the others of how she saved him.

"You have magic like me?" Thom asked as he looked down at the crystal hanging around his neck.

"Not really. What Elves, especially a Wild Elf, can do is a little different than your crystal," Essej said as he saw Nat flinch. Essej did not mean to sound short but there has always been a natural divide between the civilized Elves and the wild Elves.

"I can't do magic, like you can. My Wild Elf heritage gives me the ability to be more at one with nature. Almost become in synch with it and the animals. Now you, I can sense the magic inside you but that crystal around your neck must boost it and allow you to use it," Nat said trying not to tell all as she moved closer to take a look at the crystal wondering if he was the one she sought out. She was not sure, as there was something about all three humans.

"Inside me? So, I can do magic like my great grandfather!" Thom started to get real excited at the notion.

"Calm down there," Essej said as he did not know a lot and was out of touch with the dealings of pure magic and magical artifacts.

"Essej is right, you have to be careful. Where Elven magic comes from using nature, your type of magic pulls from within yourself and using it untrained can be deadly. I don't know much about your crystal there but I am sure it not only boosts your magic but has managed to keep you from killing yourself, for now," Nat remarked.

"I knew that thing was dangerous. I bet that is why you pass out every time you use it," Semaj said knowing he was not getting through to his friend.

"Maybe its best you not use that anymore until you can be trained better," Anna said not wanting to lose another friend.

"Can you train me?" Thom asked looking at both Essej and Nat.

"I am afraid I can't. Only person that could truly train you in the art of magic would be a magician or someone profound in magic abilities," Essej said, wishing he could help but he had to focus on Semaj and their mission.

"If you would allow me to join your party, I can help him. I may not be able to truly train him in the art of using magic and that crystal, but with my abilities and some knowledge of magic, I can at least train him to use it without killing himself," Nat suggested hoping she had found a way into the group to weed out the Chosen One without having to spy from afar anymore.

"I don't know if that is such a good idea," Essej said not knowing if he could trust this Wild Elf or her story.

"Please?" Thom begged.

"She did save all of our lives," Semaj added thinking if Thom was going to use that dumb crystal that someone would be there to help him.

"What say you, Anna?" Essej asked eyeing the girl who was staring hard at the new comer.

"If it's what everyone else wants," Anna shrugged trying to hide her feelings of distrust or was it jealousy?

"It is settled then," Essej said as he decided he would have to do his best to keep the details about the Chosen One and their mission secret from Nat until he knew that they could really trust her.

"How did you get these Frostites to come to our aid?" Semaj asked as the one with the scar moved closer to him and sniffed as the other three rested back at a distance, watching the direction the last Snogre had fled.

"It is part of my gift and Wild Elf heritage. I reached out and luckily felt them nearby and urged them for their aid," Nat said hiding the fact she was not sure it would work or that they would even come to her request as she was in an unfamiliar land.

"Good thing they were out there," Semaj said as he reached out and was surprised at how friendly the creature was.

"I don't know everything about Frostites, but I do find it odd for four of them to be wondering out in the middle of nowhere," Essej said as he felt something on the wind.

"I wonder what brought them out here," Anna added as she could not help but smile at the Frostite nuzzling next to Semaj.

"They're with me," a voice boomed followed by a command that made the Frostite with the scare move away from Semaj and leap up upon a snowbank to stand next to two grumpy looking figures.

"Dwarves!" Thom shouted as the other three Frostites moved closer behind the traveling party.

****

The Snogre ran as fast as it could. It only knew one thing. It had to get back to warn the others about the fleshlings. The Snogre made it half way back when something large dropped down in front of its path. It was a giant bat-like creature with large wings and sharp claws on its back legs. Its fur-like skin was black as night and shimmered like hard steel. Red stripes streaked across its large wings, matching the eyes that glowed like fire. The creature opened its mouth and a sonar-like sound emitted that hit the Snogre with enough force to knock it upon its back.

As the Snogre started to recover a figure stepped out of the shadows. The woman hid behind a black hooded cloak. The Snogre quickly got to its feet as the woman charged at him. She leapt into the air as swords made of blazing hot fire formed out of nowhere into her hands. She extended out her arms and spun like a top in the air, the fiery blades severing the head from the Snogre's body. The woman landed back upon the ground, swords vanishing as she walked past the creature.

"I can't have you, your friends or anything else interfering with my plans. At least not until I am done with them," the hooded woman laughed as she mounted the bat-like creature and took flight.

Chapter Ten:
The Lost & The Dead

"We've been traveling for days. Shouldn't we be there by now?" Lija complained from the back of the wagon.

"It hasn't been days. Quit being so dramatic," Marcus shouted at his sister, thankful the winds had stopped and they did not have to wear face coverings anymore, which made it easier to see in the dark.

"We can rest once the sun comes up," Patches added as he glanced back into the wagon.

In the back of the wagon his sweet dear Elle lay unconscious, her breath getting shallower. Her injuries suffered during the Drogan's attack had burned her worse than he had expected and the traveling through the desert did not help her condition. He just hoped they would make it to Silversword in time. As whiney as Lija got, he was grateful at how attentive she was to his Elle. She never left her side, holding her hand and praying. Young Prince Arron sat back there, also never leaving Lija's side. Watching the potentials of young love made him think back to Elle and smile.

Sitting by his side on the wagon was Bruce Peters, former student and now dear friend. He had thought of Bruce as a son and Elle had pretty much adopted him since they never had children of their own. He always felt bad that Bruce's good friend Broc had advanced and he had never made it past grounds guard. Bruce was a good fighter and Patches had trained him well, he just lacked the confidence and self-esteem to push himself higher in the ranks. No matter, Patches was glad to have him by his side.

He glanced over at the splitting image of Broc, Marcus Masters. His father had trained him well and Patches could see the boy was just as good if not better with a sword as his father was at his age. He knew the boy was scared and worried for his family back home but for his sister, the boy kept a very strong and brave face. Since they had lost one of the horses during their battle with the Vampires, Marcus rode his horse with their newest companion, Korvan Salee. Between the shelter and their supplies, they managed to fit the man with new clothes. He still did not know what to think of this man or how he survived so long in the Drol Death Desert, but for now he would keep his one good eye on him.

"I think we need to talk," Marcus finally said breaking the silence to the man seated behind him.

"The dream? It didn't mean anything and probably some strange effect of the desert that made us dream the same thing," Korvan said growing a bit nervous.

"I don't think so. My friends were in that dream and I know they have had some strange dream happenings before. I can't remember really what all happened in it but the fact you were there and hit with the same energy that my friend was means there's more to you than you've told us," Marcus said as he looked over his shoulder throwing a glance at the man.

"If you don't trust me then why let me ride behind you?" Korvan asked.

"I'm not worried. My gut tells me Patches will take you down before you could try anything," Marcus said with a laugh, "now, start talking."

"To be honest, I don't know what that dream was all about. I've never even seen or heard of anything that happened in it. All I know is that I have some common connection and power with a bunch of those people and a feeling that I'm supposed to help fight some evil. That's all I remember and still in the dark about what it all means," Korvan said telling the truth and wondering if that is why the king of the Vampires wanted him so bad. Was there something truly special about him?

"I believe you're telling what you believe is the truth. There was some weirdness going on with my other friends too that was unexplainable, so not too surprising they were in that dream with you," Marcus said and then pushed, "tell me how you really became to be in this desert and survived, especially all by yourself when it took all of us to take down just a few Vampires."

"I," Korvan started and then paused. Something in him had changed after the dream. He felt different inside, but it was hard to explain or figure out just what it was. He felt drawn to the people in the dream, like he had to find them or others like him, whatever that meant. He could sense that he could trust Marcus and should tell him everything, but he was afraid they couldn't handle his whole truth or understand how things were different now than before he had first met them. He took in a deep breath and decided to tell him a bit of an edited truth, for now.

"I was born in a small village where the Northern River meets the Bergonia River. My family was poor and didn't have much. I was an only child and they did their best to provide for me. There were some big changes going on that I didn't agree with so when I turned twenty, to make it easier for my parents, I ventured off into the Death Drol Desert. I don't know how long I was here before I decided to return home, only to find I couldn't. Depressed, I continued to wonder this wasteland, lost without a care of my fate.

"I soon met a group of Vampires. I was so beyond living that I wasn't even scared and just threw my hands up and told them to have at me. They got near and I started to fill the teeth on my neck when they stopped. I don't know why, but they knocked me out instead. I soon discovered that they had taken me back to their master, Lord Suras, where they all lived within the Lost City of the Dead.

"It wasn't so much a city but a castle, well secured with tunnels, dungeons and rooms well below ground where they could reside out of the sunlight. I had heard stories about Vampires from my parents but thought them stories to scare us away from the Desert. Being among them and Lord Suras I was able to learn a lot about the Vampires and their weaknesses. Lord Suras liked to chat and kept me alive and chained for a long time as he seemed to be trying to study me and I think he liked talking to another intelligent being. To be honest, I had given up hope and didn't care, until the day he tried to turn me.

"Most of the time they feed off of the creatures and wondering humans in the Death Drol Desert. Humans tend to be turned into one of them, if they aren't completely destroyed in the feeding. Sometimes, humans are turned by Lord Suras personally as he is the only one that can turn a human into a Drac. I think it is because he was the first turned during the time the Death Drol Desert was created and the only one to become undead but remain more human than monster, unlike everything else that got warped in the change.

"There aren't as many Dracs as there are Vampires. They are almost like Suras, a Vampire but less feral and more intelligent, stronger and gifted than the Vampires. The Dracs are Lord Suras' elite guards. They protect him and the Lost City of the Dead in case any humans tried to attack or when the other creatures of the Death Desert get too close to the city and want to feed or forget who's truly in charge.

"The time had come and I waited for Lord Suras to turn me. As he went to press his fangs into my neck I felt something stir inside me and I opened my eyes to see a ghostly image of my mother hovering over us. Moments later Lord Sirus stepped back and then left me in my dungeon so I could turn alone. Only thing, I didn't turn and I don't know if it was a freak incident or if what I felt in me and my mother's ghost had something to do with it but I didn't become a Vampire or a Drac.

"After seeing my mother and believing it was a second chance I decided I wanted to live and find my way home again. I managed to escape and I have been fleeing the Vampires ever since until I stumbled upon your group," Korvan said bringing his story to and end as the first rays of daylight started to shine over the desert sands.

"You are lucky to have survived and I'm glad you trusted me with your tale," Marcus said as he felt like the man had still held something back and there were a couple things with his story that didn't register but before his mind could figure it out the horses stopped and began to whine and stomp their hooves.

"What's going on?" Bruce asked as Patches yelled and did his best to get the horses attached to his wagon to calm down.

"Maybe they don't like the sun anymore," Arron added as he stuck his head out of the front flap to see what the commotion was all about.

"There, something off in the distance," Marcus said pointing and straining to see what it was, then turned to ask Korvan only to realize he had jumped off the horse and was getting into the wagon.

"What is that?" Patches asked as he could almost make out something sticking out of the sand.

"Here, found it," Korvan said as he stuck his head a little out of the wagon with a long strange metal devise pressed up against his left eye and then swore.

"Spit it out boy. What do you see with my far-seer?" Patches asked as he grabbed the metal thing from Korvan and placed it up to his good eye.

"I'm afraid it's a sand shark," Korvan said as he sat back nervously in the covered wagon.

"What's a sand shark?" Lija asked as panic overtook her.

"They are massive fish-like creatures that live well under the desert sand. They are mostly rotted flesh and bones. They have razor sharp fins that run up and down their backs and large teeth. They rarely come to the surface and dwell mainly towards the center of the Drol Death Desert," Korvan answered as the fin kept going down under the sand and then back up, getting closer to their wagon.

"How do we fight it?" Marcus asked as he drew his sword.

"We don't. You watch where the fin is at, and when you see more than one come up, know it's about to attack, leap out of the way and survive till it tires and retreats back deep into the sand below," Korvan said getting nervous.

"Patches, you take the wagon and move as fast as you can. Marcus and I will play bait and distract it till it tires and goes away," Bruce said as he drew his sword as well and leapt from the seat of the covered wagon.

"I will stay and fight too," Arron proclaimed as he drew his sword.

"No, you will be needed to protect my sister," Marcus said not wanting to worry about the prince in a fight with some strange sand creature.

"And you need to get your wife to safety," Bruce added with force before Patches could speak.

"Korvan can take arms and assist us," Marcus said as he wondered why the man cowered inside the wagon still.

"It's best I stay in here," Korvan said as Patches knew they did not have time to argue and commanded the horses to take the wagon away from the approaching fin.

"There's something off about that guy," Marcus said as he watched the fin dip down and then rise, getting closer.

"Maybe being stuck out here has its effect on a person. Not everyone is brave or a fighter," Bruce said trying to hold his sword steady.

They both remembered Korvan's words and they prepared themselves, Bruce on his feet and Marcus on his horse. The fin was almost upon them when it rose high and then went straight down. Seconds later about four fins in a perfect line rose up in a curve and followed each other back into the sand. At that moment, Bruce leapt to one side while Marcus had the horse gallop to the opposite side.

Seconds after, a large creature erupted from the ground, face first, into the air. It looked like a very large fish, about the size of a small Dragon. Its mouth was open, sand pouring out of it between large sharp teeth. Its body had blotches of rotting flesh along with its skeletal frame showing and poking through. On its back was a line of razor sharp fins that went all the way down to the tail that ended with two large sharp fins. The sand shark came back down, mouth biting into the sand as it went straight down with the sand filling in after till there was no sign of the creature or its attack.

"Did you see the size of that thing?" Bruce asked to no one in particular.

"Where did it go?" Marcus asked as he tried to keep the horse calm, watching the ground closely for signs of the creature and its fins.

The ground began to tremble, but to Bruce it felt more like aftershocks, as if something was about to erupt much farther away. Bruce stared towards the wagon that had made great progress and then came to a realization. Bruce knew Marcus had thought the same thing when he felt himself pulled up onto the horse and they took off as fast as the horse could gallop. A fin had moved up not far behind the racing wagon. Marcus screamed when it appeared they would not catch up in time and stared in horror at the scene that unfolded before him.

The ground exploded as the sand shark shot out of the ground. They were both still too far away to see clearly, but it looked like the creature missed the wagon with its large mouth but its massive body and sharp fins hit and sliced into the wagon. The creature curved over and plunged back into the sand and out of sight. Marcus urged the horse onward, praying with all his might that his sister was safe as the distance and the kicked-up sand made it hard to see the aftermath.

"Those creatures must feel the vibrations under the ground. Since we were standing still it picked up on the wagon," Bruce said as he saw a fin poke back out but was moving towards them now.

"Do not move and wait till I get far enough away then go check on your sister and the others," Bruce said as knew what he had to do.

Before Marcus could react, Bruce grabbed his shoulders and gave him a hard push. Marcus had been thrown from the horse, hitting the ground and rolling as Bruce shifted up and grabbed the rains. Marcus stood up quickly, ignoring the pain from his body hitting the ground and watched as Bruce steered the horse back in the opposite direction. Marcus remained still as he saw the fin approach him, raising his sword. To his surprise the fin did not go down but veered to the side and started heading for Bruce. Bruce was making great progress but it wouldn't be long before the sand shark caught up to him.

Marcus took in a deep breath, wished Bruce luck and sent his thanks and then ran swiftly to where the covered wagon had been attacked just moments ago. The thought of his sister injured or worse drove him to run as fast as he could but it seemed like he was not gaining any ground. Now that the sun had fully risen he could see clearly ahead of him and the site of the covered wagon in pieces pulled on his heart thinking of his sister and the others had been on it just moments ago. A sudden noise brought him to a stop and diverted his attention.

He turned and looked behind him. Off in the distance he saw the sand shark come up out of the ground and then plunge back in, vanishing seconds later. Marcus strained his eyes but due to the distance and the wind kicking up the sand it made it hard for him to see anything. Marcus felt his stomach turn as he saw no signs of Bruce Peters or the horse he was riding on. He waited a few seconds, watching intently but still saw nothing but the moving sand. Marcus felt tears form at the thought of his dad's old friend sacrificing his life for him and his sister.

"Lija!" Marcus suddenly shouted her name as the thought of his sister brought him back to the destruction behind him.

He had to find her. He was sure she was still alive as he would have known it if his twin had died, unless she was swallowed... no he could not think that. He finally made it to the destroyed wagon and looked around. There were no signs of the horses and the wagon was split to pieces. Smaller pieces, wheels and all their supplies and weapons were scattered everywhere. He wanted to start shouting out his sister's name again but stopped as he thought of the sand shark. He doubted yelling would attract it back but he did not want to take that chance.

Marcus lightly stepped as he neared what was left of the wagon. He peered inside one portion of the wagon and thought he saw something under a pile of wood. He moved the boards and stepped back in shock when saw the body of Prince Arron lying face down, his back was sliced and bleeding. He began to move forward to see if he was still alive when he heard a strange gasping sound. It looked like something was moving underneath Arron. He started to move in closer when the body pushed upwards a little causing Marcus to let out a scream and step back.

"Help, get him off of me. I can't breathe," a somewhat muffled voice came from under Arron's body.

"Lija!" Marcus screamed with joy as he knelt down and carefully rolled Arron over and off his sister.

"I think he's still alive. I could feel and smell his breath," Lija said as she looked at her brother with joy and then concern washed over her face glancing over to Arron.

"I got a pulse. It's weak but he's alive," Marcus said as he placed two fingers upon the prince's wrist.

"He saved my life. When the wagon began to tear apart he threw himself over me to protect me," Lija cried as she stared at Arron's body.

"He'll be okay. Look for anything we can use to clean up the wounds on his back. I'm going to look for the others," Marcus said as he glanced down and saw two canteens of water, which he kept one and threw the other at his sister.

"Where's Mr. Peters?" Lija asked as he leaned over and picked up a container that had Elle's salve and bandages inside.

"He raced off with the horse to lead the sand shark away," was all Marcus needed to say as Lija stifled a cry, nodded and took the water and first aid supplies over to Arron to tend to his wounds and make him comfortable.

Since his sister was safe, Marcus started to worry about the others in their party. He passed between the wagon debris and saw a few feet away was a figure hunched and rocking. As he got closer, he saw it was Patches holding his wife. Even with all the sand and dust Marcus could tell she was cut up and bruised pretty badly, on top of her previous burn wounds. Marcus stepped up behind him and placed his hand upon the old man's shoulder. Patches glanced up with his covered eye and then turned back down to his wife.

"She's a tough ol' bird. She's still holding on but I don't know," Patches started to say and then trailed off into silence as Marcus knelt down next to him.

"I'm sorry," was all Marcus could say as he saw Elle's lips barely part and a feint rasp escaped her body.

"I was thrown from the wagon the second that monster exploded up from the ground. Landed on my leg pretty hard, not broken but can hardly walk on it," Patches said as the pain he felt for his wife still outweighed the pain shooting through his lower body.

"We'll come up with something. My sister is fine and tending to the prince," Marcus said as he told Patches about Arron and about Bruce's sacrifice.

"A wife and *son,* all in one swoop. Not fair, it should've been me," Patches said as he finally wiped a tear from his good eye.

"It's all our fault. If my sister and I had never gone to the king, none of this would have happened," Marcus said as Patches gave him a look that instantly silenced him.

"Boy, it's not your fault. The blame goes to the evil monster that sent those creatures to your home setting all this into motion. We will find out who is responsible and we will make them pay for all this," Patches said as he finally got himself together as he knew what needed to be done. "Suns getting high, we need to make some kind of shelter."

"I still need to find the horses and Korvan," Marcus added as he stood up and looked around, sweat pouring down his back and the sun's heat started to wear down on them.

"Horses are gone. Unfortunately, the sand shark got them. They got cut lose and as I hit the ground I managed to see both horses galloping away but not fast enough to be swallowed as the giant monster came down mouth first around them and then back under the ground," Patches said as he tried to move out from under Elle and winced at the pain. A moan sounded, but he knew it had not come from him or Elle.

"It's Korvan," Marcus said running as he saw a figure crawling slowly on his hands and knees towards them.

"I'll be fine, just need to get out of this sun," Korvan said in a whisper as he dropped and Marcus helped roll him onto his back.

Marcus, being concerned, started to check the man over to see how bad his wounds were. Despite some protest, Marcus was able to get a pretty good look and was shocked to find that with so many tears in his blood-stained clothes, there was not a cut, mark or bruise on his body. There's no way that could be possible. Things didn't quite add up, especially the surviving an attack by the Vampires. He almost suspected he was one of them if it wasn't for the fact he was laying here in the sunlight. The more he stared at the man, obviously in some kind of pain and wanting to go into the shade, the more questions he had.

"How's Korvan?" Patches shouted from where he sat with the slowly dying Elle, trying to make her comfortable.

"He seems to be in a lot of pain but there's not a mark on him," Marcus said stepping back from the man and watching him squirm in the sunlight.

"Oh?" Patches asked picking up on the tone in the boy's voice that told him that Marcus was not being concerned but questioning something about their new *friend* that mirrored his own intuitions.

"Something about his story of being in the desert and fleeing the Lost City of the Dead isn't adding up," Marcus said as he told the old man the tale Korvan told him earlier.

"Well, at age twenty I can tell you he didn't leave his home and get lost in the desert since where he said he is from is actually located in the Kingdom of Tallus, and they've had the border wall up for at least a few hundred years. So, either he is lying about where he is from or his true age," Patches said as he held up a shiny object from his pocket, catching the sun and reflecting a sun spot right on Korvan's face.

Korvan hissed moving his face revealing a red sun burned spot on his cheek and what Marcus could have sworn were fangs that quickly retracted. Marcus took a fast step back and he stared eye to eye with the man in front of him. After a few seconds the red burn mark began to heal and fade. There was definetely more to this man's story then he was letting on. Marcus turned back towards Patches, "it burned his face and I swear I saw fangs, but if he was a Vampire wouldn't he be dust by now?"

"I've grabbed what wagon covering I could and should be able to make a tent to shade us from the sun," Lija said as she walked over to the ground and froze not sure what she was interrupting.

"We will get our answers, but first, let's get Elle out of the sun," Patches said as he glanced from Korvan, to the twins and then back down at his wife.

****

Bruce Peters had never been so lost in his life. It seemed like he had been walking for days, but in reality, it was more like hours. The blazing hot sun just made it seem like eternity. Bruce chuckled at the thought of surviving the sand shark attack to only die of heat and dehydration hours later. It was only a miracle he was alive. As he charged the horse onwards to lead the creature away from the rest of the group, he knew it would only be a matter of time and he would be making a brave sacrifice.

As luck would have it, the horse stopped and let out a strange cry before bucking him off, seconds before the sand shark came up and swallowed the horse. Bruce hit the ground but did not waste time, he started running in the opposite direction from where the sand shark landed. When he was a short safe distance from where the large desert monster dug its way back into the ground, Bruce found a spot and sat perfectly still, catching his breath and resting his sore body, as he masked his presence from the creature until it went away. After a few minutes he thought he saw a small fin poke up and then vanish never to be seen again. They were all safe.

Bruce began heading back to the group but with all the dust the sand shark had kicked up it made it hard to see. It wasn't long before Bruce realized he must have got turned around and had gone the wrong direction as there was no sign of his friends or the wagon anywhere. Bruce took in a deep breath and began walking trying to do his best to find his way back to his party. Hours later, shirt tied around his head and armor long discarded, he knew he was lost and soon to be dead.

Bruce was ready to collapse and give in to the desert heat when he saw what looked like stone structures off in the distance. Mirage or not, he found some inner strength and continued moving in that direction. He was not sure what he would find, but if there was shelter from the heat then that is all that mattered. He managed to make it halfway to his new destination when a strange sound and movement snapped him sober and come to a complete stop. He gripped his sword and looked from side to side trying to determine reality from imagination.

He heard the sound again and turned to see sand swirling a few feet away from him. A mini cyclone of sand formed around the desert ground as a figure began to rise from under the sand directly in its center. Once the creature had fully risen out of the ground the cyclone of sand vanished making it easy for Bruce to see what had risen. It looked human, but the flesh all over its body was rotting and was either torn off in chunks or peeling off and hanging from its body. It made a strange moaning noise as it slowly limped toward him, eyes dead and vacant with drool made of sand coming from a mouth full of pointed teeth.

"Stay back," Bruce shouted as he waved his sword, blade shinning red off the sun's light.

The creature didn't hesitate or flinch. It kept moaning and walking towards him. Bruce lunged forward and drove his blade into its chest. He pulled his sword back out and stepped back as he saw that it had no effect on the creature. Not only did it not slow the creature down but there wasn't even any blood coming out of the wound, just sand. The walking dead opened its mouth, sharp teeth exposed, lunged forward for a bite. Bruce sidestepped and brought his weapon down taking off its head.

"That's what I thought," Bruce laughed as he watched the body and head hit the ground.

Bruce started to walk towards the stone buildings when he heard the moaning again. He turned and gasped as he saw the head and body were still moving but now the desert sand under them were swirling and somehow pulling the two body parts back together. Bruce couldn't move as he stood frozen in horror as the head soon reattached to the body and the creature got to its feet and started moving towards him again. Bruce raised his sword ready for a second round when he heard more moaning sounds.

Bruce slowing turned his head as he saw swirls of sand forming in the desert sand all around him. It didn't take long before seven more creatures rose out of the ground. Some looked like men, some looked like woman and two sadly looked like children, but the one thing in common was that they were all dead, rotting and slowly walking towards him. He had his sword raised, but if these things could not be killed he would not last long. Feeling the heat and exhaustion, Bruce tried to map an escape route when he felt something zip past his head.

He reached up to his ear and confirmed no wound or blood as he watched a shiny object fly through the air towards one of the dead creatures. It was a curved sword, shaped almost like a scythe. It sliced through the air and hit the top of the creature's head slicing it right off, brains and all. The creature and the very top of its head fell to the ground and immediately began to melt and dissolve back into the desert sand. Bruce then watched as the blade continued to move through the air, arc and head back in the direction it had come from. Bruce rotated as he saw the blade return to the hand of its thrower.

The owner of the curved blade appeared to be a tall man completely wrapped from head to toe in a strange cloth material that had a glossy white color to it. He almost looked like a mummy. Not an inch of skin or anything of the man could be seen. He wore strange goggles where the eyes would be and even his boots and gloves were made of the same glossy white material. It almost looked as if it helped reflect the sunlight off of him. Bruce figured it was to keep him cool out in the desert heat. The man then leapt through the air, almost as if he were flying, landed near Bruce and swung his blade piercing the head of another causing it to melt back into the sand.

"The only way to kill them is to puncture their brain by stabbing it through the head or slicing a chunk off," the man said with a muffled voice.

"Who are you?" Bruce asked still trying to comprehend what was going on around him.

"No time for that. If you don't help me finish these Sand Walkers off there will be more and we won't be able to make it to safety. Whatever you do, do not let them bite you," the man said as he leapt up and charged another Sand Walker.

Bruce was about to ask more questions when he felt a hand grab him. Bruce turned with a start and managed to push the dead creature back moments before it could take a bite out of him. Bruce quickly thrust his sword and plunged its blade deep into the Sand Walker's head. Before he could pull the sword out, the creature had already begun to melt back into the desert sand. He turned to see his new friend take out the last two Sand Walkers and then motion him his way. He appeared to be slowing down in his movements and was looking a bit sluggish.

"Hurry, we can take shelter in the ruins of the old city. You will be safe from the Sand Walkers in there," the man said as he moved in the direction Bruce was originally headed.

"Don't have to tell me twice," Bruce said as he looked back and saw more Sand Walkers starting to form and ran after the wrapped man.

****

It had taken a few hours but Marcus and his sister had managed to use the broken wood and canvas from the wagon to make a decent tent big enough to hold the lot of them and protect them from the sun's rays. They got Elle and Arron placed comfortably inside, and while Patches looked after the two, Marcus and Lija searched around for anything salvageable. Luckily, they were able to find most of their supplies including their food and water. Despite his pleading, they kept Korvan out in the sun as it seemed to keep him pretty weak and out of their way until they were ready to deal with him.

"This is torture. Please let me out of the sun. I won't hurt any of you, I swear," Korvan said as his body ached from the touch of the sunlight.

"Lija, dear, please look after these two while me and your brother have a chat with our friend there," Patches said as he limped, making his way out of the tent. Leaning on Marcus, they made their way over to Korvan.

"You're a Vampire?" Was the first thing Marcus asked as he studied the man lying before them, feet and hands tied together.

"Not exactly," Korvan said through gritted teeth.

"Then what are you?" Patches asked as he sat down, aiming a small handheld crossbow with a stake loaded in it at the man's heart.

"How do we know he'll even tell us the truth after the story he fed me this morning?" Marcus added.

"What I told you was the truth, just not the whole truth," Korvan said wishing he could get into the shade.

"If you want us to trust you, then get to talking. I want to hear everything and if I sense you are lying or pulling a fast one on us, I will end you here and now," Patches said staring right into Korvan's eyes with his one good eye while holding the mini crossbow steady and trigger finger ready.

"I was born in that village in Tallus but it was not twenty years ago, more like three hundred and twenty years ago. My family was poor but outcasts as well. We lived in that small village because many thought my mother a witch and that wasn't true. She just liked visiting this old woman who liked to tell stories of the days of the Magic Wars. My father wouldn't allow me to go because people all over were starting to get worried about magic and magical creatures.

"On my twentieth birthday, one hundred years after the Magic Wars. The land of Bergonia was divided into five kingdoms and the kingdom our village resided was given to and named after King Tallus. There was all this talk of hunting and exiling magic creatures or anyone associated with magic. That was the day my father had officially forbid my mother to ever go near that old lady again.

"My parents had gotten into a huge fight over this. While they were fighting I found a strange blue book with an odd symbol hidden in my mother's craft box. On the inside it said, "With all my love, Shirlynn." At first glance, I thought it was some kind of witchcraft book. I was going to look further when I heard a big commotion. I peeked to see the village people had come to search the house for proof my mother was a witch.

"I couldn't let them find this book so I snuck out of the house and ran like crazy. I figured I would go into the Desert and bury it where no one would find it and then return back home. I made it safely undetected into the Drol Death Desert and went as far as I thought safe to bury the book. Once I had the book hidden, I headed back only to find I had lost my way. I wondered around for days till I found that shelter, I had lead you too, stocked with rations and supplies. It had belonged to someone but to whom, I did not know.

"I stayed there for a week or two, venturing out but not far trying to find my way back home but I couldn't and always ended up returning to the shelter. Then one day, I headed in what seemed a new direction and soon found myself lost. That is when I decided that I was unable to return home and had given up hope and came across the Vampires. The rest of what I had told you after that was true. Only thing is, I had been captive of Suras for a few hundred years before I managed to escape," Korvan said finishing his story.

"And that's when we found you being chased by Vampires," Marcus said as more of a statement as Korvan nodded.

"That's all fine and dandy with your story, but you haven't explained exactly what you are, Vampire or human," Patches said as he lowered his weapon, but only a little.

"Actually, I really don't know, but with recent events in that dream I might have an explanation of sorts," Korvan said as the others nudged him to continue.

"When the original Vampires went to bite me, they tasted or sensed something in my blood and that is why they took me back to their master where Suras studied me for months before finally deciding to turn me. But when I didn't fully turn and ended up like this, that sealed my fate. The next few hundred years I was interrogated, studied and experimented on. It seems I remained human taking on some Vampire traits.

"I have slightly enhanced strength and speed, I never age or I age very slowly and I heal pretty fast. Unlike Vampires, the sunlight does not instantly kill me. It does make me very weak and my body shrieks with pain but I can survive in the sunlight. That was the case when you guys found me. I was severely weak from being in the sun that I was not fully back up to strength. Now, after that dream, something inside me has stirred and being in the sunlight is not as bad as it was before," Korvan explained.

"So whatever special gift you have inside you, it keeps you from fully turning and allows you to be in the sunlight and that is what Suras wants you for," Marcus said looking at Patches.

"Last thing we need is Vampires roaming during the daytime and then being able to make it out of the Desert," Patches said as he looked at Korvan and then lowered his weapon. "What about feeding on blood?"

"I have the craving, but it's not a strong feral urge. I have no desire to feed on human blood and when I need to feed, animal blood does just fine," Korvan said as Patches nodded with approval as Marcus suddenly thought about the missing horse Korvan could not find and decided it was best not to ask.

"Looks like we're stuck with you until we get you far from Suras and the Vampires," Patches said as he started to put his weapon away and get to his feet, "but if you do anything to cross us or try and hurt us I will stake you."

With a mutual understanding, Marcus helped Patches back to the shaded tent and then went back and helped Korvan. Once in the shade, it seemed Korvan was gaining his strength back pretty quickly. Marcus watched him carefully as Patches made his way to Elle's side. Korvan didn't make any moves and Marcus's gut was telling him that they may not be able to fully trust the man but they were safe and he would do them no harm.

"I wish there was something more I could do," Lija said as she dabbed Elle's forehead with a cloth.

"I don't know if I can, but I could try and turn her," Korvan offered but retreated at a glare from one eye.

"No, as much as I love Elle, I could never risk her becoming a monster like them and she would never want that life. We'll be together again soon," Patches said as he bent over and kissed her forehead, wiping a tear from his eye.

The sun had finally started to vanish when Marcus and Korvan began to bury Elle's body. Patches hated to leave her out in this wasteland, but he knew there was no way they could carry her body around. Marcus and Patches, mainly Marcus, dug a grave deep into the desert sand. Lija and Korvan nicely wrapped her body in cloth from the covered wagon tent and then they laid her to rest. Patches gave a silent send off to his wife and when he was done, Marcus and Korvan took care of the open grave while Patches limped off to be alone for a while.

"I feel for him. That's two loved ones he's lost," Marcus said as he felt a twinge of guilt as if it was not for him and his sister this would never have happened to Elle or Bruce.

"Marcus, look!" Lija shouted as she stood off to the side pointing.

Marcus glanced up and saw a figure lying face down in the desert sand. Marcus and Korvan made a dash for the body as Patches limped his way after telling Lija to stay back. Korvan, with his speed, reached the body first. He recognized it right away. It was one of the Dracs. He wondered why it had ventured this far from the Lost City of the Dead at the price of its life as Korvan could tell that the cloth wrapped body was now going flat as the Drac turned to dust from the exposure to the sun.

"It's a Drac, but he's gone," Korvan said to Marcus as he pressed down on the material with his foot, oozing out ash and sand to demonstrate his point.

"Luckily the sun got it before nightfall," Patches said as he approached the two, lighting his makeshift candle so they could see with the darkness starting to take over.

"You think there's more of them?" Marcus asked looking around.

"No, he was sent to deliver a message," Korvan said fishing something out of the gloved hand.

"They've got Bruce," Patches said as he recognized the ring he had given his *son* with a note attached that said, "come get him."

185

"Did I miss anything?" Came a voice that startled the three men as they turned to see Prince Arron sitting up, scratching his head.

Chapter Eleven:
Escape To The Frosted Waters

Lucian Darkheart sat staring out his window at the glow of the Fire Mountains off in the distance. It was hard to believe that something so beautiful represented something so terrible. During the Magic Wars, when the battle between good and evil came to the end, the world had changed in one final act. His mentor and adopted father, Docanesto, had given him the history lesson. This act had not only caused the Drol Death Desert but it made an earthquake so vicious that it caused the Mountains to split in two and a chunk of land to break away. Waters rushed in separating Bergonia's now named Eastern Mountains with the chunk of the land now known as Ogra. Their half of the mountains became the Western Mountains.

No one knows how or why, but not long after, the water separating the two lands froze over and became known as the Frosted Waters. Too frosty for boats to sail in but not strong enough for anything heavier than a human to cross. By chance, almost all of the Ogre and Goblin-based races happened to reside on that section of land when it separated and there they would always remain as the mountains and specially the Frosted Waters would keep them from ever touching foot on Bergonia again. At that same time, the forces fighting against the evil Semaj and his followers were forced to retreat into the Unknown Lands. Due to the earthquake and magic explosion, part of the southern land cracked and shifted south causing the area between the southern mountains and the forest to fill with scorching lava.

Not soon after the end of the Magic Wars, the races tried to rebuild and recover but because evil had prevailed the normals took the advantage and declared war on magic and all magic users and creatures. The War of the Races began. Eighty-five years later, the normals had prevailed and the Age of Humans began. Dwarves had vanished into the Northern Mountains while all magic creatures were either exiled or killed. The Elves were relocated into what became known as the Forest of Spirits. While the normals were creating the Five Kingdoms, the Elves and remaining magical creatures created their new home within the forest.

Even with the precaution of guard posts setup all along the borders of the forest to keep anything from coming out, the king of the Elves declared it forbidden for any magic creature to ever leave the forest. Which was a big reason why his adopted father had been exiled when he was caught leaving and helping a normal, his real father, learn magic. The Elves had taken their law of new land one step further by banishing any that opposed their rule or had sided with evil to the Unknown Lands and then cast a great spell that turned the Southern Mountains into the Fire Mountains which now made it impossible for anything or anyone to leave the Unknown Lands.

Little did the normals or Elves know that the Kingdom of Drol was building the Unknown Lands into the force it is today, with him, his real father and adopted father to rise up to their destiny to do what the Elves and others were too afraid to do, take Bergonia back. When they did that, the magic creatures would shower them with praise and worship them as gods. They have, with magic and a few allies, created a hidden underground passageway that leads from the Unknown Lands, through the Fire Mountains, under the Forest of Spirits and right into the Old River Gorge that separates the Forest of Spirits from the Kingdom of Argoth.

Normally the guard posts would stop and kill anything coming out, but they had an inside ally in Argoth who has given Docanesto and their forces a free pass out, but they still had to be careful as the Elves above their passage and other normals in Argoth could foil their plans if spotted and caught. Now that they had taken Soré, they had a place to send their Drogan forces. With the exception of a few parts of Sorran, Argoth was the only kingdom they were safe to pass through at this time as the magic alarms were dismantled. With these forces out there, including his spy Natureza, Lucian felt a twinge of jealousy and anger as he has been isolated in the Unknown Lands all his life and has never been able to leave or have contact with the outside lands of Bergonia. Hopefully that would change soon.

From his dream, he could only remember a few descriptions, but for some reason his instincts kept drawing him to and see the land called Ogra. He told his dad that the only beings he remembered from the dream fit the descriptions of the creatures that lived there. With Docanesto needing to prepare the forces for an attack on another part of Bergonia, Lucian hoped his father would allow him to lead the mission to find and capture the Magestic in Ogra. Not only would it allow him to prove himself to both his dads, but also see a part of the outside world.

It would be an easy mission. Sneak through the hidden passage under the Forest of Spirits, then take the Eastern Sea to the southern edge of the Frosted Waters, and then from there make it to Ogra. His father would have to agree it would be easier for him to go with the chance of maybe tracking the Magestic and finding them quicker than someone else just waging war and spending too much time trying to find and weed out a creature they didn't truly know the identity of. He was the best and obvious choice.

"You can't go, it's too dangerous and we need you to stay here," Docanesto said stepping in to the room.

"You can't go either so who does that leave?" Lucian asked as he turned to face the Fire Elf.

"You are not prepared yet to go out into the outer world," Docanesto said eying the young man he had raised as his own.

"I can use a sword and what magic you have taught me, including the mastery of fire like all those that pledge their lives. I can handle myself and I can do this. You know as well as I do if anyone has a chance of finding the Magestic it's me," Lucian said, anger and determination rising in his voice.

"I will speak to your father," Docanesto said as he vanished from the room.

Lucian held out his hand, and from a vial, shook a speck of dust upon it. He then called on magic, whispered something upon it causing it to glow. He then raised his hand to the window and the wind seemed to pick it up and carry the glowing speck of dust out the window and out of sight. Lucian did not wait. Before he knew it, he grabbed his hooded cloak, the map, the book and pills he stole and copied from Docanesto and found himself running from his castle. He quickly sought out the one person he could trust, Sev.

Sev was a Fairy he met when he was a very young boy. Not many Fairies choose to leave the forest, let alone join Drol Greb's cause and take the honor of serving him. His father told him that many in the world see that as a sign of evil, but he said he ignores it and uses it to instill fear back at them and strength into ourselves to rise up on the side of right and free our people. Sev had pledged himself at a very young age and had taken the fire becoming a Fire Fairy.

Sev had then been immediately assigned to Lucian who was about ten at the time, to watch over him and report back to Docanesto. As the seasons went by, they grew very close as friends and Sev did not always report everything back to Lucian's fathers. Now that Lucian was an adult he did not need a watcher or sitter so Sev had been reassigned as watcher over the soldiers being trained. Even though times have changed and they had gotten older, they did make time to see each other whenever they could. No one but them knew of their strong lasting bond.

"Sev, you there?" Lucian called out once he reached one of the empty stone living quarters that they provided to their soldiers.

"Is everything okay? I felt something strange in your summons," a small voice said from somewhere above Lucian, referring to the magical message that Lucian had just sent out upon the winds.

"Sorry, I don't have a lot of time to waste," Lucian said as he looked and then gave a hand signal to ensure the coast was clear.

"What's going on?" Sev asked as a small figure with fast beating wings moved into sight and with a swirl of glowing dust his body began to grow while his wings shrunk out of sight.

Lucian watched as the small Fairy enlarged to about five feet tall. He had a slender body but muscular. His skin had a grayish hue and his eyes were red from the effects of going through the process of swearing himself to Drol Greb. His hair was short, blue and barely covered his pointed ears. He wore only a black pant made of cloth that covered him from his waist to his knees. The rest of his body was exposed showing off red swirl symbols painted all over. He had a string-like belt wrapped around his waist to hold his small dagger. Sev smiled brightly as he walked up to Lucian, shifted up on his tip toes and kissed him hard.

"It's good to see you too, but we have to hurry before they notice I'm gone," Lucian said as he pulled away from Sev, smiled and then got serious.

"You have me worried," Sev started to say when Lucian held up a finger signaling him to listen.

"What I've told you is happening. The Chosen One has surfaced and it appears he has a group called the Magestics he is recruiting to try and keep me and my fathers from freeing the world. I believe at least one Majestic to be on Ogra and someone needs to go find them," Lucian said in one quick breath.

"Let me guess, you're going with or without permission. You've never left this place. It's too dangerous to go alone," Sev said as he knew from the look in his love's eyes that the decision was already made.

"That's why I must go. How can I rule a land that I've never seen? If I can pull this off I can show them both I am more than capable in helping free and rule this land. Plus, I won't be going alone," Lucian said as a hint of a smile escaped his mouth.

"You know I'd go anywhere and do anything for you," Sev started to say when Lucian grabbed him by both his shoulders.

"Good, I need you to find some soldiers we can trust and meet me by the hidden entrance through the Fire Mountains," Lucian said as he stared intently into the Fire Fairy's eyes.

"I'll do it," Sev said knowing better than to say no.

"Go!" Lucian commanded but not before he gave him one last kiss and then ran out as Sev shrunk down, sprouted wings and flew off.

Lucian made it to the wall that surrounded his city. He pulled his hooded cloak closer around him to help hide his identity. He knew it would be difficult to leave the city without someone noticing and reporting back to Docanesto. He didn't care if his fathers found out, but he wanted to be halfway through the hidden passageway before they did. As he moved closer to the wall he felt a shadow fall upon him. He turned to see a figure about six feet tall, very muscular and head shaved bald. This was one of their Barbarian Warriors, a barbaric race of humans that dedicate their lives to fighting, battle and training for war. He would have mistaken this Barbarian for a man if it wasn't for her outfit.

Like all Barbarians, she wore black furred boots, matching waist cloth and straps that went across their front and back to hold their weapons of choice upon their backs. She had a cloth as well to cover her chest, which is what distinguished her gender. The Barbarian woman stepped closer, arms crossed but ready to grab the large double-bladed axe resting on her back. Lucian took a step back and smiled under his hood. "What are you doing here?" The Barbarian asked sounding more like a threat than a question.

"Is that any way to talk to your king?" Lucian asked removing his hood.

"I could not talk and just take your head off instead," the Barbarian said reaching her hand back towards her battle-axe.

"Fylla, I would have you burned alive before you even reached me," Lucian countered with his hand stretched out and ready to call upon his magic.

"Shall we test that?" Fylla asked as she charged forward, grabbed Lucian in a bear hug and squeezed.

"Damn it, put me down," Lucian swore trying to catch his breath from the tight squeeze.

"You really thought you would go off to battle without me? I really should take your head off," Fylla said giving Lucian a very serious and angry look.

"Why am I not surprised Sev spoke to you?" Lucian said as he pulled his hood back up so no one else would recognize him.

Lucian found it hard to trust anyone. You could not if you were the master over an entire land. If he had to give trust to someone, besides Sev, that would be Fylla. She was a couple years older than him and he had known her just as long as he had known Sev. He met her when he was younger and was sent to the Barbarians to learn to fight. She had been assigned as his sparring partner. During his time of training, they had grown a strong and secret friendship. Unlike other Barbarians that take no last name and denounce all family and commit only to the battle, Fylla wanted a family. She wanted to find love. She wanted to kill and live for the battle. She wanted it all, but she could never admit that because love and family was not the code of the Barbarians.

For now, Fylla could only channel her love towards animals, so she had taken on the role of animal trainer. She helped train, control and prepare the many creatures at their disposal for battle. Her specialization was in Fire Hounds and Tazarians. She had just put in a request to become a member of the Tazarian Riders. Barbarians didn't fly and believed in the battle on the ground. While the position of Tazarian Riders was mainly held for Fire Elves, Fylla had proven to be good and was determined to be the first Barbarian Tazarian Rider. If her request was granted she would have to battle in the air against five other Riders. If she prevailed and lived, then she would be admitted.

"I will go with you," Fylla informed Lucian.

"No, your trial to be a Rider is coming up. I cannot ask this of you," Lucian said feeling better about his mission with two of his best friends by his side.

"It's already decided," Fylla said as she pulled a bundle off her back and threw it at Lucian's feet.

Lucian quickly looked inside and saw a sword and traveling armor. He had not thought of that when he raced out. He quickly put it on. The black armor with red accents was light but provided protection. The matching boots and gloves fit perfectly. He then picked up the sword and swung it with ease. It had great balance and would work just as well as his personal sword. Fylla knew him well. He slid the sword in the side holster and then put his cloak and hood quickly back on to conceal him. With a nod he gave his approval and thanks to Fylla.

"Now we need to get past the gates without being recognized," Lucian said as he looked back and forth at the wall that closed out the outside world.

"Follow me. I have a pass for Fire Hound training outside the grounds. Keep the hood pulled tight and they'll think you're my trainee," Fylla said as she led the way.

Lucian followed Fylla closely as they approached the gates that led out to the fields where training was done with certain creatures of the Unknown Lands. The guards looked at her pass and motioned them through as the gates opened and then closed behind them. Off to the left Lucian could see creatures being trained with other warriors and fighters. He was about to step that way when Fylla looked up and then motioned him in the opposite direction. After a few minutes she stopped and blew a wooden devise around her neck. It did not make any noise but it was a whistle of some kind.

It wasn't long until two large beasts came running towards them. Lucian recognized them instantly as Fire Hounds. Dogs the size of a cow covered in black fur. Their eyes were red as blood and teeth as sharp as blades. Their legs were muscular with sharp claws that allowed them to run at great speed and dig into most anything. Their main feature, the one they're named for, is that their fur is resistant to heat and flames, but only while attached to the creature's body. If the fur is removed it turns to ash, which Lucian knew from experience when he was young and he removed a patch from a hound.

"Frrr!" Lucian shouted when he saw that one of the Fire Hounds approaching had a patch of fur missing from the right side of his neck.

The huge beast pounced on Lucian, knocking him to the ground. The second Fire Hound began to snarl but Fylla slammed her hands together getting its attention and commanding it to heel. Lucian got to his feet, grabbed, ruffled and patted the large hound's body. Fire Hounds were never named, but Lucian had named this one. It was his first Fire Hound he encountered and later trained with and the only one he would ever associate with. They had bonded after Frrr allowed him to try and burn off a patch of fur and unlike any other, the Fire Hound took Lucian as a personal master and friend. At age seven, Lucian had named him Frrr.

"Hurry, the others should be there by now," Fylla said as she leapt up on top of the Fire Hound while Lucian did the same with Frrr.

"Go!" Lucian commanded as he grabbed handfuls of the beasts main and Frrr leapt forward with Fylla following right behind.

With their muscular legs and sharp claws, the Fire Hounds moved with great speed away from the great city and towards the Fire Mountains. Lucian was grateful for their speed. Otherwise, it would take way too long to reach the hidden entrance into the mountains. Lucian noticed as they got closer to their destination, the temperature got hotter and the grass on the ground got lesser and darker. Due to the intense heat off the Fire Mountains, not much could live or survive for long near them. After a few hours Lucian saw a group off in the distance. From the way they were moving he suspected they had just gotten there.

Lucian could not believe how Sev was able to assemble a group so fast and secretly. If he did not like him so, he might be a little concerned about how easy it had been for him to arrange all this. As they got closer, Lucian counted seventeen members, including Sev, waiting for him and Fylla to arrive. There were five Fire Elves, each sitting upon a saddled Fire Hound, wearing their black hooded cloaks, which were resting back to show their pointed ears, grey skin and red eyes while each holding a bow.

Standing off to the side were ten Drogans, each in their more human forms waiting further commands as their swords remained holstered at their sides. Lucian wasn't sure they needed that many, especially if this were a stealth mission to Ogra. Then again, depending on what they might encounter in the land of Ogres, they might be well needed. As Lucian nodded in approval at the assembled party his eyes rested upon Sev who was now standing there talking to a figure off to the side. It was this last member of the group that almost sent Lucian into shock.

"Aksurh?" Lucian said out loud as if what he was seeing was not really there.

The man standing next to Sev was about the same height as Lucian and on the stocky side. He wore brown leather boots that matched the material that covered his body from the knees up to his belly and held up by a strap that crossed over his left shoulder and attached to the back. He also wore wristbands that were the same color but had some metal spikes all around the center. Lucian saw that he still had his brown curly hair and bushy eyebrows and wore his shiny pendant around his neck.

Most would think Aksurh was no threat but it was that pendant that held his biggest secret. Aksurh was, as far as they knew, the last of his race. He was a Giant. Lucian met him one day, when he was younger, while he was out training with Frrr. He had seen a figure walking and went out to great him. At first, he thought it was an older kid or young adult by his size but once he approached him soon found out he was just a few years older than him. Lucian had asked why he was so big for his age and that's when Aksurh introduced himself and said he was a Giant.

Lucian had heard that name from Docanesto. Giants were now considered a myth to most and extinct to others. They were a race, much like the Ogres but smarter and more human looking. According to his fathers, giants opposed the Ogres and had always sided with the cause of evil. It was rumored they had all been slaughtered and driven away from Bergonia, deep into the Unknown Lands. Lucian never thought he would ever meet one until he had run into Aksurh.

Aksurh said he had been separated from his family and had been wondering for seasons, lost until now. Lucian felt bad that someone so young had been wondering on his own. Lucian sat and talked with him and really grew to like him but knew if his fathers found out about him he would be put to death or experimented on. Lucian took him to his secret hideaway, where he and all his friends would meet in secret. That day he introduced Aksurh to Sev, Fylla, Frrr and Natureza and he became the last of his secret group of childhood friends.

They all grew up together, always looking out for each other and forming that bond of trust. With everyone's help, they managed to create a pendant that would magically turn Aksurh from a giant to a human and he could pass without anyone knowing. Natureza had found the pendant amongst the Elves but never said anymore on how she came across it, but they did not ask, for it helped protect and conceal their friend's identity. They remained close until a few years ago when Aksurh decided to wonder off back into the Unknown Lands in search of his family. He had left and that was the last they saw of him until now.

"Lucian!" Aksurh called out with a wave once they had reached the group.

"When did you get back?" Fylla asked with a grunt and a glare.

"Good to see you too, Fylla," Aksurh said nervously as the day he had left was the same day Fylla had admitted her feelings for him and took his leaving as a hard rejection.

"Did you find your family?" Lucian asked.

"No," Aksurh said after a brief hesitation.

"What happened?" Lucian asked.

"Not much to tell. Journeys over and I'm back. I had actually just gotten to the city when I ran into Sev preparing to leave," Aksurh answered, quickly changing the subject.

"Once I told him what we were doing he insisted on joining us," Sev said with a smile.

"Wonderful," was all Fylla mumbled.

"Where's Natureza?" Aksurh asked realizing she was the only one not present.

"She's off on a different mission," Lucian said in a tone they all knew as best not to ask any further questions.

"We better get moving before we are noticed," Fylla said as she moved her Fire Hound forward towards the Fire Mountains, keeping her eyes away from the giant.

The Drogans shifted form and took flight, keeping an eye out high above them. Aksurh mounted his Fire Hound and road behind Lucian as he followed Fylla. The five Fire Elves rode their hounds in a circle pattern surrounding Lucian to provide protection from all sides. Sev, not too fond of riding, shrunk down to his Fairy size and flew near Lucian. It did not take long before the party reached the base of the Fire Mountains.

The mountains were black with a faint red haze to them. They looked redder from a distance but up close they didn't look so hot or on fire. Make no mistake, Lucian could feel the heat generating from them and knew direct contact with the mountains would result in burning tragedy. Lucian leapt off Frrr and moved to the spot where the secret entrance was supposed to be. He held up his hand and recited the words he had learned from Docanesto's books as they all watched and waited.

After a few minutes the red haze from a small area vanished and the black mountain base behind it shifted inward and over to reveal a passage way. To make sure, Lucian instructed the Drogans to enter first. One by one they entered the passage way. When none of them burst into flame they all dismounted their hounds and entered in single file. Fylla, followed by Sev, then Lucian, Frrr, Aksurh, three Fire Elves and then bringing up the rear were the Fire Hounds and the last two Fire Elves. Once they were all in, the entrance sealed up behind them.

Lucian, if he doubted before, he did not now. This passage was created with some very complicated and powerful magic. The sides of the passage glowed red enough for them to see but something was keeping the heat away. It actually felt quite comfortable within the passageway, but Lucian knew better than to reach out and touch the mountain walls to see if it felt cool as well. As they all kept moving forward quickly and quietly, Lucian noticed a strange sensation from the ground below them. It was as if it was moving forward making them move faster and cover more distance than it seemed. His theory was correct when they suddenly came to a stop and reached the river of lava that separated the Fire Mountain from the Forest of Spirits.

"Now what?" Fylla asked as she stepped to the edge of the mountain passage and looked across a very wide river of flowing lava.

"The secret passage is directly in front of us over there. Once we get to the other side, I will open the passage and we will head down below the ground through the secret passage that will take us past the forest and come out in the Old River Gorge," Lucian said as he opened his book that had a sketched map of Bergonia.

"The instant one of us touches down on the forest land, *they* will know we are there," one of the Fire Elves said.

"That's why I have these." Lucian pulled out a small pouch. "Once we swallow them, we will be magically cloaked, but it won't last long so we will have to hurry," Lucian said opening the pouch.

"How long do we have?" Sev asked worried about being caught by Elves or the creatures in the forest.

"We should have long enough to get past the Elven City and almost to the exit entrance. At that point, by the time they detect us we will be at the exit into the gorge before they can reach us," Lucian said as reached into the pouch.

"If need be, we can handle them," Aksurh said touching his pendant while glancing at Fylla.

"Ready?" Lucian said as he mounted Frrr.

Lucian swallowed the pill and tossed the pouch to Sev. He then grabbed a hold of Frrr and the mighty beast backed up, ran and leapt with all his might. They both flew through the air with ease and landed upon the edge of the forest. Lucian jumped off and quickly invoked the enchantment from the book and waited. Shortly, an entrance appeared in the side of a huge tree that revealed a path that lead straight down. Lucian motioned for the others before he and Frrr entered and headed down.

Sev passed out the pills to everyone, swallowed his and then shrunk down to Fairy size and flew off after Lucian. The Drogans shifted form and flew next, quickly landing, shifting back and entering the next hidden passageway. Fylla went next and with her weight, almost missed the edge but the Fire Hound caught its balance and stayed on the edge. Aksurh went next and was a bit nervous. His hound ran and leapt but came up short, missing the edge and sliding down towards the lava. There was a chance the hound would survive but hounds were not lava proof.

Aksurh felt a strong hand grab him and hoist him up and safely onto the edge. "I've got you, as always," Fylla said as she glared at him.

Aksurh looked over the edge and saw his Fire Hound slipping and then dig his front claws into the ground to stop its decent. Unfortunately, its back-left leg had slid into the river of lava. The creature growled in pain but managed to pull itself up a little further to bring its leg out of the lava. Their fur was fire proof but not lava proof as the foot looked melted and deformed. The remaining Fire Elves had landed next to him with their hounds as one of them turned, drew his bow as an arrow made of fire appeared and went soaring down hitting the ground in front of the hound causing it to fall back and plunge into the river of lava.

"Creature does us no good crippled," the Fire Elf said as he turned, dismounted and lead his hound into the tree's passageway.

Aksurh took a final glance back and watched as his hound vanished deep under the river of lava. "Don't worry, you can ride with me," was all Fylla said as she turned and entered the secret entrance that soon closed after Aksurh slowly stepped in and headed down.

The passage leading under the Forest of Spirits was different from the one they had just come out of from the Fire Mountains. This one was a lot narrower and not as high as some had to hunch over a little. The sides glowed like the last one but it was a whitish light this time instead of red. As Lucian walked he realized the ground had the same effect as before and they were actually moving at a faster rate. He knew they would not be out before the magic pills wore off but he hoped they would at least be real close to the exit and far from the Elven City.

"When we get to the exit how do we get past the guard posts?" Sev asked as he flew up next to Lucian and then returned to human size.

"By the time we get there it should be close to sundown. That will shield us some, but I will approach the guard alone and once he sees who I am and the seal of my father, our ally at the guard post will let us through," Lucian explained as he thought of the seal he had hidden.

"Then what? We just walk through the Kingdom of Argoth?" Aksurh asked from behind them, mouth full of bread and jerky that had been passed around to everyone earlier.

"The magic alarms no longer function in that kingdom but we won't be traveling up past Argoth. Once out of the Old Royal Gorge we will head straight east to the Eastern Sea. From there we will take a boat up to the Frosted Waters and then on to Ogra," Lucian said making it sound easy.

It seemed like forever as they all moved in silence through the underground passageway. Lucian was not surprised, but was glad that his friends were with him and following him without doubt or hesitation to his orders and plan. It seemed almost too easy to have made it this far. He was sure by now Docanesto and his father would notice him missing and put two and two together on where he had gone. If he succeeded he would be praised by his father for sure, if he failed, well that was not an option.

"Lucian!" Sev shouted suddenly from behind him in a muffled shout.

Lucian turned and saw tree roots had wrapped around Sev's throat and was pulling up and strangling him. More noises sounded and he could see that two Fire Elves and a Drogan were meeting the same fate. Lucian was about to respond when he saw roots growing down towards him.

"The cloaking has worn off sooner than expected," Lucian said as he pulled out his sword and sliced at the roots.

"We need to get you out of here," Sev said as he shrunk down to escape the roots and flew past Lucian.

"They know we're here. Go, we will cover you," one of the Fire Elves said as he raised his bow, moved his hand creating an arrow made of fire out of thin air and releasing it. The arrow hit the base of the roots that were holding one of his own, causing it to burn and release the Fire Elf.

Lucian moved quickly with the others as the Fire Elves freed the others and followed behind lighting up the passageway ceiling with fire to keep back the tree roots. It was an intense and exhilarating moment of running, chopping and avoiding the tree roots. It did not take long before he came to the exit and went sliding down a short distance to the bottom of the Old River Gorge. Lucian quickly got to his feet and turned to see the rest of his party sliding his way. The sun was setting making it hard to see but he was able to count that they had all made it but one of the Drogans.

"Stop!" Shouted a voice from above the gorge's edge where several Elves were standing back within the trees with arrows at the ready.

"We and the Drogans can take them out and provide cover," one of the Fire Elves said as they turned to ready their bows.

"Won't this draw attention to the guard posts?" Sev asked looking at Lucian.

"Allow me," Aksurh said knowing this would be the quickest way to avoid unneeded battle and bloodshed.

Aksurh grabbed the pendant around his neck and took it off, placing it securely in his pocket. As soon as he felt the tingling sensation he began to inhale. As he started to shift and grow taller he was able to take in more air. It did not take long before he reached his fifteen-foot-tall giant status, his chin now level with the forest edge. He saw the Elves in the trees and before they could release their arrows, due to their surprise at seeing him grow, blew out his breath as hard as he could, sending a gale of wind at the Elves blowing them all backwards. He then brought his arms up and around slamming them on the ground causing the ground to shake and trees to fall. The Elves would be distracted for a bit.

Aksurh then turned, scooped his party up and placed them all on the Kingdom of Argoth side of the gorge. He quickly leapt up, crawled over the edge and stood up. The guards in the guard post were already crying in alarm. Whatever stories they may have heard about the creatures of the forest, they probably never heard or imagined coming face to face with a Giant. He knew there was little time as one of the guards was preparing to ride for help, and ally or not, there was no other choice but to stop them. He brought his leg up and brought it down with great force causing the ground to crack and spilt apart, the guards, post and man on horse to fall in between.

"That could have gone better. Hurry, it shouldn't take us long to reach the Eastern Sea from here," Lucian said as the Drogans took flight and the others mounted their hounds taking off in a dash. Aksurh followed after, easily covering ground running at his height and size.

****

"Your majesty," Docanesto said bowing on one knee.

"Have you received word on that stupid boy?" Drol Greb asked when his spirited head appeared in the room, thanks to the four witch sisters.

"They have made it to the Eastern Sea and should be sailing up towards the Frosted Waters soon. Shall I try to stop them?" Docanesto asked raising back up onto his feet.

"No, I've allowed them to go this far thinking they would fail, but the fact Lucian managed to make it onto the waters makes me think he might actually pull this off," Drol Greb responded.

"Are you not concerned with him being out there?"

"They are going to Ogra, a land completely cut off from Bergonia. We have nothing to worry about for now and our spy is with them to be our eyes and ears," Drol Greb said, his face showing signs of deep thought and contemplation. "Did all in his party make it?"

"From what I've gathered, they are down one Fire Hound and one Drogan. The rest are all there and unharmed, despite the commotion they have caused," Docanesto said catching his master's eye and raised eyebrow.

"Commotion?" Drol asked.

"They weren't quite out of the passage under the Forest of Spirits when the cloak wore off and the Elves tried to stop them at the Old River Gorge. It seems, thanks to Lucian's Giant, the Elves were blown back and the Argoth Guard Post was stomped out of sight," Docanesto answered.

"What!" Drol Greb screamed, his eyes flaring.

"Don't worry, our ally in Argoth will help cover this up. As for the Elves, our passageway may have been compromised but they won't dare come here," Docanesto responded quickly.

"That I don't care about. What concerns me is how Lucian has a creature amongst his party that is supposed to not be in existence anymore," Drol Greb said with concern in his voice. "Find out more about this Giant but don't do anything till I say, Lucian may need him against the Ogres."

"Yes, your majesty," Docanesto responded with a bow.

"What of the Chosen One?" Greb asked.

"Lucian's spy has made contact with the group and has now encountered the Dwarves. We don't know who the Chosen One is yet, but my daughter is there and keeping a very close eye on the situation," Docanesto answered as Drol Greb dismissed him with a final command and then vanished back to the realm he was trapped in.

Chapter Twelve:
The Dwarves

Semaj, Anna, Thom, Essej and newly met Wild Elf, Nat stood grouped together looking up at two Dwarves and a Frostite, while also keeping an eye on the three Frostites positioned behind them. It seemed like they had been staring at each other for hours as the sun shifted in the sky. If it was not for the cold stares from the Dwarves it might have felt a little warmer from the midday sun's rays. Semaj was not sure if one side was waiting for the other to make the first move as he shifted his gaze back and forth between Essej and the Dwarves. Semaj tried to study the Dwarves closely as he was getting a strange sensation from one of them.

One was female and the other was male, but from the looks the male Dwarf gave the female it was clear, she was in charge. The male Dwarf had black hair and a short beard, barely off his chin which signified he was still fairly young. The female Dwarf had brown hair and was braided around the sides and to the back of her head. By looking at her face she appeared to be slightly younger than her male companion. Both Dwarves were stocky and on the short side. They were both wrapped from neck to toe with fur and clearly dressed for the weather and each carried a battle axe.

"So, are we going to stand here all day until someone freezes to death?" Thom finally asked breaking the silence.

"How is it two Elves accompanied by thee young humans are wondering around the Northern Mountains?" The female Dwarf asked as she rested her eyes on Semaj and stared oddly at him.

"One could ask the same of two rival Dwarves," Essej countered as he recognized that each Dwarf had a different clan crest on their axe but then continued speaking.

"I am Essej and my traveling companions are Semaj, Anna, Thom and Nat. We seek shelter and an audience with the great Dwarf King of Norax."

"I am Noraxa and this is Lorax. Why do you wish to see my father?" The female Dwarf asked, despite Lorax's look, she had a feeling the tall half-Elf knew who she was and something in the back of her mind felt like she should know him.

Essej stepped closer, glancing quickly at the Wild Elf, Nat, "May you take us to him and once we are out of the cold we can talk further?"

"I don't know if we can trust them," Lorax mumbled, shifting from side to side.

Semaj looked at Lorax and almost got the impression he disliked confrontation and by the way he was holding his weapon, had never really used it or was uneasy with it. Semaj then looked back at Noraxa. He was definitely feeling a connection to her and he could almost swear she was the Dwarf from his dream. Without realizing it he began to move closer to the female Dwarf when the Frostite next to her leapt out to block his path and growled.

"Easy, Freezia. Don't eat him just yet," Noraxa said with a smirk as she rested a hand on the Frostite's side keeping eye contact with Semaj.

"You don't scare us," Anna said as she quickly had her daggers in her hands.

"Freezia's friends there would devour you all long before you even got close to me," Noraxa said, battle axe ready.

"Anna," Essej said trying to prevent the girl from displaying her gift but was too late.

Anna closed her eyes and felt the power within and then reached out to the area between them and the three Frostites. The snow on the ground began melting pretty fast from the gathering heat. It did not take long before fire erupted between them and the creatures. From the shock and surprise of the fire, the three Frostites took off in a dead run and out of site. Anna saw Nat staring after the creatures with her fingers on her temple that gave hint she may have helped in the nudge to run away. Anna swayed, as her release and the cold allowed her fire to diminish back into nothing.

"She's a witch," Lorax said in a panic, raising his axe and stepping back.

"No, I don't think that was magic," Noraxa said as something deep in her stirred.

Noraxa did not get scared easily, but something about what the female human just did and the weird vibe she was picking up on from the boy that had tried to approach her, made her shiver. There was more to these two. She knew their visit here in the Northern Mountains and wanting entrance into her father's kingdom was about more than they were letting on. As this fear of unknown built up in her, she began to think about her father and being out here with Lorax. She hated this feeling and felt like something deep within her was taking over.

"Do you feel that?" Thom asked looking at the others.

"What's happening?" Lorax asked as he started to become unbalanced.

"Something is causing the earth itself to unsettle," Nat said as her Wild Elf side allowed her to be in tune with nature and the animals.

They all looked around as they felt the ground shake. Essej looked up and gasped as he glanced over at the mountain side and saw the tremors beginning to trigger an avalanche. No one else seemed to know what was going on but he did. He looked over at the female Dwarf. The eye contact with Semaj told him that the boy had figured it out too. They had found the Magestic and if they did not do something soon, her gift would bury them alive.

"Am I doing this?" Noraxa asked quietly as the more she panicked the stronger the tremors got.

"Don't come any closer," Lorax said as Freezia prepared to pounce upon Semaj.

Semaj knew in his gut that Noraxa was the one they were searching for and, with the tremors mimicking the dream, confirmed all signs were pointing to her. Semaj held one hand out to the Frostite while extending the other towards Noraxa. "Trust me, I can help."

Noraxa stared at the extended hand, her mind said chop it off while her whole body and soul said to reach out for it. She glanced up and saw the avalanche building and heading their way and knew she was causing it. She had no idea how to stop it. The tremors were getting worse and she decided to give in to her inner feelings and she stumbled forward, pushing past Freezia and grabbing Semaj's hand. Upon contact, a strange, invisible force passed between them and Noraxa suddenly felt calmer and as if something had been triggered within her.

"I," Noraxa began to say when she suddenly got dizzy from a flood of memories from what she thought was a dream came flooding back.

"It's real and we can explain more later, but you must do as I say," Essej said as he stepped up and began to guide and instruct the Dwarf in the use of her Magesti.

Noraxa tuned all the staring eyes out and focused only on the half-Elf's voice and the feel of Semaj's hand, which seemed to make things a lot easier. As she found her center, per Essej's instructions, she reached out to feel the earth all around her. She was then told to focus on the area around the avalanche and push with all her might. Her gasp of awe was not the only one heard as the falling snow seemed to shift and head away from them. Once that was done, Essej guided her on taking that connection to the earth and pull it back and calm it till there was nothing left. She exhaled in relief and then passed out as the tremors stopped completely.

"Noraxa!" Lorax shouted as he moved to help catch her.

"What have you done to my daughter? Unhand her this second," a voice commanded causing them all to look past the Dwarves.

There, standing in formation, was about twelve Dwarves. All of them were clad in helmets and armor while holding various styles and sizes of axes. Each Dwarf sat upon a large snow ram covered in pieces of armor and bore large solid horns that curled, coming to a point that could be used for colliding with the enemy or shifting heads down to stab them. In between the Dwarves stood a very large snow ram with gold fancy armor and upon it, was a Dwarf with a long bushy beard that was now more grey than black and wore a very mean scowl upon his face.

"Your majesty," Lorax began to say when he was instantly put into silence.

"Lorax, I should have known you were involved with my daughter's kidnapping. What is this, some kind of move from your father against us?"

"Great King Norax, if I may interject," Essej said stepping forward to address the king.

"Take them!" King Norax commanded as the group of Dwarves charged the group around his daughter.

Everyone looked at each other and then to Essej, nervous and preparing for battle. Essej called on his gift and whispered into the open air as a small gust of wind carried his words into the ears of each of them, telling them not to fight. That going with the Dwarves is what they actually want. Not sure if it was wise, the group decided to trust the Huelgon and they surrendered themselves to the Dwarves. Without resistance, they were bound and slowly escorted as the party moved towards the Dwarven City of Norax.

The male Dwarf, Lorax was placed amongst Semaj and his group. It was obvious the king disliked him. His daughter, Noraxa, rode upon Freezia next to him. With exception of her occasional plea to her father, which was cut off with a stare, the party moved in complete silence. Semaj was amazed how beings so short could look so mean and dangerous. Even Lorax had a tough look about him, despite his bouts of sniveling and worry in his eyes. Semaj wanted to ask the Dwarf what the story was between him and the king's daughter but his attention was diverted when a large shadow fell upon them all.

At first glance, Semaj thought it was another large section of snow covered mountains until they came to a stop and he got a real good look. What he was looking at was not mountain side but solid stone walls. Then, what he thought was a large boulder high up covered in snow, was what appeared to be a Dwarven face carved dead center in the wall. It was hard to make out who it was a carving of since it was so high up and Semaj had no knowledge of Dwarves, let alone seen any until now.

"That's the late king, Thorax, Noraxa's grandfather," Lorax said as one of the Dwarves near the king blew into some kind of object making a low toot sound causing the eyes within the carving to light up with what looked like fire.

The ground shook as the wall under the face carving seemed to crack and shift. Soon a small section of the wall had moved back and to the left revealing a large gap, an entry way through the stone wall. Semaj stepped forward to get a good look and was amazed at what he saw. There was a large mountain range that continued on in all directions with what looked like a castle of some kind built within the center of it. The big thing was that there was a very large chasm that separated the mountains from the stone wall that stood before all of them. Anyone who attacked and made it over or through the wall would immediately fall down into what appeared to be a bottomless abyss.

The king raised a large horn like object made of stone to his lips and blew, making a long loud sound that shook the ground around them. Not long after he lowered the stone object the ground on the other side of the chasm shook and shifted as the earth itself seemed to move up and form a solid stone walkway. The earth kept moving up and along the bottom of the walkway making it longer and longer as it quickly approached them on the other end of the chasm. Once the walkway fully connected them to the other side, the king gave his command and they all began to walk across.

"I thought all Dwarves forbade the use of magic?" Thom asked as he thought back to his books.

"Dwarves don't forbid it, they just choose to rely on their fists and their weapons. This, though, isn't magic," Lorax clarified waving at the stone bridge that had formed before them.

"The entrance could be setup with mechanisms, but the walkway forming like that has to have some kind of explanation to it," Anna said as she looked at Semaj whose expression told her that he was having the same weird sensation.

"He's telling the truth. This isn't magic, it's something else," Nat added as she knelt down, touching the stone walkway and looking over at the object in the king's hand.

"Like what?" Thom asked looking from Nat to Lorax for an explanation.

"No one truly knows. All Noraxa knows is what her dad told her. This was like this when Thorax led the Dwarves here and, on his death bed, gave Norax the horn saying it wasn't magical but it was the key to enter their kingdom," Lorax said knowing how frustrated Noraxa was at not knowing the truth about her homeland.

"Someone has to know," Semaj said glancing at Essej, making eye contact but not exactly expecting an answer, which he didn't get.

"We have arrived," Essej finally spoke diverting the conversation to the path ahead of them as they heard Dwarves shouting.

The sight of the mountain side was more impressive up close than it had been from afar. The craftsmanship was astounding. It was as if the castle and the mountain were merged as one. Whoever carved this out of the mountainside must have been a master craftsman and took them years to do this. It was clear that there were no windows or visible way inside but there appeared to be a gate-like design carved in the mountainside in front of them. The one Dwarf guard blew into his stone object, and like the entryway, the gate shook and shifted until a doorway opened leading into a dark tunnel lit by torches.

Once they were all in the tunnel, the king turned and blew into his stone horn causing the stone walkway across the chasm to shake, crack and then crumble completely falling into the abyss cutting them off from the outside world. As the king moved forward, the other Dwarf guard blew into his stone object causing the entry in the wall beyond and the gate behind them to shift and close. Semaj and the others knew they were now trapped inside with no way out. The group continued on for a little bit before light exploded in their faces letting them know that they have now entered Norax, the great City of the Dwarves.

"This is amazing!" Anna exclaimed as she looked around.

"How is this possible? It's like someone took a whole kingdom and placed it inside a mountain," Semaj added as they were urged to keep moving.

As they traveled the stone pathway downward they could see all around them as somehow sunlight from far above was filtering down and casting light upon the city in the mountain. It literally looked like any other outside city. Houses, fields growing food, flowing rivers, everything you could think of and it went on forever in all directions connected by stone pathways, tunnels and ladders. Then, a bit off in the distance was a large stone castle that bore the face of the late great Thorax carved above the castle gate.

Semaj noticed Dwarves, young and old, staring at them as they were led to the front of the castle gate. He could tell by their glances they held distrust towards them. The fact that they were real meant that the old stories were true. If the humans did drive all the magical creatures away, he almost felt they had the right to blame and not trust him and his friends. Semaj brought his thoughts back when all the Dwarves dismounted from their rides and at the king's command, moved the whole party into the castle. Noraxa was the only one that kept her ride as Freezia refused to leave her side.

"Take them all to the dungeon. I need to have words with my daughter," King Norax commanded.

"King Norax," Essej began to protest.

"I am not ready to deal with you," King Norax said as he glared deep into the Huelgon's eyes cutting him off.

"I say we take them," Nat said looking around at the Dwarves surrounding them.

"No, they will not harm us," Essej reassured the group as they were taken down a corridor and then down a flight of stairs that led deeper under the castle.

The dungeons were dark and barely lit by torches on the wall. The air felt and smelled damp and musty. The cells were made of stone and looked as if no one had been down here in ages. One of the Dwarfs unlocked a cell and ushered them all inside. The cell was big enough to hold them all comfortably, but only had two beds, two chairs and a waste deposit all made of stone. The guard closed the cell door and locked it leaving Essej and his party alone.

"Why didn't they take our weapons?" Anna asked, feeling her boots to reassure that her daggers where still there.

"The king knows we're not a threat and I may have sent a suggestion upon the winds to their ears to overlook what we carry," Essej said with a smile as he sat upon one of the chairs and looked upon the group before him, that just stared back with questioning eyes for answers he left unanswered.

"What's the deal between you and the king?" Thom asked walking towards Lorax when Essej and the others settled into uneasy silence.

"I am in love with his daughter. We want to be together but he forbids it. He thinks I am using her so that my father can gather information and attack," Lorax answered with a sigh. "Which I'm not. We are truly in love."

"I take it you're not from here?" Semaj asked noticing a softness in the Dwarf's gruff looking face.

"No, my father is King Mirax. He rules the Dwarven City of Mirax on the far eastern side of the Northern Mountains. That is where I was born and raised," Lorax answered as he kept looking outside the cell, as if he expected someone to come for him at any moment.

"Seems, Dwarves, like humans, need to feed their egos by naming their cities after themselves," Nat mumbled to herself and blushed when she realized Semaj had heard her and nodded back with a slight smile and chuckle.

"If this city is in isolation and you both live on opposite sides of the Northern Mountains, how did you two Dwarves fall in love?" Anna asked, always interested in a love story despite her tough adventurous exterior.

"Twice a season the two kings and their representatives from both cities meet at Steam Lake, that body of water that resides in the middle, to talk, negotiate and eventually end up arguing and fighting and going once again their separate ways.

"About thirty seasons ago, my father deemed me old enough to come along. I almost didn't but glad I did, for that day was when I laid eyes on Noraxa. It was her first time coming and the moment our eyes locked it was love at first sight. We would visit quietly while our fathers talked and argued, growing closer. It was about four seasons ago when our fathers found out and forbid us to see each other and stopped taking us," Lorax said as he smiled, remembering the first time he spoke to Noraxa and she punched him in the face telling him he was breathing on her.

"You mean you haven't seen her till today?" Thom asked.

"That is correct, as we've been only sneaking out messages for the past two seasons. We were actually set to make plans to permanently leave our homes to be together when we stumbled upon your group and then got caught by her father," Lorax sighed.

"Wait, how is that possible when there is no way in and out of here except by what those objects do?" Semaj asked as he knew there was something more to this city and those stone objects. He felt it.

"Noraxa said that she found a secret passageway that leads out of the city and I didn't believe her till I saw her at the lake earlier," Lorax answered.

"Where is this passageway, we can escape," Nat finally spoke up looking at the Dwarf.

"I don't know. She never told me any more details than that regarding her escape from here," Lorax said stepping back from the Wild Elf.

"I have a feeling it has something to do with," Semaj began to say when a stern look from Essej with darting eyes to Nat silenced him.

"I think it's time we rest as I assume King Norax will make us wait and retrieve us in the morning," Essej said as he laid back and closed his eyes.

Semaj could not believe Essej wanted to sleep at a time like this. They were prisoners of the Dwarves and there were so many unanswered questions about this city and Noraxa. Semaj did feel tired but he wanted answers and he had a feeling Essej had them. Semaj, feeling angry, tired and longing for his parents and home, rubbed his slightly moist eyes. When he opened them back up, he was standing atop a ledge, looking out amongst the mountain range. How did he get out here and why wasn't he cold?

"Finally, didn't think you would ever fall asleep," Anna said, coming up from behind and punching his arm.

"How?" Semaj asked in confusion as he saw Thom and Essej standing off to the side.

"As you slept, I sent a suggestion upon the wind into your ear hoping to trigger your ability as the Chosen One and then with my guidance and Thom's crystal, synch together and pull us all into your dream vision as he's done in the past," Essej explained.

"So, it's not just visions or a onetime thing with the Dragon spirit Dwin? I can use my gifts to communicate whenever I want?" Semaj asked, still not understanding all that Dwin and Essej had taught him and once again feeling overwhelmed by the whole Chosen One and Magesti power thing.

"Yes, with more training you can summon and communicate with any of the Magestics, but you have to be careful, as there are evil forces out there that can track you and break in when you use it. Since this is a controlled use, with me and Thom's help we should be protected long enough to talk away from untrusting ears." Essej said as he looked over to an entrance leading into the mountain side.

"I know you vouch for her, but we can't trust Nat with all this, not yet anyways," Anna said as she saw that look in Semaj's eyes accusing her of jealousy, which was absurd.

"If we can talk, then I want some answers, real ones. I know you know more than you've said about the Dwarves here and their *non-magical* stones," Semaj said biting his tongue and diverting his anger from Anna to Essej.

"Ah, now we can begin," Essej said as the rest of the group turned towards the entrance he was staring at.

"Where am I? How did I get here?" A figure asked in confusion and then froze with fear and anger at the sight of the group of four. "How did you escape? Where is the Wild Elf and Lorax? I swear, if,"

"Calm down my dear young one. We did not escape. We are in a Magesti dream state," Essej said with a smile at the female Dwarf as she slowly moved towards them.

"Like the Dragon in the cave. It isn't a dream, this is all real," Noraxa said as her eyes met Semaj's and suddenly a wave of calm rushed over her.

"It's a bit to get used to, but you have a power called the Magesti and I'm the Chosen One destined to lead you all to fight a great evil," Semaj said with a bit of sarcasm and disbelief in his voice.

"And you have the ability to weld the Magesti of Earth," Essej said as he and Semaj filled her in and the memories of the dream with Dwin flooded back into her mind.

"Then that explains the secret passageway," Noraxa said more to herself.

"We were wondering how you managed to sneak out of here," Anna commented.

"Not long ago I felt a pull to a section deep under the castle. I would feel tremors and then discovered a secret passageway. It was after the group dream that I touched the wall and a tremor moved the wall away revealing a tunnel that lead secretly across and to freedom," Noraxa said as she looked past them and out into the mountains.

"So you could send word to Lorax and be able to meet once again," Anna said with a smile.

"Yes, but it appears my father had found out about my leaving and wasn't pleased about the secret tunnel. He still thinks this was all Lorax and his father's doing," Noraxa said realizing her lover must be talking openly with these strangers.

"Why is your father so intent on keeping you here?" Thom asked.

"He is afraid of the outside world," Noraxa said in the tone of a stubborn daughter not getting her way.

"No, he's afraid of what you can do and the dangers you face because of that," Essej said as he suddenly looked up into the sky and listened to the wind.

"Okay, you seem to know more than what you've been letting on," Semaj said with anger rising in his voice as he glared at the old Huelgon.

"No more lies," Anna said taking sides with Semaj.

"I apologize if it seems that way. I truly didn't know which group of Dwarves the Magestic lived with. A lot of time has passed and my memory isn't what it's used to be. Many, many seasons ago, during the battle against Drol Greb, there were two Dwarves, best friends. One was a Defender of the Magesti that went into battle with me and the great Semaj Lightheart, while the other went off on a mission with another group.

"I truly couldn't remember which one was which. All I knew was that after the war the two were reunited and then retreated into the Northern Mountains and over a quarrel split into two clans. Until we saw Noraxa in person I remembered it was her grandfather, Thorax who was the Magestic and Lirax, Lorax's grandfather, was the other Dwarf," Essej said as he thought back to the look he got from King Norax which told him that, whether he knew who Essej was or not, that he knew they were here for his daughter.

"What about those stone objects the king and his guard use?" Thom asked looking at Noraxa.

"I don't know how they work. My father won't tell me anything," Noraxa answered as she noticed the wind picking up and looked over to where Essej had kept watching.

"Then maybe I can fill in some of the blanks," a voice said as a form materialized right in front of where she and Essej had been looking.

"Thorax," Essej said with a smile and a bow.

"It's been a long time, Huelgon. My dear granddaughter," the ghost of Thorax said to Essej and then to Noraxa.

"How can this be?" Noraxa asked of the Dwarf that had died before she was born.

"My spirit is tied to these mountains and the Magesti that flows through them and you. It seems I have been called forth, but briefly in this dream of yours," Thorax said as he hugged his granddaughter, despite that they could not physically touch.

"We and you don't have long," Essej said urging the great, late king of the Dwarves to speak what he had come to tell.

"Let me see, where to begin, ah yes. After the defeat of Drol Greb, me and my best friend, Lirax Longbeard were reunited and glad to see that we both had survived, even though many of our friends had not or were severely injured. Since we had gone our separate ways on separate missions we had not seen each other in a very long time.

"He was amazed in my abilities of the Magesti as I was with his newfound courage, strength and shiny battle axe he had found. It was clear we needed to rally the Dwarves together, and agreeing to keep my abilities secret, we helped to recover and rebuild a home for the Dwarves in the land to the north of the newly formed Drol Death Desert.

"About ten seasons after the battle of magic, I got word that the humans had formed a council made up of five human men. They were pushing that magic was evil as well as anything not human. Lirax and I had our first disagreement. I wanted to leave and he wanted to wait out and believe humans were still good and would not harm us.

"About five seasons later, the humans declared all-out war, banning magic and hunting any beings of magic. With great hesitation, I managed to get Lirax to help me unite the dwarves and we moved into the safety of the Northern Mountains. Once

there, we knew we would be safe from the human's war, but we couldn't survive living out in the cold wilderness of the mountains.

"Because of my gifts, I sensed a pull to the west, but Lirax insisted we go to the east to build a city. I ended up going off to the west with a small group where we traveled for days, faced many dangers and lost most of our party until me, and three others, one of whom became my true love, finally stopped at the barren, snowy spot that would soon be the great city you call Norax.

"In my frustration I screamed and the power I held in check and secret came free and ripped apart the snowy ground and the great chasm was created. Everyone fled in fear except my dear Roz. She kissed me with such gentleness and gave me the courage and incentive that if we couldn't find a home, then BUILD one. And with that, I called on my powers of the Magesti and created from the earth itself, the great city you, my dear Noraxa, now live in, including a great stone bridge to cross the chasm.

"Leaving Roz behind, I quickly traveled back to the other Dwarves. When I finally found them, Lirax had declared himself king and had already started to build their new home. We argued for hours before it was made clear that those who wanted to follow me were to leave and those that wanted to stay would stay. It was about eighty seasons later before I would see my best friend again.

"Word had reached me that he had taken a wife and had given birth to their son Mirax, just as me and my Roz had too given birth to our son, Norax. Just as best friends do, thinking alike, we had both named our sons after each of our established Dwarven cities. So, I had sent word and we had agreed to meet on neutral ground, half way between our cities. A few days later we came face to face, each of us bringing a few of our best warriors just in case, to catch up and try and bridge the gap between the two groups of Dwarves.

"It was good to see him again, and I could tell he missed me too. Since I was more isolated from the world, Lirax filled me in. The Age of Humans had begun. The descendants of the human council had divided the large central land of Bergonia

into five kingdoms that they would each rule. Magic creatures had to go into exile or they would be killed as all magic had been banned. The Elves and most magical creatures had fled into the southern forest and rumors said that the people of Tallus had taken the Minotaurs into slavery.

"I had decided, now more than ever it was best to isolate ourselves from the humans but to my surprise Lirax felt they could still mend fences with the humans and was working on deals of trade with a group of them. I told him he was crazy and we got into a huge fight and when I mentioned that his axe he still gripped seemed to almost possess him, he took an angry swing at me and cut me.

"It had taken me by surprise as it did my dear friend, but it didn't stop him from bringing that axe high above his head for a final attack. I pushed out with my powers and it seemed they collided with his axe as it sliced through my abilities causing a strange reaction. The axe left his hands, engulfed in my Magesti power hit the ground with a large explosion as the ground caved in, taking the axe with it and soon filling up. A very large lake formed, steam rising above from it. Our final fight had created the lake that solidified the division of the Dwarves, Steam Lake.

"We both went our separate ways never to speak or see each other again and once I returned home I used my gifts to collapse the stone bridge and create the great wall so no one could ever get in or out of Norax, placing us in safe isolation. As my son got older, I knew we needed some escape, so I created a secret passageway, which Noraxa found, and I told people that the two stone objects held the key to opening the gates and creating the stone walkway, as a way to mask my abilities.

"Then, about twenty seasons before Noraxa would be born, I laid on my death bed. On that day I told my son all about the Magestics and my abilities and how one day, when the time came, a descendant of mine would inherit my gifts. My son refused to hear this and vowed to not allow such evil magic in his kingdom. Before I died, I willed my power into the stone objects so they could be used to do what I used to do to leave the city. Knowing there was no other choice about the exiting of the city, Norax accepted them along with my final breaths," Thorax said as he finished his tale of two cities.

"And that time has come," Essej said looking at the two Dwarves.

"But," Noraxa started to say looking from her hands to her grandfather.

"The gift of my Magesti is now in you. You may not trust them but trust me when I say you and your gifts are needed. Follow Essej for if Drol Greb enters back into the world, then all we fought for long ago and all you hope to have will be lost, forever," Thorax said as he looked at his granddaughter, kissed her on the forehead and vanished. *"Go, my dear Noraxa, it is now your destiny."*

"Yes sir," Noraxa, the strong-willed Dwarf that she was, finally stood up strong and took the honor from her grandfather and turned to the others. "What now?"

"I, with Semaj's help will guide you and train you in the use of your gifts so that you can be as great as your grandfather was," Essej said with a smile.

"Until then, we will have to use the secret passageway. I can't do anything like my grandfather did and there is no way we will get our hands on those stone keys," Noraxa said as she looked to Essej.

"I'm sure if I talk to your father he will understand and let us go," Essej said confidently.

"No, I don't think so. After our argument, he said in the morning he was going to drop you all into the chasm and make an example of Lorax by sending a clear message to Mirax and his followers," Noraxa said as her initial plan to save her true love now included the whole group in his cell.

"Then we must escape and soon," Anna said looking to Thom and Semaj.

"Where will we go?" Thom asked.

"Can we go to Mirax?" Semaj asked looking from Essej to Noraxa.

"No, that will be the first place my father would look and if found there he would truly blame Lorax and wage all war against the city. Before being caught we were thinking of heading down into Sorran or possibly to the mountains to the east near Mount Semaj," Noraxa said and then paused at the similar name the mountain shared with the boy in front of her.

"We came from Sorran and they are being attacked by the Drogan forces," Thom said as they filled in Noraxa with their escape and the mission she was now a part of.

"Maybe I can use my abilities to find where to go next?" Semaj asked looking at Essej.

"We can try. Let me guide you to open up and pull a vision of where we must go," Essej said as he knelt down next to the boy and guided him.

Semaj closed his eyes and reached out, searching for the Magesti and clues to where he needed to be next. What happened was unexpected. It was like a great force struck the mountain causing it to shake. Semaj opened his eyes and saw those around him trying to stay upright as the whole mountain rocked back and forth. It was not long before they suddenly found themselves standing in a dark cavern and their bodies were almost translucent. Then they saw a man scream as he and a group behind him was being attacked by strange creatures.

"Wait, I recognize him," Anna began to say when a large force shook them all and she felt herself yanked sideways.

Suddenly they were all deep under the water. As they all panicked, especially Noraxa, to hold their breaths and swim up towards the surface they saw a strange figure coming towards them from the bottom depths of the water. The water seemed to shift and move at the creature's will as it got closer. Semaj knew whatever it was, it was a Magestic. He tried to focus on the creature when suddenly another force pulled at him and he gave in to it and they were all yanked in another direction.

"What is going on?" Anna asked as they were now all on dry land.

"Semaj, concentrate. You're allowing us to be pulled in too many directions at once," Essej said as he tried to guide the boy in his gift.

"Look!" Thom screamed as they all turned and saw all these strange creatures in what seemed like a strange war as they suddenly sensed loud screaming in their minds as they soon saw blood and decay everywhere.

"It's too much, I can't take it," Semaj cried as the sensation was too overwhelming for his mind and body. "Please, make it stop!"

"What do we have here?" A voice asked as they all turned to see a familiar dark figure of a man standing upon a boat of some kind off in the distance.

"Is that?" Noraxa started to ask.

"Yes, he's part of the evil we are up against," Essej said as he turned to Semaj and quickly started to coach him into breaking their connection before it was too late.

"You are already too late, Essej. Yes, I have been told of your name and what you are trying to do and your evil will be stopped. As we speak, I am about to pounce upon your Magestics and take them before you can reach them," the figure laughed as he motioned his hand at the battlefield of death before them.

"He's starting to reach out to us, we have to hurry," Anna said as the Magesti within her seemed to be reaching out in an odd way to the dark figure.

"You won't win!" The dark figure screamed as the ship flew towards them and was almost upon them when Semaj screamed and an explosion of light sent the darkness back.

"Are you okay?" Lorax asked as Semaj started to scream, causing him to jump up and look over at the young human.

"I think so," Semaj said in a whisper as he sat up, drenched in sweat and looked around in relief to be in a dungeon cell.

"What just happened?" Nat asked as she looked at the half-Elf and three humans who had all suddenly woken up at the same time, all sweating.

"Bad dream," Thom laughed nervously as he covered his crystal that was now dimming.

Nat thought she had seen his crystal glowing and had felt a strange energy coming from the three humans. They were connected so she couldn't tell the source but she knew for sure, one of them was the Chosen One but which one? Nat looked closely at both Anna and Semaj. It had to be one of them, unless the crystal was throwing her off the scent of Thom. For a split second she thought she had felt Lucian but did not know if she was missing him or if it was just her needing to get word to him with an update and receive further instructions.

"We need to talk about what just happened," Anna said looking at Semaj and moved to help calm his shaking body.

"You can talk later. We need to move before my dad notices I'm gone," came a voice followed by the clicking of a cell lock.

"Noraxa!" Lorax screamed in joy and relief at the sight of his dear love.

"Lead the way," Essej said as he motioned everyone out the cell and quickly following Noraxa down a corridor and then onto a set of stairs that led them deeper into the darkness under the castle's dungeons.

Chapter Thirteen:
Lord Suras

The sun was all but gone as the moon began to take its place in the night's sky. Despite some minor bruises and lingering aches and pain, the group was well enough to travel on by foot. Marcus and Lija had managed to recover as much food and supplies as they could and divided it amongst the group so each carried their weight, except Korvan, who was now up to full strength in the night sky, carried more. Prince Arron, excited he still had his sword, walked on as if nothing had happened to him while Patches limped on claiming to be up to par and hiding his pain with pride. Marcus knew they were all well enough to walk, but wished they still had their horses to make it easier for their journey.

"Are you sure this is wise?" Korvan asked as he led the way.

"I lost my wife, I will not lose my son," Patches said flatly.

When they had found the note and the ring, Patches declared without a doubt he knew Bruce Peters was still alive and that Suras had him and he was going to rescue him. There was some debate from Korvan and Lija about going to a city full of Vampires. Patches said he would go but expected none of them to follow. He just asked that Korvan lead him as close to the Lost City of the Dead as he could and then he would continue on alone. That was the plan, but deep in his gut, Marcus knew he could not let Patches do this alone and that Korvan would help as well. He would just make sure Arron took his sister and headed in the direction of safety.

Marcus still found it hard to believe Korvan was some kind of Vampire hybrid. That the only thing keeping him human was some kind of unknown power within him. If it was not for the dream they shared connecting him with his friends, Anna, Thom and Semaj, he would have done away with this man. Well, if he could call him a man. This made him start thinking of his friends, wondering how they were doing and what they were up to with the old man. Was that dream real and had they really met a Dragon? Then his thoughts weighed very heavily upon his heart.

He looked over at his sister as he thought about home. He wondered if his parents were okay. Marcus was pretty sure his dad was sending those vicious creatures running back to wherever they had come from, but he still feared the worst. While he left his home behind and his other friends went off on their mission, he was supposed to keep his sister safe and alert King Sirus to send reinforcements back home. A mission he has so far failed and come so far from achieving.

Instead of sending help, they managed to get chased out of Sorran and branded kidnappers of the prince from Argoth. To make matters worse, they have ended up stranded in the Drol Death Desert and now were on their way to a suicide mission to rescue their friend and companion, Bruce Peters from a city full of the dead and led by the king of Vampires, Lord Suras. If they managed to rescue their friend and escape alive, it would be a miracle.

"It'll be okay," Lija said suddenly breaking his deep thoughts.

Marcus looked at his sister. At least he had managed to do one thing right so far, keep her alive. As he watched her smile behind her sand dusted face, he could only help but be proud. This once proper girl who would go running from work or avoid getting a speck of dirt on her now walked in a torn dress covered head to toe in dirt and did not even seem to give it a second thought. He was even surprised, without so much as a whine, his sister was helping and doing what was needed to help someone other than herself. She had really grown up. With this he smiled back with ease.

"I know," Marcus paused before getting serious, "once we get close enough to the Lost City, you and Arron will head straight south."

"I can't leave you," Lija began to protest.

"Lija, you have to. No matter what happens to me and the others, you have to go. Mom and dad, and all of Sorran are counting on you. You and Arron will keep going and don't stop for anything. You will eventually exit the Desert and end up in the Kingdom of Erikson. Once there, head straight for the city and find the king and tell him everything. With Arron, you can clear our names. You can do this," Marcus stressed upon his sister to do what he had failed to do, save their parents and their home.

"Fine, but once I get help, I will come back for you," Lija responded as she then moved forward as to not let her brother or anyone see her tears.

The group of five traveled through the desert night, slowly and with caution. No one really said a word as they concentrated on their own private thoughts on what was coming next, as well as watching out for the Vampires. Patches was pretty sure they would be left alone as Lord Suras wanted them to arrive into his city in one piece. After a few hours had passed, Korvan raised his hand bringing them to a stop. They all turned, eyes watching him while he closed his and *gazed* out into the darkness ahead of them.

"What's he doing?" Arron whispered to Lija who shrugged.

"The Lost City of the Dead is straight ahead. Whatever this power within me is, I can sense, in a spot of nothingness, a soul. I don't have a handle on my gift, but my gut says it belongs to Bruce," Korvan said as he turned, looking at the others and almost sensing the souls within each of them as well, but managing to shut it down before it got overwhelming.

"That is the direction you will need to go to reach Erikson," Marcus said pointing towards the south.

"I'm not afraid to fight. We are about the same age and I'm just as brave and capable as you are to take on the Vampires," Arron said stepping up, a little wobbly, to Marcus.

"I know, but I need someone who can get my sister to safety. Who better to protect and keep her safe than a prince?" Marcus said putting on the right amount of charm as he clasped Arron's shoulder.

"You're right. My lady, shall we?" Arron asked as he bowed at Lija, who rolled her eyes as she moved to her brother and gave him a deep long hug.

"Be careful and don't do anything stupid," Marcus said, kissing his sister's forehead.

"Same goes for you," Lija said as she patted her brother's cheek and began walking off with Arron.

Marcus took a step forward but stopped. Compared to where he was headed she would be just fine. Marcus turned to see Patches and Korvan marking the spot they had buried some of their supplies and rations. What they hadn't sent with his sister and the prince, they wanted to keep here to pick up later so they wouldn't be weighed down for the fight ahead. Marcus padded his Drogan blade resting on his hip and joined the other two.

"All set?" Marcus asked.

"As we can be. Let's take out some Vampires and get my boy back," Patches said as he adjusted his satchel and headed east.

The three companions moved as quickly as they could in the sand as the desert's night sky shined bright with stars. Marcus could tell that Korvan moved better and was a lot stronger without the sun around. He even offered to carry Patches from time to time but always got the evil eye and would move back. It did not take long before they could see the ruins of a city. It was hard to make out the details at night but knew they had just found the Lost City of the Dead.

"I don't like this. It makes me even more uneasy that we haven't encountered a single Vampire," Korvan said as he scanned the ruins with eyes that allowed him to see better than most humans at night.

"You're gift still pick up Bruce?" Patches asked without taking his eye off the ruined city.

Korvan closed his eyes and tried to find that strange feeling or power within himself. It took a little bit but he finally found it and then reached out. Now that he remembered his dream, he recalled the Dragon indicating *soul* at him, so his gift must have something to do with souls, which was probably a big factor in him keeping his and not fully turning. He could sense dozens of dead spots, which he assumed were Vampires but nothing else. He was about to quit, as he felt himself getting a little weak when he felt something, a living soul.

"Got him, he's still in there and alive, but how alive I can't tell. Still getting the hang of this," Korvan said as he let go of the power and released his ability to track.

"How do we proceed?" Marcus asked as he drew his sword, red blade shinning in the moon light.

"They know we're here and are waiting for us. No point in playing games and just walk in," Patches said as he loosened the top of his satchel. "You sure you don't need a weapon?"

"I am a weapon," was all Korvan said as Marcus saw fangs and claws extend from the man's mouth and fingers.

"Good, then these are all mine," Patches responded as he now had two small hand-held finger triggered crossbows in each hand. Both were loaded with six small wooden stakes.

"Best way to kill them will be wooden stake to the heart or decapitation," Korvan said glancing from Patches' weapons to Marcus' sword.

"Got it," Marcus nodded as he had a feeling that his sword would be lethal no matter how or where he used it on the vicious creatures.

The three moved forward, Korvan slightly ahead and in the center, Patches on the left and Marcus on the right. They made it to the ruins and looked around. What looked like houses or building were worn, rotted and mostly buried under the desert sand. Scattered in various spots were bones, to who or what, they could not tell. As they carefully moved further in they looked for signs of the living or the dead, but nothing. Marcus and Patches felt lost but trusted in Korvan that he knew where they were going.

"I wish we were heading in closer to sunrise," Marcus mumbled as he suddenly felt like he was being watched.

"Company," Korvan said as he instinctively made a hissing sound and bared his fangs.

Coming out of the ruins and darkness, about a few dozen Vampires surrounded them. Marcus took a step back as the three of them took a triangle formation with their backs to each other. Patches mumbled something about them just toying with them as both sides stared at the other but not making a move. Korvan agreed adding that they appeared to be waiting for something or someone. Out of the darkness, in a low and creepy tone, came a voice, "attack!"

The Vampires moved fast as they were upon them instantly. Their pale grey skin, hairless bodies and sharp fangs and claws ready to tear into each of them. Patches, without even bating an eye, raised his weapons, one arm aimed in one direction and the other arm pointed in the opposite. Twisting his wrist slightly each time, Patches pulled the trigger rapidly and with perfect accuracy twelve Vampires exploded into ash as the wood stakes each hit their hearts. He then reached into his satchel and pulled out two small greyish balls that he threw down causing an explosion of fire that held the Vampires back to give him time to reload the stakes.

Marcus saw Patches making short work of the Vampires while Korvan, using his own fangs and hands, tearing into the creatures near him. He hoped that they continued to prevail but at the moment he had to concentrate on the batch of Vampires approaching him. They seemed to be leery of his sword and its red blade. This hesitation worked in his favor as he could quickly strike out with his sword. Marcus did not know what the blade was made of but the moment it cut the neck or sliced through the body and heart the Vampires instantly exploded in ash.

"Tell your master we want our friend back," Marcus said as he swung his blade taking two heads off at once.

"These Vampires are too feral to talk. The only way to deliver a message to Suras is by killing every last one of them," Korvan said as he ripped the heart out of a Vampire with his bare hands turning it to dust.

"I have no problem with that," Patches added as he fired off more rounds of stakes with one hundred percent accuracy.

The three companions fought on, ignoring pain and exhaustion as they finished off Vampire after Vampire with their weapons. It didn't take long before they all stopped, swayed and looked around while trying to catch their breaths. Covered in ash, the battlefield was now void of Vampires. They had won this round.

"That's all of them," Korvan said as he quickly scanned the area.

"That was easy," Marcus chuckled as he kept his eyes alert and his sword ready.

"Yes, too easy. I could tell by their attacks, they were instructed to play, not kill," Patches spat as he had his weapons reloaded and ready.

"Why would they do that?" Marcus asked already knowing the answer.

"Out of pure entertainment and to test us so Suras can see what we can do," Korvan answered as he reached out with his abilities to locate Bruce Peters.

With a nod, Korvan lead them to the center of the city where a castle used to sit, but now was buried under sand with only the top of its towers rising up and exposed. They noticed any doors or windows were all boarded up except for one. With the way the top of the center tower looked sticking out of the sand, the entry in almost looked like a tomb. Korvan stepped up to the window turned doorway, listened for a bit and then pushed the door inwards.

"Pretty dark in there," Marcus said as he looked over Korvan's shoulder and into the room.

"I can see clearly in the dark so I will take lead," Korvan responded as he leapt through the entryway.

"Wait, this will help," Patches said as he pulled out a wooden stake, rubbed something on it and then ignited the top turning it into a torch.

"I don't need it, and better I keep my hands free to fight," Korvan called back as Patches handed the torch to Marcus.

"You go next with the torch. I need both my hands," Patches said as he gripped his stake shooters tight.

Marcus swallowed hard and thrust the torch forward into the room. He could see that it used to be a bedroom of sorts. He carefully stepped in and onto a stone bench that rested under the window and then down onto the floor. Marcus then shifted, so Patches could see and slowly make his way into the room. Once all three were in, Marcus took to the middle of the room and held the torch high so they all could get a good look at their surroundings.

There was not much left of the small room as it was pretty empty. With the many passing years, what remained was pretty dusty and worn with age. Korvan and Patches looked around the room making sure nothing was hiding anywhere as Marcus closed the makeshift door into the room so nothing could sneak in behind them. He even placed an old vanity with some of the glass still intact in front of it. That way if something did come in, they would hear the crash of the glass and warn them.

"Only one way to go," Patches said as Korvan was already at the door leading out of the room and further into the castle.

"Clear so far," Korvan said listening carefully as he stepped out of the room.

The hallway was pitch black and the only one who could see in the dark was Korvan, so he took the lead with Marcus bringing up the rear with the torch. Luckily it was a narrow hallway and the only thing to their backs was the door back into the bedroom. Marcus was worried about being attacked in the dark with so little light but Patches and Korvan were both reassuring that Lord Suras wanted them to reach him alive. Marcus wondered what their actual chances were with a creature so confident in them walking right into his laier.

The three kept walking in silence, watching every corner with intensity. The torch gave off little light but it was enough to see that they were traveling a narrow hallway that was going at a downward slant. There appeared to be no doorways leaving the hall with only one option of continuing forward or going back in the direction they came. Patches noted it appeared that someone may have restructured this hallway that way.

They walked on slowly and carefully before they finally came to a large steel door. Korvan put his hand upon the door and closed his eyes and reached out. "We're here."

"Let's go get my boy," Patches said swallowing hard and raising his two weapons.

"Wait, shouldn't we have a plan? We just can't go barging in if they're all waiting for us," Marcus added trying to control his fear.

"The more reason to. Just be smart and watch each other's back," Patches said as he nodded at Korvan.

With a swift kick, Korvan sent the metal door flying inwards and leapt inside. Patches followed right after, moving his head from side to side swinging his weapons left and right ready for the attack. Marcus darted in after the two, sword and torch raised high and ready to swing. All three came to a puzzling halt when they found themselves in a very large room that was well lighted by candles and metal crafted torches. There

were archways to the left and right of them that clearly lead to
other parts of the castle with stone pillars that ran down the
center to the far end of the room. In front of them was a large
stone stage area with a man hanging from the wall by chains.

"Bruce!" Patches called out as the chained man moaned and
barely moved.

Bruce Peters, friend and son, looked as if he had seen better
days. He had been stripped down to his undergarments. His
clothes and weapons were nowhere in sight. Cuts and bruises
appeared all over his body as if he had been tortured. Patches all
but ran towards Bruce when he saw two marks on his neck with
dried blood running down from them, but Korvan grabbed his
arm. "Wait."

"Welcome, I was almost afraid you wouldn't join the fun,"
a deep voice said from all around them.

"Suras," Korvan growled under his breath.

"You better not have harmed him," Patches called out,
swaying from side to side as he knew they were all around them
but hiding from plain sight.

"Don't worry, he's not turned. I was just having a little
sample," Lord Suras laughed.

"I got him," Korvan said as he ran towards the stage but
was suddenly sent backwards with a huge impact of force.

"Now, now, I know it's been a long time since I've hosted
people in my home, but I believe its rude to start the festivities
before the host is ready," Lord Suras proclaimed as he was
suddenly standing on the edge of the stage blocking the three
from their chained friend.

Marcus stared at the figure on the stage as Patches stepped
over to check on Korvan. The lord of the Vampires looked
nothing like he imagined. Marcus thought Lord Suras would be
some hideous looking monster but instead he looked as human as
Marcus himself. Suras looked to be in his mid-twenties with
flawless, but pale skin. His hair was a dark brown color that had
a hint of curl to it and rested upon his shoulders. His shirt and
pants were the color of blue with black leather boots to match his
cloak-like cape.

"I'm okay," Korvan said getting to his feet and rubbing his
jaw while the cut on his lip was already healing.

"Sorry, I do tend to forget my strength," Lord Suras smirked showing off his white fanged teeth.

Patches, wasting no time, raised his weapons and fired off several wooden stakes from the weapon in his right hand. Suras scowled as he, with great speed, dodged and batted away the incoming stakes. The lord of the Vampires then flew off the stage and in seconds had Patches pinned up against a pillar, raised by the neck with one hand and the other crushing the old man's wrist making him drop his loaded weapon.

"I wouldn't or he'll be dead before you reach me," Lord Suras said over his shoulder causing Marcus and Korvan to freeze in place.

"Let him go," Marcus demanded as he held his sword ready.

"Why do you care? He's old and weak," Lord Suras declared as he tossed Patches off to the side, hitting the ground while stepping on and crushing both stake shooters.

"Leave me, save yourselves," Bruce Peters managed to whisper from a broken and shaky voice.

"Never," Patches responded as he laid there, holding his wrist and trying to overcome the pain that kept him from getting up.

"If I surrender to you will you let them all go safely?" Korvan asked the Vampire lord while keeping watch on what was hidden in the shadows.

"Oh, silly me, did I somehow give the impression that you were in a position to negotiate? No, no, no. I want you and will have you and there's nothing you can do to stop me. I am all that stands between my hoard of servants pouncing and feasting upon your friends," Lord Suras laughed as he moved with great speed right at Korvan.

Korvan watched as Lord Suras came right at him and knew he would not be fast enough to dodge the attack. Korvan suddenly felt a strange sensation in his body, similar to the one he had right before the sand shark attacked. Closing his eyes, he gave into this sensation and allowed his mysterious power to take over just as Suras's finger tips were on him. Korvan awaited the impact but was surprised when it never came and opened his eyes when he heard a loud crack.

"What the?" Was all Marcus could say as he stared at, or more accurately, through Korvan's body with a fuzzy view of the Vampire lord crumpled against the side of the stage.

"Korvan, how did you do that?" Patches asked as he wrapped his wrist with material he had pulled out of his pouch after resetting his hand the best he could.

"I'm not sure but I think it is part of that power within me. Same thing happened during the sand shark attack but I thought I imagined it," Korvan said as he suddenly went solid with a weird sensation as if his soul was trading places with his body.

"Then it makes it more important than ever that I have you," Lord Suras said as he got to his feet, broken bones already healed but feeling a bit weak as if passing through Korvan had affected him in some way.

Korvan turned to face his enemy while Marcus made his way over to Patches. In the back of his mind he began to remember things like the white Dragon spirit and what he had said to him, *soul*. His Magesti was power over the soul. It made sense now. He had reverted to his soul form, that is why he had become translucent and when he used his abilities to track, it was reaching out and feeling for souls.

This power of the soul was definitely what had kept him from turning into a true Vampire. His Magesti gave him control and possession of his soul. He could not be turned. With this revelation it made him wonder what more he could do. If they survived this he would have to search out the Chosen One and learn more about his abilities. Until then, he had more serious things to worry about.

"Problems, Suras?" Korvan asked as he noticed the Vampire lord swaying and having trouble moving.

"I don't know what you did to me but I still have more power than you," Lord Suras declared as he waved his hand causing a horrifying hissing sound to boom from all around them.

Dozens upon dozens of Vampires leapt from the shadows from both sides of the room. The noise in the room growing louder as they all prepared to launch an attack but froze instantly in place the moment Lord Suras waved his hand again. Every Vampire stood perfectly still as if some force was holding them while they stared at their prey with hunger in their eyes and saliva dripping from their fangs. Lord Suras laughed as he leaned back against the stage.

"I have a feeling I can reach you before your minions can," Korvan said as he slowly positioned himself for a leap attack.

"You forgot something," Lord Suras smiled as he snapped his fingers and five members of his elite guard, the Dracs, dropped from the ceiling and to the ground, two on the stage in front of Bruce, two behind Korvan and the final one between Korvan and Lord Suras with swords drawn and ready.

The Drac right in front of Korvan darted forward, sword swinging with all his might. Korvan was starting to feel the effects of using his gift but had to do it one more time. Concentrating on the power within, he focused on his soul and willed it to dominate over his body. Just as the sword was inches from his neck, Korvan shimmered and became translucent causing the sword to pass through him and take off the heads of both Dracs moving in right behind him causing them to explode in a burst of ash and blood.

The Drac paused in confusion as he looked through his prey and the space where his two fellow Dracs had once been. Korvan felt a weird sensation come over him and he realized he had started to rise up off the ground. With determination he decided to try something and soon found himself flying up in the air. The Drac looked up and leapt into the air after him. Korvan, remembering what had happened to Suras, turned and dove straight for the Drac. The elite guardsman screamed as Korvan passed right through him and landed on the ground, turning solid out of exhaustion while the Drac slammed back down upon the floor.

"Their bodies can't take the shock of feeling a soul and then having it ripped away again," Patches said as he was finally on his feet, wrist wrapped and holding a circular object while fighting back the pain. Between the sand shark attack and Suras, he was amazed he could even stand, but one look at his *son* was all the explanation he needed.

Patches threw the object hitting the fallen Drac causing an explosion that engulfed the creature in flames. The Drac rolled there screaming in pain as it tried to put himself out. Short of a huge douse of water, there was no way to extinguish the fire caused by the chemicals that Patches had mixed together. It would not be an instant death for the Vampire, but a slow and eventual one. Korvan used his strength and kicked the burning Drack towards a group of waiting Vampires causing them to retreat back a few feet.

"Kill them all but Korvan. I still need him alive!" Lord Suras commanded as his hoard of Vampires raced forward and the last two Dracs leapt off the stage towards Korvan.

"There's too many," Marcus said as he met the first Vampire, stabbed it in the chest with his sword turning it to ash.

"It was good fighting with you kid. Your dad would have been proud," Patches said as he threw some more objects causing fire to help keep as many of the Vampire back as he could. "I'll see you soon, Elle."

Korvan glanced back and could no longer see his two friends as the swarm of Vampires filled the gap between them. He wished he could help them but he had his own fight to worry about. The Vampires were steering clear of the stage area where Bruce remained chained. Lord Suras stood there, gaining back his strength while his two Dracs moved to engage him. Korvan eyed the two Dracs carefully anticipating their attack knowing he would have to use his Vampire skills while his new abilities recharged a bit as to not weaken him any further.

"You can't win," one of the Dracs said as he swung his sword, Korvan dodging barely.

Korvan twisted and grabbed the arm holding the sword and began to wrestle the Drac for control. The second Drac stood back watching the two struggle, waiting for his moment to strike. Lord Suras could be heard in the background laughing and declaring his victory. All seemed to be swaying in the favor of the Vampires when a strange sound and rumbling caused everyone to pause. Lord Suras opened his mouth to speak but did not get the chance.

The sound of a roaring wind broke into the room and was quickly followed by sand, desert and debris. Somehow a huge sandstorm had erupted inside and continued to flow throughout the room. Sand blew everywhere making it hard for even the Vampires to see or move. Marcus feared the worst until the sand within the storm began to shift and take the shape of sharp, pointed stakes and then plunged into the Vampires. Marcus didn't know who to thank but the tide seemed to be turning as lots of ash joined the sandstorm.

"I don't know who is helping us but this sandstorm is driving back and killing those creatures," Marcus said as Patches reached into his pouch and pulled out protective eyewear for the both of them.

"While there's cover, get to Bruce and free him," Patches said as a Vampire suddenly leapt at him but was instantly turned to ash by a forming sand stake.

"I can't leave you here," Marcus began to protest.

"I'll be fine. All that matters, is you save Bruce for me," Patches said as he leaned against a pillar, choking back the pain his body was producing all over. "Go!"

Marcus nodded and began to make his way to the stage. His sword made quick work of some Vampires in his path as others were staked or blown back by the mysterious sandstorm. It was hard to see but the goggles helped and soon he had made it to his destination and climbed up on the stage. He could hear and almost make out Korvan as he battled two Dracs nearby, but no sign of Lord Suras.

"Bruce, don't worry, I'll have you down shortly," Marcus said as he reached the chained man.

"Bnd ou," Bruce mumbled painfully.

"What did you say?" Marcus asked not being able to understand the man.

"He said, 'Behind you'," Lord Suras growled as he backhanded the boy across the stage and away from his chained prisoner. He still felt weak but he was quickly gaining his strength back as the effects of whatever Korvan had done wore off.

Marcus laid on his back, the wind knocked out of him. He managed to spot his sword and reached for it until a sharp pain shot up his arm. Lord Suras stood over him with one foot pressing down upon his wrist. The lord of the Vampires quickly reached down and picked Marcus up by the neck and held him dangling in the air.

"Any last words?" Lord Suras asked as he bared his fangs.

"Yeah, leave my brother alone," a voice shouted from behind him as the tip of a red blade suddenly poked out from his chest.

Lord Suras dropped Marcus and turned, falling to one knee while touching the tip of the blade with one hand and reaching for the sword handle behind his back with the other. The burning pain overwhelmed his body as he struggled to remove the sword from his back. He soon yanked it out and fell to the ground as he stared at the owner of the weapon.

"Lija!" Marcus shouted as he saw his sister standing before the Vampire lord with a wooden stake in her hand as Aaron left her side and was already moving over to assist Bruce.

"Why didn't that kill him?" Lija asked as she stared at Suras who laid there in a pool of his own blood but still alive.

"Because he is the original, but I hereby claim leadership over the Vampires," the Drac near Korvan declared as, to Korvan's surprise, beheaded the Drac wrestling with Korvan, leapt upon the stage and sinking his teeth into Lord Suras' neck before rolling off the stage with him and into the darkness of the sandstorm.

"What are you doing here?" Marcus said as he got to his feet and grabbed his sister into a tight hug.

"We were on our way when we ran into someone that insisted we come back and help you," Lija said with a smile as her brother finally let her go.

"Who?" Marcus asked staring at his sister.

"The creator of this sandstorm," Aaron said with excitement as he helped Bruce Peters walk slowly, making their way over to the twins.

Patches could hear a lot of commotion but unsure what was happening over near the stage. The same thing that was keeping him from seeing was the same thing that was keeping him alive. He all but thought he was in the clear when a large figure approached him, it was the Drac he had set on fire. It appeared that the wind and sand had snuffed out the fire but left the Drac very weak and badly burned and disfigured.

"I will have the pleasure of feasting upon your blood," the Drac hissed as he reached out his right arm and grabbed the old man.

Patches knew he did not have the strength to fight off a Drac so he closed his eye, whispered something to his late wife and awaited his fate. He felt a sharp jerk but no pain. He slowly opened his eye to see the Drac's arm still holding his neck but it was no longer attached to the creature's body. Between the Drac and its arm was a large sword made out of sand. Patches loosened the grip and tossed the arm to the side as he watched in amazement.

The Drac shook violently as a hand formed out of the sand, grabbed him and held him tight up in the air. Then in the next moment, the sword of sand swung with great force taking the Drac's head right off causing the creature to burst into ash and blood.

"I never thought I would see the day you would give up so easily," came a sandy and gritty voice but with a tone that Patches would know anywhere.

"Elle?" Patches asked with watery eye as the hand and sword began to swirl and break apart.

Patches watched intently as the whole room began to follow suit as the sandstorm quickly faded. Soon the room was back to normal, no Vampires in sight as they were either part of the ash on the ground or had vanished into hiding. He smiled when he saw Korvan up on the stage where Marcus, Lija, Aaron and Bruce Peters all stood watching what was happening in front of him. Another movement made Patches refocus and gasp at the sight in front of him.

"It can't be," Patches whispered as a chunk of remaining sand swirled quickly and began to take a new shape.

It happened quickly, but to Patches it seemed like everything was moving in slow motion. All the remaining swirling sand came together and started to form one solid shape. As the sand took shape, Patches started to recognize the features and smile of his late wife. He didn't know how it was possible but his wife was now standing in front of him. He reached out and touched her face. It was solid, but it felt cold and like sand. A hand made of sand, raised up and touched his face in return.

"My love," Elle said in a voice that was hers but laced with a gritty sound.

"How are you alive? Why do you look like this?" Patches had so many questions.

"I have somehow become one with the desert. Normally those that die here become creatures of the desert, like the Sand Walkers, but when I was being buried, something passed between me and Korvan and my soul was tied back to my body and I became something different, a Sand Wraith. My spirit is now a part of this place," Elle explained and then turned to the rest of the group that had joined her and her husband.

"We were so glad to see Elle when she appeared to us and convinced us to come back and help save you," Lija said giving a sad smile to the sand form of Elle.

"I," Korvan started to say when he saw Elle.

"No, it's not your fault. This is my destiny now," Elle replied stopping Korvan's apology.

"Wait, you can't stay here," Patches started to plea.

"I have to. I am bound to the Drol Death Desert. I can't leave this place," Elle said.

"Then I will stay with you," Patches said with love and pain in his voice.

"No, your destiny isn't done yet. You must lead this group and our boy out of the desert and help save Bergonia from Drol's return," Elle said as she glanced over at Bruce.

"I would slow them down, I can't continue on," Patches said knowing that he must.

"I can help with that," a deep voice came from behind them as they all turned to see the Drac that had betrayed Lord Suras.

"Stay back," Marcus shouted as he drew his sword and Korvan prepared to attack.

Without saying another word, the Drac moved with great speed and grabbed Patches. He then slit his wrist and forced his blood to drip into the old man's throat. The Drac then stepped back as Patches swayed and then removed his bandages from his wrist and hopped from one foot to the other. "I'm healed."

"What did you do to him?" Arron asked.

"Lord Suras as the creator and me a Drac, our blood has healing properties. We use this to prolong our tortured victims. Since I took down and feasted on Suras, his blood is mixed in mine so I can heal faster and now have control over any Vampire created up until this point," the Drac answered as he quickly moved over to Bruce Peters and provided the same healing for him.

"Why did you kill Suras?" Korvan asked.

"I may now be lord of the Vampires, but he is not dead. He managed to escape in the sandstorm confusion. Since the day he turned me I have vowed to bring him down and now I have," the Drac said as the group eased up a bit.

"You won't feast on humans anymore?" Lija asked.

"I can't promise you that but I will promise you safe passage out of the Desert, at least from the Vampires," the Drac vowed with a bow.

"And I will guide you out of the desert and help keep you safe from everything else," Elle said as the Drac faded back into the darkness so the group could rest and make their plans to leave the Drol Death Desert once and for all.

Chapter Fourteen:
Greybeard's Ghost

Lucian was the first one up, except for the Drogans who didn't require much sleep so were spaced evenly around the boat to keep watch from all sides. He wanted to sleep longer but the dream he had of the Chosen One and his party had shaken him. It seemed the Chosen One had found another Magestic but before he had been forced awake, Lucian had made it clear he was after and close to a Magestic as well.

Lucian took a deep breath, calmed himself and then snuck out of his sleeping quarters as to not wake Sev. He made his way up the stairs and out onto the deck. The sun was starting to rise and he wanted to see the first light upon his first day of freedom from the Unknown Lands. He made his way over to the edge of the boat and looked out upon the big vast waters of the Eastern Sea. He still had trouble believing they had made it this far.

It took most of the night but they had made it to the edge of where Argoth touched the Eastern Sea. That time of night and so far south of Argoth there were only a few ships docked. Lucian prepared to lead a takeover of one of the boats when one of the Fire Elves recognized the captain of a smaller ship, an ally of Docanesto who had assisted his adopted father on several occasions. The Fire Elf slipped away and had come back with the confirmation that the captain would help them cross the Eastern Sea to as close as they could come to the edge of the Frosted Waters.

Lucian was amazed how the captain and the ship's crew of twelve never gave a second look at his party, especially the Fire Hounds as they quickly boarded the *Ghost*. Then again, if you were an ally of his fathers, then you learned to look the other way if you wanted to live. They were all stored and hidden away below deck until they were out deep and away from land. When all was clear and secure, the Drogans were placed on watch while the rest of them got some well needed rest. Lucian was too excited to sleep but had managed to get some rest.

"Beautiful isn't it," a soft voice came from behind him.

Lucian turned to see a woman of great beauty approaching him. She looked to be a few years older than him, a tad shorter, very slender body with green eyes, red lips and long black curly hair that went slightly past her shoulders. She wore black boots, black leather pants, white blouse with a black leather vest and a black glove on her left hand. She had a silver hook where her right hand used to be and a black patch with stones covering her left eye. She appeared to carry no weapons but wore a brown pouch on her right hip that had the pattern and shape that almost made it look like a treasure chest.

"Captain Greybeard," Lucian said keeping his eyes locked with hers.

"Lucian Darkheart," the woman nodded.

"You know who I am," more a statement than a question.

"Just as you know Captain Greybeard is my father's title. Don't worry. I am the only one who knows who you are and that you are on my ship," the woman said as she walked closer to him and then looked out upon the sea.

"Good, I'd hate to have something happen to the captain so soon after taking over for the previous one," Lucian said with a smirk, impressed that she had not flinched or even showed signs of a pause about who he was or his features.

"You don't scare me, boy. My father has been dealing with Docanesto and his types long before you or I were born. He taught me everything I know and I inherited more than just his name and ship," the woman said glancing at him from her uncovered eye and returning a half smile. "Captain or Gabrielle will do just fine."

"When my Fire Elf told me of your ship, I remembered Docanesto mentioning a pirate and his daughter in his employ, but he never said much more. It was a few years ago he went on a mission with your father but when he came back he never mentioned you again, Captain," Lucian said watching the sun continuing to rise.

"Because that was the day my father, Docanesto's friend, died," Gabrielle said with a heavy tone in her voice.

"What happened?" Lucian asked finally getting answers that his adopted father would never provide.

"My father was one of the most famous pirates out on these waters. No job too small or dangerous that he wouldn't take and succeed at. Even to this day it awes me how much he was feared and admired. He had a code of honor and could be trusted with anyone's secret or paying job. When hired, you got more than your monies worth and all of these traits was why Docanesto hired him and remained one of his best customers and friends," Gabrielle started, took in a deep breath and continued her father's tale.

"There were very few men out there that would sail across the Eastern Sea through the Unknown Oceans to the Western Sea to do trades with the Kingdoms of Tallus and Silversword. What other dealings they may desire, especially unsanctioned and in a sneak in and sneak out job, my father never said no. My father loved danger and adventure and refused to get authorization from the Western Kingdoms to sail the open sea because he felt no one peson or kingdom had ownership of the open seas.

"Making this kind of trip through the Unknown Oceans was very dangerous and risky and my father had only done it a handful of times. The first time and last time my father had made that trip was upon the request of Docanesto. My father's first attempt was when he and Docanesto had first met, years before I was born. The last time, with Docanesto, was also my father's final voyage and the trip that had killed him. Docanesto had sailed with him both times and those were the only times they had sailed together."

Lucian glanced over at the woman and smirked. She was pretty but he knew she was very smart and dangerous too. The fact that he, for the first time, stood out in the open with nothing covering his disfigured body without feeling self-conscious or the need to kill the person who laid eyes on him, moved him. Yes, there was his friends and Sev, but that was different. This pirate, this woman, genuinely treated him like he was anyone else and his scars, as well as who he was, mattered little to her. He found himself intrigued by her. "Tell me more about your father."

"My father grew up in a small village in the Kingdom of Erikson, near the only bridge that grants safe passage over the Old River Gorge and into the Kingdom of Argoth. My grandfather was a tradesman and traveled to the capital city of Argoth constantly and would take my father with him. While my grandfather traded in the city, my father would sneak off and see the Eastern Sea and dream of living upon the waters.

"When my grandparents died in an accident leaving my father an orphan at the age of fourteen, he sold what they had and moved to Argoth. It was a few years later when he joined the crew of a ship and lived upon the seas. The captain, who was very well known shared the same name as his ship, Greybeard. Captain Greybeard took my father under his wing and treated him like a son and on his deathbed gave my father his ship and his name.

"You see, that is why the name is so feared, everyone believes the ship's captain is immortal or a ghost. Not only did my father live up to the name but encouraged the rumors and helped make the name one to be feared. It was the day he met Docanesto that changed everything for my father and brought the name Greybeard to a legendary status. It was the day Docanesto hired my father to take him to the Western Sea.

"My father was impressed by Docanesto, for he was the first person to ever sneak aboard his ship. He had been sitting in the captain's quarters waiting for my father when he had retired for the night. My father saw he was an Elf but didn't feel threatened as he didn't judge anyone willing to hire him and feared nothing as he was brave. My father also had ways to defend himself as he had collected many items, skills and weapons upon his many adventures upon the seas.

"Docanesto said that he needed to be taken to the Western Sea. That he needed to go to a place called the Forbidden Isles and traveling by ship was the only way to reach it. He promised to pay my father well but no one must know where they were going, who his paid passenger was and to never speak of this mission to anyone ever. The brave, adventurous and honorable man my father was, jumped at the chance to cross the Unknown Oceans and accepted the job.

"Of course, my father had a little concern about sneaking into seas he had never been before and had heard they were highly watched by the western kingdoms. Docanesto put those concerns to rest by giving my father part of his payment early.

The Elf cast a fire-based spell upon the wooden body of the Greybeard.

"Not only was the ship now resistant to fire but could heat up the waters to either move through more frosted waters or make a steam-like foggy haze to help mask the ship. The spell also caused light to be reflected away to almost make the ship become invisible. That spell is what made Greybeard's legend flare and the ship to become known as the *Ghost*," Gabrielle said as she rubbed her hand along the edge of the ship.

"Go on," Lucian urged her to continue.

"I don't know many details as my father kept his word and went to his grave with Docanesto's secret. All I know is that they made it to the Western Sea and found the Forbidden Isles. They had been there for days as Docanesto vanished off to do what he had gone to do while my father and his crew remained on board the ship, well until a few days before Docanesto came back.

"My father was sitting on deck when he saw a figure on the beach and it appeared to be a woman. He took a small boat to shore and that is when he met and instantly fell in love with my mother. For the next few days he would go back and forth, meeting her in secret. My father never spoke much about my mother or where she came from but always said it was love at first sight," Gabrielle said as she saw the question on Lucian's face.

"What happened to your mother?" Lucian asked.

"On that last day, when Docanesto came back ready to go, my mother had snuck on board our ship to forever be with my father. Docanesto declared it was too dangerous to travel back to the island and my father either had to throw the woman overboard or swear responsibility for her. With that, my mother joined my father as his companion and fellow pirate. They had many adventures over the years until the day she died giving birth to me out in the open seas," Gabrielle said with a heavy sigh but kept her emotions in check.

"If she's anything like you I bet she was beautiful," Lucian said with a smile, knowing what it was like to lose a mother you never knew.

"Thank you, she was. My father told me of her beauty every day as I grew up but little of anything else about her origins.

That is why I was so eager to go on that last trip with my father and Docanesto. It was a chance to go back to the Forbidden Isles and maybe learn about where my mother had come from.

"At first my father protested but knew I was as stubborn and strong willed as him so I remained with the crew. With the *Ghost's* abilities we easily moved out into the Eastern Sea and headed towards the Unknown Oceans. I was worried about getting lost but my father had a reliable compass that kept us going in a straight line. For about a day or two into the Unknown Oceans I laughed at the worry people had about crossing it, as the waters were calm as could be, until that third day.

"A storm came out of nowhere. Dark clouds with lightening formed as rain and strong winds rocked the *Ghost*. I had never seen a storm like this before. My father shouted commands to his crew who moved without hesitation. They had all been through this before and had been expecting it. Even Docanesto was doing what magic he could to try and help calm and divert the waves.

"The crew used all their skill and might to keep the ship from being torn apart while staying the course. I saw a wave the size of a Dragon roaring up upon us but then blacked out as something hard hit me. When I came too, we were back in the Eastern Sea. It appeared I had been knocked out cold for days. My father tended to me while Docanesto took care of his business. I was angry I missed my chance to see the Forbidden Isles, but I did not have time to dwell on that as our ship was soon attacked by a group of pirates.

"Two ships came at us from both sides. I was still weak but refused to sit by so I had my sword and joined the fight. They wanted whatever treasures we had returned with from the other side of the world but hadn't counted on an Elf being on board. It wasn't much of a fight but it came down to the captain of the other ship and Docanesto at the end. Their captain pulled out a bow and fired a poisonous arrow at Docanesto's back.

"He noticed too late and turned just in time to witness my father push him out of the way and take the arrow for him. Docanesto screamed as he dealt a quick and horrible death upon that pirate bringing the battle to an official end. I ran to my father's side but there was nothing anyone could do. The poison was fast acting and my father just had moments before he left us.

"In those final moments he told me he loved me and passed on his secrets, the ship with all its treasures and weapons as well as his legacy to me. I vowed to take over the *Ghost* and carry on the Greybeard name. Docanesto, for saving his life, vowed to watch over and protect his daughter. Which he did by giving me a few things and a promise to call if I ever needed help as I promised to carry on my father's agreements with him and those he served," Gabrielle said finishing her tale.

"And you never learned why Docanesto wanted to go to the Forbidden Isles or what was there?" Lucian asked as he looked away from the water and rested his eyes back on her.

"Guess you will need to get that information from the Elf himself," Gabrielle said with a tone in her voice that made Lucian think she knew more than she let on.

"So, that story you told, was that how you lost your hand and eye?" Lucian asked as he waved his finger at the hook and eye patch.

"No, I lost my hand to the first and last sword fight I ever lost. As for the eye, a girls got to have some mystery about her," Gabrielle said as she lifted up the eye patch, revealing a perfectly fine eye in which she winked at him with, then replaced the patch and walked away with a smile after blowing a kiss Lucian's way.

"Do I need to worry?" Sev asked walking up next to Lucian as he watched the captain vanish off to another part of the ship.

"You know I hold a special place for you in my heart," Lucian said as he kissed Sev. "I do have to say, there is something about her," Lucian added as he walked off to the front of the ship to get another view of the sea.

"Having your heart isn't what I worry about," Sev whispered as he glared off in the direction of the captain before moving after Lucian.

****

"Are you okay?" Fylla snorted as she walked over to a figure hunched over the side of the ship.

"I've never been fond of boats," Aksurh said as he straightened up and then slid down to sit against the edge of the ship.

"A big ol' Giant is afraid of water?" Fylla taunted as she stood there looking down, arms crossed.

"We usually walk or wade through bodies of water and with my pendant, I am the first Giant small enough to travel by ship over the sea," Aksurh said slightly jerking to get up but then relaxed as it was a false alarm.

"According to Lucian, Captain Greybeard says we should arrive near the Frosted Waters by nightfall," Fylla said as she looked up at the sun sitting high up in the sky.

"Not that I'm complaining, but I can't believe how much distance we've covered and even with no wind, the sails keep us going in the direction we want to go," the Giant said as he thought about standing up but decided it was safer to remain sitting.

"I'm guessing there's more to this ship than meets the eye," Fylla said leaning over the edge and noticing a red glow coming off the ship as it touched the water below and making some steam rise up despite the cold of the sea and season they were in.

"I want you to know that I'm sorry I," Aksurh started to say when the blade of an axe suddenly at his neck cut him off.

"Don't, you made your decision and I've come to accept it," Fylla said through gritted teeth.

"But," Aksurh swallowed hard, the pressure against his neck making it hard to speak.

"Say no more or I will make it so you can't bring it up again," Fylla said with finality, and with a nod from Aksurh, she placed her axe back upon her back.

Aksurh looked up at the female Barbarian as she now stared out towards the sea. As tough and mean as she looked, he could see the hurt in her eyes. He just wished she would let him explain. His leaving had nothing to do with her or the feelings she had for him. He left because he had to search for his family and the rest of his kind. He meant to get word back to her or return sooner, but too much had happened and time had slipped away. Now it was too late. He knew if he tried to tell her how he felt, she would cut off his tongue before he even got the words out.

Now that his stomach ached for another reason, Aksurh managed to compose himself and get back on his feet. He started to walk away to give Fylla her space when something caught his eye. He stepped up to the edge of the ship and squinted to try and focus on what was out there. It was hard to make out but he knew something was moving towards them.

"What's with the face? Going to get sick again?" Fylla asked and then froze as she finally saw what he was looking at.

What had originally been a single speck now appeared to be an object followed by five more. As they got a little closer, she could tell it was a fleet of six ships heading for them from the direction of the Unknown Oceans and fast. She turned to a Fire Elf that was moving their way and told him to notify Lucian and the captain immediately. The Elf was gone before Fylla could blink. She then turned back to face the sea, drawing her axe.

"Let's make this a little harder on them," Gabrielle said as she leapt up in front of the ship's wheel and placed her hand upon an object in its center.

Lucian and Sev were soon at her side to witness her whisper something and the object under her hand began to glow. The ship began to make a strange noise as steam rose up from the water all around them. In a matter of moments, they were engulfed in what seemed like a thick fog. To anyone watching the ship from the outside would have sworn that the ship sailed into smoke and vanished from sight.

"Now we can't see them coming," Lucian said as he could barely see through the fog-like steam.

"If we can't see them, they definitely can't see us," Gabrielle said with a smile as she removed her hand. "We should be a long distance away from them before I make us visible again."

"How did they even know we were out here? Who are they?" Sev asked looking at Lucian and trying not to glare at the captain.

"Hard to say. Out in these pirate infested waters there are no magic alarms or rules," Gabrielle said with a shrug. "I've drifted us off course a little. They'll give up and turn around now that they can't see us."

"We can't take that chance, I'm afraid," Lucian said as he moved to the side and called out to a Fire Elf with instructions.

The Fire Elf darted off with a bow in hand and soon after, five Drogans came running to the side of the ship facing where the unknown enemy had been sighted. Just before they reached the edge, they shifted form and sprouted wings. Gabrielle smiled in awe as she saw the five creatures take flight and vanish into the steam towards the fleet.

"No matter how many times I see those creatures, I'm still amazed by them," Gabrielle said as she turned back to face Lucian.

"You've seen a Drogan before?" Lucian asked.

"Like I said, I've helped Docanesto with anything he has needed," was all Gabrielle offered before something off in the distance demanded her attention.

"What was that?" Fylla asked when they heard a loud explosion followed by a monstrous scream.

"Captain Greybeard, just as the flying creatures approached those ships, they blew one out of the air with," the *Ghost's* crewman, who was positioned clear atop one of the masts watching with a special telescope, started to report when he was cut off by the sound of another Drogan being blown out of the sky.

"It can't be," Gabrielle whispered as she placed a telescope right up to the patch covering her eye.

"Who is that out there?" Lucian asked as for the first time he saw this strong woman shiver a little.

Before she could answer her crewman shouted in panic. "They're headed right for us and there are no signs of the winged beasts."

"I thought your ship's magic kept us hidden," Sev mocked the captain.

"Not from him. It's very rare for him or any magical beings to venture out of the safety of the Unknown Oceans and come this far into the Eastern Sea," Gabrielle said as she hopped down and started barking orders at her crewmen to get the ship moving faster.

"Last time I will ask. Who is after you?" Lucian demanded as he realized his first assumption that someone had come for him was wrong.

"His name is Drache. No one truly knows what he is. Some say he is a ghost, a water wraith or some kind of spirit or creature bound to the waters of the Unknown Oceans. No one knows how old he is but the legend goes that he hunts the waters looking for something and those that cross him became a part of his ghost ships. I always believed it as what it was, a story to scare," Gabrielle laughed nervously.

"But you know it's not a story," Lucian said glancing over his shoulder towards the advancing fleet.

"I did until I saw him eye to eye. I was fairly deep out in the Unknown Oceans, sending my father's ashes off to his requested resting place, out into the waters. Luckily, it was only in passing as his ship went past mine. Seems he was after a ship out farther from me so I finished my business and headed back home," Gabrielle said remembering with a small shiver.

"And exactly why would he be after you now?" Sev demanded already knowing the answer.

"I may have stolen the item legend says he is hunting for," Gabrielle said with a nervous smirk.

"Then you have to give it back," Aksurh pleaded.

"Well, I would but I don't know what it is. That ship he went after, before I scattered my father out to sea, I kind of attacked and stole everything in its treasure room as a tribute to my father who had robbed that same ship before. The captain of that ship, before he accidentally died, had started to warn me about Drache. I laughed it off at that time but now… I truly doubt Drache would politely search my ship then leave. I don't want to risk becoming part of his ghost fleet and what is mine is mine," Gabrielle rambled and then resumed her tough tone.

"That is the real reason you have yet to return to the Unknown Oceans," Lucian added remembering hearing a crewman mentioning something about the last time they went into those waters was the captain's burial at sea.

"Yes, I wanted enough time to pass so whatever that thing is would be off my trail and far away," Gabrielle confessed.

"If it's bound to the Unknown Oceans, then how is he here in the Eastern Sea?" Fylla asked.

"Because we are not in the Eastern Sea, somehow we have drifted off course so that we have been traveling slightly within the dividing border of the Sea and Ocean," a crewman added bowing his head in forgiveness.

"How is that possible?" Gabrielle screamed as she ran to her father's compass mounted above the wheel to see it pointing to the left and not straight ahead.

"I'm sorry, I," was all the crewman got out before Captain Greybeard did a high kick sending the man flying back and overboard, plunging into the cold waters below.

"All we have to do is cross the border and we will be fine," Gabrielle said as she grabbed the wheel and shouted orders getting the ship back on track toward the Eastern Sea and the Frosted Waters.

"They are advancing pretty fast, I don't think we'll make it," Sev said as he noticed how close the fleet of ships were getting.

"Should we send the rest of the Drogans?" Fylla asked her friend and leader.

"No, we have only four left and I don't want to risk losing them too," Lucian said trying to ponder a way to keep their mission from ending so tragically.

"Captain, perhaps Besse could help?" Another of the crewmen suggested.

"I don't know if she would make it here in time," Gabrielle said giving the crewman a look reminding him of their vow to never speak of her treasures, weapons or secrets in front of anyone not a sworn member of her crew. She thought about kicking him over but right now she needed all hands on deck.

"Who or what is Besse?" Lucian asked moving to the captain's side watching the approaching ships while Gabrielle worked the ship's wheel and controls.

"My father acquired an item that calls forth a sea monster to do its master's bidding. I call it Besse. I have used her a few times but only in desperate measures as my father warned using it too much could be dangerous. I noticed last time I called her she was harder to control and send back and almost destroyed my ship," Gabrielle said knowing that out racing the fleet was their only option.

"It's still worth a try if only to buy us the time to cross safely into the Eastern Sea," Sev added looking from Gabrielle to Lucian.

"What if he does to her what he did to your Drogans?" Gabrielle spat back at the Fairy hating the thought of losing one of her best treasures and gifts from her father.

"Give back what's mine!" Came a creepy and water gurgling voice from across the waters.

They all turned to see that the fleet was almost upon them. Lucian noticed that the mix of crewman on the ships appeared to be that some were flesh and others had a watery ghost-like appearance. Standing at the very edge of the ship was a figure, ghost-like in appearance and the color of deep blue. Drache's ghost looked like a pirate with the beard, hat and all. The story of him being a spirit was true but it seemed he needed living crewman as well to do physical tasks the ghosts were unable to do themselves. Just as Lucian was trying to form more of his theories, Drache made his move.

The pirate ghost raised his arms, palms upwards causing a strange energy to pull water up from the ocean, forming a ball. Lucian felt a strange sensation coming from the water ball and tried to figure what kind of magic this was. Lucian did not get a chance as Drache twisted his palms outward and thrust his arms towards them causing the ball of water to shoot forward, growing bigger and bigger as it pulled and absorbed more water from the ocean as it soared towards the *Ghost*.

"Evasive maneuvers!" Gabrielle shouted as she and her crew worked to get the ship to move out of the way.

"That's what hit the Dro..." was all the crewman standing atop the platform high above the sails got out when the ball of water made explosive impact with the sail causing it to break in half and then plunged back into the ocean waters, absorbing and taking the top of the sail and the crewman with it.

"The sails are gone," Lucian said as he looked up and then back at Gabrielle fearing the worst.

"The sails are more for decoration and adds a little speed. Don't worry, we're almost to the Eastern Sea border," Gabrielle said as the ship rocked from the impact but kept moving forward.

"We won't reach it in time and there's no way we can survive another hit like that," Sev said as he glanced over and saw Drache, stagger a little but preparing for round two.

"Elves, attack!" Lucian turned and shouted over his shoulder.

All five Fire Elves ran to the side of the ship and pulled out their bows. Arrows made of fire formed and in several quick motions, a few dozen arrows were now soaring across the ocean and heading for the attacking fleet. The arrows of fire made contact with every ship and cast them aflame. Lucian and his friends took a moment of victory as the Elves let loose another round of flaming arrows. Lucian stopped cheering as their victory was short lived.

Drache turned to the side of his ship and raised his arms again, but this time something different happened. The ocean's waters began to rock violently as waves began to form and hit the ships. Then, as he made an arching motion with his arms, a huge tidal wave lifted up and over all of his ships and then came crashing down. When the wave settled, the ships still stood but were no longer on fire as the flames and the new oncoming arrows were extinguished. He then kept the waters rocking with small waves and turned to face the *Ghost* and smiled.

"That doesn't look good. He's going to send one of those tidal waves at us," Aksurh said as he realized how much he really hated being on a boat.

"This is desperate measures. Call your sea monster, now!" Lucian commanded Gabrielle, who almost lashed out but remembered who she was talking to and knew he was right and bit her tongue.

Gabrielle reached under the front of her shirt and pulled out an object that was concealed and hung from a leather string around her neck. The object was blue, long and thin and resembled a sea shell. She placed the object to her lips and blew into it. No sound came out but Lucian felt a strange vibe in the air as Gabrielle blew three more times before placing the object back underneath her shirt.

"It didn't do anything," Sev tried to cover his fear with a mocking tone.

"I'm hoping she isn't far. She should be here soon," Gabrielle hoped for if they even made it past the border, a tidal wave or water ball could still follow after and do in her ship.

"I hope so," Lucian added as he watched Drache preparing to move his arms to bring up the tidal wave.

"You won't escape me. I will have what's mine!" Drache's voice bellowed across the waters as he moved his arms up and then froze.

A loud roar began to rumble from deep below the ocean. Suddenly, a very large form erupted from the water between the fleet of ships causing two to be ripped apart. The creature's body was almost as big as a Dragon but had twelve large tentacles that sprouted from it. From one end, a long neck extended out which was attached to a large head with small eyes and a mouth full of razor sharp teeth. A large tail extended from the other end. The beast was a pale blue color and looked terrifying.

Lucian watched as Besse hovered in the air for a second before it dove back down upon the remaining ships destroying all but Drache's as it went back into the ocean. Drache stood there, unmoving, as if the sight of the beast had put him into a trance. Lucian could almost see the ghost pirate trying to say something when twelve large tentacles reached up and around his ship and tore it apart. In a matter of moments, the entire fleet was floating in pieces in the ocean's waters.

"Amazing," Fylla said as she fancied the large beast that had just saved them.

"Shall we go back and save them?" Aksurh asked as he stared at the people flapping in the water calling out for help.

"No, we need to get to the border," Gabrielle said as she commanded the ship to keep going.

As her crew began to move with great haste, a strange sound came from behind them. Lucian turned to look back out to where the fleet laid in pieces. It was getting harder to see as they were covering ground and putting distance between them and the battle area. Water began to swirl and mix with a strange mist. Lucian at first thought it was Besse coming back up but he was wrong, very wrong. He glanced at Gabrielle and with the look she had, he knew why she was racing for the border of the Eastern Sea.

Piece by piece, a ship began to form within the swirling mix of water and mist. Before long a ship had reformed in perfect condition as if it had never been torn apart. Shortly after that, swirling mists appeared on the ship as six figures took shape, five pirates and Drache. They appeared as they did before but with a fainter blue glow. Drache screamed and sent a ball of water directly at them.

"We're almost there," Gabrielle said as she glanced behind her.

"It appears that since Drache and his ship are bound to the Unknown Ocean that they can't be destroyed so easily," Sev said as he nervously looked at the ship being left behind and the water ball approaching them, but at a lesser speed than the first one.

"But it weakens them, that ball of water isn't getting any bigger and isn't as powerful as the first one," Lucian said as he stepped up upon the edge of the ship to face the oncoming ball of water.

Focusing with all his might he called upon the magic he was taught. Stretching out his arms and cupping his hands towards each other he spoke in the tongue of magic causing a ball of fire to start to form between his hands. Calling on more of his energy and magic he chanted and moved his hands slowly apart causing the fire ball to grow in size. Taking his queue, the Fire Elves sent a few dozen arrows of fire, round after round, at the ball of water. It did not stop it but it caused it to lose some mass as the fire turned the water to steam. Just as the last arrows hit, Lucian released his fire ball at the water ball causing it to vanish in a big explosion of steam.

"You did it," Sev said as he was right by his lover's side, using his embrace to help mask Lucian's sway after unleashing such a powerful spell.

"And it looks like Drache is too weak to do that again," Aksurh added with relief.

"Thankfully, but I have a feeling why he keeps living people with him," Lucian pointed and they all looked back out at the single ship floating back behind them.

Drache moved to the side of his boat and looked out upon a bunch of his crew still alive and screaming in the water. Drache reached out his hand, pointed at them and then opened his mouth. Then men in the water quit screaming as swirling vapor came out instead of sound. As the vapor reached Drache, he began to glow a brighter and stronger blue as his former crewmen seemed to dehydrate, shriveling up and then sank below into the ocean. The ghost captain was now fully revived as the crewmen he had drained reappeared on his ship as spirits themselves, forever bound to the ship and the Unknown Oceans.

"I don't like the looks of that," Sev said as Drache, as far back as he was now, glowed bright enough to be seen perfectly.

"We're about to cross the border so we will be safe from him," Gabrielle said with relief.

"What about Besse?" Fylla asked as Gabrielle turned white forgetting about her beast and hearing a large roar.

She turned and looked and saw Besse sitting there staring at Drache. Neither moved for what seemed like an eternity before Besse roared one last time and then turned and dove right for the *Ghost*. Besse was moving with great speed, growling with intensity in her eyes. Gabrielle pulled the shell out from her shirt and began to blow the signal to calm and send Besse back to where she sleeps in the ocean. Besse seemed to fight the command and growled even harder with more ambition to reach the *Ghost*.

"Make her stop. At that speed she'll destroy us," Fylla said as she studied the creature coming at them.

"I'm trying but it's as I feared, she is resisting," Gabrielle responded as she kept blowing. They had made it to the border and into safe waters to only now be destroyed by her own pet.

"Well, if Besse doesn't do us in, that will," Aksurh said with fear in his voice.

Lucian looked back and past Besse to see the faint form of Drache, arms up in the air and behind him the largest and tallest tidal wave anyone had ever seen. The wave slowly passed through Drache and his ship without causing any damage or harm. Then Drache swung down his arms causing the huge tidal wave to take off moving with great speed and intensity towards them. It was moving so fast that it was catching up to Besse.

Lucian laughed nervously as he wondered what would get them first, Besse or the tidal wave.

"Even if she called off that creature, that tidal wave will still cross the border and hit us. A wave that size, it would take a miracle if this ship survives the impact," Sev said slipping his fingers between Lucian's and squeezing tight.

"Sev, there are still four Drogans left on board. You fly high above the ship while they grab me, Fylla, Aksurh and Gabrielle and take us safely above," Lucian said in a low whisper.

"Why are you saving her? What about the Fire Elves or even Frrr?" Sev asked, stepping back appalled and glaring quickly towards *Captain Greybeard*.

"As much as I care for Frrr, one Drogan can't lift him. I can't sacrifice Fylla or Aksurh as we will need them. I choose to save Gabrielle and you should never question my decisions," Lucian snapped as Sev flew off in a huff to give instructions to the Drogans.

"Incoming!" One of Gabrielle's crewmen screamed as it appeared both Besse and the tidal wave were about to hit the *Ghost* at the exact same time.

"Where are those blasted creatures?" Lucian panicked as he finally felt a tug and looked up to see a Drogan grabbing him.

As he was lifted high into the air he looked around and saw Fylla and Aksurh being grabbed as well. He glanced over to where Gabrielle was standing to see she was still there with no Drogan in sight. Cursing, Lucian opened his mouth to call out to her when the roar of the tidal wave drowned him out. He then saw Besse grab the *Ghost* with her tentacles just as the top of the tidal wave slammed down upon him and the ship causing everything to go dark.

Chapter Fifteen:
Crossroads

Semaj was amazed it was daylight already when they had come out of the secret tunnel. What had seemed like a few moments in their shared dream had actually taken all night. He felt unrested and wanted go back to sleep but there was no time for that as they were on the move to try and make it as far from Norax and the Dwarves as they could. Especially now that they had two specific Dwarves amongst their party, the king's daughter and her lover from a rival clan. If they got caught, it would be the end for all of them and their mission to save his parents, his home and all of Bergonia.

When Noraxa had provided their escape along with appropriate attire for the cold, they followed her without question through the dark lower tunnels of the Dwarven city until they reached the spot where the secret tunnel out resided. To their surprise, King Norax had posted two guards there to keep his daughter from trying to sneak out again. Unfortunately for the guards, Essej and Anna used their gifts together to cause a warm vacuum of air around their heads so that they would pass out safely and without harm.

Noraxa then placed her hands on the wall and pushed to make the wall separate and reveal a passageway out. Once they had all crossed through, Noraxa closed the entry way so no Dwarf could follow them. They quickly moved across the secret tunnel until they came to a path that lead upwards at a slant. After a bit of uphill hiking they came to a dead end, where Noraxa once again opened a hidden doorway out of the secret passageway and into the open air on the other side of the chasm.

Semaj looked around nervously, wondering how they would get far enough away from the city traveling by foot. His fears were soon squashed when, thanks to the help of Nat, Essej and Noraxa, a bunch of Frostites heard their call for help and were headed their way. There was one for each of them, except Noraxa who had her own, and they quickly mounted their Frostite and dashed off across the snowy terrain. Noraxa took the lead while Essej took the rear so he could use his power over the winds to cover their tracks.

Semaj was impressed by the strength and speed of the creatures they were riding upon. They would reach Steam Lake a lot faster than it took them to reach Norax by foot. They were not sure where to go first after their escape, but they would have time to contemplate that once they had reached a safe distance from Norax. They had agreed to head to Steam Lake where they would have time to rest and decide the next course of action. Everyone had their suggestions but it was harder on Semaj, as a result of the dream, he was being torn in too many directions.

Just as Semaj seemed to get lost in his thoughts and felt his eyes starting to droop, he heard Noraxa shout out bringing all their Frostites to a stop. Semaj looked up ahead and saw that they had finally reached Steam Lake. The top looked slightly frosted over but not completely frozen as you could see the steam rising up off of it. Everyone dismounted as Noraxa commanded Lorax to herd the Frostites together while they planned their next move.

"I still think we should head straight to Mirax. My father would help us with anything we needed," Lorax called out as Noraxa shot him an irritated look.

"No, that would be the first place my father will go and if there is any sign we had been there then all-out war would erupt between our clans," Noraxa said as she turned back to the group she had just helped escape.

"Where do we go then?" Thom asked looking to Anna.

"We have to," Anna started to say when she looked at Essej and then Nat.

"As I said before, I am out looking for adventure. If you're willing to let me, I will help you in any way I can," Nat said pledging herself to the group as she held back her smile.

"I," Essej paused as he looked the Wild Elf over. There was something about her he could not place.

"Essej, she saved my life and helped us so far with no ill intent. I think she can continue to be of help with what we're facing. I think we can trust her," Semaj said and then whispered so that only Essej could hear him, "I feel a familiar connection to her and I don't think it's a bad one."

"She can help me with my crystal and who knows, maybe she can be our link to the Elves if we need them," Thom added in support as he imagined how neat it would be to see the homeland of the Elves in person instead of reading about everything in his books.

"We need to decide as we're running out of time. We cut her loose or we let her in and if she proves false, take her down," Noraxa said grazing her axe with her finger as she grew impatient, staring at the Wild Elf.

"I'll help keep an eye on her," Anna said more to herself than anyone.

"Fine, against my better judgement we have to start trusting somewhere if we are to succeed in stopping Drol Greb," Essej said with a sigh of defeat, fearing Semaj was mistaking his connection with one of the heart.

"Drol Greb? Wasn't he killed a long time ago," Nat questioned as she put on her act.

"Many thought he had been killed but he had survived and was banished to another realm," Essej said as the group filled her in on their mission and what has happened to them while leaving out the identity of the Chosen One as Essej had indicated by secret wind whisper, that only the select few should know that for now.

"In order to stop his return, you must find and gather all these Magestics?" Nat asked more to herself as a notation than a confirmation from the group.

"Yes, and the Chosen One will lead and guide them and their abilities to victory," Thom said with an excited grin that made Nat eye him more suspiciously than any of the others.

"Now we need to determine where to go next from the clues we all saw in the dream," Essej said looking up at the sky, deep in thought.

"I recognized the man being attacked in the cavern from that group dream with Dwin. He had been standing with Marcus," Anna said suddenly with worry as they started to eat their rations and discuss their pending destination.

"That cavern could be anywhere," Thom said thinking of his friends and dreaded the thought of losing them too.

"All I can add is it's not a part of the Northern Mountains," Noraxa explained that the cavern looked more man built than a mountain side or Dwarven architect.

"What do you think?" Essej asked Semaj carefully.

"My gut says it's somewhere south of here, but it's not a very *strong* feeling, like that of the other two towards the east," Semaj answered.

"My thoughts exactly. The figure in the water I'm guessing is water folk and the battle scene consists of the Ogres and since Ogra and the Frosted Waters are both east I think that is where we need to go," Essej said as he got up and mounted his Frostite.

"What about Marcus and Lija?" Thom asked looking at Semaj.

"Marcus is tough. I'm sure he's already notified the king and they are just fine," Anna said trying to put belief into her words.

"Anna's right, they'll be fine. We need to follow Essej and head east," Semaj said as he could feel the pull in that direction the more he thought about it.

"We are not seriously going to try and cross the Frosted Waters and go to the land of Ogres?" Lorax asked with pleading eyes to his one true love.

"Lorax, I can't explain it but I know I must follow them. I won't ask you to come with me," Noraxa trailed off showing true signs of softness for the first time since the small group met the two Dwarves.

"I may not agree with it and urge you not to go but I will follow you anywhere you choose to go," Lorax said as he leaned in and kissed her.

"Looks like we are all headed east if you still want to join us," Semaj said to Nat who agreed to go with a smile, ignoring the glare from Anna.

"It's settled than, but before we go," Essej said as he turned to the lake and called on his powers.

The wind began to pick up and seemed to be blowing from all sides. Moving his hands in a circular motion, the winds moved towards the lake, merged over the center and began to rotate in a strong clockwise direction. Soon after, a small cyclone formed above the water, growing bigger and wider till Steam

Lake itself parted in the middle with a larger rotating hole. Essej then called back to them over his shoulder.

"Noraxa, I need you to grab Lorax's hand and then reach out with your gift to feel and familiarize yourself with the earth he stands upon. Once you got that, I want you to reach out down to the bottom of this hole and feel for the earth that seems identical," Essej instructed as Noraxa did as he asked.

Everyone watched in amazement as Noraxa reached deep within herself and then reached out with her Magesti. She had her doubts about what she was doing until she felt a certain signature to the earth Lorax was standing on. Locking on to that, she reached out and focused on the center of the whirlpool and then straight down till she felt the earth at the bottom of the lake. Using the signature under Lorax, she tried to find something familiar within the earth below the lake. She was about to give up when she felt something odd but familiar. "Got it!"

"Good, now I want you to focus all your power into that section of earth and push with all your might, willing it to shoot upwards," Essej instructed as he kept his concentration on containing the cyclone above the lake.

"I don't know if I can," Noraxa said feeling the sweat form on her brow.

"You can do it," Semaj said as he placed his hand on her shoulder.

Noraxa felt a sudden spark of energy and a wave of calm come over her from Semaj's touch. She closed her eyes and instantly pictured a fist and punched upwards with everything she had. She felt a strange surge and opened her eyes in time to see a large chunk of earth shoot out of the lake, into the cyclone and then up and out the top landing between the group. Sticking out of the top of the rock was a shiny silver axe with strange markings on the blade.

"It appears the story is true," Essej said with a smile as he dropped to one knee in exhaustion as the cyclone and winds vanished and the lake closed back up.

"Is that the axe my grandfather told us about?" Noraxa asked as she reached for the handle.

"Yes, but I believe that belongs to another," Essej said as he pointed at the female Dwarf making her pause as he then looked right at Lorax.

"Me?" Lorax asked with confusion.

"That axe belonged to your grandfather and so rightfully belongs to you and where we are headed next you will need it," Essej said as he encouraged the Dwarf to take the axe.

Lorax saw a little jealousy in Noraxa's eyes but with her nod he stepped forward and put his hand around the handle. He felt a strange tingling sensation run from the axe and up through his arm. With ease he pulled the axe from the rock and swung it back and forth. He was amazed how light and balanced the weapon was. It was as if it was made specifically for him and he even felt confident holding and using it. He smiled, staring at the markings on the blade as Noraxa told him the story of their grandfathers and how it came to be in the lake.

"My father never said anything about this part when he told the story of the Dwarves dividing," Lorax said as he felt something within him telling him that this was more than just a battle axe, it scared him but he would honor his grandfather and use it proudly.

"We better get moving before the king catches up to us," Anna said as she took Lorax's old axe and adding it to her arsenal. She liked the feel even if it was a tad heavy.

Everyone mounted their Frostite and followed Essej as he took the lead. It had begun to snow so the need to cover their tracks was gone and Essej needed a rest after the display he had just performed in helping get the axe from the bottom of the lake. The rest of them followed two by two behind him. Noraxa and Lorax next, then Semaj and Nat with Anna and Thom bringing up the rear. Semaj was definitely grateful for the winter clothing as the snow fell and the wind got stronger.

"I can't believe winter is hitting already up here," Thom said with a chill trickling into his body.

"Winter? This is our fall season. This is nothing compared to what we get when winter sets in," Lorax called back with a chuckle as they kept pushing onward.

"Can't you do something with the wind?" Semaj called out to the leader of their group after the wind had started to pick up more, making the long journey unbearable.

"Sorry, I'm still a bit drained. I'm not like I was back in my younger days," Essej said, thankful that the wind and cold really had no effect on him like it did the others. He wished he could do more for them, but he needed to keep his strength for what lay ahead.

"Where are we headed?" Nat asked as she noticed that they had started to veer off and head into the mountains and she was losing her bearings.

"There is a nest of Snowpedes a little more south of here. Essej said we can ride them the rest of the way to the edge of the Frosted Waters," Lorax answered.

"Will you have the strength to help them fly us all there like you did before?" Semaj asked the Huelgon.

"There should be enough of them for us to split up allowing them to fly higher and farther without my help. We won't need to be up above the mountains, just glide through the passways between the mountains to the Frosted Waters, keeping us ahead of King Norax and out of reach of..."

"Snogres!" Thom interrupted with a scream.

"Yes, Thom, out of reach of the Snogres," Essej chuckled.

"No, Snogres," Thom said again this time pointing upwards to one side.

"There too," Anna added pointing to the other side.

They had been traveling for so long on the path between the mountains watching ahead and behind them that no one thought to keep watch higher up, especially with the blowing snow. Semaj glanced back and forth and saw about part way up the side of the mountain, on both sides, were about ten Snogres each. Semaj knew they were in trouble as there were way too many for them to take on if they charged at them. He looked to Essej for the answer. "What now?"

"We keep riding and pushing forward. If we can make it past them and a little further up this path we should be able to avoid direct confrontation with the beasts," Essej said as he urged his Frostite forward with all its speed and strength.

Following the Huelgon's lead, the group pushed their mounts with everything they had. At the sign of their prey moving faster, the Snogres let out a loud primal roar and then began stampeding down the mountain side, kicking up snow and rocks along the way causing the group to slow a little to avoid being hit.

"We'll never make it. They'll be on top of us in a matter of moments," Lorax panicked as he looked up and saw them getting closer.

"Just a little farther," Essej wished as he gripped his Frostite tighter leaning forward as if that would help.

Essej tuned out the comments of fear and panic as he kept focus on the path ahead with the occasional glance up and back. Using the wind blowing past him, he called on his gift and sent a little message into the ears of their newest Magestic. He glanced and saw her nod, despite everything thrown at her, Noraxa was brave and would be ready for what she had to do next. Essej glanced back again and saw that they had made it out of the direct path of the Snogres but the first few were touching ground. "Now!"

On command, Noraxa leapt off Freezia, rolled and came up facing the direction of the Snogres as the rest of the group shot past in surprise. Knowing if she wasted time she would be these creature's dinner, she looked up at the sides of the mountains and reached out with her Magesti. Essej told her not to worry about being careful, she just had to do it. With that in mind, she felt the earth connected to the mountains and pictured a sledgehammer hitting both sides with all her might.

The Snogres who had landed on the ground all stopped and stared at her. With a smile they prepared to charge when something else caught their attention. Looking up, the Snogres saw a huge avalanche pouring down from both sides of the mountains. There was no out running it as their confusion and the rest of the Snogres coming down not paying attention and crashing into each other had sealed their fates. In moments, the huge double-sided avalanche had hit, covered and buried the Snogres completely as well as sealing the path back out of the mountains.

"You saved us," Lorax said as he ran to Noraxa, who had dipped down to one knee in exhaustion, helped her up and hugged her tight.

"Let's keep moving. They may not stay buried for long, but it will buy us enough time to reach the nest of Snowpedes," Essej said as the group waited for the Dwarves to remount and then darted off along the path again.

"There it is," Lorax pointed out as they soon came out between the mountains and into a large clearing.

"I'm glad to finally be out in some open space but I wish the wind and snow would let up," Semaj said as he slid off the back of his Frostite and gathered with the rest of his friends.

"I can warm things up a bit," Anna said as she stepped between Nat and Semaj and prepared to show off a little.

They had been riding for so long that it felt good to stretch her legs and body a bit and to let loose some pent-up energy. She stood there and reached out with her Magesti, searching for heat, which was hard in the cold. She then thought about what Noraxa had been instructed to do and reached down into the earth and soon found plenty of heat. Using her gift, she carefully pulled the heat upwards as the snow on the ground under them all melted and you could feel the warmth.

"Well done, now sustain that and don't pull any more as we don't want the ground to burst into flame burning us all," Essej said with a soft and stern tone.

"Or give off our location to the Snogres," Thom added as he kept looking back from where they came.

"You're getting better at this," Semaj said giving Anna a smile of confidence.

"The nest is just over there," Nat interrupted bringing all attention onto her after she felt the presence of the creatures deep below the ground.

"Can you urge them upwards?" Essej said as it would be easier on him to talk to the creatures above ground than below.

"How do you get them to obey you?" Thom asked stepping up to Essej.

"Oh, they don't obey me, I merely ask them for help. Since we are both descendants to the Dragon, we speak the same language," Essej responded with a wink and a smile.

Nat glanced quickly and then away as to not let on what she had just overheard. It confused her why the half Elf would claim to be connected to the creatures unless... Nat's eyes went wide as she realized what Essej really was. She had heard stories but never thought she would ever truly see a real one. Definitely not good, Magestics and the Chosen One being led by a Huelgon. She felt she should report back, but something was causing her to second guess herself and her mission. Nat kept going back and forth as she kept glancing towards Semaj.

"They're headed to the surface," Nat said as she realized they were all staring at her and she quickly reached out to the beast asking them to emerge.

"Do all Elves talk with the animals?" Semaj asked as he stepped closer to the Wild Elf.

"Almost all Elves tend to be in touch with all manors of nature but the Wild Elves are more deeply connected, especially with the animals. We don't so much as communicate by talking but more with feelings and impressions. Some of us are more skilled at it than others," Nat tried to explain as she kept glancing at Essej, nervously.

"Our rides are here," Anna shouted as she moved between her friend and the Wild Elf.

Essej was already standing near where the ground began to shake and cave inwards. Four Snowpedes erupted from the earth showering everyone with dirt and snow. Essej raised his arms up and began to speak in a strange tongue as he used a little of his powers to carry his words upon the winds to the creature's ears. The large creatures hesitated for a minute before they made a strange noise and then slowly glided down laying themselves flat against the snowy ground.

"They will take us to the edge of the Frosted Waters," Essej said as he began to climb atop one of the Snowpedes.

"What about the Frostites?" Thom asked as he scratched behind the ear of the one he had rode upon.

"They can't follow us where we are going," Essej said.

"They'll find their way back," Noraxa said as she rubbed Freezia's fur and said her goodbyes. As much as she didn't want to leave her friend, she knew it was too dangerous for her to follow.

"I still can't get over this," Thom said with excitement as he mounted the Snowpede and the little legs extended up to grip and hold him in place.

"I know," Anna said as she quickly moved past Nat and climbed on top of the Snowpede Semaj was getting on.

"Looks like I'm with you," Nat said with a forced smile as she joined Thom. She did not care that Anna beat her to Semaj's side, and why would she? It's not like she liked the boy. Yes, she was older, but in relation to human and Elven years, she was the equivalent to his age. There was something about him, but she had to let that go. She was here for one purpose only and being with Thom would give her a chance to decipher if he or Anna was the Chosen One.

"Are you sure about this? It's not too late to go to my father," Lorax suggested as he helped Noraxa up and onto the Snowpede he was on.

"You can go if you want, but I've always wanted to be a part of something bigger than my dad's kingdom, and this is it. I have to follow mine and continue my grandfather's destiny," Noraxa said as whatever this Magesti was that was inside of her, it was pulling her to follow Semaj.

"Whether I agree or not, you know I go anywhere you go," Lorax said as with a jerk, the Snowpede glided up and took flight.

The Snowpedes quickly reached a good altitude, not too high up but far enough from grounds reach. Essej took the lead as the other three Snowpedes glided almost side by side as they moved in between the mountains. The snow had let up but the wind and air still felt much colder this high up. Wrapping their coats tight for warmth, the group quickly made their way to the Frosted Waters. Essej had told them that at this pace they should be out of the mountains and near the water's edge by nightfall, where they could safely make camp for the night.

Semaj sat back a little and watched in amazement at the scenery. He had seen mountains before but never this close and now he would be traveling over the Frosted Waters. This would also be his first time seeing the ocean. If it was not for the fact they were trying to save Bergonia from Drol Greb and his evil forces, he might actually enjoy this as a vacation of sorts. He felt a weird sensation inside of himself. Could a simple farm boy with no desire for world travel actually be enjoying this?

"Look out!" Came a scream that brought Semaj back to reality.

Semaj panicked as his Snowpede made an alarming noise. A huge snow ball the size of a large boulder was coming right at them. The Snowpede tried to move but was hit dead in the chest causing it to convulse and loose altitude. The shock of the attack had caused the creature to release its hold on him and Anna. When the Snowpede shifted to regain composure and flight, Semaj lost his holding and began to slip and fall. Anna reached out for him but the Snowpede's small hairs reattached to her legs, grabbing hold and jerking her back making her miss Semaj's hand by an inch.

"Semaj!" Anna screamed in horror as the Snowpede regained altitude and flight as her dear friend quickly fell to his death.

"I got him," Thom said as he felt words form in his mind and his crystal began to glow.

Nat watched her riding partner with interest as he went into action. Twisting his body so he had a clear view of his best friend, he raised his left arm up with the palm of his hand cupped upwards while he extended his right arm and pointed directly at Semaj. Nat found it hard to understand what Thom was saying as strange words came out of his mouth. His eyes started to glow to match his crystal as an orb of magical energy formed in the palm of his cupped hand.

"Owsl Ish Entdec!" Thom shouted as the orb made of energy shot from his hand and quickly went in the direction he had been pointing.

The orb made it to the falling Semaj in mere moments, hitting him and engulfing him in a bubble of light. Nat's eyes were as wide as Semaj's as he was no longer falling and just hovering in the air. Nat turned suddenly as she saw Thom sway, the light from his eyes fading along with the glow from the crystal. As Thom felt light headed and tried to catch his breath, Nat turned to see that Semaj was starting to descend again, but this time slowly like a leaf falling from a branch.

"We still have to get him. Move darn you," Anna said as she tapped the side of her Snowpede who, like the others had started gliding from side to side as more large snow balls came hurling at them.

"We have to," was all Essej got out when two very large boulders of snow hit him and his Snowpede causing them to be pushed off towards the side of the mountains and out of sight.

"Who's throwing those?" Thom asked as he finally regained his strength and tried to spot any signs of Essej or their attackers.

"I don't believe it. I thought she was just a story my mom made up to scare us from ever wanting to wonder off into the mountains," Lorax said as his eyes finally locked onto a form in the distance.

"What is that?" Nat asked as she saw what looked like a Snogre but almost five times their size, very hairy and a darker hue standing upon a large cliff on the side of one of the mountains.

"That's Edopha, queen of the Snogres. She's as mean as they come and I'm sure she's going to do everything she can to keep us from reaching the safety of the Frosted Waters." Lorax said as he eyed the monstrous queen.

"You declare war this day!" Edopha shouted as she, with ease of picking up a flower, scooped up and formed a very large boulder of snow and hurled it at them.

"If she's here, that means there must be dozens or more Snogres down below and on the ground," Lorax said as they realized landing or even falling close to the ground could not be an option.

"Where are you going?" Thom asked as he turned to see Nat rub the side of the Snowpede causing the hairs to release their hold on her.

"You deal with that thing, I'll go get your friend," Nat said as she stood up and started running.

She didn't know why, but something seemed to draw her to him, like a familiarity. She ran as fast as she could till she reached the back end of the Snowpede and then dove off the creature. Nat cut through the sky as she then twisted, flipped and somersaulted until she landed with amazing grace on a one knee crouched position upon the back of another Snowpede. Without hesitation, she ran up the length of the body till she was in front of Anna then sat down allowing the hairs to attach and secure her to the Snowpede.

"Excuse me," Anna started and then was silenced by look she received from the Wild Elf.

"Not now, or your friend will die," Nat said as she laid her hand upon the body of the Snowpede and whispered for it to dive towards Semaj.

Thom felt better as he watched Nat and Anna gliding down towards his best friend. This allowed him to focus on the task at hand, take down the Queen of the Snogres. He lost sight of where the Dwarves had gone but he assumed they went looking for Essej. It was up to him. Thom swallowed hard as his Snowpede swayed back and forth dodging large snow balls as it moved a little closer to the queen.

The beast was not only large but had to be the ugliest looking creature he had seen so far on this journey. She had two large sharp fangs sticking up and out of her mouth as well as two going out and down. She had a large nose and her face, like her body, was completely covered in hair. She took one look at him and growled a hideous sound and he could almost smell her bad breath from where he sat upon his Snowpede.

"I know Dwarves are with you and help you attack my warriors. The truce is no more," Queen Edopha, leader of the Snogres, declared as she bent down to scoop up more snow from the mountain side.

Thom glanced and knew it was a long way down to the ground from this high up. He had to do something, but knew he had to not go all out as big bouts of magic drained him. He looked at the ledge the queen was standing on and got an idea. As he touched his crystal it began to glow. This time he concentrated on what he wanted to do Words began to form in his mind and he listened and stared at the ugly beast in front of him.

"What you do?" Edopha asked pausing in confusion as she saw the boy's eyes glowing along with an object around his neck.

"Athe Ltme Het Owsn!" Thom shouted as he waved his right arm in a sweeping motion in front of him from left to right.

A strange wave of heat soared out from his arm and headed towards the Snogre Queen. As soon as the heated energy hit the ground, the Snogre Queen started hopping in the air to avoid her feet being burned. As she hopped, the remaining heat caused the snow on the ledge to melt and become slippery. Edopha screamed as she tried to keep her balance and not fall off the edge. Thom's magic faded and he started to form another spell when a small burst of wind came from nowhere and gave the Snogre Queen the needed nudge to send her falling off the ledge and down to the ground below.

"That takes care of her," Noraxa said as Thom turned to see the two Dwarves flying back from around the mountain upon their Snowpede with Essej standing behind them.

Nat and Anna were oblivious to what was going on with Thom and the Snogre Queen as they moved quickly towards the slowly falling Semaj. Nat noticed that Thom's magic was starting to wear off as Semaj was descending a little faster. Nat got the Snowpede to dive under Semaj as Anna reached up and helped pull him safely onto the back of their flying creature. "Thanks," Semaj said with relief.

"Glad you're okay," Anna said hugging Semaj tight as Nat instructed the Snowpede to glide around the edge of a mountain clearing so they could navigate back up and over to where the others were in battle.

"That was some fancy work there, saving my life again," Semaj said as he pushed back from Anna and called over to his new friend, the Wild Elf.

"Someone had to save you," Nat began to say when a loud screeching noise pierced their ears causing the riders to cup them as the Snowpede whipped about in agony before sending them crashing down upon a clearing that resided between two mountain peaks.

"Anna? Nat?" Semaj called out as soon as he was thrown from the Snowpede and hit the snowy ground.

"I'm over here," Nat said as she climbed out of a snowbank and walked his way.

"Any sign of Anna?" Semaj asked looking frantically as there was no sign of his friend or the creature they had been riding upon.

"No, but whatever made that sound caused the Snowpede to burrow back down into the ground. There's no way to call it back," Nat said as she tried to see who attacked them.

They felt a slight puffing of wind as a shadow fell upon them. The two of them looked up to see a very large bat-like creature with black fur that shimmered like steel with large wings beating back and forth to keep it airborne. The creature's eyes glowed red like fire to match the red stripes running across its wings. Semaj noticed sharp talon like claws on the tips of its hind legs. It was when the creature made a strange clicking noise that he realized there was a figure sitting upon its back.

"Drocana," Nat whispered as she made eye contact with the figure that slid the hood of her cloak back to reveal her face.

The woman's skin was an ashy grey color but looked smooth and glowed with beauty. Her long hair was dark black with red streaks and tied back behind her in a braid to keep it out of her face. Semaj noticed she had pointed ears so she had to be an Elf of some kind, like Nat. Under the cloak they could almost make out her black and red armor. The female Elf stared at them with eyes of red fire.

"Natureza, always a wonderful sight, despite the color," the female Elf sitting upon the winged creature sneered.

"You know her?" Anna asked as she came walking towards them from where she had been tossed off.

"Yes, she is the Fire Elf known as Drocana and she is as dark and evil as her father," Nat said realizing that her cover might have just been blown. But then, why was she here?

"Who's her father?" Semaj asked as the female Elf on the flying creature sat up higher with pride.

"My father is the great Docanesto. Now hand over the Chosen One," Drocana demanded looking straight at Natureza.

"I'm not scared of you," Anna said as she reached for the axe to find it must have gotten lost it in the fall. With quick movement to her boots she had her daggers in her hands.

"Wait!" Nat started to say but was too late as the daggers had already left the girl's hands and flying towards the bat-like creature, making contact and then bouncing off.

"That is a Tazarian. They were magically bred. Their fur is like steel, very tough and resistant to most weapons," Nat informed her companions as she kept her eyes on Drocana. "You must go for the eyes or wings."

"Which one is it? One of the two boys or this girl?" Drocana asked as she glanced at the girl who had thrown the daggers. She knew it either had to be the one with the glowing crystal or this one. There was something about her ability to summon fire that drew Drocana to her.

"Concentrate," Anna said to herself as she focused on the heat around the Tazarian and then causing a burst of fire to erupt in front of it.

The creature made a loud screeching noise as it moved back and up, moving away from where the fire blast had occurred. Drocana, as her Tazarian flew backwards, raised her left hand as a bow made of fire materialized and then moved her right hand as if she was firing the bow. Anna gasped in surprise as three arrows made of fire formed and suddenly were released right at her.

Semaj dove at Anna, hitting her from behind and moving her out of harm's way as the arrows hit the ground beside them, vanishing in a hiss as the snow melted. Drocana screamed and the Tazarian flew at Nat, grabbed her with its feet and lifted her high up into the air. Nat struggled to free herself when she was suddenly released and fell hard into a snowbank. She turned around just as Drocana leapt off, summersaulted and landed right in front of her.

"Seems like you're getting a bit friendly with the enemy. Do they even know who you really are or that you're using your unique gift to mask your true appearance?" Drocana said as a sword made of fire formed in her hand, blade's tip almost pressed into Nat's throat. "I always suspected you weren't truly one of us."

"Are you spying on me? Does Lucian know you're out here?" Nat asked as the heat from the blade started to subside as her skin adapted and became resistant from it. Since she never became a full Fire Elf, she was very limited to what she could do with *that* power.

"You may be able to use your gift of the fire to survive the elements but my blade can still remove your head," Drocana laughed as she pushed the tip into the Wild Elf's neck enough to make her wince. "I was sent here by my father, orders of Drol Greb to see what Lucian and you were up to."

Nat stared at her attacker as she now knew Drocana was here without Lucian's knowledge. She had assumed Lucian had sent her with both his *fathers'* permission but now maybe there was something else going on. She had known Lucian since they were younger, even been together a few times. She was sure he would have said something to her if he was making a play against his father or Docanesto. She was completely loyal to Lucian. That's way she never fully swore herself to Drol and made it look as if she was a full Fire Elf.

"As instructed, I am just here to find and report back the identity of the Chosen One," Nat said as she now remembered Lucian's specific orders, to only disclose the identity to him and only him.

"So which one of them is the One?" Drocana asked pushing the blade a little further into Natureza's neck, this time causing a red mark to form.

"I don't know," Nat answered, for that was the truth. The Chosen One's identity was still unknown to her.

"All this time hanging out with them and you don't even have a hint?" Drocana asked and then smirked. "Oh, but you do have a suspicion, don't you? It's the girl with the strange fire ability, isn't it?"

Nat leaned back and closed her eyes and concentrated. Using her Wild Elf heritage to reach out to her surroundings. Nat then leaned forward, opened her eyes and smiled. Drocana opened her mouth to speak when a flock of snow birds flew right at her, causing her to step back. Not missing her opportunity, Nat swept her leg, knocking Drocana's feet out from under her. Nat then quickly leapt up onto her feet, blades extracted from the bands on her arms ready to fight as Drocana was already back up on her feet with two swords made of fire, one in each hand.

The two lunged back and forth in a match of sword play, moving and turning in circles. Nat had almost lost her bearings when she glanced back behind her and saw that she was near the edge of the mountain side. Nat knew Drocana was stronger and had more access to magic so she would have to make a calculated move if she wanted to survive this encounter.

"You'll be branded a traitor," Drocana said as she stood up, swords vanishing as she prepared her magic for a different attack.

"I only report to Lucian. I am no traitor," Nat said as she had to think fast.

"I don't know why, he is worthless," Drocana sneered as she began to call forth a spell.

"You only say that because you're jealous," Nat spat back, holding back her smile, she had her.

"Jealous, of what?" Drocana asked as she hesitated, staring at Nat intently.

"Because your father thinks of him as more of a son than he will ever of you as a daughter," Nat answered, letting her smile show though brightly.

A strange growl left Drocana's throat as she suddenly charged Nat with all her might. Waiting for this, Nat dropped to her back at the last second, using Drocana's momentum, hit and propelled her attacker up and over with her feet, sending Drocana over the edge of the mountain. Nat's smile of victory only lasted a second when Drocana surprised her by grabbing her ankle and pulled her over with her.

Using her blades, Nat plunged them forward and managed to stick them into the side of the mountain to keep her from falling to her death. She felt a short tug and pain through her arms as her body jerked from the sudden stop and from Drocana continuing to hold on to her ankle with one hand. Nat knew she had to shake her off as she nor her blades had the strength to hold the both of them for much longer.

"I will take you with," was all Nat heard when Drocana screamed and suddenly let go.

Nat glanced down and saw a fiery glow vanish from her ankle and looked up to see Anna standing there while Semaj was already on his knees extending his hand to her. "Hurry, take it. I'll pull you up."

"Thank you," was all Nat managed to say when she was safely back up on the ledge.

She stared into Semaj's eyes and suddenly felt as if something had suddenly changed. He had saved her and Drocana had tried to kill her. She was now at a crossroads with her emotions. She did not know what to say or how to explain any of this. "You saved me."

"And you saved me. We will talk more later when we get back to the others. For some reason, something in my gut makes me trust you," Semaj said as they began to head away from the ledge.

Nat felt relief until she passed Anna and heard her mumble under her breath, "but I don't."

Chapter Sixteen:
Patches & The Kingdom Of Erikson

Marcus made his way out of the underground castle where everyone else still slept but one. He winced and covered his eyes from the rising of the sun as he found their missing party member. Patches was sitting on the edge of an old sand covered fountain not far from the castle's entrance they had entered the previous day on their quest to save Bruce Peters. At first, Marcus thought the old man was alone but sitting next to him was a figure made of sand, his reborn wife, Elle.

"Come join us, my boy," Patches said without turning around.

"The others are still sleeping. I noticed you were gone and you know," Marcus mumbled as he walked up to the couple, trying not to stare at the sand woman.

"It's okay, I have always loved sticking out and being stared at," Elle said with a gritty voice as her wink made both Patches and Marcus smile.

"We should wake the others and get moving so we can reach Erikson by sundown," Patches said not wanting to move as he kept his eyes on his still beautiful wife.

"How are we going to do that?" Marcus asked as he thought of the desert, the distance and the creatures out there like the sand sharks and Sand Walkers.

"Elle here will provide us quick and safe passage out of the Desert," Patches said as he placed his hand over hers and squeezed, sand reforming to replace what broke off.

"Since I am now a part of the Desert, I can call on and control the sand itself to make it do what I need it to do," Elle said answering the question that had formed on Marcus' facial features.

To demonstrate further, Elle stood up, looked out upon the Desert's sand and sent a mental summons to it. Elle slightly raised into the air, sand swirling off her body, joining the swirling sand pulled from the ground. Raising her hand slightly, the sand on the ground in front of her lifted up and started to reshape itself into a square object. Marcus thought it looked like a floating rug made of sand. He walked over and touched it.

"I will make one for each of you to sit upon. As long as I accompany you, it will remain solid and carry you to the edge of the Drol Death Desert's southern border in no time at all," Elle explained as she looked over and saw the rest of the group emerging from the underground Vampire lair.

"We get to ride on flying carpets?" Arron asked with excitement as he ran over to the floating sand rug, touching it and waving his hand underneath it where the sand swirled rapidly to cause the rug to hover.

"Any way you can make those with a canopy to block the sun?" Korvan asked as he looked away from the sun, swaying a little and stepped back into the protection of the castle entrance.

"That'll be nice," Lija said after Elle snapped her fingers and sand flew up from the ground, merged with the sand rug forming a canopy of sorts that went from the back of the rug going up and over half way to provide shade to the rider.

"We better get moving. Don't want to risk any creatures deciding to make a visit here while the Vampires are regrouping from last night's events," Korvan said, slowly making his way to the rest of the group as the sun drained his strength.

"Thanks again for coming for me," Bruce Peters said as he walked over to the man who had been like a father to him.

"No thanks needed," Patches said as he reached in his pocket and returned Bruce's ring to him, patted him on the back and then walked over to where is wife stood leaving Bruce with his smile and to avoid getting sentimental.

It did not take long for Elle to construct six additional sand carpets giving them a total of seven. One carpet for each of them in the group and a seventh one to carry all their supplies. Elle would merge herself with the one carrying their supplies as she made an enclosed box instead of a canopy to protect it all from falling off in flight. Each of them slowly climbed aboard their floating sand rug, which remained floating above the ground even with them on it.

"After you," Patches said with a wink as Elle moved forward, commanding all the sand rugs to follow her as they made a pit stop at where they had buried their supplies before going to confront Lord Suras and save Bruce Peters.

Marcus could not believe he was sitting upon a flying carpet made of sand. As he leaned and glanced over the edge, he could see the sand swirling up and pushing forward as if it was passing the rug onto another patch of sand swirling up and then pushing forward as well. As time passed, it seemed that they moved faster and faster. Even when the occasional Sand Walker formed they were well past and out of its reach. He had no doubt they would be to the southern edge by nightfall and into the safety of the Kingdom of Erikson.

"Isn't she amazing? I think she is even keeping the sandstorms and winds from touching us," Prince Arron said as his sand rug moved closer to Marcus's rug.

"I find it a little sad," Lija added quietly as she moved along her brother's other side thinking of Patches losing his wife, getting her back but having to lose her all over again.

"What do you know about the Kingdom of Erikson? I knew very little of it even before vanishing into this place," Korvan said as he still felt a little weak despite the canopy providing some protection from the sun's rays.

"All father ever said was that they were fierce warriors. Most were mean and fearless and that they take their job serious in defending the borders to make sure nothing ever comes out of the Forest of Spirits," Marcus answered as their kingdom, being so far and cut off from the southern half of Bergonia, that much of what he knew was based on stories and assumptions.

"That is true, lad. You will not meet a more barbaric group of people," Patches said as he kept his eye on the path ahead and occasionally over to his wife.

"Have you ever been there?" Bruce Peters asked, as he himself had never heard anyone really talk of the largest kingdom in the southern part of Bergonia.

"No, just stories my father told me. I bet Prince Arron would know more being from the kingdom next to them," Patches said thinking back to his father and moving the attention away from him.

"They aren't too friendly and we don't have too many dealings with them as the Old River Gorge divides our kingdoms. There is a bridge that allows safe crossing for when my father sends men there to trade but most who go never want to return again," Arron said as he liked the attention of everyone looking to him for information. He took a deep breath and continued.

"Like Patches said, they are a barbaric people and very ruthless and strong warriors. They do not wear a lot of armor, mainly chest and back plates and steel helmets that cover the tops of their heads. They'll use anything as a weapon and kill you with it if they have to. Rumor has it one of their warriors killed a man with just a chicken feather. They stick to large battle-axes or broadswords though.

"Like all kingdoms, they outlaw magic and have the magic alarms set in place. They have zero tolerance when it comes to magic. If you are caught doing magic, associating with anyone doing magic or with some kind of magical creature they will slaughter you, no questions asked, even if you are related to the king," Arron said trying to add a dramatic flair to his story.

"They really kill their own family?" Lija asked in disbelief.

"If not, they banish them into the Forest or right into the Drol Death Desert," Patches added without looking back or saying anymore to waiting ears.

"Mostly that's the rumor as no one dares even talk about the subject in their presence," Arron said breaking the silence as he continued with his tale.

"What makes them so barbaric, in addition to their fighting, is how the kingdom is setup and run. Men dominate and are the only ones allowed to be warriors and fight. Woman must serve them and cater to all their needs. Don't worry, I or my family, especially my mom, do not believe in that," Arron said glancing towards Lija who gave him a dirty look.

"Anyways, those men who want to be warriors must train and battle for the honor to fight for the king and his kingdom. Then there are the king's elite warriors, the Death Bringers. Only the best, strongest and deadliest of warriors make this cut. These men have literally battled to the death to make this status. You never want to cross them.

"As for the king, he of course is no weak man who sits behind a crown. Rumor has it that even at his age, took down a member of the Death Bringers for disobeying him. King Merrik is not afraid to fight or show his muscle and expects no less from his sons. Which, only one of them will one day take his place," Arron said as they all sped swiftly across the sands.

"What about the queen or the princesses?" Lija asked wondering how they were treated if the men treated the woman so poorly there.

"There are no queens or princesses. From what I understand, when the selected prince, after five years of seclusion, grooming and training reaches the age of twenty-five he must start his coronation of becoming king. First, he must choose a woman to bear his heir or potential heirs. He can choose more than one woman for better odds. Then for the next five years, the women will fight and beg for the honor of being selected. Many will come to him or the king-to-be may just spot one and choose her. Those chosen will go through a five-year process of trials, tests and courtship so that only the worthiest will be picked.

"Second, he will train and battle personally with his father, the king so that he can replace him and lastly, will work personally with the master of the Death Bringers to know and gain the respect of his warriors as well as his subjects. Then, when all this has been completed, on the prince's thirtieth birthday, two things will happen.

"The selected women will go off to a secluded location where the prince will be intimate with all of them for a period of three months. After three months, the women who are with child will be moved on to another location where they will be watched over and cared for until the children are born. The women, who fail, are never seen from again.

"The last is a huge coronation a few months later as the currant king steps down and crowns his son. The former king then acts as consort to the new king and is responsible for overseeing the women and future heirs. They send out invites to all kingdoms but I'm not sure if any ever attend. After this, things move on as normal until the women all give birth to their babies," Prince Arron said as he then went quiet and looked down.

"We're not going to like this are we?" Lija asked looking over at her brother while everyone else remained silent, listening to Arron while they traveled on.

"Well, um, once the babies are born, the former king goes to inspect the children. Any that are born with defects or signs of magic or witchcraft are, along with the mother, never seen again. Any girls, along with the mothers, are tossed out. Never heard from again. The remaining male babies are watched and cared for until they reach the age of five.

"At this point, the mothers are removed and placed into servant roles around the castle and kingdom, knowing that from that point they are no longer mothers to the children and forbidden to ever acknowledge them or see them. The children then are schooled and trained until they reach the age of fifteen, where at this time, they are presented to the kingdom as the potential heirs and the king officially meets them as father and sons.

"After this, the sons compete and train to be warriors by the former king with the prize to be named sole prince and heir. When they turn twenty, they will be pitted against each other in an epic battle. Once again, it becomes a big event where all are invited to see who will become the next in line for the throne. The sons will battle nonstop until one is left standing and is proclaimed the one and only son and heir to the Erikson throne. This right is finalized by the prince battling and ending their grandfather, the former king's life," Arron said explaining the Erikson Kingdom's social structure.

"I am at a loss for words," Lija responded, almost sick to her stomach.

"Yup, sounds like nothing has changed," Patches mumbled as everyone glanced his way.

"If they are so against woman and magic, why go there? Korvan and my sister are not safe," Marcus said, having heard stories but never the full details of what the Kingdom of Erikson was truly like.

"They won't harm your sister. Most she would have to be worried about is being picked to carry the heir of the prince," Arron started to say when Lija gasped loudly.

"I don't think so!" Lija shouted looking a bit worried.

"You'll be fine. We got an invitation for the battle of the princes not long before we left Argoth. The potential princes will turn twenty next year so there is no women selection going on at this point," Arron assured Lija with a heartfelt smile.

"Korvan will have to be careful to conceal his Vampire attributes and under no circumstances use your abilities as to not risk setting off the magic alarms. They may be barbaric but they are the only ones fierce enough and hopefully willing to come to our and Sorran's aid," Patches said with a hint of nervousness in his voice.

After that, everyone sat in silence. Elle eventually informed them that they were making good time but still had a ways to travel and suggested everyone nap so they are well rested and ready for what was to come next. Marcus had trouble relaxing, as he saw his sister's worried face. Coming from such a strong and privileged family, they have really been exposed to a real dose of the real world on this journey. Even when they survive this and save their home, things would never be the same for him or his sister.

It seemed Marcus was just drifting off thinking about home when a shout woke him. The sun was almost gone as night started to take over. He did not realize he had fallen asleep or had slept for as long as he had. The sand rugs had come to a stop. He quickly looked around for danger or an attack but saw nothing. Without warning, the rugs of sand dissolved and Marcus plopped down upon the sandy ground below.

"We've arrived," Patches said as he stood beside Elle holding her hand while looking at the rest of the group.

"We made pretty good time," Bruce Peters commented as he stretched his legs from sitting so long.

"We are close to the southern border of the Drol Death Desert. I dare not move us any closer without risk of being spotted," Elle explained.

"Good thinking. Even with the haze, if they by chance saw you or us riding on flying carpets we'd be executed before we stepped upon their land," Korvan said as he looked south. It had been ages since he had stepped out of the Desert and it made him a bit nervous.

"Lija, if you and Arron could get our rations I suggest we eat something and discuss our plan and story before we cross into Erikson," Patches instructed as the two nodded and walked over to the pile of supplies.

"You're sure they'll believe our story?" Marcus asked.

"Easily, but what makes me nervous is their belief in how we crossed and survived the Desert in such a short time with our rag tag group," Patches answered with a chuckle.

"Easy, keep your story as is but leaving out the part about Suras and the Lost City of the Dead. I will be a farm hand of Patches and we'll say Elle was killed by the Drogans right before we were forced into the Desert. We all had horses and a wagon and road nonstop till we got almost to the border where we lost our horses and wagon to sand sharks," Korvan added as everyone agreed that story would be the simplest and have to work.

"I wish I could stay," Patches said as he tried to take a bite of the food Lija had handed him.

"You can't, you're still needed," Elle said as she touched her husband's face with her cold, rough fingers made of sand.

"When this is done, I promise to come back to you with a way to change this or join you," Patches said as his wife smiled and then kissed him gently on his lips.

"Love you," Elle said as she began to dissolve and fade back into the desert landscape.

"Always," Patches whispered as he wiped his eye and then turned around, "better get moving."

Patches started walking straight south as everyone else quickly divided the supplies to carry and followed him. Patches was not too worried about Vampires or sand sharks as the Desert's dead stayed clear of the border into the land of the living. The only ones not truly bound were Vampires but even they knew it would be instant death to cross over the border. The closer they got to the edge, the farther Patches and his heart got from his dear sweat Elle.

"Oh no," Lija cried as she stepped down and then hopped back.

"Well, now we know what happens to those in Arron's story," Korvan said as they saw several bones scattered across the desert's sand around them.

"Looks like we've arrived," Bruce called out as the edge could now be seen a short distance in front of them.

Patches took one last look behind him and then turned to his small group of travelers. There was a brief moment of silence as they all looked at each other. They then went over their story one last time, swallowed hard and breathed in before taking their next steps forward. Once they crossed the border, the sand instantly turned into grass beneath their feet. Once everyone emerged from the Drol Death Desert, they all paused and took in their surroundings.

"The stories of the southern kingdoms flourishing better than the north appear to be true," Marcus said as he saw the abundance of grass, trees and even a pond off in the distance.

Most of the trees had already changed to their autumn colors and the smell of rain was in the cool crisp air. The season was perfect but it would not be long before winter would take over. Patches tried to get his bearings, as there was not much around them but grass, hills, fields and trees. Elle told him that she was taking them southwest so that when they came out of the Desert they would be directly north of the capital city.

"Looks like it could rain," Patches said looking up at the dark clouds forming.

"Halt in the name of King Merrik!" A voice shouted and they all froze as several warriors stepped out from behind the trees and quickly spread out to trap them.

Just as Arron had described to them, they all looked barbaric with green highlighted armor covering their chests and back with the kingdom's crest of an "E" in the middle of their breastplate. Each of them carried either a large battle axe or broadsword. If anything, they looked mean and Marcus almost preferred battling the Vampires than facing these warriors. Everyone glanced at Patches, waiting to follow his lead.

"We," Patches began to speak when a man stepped forward, pointing his broadsword and shouted.

"Silence! Search them and take their weapons," the man interrupted, barking orders.

"Don't argue or struggle, keep quiet and let them have your weapons," Patches quickly instructed the group as three of the warriors, all sporting full bushy beards, moved towards them with weapons raised and ready.

"Be careful, I saw them come out of the Desert and no one has ever emerged from there before, well except those sent in there and tried to come back out," one of the warriors called out and then chuckled with a snide remark while making a slice motion across his throat with his finger.

One of them took weapons only letting them keep their supplies, while the second gathered them from the first while the third kept his weapon ready and inspected each of them. Patches gave up his pouches and satchel, which carried his gadgets and weapons while they took Arron, Marcus and Bruce's swords. Lija carried no weapons while Korvan did his best to keep his Vampire traits hidden. It did not take long and the three warriors moved back joining the others who had been waiting and watching.

"What do they have?" The warrior who had been shouting out commands asked of the one carrying the group's weapons.

"These are just full of what looks like gadgets, tools and stakes. The one blade is pretty weak but I've never seen anything like these two swords with red blades. I'm guessing their painted because if any of this stuff was magical the alarms would be going off," the warrior said as their leader huffed and stepped forward, looking at each of them and then addressed Patches.

"Where are you from and what were you doing in the Drol Death Desert with one of the Princes of Argoth?" The leader of the warriors demanded.

"You know me?" Arron asked surprised and then gasped as he finally recognized the large muscular man with the dark red beard and hair that stood a foot taller than all the other warriors.

"Ah, you finally recognize me? Then you know that it's my duty to know everything and everyone in this kingdom and much of the kingdoms that surround us," the leader bellowed in a voice that carried pride and induced fear.

"Who is that?" Lija whispered to Arron.

"That's Terrik, the master of the Death Bringers," Arron swallowed hard.

"We come from the Kingdom of Sorran, which has been attacked by fowl creatures as we were forced to protect Prince Arron while driven into the Desert to survive. We graciously ask for an audience with King Merrik so we can plead for his protection and help against the evil forces invading Sorran and Bergonia," Patches said as he bowed his head to the great master warrior.

"You all must be pretty tough or lucky to have crossed the Desert and lived. What makes you think I should believe you and grant your request to bother our great king?" Terrik asked glaring at the old man with one eye.

"Because the current king will want to speak to me as his father, the former King of Erikson, who should still be alive to validate, is my uncle. I am the son of Logan Erikson, brother of former King Mogran Erikson," Patches said lifting his head high as everyone stared in surprise. Patches' group was in shock at the connection and Terrik's group was shocked because of something more behind the mentioning of Patches' father's name.

"Good thing I decided to do a routine check after the training session with the potential princes. Round them up and take them to the women's holding quarters. Since it is not choosing or breeding season, they are completely empty and will be used as a holding cell for them while I rush off to inform King Merrik. Watch them and death to anyone who lets them escape," Terrik commanded as the warriors rushed the prisoners while he ran to his horse and rode off towards the south as fast as his horse could go.

"Let's go before we lose sunlight," one of the warriors said as they surrounded the party and pushed them slightly southwest as the sun began to set.

They walked a short distance before they reached the top of a hill that was high enough to let them see in the distance three areas, each completely closed off by large, tall walls of stone. The three walled areas formed a triangle pattern. There was one at the top more towards them with the other two behind that one. Between them and upon the outer area were no trees and completely barren. Marcus figured it was made that way so they could see everything going on outside and around these walled in areas.

Arron informed them that the top one was strictly for the pronounced prince. The new prince lives and trains there from the age of twenty until he turns twenty-five and is not allowed to leave until he goes to the main castle for the choosing of the women. The other two are for the chosen women and the potential heirs. The one they are going to is where the women are kept after they are chosen and until they give birth and their children reach the age of five. The other facility is where they keep the children from the time they are five until they turn twenty.

As they got closer, they could see that guards stood post in towers atop of each corner of the walled facilities. Three guards walked the perimeter of the walled facilities as well. It was clear that there was no way to get in or out of these structures without being spotted. Marcus noticed, as they got closer, every guard kept their eyes on them, almost hoping they would give them a reason. The warrior leading them to their holding area ran ahead and spoke to a perimeter guard who had come running towards them.

After a brief conversation, the guard waved towards them and the warriors surrounding the small party pushed them forwards. Everyone stayed quiet and Marcus noticed Patches had, for the first time, a very nervous look on his face. This news about Patches being related to the Erikson bloodline was surprising. Marcus wondered if his dad knew this or King Sirus himself. There was a story here and Marcus hoped the old man would spill it before they all ended up dead.

They came to the holding facility for the women and it looked just like the others, one continuous square wall made of stone, no doors or windows. Marcus was starting to wonder how you get into the place when one of the tower guards shouted out a command and a small door size section in the wall began to lower down in front of them like a drawbridge. With a shout, they were forced to step onto the lowered stone doorway and pass through the wall and into the facility behind it.

"You suppose that is where the women sleep?" Lija asked no one in particular and received no answers.

Inside the wall, exactly in the center of the area was a large, one level living quarters made out of stone. There was one door and a handful of windows along the sides but had bars to keep anyone from getting in or out. Scattered throughout the area there were trees, bushes, flowers and a small area that almost looked like a playground for toddlers. Because there was no one staying here at this point and time, it looked abandoned with no guards at all inside the walls.

"You will stay in here till we hear word back from King Merrik or Terrik," the warrior that had led them into the place said as he opened the door leading into the women's facility and then closed and locked it once they had all stepped inside.

"You two stand guard outside this door. No one gets out for any reason. The rest of us need to head back to border patrol in case there are more coming out of the Desert," a voice boomed from the outside as the small group stood facing the locked door.

"They could have at least given us something to see with," Bruce mentioned, as the only light they had was the light from the moon coming in the small windows.

Marcus noticed they were in a small room with a large table with chairs that went all the way around. It looked like the women's eating area with a space on the side for heating and preparing the food but at this time was empty and void of any knives or utensils. It was plain, as there were no flowers or decorations of any kind on the walls. Marcus walked in a little further and saw a door in the middle of the far wall. He opened it and looked in.

"What's back there?" Arron asked.

"It's a hallway, from what I can tell with little light. It must lead to all the rooms the woman and their infants stay in," Marcus answered, as directly to his left and right were two doors and when he opened the doors, they revealed a room with a bed, crib, two chairs and a table as well a couple empty shelves.

"Patches, I hate to pry and I would never dig into your personal business, but how are you related to King Merrik?" Bruce asked as the old man pulled out a chair and sat down.

"It's a story I thought forgotten and would never have to tell," Patches said rubbing his chin between his fingers.

"The simple fact that this story may or may not be the end of us, we have the right to know. I mean the minute you said your father's name, I saw the look they all gave each other," Korvan said feeling it was only fair since he had to own up to his past.

"My grandfather's name was Torran Erikson. Besides the current King, Merrik Erikson, he was the most vicious and iron fisted rulers of this kingdom. During the birth of potential heirs, a woman gave birth to my father. When the time came for naming the sons, he was named Logan and from birth, he proved to be a strong fighter.

"This made his fellow brother, Mogran very jealous and was always trying to do things to bring my father down. As the boys reached their teens, my father and Mogran were favored to be final two for the crown by their trainers. My father was even encouraged more than Mogran was and that made him furious. My father was near perfect, but he had one flaw, which led him to make one fatal mistake.

"My father found a way to sneak out of the facilities here, which is probably why they are now more guarded. Logan had met a girl and fallen in love. Not only was that forbidden, he pledged himself to her and became intimate, an act that was forbidden until the age of thirty. One night, when my father snuck out to meet his true love, my mother, she told him she was with child. Panic hit my father with this news. Unfortunately, Mogran had snuck out, followed him, and heard everything.

"Before my father could come up with a plan, Mogran had turned my parents in to the king, where they were imprisoned to await sentencing. Mogran was excited and declared that he had just secured his spot as the next prince. My father did not care. He just wanted to find a way to save his true love and unborn child. Alas, King Merrik sentenced them both to death, as an example had to be made of defying the law of the land.

"Not only was my father a strong and superior warrior, even for his young age, he was also skilled in creating gadgets. The eve of their death, he managed to escape with a gadget he fashioned in his cell to undo the cell door and blind the guards. He then grabbed a sword and led my mother to freedom, driven by pure rage and determination to keep her and his child safe. He cut down any warrior that got in his way. He had almost made it to safety when the king had sent his elite warriors after them, forcing my parents to flee towards the Drol Death Desert.

"With no hope to survive against the king and his Death Bringers, they vanished off into the Desert where no one dare follow. My father never talked much of his journey through the Desert but he said it had been a long and terrifying one. The day I was born was they day they finally emerged from the Drol Death Desert and into the Kingdom of Sorran. My father was exhausted, wounded and near death. My mother, just as injured, went into labor and used the last of her energy to scream out in pain and in fear for her unborn child.

"It was those screams that brought the aid of a very kind young couple. The man attended to my father while the woman helped deliver me. My dad lived, even though he lost the use of one of his legs and had chronic pains in his arms. I was born healthy despite only having one eye. Unfortunately my mother passed during my birth," Patches said as he stared off into the corner, as he tried to hold back the tears from his parent's story of love and loss.

"That's terrible," Lija whispered as she walked over and sat next to Patches, taking his hand in comfort.

"Go on," Bruce encouraged the man who had been like a father to him.

"Not much else to tell really. Despite my father's handicap, he did chores for the young couple in return for a place for us to stay. I grew up loved by all three and as I got older, my father taught me everything he knew about fighting, making gadgets and weapons. When I was ten, my father fell ill and passed. Before he died, my father told me all about my mom and our journey to the Kingdom of Sorran.

"On that day, I vowed revenge on King Merrik. The next day when we buried my father, I also learned that the couple that had took me in were expecting their first child. Knowing they could barely feed themselves in their small cottage, I decided to leave. I went to the great city of Sorran where I learned everything I could about fighting and prepare myself for the day I would return to Erikson to get justice for my parents. I would even sneak off into the Desert to better myself fighting its creatures," Patches said as he looked down and then at the audience in front of him.

"You didn't bring us here for revenge instead of help, did you?" Marcus asked suddenly feeling angry and betrayed.

"No, no, my boy. I let that anger and desire for revenge go a long time ago. Mind you, I had every intention of doing so when I was about twenty-five and went back to the cottage to say farewell to the couple that had took me and my father in all those years ago," Patches started to explain.

"What changed your mind?" Arron asked anxiously to hear how the story ended.

"Well, I met their daughter who had grown into a beautiful young woman," Patches started to say when a squeal interrupted him.

"It was Elle, wasn't it? Oh, and the cottage we saw was her parent's home," Lija clapped with joy.

"Yes, that was when I met my dear sweet Elle. She looked up at me and said, 'Hey Patches' and it was love at first sight. At that moment, I vowed to make something of myself and let go of my past. I returned to Sorran and worked for the king and eventually we got married and lived out our days in that cottage," Patches said with a smile full of joy and sadness.

"Then why bring us back here? If what you told us still carries weight here, they'll execute us all," Korvan said growing worried and moving towards the door.

"Stop, you go breaking out of here then we definitely are done for, especially if they discover what you are," Marcus scolded the man while keeping his voice down, fear for his sister's safety now pushing at him.

"You all need to relax, the king will help you, even for the simple fact that Prince Arron is with you. He will not pass up a chance to finally battle creatures like the Drogans. Whatever fate befalls me, you all will be safe," Patches said looking at them with a look that spoke volumes.

"You brought us here knowing you would," Lija began and then started to cry.

"My destiny was to get you to the help you needed," Patches said as he looked at the girl sitting next to him.

"No, this is not what Elle would want. She would want you to help us see this through to the end. You don't even know if your life is even in danger. Years have passed," Bruce said, but not very convincingly.

"Unfortunately, the story of your father lives on and used as an example that no one, not even an Erikson will escape their fate for breaking any of the major rules," a voice said from the shadows of the kitchen space.

They all looked over and saw a young man, maybe a little older than Marcus and Lija, step towards them. It was hard to make out his facial features but he had short hair, was clean-shaven and about the same height as Lija. He wore what looked like training attire with an "E" on the front of the chest armor. Stepping out from behind him was another boy, almost identical in appearance to the first but just a little taller with a slightly bigger build.

"Who are you?" Marcus asked as he stood up, ready to defend his sister.

"Hey, calm down, we aren't here to start a fight," the second boy said.

"How did you get in here?" Korvan asked in hopes of a secret way out.

"We were already here when the guards let you in," the first boy said as if they were the ones that had been intruded upon by the group's arrival.

"I recognize the armor, you two are potential princes. Why are you in here? I thought until you turned twenty and headed for the battle that you were locked up in the other facility?" Arron asked as he stared at the two young men.

"You guys are princes?" Lija asked trying to compose herself a little.

"Not yet, well not till next year. I'm Chadwick and this is my brother, Lark," the second boy introduced with a bit of a smile.

"I'm Marcus and this is my sister," Marcus started to return the introductions when Korvan stepped up.

"Wait, what makes you think we can trust them? They could be spies placed in here to get more details and incriminate ourselves," Korvan said as he got a strange feeling from the first boy.

"They don't know we are in here or that we have a way to sneak out of isolation. As potential princes, if they found us in here with you we'd be killed for sure," the first boy, Lark, said stepping back as he was getting an odd vibe off the man with pale skin.

"I think we can trust them," Arron said looking at the two and then to his group.

"You can. If you tell us why you are here, every detail, and promise not to out us, we won't say anything to the guards," Chadwick assured them.

"I don't know. What makes you so sure we won't tell them you are in here?" Korvan asked as he locked eyes with the one named Lark.

"Well, as sure as we won't tell them you are a Vampire of some sort," Lark said without blinking or flinching.

"How," Korvan began to say when Patches stood and held his hand up.

"We've snuck out enough and been into the Desert to know what one is and your reaction just confirmed our guess," Chadwick said ready to challenge whatever the man in front of them was.

"They call me Patches," the old man with an eye patch said stepping between his group and the two young men and eyeing them carefully and then smiled with a nod allowing the rest of the group to continue with introductions. Then, with a brief pause and encouragement from Patches, Marcus and Lija told them everything.

"Lark," Chadwick turned to his brother in excitement after the story but the look he received from his brother stopped him.

"I assure you, that when you meet King Merrik, if you tell him about the Drogans but leave out some of the details about your friends and the magical stuff, he will help you. He may even let most of you leave here," Lark said cutting off his brother while turning his gaze to Korvan and then sadly to Patches.

"Now, about you two," Korvan started to say as there was more he needed to know when a strange sound could be heard outside.

"We have to go," Chadwick said.

"Good luck. Your secrets are safe," Lark said as he grabbed his brother and slipped into a room next to the kitchen area.

"Where'd they go?" Marcus asked as he and Korvan followed to find the room was empty with a large hole for waste.

"Better get some shuteye, dawn will be here soon enough," Patches said as he headed off to a room to sleep in, leaving the others to stare at the empty room in confusion.

Chapter Seventeen:
Ogra

A sudden warmth and brightness caused Lucian to jerk awake. He looked up and saw the sun rising, it was morning. He began to feel sleep reaching out for him when a brisk chill snapped him back awake. He sat up and realized he had been lying on ice. Not just regular ice, he was sitting upon the frozen water of the Frosted Waters. Clothes damp, his bag of supplies and stuff gone and needing to warm up, Lucian muttered a word of magic and felt a wave of heat flow through his body. The spell may not last long but would be enough to keep him alive without risk of melting the ice below his feet.

With a little struggle, Lucian stood up and looked around as he tried to piece things together. The last thing he remembered before blacking out was Gabrielle still on her ship as the sea creature and the tidal wave struck it. He knew a Drogan had lifted him up, but not before the tidal wave hit causing him to black out from the impact and shock of the cold. He tried to dig deeper into his memory but paused when he saw a body lying a few feet from him. He could not tell whom it belonged to and carefully made his way over to it.

"Just you," Lucian said in relief when he saw it was the Drogan and not any of his friends.

Lucian saw one wing stretched out, torn and broken with no sign of the other one. The creature must have suffered grave wounds against the wave, but managed to get Lucian to safety before dying. As Lucian bent down and removed the creature's sword, he looked around for any other signs of life or bodies. There was nothing. No sign of his friends, Gabrielle or anyone. He was all alone upon the Frosted Waters with no sense of what lay in what direction. If he went the wrong way, it would certainly be a death sentence. He also knew staying here, cold and in the middle of nowhere, would be the end of him, despite his magic.

Thanks to his magic, the cold and empty howl of the wind was tolerable. His spell had done its job, for now. His clothes were dry and heat was flowing around and through his body. He had to figure out which direction to go and start walking. Lucian closed his eyes and tried to concentrate, tuning out the wind. He was about to give up when he felt a split second tug behind him. He turned and found nothing. Had he just imagined it? With a shrug and trusting his gut, Lucian began walking in the direction the tug had pulled him in.

Lucian walked and walked, for what seemed like hours. Whether it was because he was afraid of falling through the ice or just growing tired, each one of his steps was getting slower and slower. He felt the heat spell wear off and feared the strength needed to cast another one may not be within him. He came to a stop when he heard a strange growl from behind. Lucian turned around to see a fast moving beast coming right at him. At this point, Lucian welcomed death be it beast or the cold and dropped to his knees and closed his eyes.

He could feel the breath of the creature on his face. He welcomed the pain of being torn apart so as to feel something other than the cold. When the creature bit down on him, Lucian was surprised when he felt the teeth snag his shirt instead of his flesh. With force, the creature yanked him up on his feet causing Lucian to open his eyes and look at something very familiar. "Frrr!" Lucian yelled as he hugged his Fire Hound and friend.

Frrr growled as Lucian stepped back and looked at the large beast, guilt washing over him for leaving him behind. "How?"

"There he is," a voice called out from behind his fury friend.

Lucian looked past Frrr to see six figures riding upon the backs of six other hounds coming right towards him. Straining his eyes, he noticed that three of the riders were Fire Elves, two were *Ghost* crewmembers and the final lead rider was a patch-wearing pirate. "You made it," Lucian said more to himself as he stepped past Frrr.

"Lucian, I feared the worst when we saw the dead Drogan," Gabrielle said as the party of riders came to a stop in front of the man they had been looking for.

"I thought I was the only survivor. Last I remember…how did you survive?" Lucian asked as the woman dismounted and walked towards him.

"Can't get rid of me that easily," the captain of the *Ghost* smiled.

"Is this all of you?" Lucian asked as he looked past her to see if any more figures were coming, but nothing, they were all there was.

"There are a few of my crewmen still alive, back at the ship working on repairs," Gabrielle said as she handed some food to Lucian and a fur coat to wear for warmth that matched the one she and her men wore.

"Your ship survived a double attack?" Lucian was impressed.

"Only thanks to Besse. It appears she wasn't attacking the ship. She was only trying to reach us in time. If it weren't for her grip on my ship, the wave would have destroyed the *Ghost*. Besse held tight and the ship remained whole for the most part and upright," Gabrielle answered, and then when Lucian took a bite of his food, she continued.

"When that tidal wave hit I saw you vanish within the water but before I could see if you and the Drogan had pulled free, I was knocked over by the wave. Luckily, a Drogan caught me and started to lift me up. I thought I was in the clear but something hit the Drogan and we went down, hitting hard upon the ship's deck. I got up, but I couldn't see where the Drogan had gone.

"I tried to get my footing, but an after wave tipped the ship and sent me towards the edge. A Fire Elf quickly had a rope around my waste saving my life as he took my fate and went overboard. I held onto the rope and soon the wave settled and my ship finally stopped moving," Gabrielle finished.

"And you came looking for me?" Lucian asked, locking his eyes with her and not looking away.

"Not intentionally," she teased, "it seemed the wave pushed the ship quite a distance forward and then Besse dragged the *Ghost* till we hit the edge of the Frosted Waters. She then let go and vanished back into the waters. I realized my ship was in bad shape with only a handful of survivors, including six of your Fire Hounds, three Fire Elves and your pet there who immediately dove off the ship and raced off.

"I pulled out my scope and when I looked out I saw a figure on the ground off in the distance, too far to see what it was. I knew we needed supplies to rebuild my ship, which we could gather in Ogra, so I left what remained of my crew to start repairs except two. We mounted the Fire Hounds and headed out. When we got to the body, we saw it was the Drogan that had carried you away. I also noticed footprints leading in this direction. We pushed onward in hopes of finding you," Gabrielle said as her fingers had grazed Lucian's hand.

"What about my friends?" Lucian asked thinking of Sev, Fylla and Aksurh.

"No, sorry," Gabrielle started to answer when Lucian turned from her and mounted Frrr.

"Looks like we're headed this way then," Lucian said as he pushed Frrr in the direction he was originally going and his Fire Elves followed.

"After you," Gabrielle shook her head as she leapt up upon her Fire Hound and followed after with her two crewmembers.

They quickly covered the distance north upon the Frosted Water between the Eastern Sea and the land of Ogra. They were half way there when Lucian started to see the Western Mountains rising above the horizon on the western edge of Ogra. To the east was nothing but flat lands and some hills. Gabrielle raised her telescope to her eye patch, raising her hooked hand signaling them to stop. Lucian defiantly had to find out more about her and her toys.

"That thing lets you see farther?" Lucian asked moving Frrr up beside the woman.

"Among other things," Gabrielle smirked as she moved the scope side to side.

"What do you know about Ogra?" Lucian asked, as his knowledge of the land of Ogres was very little.

"Just what information I have gathered over the years from other pirates and sea travelers. The Western Mountains are the home of the Ogres. They are large, mean, strong and very dangerous. Rumor has it that there is no snow there because the Frosted Waters pull all its cold from them making them and most of Ogra dry, humid and rainy from time to time. The Ogres mainly stay in the mountains but some of the smaller ones tend to come out to hunt and scavenge for food but rarely venture too far away from the mountains.

"The land more central to northeast of the mountains is more marsh country, made up of marshes, mud and swamps. Various ugly and nasty creatures populate this area. The most common are the Goblins and Hobgoblins. To the very northeast of Ogra is a higher class of creatures calling themselves Gooblyns. They are basically Goblins but more intelligent and civilized than their cousins, but not by much. They live in what they call the Gooblyn City, which is ruled by their master, King Snoog.

"Mind you, this is all just what I've gathered and not knowing much more details or how true any of it is. One aspect I do know, just because they do some trading with pirates, is the Orgites Colony of the southeast lands of Ogra," Gabrielle informed as she placed her scope away and turned to look at Lucian.

"Orgites? I have not heard of them at all," Lucian said, as they slowly started moving forward again.

"They are descended somehow from the Ogres. Some think they are half human and half Ogre. They have many of the same features of an Ogre, like strength, but are only about eight feet tall and have a stronger intellect. They have built a very tall and impenetrable wall that closes them off and keeps them safe from the Ogres and other fowl creatures living on Ogra. The Frosted Waters actually end and turn to slush right where their wall and land touch the edge of the Eastern Sea," Gabrielle answered as Lucian saw the ice below them start to soften and turn to slushy water as they got closer and veered more to the west to stay upon more frozen footing.

"Are you planning to get your supplies from the Orgite Colony?" Lucian asked.

"It is the safest place for us to go. They are friendlier, as in, they will talk first before attacking. From what I'm told, they have a king and queen but it's the queen that makes the rules. Queen Ola and her mate, Oltar. We will seek an audience with Ola," Gabrielle confirmed her plan. "Where are you headed once there?"

"I'm not sure. There are one or more people I am looking for but not really sure where they are located. I just know they are on the land of Ogra," Lucian said as he tried to remember the fading dream and could not remember what manor of creature or creatures held the title of Magestic.

"If you don't mind, we can both start with the Orgites," Gabrielle offered with a smile, "unless you're ready to be rid of my company." Lucian smiled back and nodded.

"Wouldn't it be safer to enter through the slush and water than Ogre country?" Lucian asked as they were soon to the border where the ice touched Ogra.

"Only those with approved access can take that small route in. If we want access, to be trusted and not cause unwanted problems, we have to enter though the proper outer gates," Gabrielle said as she stopped her Fire Hound.

Lucian stopped next to the woman and glanced at the new land ahead of him. Ogra, he had made it. Where they had stopped placed them right in the middle. To his left he saw the massive mountains that made up the Western Mountains of Ogra. To his right was a very large wall that stretched from the Frosted Waters and headed straight north for as far as he could see. He could tell the wall was made of an unfamiliar material, but it appeared to be solid and sturdy. Directly in front of them was grass and mud, which led straight into more of the same with areas of swamp and marsh according to Gabrielle. He looked at the mud and, "look!"

"What is it?" Gabrielle asked as Lucian leapt from Frrr and knelt down to look at the muddy ground, the Fire Elves instantly by his side, bows drawn.

"Foot prints, four sets. Looking at the size and pattern, I would almost bet they belong to Fylla, Aksurh and their Drogans," Lucian said as the Elves looked and nodded in confirmation.

"Appears there was a struggle not far from here," one of the Fire Elves said kneeling down and looking further ahead.

"There was, the Goblins took them prisoner," a voice said causing Lucian to stand up and see a small form approach, and then take on a more human size.

"Sev," Lucian exhaled as the Fairy had moved right into his arms, hugging him and kissing him tight.

"What happened?" Gabrielle asked clearing her throat causing Lucian to break contact and step back a little from Sev.

"After you gave the order for the Drogans to grab everyone," Sev started and noticed an accusing look shot his way from the female pirate, causing him to hesitate, which generated another look from his lover. Taking in a deep breath he quickly continued.

"I flew as high up as I could to avoid the water that would surely drown me. I saw two Drogans fly off with Fylla and Aksurh. I started to follow and then stopped to look for you, Lucian. I saw the water hit you and then realized I was too close and my wings got wet. I thought I was done for but Fylla's Drogan came back around and caught me.

"I stayed small so the Drogan could carry me and before I knew it we were at the edge of Ogra. The Drogans were too afraid of falling though the ice to land on it, so went for dry land. I remember Fylla demanding to go back and look for you, but the Drogans wouldn't listen. Once we touched down I grew in size since my wings were wet and I was too weak to fly," Sev said with an apologetic look on his face.

"It's okay, you wouldn't have made it on your own crossing back across the Frosted Waters," Lucian said touching Sev's cheek and then got serious. "What happened to the others?"

"We were standing here, arguing about what to do when we heard a loud thump and Aksurh went face first to the ground. Before we knew it, we were surrounded. Fylla wanted to fight but they had Aksurh and I thought it wise to wait, maybe they would take us to you. She reluctantly agreed as they took us prisoner and led us off to the north. I waited until I was sure where they were headed and then shrunk down and bolted back to look for help. That's when I stumbled upon you guys. I have no idea if they followed me or not," Sev said just caring that he was with Lucian again.

"Can you lead us back to where they were taken?" Lucian asked.

"Yes, if you want," Sev answered with a little hesitation in his voice.

"I don't think it is a good idea," Gabrielle said shocking both Sev and Lucian.

"We can't leave them to the Goblins," Lucian said growing angry.

"I'm not saying that. We need to get to the safety of the Orgites first, before it gets dark. I would rather face an Ogre in the daytime than a heard of those creatures at night," Gabrielle countered.

"Why is that?" Sev asked.

"Because you can see the Ogres coming," Gabrielle answered as she got her Fire Hound and headed towards the north, parallel to the wall, in the direction of the main gate.

"As much as I hate to say this, she's right. We should get to the safety behind that wall. Fylla is tough and she has a Giant with her. They'll be safe till morning," Sev said as Lucian finally agreed and urged his group to continue on after Gabrielle.

Lucian was starting to sweat, it may be getting close to the winter season but here it was warm and humid. Lucian was used to the hot but where he was from it was more of a pure dry heat, this was slightly different. It was this humid moisture that contributed to the wet lands of this country. He could hear the slap of mud as the Fire Hounds moved through the mud and marsh.

"We're being watched," a Fire Elf called over to their master.

"I see them," Lucian said as he glanced up and saw a shape moving along the top of the large wall.

"No, not them, over there," the Fire Elf nodded to his left causing Lucian to glance over towards the mountains where he saw a very large creature, skin a mix of green and brown standing behind a bolder on the side of the mountain. It was a good distance away so it was hard to tell just how big the creature actually was.

"Don't worry, the sun will be setting soon. The Ogres prefer only coming out during the day. They are probably just watching us, taking inventory," Gabrielle said as she finally saw the front gate ahead and would be grateful to get behind those walls before dark fell.

"State your business," a voice came from above them.

They all looked up to see several figures standing atop the large wall, many holding large rocks above their heads, waiting.

"I am Captain Greybeard, of the *Ghost*. My ship was attacked by sea pirates and a sea monster. It is stranded up against the Frosted Waters' edge. I am here seeking supplies to repair my ship," Gabrielle called out as she moved forward to place herself well ahead of her group.

"We have heard…stories of you and your ship…you look much thinner and less hairy," one of the Orgites said looking down puzzled.

"That was my father who had dealings with you. I'm captain now and ask entrance," Gabrielle responded bowing her head slightly.

"We will consult with the queen," the Orgite said and vanished.

"Now what?" Sev asked.

"We wait and hope they let us in," Gabrielle said keeping her eyes strictly on the gate that was made of the same material as the wall and just as solid.

"If they don't?" Sev asked mockingly at the female pirate.

"That won't be an option," Lucian answered with a smirk.

"Give the word and we can force our way in," the Fire Elves said, rallying behind their master who held his hand up in a hold and wait motion as he kept his eyes on Gabrielle and the gate.

After a little time had passed the Orgite returned and this time dozens of other Orgites appeared all along the wall with large rocks raised above their heads. Sev began to panic but Lucian knew those rocks were not for them, they were for anything else that might want to follow them into the colony beyond the wall. Lucian was correct as a strange loud noise rumbled from the gate as it began to swing inwards allowing them passage. The Orgite shouted one last command before vanishing from the top of the wall. "Hurry."

Gabrielle had her two crewmen go first followed by a Fire Elf. Gabrielle, Lucian and Sev followed next as the last two Fire Elves brought up the rear. Each of them stayed on their Fire Hound and made sure they moved cautiously and slowly through the gate and into the Orgite Colony beyond the protected walls.

Once they were in, the gate began to rumble as it closed quickly behind them thanks to the assistance of a few Orgites turning a wheel contraption that made the gate open and close.

Lucian looked around and saw on both sides of the wall that there were stone steps that lead up to the top, spaced evenly apart, so that the Orgites could easily go up and down at any point or distance. The Orgite that had first spoken to them was already down and on her way to them with a group of ten other Orgites, each carrying a large stone like shield in one hand and a large weapon made out stone and cut to serve as both a sword or throwing spear.

As they got closer Lucian could tell they were descended from the Ogres but with a few minor differences. They all averaged about eight feet tall, less than half the height of an average Ogre. Because they were shorter, they looked more plump than muscular but still displayed strength. Their skin was more of a lighter green with a touch of pink hue to it. They had strange ears, smaller than a human and, unlike the Ogres, had hair. The males had brown and the females had a darker blond color. Their outfits looked similar to what humans wore, but not as well cleaned.

"Queen Ola has agreed to see you, but only you two humans. The furry beasts and Elves must remain here with the other humans," the female Orgite said glancing at the Fire Hounds, Elves and Gabrielle's crewmen.

"We must go," a Fire Elf started to protest making the Orgite guards grumble and raise their weapons.

"I'll be fine. If I need you I'll let you know," Lucian said with a smirk as Sev, before entering the gate, had quickly shrunk down and hid underneath Lucian's shirt.

Lucian and Gabrielle slid off their hounds and followed after the female Orgite as a few of the guards followed behind them leaving the rest to watch over the remainder of the group. No one spoke as they moved away from the gate and headed into the heart of the Orgite Colony. Lucian kept his eyes open and took everything in. He was amazed at what these creatures had built.

Just like any of the upper races, they had their own livable community. Dwellings to live in, land where they grew food, even shops and what Lucian thought looked like a school of sorts. They were definitely more civilized than Ogres or similar creatures. As they made their way to the center of the colony where a large castle was built, Lucian saw several Orgites going around and lighting lanterns throughout the area to provide light as the sun started to set.

They eventually made it to the castle were a male Orgite, dressed in what looked like royal attire, cleaner and brighter colors along with a crown on his head made out of stone. He had a big smile and opened his arms wide as they approached him. The female Orgite and the guards behind them took a stance, ready to protect the male Orgite if needed.

"Welcome to the Orgite Colony. I'm King Oltar and I will escort you to my wife," the Orgite said in a voice that Lucian thought was slow and groggy but still understandable and articulate.

"I'm Lucian," Lucian introduced himself, feeling a strange vibe coming from the king as he reached up and shook his glove covered hands, and from the expression on his face, the king felt it too.

"Captain Greybeard," Gabrielle said extending her hand trying to be more formal.

"Nice to meet you Gabrielle, your father was an honorable man," King Oltar said with a smile as he took and patted the top of her hand then released it quickly. "This way."

Lucian looked around and saw the castle was simple and mainly made of stone and the stuff the outside wall appeared to be made out of. He was not sure what the material was but he made note that it might be worth looking into later. They were led straight down a corridor until they reached a set of large stone doors. Two Orgite guards pulled open the doors while bowing to the king. They all stepped into a large room lit up by dozens of candles and torches. The room was simple as well with not much decorations but housed two large stone thrones where one was occupied by a female Orgite wearing a nice dress and a stone crown atop her nice long brownish blond hair.

"I present to you, my wife, Queen Ola," Oltar said bowing to the female Orgite.

"Your majesty," Gabrielle said as she bowed and then reached over, yanking Lucian into a bow as well, who gave back a look that could kill. Gabrielle gave him a little wink and that seemed to soften his scowl towards her.

"Gabrielle, I only granted you this audience because of our honorable dealings with your father. Sorry to hear of his passing, he was a good man," Queen Ola said in the same slow speech patterns as all the Orgites.

"Thank you, your majesty. I come here as my ship was badly damaged while at sea. I hoped to secure the supplies I need to repair my ship," Gabrielle said as the queen seemed to be staring only at Lucian.

"What of this man with you and the company you keep?" Queen Ola asked referring to the hounds and Elves.

"I am Lucian," he said as he stepped forward, calculating what to say or reveal to the Orgite Queen. "The hounds and Elves are part of my party that hired Captain Greybeard to bring us to your great land."

The queen didn't speak but the king, who took a seat in the second throne motioned for him to continue on. "I come from the Unknown Lands, where my father and many of the magical beings and creatures of Bergonia had been banished by the magic hating humans, now isolated like yourselves. We have learned of a being calling himself the Chosen One who is on a journey to find a select few beings that have the power to once again wage war upon the creatures of magic and those who are not human or support them.

"I came here because two of these Magestics are on Ogra and I hope to find them and save them before the Chosen One finds them and turns them evil. I hope to find them first and get them to join me in the fight to save and give Bergonia back to creatures of magic. Unfortunately, some of my friends have been kidnapped by the Goblins and I must try and rescue them," Lucian finished with a slight forced bow while noticing that Oltar was fidgeting and staring at him with wide eyes.

Queen Ola stared at him for a little bit before addressing them. "We've worked hard to keep the peace and separate us from the Ogres, Gooblyns and other uncivilized creatures out there. With the exception of trading, we do not concern ourselves with the affairs of the humans and outside world."

"But," Lucian began and stopped when Gabrielle and the king shot him a look. His first thought was to teach them not to silence him but gained control and bit his tongue. He was on a mission and now was not the time to be aggressive.

"Captain Greybeard, we will work out a trade with you for the supplies you need, as for you Lucian, we can't afford to assist you in risk of causing war with the other colonies. We will give you food and supplies but then you will need to be on your way at dawn's first light," Queen Ola said and then dismissed them with a wave.

"Thank you, your majesty," Gabrielle said with a bow as they were soon escorted from the room by the king.

"She is a very giving and loving queen, but she, like many of us, do not wish to risk what we've created here," King Oltar apologized.

"As someone who has lived in isolation and forcibly cut off from the rest of the world, don't you think it would be better to have the freedom to go where you want, when you want?" Lucian asked as he still felt a strange vibe coming from this creature.

"I," the Orgite King started to say and then stopped pointing to a room. "Here you can stay for the night until you make arrangements in the morning for supplies and then leave."

"That got us nowhere," Sev said flying out from under Lucian's shirt once the king left and closed the door. "Should've dropped your father's names and forced their help."

"I don't think that would have worked at all," Gabrielle said as she looked around the medium sized room with two beds made of stone and a few candles to give them added light to the moon's light from the small window.

"Gabrielle's right, forcing them would make me no different than the evil of the Chosen One. We are here to find the Magestics and can't compromise our mission. I have no doubt we will win over the Orgites and all the creatures of Ogra to our side. First, we have to rescue our friends. Sev, alert the others we leave at first light," Lucian declared as Sev gave a nasty look to Gabrielle and then shrunk down and flew out the window.

"You must really care for your friends to go save them," Gabrielle said as she looked over at Lucian.

"They are my friends, yes, but the mission comes first. I think I've found what I was looking for here and now I am getting this pull to the north. I think the other Magestic I am looking for just happens to be where my friends were taken," Lucian said trying not to sound sentimental.

"I find loyalty honorable and sexy," Gabrielle flirted as she smiled and stepped a little closer.

"Will you join us or will you stay here?" Lucian asked, changing the subject and trying not to notice the beautiful woman moving closer to him.

"I need the repairs done on my ship, my two crewmen could be capable enough of getting what I need and taking it back to the ship," Gabrielle said pausing and looking coy at Lucian, "that is, if I could be persuaded."

Lucian looked at the captain, her mysterious eyepatch and bag of treasures she kept at her side and then back to her beautiful lips. There was something about this woman and she could be very useful where they were going, let alone securing her ship to stay as well. "I think I could persuade you," Lucian said as he grabbed her into his arms and kissed her hard, moving her towards the bed.

"I need to try a little harder next time," Sev swore to himself as he glared at the captain, who had managed to survive her calculated death upon the *Ghost,* before finally leaving to report Lucian's orders to the others.

****

Docanesto moved as fast as he could. He had already sent a messenger on ahead so the four witches would have the portal opened before he got there. He had to give an update to his master Drol Greb before moving on to his next mission. They had wanted to move up the time line but had held back to see what developed in the Northern Mountains and with Lucian. He finally entered the secret chamber and saw the image of Drol

Greb emerging from the portal with his messenger lying dead at the witch sister's feet.

"Docanesto, what do you have to report?" The image of Drol Greb's face asked immediately.

"There has been a little resistance but much of the Kingdom of Sorran is under General Vex and the Drogan's control. They just wait word to launch an attack upon the capital city itself," Docanesto began.

"What of our ally?" Drol Grab asked.

"Gone out of the castle. With the commotion of the Prince of Argoth being *kidnapped* and the Giant sighting, she had to return back to Argoth," Docanesto answered.

"We could have used her in the castle but will deal with that later. No sign of the prince and his captors?"

"No, they never came back out of the Desert and we have Drogans using the old man's cottage as a look out. Only chance is if they made it to Erikson or Silversword."

"They're as good as dead. No one would be able to survive crossing that desert, especially an old couple and three inexperienced kids. What about the Chosen One? What's to report from the Northern Mountains?"

"Seems Lucian's spy, Natureza has befriended and joined the group. It appears that two Dwarves have joined their party and they are headed towards where the Eastern Mountains end and the Frosted Waters begin. It looks as if they might be headed to Ogra."

"Has your daughter or Natureza identified the Chosen One?"

"My daughter thinks Lucian's spy is going soft. It seems the female Dwarf that is with them can cause the earth to shake. There is a girl and two boys about Lucian's age still with Essej. One boy does nothing while the girl masters fire and the other boy performs what looks like magic. My daughter thinks it's one of the latter two we are searching for."

"The girl with fire and the Dwarf are Magestics. I bet the boy using magic is the Chosen One. Tell your daughter to bring the Chosen One in and kill all the others, including Lucian's so-called spy."

"I will," Docanesto bowed afraid to tell his master that against his wishes his daughter had already decided to engage the group and he has not been able to contact her since. He will give her a little more time before he worries or alerts his master.

"What of Lucian?" Drol Greb asked as his eyes burned with intensity.

"I've finally heard from our spy. The pirate Greybeard, her ship was attacked at sea and was all but destroyed. It seems the survivors have made it to Ogra. Some have been kidnapped by the Goblins while Lucian, Greybeard and the others are within the Orgite Colony's secured walls. Lucian plans to go rescue those that are kidnapped. Lucian believes he has found one Magestic and will be in pursuit of the second," Docanesto responded as he found it hard to read his master's expressions or mood.

"I am pleased, the boy has made it farther than I thought he would and may even get the Magestics before the Chosen One. Get word to the Gooblyn King with my thanks for taking Lucian's companions in and give strict orders that my son is not to be harmed. Get word to General Vex to stand ready with his forces and do nothing to setoff those magic alarms or tip off King Sirus. As for your mission, proceed as it's time we get our hands on those items," Drol Greb instructed and then faded away when finished, leaving Docanesto, moving as fast as he could to carry out his orders.

Chapter Eighteen:
The Isolation Of Tallus

Stephanie Tallus sat in her room staring out the window that over looked the great city named after her ancestors. Ever since she was little she daydreamed of traveling all over Bergonia, not so much looking for adventure but to see the world, meet other people or even help them if she could. Of course, living in the great Kingdom of Tallus, you were shut off from the rest of the kingdoms thanks to her great something grandfather. She forgot the family tree as history tended to bore her.

From what her father, King Stephan, whom she and her twin brother Steffon were named after, told her was that a long time ago that the reigning King of Tallus had decided to isolate the kingdom from the rest of the world to protect it and keep it safe. The king had a large wall constructed along the borders of Sorran and Silversword as well as the section that ran against the Drol Death Desert. The wall was very strong and built very high so that no one could ever get in or out of Tallus, except for two controlled locations.

There were mountains located along their northern border but they were taller than the wall and nothing ever came down from there. Then on their western border was the Western Sea. Tallus was more of a sea fairing kingdom and controlled most of the waters where they did their fishing. Some trading was done as there were a select few that were trained and stationed to watch the seas and run the sea operations from the port city of Tallut. Except those living in the port city, everyone in the kingdom was truly isolated.

Stephanie did not hate where she lived as it was a very rich and thriving kingdom. The only difference she really knew of from the other kingdoms was that her father, King Tallus, like his father before him and so on, did not have as strict of rules regarding magic. Magic was forbidden and if caught using it you would be tried and banished out to sea but as far as she knew, that had never happened as no one ever talked about it or tried using it.

If someone did, no one would know it as the Kings of Tallus secretly had the magic alarms deactivated. Not so people could use magic, but so the people would never find out the deep dark secret the king kept. Magic alarms do not go off in the presence of magical creatures, only if they use magic. King Stephen knew this but was not willing to take that chance. There would be an uproar if the subjects of Tallus were to find out that in the Kingdom of Tallus, the magical creatures known as Minotaurs were housed and used as slaves in the mines.

Stephanie hated this and cried at night wishing she could help them, but she could never say anything or let anyone know that she knew they existed. The only reason she knew, was her twin brother told her after he had turned fourteen last year and their father had moved him into the privilege of being the next in line to be king. As twins they protected each other and shared their secrets with each other. She knew about the Minotaurs and he knew about her sneaking off to visit the old lady who lived in the village of Tall, past the Northern River and half way to the eastern wall.

She was a nice lady whom she had met last year at the Tallus Summer Festival. The festival was something her mom and dad organized every summer to help compensate for the isolation. Everyone, rich or poor, was invited and welcomed to the festival. They held it on a big area of land south of the City of Tallus, close to where the Northern River meets the Bergonia River. Games, tournaments, food, trading and so much more went on at the festival. Everyone came and, for one day, were all equals and had a good time. Stephanie looked forward to it every summer, but last summer's festival was the one that had changed her life.

It had been a few days before the festival and Stephanie and her brother had just turned fourteen. This would be the first year she and her twin brother would have to do official royal duties. Her brother was preparing to go with their father to learn the family secret and prepare to step up as the prince to one day be King of Tallus. Stephanie was in her room, servants all around her, preparing her and making her presentable as the princess. She would go with her mother to learn her place and role, one that Stephanie cared less about.

She had sat there, staring into the mirror while she was being primped and pampered. Her beautiful long golden blond hair now pulled up and tied in a bun on the top of her head, a pretty crystal crown resting upon it. Her blue eyes popped against her flawless skin and recently applied blue eye shadow and red lipstick. She had a beautiful yellow and orange accented gown, representing the colors of Tallus, waiting for her to be placed into once the servants were down and ready to put her very slender body into a dress that made her look bigger than a boat.

Stephanie hated this life. She wanted to be free to roam the world, not tied to a throne she could never rule, nor want to. Her only role was to serve her brother when he became king and produce children who would be backups if her brother was unable to provide the next heir. The only reason she would want the power over the kingdom, would be for freeing the Minotaurs. For now, she would have to hope her brother would do that. Thinking of her brother, she glanced in the mirror, and realized how much they resembled each other.

Those thoughts were yanked away as she was shoved into an unnecessary corset and then shoved into her formal gown. Once ready, she was taken to her mother, an identical but older version of herself with matching dress and a much bigger crystal crown. She curtsied to her mother and then, without a word, taken out of the castle and to the horse drawn carriage that would take them around for all the people of the city to look upon the official Princess of Tallus.

It was this day, when they were rounding the business and trading section that Stephanie saw an old woman, long curly grey hair, clothes and robe a tattered and torn mess of rags, hunched over and trying to walk with a cracked wooden stick and no shoes. People moved past her paying no attention, bumping into her and sometimes pushing her out of the way until she lost her balance and this time falling to the ground.

"Mom, we have to stop. That old woman just fell," Stephanie said, shocked no one was stopping to help her to her feet.

"No dear, we have to keep moving. We have more ground to cover before the ball tonight," her mother, Queen Lucy said without glancing at her or towards the fallen woman as she waved to the crowd.

"We have to help her," Stephanie declared to her mother and turned away.

"Stephanie!" The queen shouted, but was too late, her daughter had leapt out of the moving carriage, hitting the ground with her knee, wincing at the pain and then getting up without brushing any dirt or mud off her dress. "Stop the carriage!"

"Ma'am, let me help you," Stephanie said as she bent down and helped the old woman to her feet.

"Thank you, child. Oh your poor dress," the older woman said as she placed her hand on the princess's knee, which had been exposed by a large tear and hole in the now ruined gown.

"No worries," Stephanie said as she noticed her knee no longer hurt after the lady removed her hand and she looked down to see, despite the hole in her dress and dried blood, the scrape on her knee was gone.

"It was very thoughtful of you, Princess Stephanie, but there was no need to bother with me. I am fine," the old woman said as her long grey hair covered most of her dirt-coated face.

"Where are your shoes?" Stephanie asked as she saw the woman had small but very dirty and wrinkly feet.

"Stephanie, what do you think you're doing? Get back in the carriage right now. You gave me a heart attack jumping out like that," Queen Lucy scolded as she started to grab her daughters arm.

"I was doing what many of these people should have done instead of standing here gawking," Princess Stephanie shot back as she bent over, removed her shoes and handed them to the old woman.

"Your shoes…what have you done to your dress?" Queen Lucy started to object until she saw the hole and condition of her daughter's gown. "Let's go!"

"Thank you," the old woman said lifting up the shoes as she watched the queen drag her daughter back to the carriage, who just waved and smiled back at her.

Stephanie had been seriously scolded and grounded that day, but she felt it had been worth it. It felt good to help that woman and it seemed to have sparked something within herself, an even bigger desire to want to help people. She had ideas, but every time she went to present them to her mom or dad, their looks shut her down. For the next few days, she kept thinking of her ideas as well as that old woman, whom she never thought she would see again and was wrong.

It had been the day of the Summer Festival and Stephanie and her brother were allowed, with guards escorting them of course, a short time to wonder the booths and games while their parents had some king and queen obligations. As Stephanie turned the corner, she saw a row of vendors selling their crafts and wares and recognized a familiar looking woman behind a booth. Her brother, wanting to go right to the games, shrugged her off as she went off on her own to visit the vendors.

Stephanie instructed her guards to stand back and give her room as she approached the old woman. She looked to be wearing the same clothes from a few days ago but her face was clean this time and she could see her beautiful grey-blue eyes. There were many items in her booth, hand sewed clothes and towels, handmade jewelry, charms and pendants. She had a lot of miscellaneous crafted items, nothing fancy or eye-catching but Stephanie could see the hard labor that went into it by a woman she assumed had to be ancient.

"Well, hello again, your majesty," the old woman's face lit up with a smile.

"You can call me Stephanie," the princess responded with a smile as she kept looking around the woman's booth at her items she had for sale.

"See anything you like, Stephanie?" The old woman asked.

"You have a lot of nice things. You know my name but I never got yours. Are you from around here?" Stephanie asked trying to change the subject politely. There really was nothing that caught her eye.

"What is with a name? I have been around so long that I don't even think about it, but you can call me Shirlynn. I live in a very small village east of Tallus called Tall," the old woman said with a sweet joyfulness in her voice.

"I have never heard of it. You lived there all your life?" Stephanie asked, feeling like she could get lost in the woman's eyes and voice.

"No child, I was born somewhere, so long ago I can't remember. Old age will do that to you," the old woman laughed, "I have lived in several places here in the Kingdom of Tallus but just settled down in Tall many years ago. Very quiet all by myself and no one ever bothers me."

"Don't you get lonely? Do you have a husband or a family?" Stephanie asked as she saw something sparkle out of the corner of her eye, stepped to her left and looked on a stool back behind Shirlynn.

"Unfortunately, I never got the chance to marry as my true love died. I never found another mate nor did I ever have children of my own," Shirlynn said with just a touch of sadness that made Stephanie look up at her.

"I'm so sorry," Stephanie said as she couldn't help but look back at the shiny object.

"It's okay, it was so long ago and he died a hero but that is a story for another day. What has your eye caught?" Shirlynn asked as she shifted off her stool, grabbed her walking stick and moved across her booth.

"What is that?" Stephanie asked as the old woman picked up the shiny object and handed it to her.

"That is a necklace with a good luck charm I placed upon it," the old woman said with a smile as Stephanie took it and then dropped it when a shock passed between the object and her hand.

"I'm sorry, I hope I didn't break it," Stephanie said as she rubbed the palm of her hand.

"No harm done. Just a wood carving attached to a string," Shirlynn said handing it back to the princess who hesitated but then took it with no problems this time.

"It is so pretty, what is this supposed to represent?" Stephanie asked as she examined the necklace and attached charm.

The wooden charm was very smooth and cool to the touch. It was in the shape of a circle with strange markings that went all around the edge. In the center of the circle was two objects that went from the bottom, intertwined with each other and stopped towards the top where a star connected them to the top of the circle. Stephanie thought the one object looked like a tree and the other it was intertwined with was some kind of animal. The star had a small strange white-blue shiny crystal embedded in the middle of it.

"It represents all living things being connected. The crystal is a chipped piece off an old staff of mine, which I added for luck," Shirlynn said with a smile as she watched the princess hold and stare at the charm in grand captivation as the crystal shined in the reflection of her eyes.

"It's so beautiful. Is it for sale?" Stephanie asked finally looking away from the charm necklace.

"It is not for sale but you can have it," Shirlynn said as she took the necklace and fastened it around the girl's neck.

"Oh, I can't just take it. Let me pay you for it," Stephanie said as she touched the charm that felt almost warm against skin but cool to her fingertips.

"No, considerate it an exchange for the kindness and the shoes you gave me yesterday. It seems it was meant for you to have it," Shirlynn said with a smile and watery eyes.

"Thank you, I will wear it and cherish it always," Stephanie said with pure sincerity.

"You're welcome, my child," Shirlynn said as she touched the girl's face and then moved to sit down again.

"I would love to come visit you sometime and hear more of your stories," Stephanie said, finding a strange connection and interest in this old woman who gave her this fascinating charm necklace.

"I would like that. You are welcome anytime," Shirlynn said with true kindness in her voice.

"I will, I promise. I better get going. I hope your day is good to you," Stephanie said leaving the booth.

"It already has," Shirlynn said with a sigh of hope.

Stephanie brought her gaze from the window and down to her charm necklace that still rested around her neck. She had never forgotten that day and never removed it, even though her mom said it was gaudy and forbid her to wear it. Stephanie wore it anyways and decided it was best to never tell her mom of her visits to see Shirlynn.

Which she did right away, as promised, the next day after the festival ended. She snuck out and went there instead of her riding lessons. She took a horse and rode straight to Tall while everyone thought she was out riding. Shirlynn had been happy to see her and they talked for hours and walked amongst nature. The old woman never told her any tales of her past, just talking about nature and the acts of kindness to help all living things.

Stephanie wanted to hear stories but was just as delighted with the lessons and talks. She felt complete when she was with Shirlynn and talking about nature and helping others. Immediately a routine was established. Once a week, Stephanie skipped riding lessons and went to Tall where she spent some time helping, visiting and learning from Shirlynn. Stephanie even noticed that as time had gone by, she was becoming more in tune with nature and animals and, like the charm, seemed to have good luck.

Stephanie got up, walked away from the window, and looked into her mirror, worry and sadness crossing her face. She had not seen Shirlynn in a long time. The week before this year's Summer Festival, Shirlynn finally stopped avoiding her plea for stories and promised that next time she would tell her what she needed and wanted to hear. Stephanie had been excited until her father caught her starting to leave to skip her riding lesson.

Her father demanded to know where she was going and why she was lying about her whereabouts during her riding lessons. She did not want something bad to happen to Shirlynn so she lied to her father and said she just went off to a secluded field and laid in the grass daydreaming. She was not sure if her father believed her but he had an escort stay with her for the whole lesson.

Stephanie had hoped to see Shirlynn at the festival and explain why she had not shown but Shirlynn never came this time. Stephanie feared the old woman was mad at her for standing her up, or worse, her dad found out and did something to her. Stephanie wanted to go and check on her but was never able to, as it seemed someone was always watching her and every lesson she received a personal escort. Now winter was approaching and there definitely would not be a way to go to Tall.

"What's wrong?" A voice asked from behind her. Without even turning or looking in the mirror, she knew it was her twin brother.

"It's Shirlynn. I haven't seen her or heard from her since before the Summer Festival. Do you think she is okay? You haven't said anything to dad or mom?" Stephanie asked already knowing the answer.

"You know I haven't. Even when dad first drilled me, I played dumb to why you were skipping riding lessons. I don't see why you waste your time and risk our parent's wrath visiting with an old woman," Steffon said a little more harshly than intended and immediately felt bad.

"And I don't see why you think it is okay to make Minotaurs slaves. They are living beings just like any of us," Stephanie shot back, not regretting her words or tone.

"I know, but there's nothing I can do about it. Maybe I can think about it once I am king," Steffon said making a promise he was not sure he could keep. His sister knowing this too, took his words anyway and hugged him.

"Thank you," Stephanie said as she stepped back and then looked out the window, touching her charm. "I really think something is wrong. I can feel it."

"If you promise to not be gone long and come right back, I will," was all Steffon got out before his sister screamed with joy and started hugging him again. "You better go before I change my mind."

"You're the best brother ever," Stephanie said as she changed into her riding outfit and bolted out the door.

Stephanie was worried about being caught, but as luck would have it, she made it to the stables without anyone noticing her. Then again, with her hair tied back in a ponytail with her pants, top and boots she did not look like a princess, but more like the common folk. She was about to try and figure out a way into the stables and borrow a horse when she saw a pretty white stallion with a long blond mane, blue eyes and black spots all over his body standing in the fields all alone. The horse had a strange bluish diamond mark on its forehead.

Stephanie looked at the horse and almost felt like it was shaking its head to let her know she could ride him. Stephanie looked around. There was no one in sight so she ran over to the horse, who did not flinch or move upon her approach. The horse then knelt down slightly allowing her to mount him. The horse did not have a saddle or anything, but she still felt safe and held on to his mane as the stallion bolted off to the east.

Stephanie almost wanted to scream in joy at the freedom of riding with the wind blowing against her, but did not want to draw unneeded attention her way. The horse went off into the grasslands and fields as if it wanted to avoid the general population and from being seen. Stephanie also realized that the horse did not need much guiding as if it knew where they were going. Stephane instantly felt a bond with the horse and knew they could both trust each other as they rode on to Tall.

It did not take long before she saw the very small run down but livable village off in the distance. Unless it truly had been a long time since her last visit or her horse was a lot faster than any she had ever ridden, she had made it to Tall in record time. She quickly rode past the few houses until she got to the most eastern edge of the village, where nothing was around but a single cottage surrounded by trees and flowers. She had made it to Shirlynn's home.

"Shirlynn! Are you there? It's me, Stephanie!" Stephanie shouted as she leapt off the horse and sprinted to the cottage door.

The door was ajar, but she did not hear anything nor even see a trace of light coming from within. Fearing the worse, Stephanie grabbed a stick she found on the ground, raised it high and stepped through the door slowly. The place looked as if it had been ransacked. The furniture, pans and dishes were all broken and thrown everywhere. She moved slowly towards the small bedroom afraid of what she might find, pushed open the door with a gasp to find it empty and just as demolished.

"What happened here?" Stephanie asked to herself as she looked around, ready to cry, picturing her old friend hurt or even dead.

She was trying to think what her next plan should be when she heard something at the front door. In fear that the person who had attacked Shirlynn and her home was coming back, she moved behind the door. Raising her stick high, she prepared to attack as the door slowly pushed inwards, a figure starting to step through. Stephanie, from the shadow, could tell it was one person and just as they stepped fully in, she jumped out stick raised high and ready to strike. "You'll pay for what you did to my friend!"

The figure screamed loud, falling to the ground dodging the stick by inches. "Dear child, what are you doing?"

"Shirlynn?" Stephanie asked as she saw the old woman now on the floor. She threw her stick down and tackled the woman in a big hug.

"Oh my, what's got you all in a fuss?" Shirlynn asked as she pushed the princess off and then allowed her to help her to her feet.

"I hadn't seen you in so long. You didn't come to the festival and then I got here and saw that someone had attacked your home, I feared. Oh Shirlynn, I am so glad you are alive!" Stephanie screamed as she hugged the old woman again.

"Yes, yes, I am alive, old and barely hanging on after the start you just gave me," Shirlynn laughed as she righted a chair and took a seat to catch her breath.

"What happened here?" Stephanie asked as she started to pick things up.

"You are right, my home was attacked, but luckily I wasn't here at the time. I just haven't had the time or strength to put everything back," Shirlynn responded as she smiled brightly at the sight of the princess, whom she had known would return.

"When did this happen? Is this why you were not at the Sumer Festival? I felt so bad because I thought you were mad at me for not coming, so you didn't come. Then I haven't been able to make it back out here until now," Stephanie said as she explained about her dad preventing her from coming here and how her brother made it possible for her to come today.

"It's okay, child. I could never be mad at you. I knew there was a reason you weren't coming but I also knew you were okay and waited for the day you would return," Shirlynn said with a smile as she watched the princess help pick up and clean her home.

"Who did this?" Stephanie asked feeling that if she had come like she used to, none of this would have happened.

"Bad people, very bad people," Shirlynn said, her gaze drifting off into space.

"What kind of bad people?" Stephanie asked as she left the main room and moved over to the kitchen area to start picking things up and put them were they needed to go.

"Stephanie, dear, while you're there, could you get a pot of tea going?" The old woman asked as she got up and moved to the small room where she slept.

"Sure," Stephanie paused, and when the old woman said nothing more, turned back to the task at hand.

Once Stephanie got the stove area cleaned off, she found a couple pieces of wood and got the fire burning in the stove. She then found the kettle, brushed it off and ran out back to the small pond near the cottage to get some water. As she headed back, she looked around to see if she could see anything out of the ordinary. Not a person in sight. When she got back inside, she saw Shirlynn moving about her bedroom as if she was trying to locate something. Stephanie asked if she needed any help, but when she did not answer, Stephanie moved back to the kitchen.

Stephanie placed the kettle on top of the stove so that the water could come to a boil. The stove was good and hot so it would't take long before it would whistle. After that, she would let it boil just a little longer before adding the herbs and ingredients to finish making the tea. As she waited, she continued to pick up and clean the kitchen. By the time she finished, the kettle started to whistle.

"Oh good, teas about ready," Shirlynn said as she moved out of the bedroom.

"Few more minutes. Find what you were looking for?" Stephanie asked as the woman moved past her and headed for the kitchen.

"Child, could you be a dear and finish straightening my room. I will keep an eye on the kettle and finish making the tea," was all Shirlynn said as she patted the girl on the shoulder on her way by.

"Sure," Stephanie said, not minding at all to do all the cleaning but really wished she would get some answers of what happened here and what the old woman was looking for in her bedroom.

Stephanie could hear the kettle whistling as well as Shirlynn humming a tune. There was not much but between whomever did this and Shirlynn looking in here, they really tore the place apart. She got all the straw piled and packed into place before placing the bed sheet over it to tuck it in and secure her bed for sleeping. She knew she was spoiled and Shirlynn did not mind it, but she could never sleep on a pile of hay. Once the bed was done she turned to the rest of the room.

She placed the candle stick nicely back on the log stump Shirlynn used as an end table after she up righted it. Stephanie's heart dropped when she turned and saw on the far side corner wall a broken pile of wood. It had once been Shirlynn's pride and joy. She had saved up a long time and a kind woodcarver had made it for her. A dresser for her clothes and personal items. Stephanie could see that there was no fixing it as it was smashed to pieces. She did her best to pile it together while trying to hold back the tears.

"Don't fret, child. It's just a thing. I'll find something else to put my stuff in. If you could just fold and place my clothes on the end of the bed that would be great. The rest of the stuff can just be put in a pile in the corner, I'll find places for them later," Shirlynn's voice sang into the room with not a care.

"Still terrible, who could do such a thing?" Stephanie asked with no response, but she had not expected one.

It did not take long to fold the clothes since Shirlynn did not own much. She then looked at all the other personal items, which was not much either, and gently shoved them into the corner making a nice pile. As she walked out of the bedroom she saw Shirlynn sitting at her table with two cups of tea waiting for her. "Sit down, while it's hot."

"Now, tell me what happened," Stephanie insisted as she sat down and stared at the woman and sipped her tea.

"It happened the day of the Summer Festival. The sun was just starting to rise and I was ready with my goods to sell and had headed out upon the road so I could be there on time before everyone started to show up. I was half way there when I got the strangest feeling so I turned around and went back.

"Just as I got within sight of my home, I saw three strange creatures sprout wings and take flight. Afraid, I sat back and waited to make sure there were no more in my home. When I saw nothing, I proceeded on into Tall.

"People were everywhere going about their business, saying nothing of these creatures as if they hadn't seen them. Some said hi or asked why I was not heading to Tallus, which I told them I was but had turned around because I forgot something.

"When I reached my home, the creatures were nowhere in sight but my home was as you saw it. I was devastated and gave up the festival so I could stay here and figure out what they were doing and make sure that nothing was missing," Shirlynn explained as she finished her tea and then poured them both some more from the kettle.

"That's horrible. What were these creatures?" Stephanie asked as she looked towards the door and windows, afraid they might return at any moment.

"They are creatures I've not seen in a very long time. They are called Drogans and very dangerous," Shirlynn said as she nervously sipped her tea.

"Drogans?" Stephanie asked, knowing that despite no one ever talking about it and her knowledge of the Minotaurs, she believed that there were other creatures of magic out there somewhere.

"Evil creatures magically spawned somehow. They are half human and half Dragon. They look human at first but then shift form, taking on a scalier appearance and sprout wings as well as most can spit fire. Very strong and very dangerous," Shirlynn said as her tea cup and hands started to settle and clam.

"They were here? How did they get here? What were they looking for in your home?" Stephanie's mind began to race as she asked so many questions at once.

"At the time, I was shocked at seeing them here. I still have no idea how they got here but the fact they are on the move from the Unknown Lands was not a good sign and I fear they may come back since they didn't find what they were looking for," Shirlynn said as she kept sipping her tea and staring off into nowhere.

"Unknown Lands?" Stephanie asked more to herself and waited for Shirlynn to continue. When she did not, she pressed for more details, "What were they searching for that they tore your place apart like this?"

"I had to make sure they didn't take anything and deal with unexpected events," Shirlynn said as she finally came back and stared right at Stephanie.

"Unexpected events?" Stephanie asked, wondering if she would ever get any answers.

"I went into the woods behind my cottage to meditate and become in tune with nature and my surroundings. I felt something I hadn't felt in a very long time and slipped into a deep meditative sleep and didn't wake for almost a month later with a vision," Shirlynn said as she continued to keep eye contact with the princess.

"Vision? What did you see?" Stephanie asked as she felt the skin where her charm rested grow warmer.

"I saw the return of Drol Greb, which explains the Drogans, as well as the prophecy of the Chosen One amongst other things," Shirlynn said sitting back, now starring at Stephanie's necklace she gave her.

"Chosen One? Drol Greb, isn't that the evil guy the Desert is named after? And he's here in Tallus?" Stephanie asked as she had to lift the charm off her chest to keep it from burning her as the crystal began to glow bright. She had so many questions with no answers.

"No, he has not returned, yet, but the fact I saw what I saw means the portal has been breached. I fear the Artifacts of Power are once again in play," Shirlynn said as she stood up and pulled a staff out from under her robe with a glowing crystal on the top that now pulsed in harmony with the crystal chip on Stephanie's charm

"Are you a witch?" Stephanie asked standing up and backing away.

"No, I am the last of the Order of Clerics, or I was until you," Shirlynn said as she reached out to the girl who suddenly feinted amongst the glowing light of the crystals.

Chapter Nineteen:
Defenders Of Magic

Stephanie woke with a start as she rubbed her head. She sat up and saw she was lying in Shirlynn's bed. She touched the charm on her neck and realized it felt cool and was no longer glowing. Then she remembered before blacking out that Shirlynn had a staff that was glowing and had said something about being a cleric. She was about to jump off the bed when Shirlynn stepped back into the room with a cup of tea.

"Sit tight and drink up, it will help," Shirlynn said as she handed the cup to the girl and then sat on a chair at the end of the bed.

"I have so many questions," Stephanie said as she drank the tea, winced at its sour taste but noticed how she was instantly starting to feel better.

"Yes, and I have so much to tell you and not a lot of time. As to not leave anything out or forget something important I might as well start at the beginning and work my way from there. Pay attention and don't interrupt," Shirlynn said as she leaned forward and spun her tale.

"As most tales go, it all started with good versus evil. Drol Greb had made his move and the Magic Wars began and would last for about ten years. It was all out war and by the eighth year of the war, Drol and his evil forces were winning and lots of lives were lost. There was a group called the Order of the Clerics. They believed in the wellbeing of all living things, human, animal, nature, plants, all that make up the world of Bergonia. They were forced to stand against the evil and do what they could to save and heal those afflicted.

"Drol hated them and issued a declaration of death on all clerics. They were hunted and no one was safe, especially if you were a member of the Order of Clerics. At this time, I was very young and had just started my training with the Order. I wanted to do more but was told to remain on the sidelines, helping who I could while the older and more experienced clerics went to the front lines and to their deaths.

"When all seemed lost, a great hope arose. A Huelgon by the name of Essej Lewin, a rare race of half Dragon, half human and Elf, and a man by the name of Semaj Lightheart had appeared claiming to have found and mastered a new source of power called the Magesti. They were ready to take the fight to Drol Greb and stop his reign of evil and needed help, which they found in twelve unique individuals.

"Over the first eight years of the war, humans and magical beings and creatures from all types, came together to fight a common enemy. I happened to be at a secret camp, helping to tend the wounded, when many of them had come together, some for first time while others reunited, to back and meet Semaj and Essej for their final assault on Drol Greb. One of my good friends and mentors in the Order was there with me when those individuals were being chosen.

"I wanted to be one of them but was told I was too young and inexperienced, so my friend was chosen instead. Her name was Korena Salle and she was a powerful human cleric. I was jealous but also happy that she got to go. Along with her, there were eleven others chosen: a Dwarf by the name of Thorax Doubleaxe, a Minotaur named Toro, a human by the name of Maryanne Baumann, a knight named Jace Stone, a brave warrior named Marrick Stevenson, a member of the water folk named Ard-Rich, a were beast named Xia, an Orgite named Olga, a Goblin named Glork, a Wild Elf named Philana and the last I believe was a centaur named Callo.

"Those twelve called themselves the Defenders of the Magesti and swore their loyalty to Essej and Semaj. They all quickly departed on their journey to face Drol Greb leaving everyone else to continue fighting on or doing their part to help in the efforts to stop evil and help those that needed it. There was a small group that remained at the camp to help support us clerics that were still tending to the wounded.

"I was tending to a man who wasn't to last much longer. With his final breaths he told me that there was a secret plan of Drol Greb's to anchor a portal to pull the dead into the land of the living. Meaning if he was killed in battle he had a way to still return. He was on a mission to find the Spirit Source to require the power needed to seal this portal off or all that the Defenders of the Magesti attempted to do would be for nothing.

"Before he finally passed on, he revealed the location of the Source. I went to the elder Clerics of the Order and told them what the man told me, but they dismissed it as the ramblings of a dying man, as there was no such thing as a Spirit Source or a means of opening portals between the living and the dead.

"I was frustrated as I felt it in my bones that what the man said was true and I needed to finish that dying man's mission to help save Bergonia. In my ranting to myself off in the woods, there was a man who claimed to be a magic user by the name of Thomas Raven, who offered to join me on this mission.

"I was torn between staying and ditching my post and going on this mission when the best friend of one of the Defenders of the Magesti, a Dwarf named Lirax Longbeard approached us and demanded his services to this mission. For me, that was the tipping sign so I grabbed my staff and some supplies and we took off in the night before any of the Order noticed I was gone. I knew I was risking everything but believed it was my destiny to carry out this quest.

"Thomas, with his flair for the dramatics and humor nicked named us the Defenders of Magic. Me with my staff to help me focus my healing gifts, Thomas with his crystal and books of magic and Lirax with his axe made of the strongest steel, set off to help save Bergonia. The man that had died said the Spirit Source was located deep in the forests located in the most southern part of Bergonia, so that is where we went.

"We battled and faced many dangers along the way, as well as people joining and leaving our group as we made our way to the southern forests. When we reached the forest, our party had become five members strong as the other handful refused to enter the forest and left. It was us original three, a slave-prisoner we had freed by the name of Mia, who wore a pair of rings that she used to mesmerize men into doing what she wanted and a man by the name of Thad Silversword who, with his fancy shield was determined to prove himself a true knight.

"The five of us made our way into the forest where, even before the great exile, many magical creatures called it their home. We had no idea what we were looking for but we ran into a unicorn by the name of S'r'h. She was a beautiful white color with a pink tipped main and her horn shined almost as bright as the crown she wore upon her head. She was a princess and her mom was queen of the unicorns, which she never let us forget. We would have ditched her but she knew what we were looking for and agreed to take us if we let her join our group.

"By the time we got to the Source, we had run afoul a few different creatures, good and bad and even added one more member to our party when we helped an Elf by the name of Ferron escape a group of Wild Elves. The Source wasn't what we expected and many of us accused the unicorn princess of not really knowing and leading us on a false path.

"What we had found, in the middle of the southern part of the forest, were three large stone pillars imbedded in the ground with a stone beam connecting them across the top. In front of this was a large empty pit about three feet deep and looked to be the size of a small pond, minus the water. We all stood there and stared at each other not knowing what to do next or whether we had failed our mission.

"Then my staff began to glow and I felt drawn to the pond, so I stepped forward and a spirit formed right in front of us. It was the image of a purple Dragon. The Dragon spirit held up a claw signaling me to stop and not come any further. I was about to speak when another form appeared atop the pillar's joining beam. It was a woman with long green hair and a beautiful green dress. To this day, I do not know if she was real or a spirit, she was just suddenly there.

"The woman spoke in a beautiful soft and kind voice. It was as if we could all hear her as if she was standing there speaking directly into each of our ears. Her name was Feli and the purple Dragon was Losu and they were soul and life mates. They resided there as they had sacrificed themselves in a grand battle to help save Bergonia and rejuvenate and bring life back to the forest we now stood in.

"Many questions arose but we knew now was not the time. We had a quest to complete with time running out. I stepped forward and Feli acknowledged me with a nod. I don't know if the Dragon spirit could speak but Feli had done all the talking as she asked us why we had disturbed them.

"I told them of our quest. That we had vowed to find and stop Drol Greb and his portal. Feli and the Dragon spirit looked at each other and after Losu nodded at her mate, Feli addressed me. She said they were aware of this great evil trying to devour Bergonia and of the portal. She told me that the portal would allow the dead to return to the living, making whom controlled it and their forces immortal as they could always die and return.

"My heart skipped a beat at the thought of Drol Greb and his evil forces becoming unstoppable and unkillable. I pleaded that we needed help and would do anything to help stop this. Feli agreed it had to be stopped and they would give us the tools to do so but each of us would have to give up something that was a part of us and make a big sacrifice in exchange for their help.

"I looked at my group of seven and stepped forward and threw the one thing I had that made me what I was, my clerical staff. Losu shimmered purple as the staff slid right under him. Thomas went next as he looked between his books and his crystal around his neck and decided the crystal was the right choice. With a tear in his eye he took the crystal from around his neck and threw it into the pit where it slid and joined my staff.

"Losu shimmered each time an item was thrown in. Lirax's axe, Ferron's sling, Thad's shield and Mia's rings. All that remained was S'r'h and she just stood there, not moving. Like all unicorns, when she spoke you didn't hear a physical voice as her magic allowed you to hear her in your head. S'r'h pleaded to us that she could not give up her crown. She just couldn't. After a little more protesting and tantrum throwing, she finally bowed her head and flicked it up causing her crown to fly off and land in the pit with the rest of our items.

"The moment that crown hit, Losu transformed into a swirling whirlpool of purple light that wrapped around the seven items causing them to melt and merge until nothing was left but a small swirling whirlpool of purple light. We all waited for this great gift of help and then nothing happened. We all looked up to Feli and she just stood there staring at us. Then Thad shouted at her about each of us making a sacrifice and why she wasn't holding up her end of the deal which caused the others to start shouting too.

"I looked at my group and then back up to see Feli was gone. I didn't understand why we were tricked. Feli's words were running through my mind when it finally clicked. The items were not the sacrifice. I knew then what I needed to do. As I ran for the edge I heard the others call after me but I didn't hesitate. I dove head first into the pit. I felt the wave of purple light as I made contact and then total darkness.

"Soon, light returned as I watched Losu rip my soul from my body, dropping my physical form into the whirlpool and releasing my soul upwards. When my body joined with the whirlpool of light an explosion went off as the pit started to fill with lavender colored water. Once the pond was full, the water raced up the pillars and over creating a water fall of beautiful lavender water.

"This lavender water then continued over the waterfall and headed through the forest northbound creating a river. The closer it got to the forest edge the clearer the water became until it shot past the forest and now looked like a normal river as it traveled north until it collided, merging and becoming one with the Bergonia River. It was the prettiest thing I had ever witnessed.

"As I felt myself floating upwards, I glanced over and saw Losu reach down into the pool of water he sat in and pulled out his closed paws, water flowing out of them as objects inside could be seen. Wishing my friends the best of luck, I turned and prepared to cross over when something grabbed me and yanked me back. I turned to see Feli in her true form. She told me, despite my grand sacrifice, my time wasn't up yet as she threw my spirt downwards.

"Just as I went racing back, Losu's tail came out of the water, throwing my body towards me. My body and soul collided in a grand flash of green and purple light. When I came too, I was laying upon the grassy bank of the pond. I remembered everything that had just happened except the image of Feli's true form. My companions were all around me, especially Thomas, asking if I was okay, and I never felt better. I felt changed somehow, reborn and more connected to my clerical gifts.

"I sat up and turned as Feli was right there on the edge of the pond, with Losu reaching down, paws open right next to her exposing the seven items he held. Feli told us that these items were now seven artifacts of power, each with their own magic abilities but when used all together as one, would seal the portal, defeating evil and saving all of Bergonia. She also warned us that when used together, in the wrong hands, could undo all we will have sought to do.

"She then gave each item back to their original owner with instructions of what the items could now do. They would have basic abilities, but when invoked of its full power could be draining on them so to do so lightly and not abuse the power. The item's part in the final battle would be revealed at that time. She turned to Thomas first placing his crystal in his hand.

"Thomas Raven's crystal would do magic, but when invoked gave him complete control and use of magic. Princess S'r'h, as a unicorn, already had similar abilities as what the crown could now, but it would amplify her natural abilities as the crown would heighten the wearers senses and when invoked could communicate with and understand all things. Lirax Longbeard's axe was strong, sharp and unbreakable, but when invoked could ultimately cut through anything. Ferron received his sling which always hit its target dead on but when invoked could bind its victim.

"Feli then turned to Thad Silversword and gave him back his shield which could defend against most attacks but when invoked would repel all form of attacks, even the strongest of magic. Mia took her two rings and placed one on each of her thumbs and was told that that the rings would allow her to hypnotize and be able to get people, mainly men, to do what she wanted but to invoke them, both rings would have to be worn together and she would have the ability to completely control and possess others.

"Feli then grabbed and picked up the last item, my staff. She handed it to me and said the staff would aid in my abilities to help heal others but when invoked I would have total control over the ability to heal, cure or fix any being from anything but warmed me to really be careful of over using or abusing this power.

"We all swore we would complete this mission and safeguard the Artifacts of Power. With that, Losu vanished and

Feli gave us one final set of instructions. The portal would be found in the most southern part of Bergonia and S'r'h could use her crown to help guide us in the right direction. When we got there a great guardian would be waiting and we wouldn't be able to defeat it unless we worked together. Once defeated we could use the Artifacts of Power to stop evil and seal the portal. She wished us luck and was gone.

"We had many adventures with many obstacles along the way but as the world entered into the last year of the Magic Wars we had found our destination, deep in the heart of what is known as the Unknown Lands. By this time, we had all mastered our Artifacts of Power and grown very close as the Defenders of Magic, which is what my dear Thomas continued to call us.

"During this time, I had fallen in love with my one true love and soul mate, Thomas. I even promised to marry him once this quest was over and we saved Bergonia. Mia and Ferron had grown close as well, but it almost seemed more one sided as Ferron wasn't as affectionate as Mia was. Thad had even fallen in love with a lovely dark-haired woman, whom I can't remember her name any more, but she was one of several that had rallied and joined us on our quest.

"We all stood looking upon a small fortress in the middle of a barren and very hot and humid area of land, twenty of us in total. We quickly made our way to the fortress, unseen and unopposed. That was until hundreds of Drogans descended upon us from the skies. It was almost as if they had been waiting for us.

"We were all afraid of weakening ourselves and over using our weapons before reaching the portal but we had no choice. I was fairly good in a fight but I spent my time avoiding the attacks and kept up with healing as many as I could, but I couldn't always get to everyone. Mia pushed herself trying to possess a handful of Drogans to have them turn and help fight for us. My Thomas was marvelous as he used his magic to fight the hordes back but demanded that we needed to get to the gate.

"We were almost there but the Drogans kept coming. Thad, his woman holding him in support as he used his shield causing a wave of energy to literally repel twenty Drogans sending them flying backwards at least twenty feet. We got to the gate and

Lirax cut us a path right in with his axe. Once we made it in, Thomas used his magic to not only seal the hole Lirax had cut but placed a barrier to make it hold. The seven of us plus Thad's girl and five others were all that were left of our party. S'r'h said that the portal was located down a stairway that lead deep under the fortress. Tired and needing to gain our strength, we still pushed on and quickly moved down the stairs.

"We soon found ourselves in a large cavern barely lit with candles. Across from us on the opposite end was a portal that was trying to be opened and sustained by seven dark clerics. On the other side of the portal you could see images of the dead swirling by and fading away. The dead were waiting for the chance to walk Bergonia again. I looked at everyone and told them this was it. We had to stop the clerics and seal that portal.

"Before we could devise our plan, three spears formed out of the darkness and shot forward, two spears impaling and killing two of our party and the third bouncing off Thad's shield and dissolved like the other two had after impact. S'r'h said there was something hiding in the darkness just as a loud growl caused the cavern to rumble. We prepared ourselves as out of the darkness a form began to take shape, a large black Dragon who looked very menacing despite its old and weakened appearance.

"S'r'h invoked her crown and verified that the Dragon before us was the great Dragon King known as K'Dra. Thomas shouted something about legends and stories of old indicated that Dragons no longer existed and all the Dragon Kings had been killed almost three thousand years ago. The black Dragon before us opened its maw and laughed. I am not sure if it could actually talk or if it was S'r'h crown but her voice was grained with age and anger.

"The Dragon King, K'Dra told us that Thomas was almost right. That she had managed to sneak and hide away in the Unknown Lands, resting, letting the world think she was dead till she could strike again. She told us that many seasons had passed till the day a man by the name of Drol Greb found her and made a deal. If she swore allegiance to him and guarded his portal he was creating, he would make her whole, strong and deadly again. She made the deal and even though she was not what she once was, she would be more than able to kill all of us.

"The Dragon opened its mouth and instead of fire, darkness came out and started forming shapes. Soon a dozen solders carrying swords, all made of solid darkness came charging at us. As we fought for our lives against these dark beings, the Dragon King taunted us and told us of Drol Greb's plans. Drol was battling Semaj Lightheart and his forces at this very moment, but no matter the outcome, Drol and his forces would win.

"If Drol succeeded in killing Semaj, he would drain the Magesti from him and use that to open the portal in front of them forever, controlling and allowing the evil dead to invade Bergonia. If Semaj were to kill Drol, thanks to the grey Dragon King Thead, whose spirit could be seen beyond the portal, would pull him right to the portal and infuse him so Drol would have enough power to open the portal long enough for Drol to step back into the land of the living. In doing this Drol could keep attacking Semaj and returning from the dead till he finally wore Semaj out and killed him.

"It was at this moment that me and my friends realized how important it was to close this portal or nothing Semaj and the Defenders of the Mejesti did would matter. It was up to all of us to truly help save Bergonia. This drove us to fight even harder against the Dragon and her shadow fighters. At this time, S'r'h sent a message to my head alone, saying she sensed a traitor amongst us and that is how the Drogans and the Dragon King knew we were here but she couldn't pinpoint who it was.

"My heart sank, but so far no one was showing signs and I told her to just watch and be ready for now, as we all had to focus on the Dragon. Thomas came up with a plan and S'r'h relayed it to all secretly. Mia stepped up and invoked her rings and fought to gain possession of the Dragon. They were locked in fierce mental battle as both Mia and the Dragon were starting to bleed from their ears and nostrils.

"While the Dragon was distracted and unable to defend itself, S'r'h invoked her crown as Thomas and I invoked our items having our powers connect with S'r'h and her power. Once our powers communicated and understood what was needed, they merged and a powerful blast engulfed the Dragon. Mia flew backwards as K'Dra screamed in horror, but before she could do anything, Lirax invoked his power and brought his axe down upon the Dragon King's neck severing the head. When the light from the blast faded, all that was left of the Dragon was a black burned mark on the cavern wall and a lifeless head and a pile of ashes.

"I heard screams of victory from our party as I instructed them to head for the portal but an immense earthquake shook the whole cavern causing all of us to fall to the ground and protecting our heads from falling debris. S'r'h started screaming how she used her crown and all of Bergonia was communicating to her as an explosion had just gone off and the land of Bergonia was changing as we speak, all over.

"I glanced over at the portal and realized what had happened. Semaj had brought down Drol as his evil spirit was now starting to form on the other side of the portal. I yelled at everyone that we had to act now but the traitor revealed himself, as Ferron pulled out two daggers and slit the throats of our last three allies leaving just us Defenders of Magic and Thad's girl.

"Thomas asked him why and Ferron said that he had been a spy for Drol and was supposed to reveal himself after we killed the Dragon. Drol wanted K'Dra out of the way once her services were no longer needed and Ferron could acquire the Artifacts of Power for Drol. I started to approach when Mia stepped in front of Ferron, still weak from her battle with the Dragon and pleaded that we had it all wrong as she tried to use her rings to persuade us not to hurt him. She said Ferron had explained to her how Drol and the portal were actually going to be used for the good of all, immortality so that is why she helped him keep his secret.

"I glanced back and saw Drol's spirit had just taken full form. We were out of time. Thomas told me to send a blind healing light at the dark clerics. I did it without hesitation causing the dark clerics to stop and deflect it, releasing their hold on the portal. Thomas told Lirax to use his axe, which he did placing a large crack in the floor. Thomas then used his magic to cause that crack to spread upon the floor where the dark clerics stood, opened up swallowing them and then resealing killing them instantly making the portal shimmer.

"Thad cheered but S'r'h, using her crown said that it will only delay as the grey Dragon spirit on the other side was attempting to hold their death back so the dark clerics could reestablish our end enough for Drol to come through. Using that moment of our distraction, Ferron shouted that he would kill us all and with Drol free they would rule the world, and then used his sling to send a rock right at Thad's head.

"Being distracted and the power of Ferron's sling, there was no way he was going to avoid the blow but as fate would have it, Thad's true love shoved him out of the way and took the blow meant for him. Thad screamed as I saw her drop limp to the ground, blood forming on her head. I then heard Mia scream at Ferron for playing her a fool and she pointed her rings at him, but Ferron was too quick as he used his knives to sever both her thumbs clean off, separating her from her rings and her power. Mia dropped to her knees in shock as she began to bleed out.

"In a fit of rage, Thomas cast a fire ball spell that hit Ferron and consumed him. Not wanting to risk losing the sling, Lirax used his axe to chop off the hand holding the sling and knock it away from the body that was now on the ground burning to a crisp. To this day, I don't know if I wanted Mia to pay or I truly believed I couldn't save both her thumbs and Thad's woman, but I chose to send a blast of healing light at Mia's hands that closed and healed the wound. She no longer had thumbs but would live and not bleed out. I then leapt to the woman who sacrificed herself for her man and invoked the staff and called upon its healing light to save the woman who was all but dead.

"My healing was cut short when S'r'h screamed that we had to use the Artifacts now or all would be lost. I stopped what I was doing and hoped it had been enough and called forth the Artifact of Powers to join together but nothing happened. Not sure why, S'r'h quickly used her crown and informed us that the reason was that each of the intended user had to be alive. Using everything I had I invoked my staff to do something that I realized I would never try again as it not only aged me but it put a dark stain on my aura.

"I attempted to bring the dead back to life and succeeded, but not how I intended. Farron rose but remained burned, charred and very zombie like in nature but the Artifacts began to glow. Mia pulled herself together, grabbed her rings and placed them on new fingers and invoked them compelling the living dead Ferron to help us as he picked up his sling. Without time to lose,

I called forth the Artifacts of Power once again, and this time it worked.

"All seven of our items turned a green and lavender color as a white-blue mist swirled around them. Thomas' crystal opened a pocket to another dimension. S'r'h's crown called Drol Greb's spirit away from the portal of the dead leading it straight to the pocket dimension. Lirax's axe breaks the barrier of the portal of the dead collapsing it shut on both ends. I then use my staff to make Drol's spirit whole, giving him back a physical form. Mia's rings forces Drol's body to step into the pocket dimension where Ferron's sling binds and traps Drol within the pocket dimension. Finally, Thad's shield repels all magic and unwanted evil sealing shut the Pocket Dimension but something was keeping the Pocket Dimension from being permanently banned from our realm.

"I quickly recalled, like in the beginning, a sacrifice had to be made to make it so that neither portals could ever be opened again and allow evil to cross back over. I was ready to make that sacrifice when Thomas stopped me and told me it was his turn. I screamed no but he kissed me hard, touched my belly and said to take care of our son. With that he handed me his books and invoked the last of his magic.

"With that final act of sacrifice, the artifacts expelled all their green and lavender light causing a huge blast of magical energy causing the fortress to collapse in on itself. Thomas, in his final act, blew me a kiss and touched his crystal. His body evaporated as two blasts of magical light left from it. One teleporting all of us out from the cavern and safely away above ground and the other completely obliterating the evil fortress and sealing the ground above making it as if nothing had ever been there.

"I remember screaming and crying out for my one true love, but I knew deep down, his sacrifice had sealed Bergonia's victory along with what Semaj and his group had done. I looked and he had saved all of us and our artifacts, as well as Thad's woman. She was stirring but still comatose, I had to complete her healing if I could but then I saw the zombie Ferron grab his severed hand holding the sling and took off running for what was now called the Fire Mountains.

"I knew none of us had the strength or power to chase after him so I called forth and invoked my staff's powers to undo what I had done and hit the zombie with a magical blast. The creature kept running but I knew in a few hours my spell would run its course and the zombie would be in the mountains of fire as it reverted back to a lifeless corpse leaving it and the sling forever lost within those mountains.

"I quickly ran over to Thad's girl and used what strength I had left and managed to finish healing her, causing her to wake. She was alive, but would not be quite herself as she would always talk with a slur and be a little slow. Thad didn't care, he still loved her and pledged to remain by her side forever and care for her. We had done it and cheered our victory as well as mourned our losses.

"We later agreed that we would take our artifacts, protect them and keep them hidden so they would never fall into evil hands or be used together to undo what we had done and sacrificed. With that, Thomas's Defenders of Magic came to an end and we would all go our separate ways," Shirlynn sighed with a heavy heart as she thought of Thomas again and concluded her tale.

Princess Stephanie sat there in awe of what she had just heard. She still had so many questions and went with, "What happened to everyone and the rest of the Artifacts?"

"Being the key leader and main Artifact holder, I have always been able to sense or receive visions of the others and their artifacts. After Semaj sacrificed his life to help banish Drol it had caused Bergonia to change creating the Fire Mountains, Drol Death Desert and the Frosted Waters separating the land known as Ogra. Now, for all of us, it was to be a new world to walk back into.

"We managed to all make it back to the forest and Spirit Falls but never saw the two spirits that gave us the Artifacts and decided that it was time to go our separate ways and vow to the protection of the Artifacts. S'r'h left us at that point and went back to rejoin the unicorns. She never told her mom what happened and used the crown as the new symbol of the queen when she took over, never revealing or using the crown's power again by using her own magic to bind its magical properties.

Even as we speak, the crown sits on the current queen of the unicorn's head in the Forest of Spirits, no one the wiser what it is or what it could do.

"Mia, who was ashamed at letting herself be played, had vanished in the night. My last vision of her was that she threw the rings in the river and wondered off into the area now known as Argoth. With the Drol Death Desert, the river soon dried up and became the Old River Gorge and the location of the rings remained lost within it for many, many years.

"Me, Lirax, Thad and his woman, traveled up the Bergonia River where we planned to loop around the newly formed desert to meet up with the Defenders of the Magesti to see what happened to our friends. We made it over half way up when it appeared traveling was too much for Thad's woman, who was still having issues after her injuries and near-death experience. They both decided to part ways and make a home in a nearby village. We said our goodbyes and me and Lirax continued on.

"It turned out that her troubles in traveling were due to the same condition I was in, she was pregnant and much farther along than I was. They quickly wed and had a son soon after who luckily was born normal despite the trauma his mother went through during her pregnancy. Thad, about ten years after the end of the Magic Wars, would be one of five men who would form a Council of Humans and declare magic evil. About fifteen years after the Magic Wars, magic would be outlawed and the humans would declare war on all magic beings. Thad died during this War of the Races leaving his son Thadius to carry on and place the shield in display at their castle in honor of his father where it still sits on display today."

"Wait a minute, you told me you had no children," Stephanie interrupted when she realized something Shirlynn had said in her story.

"I had one, but after I *lost* him and with so much time having passed, I find it easier to protect me and my heart by telling people I was never a mother," Shirlynn said with such sorrow in her voice and a tear in her eye. "I am sorry I lied to you."

"It's okay, I understand. You are trusting me and telling me now. What happened to your child?" Stephanie asked as she urged the old woman to continue.

"I will get to that. It was almost one full season after the Magic War before me, Lirax and my new child Tuc Raven, made it to the northeastern land that would one day be called Sorran. By this time the races and all of Bergonia were recovering. By luck, we ran into what was left of Semaj's group in a small tavern which included my friend Korena Salle, Lirax's best friend Thorax, Xia and Maryanne Baumann. They told us that Semaj had sacrificed his life and that Essej had now gone into hiding while five others in their group had died and the others, some badly injured, had all departed for parts unknown.

"These four had made this area their home while they healed and waited to hear word from me and Lirax. Lirax decided to leave at this point to go with Thorax to find and rally the Dwarves. It would be about twenty years later when all the Dwarves would decide to steer clear of the war on races and vanish into the Northern Mountains where a confrontation between two friends would result in Lirax's axe to vanish into a lake while Lirax would move on to build one of the two cities of Dwarves.

"Wanting to take the time to raise me and Thomas's son, I chose to settle down in the small secluded village Korena and the others were living in. With me there, Xia took this opportunity to gather her people and they headed off to an island. Maryanne had met a guy, last name was Sparks I think, and the two settled down in another village not far from ours. I did the best I could raising my child with Korena, who had met a guy of her own and moved in with the three of us.

"Tuc was about fifteen when the War of the Races began. The Council of Humans had declared war on any magic beings or those using or supporting magic. Despite all I told my son about his father, he bought into the propaganda and believed magic was wrong and in fear of my life, urged me to either denounce my Order of Clerics or leave into hiding. He said he loved me, but if I chose to remain a cleric, he would have to turn me in. After an agonizing debate, I decided to leave, and knew it was for the best to finally separate the final two Artifacts of

Power. Me, Korena and her new husband traveled west leaving my son behind.

"I would never see him again, except for in my visions, but he made a life for himself. As soon as I had left, he found a spot where he buried his father's books and crystal so no one would ever find them. He then met a girl and they settled down in a nice secluded place near what would one day be called Soré. Knowing he was doing so well on his own made it easier for me to move on with mine as well.

"We made it all the way to the west and settled down in what would become known as the Kingdom of Tallus. Because of war in full force, someone had started killing off all the clerics. Korena and I were the last of our order. Now pregnant, Korena denounced the order and decided it was best we part ways so she would not endanger her child. I agreed and kept myself in total isolation, watching over Korena and her bloodline, the Artifacts and Bergonia, waiting for the time I might be needed and to restart the Order. That is what I have done, moving from one small place to the other here in Tallus. I have tried a few times to start the Order again, but after failing with the last one and losing her son to the Desert, I had surrendered to the isolation and the death of the Order, well till I met you," Shirlynn finished and then stared at the princess, waiting for her to speak.

"That's quite a story, and taking it all in, and no offence but, you have to be ancient. How old are you and how is it you are still alive?" Stephanie asked causing the old lady to laugh.

"I have been around a very long time, but that's the price to pay being the last of your order and having a staff that tends to prolong the owner's life. Fortunately, I have one last adventure left in me and can then pass it on to the next and finally get the retirement I've only dreamed of," Shirlynn said as she rubbed her hand along the staff.

"Those creatures that invaded your home, are they looking for your staff?" Stephanie asked and then looked to the door, worried they might bust in at any moment.

"Yes, evil has returned to the land of Bergonia and we must help stop it," Shirlynn declared, standing up and staring right into the princess's soul.

Chapter Twenty:
Takes A Knight To Get To The Mines

Stephanie sat there while Shirlynn went to bring back more tea and some lunch. The day was getting late and she knew she should return home before her parents discovered where she really had gone, but something in her drew her to the woman, her stories and her staff. When Shirlynn returned, placing food down for them, Stephanie finally looked away from the staff and addressed Shirlynn.

"You talked about visions and the Artifacts, if you want my help I need to know what is going on," Stephanie said finally making her decision to do what she had always wanted, travel and help others.

"The vision I saw was Drol Greb returning with a force to wipe out all of Bergonia. I also saw the prophecy of a Chosen One, who will call together the Magestics and challenge the evil lord. I also saw quick flashes of other evil already on Bergonia, working to release Drol Greb. Then I felt something I hadn't in a long time, one of the Artifacts had been activated. I saw a woman, working with the evil forces of Drol Greb, wearing a ring, but only one ring. Then it came clear, with the vision and the ransacking of my house, someone is looking for all the Artifacts of Power so they can undo what I did so long ago and free Drol Greb once and for all," Shirlynn said, hands shaking a little as she sipped her tea.

"If only one ring was found then it can't truly be unlocked," Stephanie recalled from the old woman's story. "Maybe it's just coincidence."

"No, the Artifacts are coming back into play and that's just a part of it. Let me continue," Shirlynn said, taking a bite of her food, swallowing it down with her tea and then stared right into Stephanie's eyes again.

"Not long after I had my vision, I thought about my staff but was afraid of bringing it out of hiding and risk the Drogans coming back, unfortunately I couldn't remember where I hid it till you arrived and your charm connected with it and unlocked my memory. I thought about meditating but was afraid of getting trapped in a coma again like last time but I gently reached out, map in front of me with hands waving over the top and sought the spirits for answers.

"I immediately sensed the one ring being used in Argoth, then felt a pull to the Unknown Lands. My hand stopped over the area we had stopped Drol and sealed the portals so long ago, and I saw a breach. I didn't know how that could be possible but felt four very dark souls assisting, and in that moment, I confirmed Drol was somehow back and the Artifacts were the only things standing in his way from walking Bergonia again.

"After that I continued to look and search while keeping myself attune to the Artifacts and wait for your return. I started to wonder, when I felt a strange sensation come over me. I knew it before I reached out with my gifts that Thomas's crystal had been found. As the vision came to me I feared the worst and my heart dropped at what I saw. There, holding Thomas's books and crystal was, for the first time in many years a boy in our son Tuc's bloodline not denouncing the idea of magic.

"My first instinct, past my joy and excitement, was to run off and find him, but I knew I had to wait for you and I needed to find my staff. The fact it was the side of good and one of my kin that found the crystal set my mind at ease. The odds and fate had given the sign that we had a chance and once again it was up to me to help protect and keep the Artifacts of Power from releasing Drol Greb. I didn't have a clearer idea or plan of what the bigger picture was until a little later.

"I was outside in the woods behind my house, looking for signs of my staff when a strange sensation came over me again. It was the crystal being used again, but this time I felt the urge that I had to look in upon it. As I closed my eyes and reached out, a white-blue light grabbed hold of me and I soon found myself in a weird dream-like state. My spirit was wondering around a cavern when I stumbled upon a sight to behold all sights.

"There in the center was a large Dragon spirit, similar to Losu but this one was white. Surrounding him on all sides were ledges, each with a different being on it. Some looked human while the others were a variety of magical creatures. It was something to witness but my focus was drawn to the Dragon spirit's paws, where three forms stood. I couldn't believe my eyes as I saw a boy resembling Semaj Lightheart, the boy who was my kin and possessor of Thomas' crystal and the third, whom I couldn't believe it, was Essej.

"I stood there, unnoticed as I listened to Essej and the Dragon spirit, Dwin, fill the figures on the ledges on what they were, the Magestics, and the need for them to help stop the evil forces of Drol Greb and then unlocking their inner abilities. The rest became a blur as a figure of evil made its appearance and a blinding flash of white light fought it off and sent everyone away, but me and one other.

"I looked and saw the Dragon spirit shrink down to my size and approach me. Dwin introduced himself as one of the great Dragon Kings of long ago and said he held me in this dream vision to talk but we wouldn't have much time. He told me that Essej was leading the Chosen One to go gather the Magestics before the evil forces of Drol got to them. Then I told him my story and about the Artifacts going back into play. He already realized that and was why he had held me back.

"He confirmed that I needed to move fast and gather the Artifacts of Power and that the Magestics and my new band of Defenders would have to work together if Drol was to be stopped for good and save Bergonia. He said he would let Essej know where to find the axe and get it in the right hands and protect the new Defender of the Artifacts if I helped rescue a Magestic in my area. Not only would we get to him in time, but this Magesti would come in handy on our quest to locate and reclaim all the Artifacts.

"I agreed knowing that I could use all the help I could get and it would speed things up if my group and Essej's group were helping each other in finding what we needed to find, Magestics and Artifacts. With that, Dwin told me about the Magestic which I remembered as the Minotaur standing on the ledge who bared the Magesti connected to Dwin, the power over air and wind. I then woke with a start and knew time was running short and hoped you would arrive soon.

"I knew Dwin would keep his end of the deal as I felt the axe being freed and then placed into the original owner's grandson's hands. After that I pushed up my efforts of looking for my staff while devising a plan to rescue the Minotaur from slavery and then from there head out to gather and find the rest of the Artifacts," Shirlynn said as she brought her tales to an end for now.

"Finally, we get to free the Minotaurs," Stephanie said, her long time urge to help them coming forth.

"Stephanie, our task is to free the one that is a Magestic. We won't be able to save them all. We can't risk that right now when we have a bigger mission at hand," Shirlynn spoke the harsh truth that Stephanie had to accept.

"One day though, I will free them all, I promise. If the Minotaur we seek is a slave, then he is being held in the mines. I can get my brother to help us sneak in there and get him out," Stephanie said with confidence that her brother would help her with no problems.

"Good, once we have him free, we will head to the Kingdom of Silversword to get the shield." Shirlynn then began to mumble to herself as she quickly started to pack up supplies for the journey.

Stephanie felt a thrill pass throughout her body. Not for the adventure, but she was going to travel and not only help people but help save all of Bergonia. There was something else she could feel but couldn't explain it. Ever since her charm and the staff came into contact, her body felt different, almost charged with a very healing and soothing energy. Was this part of what the old woman had said about passing the *staff* to her? The thought didn't scare her, but it did make her a little bit nervous – what would her parents say or how would they react?

"Are we ready?" Stephanie asked as she took the packed bag from Shirlynn and put it over her shoulder.

"Almost, just have to wait for," Shirlynn said and then trailed off as she clapped at finding something and placing what looked like cloth made of wood over the top of her staff which suddenly altered and now looked like a regular walking cane.

"Wait...wait for what?" Stephanie asked as she looked from the cane to the old woman.

"For me," a voice answered as a figure stepped through Shirlynn's door.

"Who are you? Don't take another step," Stephanie said quickly grabbing a small knife from the table they had just been sitting at earlier.

"Isn't she cute?" A man said stepping more into the light and chuckling as Stephanie waved and held firm the kitchen knife.

The man looked to be maybe a few years older than Stephanie with short black hair and what looked to be the starting stages of a beard that gave his face a shadowed and slender look. He had to be close to six feet tall and wore a silver with black accented knight's armor that looked light and fitted more for movement and design. It almost seemed like a normal outfit than a regular knight's armor. On the chest plate was a letter "B". Stephanie noticed he carried no weapons and she swore one of his eyes were green and the other... purple?

"Relax, child, he is here to help us," Shirlynn said with a great smile. "You look just like him."

"Look like whom?" Stephanie asked Shirlynn but not taking her eyes or her knife off the man.

"Oh, my manors, this is Princess Stephanie, her father is King Stephen," Shirlynn waved her hand at Stephanie and then nodded at the man to continue with the introductions.

"Sir Owen Linah, Knight of Bergonia and protector of the peace for the Kingdom of Silversword, at your service," the man said with a bow to Shirlynn and shifted a smirk and wink towards Stephanie.

"You don't look like any knight I've ever seen. Where are your weapons or your helmet? How did you get past the great wall of Tallus?" Stephanie asked, lowering her arm but still held the knife tight and ready.

"The Knights of Bergonia and the Kingdom of Silversword believe in peace not war or weapons. We can defend ourselves but we do not intentionally fight or kill. Your more traditional looking knights can be seen in the castle but those of us select few that are trained in defense and posted near the borders, wear these outfits and use weapons for defense and fighting to take down an enemy without taking a life," Sir Owen explained in a formal tone, then smiled slyly, "and you, my dear, don't look like no princess or act like one."

"I know my father is real strict about letting strangers from other kingdoms into Tallus. How did you get past our wall and guards?" Stephanie asked, getting real irritated with this supposed knight, like he was more amused than honored to be in the presence of royalty.

"I have my ways, but when the legendary Shirlynn calls, you find a way. I must say, it is my honor to finally meet you and be the one to fulfill the life debt," Sir Owen said as he bent to one knee in front of Shirlynn, taking her hand and kissing the top of it.

"Wait, you've never met? Do you even know him? Are you sure he can be trusted?" Stephanie addressed the old lady who took a serious look, kissed the man's forehead and accepted his offer and instructing him to rise.

"As soon as I had my vision I sent word for *him* to come and here he is and I trust him completely," Shirlynn said as she handed the knight another bag of supplies.

"You sent word? How do you know this is the right guy if you have never met?" Stephanie asked confused, knowing there was more to the story than being told.

"Because, he's with him," Shirlynn said as a beautiful brown bird, which looked almost like a hawk, flew in landing on the knight's shoulder and bowing to Shirlynn, which Stephanie could almost swear looked like human facial expressions. "Thank you, Zain."

"Maybe I'm the crazy one," Stephanie muttered to herself and the bird flew over to Shirlynn as she walked into the kitchen, talking to the bird.

"Better get used to it. I am assuming, if your next to take over the Order of the Clerics, well, that's your future," the knight laughed as he walked past her, grabbing a few more bags and headed out the front door.

"That is not my future...or is it?" Stephanie said and then paused as she sat there and watched Shirlynn carry on what looked like a one-sided conversation with a bird.

"Horses are all set, we better get going if we want to make camp by nightfall," Sir Owen's voice came in from outside.

"Camp? We can easily make it to the castle and you all can stay there and then sneak out after dark," Stephanie suggested as she walked Shirlynn outside where Sir Owen stood petting and talking with her horse and the two beautiful brown horses with white spots he must have brought.

"Our mission is too important to risk your parent's catching and stopping us. We will camp not far away as you go in and talk to your brother. We will leave at dawn's light for I do not like and am too old to be traveling at night," Shirlynn said as the knight helped her up on the horse.

"I got it," Stephanie shrugged off the knight as she got on her own horse with ease.

"Forgive me, princess," Owen said with a mocking bow before gently mounting his horse.

"We can make camp at the Northern River, that way we won't be spotted with Stephanie and then use the river to guide us to where it meets with the Bergonia River," Shirlynn said more to the knight who nodded before urging his horse forward as Stephanie and Shirlynn followed with the bird flying far above them.

"I would really like to know how you got into Tallus without detection. Did you come in somehow from the Western Sea?" Stephanie asked as she moved alongside the young knight.

"Why, going to turn me in to your father?" Owen asked without looking at her.

"No, I won't turn you in, but I need to know for safety reasons," Stephanie said as she continued to stare without any reaction back.

"Trust me, the way I got in and the way we'll get out is a onetime thing," was all Sir Owen said causing Stephanie to huff in annoyance.

Stephanie did not know what it was about this guy but he just got to her. She had always liked helping people and seeing the best in others, but she was having trouble with the so-called knight. As much as he made her mad, she knew she had to try and get along with him as they were all here for one reason, help Shirlynn save Bergonia. Stephanie took a deep breath and let it out calming herself.

"Sad to say, we part ways here," Owen said as he brought his horse to a stop just at the edge of the Northern River.

"Don't worry, we will be here waiting for you at dawn's first light," Shirlynn assured the frowning girl and then said to the knight as he helped her off her horse, "we need her."

"What if something happens or I can't get back to you?" Stephanie worried about if she got in trouble for being gone so long and was unable to sneak back out.

"Don't worry, Zain will be keeping an eye on you and will let us know," Shirlynn said as she nodded at the bird who flew and landed on a tree branch near Stephanie.

"I'll be back," Stephanie hoped as she urged her horse across the river ignoring the comment that came from the knight about counting the hours.

Stephanie, a little angry, pushed her horse as fast as it could. Night would soon be upon the kingdom and she was more apt to be in trouble coming in after dark than before. She never intended on being gone this long. She thought she would find Shirlynn, chat and then return home in no time at all. Instead, she was in line to be a cleric and recruited to help find a bunch of Artifacts, stop evil and save all Bergonia. It was quite the day and she realized she should be more careful what she wished and dreamed for.

"Stephanie, where have you been?" A voice shouted causing her to look up and see her brother, on his horse, charging towards her.

"Steffon, I'm sorry, but," Stephanie started to explain when a different and scarier voice boomed at her.

"Guards, grab her and escort her back to the castle," King Stephen commanded. "We will talk later as supper is waiting."

"You did it this time," Steffon warned with pain in his voice as he watched the guards pull his sister off her horse and placed her in a carriage where he heard his mom start screaming the second his sister entered.

"Come along," the king called over to his son.

"Yes, father. Just as I," Steffon began to say when he turned and saw the horse his sister had been riding was nowhere to be seen, shrugged and rode off after his family.

****

     Stephanie stood in her room starring out her window. She would sit but it was still a little too sore to do so. She refused to cry and meditated bringing in a calm that helped her endure and forget the pain. It had been a very long time since her father had disciplined her. She was not sure what shocked her more, that he had done so at her age or that her mother demanded that he do it or she would, and no one would want that. She agreed that her mother's hand could be worse than her scolding, but not by much.

     No matter how much she had been yelled at and disciplined, she never once mentioned Shirlynn or where and what she really had been doing. She told her parents that she had tricked and ditched her brother so she could go riding and be by herself out in the fields, away from royal life. The fact she declared she hated and wanted nothing to do with being a princess was enough to take all focus away from where she had been. An hour later, here she stood in her room, not allowed out till she was summoned in the morning.

     "Hey," her brother said as a guard let him into the room.

     "Oh, Steffon," Stephanie cried as she hugged her brother, who tried but could never remain angry at his twin sister.

     "What happened to you? I was so mad when you never came back and really thought something may have happened to you."

     "Thank you for not telling."

     "You're lucky I didn't. When you never come back, I stayed out as long as I could looking for you. When it reached supper time I had to go back. I told dad that you took off and I tried everything to find you and he immediately led the search and never asked me any more since we found you soon after and decided to only reprimand me for losing you and saved the discipline for you."

     "I'm really sorry. I had every intention of being back but fate had other plans for me today," Stephanie said as she told her brother everything that had happened and he listened intently as

354

there were two rules between the twins – they told and trusted each other with everything and they never lied to each other.

"If I heard this from anyone else I would have them declared crazy," Steffon paused, and then sighed. "Stephanie, I love you and you know I would do anything for you, but I can't help you break out even one Minotaur. The risk of getting caught…the consequences of that alone." Steffon started to pace as he thought he kept seeing a bird continuously fly by the window.

"I have to do this, they need my help. All I need is to leave here and join them by dawn's first light and the location of the Minotaur mine. A way in would be great but we will take all the risk. You won't even be a part of it," Stephanie pleaded with her brother.

"I am already a part of it. Even if I did help you, you really think I can just let you run off with a crazy old lady and a knight who claims to have come here from beyond the wall? Oh, and a bird the lady talks to?" Steffon continued to pace flapping his arms in the air. Stephanie thought her brother was on the verge of a nervous breakdown.

"Please, I have to do this and I can do this, but not without your help," Stephanie said as she placed her hand on her brothers arm while the other touched her charm causing a sudden calmness to pass between the twins.

Steffon stood still for a minute and then breathed out slowly. "I'll give you the location and the way in but that's it. If you get caught you're on your own and I will deny any involvement." Stephanie almost shouted with joy but remembered the guards outside her door and gave her brother one last hug.

****

It was the middle of the night when everyone was asleep that Stephanie had made her escape out of the castle, wearing only her riding and traveling clothes with a bag clutched in her hand. She looked around and saw the bird, Zain. The bird seemed to be indicating which way to go so she followed and stopped when it motioned to her. It did not take long before she made it out of the castle grounds without running into any guards. She rested for a second to make sure the bag of supplies her brother had assisted in packing for her was secured to her back. Nodding to the bird and touching her charm, she ran as fast as she could, following Zain's lead.

She made it to the edge of the city but feared not making it back to the others in time. That fear vanished when she heard a snort and turned to see her white horse again. It had returned for her. Stephanie told the bird to race on a head and let Shirlynn know she was on her way. The bird darted off as Stephanie paused realizing she had been talking to a bird, shook her head and mounted the horse and bolted across the fields.

The sun had started to rise as she neared the Northern River. She could see Shirlynn and horses but no sign of the knight. Shirlynn clapped and waved when she saw Stephanie and her horse crossing the river. They made it to the other side and she was about to ask where Owen was when he came walking out from behind a bunch of trees and headed over to help Shirlynn onto her horse. "Almost left without you."

"Zain told us you were coming, and that you got the location to the slave mines," Shirlynn cheered with positivity.

"They are located north of here, where the great Mountain Falls flows into the Northern River. The entrance is hidden behind the waterfall," Stephanie said trying not to glare at the knight.

"Smart play, hidden in a location that your people won't go near and with that half of the Dwarves in isolation and it being at the edge where none of the mountain creatures will roam," Owen said more to himself than the group he was with.

"You seem to know a lot, not being from Tallus," Stephanie threw out there as she continued to be suspicious of the *knight*.

"As a Knight of Bergonia, it's my duty to know and gather as much information about our world. To be kept in isolation is being ignorant and opens you to disaster and danger," Sir Owen responded in a condescending tone.

"Let me tell you something…"

"Look, we've made it," Shirlynn chimed in bringing the party and the conversation to a halt.

Up ahead they could see where the mountain's base touched the Kingdom of Tallus' border. No giant wall was needed as nothing ever came out of the mountains and there was a guard patrol that kept watch just in case. Stephanie's brother told her that the guards change shift on a routine schedule and if timed right, they could move past without being seen and into the mountains where there was a secret entrance into the mines to avoid the hidden main entrance that was well guarded at the mountain-river base.

The bird, Zain, flew overhead and made a noise that everyone but Stephanie appeared to understand as both Shirlynn and Sir Owen nodded to each other and signaled it was clear to move on. The group quickly moved their horses away from the river and headed off to the west reaching the base of the Northern Mountains that put them a small unnoticeable distance from the mine's main entrance. Shirlynn slid off her horse with the help of Owen.

"We will leave the horses here," Sir Owen confirmed with a nod from Shirlynn and then glanced over to Stephanie.

"Will they be safe here?" Stephanie asked as she dismounted her beautiful white horse, noticing there was nowhere to tie any of the horses up.

"Don't worry, they'll return when we need them. Good ol' Diamond here will keep a watch over them," Shirlynn said as she touched the side of the white horse's face and then kissed the blue marking on his forehead.

"Diamond? This is your horse? It wasn't a coincidence that I found him, was it?" Stephanie asked the old woman who looked at her and smiled.

"He has been with me a long time, but he is your companion now. As sure as I am of you taking my place as head of the Order of Clerics, I knew you would return to see me so I had him wait for you," Shirlynn said as she gave one last rub and Diamond led the other horses away.

"How will he...?"

"Trust me, he'll know when you need him."

Stephanie stared after the horse and then looked at the old woman who kept smiling as she walked over to the knight. It was hard for her to believe what a turn life had taken in the last two days. The old lady turning out to be a cleric who's so old she was around during the Magic Wars and led a group of heroes that helped save Bergonia. Now she was part of a new group consisting of a man claiming to be a knight and a bird, destined to save Bergonia again. Stephanie was now not only a member of this group but was also destined to take over as the new leader of the Order of Clerics. Many, including herself, may have laughed at this, but Stephanie had always wanted to be out traveling and doing something to help others. She had gotten her wish and it felt right. It felt good.

"Where is this secret back entrance into the mines?" Sir Owen asked as they slowly moved along the mountains, Zain keeping watch from up above.

"Somewhere around here," Stephanie answered as she moved slowly, looking back and forth while unconsciously touching her charm. Her brother told her about where to look but she was unsure of the exact spot. Her fingers got warm as something caught her eye behind a big patch of bushes and vines along the side of the mountain. She brushed the greenery aside and saw the mountain base was slightly discolored. She pushed on it and the section went in and over revealing an entrance with a ladder leading straight down.

"I will go first, then Shirlynn and you bring up the rear," Sir Owen said as he began his decent followed by Shirlynn.

Stephanie stepped in and then glanced up as Zain flew high up into a tree branch. She assumed the bird was going to keep watch instead of joining them in the mines, which was probably for the best. As she stepped onto the ladder, the vines slid back across as she let go and helped move the piece of mountain back into place to close the secret entrance. The sudden darkness took her by surprise but carefully continued her way down the ladder.

After a little time had passed, Owen whispered up at them to halt. Stephanie stopped climbing down and waited patiently in the dark. Soon a light exploded below her that caused her to flinch. As she rubbed her eyes and looked down she saw Owen at the bottom of the ladder where he had opened a passageway. Once Shirlynn was safely off the ladder Stephanie made her way down and followed the two out closing the passageway behind her.

The three companions stood in a small mining tunnel lit by lanterns. Owen's head almost touched the top and there was barely enough room to stand side by side. To their right the tunnel went on a little ways but came to a dead end of solid mountain. With a silent motion, Owen moved them slowly down the tunnel away from the dead end. It was very quiet, dank and a bit chilly in the tunnel. So far there was no sign of anyone, including the Minotaurs. Stephanie was about to wonder how much farther this tunnel was going to take them when Owen brought them to stop.

"Another dead end?" Stephanie asked feeling defeated.

"No, below us," Shirlynn responded pointing to a medium sized hole in the ground.

"Did your brother say who or why a secret passage was made?" Owen asked as he knelt down and reached into the hole and found a handle, pulled up and brought a circular cover made of dirt and stone on the opposite side.

"He doesn't even know if my father knows about it. He accidently came across it one time he was left alone and he did a bit of exploring," Stephanie shrugged.

"Puzzling," Shirlynn said more to herself.

"Can't be common knowledge or the Minotaurs would have escaped a long time ago," Owen added as he carefully looked down into the hole then dropped down through it.

Owen suggested that Shirlynn stay behind and watch the secret escape while he and Stephanie continued on. The older woman started to protest but then realized how she might hold up a quick escape and agreed to remain behind. Stephanie dropped down through the hole and found it a short drop. Once down, Shirlynn told Stephanie that her charm should guide them back to her and then placed the cover back to hide the entry into the ceiling. Stephanie looked at Owen and then glanced at her surroundings.

They were in another mining tunnel but this time it was much wider with more lanterns providing light. The tunnel continued on in both directions, but only in front of them could they hear distant sounds of clanging, shouting and moaning. "Put this around your face, last thing you need is someone recognizing the king's daughter." Owen removed a white cloth from a pouch hanging on his right hip.

"Thanks." Stephanie took the cloth, wrapping and tying it so that only her face from the nose up was exposed. She was pretty sure with the way she was already dressed and had her hair tied back that no one would recognize her but this wrapped cloth would surly mask her identity.

As they moved forward, passing other tunnels leading elsewhere, the noise got louder until they arrived upon a balcony. Owen knelt to the ground signaling for her to do the same as they moved to the edge and looked over. Stephanie could see dozens of balconies and tunnels leading to this one giant cavern which all but made Stephanie cry out in horror. Down on the ground towards the center were dozens of Minotaurs, grunting and crying out in pain as they used picks, shovels or their own hands to move, fill or unload mining carts. There were tracks for the carts so they could move on down other tunnels as well as the Minotaurs to be lead off to other destinations to work, shackles around their hands and feet lead by very unfriendly guards. Looking at what she could see, the Minotaurs ranged from very young to very old but they all looked tired, dirty and bruised as guards yelled at them and sometimes whipped them.

"I have to stop this now," Stephanie said as she went to get up and a hand yanked her back down.

"I feel the same way, but there is no way we can fix this now. We have to find the Minotaur Shirlynn told us about and get him and us out of here alive. All of Bergonia is riding on us to complete this quest," Sir Owen said with a heavy heart.

Stephanie nodded, holding back her anger and tears, took another look over the ledge. When she first heard about the Minotaurs she pictured big ferocious beasts, but they really were no different from humans. Their bodies looked just like a human with only three differences. They had hooves for feet, a tail, and their heads were that of a bull. Like humans, some were small, fat, muscular, short, and tall as some were bald and others had hair or manes. Unlike a beast, they gave off full facial expressions and emotions that mirrored humans. Stephanie swore to herself right then and there, she would put an end to this one way or another.

Owen pointed to a hole off to the side where a wooden ladder led straight down to the cavern below. They both knew it would take a miracle to climb down a ladder without being noticed. Stephanie touched her hand to her charm and wished for one. Suddenly a voice boomed throughout the cavern demanding everyone's attention and it was a voice she recognized. "Steffon?"

"Who?"

"My brother, quiet so I can hear."

"I will be overseeing today's project as my father has other matters to attend to at the moment," Steffon said as he glanced up for a second before engaging the crowd.

Stephanie all but squealed. He had looked right at her and knew she was here. That meant her father was out looking for her while her brother had come here to help her free the Minotaur. Stephanie moved to the ladder as she heard her brother barking out his speech and instructions. "Hurry, while Steffon has all their attention directed at him."

Stephanie was already moving down the ladder before Owen could say anything. The ladder was not the sturdiest but she made it to the bottom and ducked behind a nearby mine cart. Moments later Owen was right beside her. They had done it without being spotted. Stephanie looked up and mouthed a thank you to her brother as she and Owen slipped down a mine tunnel and out of sight. She knew her brother was risking a lot just by doing that but it was enough. Now they were on their own to find the Magestic and get him out of here.

Chapter Twenty-One:
A Knight's Tale

"Do we even know if we're headed in the right direction?" Stephanie asked as it seemed like they had been moving forever down the mine shaft. She was getting tired and the smell and thinning air was starting to get to her. If it was not for the cloth she would have succumbed to her cough a long time ago.

"Shirlynn gave me something that she said would help guide us," Owen said opening up his palm showing a small compass that glowed a little like her charm but then a small puff of air pushed at them slightly from behind in the direction ahead of them.

"Where did she get that?" Stephanie asked as she stared at small object.

"It belonged to her one and only love. She said they had created it with both their special gifts. It can help you find what your looking for if you have something connected to fuel it. When she woke from the dream, some of Dwin's Magesti residue was on her and when she pulled it out, upon her wish, the compass pulled it off and is now locked on what we wish to find," Sir Owen explained as he took honor in Shirlynn trusting him with such a priceless heirloom of her true love. He would protect it and return it to her.

"If she had that, then why did she need me? She could have found it on her own," Stephanie asked feeling a bit flustered.

"Because she did. You not only found us a secret way in but can go where she is unable," Sir Owen said as he started to move onward, finished with the conversation. Stephanie started to protest but then realized he was right. Because of her and her connection to her brother, they could achieve this mission easier than Shirlynn could have on her own. Stephanie touched her charm, felt a calming connection to the old lady, and realized they all had their parts to play if they were to succeed, together, to save Bergonia. Stephanie nodded and followed after the knight.

They continued on for a few feet when Owen pushed her back up against the wall with his right arm as he jumped back quickly. Something was moving towards them as they could now hear shouting and the crack of whips. Stephanie glanced at the side of the wall and saw shadows dancing off of it giving shape to what looked like two Minotaurs followed by two men. As the group got closer, Stephanie could make out voices.

"Keep moving you filthy beast," a voice came followed by the crack of a whip and a loud thud.

"Mother! Stop it you're going to…" The plea stopped by what sounded like something being smacked hard against something else.

"I warned you cow that if you spoke again I'd whack you," a second voice laughed followed by the laughter of the first voice.

Stephanie felt her anger rising and this time she would not sit back and watch. She went to push Owen's arm off her when she realized he was already advancing. She moved quickly after him as the guards looked up in shock at the two of them charging. The first guard snapped his whip but Owen caught it and used the momentum to yank the guard forward and right into his fist knocking him out. Without hesitating, Owen used the whip and snagged the second guard's leg yanking it out from under him and making him fall flat on his back. Stephanie, grabbing the man's club, wacked him on the head making sure he stayed down.

"Nice," Owen said to the princess as he quickly used each guard's whip to bind their hands behind their backs while using some cloth to gag them in case they came too.

"What is going on?" The young Minotaur, with a muscular body the color of grey with a long black mane tied into braids asked as he rubbed a bleeding cut over his right eye that had a white patch of fur around it.

"Looks like we've found our Minotaur," Owen said looking down at the Minotaur, holding the compass out as it glowed and puffs of air kept moving from them to the creature in front of them.

"Found? Mother!" The Minotaur panicked but then swayed from the loss of blood. Stephanie could see that he was hit quite hard and the cut looked deep.

"Let me," Stephanie started to say wishing there was more she could do to help when she felt a strange sensation come over her body and her charm began to glow. She felt a part of her pass from her body and out her hand that she had cupped over the Minotaur's wound. Everyone, including Stephanie was surprised to see the cut completely healed.

"How did you do that?" The Minotaur asked as Stephanie leaned up against the wall, feeling very faint.

"She's a cleric and from the looks of it, a very young beginner," the older Minotaur said as she tried to move but winced from the pain of being whipped so many times causing her son to try and reach her.

"Hold on, let me get these off of you," Owen said as he took the key he retrieved from one of the guards, unlocking and removing the shackles from the Minotaur's hands and feet.

"Thank you," was all he said as he quickly knelt down by his mother as Owen freed her as well.

"Are you okay?" Owen asked stepping near the princess.

"Very light headed. I would try and help his mom but not sure I know how I helped him to begin with," Stephanie said as she looked at her hands, still feeling very weak.

"No, child, you need more training before you go pulling stunts like that or you'll drain the life right out of you. I'll be fine. I am Cleo, this is my son, Tor," the older Minotaur said, her smile lighting up her brown and dirt covered face.

"I'm Stephanie and this man here is Sir Owen of the," Stephanie started to finish the introductions when Owen suddenly moved over near the unconscious guards and listened down the tunnel.

"We need to hurry and get you out of here before more guards come," Sir Owen said looking back at them and specifically at Tor.

"Go where? I'm not going anywhere until I get some answers," Tor grunted with his deep voice while blowing air out his nostrils.

"We were sent here to rescue you. You have an ability inside of you that makes you special and you're needed to help us save Bergonia," Stephanie explained as she had finally started to feel her strength return to her.

"Ability?" Tor asked more to himself as Stephanie and Owen could see confusion and confirmation in the Minotaur's eyes.

"Yes, my son, you are special."

"That dream with the Dragon spirit, that was real?" Tor asked his mother as memories of the dream began to go from hazy to clear.

"The Dragon spirit is who sent us here to free you," Stephanie assured the Minotaur as Owen started to pace and grow impatient.

"I still don't understand. At first, I thought I was imagining things but after that dream it was like I was connected to the air or wind somehow," Tor looked to his mother for help, for answers.

"You know the stories that move amongst our people. About a great and powerful Minotaur that will one day come and save us? That it's more of a story to make us believe and inspire hope of our freedom? Well, the story is true. One passed down within our family from one generation to the next hoping the day will come, and it seems it has.

"Tor, most of our family believed it a story, but I know it to be true and now confirmed standing right in front of me. Legend has it a great Minotaur was chosen to help battle and sacrificed his life to save Bergonia during the Magic Wars. That great warrior was your ancestral grandfather, whom you are named after, Toro. His mate, your ancestral grandmother who was pregnant at the time, said she was told that a great power would be passed down within Toro's descendants till the day the one was needed," Cleo explained as she slowly made her way towards Owen and the opposite direction of the exit out.

"If that's the case, then I will stay here and help free our people," Tor proclaimed as his mother turned, looked at him and smiled through tears.

"No, my son, you will not stay. You will go with these people here."

"Mother."

"Our people believe in the one to free our people, but I believe and know it now in my heart, you are needed and have been granted the power not to save us, but to save all of Bergonia. We will continue to survive here until the day you come back to me, to all of us," Cleo said kissing her son on his head and then started down the tunnel.

"I can't leave you."

"Tor, you must. I do not have the strength and would slow you down. I must remain behind to cover your escape. I will be fine."

"Good luck to you," Owen said as he patted the woman's hand, slipping the master shackle key into it.

"As to you, I entrust my son's life and destiny." Cleo moved down the tunnel without looking back and out of sight.

"I will come back for you and for everyone," Tor called after his mother.

"We should go, Shirlynn is waiting for us," Stephanie said as she touched her charm knowing she really needed to talk to the old cleric.

"Shirlynn?" Tor questioned as he knelt down and took a club from the other guard.

"We need to go, explanations can be done after we are out of this place," Owen said as he moved quickly back in the direction they had come as to not let the old woman's sacrifice be in vain.

Tor took one last look in the direction his mother went and with a soft encouraging touch from Stephanie, followed after Owen. The three managed to make it back to the large central cavern that at the moment was empty except for a few working slaves. Stephanie guessed that her brother had led the guards all out on inspection of the mines in hopes of giving them a clear escape. Tor wanted to go help his people, but Stephanie had to remind him that they both will be of more value and able to help later, but the mission at hand was too important. She also vowed to come back and help him free his people.

With a gesture, Owen moved them at a sprint to the ladder that would lead them to the balcony they had originally come from. They were almost there when it seemed their luck had run out. "Stop them! We have intruders trying to still one of the cows!"

"Now what do we do?" Stephanie asked as she awkwardly held her club as a dozen or so guards came charging at them, clubs, whips and swords at the ready.

"You get Tor to Shirlynn," Owen said as he moved towards the advancing guards.

Tor and Stephanie hesitated as they watched Sir Owen spring into battle. Owen touched something on his armor that made it suddenly expand and encase his whole body, from head to toe, in shiny silver body armor. Now he looked more like the knights Stephanie was used to seeing except the armor was still form fitting and allowed for grand movement. Owen then reached behind his back and pulled loose a silver object that suddenly expanded into a large silver coated fighting staff. Owen in a few quick movements had twirled, swung and knocked out the first three approaching guards. As Stephanie and Tor moved to the ladder, Owen had fully engaged the guards, doing flips, kicks and moves she had never seen before.

Once Stephanie made it to the ladder, Tor insisted she climb up first. She moved as quickly as she could but stopped when she heard a familiar voice. "Halt or we'll shoot!" Stephanie looked over her shoulder and saw several guards standing out on all the balconies, arrows ready to fire as dozens more guards charged towards Owen who had impressively just took down the last of the original guards with his fighting stick and combat skills. Standing on one of the balconies, Stephanie glanced into her brother's eyes. She could see he was sorry and that he had no choice. His eyes also pleaded for her to surrender, but she knew out of her party, she would be the only one to come out alive if she did.

"Tor," Stephanie started to say when the Minotaur moved from the ladder and faced their enemy.

Tor could feel something deep inside him stirring and the more he thought about his people and his mother the stronger it got as did the air current in the cavern. As the power built up and he suddenly felt one with the wind, he let out a loud beastly roar which caused the cavern to explode with a hurricane level windstorm. Owen made it to the ladder just as the winds hit the guards and blew them all backwards as well as the arrows that had been released. Tor stood there glaring as the winds continued to blow holding the enemy back. Stephanie glanced up and saw that her brother, like the other guards on the balconies, were staying down as to not risk being blown off as a few had learned the hard way.

"Great work, kid. Stephanie, get moving we won't have much time before they recover," Owen said, his armor now retracted and reverting back to what he had originally been wearing.

"I will return, I promise," Tor shouted to his fellow Minotaurs before grabbing and following Stephanie up the ladder, swaying a bit from the use of his gift.

"Get them!" A voice shouted as the winds had now stopped with Tor no longer concentrating on them.

"Help me with this," Owen said as he moved off the ladder and onto the balcony taking Stephanie's club. With a few good hits from his and Tor's clubs, they managed to break the ladder free and stopping anyone from climbing up after them.

Owen looked to Stephanie and she knew it was time for her to lead them back to Shirlynn and the hidden escape route. Touching her charm, she let it guide her as she took off running, the other two right behind her. She knew they were getting close and felt relief until four guards stepped out in front of them. "We're to bring the humans in alive, the cow, not so much."

Stephanie stood there, making sure her face remained covered but not sure what to do next when Tor stepped in front of her. He pushed out his arms but nothing happened. It seemed he was unable to get the wind to attack again. He was going to try again but Owen, covered in his special armor again and using his fighting stick, propelled himself over the two of them and engaged the four guards. Stephanie watched in awe as she saw Owen disarm and take down the four guards with ease leaving them lying on the ground. Stephanie definitely knew that there was more to this *knight,* but those answers would have to be saved for later.

"You took them down without killing them," Tor commented in a tone that meant he was not sure if he was impressed or disappointed.

"I never kill when it's not necessary to do so," Owen said as his armor retracted and he urged Stephanie onward.

It didn't take long before Stephanie brought them to a stop and looked up. Tor moved to see what she was looking at when a piece of the ceiling moved and in its place was the face of an elderly woman with a big smile. Owen quickly helped lift Stephanie up into the hole. With a good leap, Owen followed with Tor easily reaching up and pulling himself up and into the new passageway. Owen turned and put the cover back into place. They had made it.

"I knew they would find you. I'm Shirlynn. I didn't know Toro very well, but looking at you, memories flow back and I'm amazed how much you look like him."

"Wait, how can you have known my ancestral grandfather? No human lives that long," Tor questioned the old lady, taking a big whiff and realizing she had an odd scent about her, not human like the girl and even odder than the scent he had gotten from the knight.

"It's a bit of a long story."

"One that can be told once we are far from here," Owen interrupted as he led the group back towards the secret passageway that would lead them out of the mines and back to the outside world.

"Where do we go once we are out of here?" Tor asked not sure why he was following this group blindly but something that had awakened in him made him feel this was the path he had to take, for now.

"We need to reach where the Bergonia River meets the southern wall, but as fast as we move it will still be almost a two-day journey," Owen said that hinted to Stephanie that there was something more he was worried about.

"We should be able to make it by sunset to the river's crossing, where the Northern River splits heading to the Western Sea in one direction and in the other merges into the Bergonia River heading south. Near there I have an old house we can eat and rest before making the final journey to the southern wall," Shirlynn said as they finally came to the secret passage in the wall, opened it and made their way in the dark up to the outside world above.

Once all four of them were now standing outside the Northern Mountains near the Kingdom of Tallus's border, Stephanie was shocked to see their three horses waiting for them. There was no sign of her father's guards but that may not last once they realized they may have made it out of the mines. Shirlynn joined Stephanie on Diamond, while Tor, a bit awkwardly, got on the one Shirlynn had ridden. Owen leapt onto his horse and Zain flew out of the trees, squawking and leading them on the race southward.

They had pushed the horses and were now well past Stephanie's home, Tallus with no further obstacles. They had stayed near the river banks and with Zain's help, steered clear of any people. Most would not care about them traveling if they were not in the company of a Minotaur. A creature no one in the kingdom knew existed, let alone being enslaved by the king himself. As Stephanie thought of her father, Zain flew low and began squawking at Shirlynn.

"It appears word must have been sent to your father. They are quite aways back but your father and some of his men have left the castle and are headed in our direction," Shirlynn said as she looked to Owen and then glanced at the sun as it started the beginning stages of setting.

"You all head on. I will double back and make sure they follow a wrong trail. That should buy us plenty of time and I will meet you at the wall," Owen said as he turned his horse around and darted back to the north.

"Don't worry, child, Zain will keep watch," Shirlynn smiled as she urged Diamond onward with Tor keeping up right behind them.

Stephanie did not know why, but she worried about the knight. She knew he was not that much older than she was but he acted as if he had been around so much longer than that. As the sun began to set she took a glance back but was surprised to see he was already gone from sight. All that was there were two horses racing off in two different directions, west and east. Stephanie took one last glance and then focused on the road ahead.

******

"Wake up, child. We need to get moving," Shirlynn said as she walked about the room and finished restocking their supplies.

"What about Owen?" Stephanie asked as she looked around and saw no sign of the knight and Tor sitting alone in the far corner of the room staring out the window of Shirlynn's home she had lived in many, many years ago.

"Don't worry about him," Shirlynn said as she went back to humming and packing.

Stephanie hadn't been the only one to have her whole life turned upside down. Tor, a slave since birth had not only found out he was part of a greater destiny and legacy but had to leave his mother and his people behind to follow it. When they had arrived at the small cottage and after they ate, Shirlynn told Tor everything, from her part and the Artifacts of Power in the Magic Wars to their rescue mission for him. That also meant revealing to him Stephanie's part, including who she was, the daughter of the royal family that had imprisoned his kind for ages. It was a lot for him to take in and sort through. Despite reassurances from Stephanie and Shirlynn, he still held mistrust in his eyes towards the princess.

"When I fell asleep, I heard you talking to Tor about doing what you could to help guide him in the training and use of his Magesti. How are you able to do that?" Stephanie asked, feeling a little jealous.

"In my vision with the spirit Dragon, Dwin, he guided me in what I needed to know to help the Magestic when I found him. It's really no different in the methods of training a cleric." Shirlynn stopped at the front door and turned to look right at the princess. "I am aware of what you did and I will train you, for you are destined to take over and restart the Order, but first, you must finish your own internal training and when you're ready, we will finish with the rest of your training."

Stephanie stared in confusion as the woman went out the door. She found it was better to not question things and to just go with it. With that, Stephanie grabbed her satchel and headed for the door. Today, if she understood correctly, would be the day she would leave the Kingdom of Tallus and enter the rest of the world. She paused and looked back at Tor. "Time to go." She smiled when he looked at her and when she got nothing back, she went out the door.

Stephanie yawned as she was still a little tired. They had only been given a few hours of sleep as time was precious and had to get moving. The stars were still shinning and Shirlynn mentioned that the sun would be rising in a few hours. Stephanie was surprised to see another horse had showed up sometime in the night and Shirlynn was already mounted and ready to go. Tor mumbled something about being easier to hide in the dark of night as he came out and mounted his horse. Stephanie looked one last time and saw no sign of Owen or Zain and then mounted her horse, Diamond.

They rode hard along the river banks, continuing to head south in the cover of night. After a few hours Shirlynn brought them to a stop so that the horses could drink and rest. Tor went off down the bank and knelt down and refreshed his face with the cool river's waters. Shirlynn said she would be right back and for Stephanie to keep an eye on Tor and the horses. Stephanie nodded and thought nothing of it until something pulled at the back of her mind. After a few minutes, as the sun started to rise, she got up and followed off into the nearby woods where Shirlynn had slipped into.

As she quietly stepped into the woods she stopped and hid behind a tree instinctively as she came upon two figures, an old woman and a beautiful black stallion. At first, Stephanie thought it was the crazy old lady talking to another animal and prepared to leave when the sun's first rays touched them and the horse began to neigh loudly. Stephanie then lost control and screamed as the sun's light fully engulfed the horse causing it to explode in a mix of light and fur and when it cleared, standing in the horse's place was a man, Owen.

"Oh, dear," Shirlynn said as she turned to see the princess standing behind them, trembling.

"What is going on?" Tor asked as he came bursting through the trees, club in hand ready for battle.

"One minute there was a horse and now the horse is gone," was all Stephanie managed to explain.

"That's what I smelled. It wasn't the horse you rode, the smell of horse is you," Tor grunted as he found himself surprisingly taking a protective stance in front of the princess.

"We don't have time for this," Owen said nervously looking at the old lady who placed a hand on his face.

"I think it's time you told your tale. Zain says we are safe and will keep watch. I will make us something to eat while you talk," Shirlynn said as she calmly led them all back to the river bank where their horses waited for them.

"I thought there was something about you with the armor and now whatever I saw back in the woods. Are you even a knight?" Stephanie asked as she remained standing near Tor while Owen took a seat and stared out into the river.

"I'm a knight but I am also something more. I am or was a magical creature known as a Centaur," Owen started, not sure where or how to tell his tale.

"A Centaur? That makes the scent clearer, but how are you in human form?" Tor asked looking the man up and down. He may have been born into captivity but his mother's stories had always kept him knowledgeable about other magical creatures.

"I want to know that too and your connection to Shirlynn," Stephanie added as Owen nodded, rubbed his chin and began to pick his words.

"My father was a Centaur and my mother was human. My mother was from Silversword and would sneak into the Forest of Spirits to be with the magical creatures. They accepted her and all adored her, including my father, until the day they crossed the line and did the forbidden act. They fell in love. Centaurs have a strict, no cross-breading law. Even though Centaurs are crossbreeds in themselves, they believe they are purebred and insist on keeping it that way.

"To be caught is to be exiled and in some cases, punishable by death. My parents, one fateful night, found themselves committing themselves to each other and fell into Spirit Falls and by some magic, my father temporarily took human form and they were able to consummate their bond. When they woke the next morning, they were on the ground, my father back to normal and my mother was with child.

"Of course, my parents didn't know that till she started to show, as it was impossible for it to be, they knew this was a magical miracle. As happy as they were, they knew it spelled trouble. My father couldn't leave the forest without being killed by humans just as my mother would be if she stayed in the forest and was caught by the Centaurs. Not knowing what to do, they did their best to hide it as my mother pretended to be pregnant by a man in her village and my father would only see her in secret.

"It went well until the day my mother went into labor. She was meeting my father at Spirit Falls, to tell him she would give birth anytime and it might be a while before she could travel back to see him. That is when the contractions started and she was having complications, which was expected given my heritage, and my father didn't know what to do. That is when a woman appeared on the Falls and offered to help and told my father to help move my mother into the water. My father started to move my mother when he got interrupted by another party, a group of Centaurs.

"It was a rival that hated my dad and when he found out about their affair he watched and tracked them and then rallied a group of elders and came at my parents when they were at their most vulnerable. When they saw the human woman pregnant it wasn't that hard for my father's rival to convince them that for the sake of the community, all three had to die. The mysterious woman who had appeared stepped forward and pleaded with them as they drew their bows and aimed it at the woman.

"That's when my mother screamed in pain and the woman moved to plead again but fell short when my father's rival fired his arrow right at the woman. Without thought, my father pushed her out of the way and took the arrow to his chest, not fatal but severe. My father than instructed the woman to help his life mate and his child and then charged the small group of Centaurs, not to win but to at least buy the woman, my mother and me some time. Arrows flew everywhere as my mother proceeded to give birth and unfortunately took an arrow to the back.

"Ignoring the pain, she fought hard and succeeded in giving birth to me, but with the arrow injury and the excessive bleeding from a human giving birth to a centaur, my mother was fading fast. The woman assisted my mom in stopping the bleeding and making her comfortable then took to tending to me. That was when my father appeared at the edge of the water, badly hurt and bleeding. My mother knew he didn't have long, she could feel his spirit fading. He had sacrificed his life to save them all but his rival and a few others had fled, injured, to get more help.

"That is when the woman revealed she was a spirit of the waters and was never in any danger, but because he had risked his life to save hers she would grant him his life in payment. My father declined, saying his life mate and son were more important and to grant that favor upon them. My mother pleaded no, but it was done. They said their goodbyes as my father passed and the woman grabbed me and my mother and moved us up the falls and up the Bergonia River towards the Silversword border.

"The woman told my mother that I was destined for greatness as she placed me into my mother's arms and moved to heal my mother, as she was near death herself. My mother stopped the woman and agreed that I was special and indicated that I could not survive as a Centaur in the forest or in Silversword. She insisted that the woman protect her son instead of healing her. This great love of another's life by my family deeply touched the spirit woman.

"The woman told my mom she agreed I had to live but she couldn't raise me nor would I make it on my own so she made a compromise to the life debt. She would make it so I could survive in the land of humans and grant my mother an extension on her life until I turned seven where she would have time to raise me and set me up to then continue on without her. My mother accepted and the woman basked us in a bright light and when it faded my mother found herself near the edge of the Bergonia River holding a human child, not a Centaur.

"Before my step-father, my mother's other life's husband found us, the spirit woman had given my mother her final words and instructions. First, she gave a reminder that when I turned seven, her life extension would fade and her spirit would cross over. There would be no exceptions or changes, she would die and she had to do what she had to do to raise me up to that point. Second, what was done to me would mask and protect me as long as I never went back into the Forest of Spirits and took heed to my new life change.

"It appeared that the spirit woman had made it so that I wouldn't be seen as a Centaur but only by dividing my life and soul into two. By day I was human and by night I was a horse. In order to avoid the magic alarms, I would have to submerge myself in the Bergonia River where its properties would mask the magical transformation that took place during the sun's first and last light. My mother took me back with her human husband where she raised me telling me everything I needed to know about my father and where I came from which I took seriously, listened and learned from my mother till I turned seven and she took ill and joined my father.

"I was angry and wanted revenge on the Centaurs and the world but discovered the Knights of Bergonia, a peace keeping order that fight without killing. I watched and learned from them till I turned thirteen and could officially enter training, which I did, becoming a knight and always living near the river keeping my real identity a secret and lived in peace and harmony until now," Owen said as he finished and looked at his audience and then back to the river.

"If what you said is true, how is it the alarms are not going off now?" Tor asked as he moved closer to the knight and took a seat.

"Her father, unknown to the kingdom, actually has them turned off. That's why once we get to Silversword I will have to really be careful and stay near the Bergonia River," Owen answered and then looked up as Stephanie had softened and joined the two of them.

"How do you know Shirlynn and where did you get your armor?" Stephanie asked wanting to change the subject from her father and what her family has done to the Minotaurs.

"My ancestral grandfather on my father's side allied himself with her during her quest to stop Drol Greb during the Magic Wars. She saved his life and he swore a blood debt to her, which every Centaur, no matter what your character is, takes seriously and honorably. The blood debt meant that at any time Shirlynn needed help or a favor, she could call upon it and he would *feel* it and come to her, no questions asked. If that favor is never needed, the blood debt meant that it would remain in effect and any descendant of Shirlynn could call on it and any descendant of my ancestral grandfather would have to honor it until it is fulfilled or one or both of the bloodlines ended.

"The blood debt was the first thing my mother told me about and I instantly took it seriously. I never thought it would happen until I felt it. The next day as I planned to leave, I was sitting at the river, right near the forest's border when Zain had arrived with a note from Shirlynn. Through the bond, I would have found the caller but she sent Zain to help speed things up and lead me right to her. Not only was I surprised by the calling of the blood debt but that the caller was Shirlynn and she was still alive after all this time.

"I didn't know how that was possible until I met her, of course. As I tried to determine how I was to get into Tallus I saw a form in the forest push something up the river. When it got to me it was the armor I now wear. It was one of two final gifts from the sprit woman that my mother told me about. She waved and was gone. The armor had instructions written on it, including that it would last though my transformations and being magic it would set off the alarms when fully activated. Which will limit me once we cross kingdoms," Owen said as he finally stood up.

"How are we going to do that?" Stephanie asked the question she had pondered before.

"By the second gift the spirit woman gave me. It can only be invoked twice, once to get here and once to get back," Owen said holding up a container that was half empty.

"Are we ready so we can make it past the wall before sunset?" Shirlynn asked as she brought each of them a cup of soup.

****

Each on horseback, they rode along the river's edge till they got within sight of the southern wall. Zain squawked and Shirlynn signaled them to stop. They would have to travel by foot to avoid being noticed by any locals around the small villages that resided in these parts. Stephanie knew they would not have to worry about any patrol guards because they only resided toward the west near the sea. Once they were all on foot the horses took off, except Diamond.

"Diamond is special enough to be able to make the trip with us under the wall," Shirlynn said walking forward next to the white horse leaving Stephanie with an open mouth.

"Under the wall?"

"You heard her, let's get moving or we won't be going anywhere if the sun sets before we cross," Owen said as he quickly moved down the river's bank toward the wall, the others falling not far behind.

"Everyone into the water, the sun will be going down soon." Owen jumped into the water that went up to his chest and pushed him towards the wall.

Diamond stepped into the water and maintained his balance as Shirlynn and Stephanie were instructed to stay close and hold on to the horse for balance. Tor got in next to Owen as Zain shot straight up into the air choosing to go over the wall instead of under. Once everyone was in the water and waiting, Owen instructed them to keep physical contact with each other as he grabbed Diamond's mane and then drank the last half of the container while grabbing hold of Tor with his now free hand.

Owen, even though he had done this before still shivered at the sudden change in his body. His body began to shift and become translucent and spirit like. Once his body had changed the effect spread onto to where he touched Tor and Diamond, where they quickly changed the same way as did Shirlynn and Stephanie when it spread to where they were holding on to the white horse. Soon all of them looked like spirits. That's when they heard someone shout and turned to see off in the distance, Stephanie's father and a group of guards riding towards them on horseback.

"We must hurry as the effects won't last much longer. To avoid setting off the alarms on the other side you must dive under the water, pass through the wall and remain submerged on the other side till you revert back to normal and can no longer breathe under water. Only then is it safe to rise up out of the water," Owen said as he prepared to dive under.

"What about Tor?" Stephanie asked.

"Another thing your father had wrong. Magic creatures don't set off alarms, only magic creatures that use magic set them off," Owen responded as he dove under.

Stephanie watched as Tor dove next followed by Shirlynn and Diamond. Her whole body felt weird and she almost hesitated when she heard her father shout again causing her to glance back and then dive under the water. It was a weird feeling as she did not even feel the water or even need to hold her breath. She swam forward and saw the wall blocking her way with several small slits that allowed the river to flow through to the other side. The others were nowhere in sight and she wondered where they went when she suddenly found herself passing through the wall and onto the other side. She felt relieved that it worked until seconds after her foot came through her body jerked and took physical form again causing her to choke.

"Thought we lost you," Owen laughed as Tor grabbed and heaved her out of the river and onto the bank where she coughed up water and tried to gain her breath back.

"I can't believe it, I'm out of Tallus," was all Stephanie could say through her coughing spasm.

"And from here on out, none can use magic," Owen said looking at both Shirlynn and Stephanie before diving back into the water just as the last rays of sunlight vanished.

"We can make camp over here," Shirlynn said as she moved towards a grove of trees Zain was already perched upon, Tor and Stephanie following after, but not before the princess glanced at the river one last time to see a black stallion leap out and trot over to an area Diamond had already settled down to rest.

Chapter Twenty-Two:
Docanesto

Docanesto moved quickly out of the castle. He had sent word out as per his master's instructions and now he had his own quest to undertake. His mission was an important one and Drol Greb instructed no one but him to complete it. He would now be out of touch and hoped everyone, including his daughter, did what they were supposed to do. He could not think of that now, as if he failed his mission, as he did long ago, he might as well not return as his life was good as forfeited. This was his second and Drol never gives second chances.

"Everyone is ready," a large muscular Barbarian said with a bow as he then led the master of all Fire Elves and the right hand to the lord and master, Drol Greb to a nearby group that had been waiting for him to arrive.

Docanesto thought back to the Magic Wars, he was a young Elf of about three hundred seasons when the war began. He had followed Drol Greb without question from the moment they had met. Drol had been gifted with power over magic and surpassed even Docanesto, his teacher. Drol was twenty in human years when Docanesto had met him. Having been frustrated with his father and the Elven community declaring him useless while rallying around his older brother Faldor as the next leader of the Elves, Docanesto had gone off into the world to find a better purpose and a way to gain the power and respect he deserved.

The aura of strong magic around the boy was what had drawn Docanesto to Drol. Drol had lived in a small city in the area of Bergonia that would one day be known as the Kingdom of Erikson. Even back then, most of the people did not trust magical creatures and frowned upon magic users. As Docanesto quietly walked the streets looking for the pull of magic guiding him, he heard the shouts of an angry mob. He moved to see what the commotion was and saw a small group of boys attacking a young human male, verbally and with rocks.

He saw the aura around the boy who had red flaming hair with one red eye and one black eye, but every time you looked the color changed locations. He was not muscular but he looked like he could take care of himself. He wore basic black pants, shoes and red top. Docanesto could tell he did not have a lot. He was begging the kids to leave him alone, not in a tone indicating he was afraid of them but more afraid for them. Docanesto leaned back and watched, knives ready.

The boy pleaded one last time warning them to stop. When they refused to leave him alone and the mob advanced, the boy with red hair and two-colored eyes screamed as he flung out both his arms towards the advancing mob. A magical blast from his right arm sent a majority of them flying backwards causing the rest to stop, except one, who had a stick raised, received a ball of fire from the other arm causing him to flop around and scream as he burned alive. The boy, looking drained, staggered allowing the bystanders to scream witch, among other words and threats and advanced quickly.

Docanesto was next to the boy before they even took two steps. Ears revealing his Elf nature caused the crowd to pause, which Docanesto did not even need, as he was upon them quickly. Within moments the remaining mob was dead, some by his magic, the rest by his blades. Blood dripping from his knives, he turned to the boy that instantly said the phrase that bonded them for life, "You and me, we could rule this world." That day forward, they left the city and would spend the next thirty seasons plotting, planning and raising an army to do just that, take over all of Bergonia.

They had setup base in what would be called the Unknown Lands. There they could train, plot and recruit without being noticed or bothered by the rest of Bergonia. From day one Docanesto knew Drol Greb would be the leader and he would follow and never questioned it. Whatever power Drol processed, which quickly surpassed Docanesto's training and power, was clearly that of a ruler, a king, a god. Docanesto committed himself and gave everything to Drol. Besides friendship and being his right hand, Drol gave something back to the Elf as well, a new taste of power.

About ten seasons before the Magic Wars would start, Drol had discovered something and offered it to Docanesto. Drol wouldn't tell him where or how he found it, but it was a fire-based power unlike magic. When Docanesto swore himself to Drol and accepted the power into him it changed him, physically and magically. His skin changed grey and his eyes red while his magic had become laced with fire. He could use his magic but when he used it with the new fire power, it was stronger. He had become the first and soon master and leader of a new race of evil and darker Elves, Fire Elves.

Not only did their army grow, but Drol magically created new creatures, the Drogans, half human – half Dragon – fueled by fire. When they were ready, they attacked and had almost won, if it hadn't been for Essej, Semaj and their champions, as well as his failure. Docanesto should have been there but he had been delayed and was at neither place - Drol Greb's side at his fortress nor their base where the portal had been setup. Because of that, Drol was defeated in an explosion that changed all of Bergonia, turning his fotress and a good portion of the land to the Desert and the guardian had been defeated as well as the portal being shut down and Drol banished away forever.

Angry, ashamed and defeated, Docanesto retreated into hiding with what was left of their forces deep into the Unknown Lands. He could never go back as even his own race would kill him on sight. Sulking and letting the world change around him, he remained in the Unknown Lands making empty promises to those that remained in his and Drol's forces as well as those that would seek sanctuary from the main world that started to hunt their kind, magic users and creatures. Without Drol, Docanesto had no real purpose anymore. Then about three hundred and seventy seasons or so after the Magic Wars ended, a voice whispered into Docanesto's mind.

It was Drol. He somehow had survived. The voice eventually led him to a specific spot, the spot where the portal had been closed. There he could hear Drol more clearly and learned his friend and master had not been killed but banished to another dimension by the group his Dragon and planted traitor had failed to stop. Right after the banishment something happened that demanded balance causing a small chip in the barrier that allowed Drol to focus on until the moment he was finally allowed to send his thoughts to the person he was bonded to, Docanesto.

Docanesto immediately went to work to figure out how to free his longtime friend and master. They could not simply reverse the spell as they did not know what had happened to the items that had been used or the item's users - except for one, the traitor who had been caught and killed. Without him or his body, Docanesto had no choice but to find another way and soon as Drol's voice in his head was growing weaker and weaker. Docanesto had all but given up when he stumbled upon a rumor of four witch sisters all born at the same time under a bizarre red moon and together could work very powerful and dark magic.

Docanesto had spent months searching for these sisters when he discovered that they not only existed but were living in isolation somewhere in the southwestern part of the Unknown Lands. Docanesto went at once and eventually found himself deep into the Unknown Lands, riding a small raft through the hot and smelly bogs towards a small cottage on a patch of land surrounded by the gross waters. As his raft touched land he heard a scream. He drew his small blades and leapt off the raft, approaching the cottage with great stealth.

He had moved to the window near the front door and peered in. He saw two old women wearing black robes laying on the floor with their arms tied behind their backs. One of them had her eyes wrapped by a cloth while the other one had her right eye sealed shut and her head hung as if she was unconscious or even dead. Over to the right of them was an ugly looking male troll about seven feet tall and hunched over. A third black robed woman was lying across a table, her left arm had just been severed. Blood flowed from the stump while the troll appeared to be sucking on and eating the arm.

Docanesto, needing the sisters, had crashed through the window, both knives released and hitting the troll in each of its eyes. The creature howled while Docanesto moved to the injured witch, placed his hand over the stump and summoned an intense ball of fire to cauterize the wound. The witch would be weak and in pain, but she would no longer bleed out. He then turned to face the troll who had pulled the knives out and was cursing and making threats. The witch with her eyes covered said he was

protected against magic but that did not matter to Docanesto as
he reached behind, pulled out his sword and with great speed and
might, plunged it deep into the troll's chest. As the creature fell
backwards, Docanesto retrieved his two knives and slit the
creatures throat finishing it off.

The witch with the cloth over her eyes introduced herself
as Tea, her sister next to her was Thea and the one on the table
was Tia. She had already known who he was, the right hand of
Drol Greb, Docanesto. He had asked if the trolls had injured
them as well and she had told him that their injuries had come
from something else a long time ago, the price of dark magic and
that being blind didn't mean she didn't see or know things. She
had told him that someone had sent the trolls to kill them as they
wore charms to mask them and to protect them from magic,
which is how they had surprised them and captured the sisters.
She then said that their fourth sister, Thia, had been taken by the
second troll out back somewhere and pleaded for him to save
her.

He agreed to save the sister if they swore a blood oath to
owe him a favor in return. After some reluctance and the screams
outside somewhere, the three sisters, as Thea had finally come
around, swore to him the oath bound by magic. Docanesto then
bolted from the cottage, weapons in hand and found the final
troll, who appeared to be eating the witch's fingers. The troll
dropped the old woman when he saw Docanesto running towards
him. Before the troll could speak, Docanesto, like the other troll,
made quick work of the fowl creature. His speed and skill with
the blades left the troll bleeding out and lifeless upon the ground.
With the troll dead, Docanesto had moved to the witch's side,
cauterized the stubs where six fingers had once been with fire
and then carried the old witch back into the cottage.

The witches thanked him as Tea demanded to know
what Docanesto wanted from them in return. Docanesto had
laughed as he told them he needed their help in freeing Drol
Greb. The other three witches started to refuse saying they
wanted nothing to do with him and that is why they stayed in
hiding the first time around. Docanesto made note of their age
and prolonged life as well as their deliberate choice not to come
out and assist Drol. Docanesto looked right at Tea who he knew

could see him clearly. Without saying any more, she silenced her sisters and said they had to honor the debt and would do so by doing what they could to assist in opening the portal.

Docanesto took the four witch sisters back to the location of the last portal and spent the next few years working to free Drol Greb. Docanesto and the witches worked on the magic to open the portal while Docanesto had Drol's followers begin the rebuilding of Drol's castle, followers and army. They had no doubt that the witch sisters would succeed and when they did, they wanted to be ready to launch their attack back on Bergonia the moment he stepped foot back into their world. That day, which they hoped would come, occurred about three hundred and eighty-three years after the Magic Wars.

By this time the Unknown Lands had become the Kingdom of Drol and the City of Greb was flourishing with Castle Darkheart standing in the center of the city and placed right over the secret area containing the portal. The castle had been named, upon Drol's request, in jest to his longtime, long dead enemy, Semaj Lightheart. It was a reminder that the light has fallen and the dark was rising. Docanesto stood in the chamber where the design on the floor had been crafted by him and the witch sisters, the sacrifice unknowingly next to him and the witches in each of their designated spots.

With a quick motion, Docanesto had slit the sacrifice's throat and threw him in the middle of the witches, him and his blood igniting the ritual. The four witch sisters went right into action and cast their darkest magic as Docanesto had watched with anticipation. He had felt the dark magic basking over him as he awaited the return of his master. After what seemed like forever and a moment of brief doubt, an explosion of light filled the chamber as the portal ripped open and a form had begun to step through. Docanesto had cheered as he waited for Drol to step though. Those cheers with Drol's screams of success ended when the opposite had happened. The portal had been breached but Drol was unable to physically come through, only his spirit could manifest.

After several months of intense spell casting, numerous sacrifices and draining the four witches to the brink of collapse, they had all discovered that Drol could manifest in spirit only, with the assistance of the witches' spell and could not physically return. Drol knew and told them that the only way for him to fully return was with the use of the Artifacts of Power, as they had trapped him and only they could set him free. Docanesto and Drol hated this setback but reveled in the fact that until he was set free, he could still manifest in this world to command and guide his forces. That was when the sisters laughed.

They had informed Docanesto and Drol that their part was done and they would be leaving. Docanesto told them they could not leave but Tea reminded him that they agreed they would break the barrier and do what they could and since the barrier was broken and it was established that they had done all that they could but it would take other means to free Drol, their part and the debt was done and they would be leaving. With that, they ended the spell and Drol vanished with the portal. Docanesto stood ready as the witches joined hands and called on their powerful magic and announced they would be leaving. That was when Docanesto laughed, loud and powerfully.

When the sister's magic fizzled and an invisible force knocked them back, Docanesto muttered two words of magic that caused rings to form around their necks cutting off their air and bringing them to their knees. That was when Docanesto informed the four witch sisters that he, with the guidance of Drol Greb, placed safeguards within the symbol the witches helped create in the ground. It not only prevented them from stepping out of it but placed a binding on their magic so they could not use it to escape or place harm to Drol Greb, Docanesto or anyone who's sworn loyalty to them. The rings were also a magical safe guard to help force their assistance in allowing Drol's spirit to visit. They were trapped and had no choice but to do Docanesto and Drol's bidding, but Drol did promise them that if they did as they were told and serve him, when he did return to the physical world he would grant them back their health and their youth, which made their forced help more bearable.

After a few months of the four sisters being made to help reunite Docanesto with Drol Greb, Drol's forces and plans continued to grow but without the Artifacts of Power there was no way for Drol to completely return to Bergonia. They had needed to find a way to obtain the Artifacts but after so much time, they could be anywhere. Docanesto swore there had to be a way to track them down and that was when Drol had an idea come to him. With the painful forced help of the witch sisters, Drol made them invoke a very old and powerful form of dark magic, necromancy.

It took three dozen sacrifices and pooled magic from Docanesto and his Fire Elves with the four sisters, but the spell was cast. They all stood there in anticipation when a strange wave pulsed through them all. Even Docanesto felt like something died deep inside of him and felt chilled. All the sisters moaned except one, Tea, who laughed. She said it was done. A creature somewhere out there had been raised with the means of leading them to the Artifacts of Power and she could not tell them where or what.

Docanesto had threatened to rip her tongue out for laughing and refusing to give him the information, but she clarified that she truly could not and that was not why she was laughing. She had been laughing because a balance had to be made and right now a prophecy had been revealed to her that a Chosen One would also be reborn to gather the Magestics to stop Drol Greb. Immediately Docanesto, guided by Drol, cast a spell that went through the four witch sisters making them unleash another dark spell unto the world. The witches screamed at him asking what he had just done as Docanesto smiled.

He told them that he had made them send a spell to merge and counter the Chosen One Prophecy. Now a force would be created to help hunt and stop the Chosen One and the Magestics. Tea looked right at Docanesto as he felt her eyes through the covered cloth as a strange sensation had crossed over everyone. She then informed him that because of that act, due to balance, a force would now give birth to a being to counter the one created to find the Artifacts. Now there were two forces of good and two forces of evil that were in play and it was just a matter of time.

For about the next five seasons Drocanesto, with the guidance, worked to recruit and build their forces. They were going to do it better this time and win, Chosen One or not. Drol had even come clean about his discovery and the location he had been keeping it. Docanesto burst with pure excitement when he went and found it. After the battle with Essej and Semaj, they now knew what they had. Filled with new ideas to better them and their army, he tried to recreate and imprivoe on what Drol had done before when he was alive. Towards the end of that five seasons, Docanesto discovered something that would change everything, and it did. After he had retrieved it, he applied it to the fire source and he, as well as all that repledged and newly pledge to Drol and the fire, became stronger and their fire based magic was now undetectable. Creatures like the Drogans, Fire Hounds and Tazarians were created differently and much better than previous incarnations. There was more they could do and there would be no one that would stop them this time, except maybe one.

It had been almost a season later before Docanesto had stumbled upon the one that would counter the Chosen One. Docanesto and Drol had named him Lucian Darkheart and would train and raise him with one mission, to help find and stop the evil Chosen One destined to stop Drol's forces. Now, about sixteen seasons later, everything was in motion with the Chosen One and their counter. Only thing left was to start the hunt for the Artifacts of Power.

Then a few months ago, they had stumbled upon the being they had been searching for that would lead them to the Artifacts. Word had come to the castle that something was coming out of the Fire Mountains. Docanesto could not believe the description and had not seen or heard anything like it so he grabbed a few of his best warriors and raced to confront it before it got near the City of Greb.

Right away Docanesto knew they had nothing to worry about as it walked very slowly with a staggering step. The creature had a human form but it was covered from head to toe in a black, charred rock like substance. There were no signs of having ears, eyes, nose or mouth as Docanesto moved towards it, magic ready, but when the creature got close to him it stopped and just stood there. Docanesto just stared and then realized this thing was the one when it muttered the only two words it would mutter in a low groggy voice, over and over – Staff. Tallus.

The staff, the main Artifact to tie all the Artifacts together was located in Tallus. Docanesto brought the creature back to the castle and instantly and periodically sent a small group of Drogans to the Kingdom of Tallus to search and look for the staff or any signs of it. Up until this day, they have had no luck but that was all about to change. Docanesto was ready to take on the quest himself and lead a group out of the Unknown Lands to find the staff and then locate the rest of the Artifacts of Power so he could free Drol Greb once and for all.

Docanesto could feel the pressure as he looked at the group in front of him. Everything he and Drol have been planning and doing would be forfeited if he could not find and obtain the seven Artifacts of Power. Seven items that were used over three hundred and eighty seasons ago, their owners long dead with no idea where they ended up. He could not even remember whom or if even his informant had told him who each item owner was. Another mistake on his part. Now he had one certain lead and his tracker.

"Tracker appears to have made a change. It is saying staff but now the second word is Silversword," informed the large muscular Barbarian.

Docanesto looked at the black charred rock creature, whom he had simply named Tracker, as it just stood there muttering the two words over and over as it stood among the assembled group. "It can't be."

"Sir?" The Barbarian asked nervously, trying not to make eye contact with the dark master of the Fire Elves.

"The other forces are on the move for the Artifacts as well and it appears they have the staff, but how did they get past the wall and why Silversword?"

"Maybe that is where another Artifact will be found," the Barbarian suggested as Docanesto glanced at him. The Barbarian was named Rayvac and was one of the commanders of Drol's Barbarian forces. He was very muscular and tall with dark black beard and shaggy hair. His weapon of choice was a deadly long sword but he usually just used his hands.

Docanesto knew the Barbarian commander was right. With the staff, their tracker must be going for the next Artifact. This changed everything, once again. Originally, Docanesto was going to travel through the secret tunnels leading under the Forest of Spirits to the safety of Argoth, but thanks to Lucian, the

Elves were on to them and those passages would be watched and trapped. Going up and over the Fire Mountains was not an option so that left using the secret passage or risk going right through the Forest itself and facing the Elves and all its magical habitants. Docanesto did not have the time or resources to waste in a battle that would start a war Drol was not yet ready for.

Docanesto decided that they would pass through the secret passage through the Fire Mountains but then at the edge of the Forest they would take the short distance run along the edge of the Forest and lava river to the Eastern Sea and then sail up to Argoth. It would be a time-consuming route but sensible one as going the opposite direction was too long and they would not survive that long on the lava river or risk getting caught by the Elves. Now with the recent revelation from Tracker, they needed to get to Silversword fast. What other option did they have other than going straight into the Forest of Spirits?

Whatever he decided, he knew this group before him or any of his followers would go to their deaths in the name of Drol Greb. Rayvac had assembled ten of his strongest warriors, a mix of men and woman ready and willing to fight. He also had numerous Fire Hounds and Tazarians at his disposal for travel, as well as twelve Tazarian Riders, seven Fire Elves and the other five humans. The humans, Docanesto trusted, as all humans that were in the Unknown Lands were those that either agreed with Drol, their ancestors had defected to the Unknown Lands when the Magic Wars ended or when the Kingdoms rose and those who supported magic and magic creatures were forced away and hunted. It helped that these lesser humans pledged their loyalty and took the fire. Since they were humans, they were only allowed enough to shift their flesh and become servants to Drol.

Along with the seven Fire Elf Tazarian Riders, he had seven more of his best ground fighting Fire Elves as well as twenty Drogans. Because of the magic alarms and this mission still had to be under the radar of the human kingdoms, he was limited and had to be careful who he brought. The Fire Elves and Drogans did not use pure magic so no risk there but that meant any other magic users would be risky to bring. Luckily, he did have three other individuals he could bring that he did not have to worry about setting off any alarms.

The first was a Draelvman, like a Huelgon, the creature is part Dragon, part human and part Elf. Like the new Drogans, they are created by non-natural means. They are nowhere as powerful as a true Huelgon but are gifted with magic laced with a source that masks them from the magic alarms. He is one of only three that exist as they are harder to create than the Drogans and the three they had were the only ones to survive the process successfully and remain alive. There was one in Sorran leading the Drogans, one back at the castle and the third, right in front of him.

He simply went by Draelv and was the first successfully created. The other two survived but Draelv was more powerful and a bigger success. Draelv had black and red streaked hair that went down to his shoulders, facial hair only around his mouth and wore red pants and black boots only so his muscular torso could be seen. He did wear a red cape that clasped around his neck and flowed down to his lower back. Next to him stood the last two members of Docanesto's team.

They were brother and sister, twin half-Elves. Their mother was a human and their father a Wild Elf. Being half human, they were shunned by the other Wild Elves and ended up joining Drol Greb's forces with the only desire to one day bring down the Elves and place themselves as rulers of their people. They looked like your normal average Wild Elf, as they denounced magic and refused to pledge themselves to Drol and take in the fire. Instead, they fought with their skills and weapons of choice, Lio with his wrist blades and Lia with her double-bladed staff. Drol did not require everyone to take the fire pledge but it was easier to trust and control those that did. Docanesto trusted these two as he never saw anyone who hated the Elves more than he did. They did have red paint markings all over their bodies to show their loyalties.

"We await your commands," Rayvac said breaking Docanesto's thoughts.

"We need to get to Silversword fast but Drol isn't ready for a full out war with the Elves and the Forest. If we plunge right into the Forest we will have no choice but to fight. I wish we had another option," Docanesto said as he started to strategize the unavoidable war with his former kin.

"I can help with that," said a voice that sounded like a light drawn out whisper.

Docanesto turned, blade in one hand and the other forming a ball of fire as every member of his party drew their weapons. "Stay where you are," Docanesto commanded the newcomer.

"I come as an ally in means of helping you cross the Forest of Spirits." The figure was that of a woman. Signs of her race or what she actually looked like was covered up by a black material that started from her feet and ran up to her head. It fit tightly to her body but showed no signs of ears or eyes. Only a silhouette of a nose was there and a mouth seemed to take shape and move when she talked. She carried no weapons and stood there looking right at Docanesto paying no mind to the others gathered.

"I've never seen you before. Who or what are you?" Docanesto demanded.

"You can call me Kae. As for what I am, you could consider me a shadow warrior."

"There's no such thing as a shadow warrior," Rayvac added and then stepped back with a glance from Docanesto.

"Oh, we exist, well at least once a very long time ago, but now there is just me," Kae said, no change of pitch or emotion in her voice.

"I've been around a very long time."

"As have I, way longer than you, Docanesto but that isn't what's important here. With my help I can get you through the Forest of Spirits."

"What's in it for you?"

"Helping retrieve the Artifacts and revenge on an old friend," the shadow warrior answered Docanesto, who swore he could feel a smile with the last half of her statement.

"How do you propose we cross the Forest?" Docanesto asked as he kept his eyes on the woman and his magic ready.

"You send some of your men along your secret passageway and while they cause the distraction, I will open up mine," Kae responded causing the master of Fire Elves to raise his eyebrows.

****

After making sure there was nothing or no one watching the area where the secret passages were on both sides of the lava river, Draelv used his abilities to raise a big area of lava and then harden it draining the heat so it was only warm to the touch. Docanesto and his large party stood upon it. Right in site, on the edge of the Forest of Spirits, Docanesto could see the tree that held the magic entrance to the secret passageway that went under the forest and to the Old River Gorge. He turned and looked at the shadow warrior who did not even glance his way. All she did was nod.

Docanesto looked at the tree and invoked the spell that would open the secret passageway. Once it was open, Docanesto gave the command and ten Drogans, five Barbarians and four Fire Elves raced down into the secret passage. Before he sealed the entrance, he, with a little help from Draelv, sent a strange glowing fireball into the passageway. A magical insurance, for once his men were attacked it would trigger the magical spell causing the fireball to soar through the passageway, incinerating all within as well as collapsing and sealing the secret passageway permanently.

"Now while they are distracted." Kae moved and faced the opposite direction of the tree, directly west. As her arms stretched out in front of her, they seemed to gather and pull the darkness from beneath the trees, merging and becoming one. It was hard to tell whether it was one long shadow or if it was actually a tunnel leading along or below the forest floor. "Go now."

Docanesto followed the command from the shadow warrior, this once, and led his small army towards the shadow passageway. Docanesto had his doubts but was surprised as he got near it was as if he was swallowed by the darkness and then was suddenly in a dark tunnel that somehow guided them forward. It was a strange sensation, as if they were not actually moving themselves, but transported forward through the darkness. After a few moments, they came to the end and found themselves stepping out from behind a waterfall, Spirit Falls.

"We must hurry before we are noticed," Kae said as her secret passageway closed and vanished once she stepped out.

"Too late, we must warn," a centaur started to say, but was silenced by an arrow made of fire to the face.

"Go!" Another centaur shouted as three of its party dashed off into the woods leaving him and three others to face the intruders that had appeared out of the darkness.

Docanesto knew they could not draw attention with a battle so he, Rayvac and Draelv moved quickly upon the three centaurs in front of them.

"Whoever they are, I think they mean great harm," a female centaur said but went silent as she glanced back at the friends they had left behind.

"As long as we make it back to the camp we can alert," the second of the three racing centaurs tried to respond before something came out of nowhere severing his head, sending it flying away from the rest of his body.

"No!" The female centaur screamed as she and the other remaining centaur came to a sudden halt as two figures stood in front of them.

"Nice one, sister."

"Thank you, brother."

With a nod, the twins separated and dashed towards their prey. Lia crouched low as she twirled her double-bladed staff slicing the female centaur's hooves. As the centaur began to drop in pain, Lia stopped the motion of her staff by gripping it firm with both hands, leaping backwards in a flip bring her lower end staff blade up and gutting the female centaur from torso to head. As Lia landed, she swung her staff back and around ready for a final blow that clearly was no longer needed.

The male centaur aimed his bow and loaded it with two arrows as Lio ran at him. Fully aware of his natural surroundings, the Elf timed his next move just as the centaur released the arrows right at him. Using a large rock in front of him as a platform, Lio leapt and propelled himself up, grabbed a low tree branch and swung himself up and over the arrows and somersaulting right onto the back of the centaur. As the centaur started to twist to remove the unwanted rider, Lio brought his fists towards each side of the centaur's head, making his blades extract from his wristbands and held them firm as the centaur fell forward, pulling the blades out once the creature had hit the ground.

Lia started towards her brother and his kill when she heard a tiny squeal causing her to turn and look up to see a Fairy floating above the battle area. The small Fairy, wondering alone in the wrong place at the wrong time turned and darted away. Lia fearing their cover blown was relieved to see her brother already in motion. Running a few steps and then punching his right arm out, Lio detached and sent his blade flying through the air like a dart hitting and pinning the Fairy to a tree by its wing. As it tried to free itself, Lia was there, staff trusting upwards hitting it and flipping the Fairy and blade up and off the tree. In the same movement, Lia then swung the bottom of her staff upwards slicing the Fairy in two while nicking her brother's blade sending it backwards as Lio moved, raised his arm up and allowed the blade to land and attach back on his wristband before retracting both blades.

The twin Elves, smiling in victory, dashed back towards their group. When they arrived, they saw Docanesto and the rest of the group standing there, unharmed and no sign of the three centaurs that had stayed behind to fight them. The twins could smell a hint of burning hair and flesh in the air but no bodies anywhere. Docanesto moved towards the twins. "The centaurs?"

"Dead," they answered in unison.

"And the bodies?" Docanesto asked as the twins looked at each other in a way that did not make him happy with the unsaid answer.

"Don't worry, they and any evidence has been taken care of," Draelv proclaimed as he landed, hitting the ground with a thud as his large red wings folded and shrank out of sight while his red scaly skin shifted back to smooth pink flesh.

"We better go before we are spotted again," Rayvac urged his master.

"We can't stay out in the open like this and we'll surely be spotted if we run for the Silversword border," Docanesto advanced upon the shadow warrior.

"We will use the water to take us. My gifts will allow the river to carry us quickly and unseen to the border's edge," Kae replied stepping towards the waters of Spirit Falls.

"You, it can't be. We will not permit this," a female voice said causing Docanesto and the others to look over and see what looked like spirits taking the shape of a Dragon and a woman.

Without saying a word, Kae swirled her hands causing darkness to flow out of them before breaking off and flying at the two spirits, hitting them both in the face and wrapping their heads in darkness. "Everyone, into the water."

Docanesto moved towards Spirit Falls as Kae stepped into the water. He watched in amusement as Kae seemed to melt into and causing the water to shift to a black hue. Docanesto quickly jumped into the water and was shocked when he did not splash or go under the water. Instead, it was as if the dark water reached up, grabbed him and pulled him into darkness. He laid there as he felt himself yanked up the falls and then the Bergonia River with great force and speed. Before long, he felt the light return as he was thrown from the river. Docanesto stood up, completely dry, and saw he was right at the edge where the Forest of Spirits gave way to the kingdom of man. Docanesto smiled and looked past the tree and onto their destination, the Kingdom of Silversword as the rest of his army one by one emerged from the river.

Chapter Twenty-Three:
What Lies Beneath

Semaj sat close to one of the several fires Anna had created the night before to keep them all warm. Winter was coming and he could feel it. Being this far north near the mountains and Frosted Waters, it was already colder than he was used to this time of year. The wind howled and felt cooler as it lifted off the frozen water and up into the mountains behind them. After they had all emerged from the mountains they had made camp right at the edge of the Frosted Waters. Being this close to the water the Snogres would leave them alone. Everyone was still sleeping after the exhausting battle but not Semaj. The farmer in him always had him up right before sunrise, plus he had another dream.

He was drowning in water but was then saved by a mysterious creature that looked almost half human and half fish, but he wasn't sure as the dream did not last long as it was interrupted by the faceless evil intruder that laughed while two Magestics stood by his side. They were not human looking, but he was not sure what manor of creatures they were. If Thom had been there he would probably know for sure from his books. He knew they had to get to Ogra before it was too late, but the underwater dream was very prominent. His gut told him they had to find that Magestic first and that would take them into water of some sorts.

Semaj shivered a little as he looked out over the Frosted Waters and then looked at the group he was with. The two Dwarves slept next to each other near their own fire while Essej half slept by his fire, closer to the mountains to make sure nothing tried to come out after them. Thom and Anna slept off to the side by their own since Anna was mad at him and Thom was keeping her safe. Semaj sat by his fire alone while Nat was off by herself with her own fire. There was a big discussion before they had all gone to bed over Nat and that had been more exhausting than any battle they had been in so far.

After he and Anna had saved Nat, nothing was said till everyone was sitting around the fire and half way through their meal. That was when Anna asked Essej if he knew who Drocana or Lucian was and filled him in on her description and the battle that took place between her and Nat. Essej looked up into the sky before he had answered. He said he knew nothing of the two names mentioned but said that Docanesto was as evil as an Elf could be and was Drol Greb's right hand and if Drocana claimed to be his daughter and was sent here for the Chosen One then she was probably as evil and dangerous as her father.

All eyes had then been on Nat, even Semaj's but as much as his gut told him that there was this connection with her and that he felt he could trust her, he wanted answers too. Nat sat there in silence until Anna finally screamed at her that she either talks or she would be thrown out of the group. Nat almost got up but paused when she had made eye contact with Semaj and her angry death filled look softened and she settled back down. With a sigh, she glanced at Anna and then had looked right at Semaj and spoke directly to him. Essej raised a hand signaling Anna and the others to remain calm and not interrupt the Wild Elf.

Nat told them that everything she had done and said to them so far was true, for the most part. She had told them that when she was younger she had traveled around and ended up in the Unknown Lands. While exploring she had met a young boy named Lucian and they had quickly become friends, along with a few others. They were a tight group and had remained friends even to this day, like Semaj and his group of friends. This friendship was the main reason she chose to remain in the Unknown Lands and not everything about the Unknown Lands was bad or evil. That was just stories humans placed upon the land the magical creatures had fled to survive. That was something Semaj was starting to see, not all magic or its creatures are evil, just like not all humans are good.

The Wild Elf then told them that there was an army building in the Unknown Lands and it was being headed up by Docanesto and Drol Greb, whom no one had yet to see in person but a select few, which included Docanesto. She told them that there was many flocking to them and joining their cause. Lucian and many of her friends wanted to join up with the cause because Lucian and the others were told that this was a fight to let the magical creatures of Bergonia to be free and live among the humans again – to take back what was taken from them – freedom. Nat said she felt this way but never fully committed to Drol Greb and refused to become a Fire Elf.

At this point, Anna started in but Essej silenced her with a look and agreed, not all from the Unknown Lands are evil. He did look right at Nat and made it clear that Docanesto and Drol Greb were the pure definition of evil and they plan nothing but world domination and destruction for all of Bergonia. He also admitted that the humans were wrong with what they had done and could see how easy it would be for Drol to manipulate those feelings to recruit people, but Drol's intentions were not for freedom but for world enslavement of all, magic and non-magic alike. Semaj could see in Nat's eyes that she was a little defensive but felt the truth of the old man's words. In Semaj's gut, he knew Nat was not evil and that there was good in her and despite what Anna thought, he believed the Elf was not currently working for Drol Greb's forces.

Nat then told them that Lucian had come to her and said that he had heard that a Chosen One meant to stop Drol's forces had been discovered and was located somewhere in the Northern Mountains. He had told her that Docanesto wanted this being found. Lucian felt that they should find the Chosen One before Docanesto and Drol did, and since she had no family and liked traveling, he had asked her to locate the Chosen One and report back. She said she knew someone in their group was the Chosen One and joined them at first to get more information but had now come to really care for the group and truly wanted to help them. Semaj noticed that she looked right at him when she made that last remark.

Nat told them that she knew Drocana and that she was evil but had no idea she was even up here in the Northern Mountains. Docanesto must have sent her to find and take down the Chosen One. An assumption that was true based on the recent attack on them. Nat said, that in her heart, she knows Semaj and his group are good and that Drol and his forces are evil, but if he gave the word, she would leave, but she hoped to stay. They had taken a vote and everyone, except Anna voted to give her a chance and let her stay. Semaj was glad and felt it was the right decision, but a small part of him hoped they would not regret it or Anna would never let him hear the end of it. Either way, he knew Essej and Anna would be watching her closely.

Essej had also, with his gift, held a private conversation with him, Thom and the two Magestics letting them know to keep the identity of the Chosen One from Nat. No matter her intentions, good or bad, she is marked by Drol's forces and they will be after her to obtain that information, willingly or not. Semaj hated keeping this from Nat as he liked and trusted her but they all made the vow to keep this part secret even to Lorax or anyone else they may encounter. The fewer who knew, the less likely Drol would find out and place Semaj in danger.

"You're up early."

"Couldn't sleep." Semaj glanced up as Essej took a seat next to him by the fire.

"Dream?" Essej asked as he called upon the winds to make the sound of their voices reach their ears only.

"Wasn't a major one but I'm sure we need to find the Magestic in the water before we go to Ogra to stop whoever is after the two Magestics there."

"She didn't know who that might be?"

"She doesn't know and nothing was ever said to her nor has she heard of a move on Ogra. She is only aware of the preparing of war upon the Five Kingdoms. You do trust her, don't you?"

"I believe, no matter what was before, she is with us now."

Semaj waited and got no further explanation. He really hated when the old man was cryptic or refused give a lot of details. Knowing it was best, he changed the subject. "Do you know where in the water this Magestic might be found?"

"Where do you think?"

"I don't…"

"Close your eyes and think about the Magestic in your dream, find a connection and then *look*."

Semaj closed his eyes and tried to remember the dream he had. Nothing was happening and he began to get frustrated and felt a little silly until he saw a small glimpse of the dream. He then tried to focus on it and soon saw the Magestic, but this time he could see that they had a fish's tail. As he tried to get a clearer look he felt as if his body was pulling him forward. He felt like he was going to go right in the water and panicked, jerking himself forward and opening his eyes to see something was glittery over the Frosted Waters. He blinked and it faded away.

"What did you *see*?"

"I saw the Magestic under the water but all I could see is that whoever it was had a tail? Then I felt like I was being pulled into the water and woke up. For a split second, I swore I saw something shiny over there but it was gone when I blinked," Semaj said as he motioned towards the Frosted Waters.

"Lucky for us, it appears this Magestic we seek can be found right there."

"Under the water?" Semaj asked, his voice getting loud in his surprise and breaking the protection of the wind.

"What's under the water?" Nat asked as she awoke from the sudden burst of sound, jumped up quickly and looked to the Frosted Waters as if something was attacking.

"The next Magestic we seek," Essej said with a smile that seemed to calm the startled Wild Elf as she joined their campfire.

"Why is there a Magestic under the water?" Anna asked as she had also made her way over to the camp fire.

"Anna, go wake the others. We can talk over breakfast," Essej said as the girl glared at Nat and Semaj and then went to get Thom and the two Dwarves.

"What can you tell us about the water folk? My books don't really have anything on them, just that there are magical beings that dwell deep beneath the waters," Thom started the moment Anna had told him and he raced on ahead of her and the Dwarves.

"Not much is really known about the water folk. They tend to keep to themselves as they rarely get involved in the affairs of the surface world. Few come to the surface and no land walker has ever gone down below and returned," Essej said as he looked past everyone and just stared out onto the Frosted Waters as Lorax helped Anna prepare food for everyone.

"I always thought that only food and fish were found out there, but then Dwarves don't tend to worry about anything past our mountains," Noraxa added as she devoured her breakfast.

"What about you?" Anna asked looking with suspicion at the Wild Elf.

"No, just rumors and stories. I've never even been on the open seas," Nat said speaking the truth.

"Right, like Drol doesn't have some kind of sea monsters at his command waiting to attack," Anna spat rolling her eyes.

"Listen here, I don't have to defend myself to you, but I would think some know it all like you would be aware that the Unknown Lands are shut away from the rest of Bergonia by the great Fire Mountains, which includes the surrounding seas," Nat said ready to gut the girl but calmed herself when she saw Semaj watching her.

"Then how did you get here?" Anna spat back.

"Enough, both of you," Semaj interjected, glaring more at Anna which made her blood begin to boil.

"In my lifetime, I've only met one," Essej threw out causing everyone to suddenly go quiet. "His name was Ard-Rich and he left his home against his people's wishes to help us fight Drol Greb."

"How is that possible?" Lorax asked licking his fingers clean.

"Water folk can walk on land, right?" Thom asked looking to Essej for confirmation from what he had read in his books.

"Yes, some creatures can survive on land and most water folk do have the ability to walk on land but if they actually do they keep it hidden. What I tell you or know is what I had learned from Ard-Rich," Essej started as he reached deep into his mind to clear his memories from long ago.

"There are many different water folk colonies and kingdoms but Ard-Rich was from the Kingdom of Coral. They considered themselves the main rulers and authority over the Eastern Waters. At the time, Ard-Rich had just turned a hundred," Essej said when Thom gasped.

"He was that old?"

"Water folk, like most magical based beings tend to have longer life spans than humans. He was about twenty if compared to a human, so quite young. Most water folk can live to as old as about eight hundred. His race of water folk is called Océans. They are half human and half fish – human from the waist up and from the waist down they have a strong powerful tail that allows them to move and swim fast under the water. Their flesh is icy blue in color while their tails all very in style, shape and color.

"The Océans in most colonies and kingdoms follow the same ruling structure. The king rules until he dies or reaches about three hundred or three-fifty and then the prince resumes the throne. If the prince's father is still alive when he takes the throne, the former king becomes the Sire, who is in charge of watching, guiding and spreading the stories and wisdom to the next generation while, if by some chance the currant Sire is still alive, retires and enjoys the comfort of his final days with no responsibilities or involvement at all. If there is only a daughter, then she, with the help of her parents, must select a mate to stand by her side and rule as the new king. If there are no heirs or blood family to step into the role, there are big battles and power plays to see who will become the new ruler of the underwater kingdom.

"Back before the Magic Wars started and we went to war with Drol Greb and his forces, Ard-Rich was the youngest of several siblings in a smaller colony where his family was considered the leader. The nearby Kingdom of Coral had a princess and was seeking out a mate for her and all eyes were on him and his siblings as potential mates. Ard-Rich did not have a desire to be king and so chose to leave the waters and explore the surface world of Bergonia.

"Water folk, specifically the Océans have natural born abilities, some stronger than others. They can communicate and to some degree control sea creatures as well as manipulate water in various forms. They can also breathe under as well as above water but if they want to walk on land they have to reject the water within and force it out of their bodies. In that moment, their tail dries out and molts off leaving them with two human legs. The process leaves them weak and vulnerable but after a little time they can walk steady and gain their strength back. The effects of living under water does make their bodies on land stronger and more resistant to harm than the average human even though giving up the water also means they can no longer control sea life or water. The only way to become water folk again is to be submerged in water and accept the water back into their bodies.

"That is what Ard-Rich had done, he became human and walked and traveled the dry land of Bergonia. He learned to avoid water and stay inside when it rained to avoid the risk and temptation to accept the water and revert back. Eventually he met me and my group about the time we were gathering to wage war on Drol. He trusted me enough and the others to reveal who he was and where he was from. He even tried to recruit the help of his family and other Océans but they refused as they had made him an outcast for choosing land over water. Despite being shunned, he joined our fight, and in the end, when we won, he gave his right arm and eye to help save all of Bergonia," Essej said with a heavy sigh as this brought back thoughts of his beloved Semaj Lightheart.

"Whatever happened to him?" Anna asked.

"I don't know. When the Frosted Waters were created and all of Bergonia was changed with the defeat of Drol Greb, he was very concerned about his family and the fate of his fellow Océans and returned to the sea. I never saw him again and the water folk seemed to go into complete isolation from the rest of Bergonia, even more than before. He'd be about five hundred or so now, so he could still be alive, but I really don't know," Essej answered as he tried to regain his composure from the trip down memory lane.

"You don't think he's the Magestic we are looking for?" Semaj asked looking at Thom and Anna whose eyes had given way to the same thought.

"No, even if he was still alive, the originals were meant as temporary hosts with access to the power, but the Magesti would have been passed down through the generations and accessible to the latest in the bloodline when all the Magestics were called upon again. I don't recall seeing him on the ledge in the dream," Essej said causing the young ones to suddenly remember the dream and that bit of forgotten information.

"Will this Coral place be located right under the Frosted Waters?" Lorax asked feeling a bit nervous about going on or even under the water.

"I don't know but it seems we are being pulled in that direction so it or the Magestic we seek is somewhere under there," Essej said glancing sideways as Semaj who gave a confirming nod.

"How do you suppose we go about getting in touch with this fish creature?" Noraxa asked.

"Or survive crossing the Frosted Waters, we'll surely freeze," Lorax added getting more nervous.

"I can use my ability to keep us warm," Anna smiled proudly.

"And melt the ice under us and cause us to fall through," Nat countered.

"Oh, no, we surely can't." Lorax turned to Noraxa who ignored him and looked right at Essej.

"You mean for us to go under the water." The Dwarf's statement caused all to draw in deep breaths.

"Maybe, maybe not, but we will need to travel across the Frosted Waters." Essej stood up and raised his arms over the iced over waters, his skin becoming scaly and almost translucent white. Wings of pure white expanded from his back and flapped as he raised up into the air. His eyes glowed white as the wind began to pick up. Suddenly the air got cooler as the wind seemed to bring the cold mountain air down and soar right over top and across the Frosted Waters.

"What is he doing?" Anna asked as she moved closer to the fire, using her gift to keep it lit.

"He's reinforcing the ice on top of the water," Thom answered as he knelt down and could see the top of the Frosted Waters getting thicker.

"I thought the ice was hard enough for us to walk across?"

"It is, Dwarf, he just wants to add extra enforcement for our rides," Nat said, her eyes looking past them towards the mountains.

"Freezia!" Noraxa screamed as several shapes emerged from the mountains and headed right for them.

"If we are going to use them, then why did we leave them behind in the first place?" Semaj asked looking between his friends and Essej who had not even wavered from his spot in the sky.

"We had to in order to make it here quickly and past the Snogres," Lorax responded as he moved towards the oncoming Frostites.

"Without riders, they can move much faster and easier through certain paths and routes in the mountains. We will definitely make it across the Frosted Waters to Ogra quicker and safer with them," Noraxa added as she grabbed and hugged her companion and friend.

"We can go," Essej said as he landed, walking towards them with a weaker movement as his wings folded back and vanished and his eyes and skin returned to normal.

The group each quickly mounted their own Frostite and moved across the Frosted Waters. As they raced at a good pace, Semaj ended up next to Essej while the others followed behind them. Essej wanted Semaj near him so he could let him know when he felt they were close or on top of the Magestic they were searching for. Semaj kept his eyes closed and tried to concentrate on the Magesti power under the water. Every now and then he would feel a tug and Essej would shift them in that direction without hesitation. Semaj hoped he was leading them in the right direction and really wished he had more confidence in his abilities as Essej did. Semaj was not sure he was doing anything right until he got a very powerful sensation that almost knocked him out.

"What is it boy?" Essej asked when he saw Semaj sway a bit.

"It was like something punched me in the gut," Semaj said which made Essej hold up his arm and bring them all to an immediate halt.

"Why are we stopping?" Anna asked, looking around for signs of trouble.

"I believe the Magestic we are searching for is somewhere directly under us," Essej said as he slid off his Frostite and walked away from the group.

Semaj started to follow but Essej pointed at him to stop. As they all sat in silence, watching, Essej raised his arms in the air, his skin turning scaly and white. The wind began to blow from all around them, moving with great speed as a small cyclone began to form a few feet in front of Essej. With a gesture of his hands, the cyclone spun fast and became very narrow, one end moving towards Essej's mouth and the other end hitting the Frosted Waters and moved as if it were drilling into the ice. No one could hear what Essej was saying but his lips were moving frantically into the cyclone.

"What exactly is he..." was all Anna got out when a loud rumbling from under them was followed by a big boom that cracked the ice all around them.

"Essej, stop," Semaj started to plea when the ice split under him.

"Semaj!" Anna and Thom both shouted when they saw their friend and his Frostite fall through the ice and down into the water below.

"Oh dear," Essej said as he turned from the cyclone that instantly faded into nothing and took flight as his wings appeared and opened up right before the ice split underneath him.

"Everyone, back," Noraxa said as the ice started to crack more and more.

"We have to save him," Nat said, almost surprised by the words that came out of her mouth as well as the feelings backing them.

"Nat, don't," was all Thom got out before she dove into the water, her body adjusting to survive the bitter cold.

Anna ran to the edge and the ice cracked and gave way causing her to slide towards the water. She was prepared to go under when she felt a tug and was lifted up into the air. She looked up and saw Essej had her and was flying her back away from the hole and cracking ice. "Put me down. The ice is already reforming, we got to save him before he is sealed under."

Thom turned to the hole and saw the Frostite pop up from under the water, trying to claw onto the iced edge, which was starting to freeze over and seal up. Thom heard the whispers and felt the pull as his crystal began to glow. Shouting words that suddenly popped into his head, Thom pointed his finger at the Frostite and then made a raising motion with his hands causing the creature to slowly rise out of the water and then placed safely down upon the nearby ice. Thom swayed as he released the magic and looked for signs of Semaj and Nat, but the hole was almost frozen over.

"Thom, stand back," Anna said as he moved away from the now tiny hole of water.

Anna was safely back on the ice after Essej put her down and ran back towards Thom and the spot Semaj had gone under. Anna closed her eyes and reached for the Magesti power that rested within her and pulled it forth, connecting with the area around the almost sealed hole. She commanded the area to heat up and she pushed with all her might. Glowing red heat could almost be seen as steam rose up and the small hole grew larger as the ice melted and parted back. Thom moved farther back as Essej remained in the air as to not fall in as the area of water expanded. Once she got a big enough circle of water, Anna stopped and maintained her focus to keep the now small pond of water from freezing back over.

"I see someone," Thom said as Nat's head suddenly emerged, gasping for breath.

"I couldn't find him, let me go back," Nat pleaded as Essej swooped down, plucking her out of the water and moving her to safety. Thom moved closer and closed his eyes trying to get the crystal to help him find and save his best friend.

****

Semaj gasped, losing his breath and taking in water as the shock of the cold hit his body. As he went under he looked up and saw the exit point getting farther away and appeared to be closing. Trying to hold his breath in hopes of making it back up to the surface, he felt something snag his foot and pull him down. He looked with panic as he saw some kind of rope made of seaweed wrapped around his ankle. He tried to shake and rip it off but it was strong and something on the other end was holding firm. He was starting to feel a burning in his chest as his lungs begged for air. Darkness started to take him over when several forms moved towards him, one of them holding the other end of the rope.

Just as he was about to succumb, he felt air instantly rushing back into his lungs. He could breathe again. He took several breaths, in and out, before he realized he was still under the water. He was beside himself. How was it possible he was breathing? Was he dead and dreaming this? Semaj then took note that he was not dreaming and was surrounded by five beings, human from the waist up and from the waist down a tail. Semaj realized that these must be the water folk Essej had told them about. Four looked to be young in appearance while the fifth one was much older, wearing a long white beard to match his pure white hair that flowed with the water's movement. The older water folk held a golden spear in his hand that matched all the others except his had three prongs on the top instead of one like the other water folk with him.

"Calm down, I have altered the water around you to allow the air and oxygen to flow through so you can breathe," the old one said as the other water folk kept him surrounded, pointing their spears at him.

Semaj noticed that the old man's right arm was missing and he wore a patch over his right eye. His tail was light blue while his fins were white like his hair. The other water folk had various colors for tails as did the female who just happened to be the one holding the seaweed rope around his ankle. Like the men, she wore a form of an armored chest piece that matched her spear. She had long wavy red hair that complimented her dark red tail with pinkish fins. She looked to be about his age and from the constant looking back and forth from him to the old guy, Semaj assumed she had never been this close to a human before.

"Sorry, I've never met someone like you before, let alone being under water and breathing," Semaj said as he was getting a tugging sensation but couldn't tell if it was from the girl or the old man. "I am here with an old friend of yours I think, his name is Essej. We are looking."

"Silence." The old man glared, paused and then softened his facial features a bit. "Essej. I haven't heard that name in a long time. I thought it might have been him who sent words through the water baring my name."

"Then you are Ard-Rich?"

"Grandpa, Sire, how does this land dweller know your name and who is Essej?" The girl asked.

"Mi-Ta, you and the others head back or your father will be worried. I will take this one back to the surface."

"We can't leave you here."

"Sire, the princess is right. We can't leave you with *him*."

"I may no longer be king but I do hold some authority. Take the princess back and I will return soon. Now go!"

Semaj watched patiently as the rope fell from his foot and the water folk swam off, the girl stopping to look back a few times before they were gone and out of sight. When Ard-Rich seemed satisfied that they were gone he swam towards him, grabbed his shirt and bolted straight towards the surface. Being this close, Semaj got a strange feeling from the Océan, not as strong as the other Magestics but it was definitely there within. Maybe Essej was wrong and the power of the Magesti doesn't always get passed down and he just found the Magestic they were looking for.

"Semaj!" Semaj heard Anna scream as he suddenly burst out of the water and landed back upon the ice, coughing as his lungs shifted back to normal breathing.

"Thank Venéah. I was sure I lost you too," Thom cried as he grabbed and hugged his friend while Anna released her powers and joined them in a group hug.

"Essej, my old friend, I thought you'd be dead or at least retired away by now, not leading another group," a voice laughed as water rose from the hole and began rotating fast enough to keep it from freezing over and closing up.

"Ard-Rich, I never thought I would see you again in this life," Essej smirked as he walked near the hole where an old man now floated with his chest and head exposed above the water.

"The time has come?"

"Yes, Drol Greb is trying to return and his forces are gathering. The Magestics are needed."

"And you are gathering them."

"With the help of the Chosen One we will stop him for good this time."

"Then I will do what I can," Ard-Rich said as he pushed the water to lift himself up and onto the edge of the ice, pulling his tail out of the water. He then closed his one eye, concentrated and made his tail shift, split and take the form of two legs while his right arm reformed right before their eyes. He then reached under his chest plate and pulled out a piece of cloth that he quickly slid over his legs that would now cover his waist down to his knees. "I'm probably the only one that still carries human clothing, then again, I am the only one that still sneaks away to take small walks upon the land from time to time."

"How is that possible? I mean, you said water folk have to repel the water to take human form." Thom stared at the man's newly formed legs and arm that were still dripping with water.

"That's true, but I have a special gift that allows me to alter my body without denouncing the water and becoming a land dweller," Ard-Rich said as he walked towards the group, the hole he came out of freezing over and sealing the entrance back to his world.

"Aren't you cold?" Anna asked looking at the barely clothed man and, who despite his age, was still pretty toned.

"Océans' bodies are made to withstand the cold depths of the seas. Even up here, the cold doesn't bother me."

Essej kept eye contact with the Océan as he studied him. He could sense the power within him and from the impression he got from Semaj, his old friend still had the Magesti power drawing the Chosen One to him. "You still host the Body Magesti. I'm surprised you hadn't had the heirs to pass it down to."

"That's why I'm confused, because he does. I mean, the other water folk that were down there with him, he commanded them to return the princess home and I swear I heard her call him grandfather."

"Is that true?" Essej asked, slowly circling his old friend.

"Yes, I have a granddaughter. When I returned to the water after the defeat of Drol, the Océans and all water folk and creatures were in disarray from geographical changes Bergonia fell under. With my experience in battle and now hosting my Magesti power, I helped gain control over and end the battles under the sea. In doing so, I won the hand of Princess Ann-Sue and established the Kingdom of Coral as the dominant and ruling kingdom of the sea with me as its king.

"We ruled for many seasons with a firm hand and a steady growing peace. We even declared the surface world off limits, especially when I got word the humans were declaring war on all magical beings and creatures. Many, even I, soon believed, that the creation of the Frosted Waters had been a sign that the water folk were never meant to touch land again. About two hundred and fifty seasons ago, my lovely bride gave birth to our one and only son, Dal-Ran.

"As time went by, I became Sire as my son became the king and had two children of his own, Prince En-Steve and Princess Mi-Ta. It wasn't long after their birth that I lost the love of my life. Despite all the time I spent with my grandchildren, I was lonely and heart broken and soon snuck off from time to time to walk upon the surface once again, a secret none of our people are aware of as well as my one other secret, the power of the Magesti that resides in me. I figured there was no point in revealing my past or this secret unless the time came, but I never thought it would," the former King of Coral said as the Huelgon finally half smiled and stopped staring him down.

"Yes, that time has come and as surprising as it is that you are still the Magestic, I welcome and plead for your help in joining us in our quest."

"Well, Essej, where am I following you to this time?" Both old men laughed as they put their arms around each other while Essej filled him in on everything that has happened and their travels across the Frosted Waters to the land of Ogra.

Chapter Twenty-Four:
The Land Of Ogres

Semaj found himself lost, trying to make his way through what appeared to be swamp land. He didn't know how he got here as last he remembered they had found the Magestic from under the water and had pushed their Frostites onward so they would cross the Frosted Waters and make it to the Ogra border before dark. He continued to look around for signs of anyone else when he saw a glowing white-blue light. He turned and saw two figures walking towards him and he smiled with relief. "Thom! Anna!"

"Anna saw you squirming in your sleep and could feel a connection, so she told me to pull us into your dream. I concentrated on connecting with you and only pulling in Magestics so Anna could join us."

"I am so glad this is a dream and that I'm not really lost out here. Then again, if this is where I am in my dream than I guess this is where we are being pulled towards."

"If you concentrated on Magestics then I have you to thank for this," Noraxa said as she made her way towards them trudging through the marsh.

"Sorry."

"Wait, Thom, if you pulled the Magestics than why isn't Essej or the new guy with us?" Anna asked as they all did a quick look around.

"Not sure. Maybe because Essej isn't a true Magestic and his powers are just Magesti based from his Dragon King father. As for Ard-Rich, something is not quite right. I sense the Magesti in him but it isn't strong like what I feel from you and Noraxa. To be honest, I still feel a faint pull back behind us. I think we have a Magestic but not the actual one we need," Semaj said as he saw in front of him a faint hazy image of Ard-Rich sleeping and when he glanced behind him he saw a faint image of the Océan girl with red hair swimming.

"Maybe you should have a word with Essej and tell him," Anna suggested.

"I tried but he stops me before I can start. I think he's putting his trust in his old friend and if Essej was concerned he would have done something by now," Semaj offered with a shrug.

"If something wasn't right wouldn't we be in the water right now instead of this disgusting place?" Thom added as Semaj agreed.

His dreams always told him where he needed to go and this time they were placed in what he assumed was the land of Ogra. "Since this is a dream coming to me, there usually is also a sign of what Magesti is reaching out to me," Semaj said as he and the others started to investigate their surroundings.

"Look!"

Everyone glanced over to where Noraxa had pointed. The area of land was decaying right before their eyes as if something was causing it all to die. It was a grave dark cold feeling that made them all shiver as it moved slowly towards them. Then a few feet to the right was a fleet of nasty looking creatures but it was hard to make them out. It was as if their heads were pulsing and with every pulse, a pain shot into all of their minds. "What is going on?" Anna asked as she rubbed her temples after each pulse.

"It seems Semaj is being led to Ogra and there we will find our next two Magestics. What you are being shown are the Magesti of Death and the Magesti of Mind. Two very powerful gifts to be left in the hands of Drol Greb's forces," Essej said as he appeared out of nowhere, walking towards them with Ard-Rich right behind him.

"How?" Semaj whispered right next to Thom.

"It was weird. I felt this strange pull and when I focused on it I woke up here," Ard-Rich said as the two boys looked at each other not sure if he heard their earlier conversation.

"It appears when the Chosen One receives his dream messages, he can pull Magestics in with him as well as Thom's crystal can pull others in too," Essej explained as he eyed them closely and glanced back to the decaying land that was getting closer to them.

"We need to get to those two before…" Anna started to say when a strange rumbling cut her off.

"You're too late. I will have them and use them to put a stop to your evil plans," a voice boomed through with grand laughter as hordes of creatures came charging at them.

"No!" Semaj screamed as he sat right up and looked around him. He was no longer in the marshes about to be trampled but lying on the shore between the Frosted Waters and the Western Mountains of Ogra.

"You okay?" Nat asked as she glanced over. She had already been awake before the sun had started to rise.

"Just a bad dream," Semaj said as he noticed the others from the dream awake and a bit frazzled. They all knew what the dream meant, to find the two Magestics meant they would be walking into a huge battle.

"Good, now that everyone is awake we can get moving again," Essej said as he started to urge the camp to eat and pack up.

"We have no choice but to go through the mountains." Noraxa commented as she eyed the massive body of mountains, tall, huge and void of any signs of snow. They may look different than her mountains but her gut told her the dangers would be the same.

Ard-Rich stepped next to the female Dwarf and looked at the mountain range and then addressed the group. "During my many travels on the surface I've explored the land of Ogra. We are far enough north that there isn't a huge section of mountains that divide us from the marsh lands. There is a straight path that will take us safely through the mountains and with the Frostites it shouldn't take long. From there, dead east is the Gooblyn City which we should make by day's end."

"There must not be a lot of danger if you can travel all over this place and explore," Lorax said hoping for confirmation that may not come.

"The danger is real. The mountains are overrun with giant Ogres and then out in the marsh and swamp lands of Ogra you will find marsh type snakes and creatures like the Goblins, Hobgoblins, that are uglier and more feral than a Goblin, as well as the Gooblyns, that are basically Goblins but more intelligent and colonized. Fortunately for me, my Magesti allowed me to blend in a bit."

"Are we sure about this?" Lorax asked looking at his dear love.

"There is something inside me that keeps pulling me towards this," Noraxa said confirming the same thing that had been coursing through Anna and Semaj, the Magesti and their destiny.

"Please, with all of our gifts nothing can stop us. We have to do this, for Lars," Thom said, the ladder bringing tears to his eyes as his heart still ached for the man he loved and lost because of Drol Greb and his Drogans. He breathed in and regained composure as he felt his two friend's hands squeezing his shoulders.

"For Lars and to save Bergonia," Anna and Semaj added before they turned and joined the others in getting ready to move out.

Ard-Rich took point riding with Essej as he led them onto the path through the mountains. The path was narrow and allowed for them to ride single file. Anna followed next, then Semaj, Noraxa, Lorax with Thom and Nat bringing up the rear. Along with her growing feelings for Semaj, Nat was also taking a liking to Thom. Despite losing the love of his life, he always seemed positive and anxious and accepting of beings of magic. She had agreed to help train him with magic and his crystal at first, to determine if he was the Chosen One, but now she truly liked being around him. He genuinely accepted her and treated her like a friend, something she never really felt from her childhood group of friends back home. The more time she spent with Thom, Semaj and this group, the more she wondered if Lucian might be wrong or misguided by his fathers.

"You shouldn't frown so much," Thom shouted back and laughed as her smile now matched his.

"Sorry, was in deep thought." Nat was not sure if Thom and his crystal were the Chosen One but either way, there was still something special about him.

"Don't let Anna get to you. Only reason she hates you is because she has feelings for Semaj too," Thom said causing Nat to suddenly choke, taken back by the shocking statement.

"I," but Nat could not deny it, could she? If it was true, would it be a betrayal to Lucian? She had always loved Lucian but deep down knew that may only be one-sided.

"Don't' worry, I won't say anything, but I think he likes you too," Thom smirked.

Nat wanted to respond but thankfully something caught her eye and took her attention away from the conversation with Thom. She thought she had seen movement and looked above her but there was nothing there. Unlike the Northern Mountains, the mountains of Ogra were void of snow and very dry and colorless. Because of this, it made it harder for things to stick out and if there was someone or something out there, they blended right into the mountainside. She could not find anything, but her gut told her they were not alone.

They continued to travel quickly through the mountains as the path led them up at a slant and soon onto a very narrow ledge. The Frostites were still able to cross but at a slower pace as to not risk sliding or falling off the side. The party noticed that their rides were not moving as strong since their thick fur coats meant for extreme cold weather were weighing down on them in this much warmer climate. Most of the riders themselves had removed their coats as the temperature was getting to them as well. Anna, who had a more direct connection to the heat seemed not to mind the change at all.

"How much further do you think?" Thom asked as even he was getting tired of the same mundane scenery.

"We should be approaching a mountain land crossing here soon. We can stop and give our mounts a rest while we eat and plan as we are over halfway through the mountains. Once we cross, it will be just a few hours decent till we reach the marsh lands of Ogra," Ard-Rich replied back.

"Mountain land crossing, is that a bridge?" Anna asked.

"Those are sections in mountain ranges where a large island of ground rests in the center of two mountains. The area can be small or large in diameter but the base that holds it extends all the way down to the bottom is often sturdy but can be narrow and not very thick," Noraxa explained.

"Usually you can reach the island from both mountain sides by a walkway similar to the one we used to get into Norax, but these are permanent and don't vanish and reform," Lorax added with an amused chuckle at his ladder statement.

It did not take long before they rounded a bend and came to a divided path. One took them around and up the mountain they were on while the second led to a long narrow pathway that was connected to a huge island mass dead center between two mountain ranges. Essej and Ard-Rich looked around, then at each other before motioning for them to all press forward. Semaj, at first glance was not sure the pathway they were crossing over would hold but it did. They cautiously made to the island where they all could spread out and relax. Semaj slid off his Frostite, stretched his legs and saw it was quite a bit further to go. You could barely see where the land mass they were on ended and the next pathway off started.

"Will we be safe stopping here?" Semaj asked as he glanced and saw Nat looking in all direction as she dismounted.

"I find it odd we haven't seen any sign of Ogres." Nat was sure they would have been attacked by now but there was not a creature or animal in sight. Even whatever she thought she had seen before had no longer popped up out of the corner of her eye. Something deep inside her gut told her this was not good.

"I agree, even when I've passed through here I've at least encountered or spotted a few," Ard-Rich added as he too started looking around nervously.

"We'll rest, eat and then be on our way. Our path will now lead us down that mountain and to the ground below," Essej replied as they had all dismounted and started to gather more to the center.

"You won't be able to cross to the other mountain, at least not this path." Everyone froze and looked up and around to see where this odd voice had come from.

"Who's there? Show yourself!" Anna demanded as she had her daggers in her hands.

"Why, we're right here silly," the voice said again, followed by a giggle and then growls from the Frostites.

They all saw that the Frostites were crouching down and staring towards the ground. As the party lowered their eyes, they saw a tiny figure standing not far from Anna. He was average in weight and barely came up past Anna's ankle. He wore clothes in the shades of brown that almost blended into the color of the ground and mountains. He wore a pointed hat the same color but his tip was dented to the side. His eyes were almost a hazel color and stubble of a beard could be seen. It was hard to tell how old the creature was but he looked young. Nat suddenly realized this was what she had thought she had seen earlier. "A Gnome?"

"Actually, we are Mountain Gnomes," he said with pride and a smile.

"Gnomes?" Semaj asked looking over to Thom.

"Mountain Gnomes," the creature repeated with a nod of his head.

"Only mention of them in my books is they are made up creatures people used to blame bad luck, accidents or missing items on. My ancestral grandfather just made note that if they did exist, they only exist to be pests." Thom shrugged looking down at the Mountain Gnome.

"We are real and surely not pests," the Gnome said with a little puzzlement on his face.

"I haven't seen your kind in a very long time. What are you doing up here in the Ogre filled mountains?" Essej asked as he knelt down closer to the creature's level.

"We have lived up here forever. Many, many seasons ago, a group of Gnomes decided to travel and explore and ended up here. Then something happened and the mountains split in two and they were stranded as frozen water now separated them from home. They decided to make the mountains home and we are now called Mountain Gnomes," the little guy answered and then waited in silence, rolling back and forth on his heels.

"Aren't you afraid of being eaten by the Ogres?" Lorax asked as he and Noraxa were both amazed by actually seeing the rumored distant cousin of the Dwarves.

"No, we have a deal with them. We travel all over to watch and report everything we see and hear back to the Ogres in turn they promise to leave us alone and try not to step on us," the Mountain Gnome replied looking up at the two Dwarves standing side by side.

"That was you I kept seeing. You were spying on us." Nat glared at the Gnome, glad she was not losing her mind.

"Yes, that was us."

James W. Berg

"You keep saying we and us, are there more of you here?" Anna asked.

"Yes," the Gnome said followed by several giggles. All around them, from what had looked like small rocks, the little objects began to move taking shape to several more Mountain Gnomes, both male and female, all looking slightly different except for the same colored outfits.

"They're everywhere!" Thom exclaimed at the creatures that seemed to come out of nowhere.

"We are very good at blending in. We are the best of all the scouting groups."

"Groups?" Anna asked.

"There is lots of land to cover, so we break off into several groups so we can gather enough information from all over to make the Ogres happy. We are known as the Terrific Twenty."

Another Mountain Gnome made a strange noise and whispered in his ear. "Oh, stepped on you say? Sorry about that, we are the Super Seventeen!" He paused as another Gnome skipped over. "Fell of the mountain? When did that happen?" He then rotated around waving his finger as he started to count and recount until he was satisfied. "We are the Fabulous Fifteen! We are their leader. You can call us Nalyd."

"All of you are named Nalyd?" Semaj asked trying not to laugh.

"No, silly. We all have different names like you. We are called Nalyd, they are called Avon…" Nalyd said as he pointed to a female Gnome near him and then moved on to several other Gnomes, pointing at each individual giving a different name than the last but always saying "they".

"They? I don't…"

"They address themselves in the plural," Anna laughed at Semaj who still seemed confused.

"Tell me, Nalyd, have you reported back to the Ogres about us?" Nat asked cutting through the foolishness and wanting to get to the point.

"No, we have not. We were waiting until you got here."

"Why here?" Essej asked as he saw Nat dart off from the group.

"Where are the Ogres and other creatures of the Western Mountains?" Ard-Rich added, his shadow falling over the Mountain Gnome leader.

"As we said earlier, you can't continue on from here so we thought it would be a break for you all." He looked back and forth between the two older humans and then glanced over to the rest of the Gnomes before swallowing and deciding to continue on. "All creatures, especially the Ogres are under strict orders to stay away from you and allow you to pass safely to the lands below the mountains."

"He's right. The path crossing from this place to the next mountain, the middle part is destroyed. There is no way to cross unless we fly or hope to jump really far," Nat said as she came sprinting back.

"Why are we to pass freely and by whose orders?" Essej asked now growing very concerned.

"You will be taken captive by the Goblins and Hobgoblins the moment you step off the mountain. All creatures, including the Ogres, were given strict orders not to harm any of you so you could be delivered to the Gooblyn City, where you will be held till Drol Greb's forces can retrieve you. Any who disobey will face the wrath of the great Fire Elf, Docanesto," Nalyd said with no change in emotion as he continued to smile and the other Gnomes nodded in agreement.

Semaj looked right at Essej with wide eyes. They were walking into a trap. "How?"

Anna glared at Nat, but before anyone could accuse or deny accusations, the Gnome named Avon spoke up. "We ran into another group who had seen you coming across that frozen water. They told us that after seeing your group they had stumbled upon a strange Elf who took them and flew off. When the Elf released them back into the mountains, per instructions, they were racing to inform all groups of Mountain Gnomes to spread the commands to all creatures."

"Strange Elf?" Essej asked to no one in particular as he seemed to go into deep thought.

"You think it was Drocana?" Semaj asked of Nat and Anna.

"If so, my guess is that her father isn't waiting for us. We are being taken there to be held till he gets there," Essej answered and then turned to Nalyd. "Why tell us this?"

"We are different from the others. We feel that you are not evil and we should help you," Nalyd replied, clearly from the looks of others in his group when he said we he did not really mean his whole group.

"Why help us?" Semaj asked.

"We want to be more than just messenger. We want to be heroic and brave like our ancestors that first set foot onto adventure."

"Food treats are traitors," a loud grumbling voice boomed from above the group causing them to look up and over to the side of the mountain they had come from to see a handful of large ugly Ogres. The large creatures were standing quite some ways upwards along the mountain side.

"It will take them a little time to reach us. We must find a way onto the other mountain side," Essej told the group as they started to turn to head away from the Ogres.

"Don't let them go, stop them," the biggest of Ogres commanded as his fellow Ogres stopped and stared at him.

"We not supposed to…" was all one of the Ogres got out before the apparent alpha Ogre grabbed him and launched him with great might down off the mountain side and hitting the crossing path with enough force to crack it.

"Ogres will not harm us, we have agreement and instructions for safe passage," Nalyd informed them all with confidence.

"I don't think they are playing by the rules anymore," Noraxa said, battle-axe in hand, as the alpha Ogre shouted again. This time he had help in pushing two very large boulders off the mountain that hit the crossing with an impact that not only shook the island they were standing upon but caused the pathway to crumble and fall away to the abyss below, taking the previously thrown Ogre with it.

"We're trapped," Lorax said as he stared at the gapping space where the pathway off the island used to be.

Essej and Ard-Rich motioned for the group to move quickly to the opposite side when a large boulder landed a few feet in front of them. Semaj realized that it had not come from behind them, but directly in front of them. He looked up and saw another group of Ogres standing on the other mountainside, but near the path they needed to somehow reach. "What now? The crossing on both sides are destroyed with Ogres on each side waiting for us."

"No fair breaking rules and taking meat for yourselves," the leader of the new group of Ogres shouted up to the Ogres behind Semaj and his group.

"No one, especially Elves or humans tells Retep, strongest Ogre there is what to do," the alpha Ogre roared back at the new group of Ogres.

"Oh my," Nalyd murmured when a boulder landed not far from him, squashing two of his fellow Mountain Gnomes. The Ogres on both sides of the mountains had begun a boulder and rock throwing fight with each other. The group on the island was now caught directly in the middle.

"They mine!" The leader of the new group of Ogres shouted at Retep as he threw a large boulder that missed, bounced back, hitting the edge of the island causing it to shake a little.

"We need to do something before we're all squashed," Anna said looking to Essej for guidance.

Thom felt a burning as his crystal began to glow. Words and instructions started forming in his mind as he raised his arms up and began to carefully move his fingers and repeat the words aloud. Thom felt a great energy pull from within as he released the spell. Suddenly a beautiful white-blue light left his fingertips and extended up and out as a magical shield formed at an arc above them and then touching down to the edges of the island they stood upon. Sweat beaded down his brow as he held on to hope that he had the strength to keep the shield up to protect them all from the onslaught of boulders being thrown, making impact with the shield, and then bouncing safely away.

"Nicely done, Thom."

"Thanks, Semaj, but I don't know how long I can keep this up."

"I can bring them down,' Noraxa suggested as she tried to reach out with her Magesti.

"No, too risky with us trapped here in the middle," Essej said causing the Dwarf to withdraw her power and huff in frustration. "Anna, try driving them back with your Magesti."

Anna nodded and stepped forward, keeping her eyes focused on the ground in front of the Ogres blocking where they needed to go. She was getting better at using her abilities as it only took seconds for her to feel and become one with the heat around the mountain floor under the Ogres. She kept pulling more heat to the area willing it to grow hotter and hotter. She heard the Ogres shout and dance backwards as the ground burned their feet. She smiled as she felt the power and became one with it, willing it now to ignite causing a wall of fire to rise up in front of the Ogres blocking them from the scene. She heard Essej quickly coaching her, helping her maintain control as she made the fire bigger, stronger but concentrated in the one spot and not spreading.

"She's driven them back but she can't hold that for long. We need to get to the other side and down before they recover and can follow," Ard-Rich said what most were thinking.

"What about the trap?" Nat asked.

"We can show you another path," Nalyd offered with pride.

"You not escape Retep," the Ogre shouted as he and a few of his ugly friends hurled large boulders at them.

"They must be getting tired. Their aim is off," Lorax chuckled nervously but soon realized what he said was wrong as the boulders that did not come close to them had all hit a central point in the pillar of rock that was holding up the island.

"This is not good," Noraxa added as the Ogres continued to hurl more large boulders at the spot causing the island they were on to shake more and more.

"Look, they're playing too," Avon smirked as she pointed at the Ogres who had retreated higher up from the wall of fire and were now throwing large boulders at the other side of the same spot, this time causing a small crack in the pillar's base.

"The ground is weakening. I fear too much more and the pillar will break and we will all go tumbling down into the abyss with the island," Nat said as she stood up from touching the ground.

"She's right, I can feel the earth weakening," Noraxa added as she felt she needed to do something.

"No!" Semaj cried out in shock as a loud booming crack caused the island to tilt to the side making everyone fall to the ground, sliding.

The tilt was not drastic as they were all able to get their bearings and stand without further sliding, but unfortunately, a couple Frostites and Mountain Gnomes had managed to slide right off the edge. With the unexpected tilt, both Thom and Anna had fallen and lost concentration causing the wall of fire and the magical shield to fade away. Not missing the opportunity, one of the Ogres ran and passed through the fading fire and leapt with all his might making the clearing and landing on the mountain island with an impact that caused the island to tilt back. Roaring with anger, Retep grabbed one of his warriors and threw him upon the island commanding him get the live meat first.

"Looks like your agreement is more than over," Semaj said to the leader of the Mountain Gnomes as he looked from side to side at the two Ogres that now stood on each side, towering over them with their massive height and each holding very large clubs.

"We will stand by you," Nalyd declared with no fear in his voice at all. Semaj admired this race of beings that had a childlike innocence and fearlessness about them.

A loud roar returned Semaj's attention back as the two giant Ogres charged from both sides. Gnomes were running everywhere as the Frostites split up and charged the Ogres with Noraxa on top of Freezia, axe held high. Lorax pulled his out and ran after as he tried to hold his axe steady. Anna followed the Dwarves against the Ogre sent by Retep while Nat, Ard-Rich and Essej moved towards the other Ogre. Semaj moved next to Thom who seemed to be catching his breath and energy from the magic shield he had created earlier.

"You okay?"

"I'll be fine. You go left I go right?"

Semaj swallowed hard as he pulled out his sword, gave his best friend a nod and ran towards Essej while Thom went in the opposite direction. Semaj would rather be anywhere else than charging towards a giant Ogre but he could not let his friends down or let another friend die. He looked at his sword and held it with a little more confidence thanks to the training he had been getting in with Anna and Nat. At least with their instructions he stood a better chance of defending himself than getting killed in the first few seconds of a battle. As he approached, he froze as he watched the Ogre bat off the attacking Frostites with ease. How was he to contend with that?

"We need to push him over the edge," Nat said as she leapt into the air.

Semaj could see Nat was right. With the island at a slight tilt, one good hit could send the Ogre falling and maybe roll and slide right off. Nat had her arm blades extracted and landed on the Ogre's back, driving the blades in deep. The Ogre screamed, reached back and threw Nat off, who managed to twist and summersault into a safe landing on the ground. Essej was up next, causing the wind to make a vacuum around the creature's head to make it dizzy, but it was not working. The Ogre raised its club and prepared to bring it down on Essej.

Semaj ran with all his might and pushed the old man out of the way just as the club came smashing down. By this time Nat was almost upon the Ogre again, who had raised its foot to stomp down upon her. Semaj got up and ran as fast as he could, pointing and driving his sword deep into the other ankle. The Ogre howled and put his foot down and moved towards Semaj. The creature prepared to bring his club down on Semaj. Semaj froze, awaiting his fate when two hands yanked him back. It was Nat.

"Can't just stand there if you want to survive this battle," Nat said with a bit of humor and scolding in her voice as they both moved, Nat grabbing Semaj's sword from the Ogre's ankle and handing it to him.

"Thanks."

Ard-Rich saw that the two were distracted and did not see the Ogre preparing to strike again. He knew what he was risking but knew what he had to do. Reaching deep inside himself, Ard-Rich found the Magesti, unlocked it and became one with the power. He quickly willed the Magesti to flow into his arms and hands, feeling every part that made up these body parts and then reached out and started to reshape them in his mind. Because of his age and lack of use, it took him a little longer and more energy but soon his arms began to grow, stretching out towards the Ogre with great speed. By the time his arms reached the Ogre, his hands had become pointed blades and the sides of his arms took on jagged edges. The Ogre screamed in pain as the bladed arms sliced through both sides of his ankle and then ripped them open spilling blood as Ard-Rich brought his arms back through as they returned to his body and reforming back to normal. The Ogre dropped his club as he raised his leg up to cup his bleeding foot with both hands.

"I now see," Essej frowned at his friend, who now appeared twice as old as he had a few minutes ago. Knowing there was not time, he turned away from the aged Ard-Rich and shouted instructions at Nat and Semaj, who took their blades and stabbed repeatedly at the only ankle still touching the ground. As the Ogre shifted to the new pain of his other ankle, he went off balance. Essej used this moment to sprout wings, take flight and unleash his power over the wind causing a blast to hit the Ogre and send him falling to the ground and rolling to the edge of the island.

"He saved himself," Semaj said as the Ogre went over the edge but used his fingers to grab on for dear life.

"Not if I can help it," Nat said as she ran towards the fingers that were gripped over the edge. Stopping part way, she thrust her arms out and released the blades from her armbands causing them to both fly forward, each piercing a finger, causing the Ogre to jolt from the impact, lose his grip and fall down into the abyss.

"Nice shot, but you lost your arm blades," Semaj said as he finally caught up to the Wild Elf.

"That's why you always carry backup," Nat smiled as she rotated her armbands and then jerking her arms causing two more blades to pop out from them.

****

Anna, Thom, the two Dwarves and the Frostites were holding their own against the Ogre but growing tired. It was hard to get any attacks in while trying to avoid getting stepped on or crushed with a club. The chanting and cheering from the Ogres on the sides of the mountains did not help either as Thom was trying to use his magic to deflect any oncoming boulders. She was contemplating her next move when there was a loud roar and all the Ogres stopped cheering. Even their Ogre paused and looked off into the distance. Anna turned to see Ard-Rich's arms retracting from being stretched and then Essej take flight with his Dragon wings. Anna could not believe it as Essej, followed by Semaj and Nat's efforts sent their Ogre over the edge. They had won and it was now their turn. "Hurry, while he's distracted!"

Noraxa dove hard with Freezia right at the Ogre and sliced the side of his foot with her axe. The creature howled with pain and swatted her off Freezia with one hand and raised his club with the other. Lorax screamed in fear as he ran to his beloved's side and raised his axe in hopes of deflecting the oncoming blow. Lorax felt a strange tingling come from his axe's handle and thought he saw a strange glimmer as the axe's blade met the Ogre's club. Lorax waited for the jolt of pain from the impact but was surprised when one did not come. Instead, he stared in awe as the blade sliced right through the club, severing it in two as if it were a knife cutting a blade of grass.

As the Ogre stared dumbfounded at the severed club, Anna planted her feet, called on her Magesti and reached out for the area surrounding the Ogre's chest. Pushing with all her might, she caused the Ogre's cloth covering part of its chest to ignite in flame. The Ogre ran about frantically trying to put the flames out.

"Kill them!" Retep shouted as the Ogres began throwing boulders at the pillar that was holding up the island. Not wanting to be left out or out done, the Ogres on the other side began throwing boulders at the same spot as well.

"This won't hold much longer," Noraxa said as they heard a loud crack and the island now tilted to the other side causing them to lose their balance and the flaming Ogre to slide and go right over the edge almost taking some of them with him.

Semaj looked at Essej, who was trying to come up with a plan. Like the rest of them, he was barely keeping his balance from the island shifting back and forth from the impact of the boulders. Another crack boomed and then the island started to tilt almost on its very side. They all began sliding towards the edge. There was no saving them now. Semaj tried to see where everyone was but only saw Noraxa sliding next to him. "I have to do something," the female Dwarf told him.

Semaj saw her concentrating and could feel the Magesti pulsing from within her. The island began to shake and then suddenly, with a very loud snap, the island broke free from the pillar and started to crumble and break apart itself as it prepared to fall down into the depths below. Semaj could not believe they had come all this way to die now. Semaj screamed as he grabbed Noraxa's foot and felt a powerful surge pass between them. Semaj could not let go as he stared at Noraxa, whose eyes almost seemed to take on a brownish glow.

"I will save us!" Noraxa screamed as she thrusted her arms up into the air. Small hands made of the earth around them popped up and started to grab everyone's feet to keep them from falling off the edge. Essej cried out to Noraxa to stop, but his words were drowned out by her screams and the thunder of the earth breaking free from the mountainsides. That earth then started coming together and forming hands large enough to grab hold of what was left of the island from all sides, keeping it from breaking apart further and then help guide the island mass as it rode down a slide that had also formed out of rock towards the ground below.

"How are you doing this?" Semaj asked as he could not seem to remove his hand from her foot and could feel the immense power pulsing between the two of them but Noraxa said nothing, her mouth open but no sound coming out.

After what seemed like forever, the load roar came to a stop as the island hit the ground and the hands made of rock crumbled away into pieces. Semaj let go of Noraxa's foot and moved to her side as she collapsed. Lorax and Essej were there immediately as the others were soon gathering by her side. "Everyone made it, including a handful of the Gnomes. Freezia and the Frostites bolted off to see if they could find any signs of the other Frostites and Gnomes we lost. If it hadn't been for Noraxa," Anna started reporting and then stopped when she saw Lorax cradling Noraxa in his arms, her body unmoving.

"Is she?" Thom began to ask.

"No, she still has a pulse. Semaj, quickly," Essej said as he had him place his hands on Noraxa and then guided him in trying to reach out, find the Magesti inside of her and then sooth and mend it. Semaj was not sure what he was doing but when he suddenly felt a positive sensation from the Magesti inside of Noraxa, Essej told him he could stop.

"What did you do?" Anna asked.

"We fixed and healed the Magesti within her after what she just did to save us all," Essej answered as he plopped down upon the ground and sat there staring at the Dwarf.

"Why isn't she waking up?" Lorax asked.

"She is in a healing coma. Her Magesti is healed but she won't wake till her body and mind catch up. I told her to stop. Her body wasn't ready for that kind of power," Essej mumbled.

"Could this happen to me?" Anna asked suddenly worried about using her gifts.

"If you are not properly trained and use your abilities in ways your body isn't ready for. Each Magestic will go through three phases. The first is small basic use of the Magesti, which most started to do and specifically after we unlocked the power in all of the Magestics back at Mount Semaj. With proper training, a Magestic can ease into phase two, a broader use of the gift. None of the Magestics should be able to access their full potential or phase three of their power for some time yet. At least not without intense training otherwise you could end up like Noraxa or worse," Essej said as he got back up on his feet.

"How did Noraxa access her full power?" Semaj asked almost knowing the answer.

"The Chosen One can not only find and help the Magestics in the use of their powers but in the presence or direct contact with the Chosen One, a Magestic can receive a boost, which is what happened to Noraxa. Unfotunately, she got a continuous boost and supply of power," Essej said as he patted Semaj on the back letting him know it was not his fault.

"We should get moving, who knows how soon our welcoming party will be here," Ard-Rich said as he noticed everyone was staring at him as if something was different. Essej glanced at his aged face with a look that said explanations would be coming soon.

"Halt, do not move or we will kill you," a sinister sounding voice called out to them.

"We can't kill them," another creature started to say, but was silenced when he was slammed over the head with a hammer.

Semaj turned and saw standing in front of them were dozens of short, green skinned and very ugly creatures holding spears, swords, hammers and axes. Semaj assumed these were the Goblins. Off to the sides were more of the same creatures but they had no weapons. They crouched baring their sharp teeth and claws, growling in a more feral state. Semaj heard Thom call them Hobgoblins. Semaj looked up to Essej as the Huelgon spoke, "we mean you no harm."

"Silence Elf. We are under orders to bring you all with us, preferably alive," the lead Goblin spat back.

"That goes for all of you humans and Elves," another Goblin added pointing with his spear at the group in quick jab motions.

"Wait," Semaj started to say in confusion when he looked back and saw that all the Mountain Gnomes and the Dwarves were gone.

"It seems our new friends have assisted Lorax in sneaking off safely and unseen to hide Noraxa," Essej whispered with a smile.

"One more word and we let the Hobgoblins eat you," the Goblin snarled.

"Where are you taking us?" Anna asked.

"To the Gooblyn City," the Goblin answered pointing his weapon in the direction behind him.

"What do we do?" Thom asked.

"What's your gut tell you?" Essej asked Semaj.

"I feel a pulling in that same direction," Semaj answered.

"Then we allow them to safely escort us to the destination of our next Magestic," Essej replied as the group was ushered forward by the Goblin hoard.

Chapter Twenty-Five:
The Gooblyn City

"Will you have any problems reaching the Gooblyn City?" Lucian heard one of the *Ghost's* crewmen ask his captain as she gave reassurances that she would be fine. Lucian looked from Gabrielle to Sev as he made his way to the medium sized covered cart that the king gave him to place the supplies the queen bestowed upon them. It was decent sized and easily carried by one of the Fire Hounds. With two hounds without riders, it left one to pull the cart and the other to move fast and free to scout the area for any outside dangers. His remaining Fire Elves would ride upon their hounds at a good distance to watch the perimeter they were traveling. If any creature managed to get past them, Lucian was more than confident that he would let them know he was the wrong person to mess with.

"Are you sure you want her tagging along?" Sev asked keeping himself hidden, small and near Lucian's ear.

"We can use her help and her ship," Lucian said as his thoughts drifted to the pirate and the treasures she held. "I think…"

"Me saying she stays is enough and no one, and I mean no one should ever question me," Lucian spat as Sev gasped in air and then flew off. Lucian almost winced at the harshness of his words and almost felt like calling after Sev, but he couldn't show weakness, ever, plus he was a bit confused at how he felt about the pirate joining them, him.

"Good travels," an Orgite said as the doors opened and Lucian mounted Frrr and followed his group out of the Orgite Colony.

"I'm surprised the king didn't see us off. The queen I know, but the king?" Gabrielle said as she moved her hound close to Lucian.

"He had his reasons," Lucian masked his smile as he thought back to last night.

After Gabrielle had left his sleeping quarters, he had a surprise visitor show up. King Oltar had snuck into his room, motioning for him to remain quiet and not draw attention to his arrival. Oltar had waited for the woman to leave before he paid a visit to Lucian. At first Lucian thought maybe the king had come for other reasons and was prepared to disappoint the king but it seemed he was actually there for different reasons. Reasons that Lucian had originally suspected and had drawn him to Ogra to begin with. The king was a Magestic.

****

"Shhh!" King Oltar whispered as he slipped into the room, looked back and forth outside the door and then nodded with satisfaction as he quickly closed it. "Sorry for the intrusion but I need to talk to you. I waited for her to leave. No one knows I'm down here. I feel like I am drawn to you."

"Look, I don't know," Lucian started to say to the king when he motioned him to be silent while listening to the door and then stepping closer to him.

"There is something different about me and I had this dream and I think you were in it, I am not sure as it is still fuzzy but you being here I think it might be all connected," King Oltar started to ramble nervously.

"Why don't you start from the beginning and tell me everything. Don't leave anything out no matter how silly or insignificant it might seem," Lucian instructed as he knew what the king was about to confirm.

"About a season ago, maybe a little less, I started feeling funny. I kept having bad luck or having accidents. I was embarrassed and it only made the queen that much harder on me. I would have bad thoughts and suddenly bad luck or accidents were happening to others. Like the Orgite that was supposed to marry the queen. He fell off the wall and broke his back, so the queen chose me to be her king. I never said anything because right before he fell, I was mad at him for pushing me down and making fun of me. So, then I thought bad things and then boom, he fell.

"It scared me that I might be bad so I tried real hard to not think and it stopped until not too long ago when I had this weird dream, which I had forgotten about until you showed up,"

Oltar explained slowly as Lucian tried hard to have patience with the Orgite.

"Tell me about this dream."

"It's fuzzy but it seems to be getting clearer the longer I am near you thinking about it. I was in my sleeping quarters when I saw a light coming from behind my door and then felt or heard, not for sure, something pulling me towards it. I slowly went to the door, opened it and there was now a tunnel leading out of my room. I knew I must be dreaming but still compelled to continue on, so I did. I eventually came to a balcony that overlooked a large cavern.

"I almost ran in fright as there was a huge white Dragon sitting right in the middle. I heard similar noises and glanced around noticing that there were several other balconies surrounding the Dragon, each with someone upon it. I was about to leave when the Dragon started speaking about Magestics, a Chosen One and other things I am having trouble remembering. I heard the word *death* and then something hit me, like a strange energy and I thought I was actually going to die until I woke up in my bed, the dream faded away, until now," Oltar said not taking his eyes off Lucian as he tugged on the gloves he wore.

"Continue," Lucian said trying to contain himself as he waited for the creature to say more.

"After that day, I definitely was the one causing bad luck or accidents. I was doing my best to control and hide it until I touched someone." The Orgite dipped his head in guilt.

"Is that why you wear the gloves?"

"It seems when I touch someone or something, not only can I do more than cause a mishap, but I drain or weaken the person or thing I am touching. I touched a flower once and it started to go limp. Then the other day I touched an elder and she got very sick. Now I wear these to help suppress this curse of mine."

"It's only a curse if you see it that way," Lucian said with a grin that caused King Oltar to flinch a bit.

"I was right to come to you? You know what's happening to me?" Oltar asked with both hope and fear of the man in front of him.

"It's why I'm here. Your dream was not a dream. You are a Magestic with the ability to call upon and control great power."

"You mean, like magic?"

"No, this is different than magic. This power is called Magesti, and it seems that all of you on those balconies each possess a different Magesti ability, like fire or earth. That word you heard directed at you, death, must be your Magesti. That would make sense with the accidents and things becoming weak. With training you could definitely bring death easily to others." Lucian was now talking more to himself and that worried Oltar.

"I don't want to be cursed with this. No, not at all!"

"With proper training I can help you use it. That is why I have sought you out."

"What about the others, the Dragon and this Chosen One?"

"They are evil set upon destroying this land and are after each of you. My father is working to stop them and allow all the creatures and beings of magic to roam Bergonia once again and be free of the human reign. I am trying to get to and save the Magestics before this evil Chosen One can. I found you and there is another up north, in or near the Gooblyn City. Come with us, with me." Lucian smiled and gently offered his hand to King Oltar.

"The queen would never let me leave, but the thought of going outside the walls and to learn more about what I am," Oltar's eyes glazed over as he fell deep into his thoughts about the outside world.

"Trust me," Lucian said, bringing the Orgite back as Oltar swallowed, nodded and nervously took his hand.

****

"You're not worried we'll get caught smuggling their king out of the colony?" Sev whispered once the gates closed and he, in his small Fairy form, flew up next to Lucian's ear.

"He's well hidden in the covered cart, despite his size. We'll be more than half way to the Gooblyn City before they even notice he's gone, let alone where he could have went."

"You were right. He is one of the Magestics. Are you sure he's best kept alive?" All Lucian did was smile leaving the Fairy to wonder what his lover had planned.

The group trudged on towards the north with no sign of trouble. It was mid-day when they reached a point where the wall to the Orgite Colony was well behind them and they were out of sight. By this time, the path they were on had turned to marsh and swamp. The Fire Hound's feet sloshed in murky water that went halfway up their legs and made it harder for the cart's wheels to roll forward. The extra weight in the back did not help either.

"There are Hobgoblins on the move from the southwest," one of the Fire Elves reported as he charged towards Lucian after hearing the howling of their scouting hound.

"I thought they only came out at night?" Lucian asked looking to Gabrielle.

"They prefer to hunt at night, but they have no problem trolling in the daylight."

"We better push it then. I'd like to be to the Gooblyn City before they reach us," Lucian said as they all urged their hounds to move faster through the swamp-like terrain.

The day progressed as they continued to travel north when a loud noise caused Lucian to look back. The covered cart had come to a complete stop and whatever had caused it to stop suddenly made the strap attached to the Fire Hound snap in two causing the hound to stumble forward. Lucian moved a little closer to the cart but because the water was so murky, he could not see what was blocking the cart's path. Lucian gave a gesture and one of the Fire Elves leapt off his hound and moved to the front of the cart, knelt down and reached under the water to investigate. Lucian was beginning to lose patience when the Elf's eyes went wide and then suddenly went down and vanished beneath the knee high watered terrain.

"Where did he go?" Gabrielle asked in surprise as the other two Fire Elves gathered quickly near their master watching for danger.

Lucian watched the water closely and could not see anything. Suddenly, a few feet from the cart, the missing Fire Elf shot straight up out of the water and high into the air. Moments after, a large form burst out of the water, moving straight up to meet the Fire Elf that was now starting to descend. The creature's body was dark green and was long making it look similar to a snake. Its body started to expand, getting wider and wider as it moved upwards. Its head was about the size of a Gnome with no facial features except a mouth, where a long forked tongue flickered out. As the giant snake-like creature met the Fire Elf, it's mouth opened and seemed to crack and contort as it made itself open wide enough to swallow the Elf whole. Lucian shivered as he could see the bulge of the Fire Elf as it moved down the long body before the creature dove at a slant back into the water's cover, the tip of its tale slamming down upon the water as it vanished along with the rest of the body.

"What was that?" Lucian asked looking at Gabrielle who just shrugged. The look of shock still held her face.

"We call them Snakzards. They are half snake and half lizard. They don't normally come this far west. They mainly dwell in the far central east of Ogra," King Oltar said as he pushed back the cover of the cart he was hiding under and flung his legs over the side. "I really needed to stretch my legs."

"What's the king doing in there?" Gabrielle asked now focused on another surprise.

"He's traveling with us but that's not important right now. What more do you know about this creature?" Lucian asked moving Frrr closer to the cart but looking all around the water for this creature.

"Once you are swallowed, the acids inside the Snakzard starts to dissolve you in seconds. The creatures tend to be long and skinny making it easier for them to travel quickly and unseen in the water but when they go to feed, they can expand their body and their mouth to great sizes. I heard once an Ogre was swallowed whole," King Oltar explained with wide eyes as he surveyed the area. "They almost always travel in threes."

"We need to get to dry land," one of the Fire Elves said, urging the party to get moving.

"That won't do any good. If they want to, they can sprout legs to move, crawl and climb with ease on dry land. Luckily, our walls are made of a substance they have trouble climbing. They also feed easier and faster on dry land as they don't like to swallow water," Oltar informed and then added, "that is why they throw their food up into the air."

The Fire Hounds began to growl at different directions and Lucian could see the water rippling a little. One had fed and the others were coming for theirs. Lucian prepared to use his magic when he felt a strange sensation that pulled him towards the Orgite. He looked over at Oltar and saw that he was looking back and forth in each direction and then closing his eyes with fear and panic on his face. Lucian could almost feel the Magesti reaching out from the king and extending to the areas the two Snakzards were coming from.

Suddenly the two creatures leapt out of the water at the same time, bodies and mouths expanding ready to snag them each a Fire Elf. For some reason, the creatures misjudged their attack and ended up colliding into each other. Their open-mouthed heads hitting at the right angle and impact causing a loud crack as their mouths both peeled and snapped backwards. The Snakzards rolled and both fell back into the water. Oltar made a strange noise and then collapsed upon the cart.

"You will definitely prove useful," Lucian whispered as he darted Frrr to the cart and checked on the Orgite who had just used his power to make the creatures have a little unfortunate accident. "He's out cold. We need to get him on a hound quickly."

Lucian saw Gabrielle open her mouth but he gave her a look that made her keep to herself for the moment. The two remaining Fire Elves, with a little magic, helped lift the heavy Orgite onto the back of a Fire Hound and secured him so he would not roll off. Lucian was glad his hounds were strong as he made the call to abandon the cart. They did not have time to fix the wheel and avoiding the Snakzards would be easier without it. Lucian hoped that they could make it far enough before the last Snakzard digested its food and wanted seconds. Lucian took one final look back as they pushed onwards.

"I think we're in the clear. The water is getting shallower and should be upon dryer land soon," Sev said as he returned from a scouting flight up a head.

"Maybe from those creatures but we still got the Ogres, Hobgoblins and Goblins to worry about," Gabrielle added as Sev gave her a dirty look.

"I fear nothing from those creatures," Lucian said knowing opponents he could see were easier to fight than those that hid below the water.

It did not take long before they were out of the wet lands and moving across dry solid ground. There were trees but not as many and most looked on the verge of decay. The Orgite had woken but kept himself in silence as he took in the sights around him, as this was the farthest he had ever been from his home. They were more than half way to the Gooblyn City, deep inside a dying forest when one of the Fire Elves raised his arm and they all stopped and looked around while the Fire Hounds growled deeply. "We're being watched."

A figure leapt out from behind a tree but before anyone could see what it was one of the Fire Elves released an arrow made of fire that hit the creature dead in the face causing it to howl in pain as it's face was quickly burning. Lucian noticed three more figures in the shadows growling in anger. He quickly called on his magic and uttered a word that caused the flames on the burning creature's face to spread and completely consume its entire body before casting another spell. "Ratesepa Nda Idediv Yb Eethr Ot Arspe Ym Iesenem!"

The ground shook from his spell as Lucian weakly swayed from the great forceful use of his fire magic. The burning creature levitated into the air for a brief second before its charred lifeless body dropped to the ground. The fire ripped away from the body and split into three spears of fire that shot out with great speed. The spears made of fire soared, making contact as each of the three creatures leapt out into the open. Lucian brought down his arms and used the last of his strength to shout one more word that caused the spears of fire to explode upon impact making all three creatures burn instantly. Lucian managed to stay upright as he looked back to see the Orgite King looking all around them and then bring his eyes directly to his. "Lucian, the Hobgoblins have arrived."

Lucian looked around as dozens of figures slowly emerged from all around them. They were hairless with large pointed noses and ears. Their eyes were a yellowish color to match their sharp jagged teeth that stuck out randomly from their mouths. Their teeth looked as sharp as their nails and all they wore on their scrawny hunched over pale grey-skinned bodies were dirty cloths around their waists. Saliva dripped from their mouths as they all watched, growled and anticipated their attacks. "We can't out run them but we can fight." Lucian said as he barked out commands.

Everyone quickly dismounted allowing the six Fire Hounds to spread out and engage the Hobgoblins. Frrr remained back to stand guard near his friend and master. The hounds were fast, strong and vicious. They ripped several Hobgoblins to shreds before the nasty creatures regrouped, counter attacked and eventually allowed many of their number to get past and head towards Lucian and his party. The Fire Elves were already on the move, arrows of fire hitting mark after mark while leaping and dodging with ease as they switched off between arrows and blades made of fire to kill the advancing Hobgoblins. Lucian was feeling a bit light headed from the use of his magic but he had training in more than just his special gifts.

Drawing the sword he had taken from the dead Drogan, Lucian held the red bladed weapon with great comfort as he stepped forward to meet the first of many attackers. Lucian swung the blade and without any resistance severed the head clean off the body of the Hobgoblin. He then pivoted bringing the sword around in an upward arc as the blade sliced easily through the side of another creature splitting it wide open as it screamed falling to the ground with blood pouring out of the large wound. The magically crafted blades were very effective and it still baffled him why the Drogans were the only ones equipped with them but Docanesto had said that since they were forged from the same source as the winged creatures, anyone else pledged to the fire would be drained and consumed by the properties of the blade.

Lucian looked at the sword as he sliced through his victims and realizing his adoptive father was wrong. He did not feel weakened when using the sword. Instead, he felt a different sensation. The blade did not want to drain him. It was as if it wanted to work with him or more accurately, the gift within him.

As a Hobgoblin leapt into the air towards him, Lucian gave into the sensation and felt a surge of energy flow from him and into his weapon. The red blade flashed for a brief second as a blast of fire shot from the tip, hitting the Hobgoblin and sending it flying backwards, hitting the ground smoking and smelling of brunt flesh. Lucian smiled, as this new trick seemed to take less effort or energy from him than when he actually used his magic. He and the blade worked together as one, not harming but complimenting each other.

Trading off attacks, Lucian would slice an enemy with the blade then turn and send a blast of fire from it to burn the next creature. So far, he was holding his own and managed a quick glance around him to see how his fellow companions were doing. Sev had shrunk down to his Fairy form, zipping left and right, using his dagger and abilities to blind as many of the nasty creatures as he could. He was not too worried about Sev. Instead, he found himself worrying about Gabrielle. Those worries changed to admiration when he saw the pirate fighting.

Sticking out of Gabrielle's missing hand was a blade that she used quite deadly as if she was actually holding a sword. Lucian thought she was almost as good as him and smirked thinking about a little swordplay with her sometime. His smirked vanished when he saw four Hobgoblins surprisingly jump her from all sides. He was ready to call out a warning but she moved faster than he could speak. Gabrielle thrust out and jerked back her sword arm causing the blade to go flying out and stab one creature in the chest. She then twirled slightly, grabbing the end of the blade with her only hand yanking it out and slicing the throat of a second Hobgoblin as she rotated and came to a stop.

With the final two creatures upon her she thrust both her arms outwards towards each attacker. Her sword plunging into the neck of one while the metal stump on her other hand shifted and turned and then upon contact with the fourth Hobgoblin, released an electric pulse-like explosion that sent the creature flying backwards hitting the ground convulsing and smelling like burned flesh. That did not stop Gabrielle as she met more advancing Hobgoblins, taking them out with her sword and after a brief pause, some with the devise where her other hand used to be. Every time he looked, there was always something new with this pirate and that completely intrigued him.

"Behind you!" Oltar screamed causing Lucian to turn his head around and curse himself for getting distracted, as a Hobgoblin was almost upon him. Thankfully, Frrr was there as his faithful friend snagged the creature by the neck and tore it to shreds.

Oltar watched as everyone fought, standing their ground and taking out the advancing Hobgoblin hoard with ease but as more began to show he knew it would be a matter of time before they grew tired and their luck would turn for the worse. Oltar hated his ability but decided he had no other choice if he or any of them expected to live through this battle. Closing his eyes, he searched for the power within and when he found it, he reached out with it, trying to reach and touch every Hobgoblin in the area. He had never done anything quite like this before but he pushed himself nevertheless.

Oltar could now see every Hobgoblin with his eyes closed, as he now felt the darkness of his power covering their bodies. The Magestic took in a deep breath and then pushed out with all his might wishing bad luck and ill will upon each one of the dreadful creatures. He felt a great power and energy leave his body as it raced out to meet every Hobgoblin he had locked on to with his ability. Oltar opened his eyes, swayed from the drainage and dizziness, and saw the Hobgoblins start to stumble and move slower. Oltar smiled right before he passed out.

Lucian did not have to look back to know that the King of the Orgites had used his Magesti, as he had felt a tingle within his body the moment Oltar called upon it. He had felt one final surge and then the tables had turned. All the attacking Hobgoblins were now tripping all over each other. Some accidently killing themselves or others. Lucian screamed for all to advance and not miss this advantage. With great viciousness, Lucian led Gabrielle, Sev, Frrr and the rest of his party to finish off every Hobgoblin in sight. In a matter of moments, they all stood victorious upon a battlefield of blood and dead Hobgoblins.

"The king?" Gabrielle asked as she looked over to see the Orgite laying upon the ground.

"He is unconscious but unharmed," one of the Fire Elves reported as he knelt down next to the Orgite.

"I was starting to worry if we'd all make it out of this alive," Sev said growing to human size, breathing heavy in exhaustion.

"I had no doubt," Lucian said as he looked at Oltar and then turned towards their destination. "We better get moving before more arrive."

"Too late," Gabrielle said as several creatures began to approach them. She noticed that they looked similar to the Hobgoblins but not as feral, had some form of intellect behind their eyes and carried various weapons. She realized that these must be the Goblins.

"We should kill them. Look what they did," one Goblin said waving his spear towards the dead Hobgoblins.

"Not if you want to die. We have orders to escort them back alive. If they attacked and disobeyed orders they deserved to die," the lead Goblin answered back.

"Escort us where and by whose orders?" Lucian asked as he stepped forward, preparing his magic while the Fire Elves and Hounds moved into protective stance near him.

"By orders of Docanesto, we are to bring you safely to the Gooblyn City," the lead Goblin responded.

"Seems your father found out about our mission and beat us there," Sev said into Lucian's ear as he landed on his shoulder in Fairy form.

"Do we go with them?" Gabrielle asked stepping up on the other side of Lucian.

"If Docanesto is there than we might as well accept the escort," Lucian snarled, as he was ready to have words with his adoptive father. This was his mission and what he now needed to know was how Docanesto knew Lucian was here and how he knew the location of where they were traveling.

Everyone mounted their Fire Hound after they tied and secured the unconscious Orgite to his hound. Sev rested upon Lucian's shoulder in his small Fairy form where he remained hidden and ready to fly at his lover's command. With everyone on a hound, it left two Fire Hounds without riders, but they stayed near Lucian and ready to defend him. All the Goblins surrounded them from all sides as they continued to head northeast. The lead Goblin shouted off commands as other Goblins ran off to spread the word they were not to be approached by any creature as they took route to the Gooblyn City. Lucian did not say a word as he festered in his thoughts and prepared to confront his adoptive father.

"What happened? Are we dead?" Oltar said as he finally woke from his deep sleep.

"You saved us," Lucian said to the Orgite without looking back as he kept his eyes forward for they were now approaching the Gooblyn City.

There were trees everywhere except for a torch lit path that lead up to the city gate. The gate and the walls that made up the city were made of what looked like wood. It looked simply made and was not too impressive, especially compared to the Orgite's walls. If anyone wanted to storm the city, he did not see how difficult it would be to bring it down. Lucian tilted his head to the side as he felt something land on his shoulder. "Hidden all along the top of the walls are Goblins with spears as well as numerous Goblins and Hobgoblins hiding throughout the wooded area." Lucian was glad Sev was able to scout the area to prove his original theory would have some obstacles.

"Stay," the lead Goblin commanded once they reached the gate.

Lucian watched as the Goblin walked up to the gate and shouted upwards. The creatures on top shouted down with laughter as they threw rocks to make the Goblin duck and move backwards. Lucian did not need to look back or say anything, the Fire Elves and hounds were already prepared if a fight were to break out. He even had a few spells ready to unleash if he had to.

"Don't worry, they will not attack. All the creatures on the gate and walls are Gooblyns. This is the standard treatment of the Goblins."

Lucian glanced back at the Orgite and nodded as Oltar continued. "The Gooblyns are of a higher class, followed by the Goblins then the Hobgoblins. No Goblin or Hobgoblin are allowed to set foot inside the city gates, except those chosen as slaves or given servant orders and tasks. They will open the gates while an actual Gooblyn escort will take over leading us into the city. The rest of them will all remain out here to guard and await any future orders."

"Go!" The lead Goblin shouted at the group as he stepped aside and the gate began to open. Lucian saw the gates move outwards splitting in two as four Goblins on each side pushed with all their might. Once the gate doors opened, a group of ten, what Lucian assumed were Gooblyns by their more fancier, but not by much, attire and weapons, made their way towards them. They even made an effort to try to walk more upright than the Goblins. The Gooblyns came to a stop right in front of them and pointed their spears at them as another Gooblyn made his way to the front, wearing what appeared to be trousers and a top as he held himself with pride.

"His greatness, King Snoog will see you now," the Gooblyn declared as he turned and headed back into the Gooblyn City.

The Gooblyn guards began to circle round Lucian's party to escort them inside. Lucian gave the signal to stand down and follow quietly while whispering to Sev to fly on and scout around for their friends. Sev was already gone and inside the city before they all moved through the gate's doors. Lucian kept his spells ready as he quickly took in his surroundings and kept from laughing. City was by far an overstatement. There really was not much to the place. Even the buildings Lucian assumed were for living were poorly constructed and almost looked like piles of trash. It was clear, like Oltar's words, the few Goblins in the city were clearly doing hard labor while Gooblyns, dressed in more human-like attire, walked around like royalty compared to the lesser class. Lucian made one last glance behind him as he saw the Goblins using ropes to pull the gate closed.

"It's filthier than I imagined," Gabrielle said as she moved closer to Lucian.

"It amazes me they survive here at all. Anyone, even the Ogres could decimate this city," Lucian replied.

"There is an unspoken truce amongst this land. As long as one colony or race does not bother or attack the other, we leave each other alone. We have managed to coexist for many seasons this way. We have put up our walls to make sure and protect us from outsiders," King Oltar added.

445

"Wait! I will announce your arrival," the lead Gooblyn proclaimed as Lucian brought his attention forward to see a very large building structure, slightly constructed better than all the other buildings. Lucian saw several almost hidden bodies holding spears and weapons all around the structure ready to attack at the slightest threatening move. There was no door just an opening to pass through. As the lead Gooblyn walked into the building, Lucian saw pointed spears on the other side greeting the creature upon his entrance.

"They're all inside, Fylla, Aksurh and two Drogans. They are all chained to stones and each in a metal-like cage but looked unharmed," Sev said as he landed back upon Lucian's shoulder.

"What about Docanesto?"

"No sign of him inside. Nothing but those fowl creatures."

"That's odd, tell everyone to be ready," Lucian said as Sev darted off and zipped past each of their party's ears.

The Gooblyn returned and motioned for them to proceed into the building but the hounds had to remain outside. Lucian heard protests but commanded the hounds to stay and Frrr would keep a close eye on them. Lucian wondered where his adoptive father was, but knew if the Gooblyns wanted them dead they would have tried already. Lucian smirked keeping his wits about him and his magic ready as they all entered the so-called Gooblyn Palace.

Lucian wrinkled his nose as the smell of rotten eggs and body odor met them with great force. There were Gooblyns walking around everywhere as well as a handful of Goblins running around carrying out orders or being punished for not moving fast enough. Lucian noticed that what decor there was, were things and materials stolen or scavenged from others and thrown around in an attempt to make the place look fancy. They continued down a long hallway as Sev soon landed back on his shoulder.

"Lucian, the others are glad that you are here. They have not seen any sign of Docanesto, just a document from him to King Snoog. That document is the only thing that has kept them alive and for them to wait and not try to escape. There is a passageway that leads down to an underground area where they are being kept guarded by Gooblyns and Hobgoblins, five of each."

"Tell them we are about to see this king, one way or another they will be released soon," Lucian said as the Fairy zipped away from him.

"Silence!" A Gooblyn shouted as Lucian saw they had come to a wooden door guarded by two Gooblyns, each holding a spear in one hand and a chain leash attached to a Hobgoblin in the other.

The Gooblyn walked up to the guards, grunted some words and rushed through the crack as soon as the guards pulled the door open.

"What can we expect?" Lucian asked over his shoulder as he focused on the door the Gooblyn had vanished thru.

"My knowledge of the Gooblyns ends here. We know nothing of their king except that the old king had died a few seasons ago and replaced by a Gooblyn named Snoog," Oltar answered as he stood between the two Fire Elves that looked more than ready to defend their master.

"If he's anything like the rest of these creatures we have nothing to worry about," Gabrielle smirked, her arm gently grazing Lucian's arm as she leaned to the side of him causing him to fight to hide a smile from the sudden sensation.

"Enter and bow in the presence of our great king, King Snoog!" The Gooblyn shouted as he darted back from beyond the door.

Lucian led his party past the guards and into the room, the smell going from fowl to almost unbearable. Around the room were numerous life like statues, mostly of Goblins. Sitting on a large throne was a huge obese creature with a purple robe-like cape that barely covered its whole body. His skin was an odd green with nails and eyes taking on a faded yellow color. Despite his weight, it was clear to Lucian that this king was by far bigger than and looked almost nothing like any Goblin he had seen so far. Lucian started to step forward, ignoring commands to bow, when the lead Gooblyn, the guards at the foot of the throne and his own Fire Elves motioned for him to stop.

"You do not," the lead Gooblyn started to say stepping up to Lucian only to be cut off by being backhanded out of the way causing the guards to move forward only to stop when a loud laugh came from King Snoog.

"Brave one you are. You are every bit his son," King Snoog smirked, grabbing what looked like slop from a tray holding Goblin and devouring it.

"I want my friends released this moment and I want to speak with Docanesto," Lucian demanded already knowing his adoptive father was not in the city.

"Very demanding are you, even though you are in my palace. They only reason you or any of your friends are still alive is because of my respect and promise to your fathers, but one I will contemplate breaking if you don't bow and pay your respect to me," King Snoog said spraying food upon the party before him.

"You dare!" The Fire Elves shouted as one brought forth his sword and leapt at the Gooblyn King.

Lucian prepared for a fight but none of the guards moved and only watched as the Fire Elf and his flaming sword attacked their king. Lucian winced, as with surprising speed and strength, Snoog whipped out his left hand, catching the Elf by his throat and snapping his neck instantly. The king tossed the body aside as he quickly pulled out a strange looking staff with his other hand and pointed it forward, a flash of light leaving the staff and hitting the other Fire Elf turning him and the series of arrows he had released to stone. Gabrielle glanced quickly at the Elf, the other statues in the room and then back to Lucian, as they both understood King Snoog's status.

"Shall we try this again?" Snoog growled, as he looked right at Lucian and held his staff at the ready.

Lucian glared at the king trying to get a read on him. There was a strange sensation but he was not certain it was coming from the king but he had really felt it when Snoog had taken down his Elves. It was faint and weak, but the power of the Magesti had been used. He still felt small pricks upon his senses. He was about to confront the king again when Gabrielle's arm touched his shoulder causing him to swoon his thoughts towards her as she guided him down on one knee with her. "Won't do you any good if all of us are turned to stone."

"That's better. She is right, you're the only one I'm obligated to keep alive but in a show of good faith," Snoog said as he waived his staff and in a flash of light the Fire Elf reverted from stone to flesh. "Unfortunately I can't undo that." Lucian looked over at the dead Fire Elf before motioning the other to stand down and kneel.

"Where is Docanesto?" Lucian asked again growing impatient.

"He has not arrived yet. Let us eat while we talk," King Snoog said as Lucian looked over and saw that Goblins were already bringing in a table, chairs, plate settings and food.

"What about," Lucian began to say when Sev landed on his shoulder causing him to look over and see a set of Gooblyn guards bringing in two figures chained at their wrists. Lucian glanced at Snoog, amazed at the efficiency and proactivness these creatures acted in without verbal commands from their king.

"The other two creatures I have left in their cages but have brought your friends up to join you to show I truly mean no harm to any of you. Oh, your Fairy no longer needs to hide, he has a chair at my table as well," King Snoog smiled as Lucian glanced at Sev while the rest of his party and friends took seats around the table.

Snoog did not need to move as the table had been placed right in front of him as the head of the table. Lucian sat in the chair closest to the Gooblyn King while Sev grew big and quickly took the chair next to him making Gabrielle stumble and glare before taking the chair next to Sev. On the other side of the table, Fylla and Aksurh were led to their seats as the guards removed their chains. King Oltar took the other empty seat next to Aksurh. The Fire Elf sat at the chair at the end of the table, across from Snoog so he could look directly at him, leaving one single empty chair that sat between Fylla and the Gooblyn King.

"We were so glad to hear you survived and made it safely here," Aksurh said across the table to Lucian.

"Yes, thanks to my father," Lucian said as he glanced up at Snoog.

"Well, I see one can't enjoy ones meal," Snoog said after he tipped his plate and emptying all its contents into his mouth and placing it back upon the table for the Goblins to refill.

"How did Docanesto know we were coming and why isn't he here?" Lucian demanded.

"I don't know how he knew. I just received notice that you were on your way and that I was to make sure you arrived here unharmed and detained till he arrived," Snoog said as he chugged down more food.

"What do you mean detained?" Fylla started to ask when the Gooblyn King held up a food-caked hand.

"Now, now, my turn for questions. What *are* you doing here so far from home and accompanied by the Orgite King no less?" Snoog asked as his eyes rested right on Oltar, who swallowed his food in a startled gulp. "Has the truce ended?"

"No, not at all. I mean no offense or wish a conflict. I joined them," Oltar began to plead.

"I asked him to accompany us as a guide. My reasons for being here are between me and my fathers," Lucian interrupted.

"You're looking for something or someone?" Snoog said more to himself as Lucian saw the Gooblyn King trail off into his thoughts, paused and then scowled as he glared directly back in his direction. "Explain!" Snoog demanded after another brief pause before he slammed his fist down on the table causing food and drink to rattle.

"Is he talking to you?" Sev whispered.

"Not sure," Lucian mumbled as he it appeared the Gooblyn King was mumbling and talking to himself.

"Try harder or you'll answer to me!"

"Not sure what you're playing at but I don't answer to no one, especially the likes of you. Now, if you'll," Lucian stood up ready to confront the king when the door crashed open from a Goblin rolling though and landing near its king.

"Your majesty, the other group is approaching and," the Goblin started to cry when a flash of light turned him to stone.

"Who dares interrupt my dinner party in such a manor," Snoog bellowed, as he lowered his staff and then quickly positioned his eyes at the doorway.

"I do!" A voice shouted back as a figure entered into the room.

"Drocana," Lucian, along with his other friends chimed in all at once, as they turned to see the Fire Elf, slightly battered but still looking beautifully threatening.

"Glad to see you safe, sire," Drocana said bowing in respect.

"What are you doing here?" Lucian asked as he made his way over to the daughter of his adopted father.

"Seems you're not the only one needing safe passage to my home," Snoog grunted as suddenly a bunch of Gooblyns and Goblins went racing out the door while another group quickly cleared the table to move it out of the room.

"Start talking," Lucian said ignoring the king as he began to feel a weird sensation, different from the one he had been feeling when he first arrived to this city.

"I was sent by my father to follow your spy into the Northern Mountains," Drocana said with a smirk. "Good thing I did."

Lucian's anger towards Docanesto exploded causing him to answer the Fire Elf's smirk with a backhand across her face. Drocana twisted to the side but caught her balance, spat and wiped blood from her mouth and stood locking eyes with Lucian. She did not wait for him to speak as she immediately told him everything from confronting Nat, surviving the fall and getting here and arranging the search and find to bring Nat and her group here to the Gooblyn City.

"It seems your girlfriend may have found the Chosen One but appears to have made friendly as well," Drocana finished as Gabrielle glanced at Lucian with a questioning but amused look.

"Don't worry. She is just a friend, our friend. There's only one person he loves," Sev said in the pirate's ear as he shrunk down flying by to land on his lover's shoulder.

If it was not for Sev now upon his shoulder, he might have attacked the Fire Elf but he knew killing Drocana might be considered an attack against his fathers. Taking a deep breath, he prepared his next move when a Gooblyn ran into the room declaring the group was now within sight of the city gates.

Lucian suddenly felt an overwhelming burst of energy and excitement. The Chosen One was here. With that, Lucian darted out of King Snoog's throne room.

Chapter Twenty-Six:
The Plea For Help

"Wake up!" Patches shouted down the hallway the moment he heard voices outside the door.

Patches made his way back into the main room after he was sure his fellow prisoners were getting up. He sat back in the chair he was originally in when he had gotten up early, before anyone else, to just think and contemplate what was coming next for him and the others. He kept his eye on the door and tried to make out the conversation but the doors and walls were too thick to make anything out clearly. He knew coming *home* was a risk but if anyone could help the Kingdom of Sorran and its people, it would be King Merrik and his ruthless warriors.

"Who's here?" Marcus asked as he and the others joined Patches at the table.

"Probably the guards. Whatever they say or do, do not resist or fight them or they will kill us outright. Our only chance is to remain cooperative in hopes we can make our plea to the king," Patches instructed not taking his focus from the door.

"Step away from the door!" A voice shouted as the door was thrown open and four guards charged in, surrounding the group with their weapons up and ready to attack.

As everyone looked to each other, nervous and trying to stay calm, Patches stood and made eye contact with the two figures coming through the doorway. The first was the massive form of Terrik, master of the Death Bringers. He stepped in, raised his sword and placed it against Patches' neck, who did not even flinch, as he watched the last figure step through the doorway. A man who looked much older than Patches, hair and beard as white as the clouds, moved with strong pride despite the assistance of a walking stick.

"King's Advisor Mogran, your highness," Patches greeted as he knelt to one knee and bowed his head not sure what would happen next.

Despite his appearance, former king, Mogran Erikson moved with speed and strength as he swiped his walking stick upwards hitting Patches under the chin and sending him up landing hard upon his back. "Stay!" Patches shouted without moving or showing pain, his sharp tone causing his party to freeze in place before their actions caused the guards to strike them down.

Mogran Erikson moved slowly towards the man with the eye patch, who did not move and remained laying upon his back. Terrik moved in protest but then stepped back out of the way when the former king shot him a look. Mogran reached the man on the floor, placed his stick under his chin and eyed Patches carefully. When he was done prodding the one-eyed man with his stick he stepped back, looked at the rest of the group being held prisoner and then stood against the wall near the door, slightly leaning upon it for support, holding the walking stick directly in front of him, both hands firmly on the stick. "Shall we kill them?" Terrik asked but got no reply.

"The face is old and battered, but I can see Logan in it. If you are the son of the disgraced, I would hear from your lips why you would dare return here and in the company of Prince Arron of Argoth?" Mogran asked as Patches sat up and then shifted himself to one knee before his uncle.

"Do we not get to meet the king?" Lija asked.

"Keep quiet," Marcus and Arron whispered quickly as they watched the guards near them and the old man with the walking stick.

"You best watch that tongue if you want to keep it. I will be the one to decide if any of you are worthy of entering the palace," Mogran said not even bothering to give Lija a glance as he motioned for Terrik to place the kneeling man back upon his chair and to speak.

Patches took in a deep breath, swallowed his pride and told the man before him all about his father and growing up in Sorran. He then went into detail about what was happening in Sorran and how they made their escape from the dreaded creatures, crossed the Drol Death Desert and made it safely to the Kingdom of Erikson. Patches left out certain details and only gave the basic information Mogran needed to know. When Patches finished, everyone remained quiet as the old man with the walking stick stared, in deep thought.

"Bring them," was all Mogran Erikson said as he turned and exited the building.

"You heard his majesty. If any refuse or put up a fight, kill them," Terrik said as he grabbed Arron and went out the door with him.

Marcus looked at Patches as the guards shoved them all out the door. He heard his sister whimper but knew better to make a scene. If they had a chance of surviving this, they had to play along and reach the king. He smirked a little to himself as he thought that if they had battled Vampires and lived this should be a walk in the park. Once they were outside, Marcus saw Arron up on a horse with Terrik just as they were all herded towards a barred cage attached to the back of a couple horses. Marcus worried about Patches but along with him, Lija, Bruce and Korvan, the old man was eventually thrown in the cell with them.

"Is everyone okay?" Patches asked as he rubbed his chin.

"Yes, how are you?" Lija asked as she knelt down next to the old man and looked at the mark and forming bruise upon his chin where he had been struck.

"Don't fuss over me. I think it is a very good sign that we are being taken to see King Merrik. It means there is a chance. Whatever happens when we get there, do not put up a fight. Go peacefully in and plead our case to King Merrik," Patches told the group knowing his fate may end up differently than theirs.

"What if he refuses to help?" Bruce asked.

"Then do your best to agree to leave with Arron and get to Argoth," Patches answered as he turned and looked out the bars.

The horses moved quickly as they traveled towards the city called Erikson. It did not take long before they could see the large stone walls that made up the castle. Before they were in full view, they stopped long enough for a large cloth to be placed over the cage so no one would be able to see in or out of the cell. The sun was bright enough that they were not in complete darkness, but Marcus still did not feel very comfortable. He leaned next to his sister and hugged her tight. king or not, he would die protecting her.

"Halt!" Came a voice from outside the cage. They all tried to listen but it was hard to make out what was going on. The cart started moving again and then eventually came to another stop. Suddenly, the cage door was yanked open and the guards ushered them out one by one, keeping their weapons ready if any of them made a wrong move. Marcus rubbed his eyes against the light and after he saw they were all safe and accounted for he looked up and noticed they were standing at the bottom of a long stairway that lead up to the entrance of a large building – Castle Erikson. Coming towards them were several armed guards surrounding two men. One Marcus recognized as Death Bringer Master Terrik but the other one, wearing a basic gold crown, he had to assume was King Merrik.

"That the king?" Lija asked her brother as she watched the man with shoulder length red wavy hair, matching beard with bright green eyes and looked as tough and strong as the guards around him. He wore a green royal cape with a long sword resting in a holt on his left hip. Lija felt awe and fear all at once.

"Yes, and even my dad says he is to be feared," Arron whispered from her other side and then knelt down, "Your Majesty." Patches and the others quickly followed suit.

"Forgive me if I don't invite you inside, but if my father seems to believe you are the son of the disgraced then you are not welcomed nor do I want your tarnished blood spilled upon MY family's home," King Merrik said as he, Terrik and his guards stopped a few steps from the kneeling group.

"King Merrik, my son, I would bet my life he is the son of," Mogran began to say steeping up to his son before King Merrik's stare silenced him.

"Do not say the disgrace's name. Prince Arron, please step forward and tell me why you are with them," King Merrik commanded as two guards *helped* Arron forward and placed him right in front of King Merrik.

"They helped save me from a hoard of winged monsters while my family was visiting Sorran," Arron explained keeping the same version of the story that they have told a few times over now.

"I don't see reason to believe you would lie to me and there is no bad blood between your father and I. For that, I have already sent a messenger to inform King Allen that you are here and I will send a personal guard to escort you safely home," King Merrik said as he motioned for the boy to be taken inside.

"Wait, what about my friends. They saved me," Arron started to plea waving his hand and glanced at Lija and Marcus when King Merrik stopped, turned, looked directly at the prince and then rubbed his beard in deep thought.

"From all I've heard from you and the information I've received from my men, it gives me a lot to consider. I feel something is not right here and things are being kept from me. That makes me doubt if there are really monsters whom have made it past our kingdoms without knowledge and invaded Sorran. Maybe it's a spoiled boy wanting attention and ran away or foolish enough to believe an old man who plots revenge on a kingdom that banished his father," King Merrik said causing Patches to quickly give his party motions to stop and remain quiet.

"Your Majesty, if I may speak," Patches said taking the lead.

"No, you may not," Terrik spat at the old man.

"What would you say?" Marrik asked as he held up his hand at the master of his most deadly warriors and took a step closer to the kneeling man with one eye.

"I have no malice towards you or your kingdom. There really are winged monsters attacking Sorran. I came here to plead for your help. Why else would I risk a journey across the Desert and the risk of my fate coming here if it all a lie for revenge?" Patches said hating to grovel but knew anything else would spell immediate death to all his friends and companions, especially Bruce as well as sealing the fate of Sorran and maybe all of Bergonia.

King Merrik eyed the old man, looked upon each person kneeling with him and then over to Prince Arron. His face remained stern with no sign of softness or weakness. He was quickly considering everything and had to make a decision. He then gave his verdict. "The girl and her brother will accompany

Prince Arron back to Argoth. They were his prime rescuers and King Allen will want to thank them."

"What about the others?" Lija asked sucking in a quick breath when King Merrik glared right at her.

"At this point, I can't let the disgraced kin go. I will have words with him, the Sorran guard and this other questionable person about these said creatures later after we've all cleaned you up, dined and sent you on your way. Bring them," King Merrik said as he turned and headed back up to the castle with Arron, Marcus and Lija escorted right behind him.

"At least he'll hear us out," Bruce said as he glanced sideways at Patches and saw him sighing deeply and felt the loss of hope.

"Our fate is sealed, isn't it?" Korvan asked, feeling weak from the sun's light as the three of them were grabbed and thrown back into the caged wagon and drug off to a location unknown.

"Mine is, but you two still have a chance. Don't make any struggles and keep your distance from me. I am sure he will let the two of you go," Patches said trying to convince them all of this hope.

"Come night fall, I can easily get us all out of here," Korvan said with a small Vampire growl in his throat.

"You wouldn't survive. They are vicious and strong in numbers. I couldn't face Elle again knowing our *son* was killed because of me," Patches said as Bruce took his hand.

"We will find a way for all of us to make it out," Bruce tried to assure himself more than anyone.

Time passed and they all sat, thinking and planning in silence as the sun began to set. Patches felt his stomach burn with hunger when the material covering one side of the cage was pulled up. Standing there was King Merrik, his father Mogran and at least a dozen warriors. The king nodded and the cell was opened, food placed inside and then relocked. As Bruce and Korvan grabbed their food to eat, Patches held off and looked right at Merrik.

"Prince Arron and the other two?" Patches asked.

"Well on their way back to Argoth, personally escorted by Terrik. They are no longer your concern."

"What about us?" Bruce asked.

"At least let them go," Patches pleaded.

"I wanted to make sure you all were fed and take one last look upon your face," King Merrik said as he glared upon the old man.

"You have to let us out of here. There is an invasion going on," Korvan screamed as he felt his strength grow back and grabbed hold of the bars on the side of the cart.

"I do not have to explain myself nor answer to any of you. All will be dealt with at dawn's light," King Merrik said as he turned and quickly walked away.

"Let us out," Korvan started to yell when a sharp object hit him in the chest sending him backwards.

"Korvan!" Bruce shouted as he saw a bleeding wound upon the man's chest right before the cloth was dropped putting them back into darkness.

"Don't worry, I'll heal," Korvan grunted in pain.

"You heard his majesty. Take them to be prepared for dawn," Mogran's voice came as the caged cart began to move forward.

"What does that mean?" Bruce asked already knowing the answer, trying to make his way in the dark to his injured companion.

"I'm sorry Elle," Patches whispered as he looked over to the direction of Bruce and then fell to the side as the cart suddenly jerked and came to a stop.

"What is going on?" Korvan asked as he could already feel the wound closing up as the night sky and his Vampire abilities kicked in stronger.

"Keep quiet back there," a strange but somewhat familiar voice came from outside the cage as the cart was suddenly yanked to life and propelled forward with great speed.

****

"We're making good time. We'll be at the Old River Gorge before dark," Arron said as he glanced back only to receive a scowl.

He knew Lija was mad at him for not being more concerned, but at this point, he was thankful that he, Lija and her brother were on their way to the safety of his home. He would talk to his parents and worry about the others later. Arron just wanted to get home as fast as possible and alive. King Merrik had made sure of it by having Arron, Lija and Marcus each ride upon the back of a horse with a Death Bringer. Surrounding them in formation were ten more Death Bringers upon horseback while their master, Terrik who rode near point, not far from the prince, making sure they made it to the Kingdom of Argoth. Arron knew it would all work out for them all and Lija would forgive him.

"I hate traveling without my sword," Marcus said after more time had passed and he kept his eyes moving all around watching out for danger.

"You have nothing to worry about child. There is nothing out here that would dare challenge us or survive if they did. We are almost there and our messenger should have already alerted Argoth's King to have an escort waiting for you," the man in front of him responded with great assurance.

After a little more time passed, the horses came to a halt when Terrik whistled loudly while holding his hand up. Marcus glanced at his sister and then tried to see past the front of his horse and rider to see what was going on. They had reached the bridge that allows safe passage over the Old River Gorge from the Kingdom of Erikson to the Kingdom of Argoth. Standing a few feet from the edge of the bridge on the Argoth side stood a single guard wearing the colors and emblem of Argoth. The man stood firm as he waited for them to proceed over the bridge.

"I thought there would be a bigger reception," Lija half mocked as Terrik led the group single file across the bridge.

"As did I," Arron said as he kept looking to see if maybe more were hidden somewhere or on their way in the distance, but alas these was not.

"State your business," the Argoth guard demanded once Terrik was halfway across the bridge.

"On behalf of King Merrik, we bring Prince Arron back to your kingdom in peace and unharmed," Terrik responded.

"Did you not receive word, Brick?" Arron asked once he recognized the bridge sentry.

"The queen did receive word of your arrival as well as some tale of winged monsters," Brick laughed as Terrik swore on their messenger's loose lips on details he was not authorized to share. King Merrik was going to leave that possible fairytale up to the young prince to explain.

"Where is our messenger?" Terrik asked as he saw a familiar horse off in the distance but no rider. "I don't recall passing him on our way here."

"Marcus!" Lija screamed once they were all fully across the bridge and she took a glance back. There on the other side of the gorge, part way down the side, was a man hanging lifeless on a rock.

"What is going on here?" Terrik asked as he recognized the man and leapt off his horse drawing his sword.

"How unfortunate, you weren't supposed to discover him. We were hoping to have you on your way before we disposed of the prince and his friends. Guess we will have to kill you all," Brick said as he started walking backwards making a strange whistling noise.

"Kill us?" Marcus asked directly at Arron.

"My mom will."

"She mandated the order. Your brother will take the throne. With you dead and it pinned on the Kingdom of Erikson, all the people of Argoth will rise together as well as the other Kingdoms of Bergonia isolating Erikson and reducing the most powerful kingdom into nothing," Brick laughed as a strange sound came from within the gorge.

Arron sat in shocked disbelief. Trying to keep tears back as everyone else turned to see dozens of winged figures shoot up from the Old River Gorge. Marcus and Lija recognized them instantly as the creatures that were invading Sorran and had killed their good friend Thom. "Drogans, kill every last one of them!" Brick shouted as he leapt upon a horse and darted off towards the City of Argoth.

"These are the creatures we told King Merrik about," Marcus said as he made eye contact with Terrik and received a look back that spoke volumes that his king should have taken them more seriously.

Terrik started shouting commands at his men as they raced to fight the creatures head on. "Get them out of here and to safety. We cannot have his death blamed on us. Get word to King Merrik and do not stop till you see his face," Terrik said to his three warriors that had Marcus, Lija and Arron and then turned to the Death Bringer closest to the bridge whom all four commanded their horses onwards without hesitation.

"I have to help them," Marcus said as he looked back to see all the Drogans completely surrounding Terrik and his Death Bringers, except one that had taken flight and pursued the Death Bringer that had made it back across the bridge and was heading towards the City of Erikson.

"You have no weapons," Lija reminded her brother.

"I can't believe this. Mother would never," Arron was mumbling to himself as he stared at Brick who had grown tiny off in the distance.

"Sorry, I have to. I love you, dear sister," Marcus said as Lija screamed in protest when he leapt from the horse, rolled and began running back toward the fight and three Drogans that had already taken flight towards them.

"What are you doing, stupid child? Go, we need to keep the prince safe. I will let no kid be braver than I," the Death Bringer commanded to the other two as he turned his horse around and raced towards Marcus and the oncoming Drogans.

Marcus could hear a horse coming up behind him but he was too focused on the enemy in front of him to turn around or stop. The three winged creatures landed a few feet in front of him, opened their mouths and each sent a blast of fire like the one that had killed Thom. Marcus dove out of the way and turned to see that they had not been aiming at him. One hit and set the Death Bringer that was behind him on fire while the other two hit the ground near Lija & Arron's horses causing the startled animals to throw all four riders off and bolt in fright. Marcus ran toward the burning man to find it was too late for him. Marcus reached down, grabbed the dead man's sword and turned back to the three Drogans just as one of them took flight and headed right for his sister.

Marcus did not have time to contemplate his next move as the first Drogan came at him swinging its red bladed sword down upon him. Marcus blocked it with his sword, which barely held against the might of the red blade. The creature was strong, but Marcus was not weak himself. He punched the creature in the throat and used that momentary startle to swing his sword and knock the red blade from its hand. The creature growled as its companion let out a roar and opened its mouth to let loose its fire. Marcus scooped up the red blade, swung it and smiled as the red blade easily sliced off its owner's head. With grace and speed, Marcus spun and hurled the sword directly in front of him causing the red blade to pierce through the Drogan's mouth before it could let loose its fire.

"Thanks, dad," Marcus applauded his father's training as he ran over, grabbed the sword hilt and jerked it up slicing the head in two. With two Drogan swords in each hand, Marcus looked back and forth to see how the battle on two different fronts were playing out. Two Death Bringers stood protectively in front of his sister and Arron while they battled the Drogan to the one side while on the other he saw a massive battle between Terrik and his men with the large group of Drogans. Knowing where he was needed most, Marcus sprinted towards Terrik and his men.

"While they're fighting, we should get to the palace," Arron said as he pulled at Lija's arm.

"Are you kidding me? I cannot leave my brother and your mom is the one wanting us all dead. Your palace is the last place I want to go," Lija cried in frustration and fear.

"Brick is lying. There is no way my mom would do that. Once we get there and tell her what happened all will be cleared up," Arron defended.

"You can go if you want to," Lija declared as she reached down, grabbed a large rock and made her way to the Death Bringers that were assigned to protect them.

"I don't know what manor of monster this is but they do present a challenge," one of the Death Bringers said as he dodged a blast of fire and tried to find an opening.

"The fire does make it hard to get a close attack in," the other Death Bringer said as the Drogan blade collided with his causing him to lose his grip and his sword to fly off to the side.

"Die," the Drogan growled as it turned its head at the unarmed man and opened his mouth.

"Hey, ugly!" Lija shouted as she threw the rock as hard as she could hitting the creature in the face. The Drogan, distracted, looked over at Lija allowing the other Death Bringer to bring his sword down hard with all his strength and sever the creature's hand causing it and the sword it held to fall to the ground. The Drogan howled in pain as it grabbed the Death Bringer by the throat and lifted him up in the air squeezing tight with his other clawed hand while looking at Lija and opening its mouth to spew fire.

Lija stepped back and then heard a loud battle cry. Arron had picked up the Death Bringer's sword and brought it down upon the Drogan. It was not a killing blow but the blade did lodge into the creature's collarbone making it drop and spin around to face the young prince. The Drogan was ready to attack when a red blade sliced through its neck sending the head in one direction and the sword in another. The headless body sank to the ground in front of Arron making him swallow as he looked up at the man who had just saved him. "Thanks."

"No, it is you, I thank," the Death Bringer said as he turned the red sword around and offered it to Arron with a slight bow of his head.

"Why are you giving me that?" Arron asked as he reached for the Drogan sword.

"It was you that struck the blow that saved me and allowed for the opening to kill the creature. You earned the bounty," the Death Bringer said not wanting to admit the shame for having touched and used a weapon of magic. He felt glad to have the cursed sword out of his hand.

"We must continue on and get you two to safety," the other Death Bringer said as he and his fellow warrior each now held their own swords and looked to the direction of Argoth.

"We can't leave my brother," Lija said looking over to the battle off in the other direction.

"Our orders," one of the Death Bringers started to say when Arron cleared his throat.

"She's right. I am not sure what truth is going on with Brick and my mother but we make that decision after we help the others. I do not want to sit back or run and let others die for me," Arron said as he raised the red blade and ran to battle. Lija smiled and followed with the Death Bringers joining the call to battle.

****

Marcus swung both his red bladed swords in a dance of combat as he finally managed to take down another Drogan. The odds were against them and he was feeling tired but the thrill of battle excited and drove him onwards. They were outnumbered and the Drogans were a bit tougher to take down with normal swords, and the fact they breathed fire. Marcus had the advantage with two red blades at his disposal. He had offered one to Terrik, but the master of the Death Bringers refused. He proclaimed that it went against their code to touch an item of magic. Marcus respected the man and saw that Terrik could hold his own with his weapon. Marcus had no problem using the Drogan's swords.

Marcus looked around and saw that along with him and Terrik there were only two other Death Bringers left alive against ten remaining Drogans. It did not look hopeful for them but they fought on until a strange booming noise caused all of them, including the Drogans to stop and look back across the Old River Gorge. Off in the distance, they could make out that the flying Drogan was just about to reach the Death Bringer. That was not what made the noise, it was something else coming right towards the two. Marcus squinted his eyes and could not believe what he was witnessing.

The object flew with great speed and hit the Drogan causing a second explosion as it sent the Drogan flying back hitting the ground rolling and smoking. The Death Bringer on the horse kept going as another object speed right past the rider and headed right for the Drogan. Marcus could now make it out. It was barred wagon cell of sorts attached to two horses. Two figures sat in front directing the wagon while several figures appeared to be in the celled wagon. Just as the wagon passed the Drogan, a figure pointed his arm out and fired off something that hit the Drogan in the head making it go still. As the wagon got closer, making all the Drogans start towards it, Marcus almost screamed with excitement.

"What is the meaning of this?" Terrik asked feeling the opposite of Marcus.

Marcus now recognized the two driving the wagon were the two potential heirs they had met in their holding cell back in Erikson. Inside the wagon were seven people, four he did not recognize and three he knew well - Bruce Peters, Korvan Salee and the one that had killed the Drogan, Patches. The other four looked like the splitting images of the other two and knew those must be the other potential heirs. He wondered how they got here, but for now, he was glad for the reinforcements, especially now that the sun was setting and it was beginning to get dark.

"Not at full strength but good enough," Korvan hissed as he leapt out of the wagon and hit a Drogan with all the speed and strength he had.

"Is that?" A Death Bringer started to ask when Terrik's voice boomed over his with a strong curse.

"We'll settle all this later. Do not waste this opportunity. Attack!" Terrik shouted as he advanced upon a Drogan as his men followed suit.

Marcus raced in with new energy as Patches, Bruce and the other warriors soon joined him. The two driving the wagon brought it to a stop at the edge of the bridge and raced into battle as well. "Boy am I glad to see you."

"Can't seem to let you out of my sight for a minute and you are in need of rescue," Patches joked as he threw two objects at a Drogan causing an explosion in its face.

"What happened after we left? Did the king send these warriors with you?" Marcus asked swinging his red blades to end the life of the Drogan Patches had just distracted.

"I am afraid not. Unfortunately, Merrik had us scheduled to be executed, but our two friends showed up and captured the wagon cell. We did not know what was happening until we got out of the city and their brothers joined us. We rode on to catch up with all of you," Patches said as he dove to avoid a blast of fire.

"Brothers?" Marcus asked as he helped Patches to his feet and deflected another blast with his swords.

"It seems the entire group of heirs has decided to believe us and want to help. How they snuck out and managed to get us here, I don't know, but you do not knock a gift horse in the mouth," Patches laughed as he looked into his satchel, thankful they had managed to get a hold of and return all off their possessions and weapons back to him and his companions.

Marcus was impressed with the Erikson heirs. They were trained well and it showed in their fighting. The tables were turning as one by one the Drogans fell. When the last of the evil creatures were slain, Marcus and the others gathered upon the command of Terrik. Terrik stood in the middle while his last two remaining Death Bringers and the Erikson heirs stood to his left while Marcus, Patches, Bruce, Korvan, Lija and Arron stood to his right. It was hard to read the face of the leader of the Death Bringers so they all waited in silence until he spoke.

"Does King Merrik know you are here?" He asked looking right at the six sons of King Merrik.

"No, he does not, sir," said the one that Marcus and his party had met previously.

"Why am I not surprised, Lark, that you'd be behind this disruption and disregard of rules," Terrik scolded the boy.

"We were all in agreement. If it wasn't for us, you may not have won against those fowl creatures," the other boy that Marcus had met along with Lark had spoken up in defense of his kin.

"You would be wise to bite your tongue, Chadwick, least you lose it," Terrik threatened as he took in a deep breath and then looked right at Korvan. "Explain!"

"What would you have us explain?" Patches asked as he and the others inched their way in front of their companion.

"Do not play me a fool, son of the disgraced. I saw what he did. How does a Vampire survive in the sunlight and come to be in your company?" Terrik demanded as he and his two guards readied their swords.

Patches glanced at his friends and decided to tell the Master Death Bringer everything, including their survival in the Desert and Korvan not truly being a full Vampire. Korvan added his story about the Dragon in his dream and having strange abilities. As they told their full tale, Terrik stared with no emotion while Marcus thought he saw the boy, Lark, react oddly to Korvan's part of the story. Marcus was good at reading people and he had a feeling that there was something more to the boy. That he was hiding something.

"You don't believe this garbage do you?" One of the Death Bringers asked their Master.

"My instinct is to say no, but look what we just witnessed," Terrik said as he waved his sword at the battlefield of dead Drogans then turned on Lark. "How did you escape your holding area?"

"We have a secret tunnel out," one of the heirs spoke up before Lark could.

"Tork, I find that hard to believe. Either way, the king will be furious. I have to get you back before anything happens to you all. Of all things, a year before one of you becomes the official heir to the throne," Terrik started swearing to himself as he walked back and forth.

"We can't go back, we have to help them. If not to prove Arron is alive, but if these creatures are trying to invade Sorran, to help our fellow kingdom. It is also in our code to stop these monsters of magic," Lark said, continuing to stand strong in front of the Death Bringer Master.

"Whether you help us or not, please let us go. My friends here will accompany me back to my home and," Arron started to say when Lija stepped up.

"We can't go there. What if your mom is waiting there to kill you, us?" Lija interrupted.

"We refuse to go back. How can we take the throne with honor knowing we turned our backs on a kingdom in need? That we could have done something to stop an attack by magical creatures," Chadwick added stepping up next to Lark as his fellow brothers chimed in with agreement.

"Your messenger will report to the king and will surely send help," Bruce said nervously.

"I will have one of my men stay here by the bridge on the Erikson side to await word from King Merrik. The rest of us will proceed to Castle Argoth and present Arron to King Allen and then we can proceed to Sorran to investigate as we await word from our king," Terrik decided as they went to round up as many horses as they could to travel onward to deliver Prince Arron home.

****

The sun had set and now the moon lit the night's sky. The surviving group had managed to round up a few horses. Terrik, Marcus, Lark and the remaining Death Bringer rode point on horses. Chadwick and Patches steered the horse drawn wagon as everyone else rode in the wagon's cell. Lija felt bad about leaving the other Death Bringer behind with no horse while having to hide out near the bridge, but he and Terrik assured her he would be more than fine. To be on the safe side, Arron directed the group onto a lesser road to avoid being spotted. This way they could reach the City of Argoth with no troubles. Lija sat next to Arron inside the wagon closer to the front. Bruce and Korvan sat to their right while the other four potential heirs sat spread out from the left to the back end of the wagon.

Before they had left, they had managed to push all the dead Drogans into the Old River Gorge and bury the fallen Death Bringers in an area on the Erikson side of the gorge. Because of their beliefs against magic, those from the Kingdom of Erikson did not take the red bladed swords of the Drogans. Lark and some of the heirs wanted to but a look from Terrik made them think otherwise. Lija and Arron had retrieved a red sword for each of their group except for Marcus who was the only one to keep two. The rest of the swords were thrown into the gorge with the bodies.

Lija was tired and finally gave in and rested her head upon Arron's shoulder. She could feel the prince smiling as he casually put his arm around her. She still was not fully sure what she thought of the prince, but the one thing she knew was at this moment she felt safe. As she drifted off to sleep, she heard everyone talking with the four brothers of Lark and Chadwick.

Last thing she remembered was the heirs introducing themselves as Brock, Tork, Lorrak and Sedrik before the world went dark.

"What is going on?" Lija asked with a start when the wagon jerking woke her from her very pleasant dream.

"We're almost to my castle," Arron said as he noticed Lija blushing a little when she looked at him after waking.

"Prince Arron, I think you should be visible as we go in so they see you are safe and unharmed," Terrik said as they all got out of the wagon with the Prince of Argoth.

"What if they try to kill him?" Lija asked.

"We won't let that happen. He'll ride behind me," Terrik said as he helped Arron up on his horse.

"If we merge onto that road there it will lead us directly to the city. We will pretty much go unnoticed until we hit the road that leads up to my parent's castle. The castle sits high up on a hill, overlooking the kingdom. It will be hard to see how pretty it is at night but it is a sight to see. Matches my mother's expensive tastes," Arron rolled his eyes a little at the thought of his mother.

"Is it really that easy to access the castle?" Patches asked from where he still sat with Chadwick.

"We will be met by a guard and once cleared, which we should when I am identified, we will be escorted up the road to the castle. At the castle there will lots of guards as well as hidden archers all along the road up," Arron answered.

"How do we know Brick or your mother won't have us killed the second we arrive?" Lark asked with agreement from Marcus.

"Once we are seen, word will already reach the castle and my father. Brick or anyone would know better as there will be too many eyes on us until we get inside the castle to risk being caught trying to harm us," Arron said confidently.

"Then let us ride," Terrik said as Lija and the others got back into the wagon and they moved forward at a calm and non-alarming pace.

They entered the city and found very few people were out at this time of night. Korvan could see very well and mentioned that they were being watched and Terrik and Arron confirmed that word was already being sent to the king of their arrival. Arron made sure he sat behind the master Death Bringer in clear view, so anyone looking would not only recognize him but also see he was okay. It did not take long to pass through the city itself and reach the road that lead up the hill to Castle Argoth. Lija's inner princess made her strain to see the castle but Arron had been right. She could tell it was large but at this distance at night, it was hard to see any details.

The hill was covered in large trees making it hard to see anyone who might be watching them. A single winding road lead all the way up to the top where the castle sat. At the bottom of the hill stood two guards who appeared to have been waiting for them. Once they got to the road leading up, the guards stepped out and held their weapons ready. "Halt and state your business."

"I am Terrik, Master Death Bringer from the Kingdom of Erikson. On behalf of our king, we have escorted Prince Arron safely home," Terrik said with a formality in his voice and demeanor.

"Hey, it is me. I need to see my dad immediately and grant safe passage to all my friends here. They are under my protection and to receive gratitude for delivering me home," Arron said leaning to the side and grabbing the attention of the guards.

"Prince, we did not see you there. We will alert your father that you have been rescued and returned home," the guard said. Arron and the others knew that the guard and King Allen were already aware of his return.

They were waiting patiently when another guard stepped out of nowhere, whispered something to the main road guard who then motioned to them all. "Prince, your father awaits. You all may head up to the castle."

"Thank you," Arron said as they all urged their horses onward, following the road up to the castle. Arron knew that even though they were not being escorted, they were being watched and followed all the way up.

"It is magnificent," Lija said as she looked out of the wagon and up at the huge castle in front of them. Being dark, she still could not see all the details but there had to be at least seven towers. There were also bushes and trees all around the front and she just imagined how it must look, the fall colors against the sunlight. She could almost imagine herself living here.

"Everyone out," Patches said as he and Chadwick got off the front.

Lija and the rest of the party in the wagon got out and made their way over to where those that were on horseback had dismounted and been told to wait. She saw that Arron was by himself visiting with the guards positioned in front of the entrance to the castle. Lija was about to ask her brother what was happening when Arron turned and headed their way. "Everything okay?" Lija asked him.

"My dad is waiting for us. The guards will tend to the wagon and horses," Arron said with a smile as he waived for them to follow him though the now opened castle entrance. "We have nothing to worry about. My dad will take care of everything."

"I find it odd we have had no trouble getting here and going in with open arms," Patches said to Bruce who nodded as they entered the castle finding themselves in a large entryway with three stairways leading up, one in the center and one to the left and right of them that lead to higher levels. There were closed doors all around the area and beautiful red rugs and tapestries hung all around. Most embroidered with the Arogth emblem. Lija commented on the beauty of the decorations, which included a beautiful chandelier that hung above them that lit the entire room.

"Greetings, master Arron. We are so glad you have arrived safely home," a tall slender man dressed in a nice burgundy suit said as he moved to greet the party.

"Glad to be home," Arron said as he ran up and gave the man a hug, who to Lija appeared to be a bit stiff. "This is Herb."

"Sir, your father is waiting upstairs in his quarters. He would like to see you right away."

"What about my friends?"

"He wants to visit with you alone. Your friends are to be taken to the dining hall where they will be fed and tended to."

"I don't think it's wise to go by yourself, you know?" Lija whispered behind Arron referring to what Brick did allegedly on behalf of his mother.

"I have to agree with my sister," Marcus said stepping up to Arron.

"The king has spoken," Herb glared at the two siblings.

"What if I just go with you?" Lija asked as she batted her eyes at the man.

"Herb, we will honor father's wishes but I demand that I be accompanied by my heart's desire. He is required to meet her," Arron said as Lija, not sure, if he meant it or not, did not want to miss a beat and curtsied.

"I would so desire to meet his majesty," Lija channeled her inner princess.

"So be it. Come you two, we do not want to keep your father waiting. The guards will take the others to the dining hall where they will wait for you to join them later," Herb said as Lija followed him and Arron up the stairs. She paused, looked back and waved at her brother, as he and the others were lead down the hall to a set of doors.

"Where is everyone?" Arron asked.

"The hour is late and your father didn't want your homecoming disturbed or you to be overwhelmed. He and your mother will make a formal announcement in the morning."

Lija was half way up the stairs before she realized she was holding Arron's hand. Her instinct was to pull it away and then she realized they had to keep appearances for the king. After climbing three flights of stairs, they had arrived at their destination. Lija was slightly out of breath but not as bad as she had once been. This journey of hers had started to get her into better shape. She had even noticed her clothes were starting to feel a tad loose. Herb gestured and Arron led her to a room at the end of a hallway. Herb knocked, stepped inside and then opened the door to grant them entrance.

"Dad!" Arron screamed as he dropped Lija's hand and plowed into his father's embracing hug that lifted him off the ground.

"My boy, I thought you dead," King Allen said as he looked at his son and then over at Lija.

"You, the one that kidnapped my son?" King Allen questioned as he recognized the slightly plump girl in dirty clothes.

"Your majesty, I did not kidnap Arron," Lija started to plea.

"Silence, you will not address him by common name," King Allen scolded the girl.

"Dad, wait, she is telling the truth. I went with them willingly. It is true about the winged monsters. I have seen them. She and her brother helped me escape and brought me home. Brick, he is a traitor. He tried to have me killed and said mom told him to do it," Prince Arron rambled on to his dad trying to fill him in on the basics of what he had been through on his journey back home.

"Why would you expect me to believe this story? Why would your mother want you dead?" King Allen asked as movement in the shadows caught Arron and Lija's attention.

"Because it is all true," came a sinister voice as a woman with green eyes stepped forward and placed her hand upon the shoulder of King Allen. "Must say, very disappointed to learn you survived."

"Mother?" Arron asked in shock as the queen's evil smile shinned like the ring that rested upon the hand she had placed on her husband's shoulder.

"Why would you want to kill your own son?" Lija asked in fear and disgust.

"My dear, your brother will be king. You are a dispensable annoyance. We went to see King Sirus to solidify your brother's marriage. With him as the new king, the Kingdom of Sorran would be mine. Making it easier to control and hide the army of Drogans that are gathering in your little home town," Queen Illyria said, as her husband seemed to just stand there in utter silence.

"You're the one responsible for attacking my home and killing my friend?" Lija asked as sadness and anger started to overwhelm her.

"Mom, you, why?" Was all Arron could stutter.

"The time has come for a new era in Bergonia. Drol Greb and his forces are planning to take back what the humans stole and I have sworn my allegiance to him and Docanesto. I will be made the Queen of the Kingdoms. The first step was taking Sorran but your arrival, dear girl, threatened my plan, but I easily saw a way to turn it to my advantage.

"When King Sirus sent you away and allowed my son to be with you. I knew if you ran, he would follow. So I persuaded Bruce to help you escape as well as stage a show and pursuit to make sure you all fled the castle," Queen Illyria laughed as she watched the two kids, moving from side to side behind her husband but never releasing her hand from his body.

"You were the voice in the room we overheard," Lija gasped in realization.

"You all took the bait and off you ran. With you *kidnapping* my son, King Sirus had no problem dismissing your plea for help and putting all focus on making it up to us and bringing our children closer together. Whether my son survived the *kidnapping,* I had his attention away from the Drogan army that was gathering in his southern kingdom. I was thrilled when you all fled into the Desert so my plan could continue without any more problems," Queen Illyria smirked looking right at Lija.

"We survived and here we are to stop you," Lija said looking at the person who might be responsible for her parent's fate.

"Actually, I was very upset when I heard you were in Erikson and on your way here but then it gave me an idea to advance our plans. When word gets out that the Kingdom of Erikson killed my son, well that will completely isolate that strong kingdom into nothing. All the kingdoms will be too focused on taking out Erikson who broke the truce. They won't even see me and my take over coming," Queen Illyria cackled.

"Father, say something!" Arron pleaded at the man who suddenly seemed emotionless.

"Jokes on you. By now, King Merrik is fully aware what has happened and where we are and help is on the way. Not only do we have a whole group full of witnesses but your son is still alive," Lija spat back as she found her fingers intertwining with Arron's.

"If you are relying on the messenger heading back to Erikson, well dear, intercepted and dead. Or maybe the guard hiding under the bridge by the gorge? Also, dead. No one knows you are here. As for the rest of your companions, I believe Brick is taking them down as we speak. Those that survive will be presented to my subjects as the ones that killed my son and will be executed at dawn. Oh, that reminds me, as for my son. Dear, if you would?" Queen Illyria smiled, sliding her fingers up her husband's cheek as her ring flashed with a mysterious white-blue light.

Lija suddenly found herself screaming as Arron looked at her, smile fading and turning to confusion as he looked at his father and then down to see his dad, the king, holding a sword now buried deep in his chest. The king pulled his arm back as Arron slid off the sword and fell to the ground trying to cover the deep bleeding wound while Lija was instantly on her knees cradling him in her crying arms.

"Lija, we," Marcus shouted breaking open the door and coming to a complete stop when he saw his sister holding Arron and the king standing over them with a blood dripping sword.

"And there is the brother. Can't Brick do anything right?" The Queen of Argoth snarled.

"They killed him! They killed him!" Lija screamed.

"No dear, you all killed him. At least that is what everyone in my kingdom will be told, as well as the messenger that should soon reach the Kingdom of Silversword to bring them to our aid in the attack on Erikson.

"Lija, we have to go. We were attacked. We have to go," Marcus said as he moved towards his sister, his heart aching for her and Prince Arron.

"Arron, please don't die," Lija said cradling her prince.

"Lija, I've loved you since the moment I first saw you. Here and now I proclaim my love for you and make you now and forever my princess," Arron said as he cuffed his hand in hers and brought his lips towards her.

"I love you too!" Lija said as she kissed him on the lips as his hand left hers and his body went limp. "No! First Lars, then Elle and now my sweet, sweet prince."

"How could you?" Marcus asked as he tried to help his sister.

"Kill them, I have to go mourn our son," Queen Illyria said as she touched her husband's face with her ringed hand before turning and beginning a dramatic sob about her son while leaving the room from the opposite end calling for guards.

"Lija, he's gone. We have to go," Marcus said as the king's face turned to hatred while raising his bloodstained sword.

"Why did I act the way I did. I should have told him I loved him sooner and now it's too late," Lija cried, looking up to her brother.

"Lija, I wish there was something I could do to help you, I really do," Marcus said as the king charged and Marcus sidestepped and knocked him down.

"There is, teach me," Lija said standing up, drawing her sword.

"I will teach you to use that sword," Marcus promised.

"No, teach me to kill," Lija said glaring off in the direction the queen had gone.

"Lija, I will teach you to fight and defend yourself. Revenge is not what you need, especially not now. We have to go," Marcus said as he let his sister whisper one last goodbye and then drug her by the hand out the door.

"There you are. Where is Arron?" Patches asked as he looked at Lija's face and realizing the answer.

"Was all a setup. We need to get out of here," Marcus said as he held his sister who had gone cold and distant.

"We've bought us some time but more guards will be on us. We have to get out of this castle," Terrik said as he and the others met up with the group. Marcus noticed right away that the final Death Bringer, Brock and Lorrak were missing and the look on Terrik's face told him that they had met the same fate as Arron.

"How do we get out of here?" Bruce asked.

"I can help you. You cannot go back home, they will be waiting. I can take you to a hidden place in the north that they won't find us," the servant known as Herb said stepping up to the party.

"We can't trust him," Lija said starring at the man with hate teared eyes.

"I assure you, you can. I had no choice. I did not know the evil witch would kill him. I can get you out of here and to safety," Herb assured them.

"What's in it for you?" Patches asked.

"Take me with you. I am the one person that will be able to verify your innocence and I hold the proof of the evil queen's treason," Herb said holding a small box. "I loved that boy like a son. He will be avenged."

Lija nodded to her brother. "Fine, show us out of here."

Herb pulled a sconce on the wall and a passage way opened up. They all quickly fled into the wall as it closed behind them and ran down a hidden hallway that then turned to stairs leading down. After several flights, they came to a stop and a doorway opened up. They were now outside the castle facing north. Herb already had several horses for all of them. A handful of them had to double up as everyone quickly mounted and dashed off, following Herb, who showed to be quite the rider. They made it out of the city when dozens of Argoth soldiers stood between them and freedom.

"Now what?" Patches asked.

"We fight," Terrik said pulling out his sword.

"No, we won't survive. Even if we prevailed, another mass of soldiers will soon be coming right behind us," Herb panicked.

Marcus, sister holding tight to his back, looked around for answers when Lark rode up next to him. "What happens next, do not stop. Get everyone to safety."

"What are you doing?" Chadwick asked as Lark jumped off their shared horse.

"Lark, I can't risk losing anymore of you," Terrik said when Lark flashed him a look, eyes of dark, silencing him.

They all watched as the boy stepped between his escaping group and the oncoming soldiers. Things had become clear after hearing Korvan's story and the Dragon dream he had. The powers he held were meant for greatness. He felt the power in him stir as he reached out, touching every shadow in the vicinity. It helped that is was night as the sky lent its power to him. When he was full and ready to explode, he scooped his arms down and up causing everyone, including the soldiers to become engulfed in complete darkness. Even Korvan swore that his vision was a complete haze.

"What manor of magic is this?" Terrik swore in the dark.

"It can't be magic, the alarms would be going off," Bruce responded.

"I think it's connected to my dream and what I can do," Korvan said as he felt a strange connection to the boy, reaching out with his gift to get a sense of where every soul was positioned. "The solders are still getting close to us."

"Go!" Lark screamed as a small portion of dark parted showing them a small tunnel of light. Patches yelled for them to move and they all raced off with their horses at full speed down the tunnel of light. Marcus looked back and saw that when the last of their party had entered the darkness swallowed up the parted tunnel and continued to close up behind them. He did not know how long they had traveled but soon they broke out of the field of darkness and rode in the open under the natural night's sky.

"Where is Lark?" Terrik asked looking back at the wall of dark that was now growing far behind them.

"Don't worry, he'll be fine. Keep going," Chadwick said as he nodded at Herb, who continued to lead them north.

They managed to travel for a few more hours before Herb brought them to a stop. They were now at the edge of the Death Drol Desert. There was a path that became narrow heading east and north between the Desert and the sea. Herb dismounted and led his horse towards the Desert. Everyone did the same thing but stopped right before the edge.

"We can't go in there," Terrik proclaimed.

"We have to. There is a small hideout where we can safely hide. It is far enough in that they won't follow but not far enough that the creatures of the Drol Death Desert will bother us," Herb said as he crossed over into the Desert.

The others followed after the old man, with a reluctant Terrik, and saw that after a few feet they had come to a large rock. Herb pulled out a key, placed it into a hidden lock and then pushed open a door that revealed steps leading at a downward slant. Herb lit a candle and gave it to Patches, who started leading everyone down. Once everyone and their horses were in, Herb closed the door, lit a candle for him and followed the rest.

"It almost looks like your old place," Marcus said to Korvan as they stepped into a large room with several chairs, beds and shelves with supplies.

"My father, who served the previous king, helped build this as an emergency hideout. The current king and queen are not even aware of this place. My father never trusted Queen Illyria and before he died, told me of it in case I ever needed it," Herb said.

"Now what?" Bruce asked.

"We wait and plan our next move. Soldiers and those winged monsters are now everywhere looking for us," a voice said as a figure appeared to walk out of the shadowed corner of the room.

"Lark!" Chadwick exclaimed as he hugged his brother.

"How?" Terrik started to ask.

"Not now. I am very drained and need to sleep," Lark said as he fainted upon the bed leaving the others to figure out what they were to do next.

Chapter Twenty-Seven:
Silversword

Stephanie woke to birds chirping just before the sun started to rise. She looked over at the large wall that now separated her from her homeland. Excitement, fear, you name it, she was feeling it all. Mostly, she worried about her brother and her father. There was no going back now. She just hoped they would understand when this quest was over and she had helped save Bergonia. She yawned, wiped the sleep from her eyes and stood up from the ground she had been sleeping on. Shirlynn was still sleeping near her as she looked over and saw next to the riverbank was her horse Diamond and the black stallion form of Sir Owen. She waited and watched as dawn broke and the black horse dove into the water, submerging himself.

"Quite the sight," Tor said coming up from behind the girl as the sun's rays seemed to make the river's water sparkle for a split second.

"Um, yeah," Stephanie stuttered in surprise as she took her eyes from the man getting out of the river and looked up at the smiling Minotaur. "I love the sun's rays at morning's first light."

"Do we know the plan from here?" Tor asked pretending to believe the princess's replay.

"We need to get the shield. Once Shirlynn wakes I'm sure she'll tell us," Stephanie answered trying not to blush or look towards the river.

"I still feel like this isn't real. Me, the Minotaur savior with special abilities," Tor said looking at his hands and then at the wall where he imagined the continued suffering of his people and mother.

"Try going from being a princess isolated in a castle to traveling the world as the next leader of clerics," Stephanie added with a sigh.

"Exactly the same," Tor snorted, hot air from his nostrils hitting the girl in front of him.

"Tor, I am truly sorry about your people. Since the day I learned about them, I have pledge to find a way to free and help you all. You have to believe me. It's not my fault," Stephanie pleaded, trying to hold back the tears.

"I should be using my abilities right now to free them," Tor said trying not to stay angry with the girl whose family was his people's enslavers.

"I wouldn't recommend that, either of you. Don't need the alarms to call us out," Sir Owen said as he walked up to them, Diamond trotting next to him, as he ran his fingers through his wet hair.

"What are these magic alarms?" Tor asked as he closed his eyes and lifted his head taking in the warmth of being free outside the mines.

"Sometime after the Magic Wars, when magic and its kind were outlawed, the kings of each kingdom forced a magic user to create a way to detect anytime magic was used. Once these detectors were placed all over the kingdoms, hidden and immune to magical means to destroy them, they killed the magic user to ensure the spell from ever being undone," Shirlynn chimed in as everyone jumped and turned to the woman still laying upon the ground.

"Many believe it detects creatures of magic as well but they only go off if that creature actually uses magic or a trait of theirs based on magic," Sir Owen added as he helped the old woman to her feet.

"If these alarms are permanently active, how is it they don't go off back in Tallus?" Tor asked.

"The ones in Tallus are turned off to not risk anyone finding out about," Stephanie started to answer and then trailed into shameful silence.

"I knew they were off but how did he manage it?" Sir Owen asked knowing what this could mean for all kingdoms and the magical world.

"Each king, hidden in their castle, has a totem that acts as the power source for the magic detectors. They too are immune to magic and harm. Anyway, my brother told me that my father told him that the alarms were turned off a very long time ago. It was at the same time that my ancestral grandfather made a deal to create a place for the Minotaurs to live safely in exchange for working the mines," Stephanie started to say, cleared her throat at how that sounded and continued without looking at Tor.

"The King of Tallus met a man who came by sea selling wares. The item spoke to him so he bought it for his bride. He was in the secret chamber next to the totem, looking at the item he just bought when it started to glow in his hand. The magic alarms started to go off and he touched the totem and wished it to stop, and it did. That's when he realized he was able to turn off the magic alarms. Justified in doing so to keep the Minotaurs hidden, he placed the object on the totem wishing the alarms to never turn back on and never told a soul. Except for his son and with that the tradition began of passing the family secret down to the next generation's king," Stephanie explained fighting her tears of guilt.

"Interesting," Shirlynn whispered as she seemed to be in puzzled thought.

"What was the object?" Sir Owen asked, thinking of the great use it could serve.

"I don't know. My brother didn't say. Since we tell each other everything I assume he hasn't seen it or my father didn't tell him," Stephanie shrugged as she had never given it any real thought before.

"Where do we go now?" Tor turned to the old woman wanting to change the subject away from the princess and her enslaving family.

"Zain," Shirlynn sang when she saw the hawk land in a tree branch above her. Everyone watched as she seemed to carry on a conversation with the bird. Stephanie almost chuckled at the observation that she was the only one who found it odd. "We go southwest about a half day's journey. The path is pretty clear. Should put us there about midday."

"Where is there?" Stephanie asked.

"City of Silversword."

"Isn't that a little more than a half day's journey from the river?" Owen asked looking at the old cleric.

"Yes, that is why we will part ways when we get close to the city. You and Tor will split and head east and camp safely by the river while me, Zain and the girl head to the castle," Shirlynn said as she began pulling out rations for a quick breakfast.

"You can't go to the castle alone," Sir Owen protested. "As a Knight of Bergonia, I can get you in with ease."

"You have to stay by the river and Tor would stick out immediately. We can get in safely," Shirlynn countered as Sir Owen swore, remembering his condition and why he was stationed by the southern guard posts near the river.

"And us girls can take care of ourselves," Stephanie added with a teasing smirk.

"I don't like it but she's right," Tor said looking at Owen.

"If we get in trouble ol' Zain here will come for you," Shirlynn assured the knight.

"We better get started then if we want to make it in time," Owen said as he helped the old woman pack things up.

"Wait, where's Diamond?" Stephanie asked as she noticed her horse was missing.

"Don't worry about him. He should be, ah, there he is now," Shirlynn clapped as the white horse with black spots came trotting towards them with three other beautiful brown and white horses.

****

The sun was high in the sky when Stephanie could see the top of a castle in the distance. Thanks to Zain and the horses, they had managed to travel through the trees and off roads to avoid any detection or small towns and villages. This being her first time traveling beyond the wall, Stephanie wanted so much to see all she could see and take it in, but she knew their mission would not allow her that luxury. As they neared the edge of the trees that resided before the road leading to the City of Silversword, Shirlynn brought them to a stop. Stephanie rubbed the side of Diamond's neck as the horses rotated so everyone was facing each other.

"This is where we part ways. This road will take you directly into the city. We'll keep to the trees and make our way to the river and wait," Sir Owen said, still not overly pleased with the ladies heading off by themselves.

"We'll be fine. No one will recognize either of us or pay much attention to an old woman and her granddaughter," Shirlynn smiled as they said their goodbyes, Owen and Stephanie trading horses as Diamond might stick out, and then moved onto the road and headed west for Silversword.

As Stephanie and Shirlynn moved along the road, they only met a few other travelers who did no more than nod, wave and smile. Even though there was a slight chill in the air, as winter drew closer, Stephanie noticed the temperature was still warmer than back home. She noticed it made a difference not being near the mountains and farther south. Most of the leaves had already turned and many were starting to fall. Stephanie hated the cold and hoped their mission would be done before winter hit. Unfortunately, Stephanie had a feeling she would not be that lucky.

"Do you know exactly where the shield is located?" Stephanie asked trying to get her mind focused on other things.

"It is displayed somewhere in the castle. As for where, I do not know. Now that we are in the Kingdom of Silversword I dare not try any kind of tricks or meditation to locate it and risk setting off the alarms," Shirlynn explained causing Stephanie to sigh a little.

"Will it be easy to get into the castle?"

"I've been thinking about that and think maybe I've an idea," Shirlynn paused and when received no reply continued, "I present you as yourself, Princess Stephanie from Tallus."

"Is that wise? How do we explain my being here?" Stephanie asked, her heart starting to race.

"You snuck off onto a boat and something happened out at sea. You woke up not knowing where you were and I found you and nursed you back to health. I then decided it would be wise to bring you to the king. Once inside, while they all cater to you, I can sneak off and find the shield," Shirlynn said smiling with cleverness.

"That could work. I am wearing my royal crested ring to help with proof of my identity, but they should at least have an idea of who I am," Stephanie, thinking to herself and then gasped, "once we have the shield, how do we get it or us out?"

"I have not thought that far yet," Shirlynn chuckled when a squawking sound made both of them look up.

"Zain, you're brilliant. Giving you the shield will at least get it out of our hands and on its way to Owen and Tor," Stephanie cheered and then paused. "Did I just understand the bird?"

"Don't worry dear. It startled me the first time I communicated with nature and the animals it houses," Shirlynn said with a joyful laugh.

"Wait, why aren't the alarms going off?" Stephanie asked in a panic, looking all around.

"You are not using magic or your actual gifts. Part of being a Cleric of the Order is your brain synchs with nature and the animals and allows you to pick up and learn tongues and languages. No magic, just an enhanced skill of your natural human capabilities," Shirlynn explained even though Stephanie still did not quite fully understand. "It'll get easier as time passes and become more natural."

"Still, this all seems more than I asked for," Stephanie mumbled with a smile as she found she liked it.

As they got closer to the City of Silversword, the roads became smoother and not so hard to travel on. Stephanie noticed on both sides of the road, spaced so many feet in distance, were banners of black and silver. Each held the Silversword crest towards the top with the words, "We believe in and defend Peace ~ Knights of Bergonia" in bright silver letters. What Stephanie did not know about the Kingdom of Silversword, Sir Owen had filled them in during their journey together.

The kingdom believed in peace and was against war and killing. They enforced this motto and over all, the citizens were non-violent people. The Knights of Bergonia were well trained in defense and taught how to effectively take down or disarm an opponent or attacker without killing them. The king did have access to guards and lethal weapons like swords but never used them. Swords were more of a symbol to the Kingdom than a weapon. Not only did the king's guards and subjects know how to use weapons, they made them as well.

Silversword was rich in food and prosperity as well as being rich in silver. There were several mines in the southern part of the kingdom. Here the material was gathered by the mineworkers and brought to nearby mining towns. The craftsmen there then took that silver and made everything from weapons and armor to home decorations and jewelry. One of the greatest mining towns was the town of Silver. The kingdom's master craftsman lived there and that is where most went to train and be mentored. There they mostly made weapons, which were used to trade with the Kingdom of Erikson for various things but mainly for their ability to kill and protect against the creatures of the Forest. Sir Owen had laughed at that part. Why kill when others can do it for you?

"When you are a kingdom of peace and acceptance, you don't need walls," Shirlynn said over to the princess as they now approached the capital city.

There were homes and businesses all about with people everywhere but not very many guards. Stephanie was sure there would be some kind of checkpoint or security to stop them from entering the city, but not a one in sight. Everyone, including guards waved with a smile as the two travelers entered the City of Silversword. Stephanie looked around and truly could not tell who was poor or who was rich. Everyone seemed to get along, respect and treat each other with kindness. "So different than the *beauty* my mom promotes."

"Here we go," Shirlynn said as they approached a large above ground tunnel with two guards on each side.

Stephanie noticed that candles behind a silver holder projected a beautiful silver reflection throughout the long tunnel, lighting the pathway. On the other side was the castle, which was huge and shimmered with silver. The Silversword crest and banners could be seen all over the structure and it's three towers – two in front and one in the back, all connected by a small walking bridge of stone and silver. Stephanie knew her castle was bigger but the silver sure did make this one more breath taking. Stephanie's attention was brought back when the guards stepped forward. Each with a shield on their backs but not armed. They wore black pants and tops with silver boots, gloves and the Silversword crest upon their chests.

"Welcome, travelers. What brings you to the castle?" The guard on the right asked as you could almost see his smile from beneath the silver hood that covered all but the front of his face.

"Greetings, I bring with me, Princess Stephanie from the Kingdom of Tallus. She has unexpectedly found herself here in Silversword and I thought to bring her to the king," Shirlynn said as she smiled and bowed her head ever so slightly.

"Is this true?" The second guard asked more to himself than to Stephanie.

"Yes, I am Stephanie. My father is King Stephan of Tallus. This kind lady, Shirlynn, found me and personally escorted me safely here," Stephanie said as she raised her hand and showed her ring.

"I will go alert the king," the first guard said as he sprinted through the tunnel leaving the other guard to watch over the two women as they waited.

Stephanie noticed the sun was starting to set when the guard came walking back with two figures behind him. One was an older man with slightly graying hair while the other, a boy who looked to be in his early twenties with dark wavy black hair. He wore a silver top with black pants and a mini side cape that draped off his right shoulder. The cape was black underneath and silver on the outside with the same crest on the back as what the guards bore on their chests, a black "S" with a silver sword running through it. The top of his head was accented with a small silver crown signifying lower royalty.

"Good evening, ma'am, your highness," the young man said as he slightly bowed to Shirlynn and then Stephanie meeting each with his eyes and charming smile.

"Good evening," both of them responded back with smiles to match.

"This here is Kyle. He will tend to your horses. I am Prince Thadios. I will escort you into the castle where you will be allowed to freshen up and then my parents, the King and Queen of Silversword will listen to your story over a nicely prepared meal," the prince said as he snapped his fingers and the two guards moved to assist Shirlynn and Stephanie off their horses.

"Thank you dear," Shirlynn said shooting a glance to Stephanie that it was okay and let the man take their horses.

"Yes, thank you," Stephanie added, as she was now glad that they left Diamond behind but also worried about how they would escape without horses.

"I would ask you how you came to be here, princess, but that is a tale to be told in the presence of my father. Instead, tell me about yourself," Prince Thadios said as he engaged conversation with Stephanie making Shirlynn glad her plan worked and all attention was away from her or whether she was truly a citizen of Silversword. Shirlynn started planning while the other two talked on their walk to the castle.

****

"Welcome!" A voice boomed as Stephanie entered a grand dining hall, beautifully decorated with objects and accents of silver.

"Thank you," Stephanie said feeling much better after she and Shirlynn were allowed to clean up, but was slightly uncomfortable in the fancy dress she was given to wear. Luckily they let Shirlynn keep her same clothes as she insisted her old age made her tired and was allowed to eat and retire in her own private chambers. Being a princess, she could not refuse wanting to look all dressed up, no matter how much she hated it. She had a part to play while Shirlynn played hers as well.

"Join us, Princess Stephanie," a woman said motioning to an empty seat at the table. "Too bad Shirlynn couldn't join us but I understand such travels for a woman her age can be trying. She will be well taken care of and awarded for bringing you here safely when she leaves in the morning to head back to her home."

Stephanie nodded a proper thanks and headed for the table that was full of food and drinks, all served on silver platters and cups. Seated at the head of the table was an older man, in his forties Stephanie guessed, sitting with a large silver crown upon his head. Slightly greying hair mixed in his beautiful black hair and goatee. Across the table on the other end was the queen wearing a silver crown with jewels upon her loosely curled brown hair. She sat alone on her side of the table but across from her was Prince Thadios and a girl, maybe a few years older than

Stephanie, who was a much younger splitting image of the queen.

"You've already meet my son, Thadios. Next to him is my beautiful daughter, Maria. I am King Thadius and this is my lovely wife, Queen Marcia," the king introduced his family.

"Nice to meet you, your highnesses. My father would be honored and thankful for welcoming me into your home, as am I," Princess Stephanie addressed as she tried to put herself in her best royal princess mode.

"Did you really come from the other side of that *wall?*" Princess Maria asked in a tone that showed Stephanie that she was not in favor of the border wall that isolates the Kingdom of Tallus from the rest of Bergonia.

"Now, dear, is that any way to address a guest?" Queen Marcia scolded her daughter.

"It's okay. I hate the thing myself," Stephanie answered and then started to put some well-wanted food in her mouth after the king finally took his first bite.

"So, tell us, how did you come to grace us here in Silversword?" King Thadius asked with a raised eyebrow.

"My father and I had a disagreement about skipping riding lessons to seek out adventures. Against my father's wishes, I kind of stole a boat and while I was out in the Western Sea I ended up shipwrecked upon your shores," Stephanie started to tell the story she and Shirlynn had collaborated between mouthfuls of food.

"We will have to send word to your father that you are safe here with us." Shirlynn heard the princess choke a little on her food but had faith she would keep the king occupied with her tales. As for her father, by the time word was sent to King Stephen they will be long on their way to the Forest of Spirits. Shirlynn nodded with confidence and moved away from the staff's door into the dining hall.

It had been a long time since Shirlynn had been on an adventure like this. It almost made her feel young again. Being old had its advantages, as she was easily able to make her way to the kitchen to return her own eating tray. Here she was able to strike up conversation with the staff and learn where the shield was being kept. Normally it is on display in the king's treasure room, but she had just learned that it, along with many other items, were currently in one of the servant rooms being cleaned and polished.

Shirlynn quietly slipped out of the kitchen and met the kind lady who was going to take her to the polishing room. She had told the lady that for repayment for food and housing she would help with chores around the castle. Luck on her side, the lady happened to be on polishing duty. They came to a small door and Shirlynn was ushered inside where a half dozen women sat cleaning and polishing many items of all kind, but mostly were those made of silver. Shirlynn looked around for the shield but could not see it. It would have been easier if she had her staff but she left it in her room. She didn't want to risk setting off the alarms by something happening with two items coming in contact with each other.

"There is a pile over there that has not been done yet. Grab an item and wash it first. When done washing, you will polish it," the lady explained as Shirlynn saw the room was divided by washing side, polishing side and another section where the finished items were placed.

As Shirlynn walked to the section where the items needing to be cleaned resided, she noticed two things, the women did not look up as they all remained focused on the task they were doing and a nice window looking upon the night sky. Shirlynn walked by the window, looked out and whistled an innocent tune and then stepped over to the pile of items. She glanced through the pile and was about to give up when something shimmered and caught her eye. There it was, Thad Silversword's shield. She would know it anywhere. Shirlynn breathed in deep as memories of her old friend came flooding back while she reached down and picked up the shield and one other item.

As Shirlynn walked past the window she heard a squawk that told her Zain had heard and found her. The old cleric looked around and with no one watching, quickly tossed the shield out the window. Seconds later, a squawk was heard letting her know the bird had the shield and was on his way. Shirlynn smiled and found a seat and started washing the goblet she had picked up. No one noticed what she had done, and with the pile so high, it would be a little while before the shield was noticed as missing. Even though, she would have to make haste and get her and Stephanie out of the castle before dawn.

When Shirlynn finished washing and polishing three items, she proclaimed old age fatigue hitting her and was escorted back to her room. Once her door was closed, Shirlynn walked over to her window and looked out at the night's sky. They had the shield and the next best route would be to head into the Forest of Spirits for the crown. Once they had that, with her staff and axe and crystal, that made five of the seven Artifacts of Power secured. They would have to then figure out how to get the sling and rings and then she would have them all. Shirlynn continued to plan when a knock at her door broke her train of thought.

"Yes?"

"You have a visitor," the guard said opening the door and revealed Stephanie with the Queen and Princess of Silversword.

"Greetings, Shirlynn," Queen Marcia said as the three women entered her room.

"Is something wrong?" Shirlynn panicked as she wondered if the item she stole had been discovered missing.

"Not at all, Shirlynn. Princess Stephanie here wanted to check on you before she retired to her quarters. I as well, wanted to thank you for bringing her safely here," Queen Marcia said with a slight smile that told Shirlynn that all was not quite innocent with this visit.

"It was my duty, your highness," Shirlynn responded with a slight bow and curtsy.

"I realize I should not have run away but I thank you for getting me here so I may return home. I am glad all is well with you?" Stephanie said turning the last statement into an undertone question.

"Yes," Shirlynn started to responded and then started to make a strange animal noise disguised as a cough. "Sorry, at my age the throat gets dry."

"Let me help," Stephanie said, grabbing a nearby glass of water and handing it to the old cleric trying to hide the fact that she understood the animal sound. *"Zain has the shield."*

"We should get going," Princess Maria said with great impatience.

"I agree, we all need our rest. Big day tomorrow. Before we go, where did you say you lived? We want to make sure you get back home safely," Queen Marcia inquired staring right at the old woman.

Shirlynn, trying to come up with a response, was saved by a loud commotion in the hallway. Stephanie moved towards Shirlynn as Queen Marcia pushed her daughter behind her and looked into the hallway. A guard soon came running up to his queen, completely out of breath. "Your majesty, the king needs you right away!"

"What is going on?" Maria asked only to be silenced by her mother's glare.

"Speak," Queen Marcia instructed the guard.

"A messenger just arrived from the Kingdom of Argoth," the guard said as the queen stepped into the hallway and then stepped back into the room. "If you will pardon me, I am needed. I can have a guard show you to your room."

"That is okay, your highness. I can find my way to my room," Stephanie said as the queen nodded and she and her daughter quickly followed after the guard.

"We need to go," Shirlynn said as her face looked very pale.

"Are you okay?" Stephanie asked.

"I may be old, but my hearing is quite in tune. If what I heard is true, we need to get to the others and make it to the Forest of Spirits," Shirlynn said as she gathered her stuff and grasped her staff tight.

"What did the guard say?"

"The youngest prince of Argoth has been murdered."

"What? Why? Do they know who did it?" Stephanie started shooting out questions while she tried not to cry over the news. She did not know Prince Arron personally but the thought still hit her heart.

"The King of Argoth claims his son was killed by agents working for King Merrik," Shirlynn said turning to the young princess and throwing her original outfit at her.

"That can't be. If it's true..." Stephanie went silent as she quickly changed out of her dress.

"It means the Treaty of the Kingdoms is over. That is why, more than ever, we need to get out of here and complete our quest before Drol Greb's influence can expand any further," Shirlynn said as she looked out the door and then back at the newly changed girl. "We're clear."

Shirlynn moved quickly down the hall with Stephanie right behind. It seemed like with what was going on with Argoth and Erikson that attentions were elsewhere making it easier to slip through the castle unnoticed. They finally found an exit that led them into the royal garden behind the castle. There were lots of beautiful flowers and large trees. Shirlynn moved forward slowly as she looked carefully around the garden's edges.

"There are no gates or walls. We can cut through the trees there. Once we get back to the others we can let them know about the messenger from Argoth," Shirlynn said as she thought she heard something in the bushes.

"I still can't believe King Merrik had the prince killed," Stephanie added when two figures stepped out from hiding.

"None of that will be of your concern," one of the figures said as it shifted and sprouted wings.

"A Drogan and a Tazarian, here at the castle?" Shirlynn gasped in shock at the creature holding a red blade and the large bat-like creature behind him.

"What are these things?" Stephanie asked as she inched backwards, away from the horrid creatures.

"They are spawned creations of Drol Greb," Shirlynn answered as she held her staff tight and protectively stepped in front of Stephanie.

"Is that the staff?" the Drogan asked looking right at the item in Shirlynn's hand.

"That's the creature that attacked your home," Stephanie gasped.

"I feared reporting back to Docanesto of my failure. When I came across the Tazarian using its strength and speed to carry the human messenger here I chose to catch a ride to assist and am I glad I did," the Drogan smiled, eyes never leaving the staff.

"You will never have it," Shirlynn declared as the Drogan raised his sword. Shirlynn eyed the creature from her past that seemed different, more intellegant than she remembered.

"What is going on back here? I knew you two were up to no good," Princess Maria demanded as she stepped up next to the gathered group and then started to scream at the sight of the creatures, but was instantly silenced when the Tazarian swiped its claws and throwing her backwards.

"Maria!" Stephanie cried as she knelt down next to the girl who was bleeding out from a deep wound that went across her entire chest.

"Give me the staff and no one else has to die," the Drogan said in his slow raspy voice.

"Shirlynn we have to do something, she's dying," Stephanie cried as she put her hands on the princess to try to stop the bleeding.

"I," was all Shirlynn could say as she kept her eye on the Drogan and then felt a weird sensation and turned towards Stephanie. "No!"

Stephanie cried as she pushed her hands down on Maria's wound and stopped when she suddenly felt a weird warming sensation overcome her body and hands. At that exact moment, three things happened all at once. Stephanie's entire body began to glow with a light that then shifted to her hands. Stephanie felt the tingling warm sensation leave her body as the wound on Maria's body glowed and then closed, healing completely. Finally, the magic alarms exploded into the night's sky causing Shirlynn to jump and the two evil creatures to take flight and vanish from sight immediately.

"You're a witch?" Maria asked quietly as she examined her chest seeing no sign of her wound.

"No, I don't," was all Stephanie managed before swaying from fatigue.

"Stephanie, we have to go. The alarms won't stop till the cause is found," Shirlynn said, holding the girl up who now pulsed with a feint white aura due to the effect of the magic alarm.

"I can't let you leave," Maria said as she looked at the two women before her. Her eyes also darted to where the monsters had once been before attacking her and leaving.

"You have to, we are on a quest to save all Bergonia from creatures just like those," Stephanie pleaded as her strength slowly began to return.

"Your highness, whatever they are, they are not the enemy. She just saved your life," Kyle, the man they met earlier that day, said stepping into the garden with their horses.

"I don't know what truly happened, but those creatures came with the Argoth Messenger. We have to go, please, dear," Shirlynn pleaded as she looked into the eyes of the Princess of Silversword.

"I heard the whole conversation, she speaks the truth, your highness," Kyle added as he moved the horses closer to Stephanie and Shirlynn.

"Go, the guards will be here soon," Princess Maria said with a huff as Shirlynn and Stephanie mounted their horses and bolted out of the garden and through the trees leading out of the castle grounds.

Shirlynn moved her horse as fast as it could go with Stephanie keeping up right behind her. She was glad that at this late hour, most people were inside their homes and the shock of the alarms would not draw them out too fast. This allowed them to clear the City of Silversword quickly and without a lot of notice, especially with Stephanie still giving off a lighted pulse. Shirlynn was not completely sure what direction they were going but when she thought it was safe and they had traveled far enough, she stopped within a thick grove of trees. "Good, looks like we are not being followed. I hope the girl convinces her father that the alarms are due to the Drogan and Tazarian to buy us more time."

"How do I make this stop?" Stephanie asked as she held her arms out and watched the pulsing aura around them as the sound of the alarms still filled the air.

"We can't, my dear. The way the spell of the alarms works is it will only go silent when the cause is found and either detained or killed," Shirlynn said when Stephanie shrieked.

"Killed? I have to die?" Stephanie interrupted.

"Not at all. There is one other means, passing out of the kingdom that it was triggered in," Shirlynn finished placing a gentle hand on the panicked girls arm and then started to plan. "We can't go east towards Erikson with the alarms going off and the situation that has arose with the death of the prince. Seems we've already begun traveling south."

"What about the river? I can dive in it like Owen," Stephanie suggested.

"No, that only works to mask the effects of magic use while under it. Since the alarms are already triggered it won't work to turn them off," Shirlynn said and then looked up when she heard a squawk.

"Zain!" Stephanie clapped when she saw the hawk, minus the shield.

Stephanie watched as Shirlynn and Zain quickly carried on a conversation and then flinched when Zain darted off past her head and soared back in the direction he had come. "Where's he going? Did Owen get the shield?"

"Calm down, child," Shirlynn said as she gathered her thoughts and then addressed the girl. "Owen has the shield. Zain just reached them when the alarms started. He sent Zain back to check on us. He said to travel southeast and they will meet us near a mining town called Silver. It's not too far from the river, as they will be traveling down that way. Zain will confirm we are fine and headed there so they don't risk their exposure coming for us."

"How will I hide this?" Stephanie asked, wishing the alarms would stop.

"I think this should do the trick," Shirlynn said as she slid off her horse, opened her bag and pulled out some clothes.

"What are you doing? Stephanie asked as she dismounted and looked at the old woman.

"Remove your clothes and put this on. The spell has marked you, my stuff is not effected," Shirlynn said as Stephanie removed her outfit.

She threw what she was wearing in a pile on the ground and watched as it pulsed in unison with the glow about her body. She grabbed the tattered dress and undergarments that Shirlynn had given her and put them on, making a few adjustments so they would somewhat fit her. She noticed after she slipped on a pair of stocking over her feet and slid them into snug shoes that the only thing that could be seen glowing was her arms, head and a faint glow from under her clothes. Shirlynn then took the material torn from the clothes and rags she had and started wrapping up Stephanie's arms, hands and head only leaving a slit for her eyes, nose and mouth. Lastly, Stephanie was handed a hooded robe that hid any sign of her glowing body under the outfit and nicely masked her face.

"There, unless someone gets too close they won't question the bandages or see the slight glow in your eyes and mouth." Shirlynn, proud of her work, packed up her things and mounted her horse.

"You think this will work getting into Silver?" Stephanie asked as she had a little trouble getting back on her horse but soon managed the challenging feat.

"No, we will stop some distance from the town and camp in a secure hidden place and sleep for the night. We will wait until we hear from Zain and arrange meeting up with the others," Shirlynn answered as she ushered her horse forward and Stephanie followed with great speed.

They rode as fast and as hard as they could keeping to the trees and less traveled paths. When they reached a good distance from the town of Silver, Shirlynn brought them both to a stop and gasped. Stephanie moved her hood so she could see better and realized taht the glow she was seeing was not the nightlife of Silver but the reflection from the fire that was burning the mining town to the ground.

Chapter Twenty-Eight:
Silver & Fire

The early morning sun was shining bright as its rays reflected off the silver support beams and framework that made up the entrance into one of the biggest mines in Silversword. This particular mine produced more silver than any other in the kingdom, which was one of the reasons it resided a couple miles from the small town of Silver. Silver was specifically built for two reasons, gathering the silver and constructing it into the many outstanding items and weapons the Kingdom of Silversword had become known for, as well as being a home for all the workers and their families. Everyone that lived in Silver worked either in the mines or in the production of the silver in return for a place to live and the basic supplies and necessities to live.

The town of Silver was greatly known for its production of silver but that was not the biggest asset of this town. Living in the heart of Silver was the greatest craftsman in all of Silversword. Not only could this man turn silver into anything, he made the best weapons in all of Bergonia. The Kingdom of Silversword believed in peace and not killing, but it had no problem making weapons that kingdoms like Erikson traded and paid handsomely for. The man simply went by the name Milo and people from all over came in hopes to study and train with him. He loved teaching and holding classes, but he only selects one to become his apprentice and learn directly from him for a whole year before they are sent off into the world.

This year was different, as Milo decided not to pick a new apprentice. Instead, he decided to keep his current apprentice to guide, train and hone his exceptional gift at the craft so he could take Milo's place. Milo was approaching seventy years and was feeling it in his body and his hands. It was time to retire and since the moment he had first met Tyson Stone, he knew the boy had something in him that made him special. Milo knew the boy's parents as they had worked in the mines leaving the ten-year-old boy with Milo, who loved watching him work and assist. Milo noticed over the years how natural the craft came to the boy and how he truly had a passion for it.

Milo, never marrying or having children, grew very fond of Tyson and when his parents were killed in a mining accident a few years ago, took him in as his own and then last year, at the age of nineteen, agreed to make Tyson his apprentice. As time passed, Milo was amazed at how quickly the boy learned and started surpassing his teacher. It was at this moment, when the boy earlier in the year had turned twenty, that Milo made a public announcement that he was no longer taking new apprentices and that he was now making Tyson his replacement, his heir to everything and his son. People were disappointed but everyone knew and loved Tyson and agreed he would do Milo's legacy proud.

Stepping out of the mines and into the sun's light, Tyson Stone stared directly into it without squinting. As much time as he spent in the dark, he loved the feel of the light upon his skin. He had been down in the mines since dawn, as he did every morning, helping honor his parent's memory by working their section and getting an incoming inventory of silver production for Milo. Now that he was done, it was time to head back into Silver and finish up a few chores before getting to work. This morning was going to be different. Today was his first day working on his own as Milo shadowed and simply watched.

"Cool glasses," a voice said startling Tyson.

"Thanks, Will," Tyson answered as he pushed the goggles made of glass and silver up to rest on his forehead revealing his brown eyes with flecks of yellow in them. "I made them yesterday."

Tyson looked at the boy, a few years younger than him, who was walking towards the mines for his shift. He was Tyson's best friend and, except for working in the mines, they were total opposites. Jay William, or Will as everyone called him since his dad went by Jay, had blond hair, blue eyes, pale skin with a slight tan, very muscular and stood about a foot taller than Tyson. Tyson was on the short side with a very thin build with clipped short black hair and dark skin with a slight lightness to it. Where Will loved attention from girls or anyone in general and was outgoing, Tyson liked being alone and the only thing that he was attracted to was his craft and the things he made.

"They're different looking."

"They help me see in the dark and if I adjust the side pieces I can change the magnification," Tyson started to say with pride and then stopped when he saw his friend yawning. "I just mainly use them in the mines."

"Cool, well I better report for duty. Want to hang out later tonight?"

"Not sure how much work I will have but you can always stop over," Tyson said as his best friend smiled with a wave and dashed off into the mines. It still amazed him that Will was his best friend, well only friend, but they had grown up living next door to each other all their lives until...Tyson sighed thinking of his parents, gave one last look at the entrance and saluted their memory and ran as fast as he could back to town.

"You are late," a voice boomed as Tyson entered a building that had a silver-plated sign hanging above it reading, *Master Milo's Silversmith Creations.* Milo never cared for the sign but Tyson had made it when he was twelve and insisted he put it up. Of course, he refused, so Tyson had hung it himself.

"Sorry, I was," Tyson apologized but then stopped when he saw the older man snickering a little and let himself relax as he approached him. Despite the grey hair and beard, Milo did not look as old as he was. He still stood tall and from many years of working, he maintained a well-built body and gave a look that instilled fear and respect.

"We have a large load coming in today?"

"Looks like it, at least a little more than yesterday," Tyson said as he saw a strange look in his mentor's eyes. "Something wrong?"

"Before we get started, I have one last order to give you then I can step back and watch. I need you to replace the sign out front." Milo kept a serious face as he handed Tyson a long piece of polished silver.

Tyson was about to speak, but fell silent when he took the item and turned it over. It was a sign that looked identical to the one already hanging, except one detail. It had his name on it instead of Milo's name. "Go hang it!" Milo shouted as he turned and walked away trying to hide his watery eyes leaving Tyson to wipe his eyes as he went and hung the new sign.

There was already a line of people waiting when Tyson finished with the new sign and officially opened the doors for business. They were easy requests and tasks that he knew he could take care of quickly. His goal was to get them all done before the midafternoon shipment of silver arrived from the mines. Once that arrived, he would have to dedicate his time to finishing the weapons supply order for King Merrik. They were expecting the order in two days and he would have to have them all finished by tomorrow morning if they were to go out and reach them by the deadline. Not only did he want this to go out perfectly, but this was also the first shipment he had done all by himself and now under his name.

"What is this?" Milo asked as he threw an object down upon the worktable. Tyson stopped polishing and just stared at the item.

"I call it a handlight," Tyson said picking up the silver hollow rod that had slits cut out in the handle and replaced with glass. At the end, the rod was bent outwards, and then flattened, with another piece of glass placed in the center of the hole. "It helps me see in the dark and navigate better down in the mines without having to use a lantern."

"How?" Milo asked as Tyson picked up the handlight and gripped it hard with excitement. His body began to tingle as he felt the power within him awaken. Closing his eyes, he reached out and connected with the light all around him, becoming one and pulling it into himself. Just as he felt his body starting to glow, he forced the light from his hands and into the handlight's glass spots on the handle. Instantly the light reflected through the rod and a beam of concentrated light shot out the end. "You foolish boy!" Milo shouted slapping the object from Tyson's hand and hitting the floor as the light vanished from it and Tyson.

"I"

"You, nothing! What if someone had walked by and seen? Please tell me you are not using your abilities in the mines," Milo tried not to scream at him but it was hard. He had known the boy was special but it was not until last year that he realized how special he truly was.

One night Milo heard the boy scream, grabbed an axe and ran to his room. As he approached Tyson's bedroom he saw a strange yellow glow coming from beneath the door. Raising his weapon, Milo slowly opened the door to see Tyson fast asleep, tossing and turning from some kind of nightmare, calling out. It was not screaming that had alarmed Milo, but that the boy was glowing. A strange yellow light was radiating from Tyson's body. Milo shook Tyson awake and as soon as he sat up and opened his eyes the glowing stopped. Milo, waited in panic, but was surprised when no magic alarms had gone off. Tyson could not remember his dream, but from that moment on, all they knew was that they discovered that Tyson could make himself glow when he concentrated, whatever the power was, it was not magic and they must keep it a secret, even from his best friend Will.

"Milo, sir, I have these gifts. If the alarms don't go off when I use them that must mean they're not evil. Every day I feel more and more that I am being pulled towards something bigger than all of this, and it scares me," Tyson said trying to calm his anxiety.

"What are you talking about? Are you not happy here? I thought this was what you wanted." Milo waved his arms about before taking a breath, walking over to put the closed sign up and lock the front door.

"I do, this is my passion, more than anything. I said I am being drawn towards something, not that I liked or wanted it," Tyson said sitting down and looking at his trembling hands.

"There's something you're not telling me. You know we agreed no secrets, please don't start now," Milo said sitting down next to the boy and making him look right into his eyes.

"I had a strange dream awhile back. I can't remember much, it is all still a haze. My head starts to hurt every time I try to remember details," Tyson started as the man in front of him nodded to continue. "I think there was a Dragon, yes, a very large white Dragon. It's like the haze is lifting some. I was in a cavern with lots of others. I think they were like me, having special abilities. I can't remember anything else, but I can't shake the feeling in my body that I am needed for something, big. And then, after I woke, I couldn't remember anything, but something changed in me."

"What do you mean, changed?"

"My powers. Not so much as changed but evolved." When Milo did not say anything, Tyson continued. "Before the dream, I could make myself glow. Now I can focus it and only make certain parts of me glow," Tyson said as he closed his eyes, concentrated and then smiled as only his teeth were glowing.

"Stop that," Milo tried not to laugh as he shook his head. "That's not all is it?"

Tyson stood up and moved to a more secluded and darker area. He closed his eyes and reached out, touching the light, becoming one and drawing it into himself. He then pointed his finger at the wall and a small, narrow beam of light projected out from it and hit the far wall making it shine with reflected light from the yellow beam. Tyson made it stop and then swayed a little. "That's all I can do for now, but I think if I practice I could grow stronger and do more."

"Absolutely not. Look how weak you are after just that small stunt. It's too dangerous, for many reasons." Milo rubbed his beard, as he was too amazed to say anything more.

"Why are you closed? Tyson? Master Milo?" A loud knock came from the door that caused both men to jump with freight. "Everything okay?"

"Will, here with the delivery of silver already?" Milo asked as he opened the door while Tyson composed himself and moved back to the working station.

"The guys are held up in the center of town. I assumed you would be there and came here to check on you when you weren't. Like the sign by the way," Will rambled as he stepped into the shop and headed over to Tyson.

"Thanks, we were just going over a few things. That's why we closed for a bit," Tyson lied as Milo removed the closed sign.

"What's going on in the center of town?" Milo asked as he tried to peer down the road where he saw many people gathered.

"A messenger from Argoth just ran into town demanding to speak with the leader of Silver. He had an important message to relay before heading to see King Thadius," Will answered as he turned to face the older man. "The guys will be here soon once their curiosity is satisfied."

"We need that silver now if I'm to finish on time," Tyson said with a grunt as he moved to the door.

"Where are you going?" Milo asked.

"To go get our silver."

"I'll come along. Find out what all the commotion is." Milo followed after but ran right into Tyson as he had opened the door and suddenly stopped. Standing on the other side was a tall slender man in the midst of knocking on a door that was now no longer there.

"Phil, we were just about to,"

"No time. Milo, I must speak with you immediately!" The man pushed past Tyson and Will and moved to the center of the room where he dramatically turned to face Milo.

"Does this have to do with that messenger in the center of town?" Milo asked as the man touched his long black mustache and stroked it from the left side making the curl bounce.

"Yes," Phil answered shooting a glance towards Will. "It seems you must halt all orders to the Kingdom of Erikson, effective immediately per Elder Robert."

Tyson started to protest but was cut off by their visitor. "The Elder has spoken."

Tyson bit his tongue as he worried about such a loss. As Phil spoke with Milo, Tyson glanced towards the center of town and saw a man upon a horse and riding off. As he got farther away, Tyson moved his glasses down and adjusted the lenses so that he could get a closer look at the messenger. They could not see super clear but the glasses did help with letting him see things very far away and was able to distinguish the colors of Argoth upon the riders clothing. Just before Tyson went to move back into the building and close the door, he saw something odd. The horse went into a grove of trees and a few moments later something large with wings shot up into the sky. When Tyson shook his head and wiped his eyes before looking again, it was gone.

"See something?" Will asked.

"No, I think my mind is playing tricks on me," Tyson said as he closed the door and pushed his glasses off.

"And you believe this messenger who just walked into town?" Milo asked as Tyson and Will joined the two men.

"He had a royal decree from King Allen. He had been riding so hard his horse failed him so he came here on foot. Elder Robert looked it over, confirmed its legitimacy, gave the man a new horse and supplies, and let him continue on to Silversword. He declined an escort but Elder Robert is going to send a messenger as well and wait to hear from the king. Until then, he sent me here to tell you to hold off on any dealings with the Kingdom of Erikson. We are halting all contact and border defense has been placed on alert," Phil answered as he nervously stroked his mustache.

"What could cause all this commotion?" Will asked, wishing he had stuck around to listen to the messenger earlier.

"It appears the youngest prince of Argoth has been murdered and King Allen states that it was by the order of King Merrik as King Allen has the murderers and agents of Erikson captured and awaiting judgement," Phil said as Milo swore.

"This can't be. We have been at peace for so long. The treaty has always been respected, no matter what." Milo swore again as he caught a few glances from Tyson and saw the same worry behind his eyes.

"We will have to wait to see how King Thadius responds, but I fear the treaty will be no more. According to Elder Robert, the messenger told him that Argoth is demanding the complete isolation of Erikson and the remaining four kingdoms to join together and make them pay for their treachery. The messenger said, as he left, the bridge connecting Erikson and Argoth was being destroyed and a full army of warriors will be stationed along the border of the Old River Gorge with instructions to kill any who approach from Erikson," Phil said as he now pulled out a cloth and wiped his sweaty brow.

"We can't go to war. There must be another way. We've always vowed to uphold peace," Will chimed in, worried, as he had never been taught to fight. The only weapon he had ever held was the ones used for mining.

"The Knights of Bergonia, just because they don't kill doesn't mean they don't know how to fight," Milo assured the group as he looked over at the workstation. "Tyson, you and Will go see where that shipment of silver is and bring it here. Phil and I have much to talk about."

Tyson knew better than to argue with Milo, so he grabbed his tool pouch, filled it with a few items, closed and tied it around his waist before he headed out the door with Will. Even if they had to stop the order for Erikson, the silver was still needed for other jobs. It was his shop now, so he was responsible for making sure the delivery arrived. He would have liked to stay and hear more, but if Milo sent him out it might be private. Tyson did not know everything about Milo, but he did know that he had dated Phil once a long time ago but never knew why they broke up. Phil was now the assistant to the Elder as well as Robert's partner. If needed, Milo might tell him later.

"What do you think that's about? The Kingdoms going to war?"

"I was just thinking the same thing. I hope this doesn't turn to war," Tyson said as they made their way towards the center of town, where it now appeared to be void of any life. "Didn't take long to empty out."

"That's odd," Will mumbled as he moved off to the left and started walking down the road leading out of town and towards the mines. "I left the others with the wagon of silver over here."

"Why would they leave?" Tyson thought to himself as he looked around and then slid his glasses down and started adjusting the side levers to help him see farther away. He was about to give up when something off in the distance, near a grove of trees caught his eye. He tried to magnify his glasses but could not see any closer, but it almost looked like a wagon. He took off running as Will called after.

"You see the cart?"

"Maybe."

By the time they reached the trees, they were a good distance outside of town. They both slowed to a walk as they cautiously approached the object Tyson had spotted, which quickly confirmed to be Will's wagon. Tyson ran up to it and saw the silver was still loaded in the back but the horses were gone as were the two guys who had been in charge of it. Tyson looked down, knelt and adjusted his glasses to see that there were small drops of blood in the grass. He stood up and wondered, what happened and whose blood that belonged to?

"Tyson, over here!" Will screamed causing Tyson to dash off deeper into the woods to find Will trembling over something on the ground.

Tyson reached his friend and froze in shock as he pushed his glasses up onto his forehead. Lying on the ground were two bodies, mutilated with blood everywhere. It was Keith and Rick. Tyson felt sickness about to overcome him when one of the bodies groaned. Will moved to him and knelt down, "Keith, what happened?"

"Something... spooked horses...ran after," Keith tried to speak between bouts of coughing up blood.

"Keith, try and relax. We'll get help," Tyson said knowing the man was too far gone to survive whatever attacked him.

"Monsters...ate the horses...attacked us," Keith finished with his last breath before his eyes rolled back and his body went still.

"Keith, stay with me, Keith," Will pleaded through tears at the man who had mentored him in the mines since the day he had started.

"Will, he's gone," Tyson said as he put his arm around his friend and helped him to his feet.

"What did this? What did he mean, monsters?" Will tried to get himself under control as Tyson led him away from the bodies and back to the wagon.

Tyson did not know what to say. He wondered if it could have been that winged shape he thought he saw fly out of the trees earlier. Tyson honestly did not know what to think but knew he had to get back to Milo. "Let's go back into town. We have to report this to the Elder."

"We can't have that now, can we?" A voice asked followed by something sharp zipping by and embedding itself into the side of the wagon.

"My side," Will gasped as he reached for his right side to see blood now coating his hand.

"How bad is it?" Tyson asked as he looked to see who the voice and blade belonged to.

"Don't worry, if my brother wanted him dead, he'd be dead," a second voice said as two figures fell from the trees and landed in front of the wagon, putting themselves between their prey and the town of Silver. "We've been placed on look out and I want to have a little fun too since the others get to play."

Tyson stared at the two attackers, one female the other male. They had strange red markings all over their exposed skin. The female held a double-bladed staff while her male counterpart had a blade on his left wrist. The right wrist was bare and Tyson assumed that was where the object in the side of the wagon had originated from. The male smiled, flicked his wrist and the band rotated and another blade extracted from it. As Tyson took the two in, it wasn't their smaller frames and appearance that caught his eye but what he saw when the wind blew back their hair. They both had pointed ears.

"It seems the boy has never seen an Elf before," Lia smirked as she looked Tyson up and down.

"Too bad we'll be his last," Lio added as he pointed his wrist blades at the two ready to fire when an explosion caused them all to lose their balance.

"Tyson, look!" Will shouted as he continued to wince and sway from the loss of blood.

Before he even looked, Tyson could smell the smoke and realized what the female Elf meant by others and play. A large fire had erupted somewhere in Silver. It was followed by more explosions and sounds of destruction. He dropped his goggles and looked and realized there were several winged creatures flying over the place he called home. The monsters were real and they were now killing the people of Silver. Tyson gasped in realization. "Milo. We have to…"

"You're not going anywhere. The people you love are as dead as you're going to be," Lio laughed as he and his sister got back onto their feet.

"What do you want? Why are you doing this?" Will asked as Tyson looked down at his friend and began to worry about the bleeding wound.

"We are simply taking back what was once ours. The human reign has come to an end and the magical races will prevail again under the rule of Drol Greb," Lia praised.

"Why aren't the alarms going off?" Tyson asked aloud as he wondered if there was something wrong with them or if this was connected to what he could do.

"You humans are so foolish. They only go off if magic is used. They don't detect magical creatures, only pure magic," Lio smiled as they could now hear the screams of the dying behind them.

"You don't have to kill them," Tyson said, tears forming as he thought of Milo and losing a parent all over again.

"To serve a bigger plan, we have to now. We were just going to bypass your town but we ran into a human riding a Tazarian. We brought him down and Docanesto had a nice chat with him," Lio said keeping his eyes on the boys, never once flinching or turning to look at the source of the massacre going on behind them.

"It seems the Queen of Argoth upped our plans of taking Bergonia back by killing her son, framing it on King Merrik and sending a messenger to King Thadius. My brother then had a brilliant idea," Lia added.

"I am brilliant," Lio chuckled. "I suggested that the messenger walk in your town, drop word of the prince's death by King Merrik before continuing on so word would spread. The messenger then tips your king off that he saw an army of Erikson warriors heading his way. We come in, kill everyone and make it look like Erikson's warriors did it and that solidifies the other kingdoms coming together to take out the Kingdom of Erikson, the strongest of all the kingdoms," Lio finished with a smile.

"We have to warn the king," Will said with mustered strength.

"That is why we shall kill you now. We were left here to kill any witnesses, such as yourselves," Lia said as she nodded to her brother to finish the kill.

"I have to stop you," Tyson said as he felt a strange energy building from within his body.

"I must be dying. I swear, you are glowing," Will said as he started to pass out.

Tyson could fill the power in him building from all his emotions he was feeling and knew he could not control it. By the look on the Elves faces, he was clearly glowing brighter than ever. Using their hesitation from the shock to his advantage, he gave into the power, letting it consume him and then released it with all his might by stretching out his arms and forcing it out in one controled blast. The entire woods exploded in a burst of yellow light as the power left him and engulfed the entire area. He heard the Elves scream in pain and confusion. When the light faded, Tyson saw the Elves lying upon the ground, blinded and barely conscious. He knew he had to get Will to safety before they recovered.

"What happened?" Will asked as he was barely conscious.

"We have to go," Tyson said as he helped his friend to lean on him and headed deeper into the woods. He knew they would not make it to Silver or the mines in time, but there was one place they could go. Not far from them was the secret hideout he and Will had built when they were little as a place to hide when they wanted to be alone. Tyson moved as fast as he could with his injured friend, but was still feeling drained from such an enormous use of his powers.

He soon found the tree marker, moved the leaves and pulled up the patch of ground that led underground. Tyson, calling on what energy he had left, made himself glow just enough so he could see and drag Will down below. Once he entered the small one room sized area, he placed Will on the bed made of hay and then ran back topside. He slowly pushed the opening up and when he was sure no one was around, jumped out. He wanted to make sure there were no traces of them coming this way. Once satisfied, he slipped back into the hiding place so he could tend to his best friend.

When Tyson got back to Will's side, he could see he had fallen unconscious again. The bleeding was stopping but he had lost a lot of blood and would need medical help if Will was going to live. When Tyson was satisfied with the make shift bandage, he sat down and tried to think of what to do next. He could not risk going back into town. Those Elves, and who knows what, would be waiting for him. He was the only one that knew the truth and if he died, then the king would blame the Kingdom of Erikson and all-out war would erupt. He could not believe any of this was happening. It had to be a dream, but he knew it was not. Feeling weak, Tyson turned off his glow and closed his eyes.

A strange noise made Tyson jump up and panic in the complete darkness. Once he realized where he was, he calmed down and took note that it was Will slightly snoring. He then realized he had fallen asleep and wondered for how long. He did feel refreshed and called upon his gift to make him glow just enough to check on Will. When he was sure he was not going to die anytime soon, he made his way out of the hideout. Listening carefully, he slowly pushed the top up a crack and peered outside. The sun was setting and it was growing dark. There was no sign of the Elves, so he climbed out and made sure the entrance was covered back up. He could slightly see and smell the fire of his burning home. He knew where he had to go next, the silver mines.

Moving as quick and carefully as he could, he began making his way to the mines. The miners always headed home at dusk. If he hurried, he could catch them before they made it back to Silver. If he rallied them together, they might be able to get word to King Thadius, help Will and save what was left of Silver. As he got closer to the mines, he started to find it odd that he had not run into the miners yet or at least heard signs of them. Could it be he was too late and missed them and they were already back at Silver? The thought of them seeing that devastation without the truth would be awful. Or worse yet, walk into a trap.

When Tyson came upon the mine entrance, the smell that hit him made him freeze in place and realize why he had not seen the miners. In front of the entrance were three bodies, and by the looks of them, Tyson knew they were dead. He quickly took cover, dropped his glasses down and looked around. There was no sign of the Elves or anything. Moving as stealthy as he could, he made it to the mine's entrance. He knew what he was going to find but he had to check. Reaching into his pouch he pulled out two gloves made of silver and slid them on. Using these, he could use just a little of his power and make it be more. Closing his eyes, he breathed in, touched his power and stepped into mines as his gloves lit up and shined the way.

Chapter Twenty-Nine:
Battle For The Staff

Stephanie woke with hours before the sun would even start to rise. Between the magic alarms and the smell from the burning town of Silver, it was hard to sleep. She noticed Shirlynn was already up and had motioned for her to join her. For their safety, they had moved farther away from Silver where they found a large hollowed log that they could both crawl into and attempt to sleep. Both their instincts were to rush into the burning city and help, but it was quickly decided that they should wait until morning.

Not long after they had come across Silver, Zain had arrived to let them know that Tor and Owen were getting close and should arrive after dawn. Shirlynn had told their bird friend that they were about to head into town when Zain squawked in protest. He had seen the fire and feared for the women and did a cautious fly by. He said that there were Drogans, Tazarians and many other people swarming the place killing and destroying everything in sight. Zain did not have to tell them that they were too outnumbered and would not stand a chance. The protection of the staff and their quest was too important to risk being killed. Shirlynn told Zain to report back to Owen and that they would take cover for the night and meet up in the morning.

"Where are the horses?" Stephanie asked as she crawled out of the log and sat down next to Shirlynn upon a smaller one.

"I told them last night to make themselves scarce and safe. I would call when we needed them," Shirlynn said, tears still streaming down her cheeks. Stephanie could feel the pain of loss as well without even looking toward the direction of what was once Silver.

"Any sign of the attackers?" Stephanie asked feeling worried.

"Zain is scouting right now. No sign of them except for a couple Fire Hounds and Barbarians picking through the town making sure they didn't forget anything. Said it looks like they arranged things to make it look like the attack happened by something else," Shirlynn answered with a heaviness in her voice.

"Why would they go to so much trouble and then cover it up?"

"So they can start a war by pinning it on King Merrik," a voice said causing Stephanie to jump up and pull her hood to help hide her face.

"Stay back, we are fierce warriors," Stephanie said as she took a defensive stance that Owen had taught her.

"I mean you no threat," the man said as he stepped forward, wearing weird glasses and strange silver gloves.

"I know child, if you had, our friend would have warned us," Shirlynn said finally turning to face the young man as a bird's call made him look up. "I am Shirlynn and this is Stephanie."

"Tyson Stone and that is, was my home," Tyson said as he pushed the glasses up and stared off in the direction that had once been lit up by fire but was now just rising smoke.

"What did you mean when you said starting a war? Do you know what happened here?" Shirlynn asked knowing things were in motion that made her quest even greater.

"I had a run in with two Elves," Tyson began as he told them everything that happened from the messenger in town to surviving the attack by the Elves and their confession of what they were doing in the town of Silver. He decided to leave out the information about his abilities since he was not sure who these two woman were. "My friend is seriously injured but I have him hidden safely at the moment."

"How did you escape the Elves?" Stephanie asked as she really wished Tor and Owen would get here soon.

"Blinding luck, I guess," Tyson tried to hide a smile, which was easy due to the circumstances. "I managed to get us hidden and dozed off. When I woke, they were nowhere in sight. I headed to the mines figuring that since I was the only one who knew the truth, it would be smarter going there than heading home where the attack was happening," Tyson said growing quiet as a sadness filled his eyes.

"They're all dead, am I correct?" Shirlynn asked already knowing the answer.

"It's my fault. In their search for me, they must have discovered the mines. When I got there, everyone was dead. I searched and searched and not even one was left alive. When I left the mines, I didn't see the Elves but I heard alarms going off. They were faint, but my gut told me they were the magic alarms. Fearing the Elves or their group had set them off, I dashed back to my hiding spot to check on Will. He was safe. I decided it was best to wait until morning, but when I woke the alarms had gotten louder, and my friend looked weaker, so I decided to go look for help. That is when I came upon you two here, talking."

"Don't blame yourself. If you had been killed, no one would have known what truly happened here this day. Elves, Fire Hounds, Drogans and who knows what else Docanesto has brought with him," Shirlynn said shivering just as much saying his name as she did when she heard it leave this young man's lips during his tale.

"Do you know this Docanesto and Drol Greb?" Tyson asked remembering the look in the old woman's eyes when he had said their names.

"I'm afraid so, but now is not the time. If he's here in Silversword, I'm afraid he's after more than destroying your town," Shirlynn said as she dismissed the boys coming questions and turned to Stephanie. "We need to get out of the open. He could still be close. With all this smoke, our scents are masked for now, but that won't last long. It's what saved them from being discovered."

"You can hide where my friend is, but I need to get him help before he dies," Tyson said putting his glasses back down to help with the smoke.

"I can help him," Stephanie offered, as she felt better that there was now something she could do to help.

"No, not with the magic alarms," Shirlynn warned.

"They are already going off because of me so I see no harm in trying to help his friend," Stephanie protested, moving away from Shirlynn and towards Tyson.

"You're responsible for the magic alarms?" Confused, Tyson looked at the girl securely wrapped up and now noticed a weird white light pulsing near the slits that exposed her eyes, wondering what she was hiding.

"Stephanie," Shirlynn started but the princess was already walking.

"Take me to your friend."

"He's not too far from here," Tyson said as he caught up to the mysterious girl and led the way back to where he was hiding Will. Shirlynn sighed and mustered the strength to follow the two.

The sun's rays began to explode through the hazy, smoked filled sky as the three reached a spot in the woods that Tyson said was where his hideout was located. Shirlynn looked around and then held out her arm as a bird landed on it. Tyson pushed up his glasses and stared at the woman and the bird. "Is she really talking to that bird? Is she?"

"No," Stephanie said as she grabbed Tyson's arm to make him stop twirling his finger near his head in a "is she crazy" motion. "You'll get used to it. Zain is a friend and has become very helpful on our quest."

"Quest?" Tyson started to ask when he was interrupted by the bird shooting off into the air with a squawk and Shirlynn rushing over to them.

"Zain didn't see any signs of Docanesto and his forces. We made it here without being spotted or followed. He will let Owen and Tor know where we are and meet us here. Then we can decide our next move. Tyson, hurry, take us to your friend."

Tyson had so many questions but knew Will needed help and he would have to trust these two mysterious and crazy women. He knelt down and soon had the hatch open. He pulled out a candle and lit it, figuring that at this point the smoke of the candle could not do harm since the smell of smoke in the air was still dominate. He gave the candle to Stephanie, who began the decent down, followed by Shirlynn and then Tyson as he carefully closed the hatch. When they reached the bottom of the pathway, Tyson was glad to see Will was still there, despite looking paler and barely breathing in his coma like sleep.

"He's burning with fever and the wound is infected." Shirlynn said after she had moved to the boy's side. "We need more light." Tyson moved quickly and lit a few more candles mounted on the walls to give them more light.

"Can you really help him?"

"I will try," Stephanie said as she freed her hands and face from cover letting the pulsing white aura from the magic alarms light up the room and Tyson's astonished face. He could not believe how beautiful she was. He assumed because of how covered up she was that she had a defect or had been badly burned. She was hiding something else altogether. "What are you?" Tyson whispered as he watched the glowing girl move towards Will.

Stephanie tore away the area of the shirt where the wound was and finished removing the make shift bandage that Tyson had made. The cut was deep and still bleeding and she noticed that it was gravely infected. She had to do something fast or they would lose him. She took a deep breath, placed her hands upon the wound, and wished it to heal. Nothing happened. She closed her eyes, concentrated and tried again, nothing. She kept trying and wishing but nothing was happening. "Do something, he's not breathing!" Tyson screamed over her shoulder.

"Shirlynn, you have to help me."

"Sorry dear, there's nothing *I* can do."

"I thought you were an all-powerful cleric!"

"So are you," Shirlynn said with a smile as the girl swore at her and turned back to face the boy who had gone completely still.

"Heal darn it!" Stephanie screamed through tears as she raised her arms up and then slammed her hands back down upon the boy's body. This time she felt something build up inside her. With all her might, she demanded that the boy heal, to live. Suddenly a strange sensation overtook her body and she felt a release as a glowing energy left her body, moving down her arms and out her hands directly into Will's wound. Will's body glowed bright as a surge of energy engulfed him causing Stephanie to fall backwards, on the verge of blacking out while the magic alarms blared louder with a renewed energy.

"Stephanie," Shirlynn moved to the girl's side, who now could barely sit up on her own as her skin and clothes glowed brighter than before.

"I don't believe it," Tyson said as he stood over his best friend's body as Will violently sat up, gasping for air. Not only was he alive but the wound was completely healed as if it had never been there.

"What happened?" Will asked, rubbing his forehead and looking down at where the cut had once been but was now just dried blood.

"She healed you," Tyson said as both boys looked over at the two woman.

"Why didn't you help me?"

"Because, dear Stephanie, you had to prove to yourself that you could. That you have the ability and can own it and use it," Shirlynn said as Tyson moved over to help her pick Stephanie up and place her on a second bed to regain her breath and strength.

"What are you?" Tyson asked looking into Stephanie's eyes.

"She is the last and the start of the Order of Clerics," Shirlynn said with pride as she moved towards the exit and listened.

"Clerics? As in magic? Is that what is making the alarms go off?" Will asked as he looked back and forth at the girl and old woman. He was not sure if he should be in awe or be scared of the two.

"It seems with your feat of healing, the alarms have gotten louder," Shirlynn said not looking back at anyone but kept her eye towards the darkened exit.

"Yes, she, we, are clerics," Stephanie said as she realized what she now was and had to embrace it now. "We are on a quest to find the Artifacts of Power to prevent those that burned your town down from getting them and releasing a great evil back upon Bergonia," Stephanie said as she tried to stand but realized she was still too weak.

"With practice and better control, you will learn to not use up so much energy when using your gifts," Shirlynn said as she then moved up the exit and out of sight.

"Where is she going?" Tyson asked wanting to follow the old woman but was compelled to remain by his friend's side.

"Silver?" Will suddenly asked in fear, remembering and getting his answer from his friend's face.

"The town was burned to the ground. Those monsters killed them all, including those in the mines. We are now all that remains of Silver," Tyson said matching Will's tears. "I thought you dead as well, but you live thanks to her.

"In that case, I thank you, my lady" Will said giving one of his charming smiles, bowing and kissing the back of Stephanie's hand. "I owe you my life."

Stephanie blushed as she introduced herself as the Princess of Tallus and that the older woman was Shirlynn. "A princess? How did you get past your wall and end up here?" Will asked, but a loud commotion stopped Stephanie from answering.

"Whoa!" Will screamed and moved towards the back wall as Shirlynn came walking back down followed by two figures, a human and what appeared to be a bull walking upright on two legs.

"What is going on here?" Tyson asked as he raised his arms up, pointing his silver-gloved hands at the creature and looking at Stephanie.

"Tyson, it's okay. They are with us. The Minotaur is named Tor," Stephanie started to introduce when Will got excited. "A Minotaur!"

"Don't worry, he won't hurt you," the man next to Tor chuckled. "I am,"

"Sir Owen Linah, Knight of Bergonia. It's an honor!" Tyson interrupted as he got down on one knee and bowed his head out of respect. Will, still staring at the Minotaur, knelt as well.

"Rise, boys. No need for such formality," Owen said as the two quickly got to their feet.

"Ever since I was little I always thought if I wasn't a minor that I could have been a knight like you," Will said in excitement while trying not to stare at Tor.

"Sorry about my friend. Your reputation is well known in Silver and though we've never meet, we've seen you pass into Silver a few times," Tyson said not wanting to admit being a knight was something he thought about as well but figured he was not cut out for such an honor and undertaking.

"Being stationed farther south, it has been a while since I've been to Silver," Owen said, his voice going soft at the mention of the now destroyed town.

"I hate to cut the reunion short but we need to get moving," Tor huffed, blowing air out his nostrils as he kept staring at Tyson. Something smelled familiar about the boy.

"Is it Docanesto's forces?" Stephanie asked, finally gaining enough strength to stand on her own.

"Zain is keeping watch while Diamond went to gather our horses and meet us at a safe location nearby to the west. We do need to hurry," Shirlynn said with urgency.

"Who is Zain and Diamond?" Will asked.

"Our bird friend and my horse," Stephanie answered as she moved towards Shirlynn.

"Wait, what?" Will looked at Tyson, who shook his head and said, "don't ask."

"It seems when you used your clerical powers it sent off a pulse waive that not only repowered the alarms but acted like a homing beacon. According to Zain, the creatures that were in Silver are on the move and heading north. I imagine to meet up with their master," Shirlynn said as Stephanie began to worry but was not sorry for saving the boy's life.

"Our best bet is to head directly south as planned and take cover in the Forest of Spirits," Owen suggested as everyone but the boys nodded in agreement.

"We can't go south with you. We have to get to Silversword and warn the king about what really happened here. If we don't then King Merrik will be blamed," Tyson said, wishing the Minotaur would stop looking at him.

"Going north will take you right to Docanesto's forces and get you killed," Tor grunted as it hit him like a club to the head. "You were in the dream. With the Dragon."

"Dream, what are you talking about?" Tyson panicked as everyone was now staring at him.

Shirlynn smiled and moved towards him. "You're a Magestic."

"A what?" Will asked staring at his friend. "What is she talking about?"

"I don't know. This is all crazy," Tyson said as something in him began to resonate with the woman and Minotaur's words.

"You are a Magestic. Like Tor here, you possess the power of the Magesti. Tor controls the air and wind. What can you do?" Shirlynn asked looking the boy up and down.

"I," Tyson went silent as his fear overtook him and he felt the power in him ignite and his body began to glow.

"Tyson, why are you glowing? What are you?" Will asked now backing away from everyone.

"The Magesti of Light," Shirlynn said as she encouraged the boy to calm down.

"If he is like Tor then he has to come with us, doesn't he?" Stephanie asked Shirlynn and Owen who both nodded.

"We're not going anywhere until I get some answers," Will said as he looked at his friend and saw that the old woman had helped him calm down and stop glowing.

"How long have you been able to use your Magesti?" Shirlynn asked, keeping eye contact with just her and Tyson.

"Not long, but they began to grow after I had the dream Tor mentioned. Milo made me keep it secret, but when I was alone I used them with my inventions," Tyson said as he held up his gloves and made them glow, pointed to show a beam of light and then made them go dark.

"Fascinating," Owen said, as a man who appreciated inventions and weapons.

"I need to get out of here," Will said but did not move when Tor placed himself between the boy and the pathway leading out.

"Tyson, you are a Magestic, and like all of us, are destined to follow a path to help save all of Bergonia," Shirlynn said as she took the boy's hand and told him everything about herself, the group and their quest.

"This can't be happening," Tyson mumbled, knowing that deep down he had always known this power he had made him a part of something bigger.

"Tyson, I'm your best friend and that doesn't change because you can do magic," Will said trying to regain his composure and stay calm, but the Minotaur was making it hard, just staring at him.

"It's not magic," Stephanie corrected, as she got a gentle but stern look from Shirlynn.

"I know that, Will. I'm really not sure what to do." Tyson wished more than anything that Milo was here to tell him what to do.

"Someone has to warn the king or all our family and friends will have died in vain," Will said, looking at Stephanie and knowing he lived because of her and felt obligated to help her and her quest, despite his reservations about the world of magic.

Shirlynn stood up and looked towards Owen when a loud squawk came from outside. Owen made a dash for the exit as Shirlynn followed after. "Everyone stay here."

"Was that your bird?" Will asked.

"His name is Zain. He called for Shirlynn. Something is happening," Stephanie said as the adrenaline seemed to bring the remaining strength back to her in full.

"So you talk to birds too?" Will asked as he got a warning look from both Stephanie and Tyson.

"Here they come," Tor said announcing Shirlynn and Owen's return.

"We have to go now!" Owen demanded.

"Did they find us?" Stephanie asked as Owen ushered her to the exit.

"Drogans and Fire Hounds are headed back our way. Zain went to alert Diamond. We'll head west to meet up with the horses and then push as fast as we can south to the Forest," Shirlynn said as the worry in her voice caused Stephanie's heart to skip a beat.

"Wait!" Tyson said grabbing Will's arm holding him back as the others ran for the exit.

"You can't stay here, they will kill you. For now, you must come with us," Owen said as Tyson ignored him.

"Will, I have something for you. I was going to give it to you on your birthday but I think you're going to need it." Tyson ran to a corner and moved a section of the wall to reveal a large hole. He reached in and pulled out a sword and a shield, both made of silver. The shield had a *W* in the center of it. He gave them to Will. "I know only true knights or members of the kings court are allowed swords but…anyway, happy early birthday."

"Tyson, these are beautiful," Will said holding the shield and waving the sword with such ease, perfectly made for him.

"You got great talent. Milo would be proud of you," Owen said as he snapped his fingers and the boys moved on out of their hideout. Will, with a smile over his presents and Tyson sliding his glasses down and making sure everything in his pouch was secured, tried not to panic.

Owen was the last to crawl out of the hideout. Shirlynn was already leading the group in a run when he pushed the boys forward to join them. The smoke from Silver was still all around them but it was starting to dissipate. They could no longer rely on it to keep them masked from their approaching enemy. As they made their way through the trees, they finally came to a clearing. Without smoke or tree coverage, they would be out in the open. Zain squawked letting them know that the horses were nearby heading towards them. Owen just hoped that they could make to the horses before they were spotted or caught.

The group kept running west when Tyson shouted. "I can see a white horse leading a bunch of other horses our way."

"You can see that far?" Owen asked as the boy tapped his glasses and smiled.

"We're going to make it," Shirlynn shouted at her group in relief when a loud animal cry pierced the air making them all come to a dead stop and removing that hope.

No one needed Tyson's special glasses to see what was playing out in front of them. As the horses got closer, two large bat-like creatures fell from the sky and dove right at the horses causing them to scatter. Shirlynn, horrified, looked at her fellow companions. "Tazarians."

"What is a Tazarian?" Will asked as he gripped his sword tight.

"They are very nasty creatures," Shirlynn started to explain.

"Fire Hounds!" Owen shouted.

"Yes, they are as deadly as."

"No, Fire Hounds!"

Shirlynn turned around and saw Owen pointing at a group of forms headed their way from the north. It was definitely Fire Hounds racing towards them, along with several others, including Drogans. She knew those shapes and old memories brought shivers down her spine. Motioning to Tyson, she had him use his glasses to get a closer look at what was coming, and as he started describing them, Shirlynn knew they were in trouble.

"There are five Drogans in the air along with seven Tazarians with riders as well as nine Fire Hounds with riders. I'm assuming Docanesto is one of them. Tyson didn't see the Elves that attacked him," Shirlynn relayed more to herself than the group as she tried not to become overwhelmed with panic.

"That's because they're over there," Will said as the group glanced back at the woods where they had come out of moments before. The two Elves each rode upon a Fire Hound while five more Drogans stepped out, sprouted wings and took to the air.

"We're pretty much surrounded. What do we do?" Stephanie asked turning to Shirlynn for support as fear and adrenaline began to fill her body.

"We fight," Owen said as he moved to face the attackers coming from the woods since they were closer.

"What are you doing?" Shirlynn asked the knight.

"Alarms are already going off, no point in hiding now," Owen smiled as he activated his magical armor. The alarms suddenly boomed with a newly energized power as Owen began to glow like Stephanie. Once he was encased in his full body covering armor he reached behind him and pulled out his weapon that immediately expanded into his silver fighting staff. "We take them first. Tor, if you could delay the advancing forces to the north that would be great."

"I'll do my best," Tor said as he moved and faced the north.

"What do we do?" Will asked Tyson as Shirlynn answered with power in her voice, "protect the girl."

Tyson and Will looked at each other and then moved closer to Stephanie, who had pulled out a long knife, determined to help fight too. Tyson felt a weird tingling that made him look at Tor. He could tell that the Minotaur was tapping into his Magesti. Tor had his eyes closed and they all could feel a breeze picking up all around them. Tyson nearly jumped when Tor suddenly let out an angry roar while thrusting his arms forward. The air howled as the breeze exploded into a massive gust of wind that hit the oncoming force with such might it knocked them all back a small distance. Tor swayed as he tried to keep the wind going. "I don't know how long I can keep this up."

"Just enough to deal with them," Owen said as he was running and advancing upon the Elves and Drogans.

"You think you can best us, knight?" Lio taunted as he released both his arm blades.

Owen swung his staff deflecting the one headed towards Shirlynn while the second hit him in the chest of his armor, deflecting off with a slight ping sound. He continued running forward, catching the Elves surprised faces, and leapt in the air holding out his staff as he went between the two Fire Hounds, hitting their heads causing them to both rear up and flip backwards. He stopped and turned and the hounds went rolling and both Elves, in unison, back flipped safely into the air and landing on the ground in front of him. Owen readied his staff as the sound of the Drogans flying past made him glance up.

"You worry about them. I got this," Shirlynn said as she closed her eyes and raised her arms up into the air. The magic alarms boomed as she started to glow. She heard a loud squawk and did not have to open her eyes to know it was Zain. Soaring out of the woods was the hawk followed by thousands of birds and insects. They swarmed into, around and completely engulfed the five Drogans in the air, forcing them to fall to the ground. The birds and insects continued to attack and keep the winged monsters grounded and distracted despite the attacks of swords and fire at them. "Thank you for your sacrifice my friends."

"Is that enchanted Elven armor you wear?" Lia asked as she brought up her double bladed staff to deflect the blow from Owen's staff.

"You know you can't win," Lio said grunting in frustration as he sent two more blades at the Knight of Bergonia that deflected off the armor without even causing a scratch.

"We will stop you," Owen responded as he swiped his staff down and up knocking the feet right out from under the female Elf causing her to land hard on her back. He then turned towards the male Elf, thrusting the staff out as it separated in the middle exposing a silver chain as the front end flew unexpectedly at the Elf, hitting him in the face and making him drop to one knee to cup his broken and bleeding nose. Owen smiled as the chain retracted and the staff became one again.

"Lio! I will kill you half breed," Lia screamed as she got to her feet and prepared to charge after getting the true scent from the human imposter.

Owen gripped his staff when he heard growling coming from behind. He had forgotten about the Fire Hounds. He looked over his shoulder as he saw the two beasts running up from behind, one leaping into the air. He was ready to defend himself when a shadow hit him making him look forward. A third Fire Hound came out of nowhere, leaping over the female Elf and into the air. Owen prepared for the attack from both fronts when to his surprise, the newly arrived Fire Hound leapt past him, colliding with the other air bound hound while its rider leapt off and onto the back of the other Fire Hound.

The man looked to be older and wore armor that only covered his chest and back leaving his arms, legs and head exposed. He held a shield in one arm and a double bladed battle-axe in the other, both weapons made of beautiful silver. The hound tried to buck its rider but the man brought the axe down with amazing strength and placing a large gash in the beast's neck. The man rolled off, turned around and swung the axe upwards gutting the creature. The man got to his feet when a piercing scream hit their ears. "Milo, you're alive!"

The man glanced back and smiled at the confirmation that he took in as his *son* was still alive. He then, without having to say a word, nodded to the knight that they had a battle to win. Milo charged towards the two Fire Hounds who had shaken off their collision. The silver harness chain he had used to force the hound to carry him had been thrown to the ground. Milo ran at the beasts as one leapt at him with a vicious growl. Milo went to one knee as he thrust his shield up in protection against the pouncing attack. Just as the hound's body hit the shield, Milo flipped a mechanism on the inside of the shield that caused the circle crest in the middle of the shield to extract out in a point driving the silver spike to impale the creature's throat. Mile retracted the silver spike and brought his axe around in a mighty swing ripping open the wound and slitting the hound's neck letting it fall to the ground.

Not wasting any time, Milo turned and threw his battle-axe with all his might causing the blade to embed itself right between the last Fire Hound's eyes. The creature howled with pain, spraying blood everywhere as it tried to shake the blade free. Milo ran, scooped up the silver chain and leapt onto the back of the wounded beast. He slamed his shield down upon the top of the Fire Hound's head, extracting the silver spike so the shield was now embedded into the creature. Then, with both hands, he wrapped the silver chain around the creature's neck pulling tight, choking the creature while trying to keep from being thrown off. After two severe wounds and the air cut off by the chain, the creature finally laid down, unmoving, allowing Milo to slide off in exhaustion. "I'm getting way too old for this."

Owen heard the older man battling the Fire Hounds behind him and hoped he could handle his own while he faced the Elf twins. The one was still on the ground trying to stop his nose from bleeding while the sister geared up for another attack. She may be smaller than him, but she was fast. The fact that she was very emotional over her brother was something Owen was using to his advantage as she was missing critical shots. It did not help that her weapon was proving useless against his enchanted armor.

"Give up yet? Hate to see you end up like your brother," Owen provoked his attacker with success as she dove right at him.

Lia gave out a battle cry as she charged Owen, who swung his staff ready to deflect the Elf's attack. To his surprise, the female Elf dropped onto her side and slide on the ground at his feet causing him to leap over and out of her way. As he turned to face her, Lia was already up on her feet. The blades on her staff retracted and then were replaced by two glowing red blades. She brought one end down and then rotated to bring the other end back across making a feint crisscross pattern on his chest's armor. Owen looked down in surprise at the slightly scorched pattern on his armor as the magic alarms boomed again causing the female Elf's staff to start glowing.

"We may have sworn off the use of magic, but unlike my brother, I have no problem using weapons of magic," Lia growled as she thrusted out her staff making the red blade detach and fly right at Owen, implanting itself in the center of the X causing Owen to fall back off his feet. He lay there for a moment, amazed that she had penetrated his enchanted armor. The Elf approached him, bringing the other end of her staff around so the remaining red blade pointed at his chest. "Now let's see how much damage this can do."

"Go ahead if you want him to suffer the same fate," Milo said as both Lia and Owen glanced over to see the tip of the old man's axe pressed against the male Elf's neck, blood starting to drip, matching the blood flowing from his nose.

"Lio! I will…"

"Nothing if you both want to live. I have reached out to all wild animals that if they want to feast upon Elven meat it's first come," Shirlynn's voice boomed with confidence as she stepped towards the group, staff raised high.

Lia looked at the old woman, then at her brother and then towards the woods. Swearing, Lia shouted up into the air commands in her native tongue. A loud roar made Milo and Shirlynn grip their weapons and turn to the north as two Drogans broke free from the bird and insect attack and flew right at them. Milo prepared for battle but was surprised when the flying creatures did not attack. They flew past, one grabbing Lio and the other Lia and took off into the sky. "I swear a blood oath, knight, that I will not rest till I feast upon your blood!" Lia screamed and was soon gone along with her brother.

"They won't be back anytime soon," Shirlynn said as she moved towards Owen. "Are you okay?"

"I'm fine. It didn't go in too deep," Owen said as he managed to pull the blade out to see a small hole in the middle of the crisscross scratch with a small slit where the blade had hit.

"Did you really offer those Elves up for dinner?" Milo asked, keeping his eye on the woods.

"No. I was hoping she wouldn't call my bluff," Shirlynn laughed causing the other two men to laugh as well.

"Milo, it's been awhile. Glad to see you made it out alive," Owen said clasping the older man's hand in a firm shake followed by a quick embrace and introduction. "This is Shirlynn."

"Pleasure, m'lady. I see these creatures are not the only ones causing the magic alarms," Milo said, kissing the back of the clerics glowing hand.

"What about the others in your town?" Shirlynn asked, looking the man in the eyes with hope.

"The attack happened without warning. They were vicious and without mercy. Over half the town were slaughtered, the rest we managed to get to safety. We have a hidden mining tunnel that goes below the town. The new Elder of our town will keep them safe. I had to come find my boy. I killed an Elf and a Barbarian before roping one of those hounds to carry me in search of Tyson," Milo said as he looked over at the boy.

"We better join the rest of the group," Owen suggested as they saw Tor drop to one knee and the wind had started to die down. The three quickly made their way back and Tyson was already in a run, soon getting a big embrace from Milo.

"I feared you dead," Milo said breaking the hug and looking at the boy.

"And I, you."

"Did anyone else make it out?" Will asked but saw the sadness in the old man's eyes.

"I'm sorry, Will. Your parents died helping in the evacuation to the hidden tunnels, as did Elder Robert," Milo said as he remembered the man he had once loved, Robert, bringing the entrance to the tunnel down so the monsters could not follow and keeping the survivors safe. Milo let Phil lead the others on while he went back through a secondary exit only to be too late. He had watched Robert being struck down and that was when he made his two kills, hijacked a hound and raced off to find Tyson.

"I'm sorry," Tyson said gripping both Milo and Will's shoulders feeling their losses as if they were his own.

"We should head south," Milo suggested as he saw the forces coming from the north, the winged creatures chasing the

horses to the west and the remaining two Drogans breaking free
from the bird attack to the east leaving one of theirs behind, dead
as the insects finished it off.

Zain flew by with a squawk making Stephanie look
horrified at Shirlynn. "We can't go south. There are three more
Tazarians down that way hidden with riders. We're surrounded,"
Shirlynn said as she looked to Owen for guidance.

"You have nowhere to run. Your messengers to the king
have already been disposed of and all of this will be blamed on
the Kingdom of Erikson," Docanesto's voice boomed as he
pushed his hound and his forces closer towards them.

"We'll have to fight," Milo said as Owen nodded in
agreement.

"Zain has been instructed to try and get Diamond and
other horses here," Shirlynn said as Owen yelled after the bird.
"You know the priority. Tell Diamond."

"Staff!" A creepy voice shouted as a strange charred
looking figure, riding next to Docanesto pointed at Shirlynn.

"Finally! Surrender the staff to me now!" Docanesto
shouted with wide, hungry eyes.

"Never!" Shirlynn shouted back as she prepared her
strength, the sound of the magic alarms almost nonexistent, as
they all grew numb to its noise.

"Kill them all! I want that staff and that witch at all
costs!" Docanesto commanded as the two forces now merged
into battle.

"Protect the clerics!" Owen said glancing at both
Shirlynn and Stephanie.

"Fight well, my boy and guard the girl," Milo said as he
cupped the boy's face with his hands, kissed him upon the top of
his head, then turned and raised his battle-axe as youth-filled
energy pushed his aged body forward.

Sir Owen, fully encased in his magic armor, swung his
staff low, tripping one hound sending it's rider flying off while
sidestepping a second hound and bringing his staff back around
and hitting the rider on the back of the head sending the Fire Elf
to the ground. The fallen riders, one Fire Elf and one Barbarian,
got to their feet and quickly moved towards Owen as their
hounds ran onward looking for new prey. Owen charged, arrows

made of fire from the Fire Elf deflecting off his armor as the muscular Barbarian raised his axe and charged to meet him.

Owen swung his staff but the Barbarian grunted in satisfaction as he used his axe to deflect the blow and then reached out, grabbing Owen by the neck, raised him high and squeezed tight. Owen wiggled for a few seconds before going limp. "What a waste," the Barbarian said as he let go dropping the Knight of Bergonia.

"Idiot," Owen laughed as he quit his façade, as the armor had kept the Barbarian from actually strangling him, and quickly scooped up his staff and jammed the end of it into the man's throat, dropping him to the ground as he gasped for air. As a Knight, he had vowed not to kill, but it would be tough if they were to all survive this.

"I see your weakness," the Fire Elf smiled as he created and sent a very small and thin arrow of fire at the knight.

Owen tried to turn and move but was not fast enough as the tiny arrow made of fire hit him dead in the chest where the Elf twin had punctured his armor earlier. He felt the heat as it entered the small hole and made contact with his body underneath. Owen dropped to the ground, his armor retracting as it exposed his body, the front of his shirt now on fire. Owen rolled upon the ground quickly managing to put himself out.

"You okay?" Milo asked as his bloody axe left his hand and embedded itself into the chest of the Fire Elf, taking his smile and life.

"I'm fine," Owen lied as he could feel the heat coming off his chest as the blisters formed. He did not have time to worry about his wounds. Calling his armor back on, he grabbed his staff and looked for his next attacker while Milo grabbed his axe from the dead Fire Elf. Owen flinched as he looked back and saw the old man run past the Barbarian on the ground and finishing what he had not done with one quick swipe.

Tor had gotten his strength back and now had two axes in each arm thanks to the Barbarian he had killed along with his hound. His weapons combined with his Minotaur strength, he managed to take down two riderless hounds that had just come at him. He prepared for his next move when shadows had drawn his attention upwards. With the Drogans and Tazarians in the air, his companions would lose any advantage or hope in defeating this small army. Feeling a strange sensation within himself, Tor gave in and closed his eyes.

Reaching out, Tor could feel his connection to the wind and very air around him growing stronger, becoming as one. He felt the wind blow as he called it to him. He looked up and wished he could reach the flying beasts on an even battlefield. At that moment he felt something he had never experienced before with his abilities. His whole body felt lighter as the wind all around him seemed to push at him with a gentle ease. Soon he no longer felt the ground pressing at his feet and when he looked down, realized he was floating upwards, as if he were flying. He started to panic and felt his body growing heavy. Quickly calming himself, he gave into his abilities and the wind and compelled himself up and towards the Drogans and Tazarians.

A Tazarian with its human rider dove right at him. Wishing the wind to assist him, Tor found himself thrust upward with great speed and bringing his right arm up, slicing his axe's blade clean up the Tazarian's under neck until it jerked from his hand as it was now lodged into the large creature's jaw. Tor willed the wind to move him to the side as the creature roared in pain, blood leaking from the wound, and dove head first to the ground below. Tor winced as he heard the sound of crunching bone when the Tazarian slammed into the earth below, crushing its human rider.

Tor smiled, letting out a roar as he flew high in the sky and turned to face the six Tazarians and five Drogans that were coming for him. With his empty hand, he reached out to the wind and the Magesti within him and pushed with all his might. The wind flowed as it raced out to meet his enemy head on. The gust of wind hit the flying creatures and sent most of them tail spinning backwards. Tor was ready to cheer when he suddenly felt heavy and realized he was now plummeting to the ground below. It came clear very quickly that he could not fly and command the wind to attack at the same time.

Knowing the ground would be soon upon him, he closed his eyes, trying to gain calm and control over his body and his powers. After several breaths, he began to feel lighter. Moments before hitting the ground, Tor gave a big hearty push as the wind rushed up beneath him, propelling him back up into the sky, giving him flight once again. Thankful, Tor gripped his axe as he willed the wind to shoot him straight up like an arrow. With a satisfying roar, he sliced through one Drogan's wing, sending him to the ground below but not before grabbing the creatures red bladed sword and using it to behead the second Drogan he shot past.

"It can't stop all of us. Fire!" One of the Fire Elves shouted as he brought his Tazarian back around leading the other Tazarian Riders in for the attack. The Fire Elf released an arrow made of fire as the other three Fire Elf riders followed suit.

Tor saw a half dozen flaming arrows head right for him and knew he could not deflect them without risk of losing control and falling. Reaching out to the wind, he willed it to pushing him sideways allowing him to fly out of the way, dodging all the arrows at the last possible moment. Tor knew he had to move quickly as he would not be able to out fly them all, especially since he was beginning to feel tired and his hold on his power weakening. As he contemplated what to do, an idea hit him as hard as the ground did his previous victims. With a smile, he willed the wind to push him up, fast and high above the other winged creatures, causing all nine remaining foes to slow and look up.

Once he was up high enough, Tor released his hold on the wind and allowed himself to grow heavy and nose dive back towards his enemy and the earth below. As he descended, he reached out to the wind and commanded it and the Magesti, making the wind and air in front of him push downwards with a penetrating force. The powerful gust of wind quickly hit all nine airborne creatures and drove them straight down towards the ground below with nothing they could do to stop their racing impact. Tor, thinking of his mother and his people, used that strength and anger to give another push making the wind slam his enemy with ground shaking force into the earth leaving them lifeless and imbedded into the ground. About to black out from the over use of his Magesti, Tor used the last of his will power and strength to ask the wind to help slow and cushion his fall. Tor grunted as the wind hit him, slowing him enough to survive his impact and roll upon the ground.

"They've taken back to the sky," Will said as the Drogans they had been fighting had taken off to join their fellow winged creatures into battle with Tor.

"I didn't know he could fly," Tyson observed as he saw the Minotaur suddenly take to the air.

"I don't think he did either," Stephanie added as Shirlynn soon interrupted them. "Stay alert!"

The three moved towards the older cleric as six hounds with riders surrounded them and crouched in attack formation. Will urged them all to stand back to back so they could watch, weapons high and ready. Shirlynn eyed the group surrounding them but kept her eyes on the Master Fire Elf directly in front of her, Docanesto. She gripped the staff tight as she saw the saliva dripping from the evil Elf's mouth, his eyes sparkling at the sight of his wanted desire. At that moment, she knew she would go to her death before she let him take the staff from her. "You will not prevail."

"You've already lost. What chance does an old woman and three children have against me and my forces?" Docanesto taunted as his Fire Hound growled with hunger.

"Staff" The charred figure muttered causing Shirlynn to glance to the side of Docanesto. She did not know why, but something about this creature gave off a very familiar aura. "Yes, my Tracker. You've led us to it."

"What are we waiting for, kill them," the female figure completely wrapped in black material demanded as Docanesto glared over at her as the Barbarian rider's voice boomed. "No shadow warrior commands our great master!"

"Rayvac, there is no need for you to speak for me but you are right. Ever overstep again and I will end you, Kae, last of the shadow warriors or not," Docanesto said, fire lighting from within his pupils.

"We're not afraid of you," Will said raising his sword and shield.

"Shirlynn?" Stephanie asked gripping her knife hoping the older cleric had a plan.

"Don't let them get the staff," was all Shirlynn said causing Stephanie to swallow hard and give worried looks to the other two boys.

"Take them," Docanesto nodded as he moved his hound closer to Shirlynn and the staff.

Tyson knew they could not survive an attack like this and knew he had the power within to do something. He felt the Magesti within tingling and calling out to him. Giving in and reaching out he felt his connection to the light all around him. He quickly pulled it in and began to glow. He noticed the hounds hesitating and used that to his advantage. He held out his gloved arms above him and spread them apart along with his fingers as he let the power out. A blinding flash of light sprayed from him and his gloves causing the Fire Hounds to real back and their riders to cringe, covering their eyes. As he started to feel faint, he released the power allowing the light to die, but not its effects as the enemy were still covering and blinking the pain away from their eyes.

"It appears we are in the presence of two Magestics," Kae hissed as she began to call to the shadows and the material along her arms began to shift and form blades.

"Light trumps dark," Tyson said as he pointed both his fingers and sent two beams of concentrated light hitting both bladed arms causing the material of darkness to flicker and resort back to normal.

"I got him," the Fire Elf said as he let loose an arrow of fire at Tyson.

"Wrong," Will said as he shifted his body bringing his shield up in time to protect his best friend from the attack.

"This fool is mine," Rayvac said as he raised his long sword, eyes still blinking away the spots of light.

Stephanie, surprised by her reaction, found herself leaping forward and throwing her long knife. The Barbarian commander roared as the knife plunged itself into him right where his right arm met his chest. "You think a knife will stop me?" The Barbarian asked with a laugh and he yanked the knife from his body and tossed it aside. He rested his eyes on Stephanie, licking his lips. Stephanie swallowed in fear when a strange sensation coursed through her body. She knew it was not her causing it so it must be coming from someone else. She turned and saw Shirlynn, her staff glowing and going on the attack.

Shirlynn felt the pains of her age but the staff was giving her rejuvenated strength for what she knew she had to do. She knelt down and closed her eyes. Her senses went out and she could *see* every living thing around her. With the help of the staff, she began chanting and sent a prayer upon the earth. Soon the very grass around them responded and began to heal, take strength and grow. She heard the hounds roar as in mid leap and movement they were snapped back. The grass was now wrapped around their legs, growing and intertwining very quickly pulling the beasts to the ground and holding them tight. She heard their riders swear or grunt as they quickly dismounted the Fire Hounds.

Shirlynn was not sure if she had the strength to hold them, but knew Stephanie had felt the same way when she felt a gentle hand touch her back. A surge of healing energy passed from Stephanie and into Shirlynn causing them and the staff to glow brighter, magic alarms roaring with madness. Not only did the grass hold firmer to the beasts but now thousands of small insects were heading their call and raced out of the ground, covering the hounds and swarming into their mouths and nostrils, blocking the Fire Hound's air flow, suffocating them.

"Do something!" Docanesto screamed as he jumped back trying to keep the insects off of him.

"What is that?" Will asked as one of the figures that had been on a Fire Hound had sprouted wings and levitated into the air. He at first looked human with black and red streaked hair, goatee and wore black boots and red pants with a matching cape but no shirt. Once the being sprouted wings, he took on a different look as his skin turned scaly and red, red glowing eyes and pointed ears could now be seen.

"Draelv is my own personal Huelgon," Docanesto smirked as he felt the fire building around them all.

"No, not quite."Shirlynn questioned as she looked at the creature that almost looked like Essej.

"Close enough. Cloning is a difficult process but with this creature he is one of three and very resourceful." Draelv paid no attention to his master talking about him as he reached out, commanded the very heat around and within him, and called forth the fire. He opened his eyes and pushed with his powers, "Burn!"

"Shirlynn!" Stephanie screamed as she and the older cleric released their power and moved closer to Will and Tyson, watching in fear as the grass holding the Fire Hounds burst into flame and then quickly spread to engulf the hounds and all the insects. Shirlynn knew that the fire would not harm the hounds but she felt the pain as the life force from each insect and blade of grass burned out. She bowed and sent a prayer of thanks to the life that had ended in sacrifice to take down the Fire Hounds.

The four companions looked to each other as the fire quickly burned and, under Draelv's command, spread around trapping them in a circle of fire. Docanesto laughed with victory as he reached out with his magic, causing the fire to shoot across and then move towards him, separating Shirlynn and the staff from the other three while forcing her closer to him. "Now!" Docanesto shouted once Shirlynn was far enough away.

Will raised his shield not knowing what good it would do as the wall of fire went up and then shot forward, directly at them from all sides. He was about to close his eyes when a commotion snapped his attention. There was a man in silver armor running right towards the moving wall of fire. He shouted upwards as a hawk gave out a call and released an object that fell into the armored man's hand. "No!" Shirlynn shouted looking over her shoulder.

"Sorry Shirlynn. I know we agreed leaving the shield in Diamond's care was the best decision but Zain knew there was no choice now," Sir Owen said as he dove through the fire, stood up next to the three kids and held the shield up high invoking it's abilities.

"Shield!" Tracker shouted as a beautiful white-blue light emanated from the shield creating a protective barrier around the four, deflecting and repelling the attacking wall of fire.

"What is this? You, delivering two of the Artifacts of Power right to me." Docanesto could hardly contain his excitement. "Where are you hiding the others?"

"You will never get them as long as I live," Shirlynn spat as the wall of fire pushing her from behind vanished and Docanesto and Tracker moved towards her and her staff.

"Oh, that can be rectified," Docanesto started to laugh when a strange wind suddenly knocked him back from the woman.

Shirlynn looked over and saw Milo and Tor slowly making their way towards them, leaning upon each other for support. Tor had his hand held out and at the slight motion of his arm, the wind started to swirl until it caused a vacuum that instantly snuffed out all the fire. Docanesto swore and commanded his servants to attack.

"Can't leave you alone for a second can I?" Milo asked returning Tyson's smile and Owen's salute after the magical berrier vanished. At this point, the magic alarms were going off intensly as magic and magical items kept being used.

"You're mine," Rayvac declared as he raised his sword and charged the old man and Minotaur.

"Milo," Tyson said as he moved away from his group of friends but was then blocked by another figure.

"I will extinguish your light,' Kae said as the material around her body shifted and grew, swirling all around her like dark banners made of shadow.

Sir Owen turned to attend to Shirlynn but suddenly found the winged Draelv flying at him while the Fire Elf raised his bow and charged from behind at Will and Stephanie. "You take him, we can handle the Elf," Will said as Stephanie nodded, pulling out another long knife.

The Fire Elf raised his bow and quickly sent off several arrows made of fire. Will held up his shield deflecting all but one arrow that managed to hit his left leg causing him to shout in pain as the fire burned his flesh. As the arrow was made of fire, there was nothing to pull out, but Will managed to smack it out with the side of his sword. He could smell the charred skin but with the Elf almost upon them, the wound would have to wait. He charged the Elf and swung his sword. The Fire Elf ducked, pivoted around and slammed his foot into Will's back sending him falling forward as he then raised his bow to make the kill shot.

Stephanie, wanting to be tough but having never killed, swiped the knife at the Fire Elf's back, only landing a small cut across his back. It was not lethal but it was enough to cause him to forget Will and turn around to face her. With a small whisper, the Fire Elf created a fiery dagger in his hand and held it out in preparation of an attack. Stephanie gripped her knife and prepared herself for battle. The Fire Elf began to lunge forward but stopped as the tip of a silver sword came piercing out of his chest. Blood formed from the wound and his mouth as he was pushed off the blade and fell limp to the ground.

"You okay?" Will asked, blood still dripping from his sword as Stephanie thanked him and then lent a healing hand to his previously burned leg.

Tor, still not quite up to full strength, managed to stand tall, axe in one hand and red blade in the other as the Barbarian Commander, Rayvac, charged right into him and Milo. Tor managed to block the knife with his sword while Milo fell hard to the ground due to the impact from the Barbarian's strength and long sword upon his shield. Tor glanced as he saw the old man shake off the blow and slowly get back to his feet, shield in one hand and axe in the other. Tor had to give Milo credit. He may be old but he was standing his ground.

"I will feast upon your meat, cow," Rayvac growled as he swung his weapon hard, knocking one weapon from his grasp and leaving Tor with only the red bladed sword he had scavenged from a Drogan.

"I am not a cow," Tor said as he swung his blade, hitting and taking off the tips of a few fingers from the Barbarians empty hand.

"I will gut you," Rayvac swore thrusting out at the Minotaur with his long sword.

Tor brought his sword up, ready to spar, when the Barbarian was slammed from behind and thrown forward, missing his mark and hitting the ground face first. Tor nodded to Milo as the old man shifted his shield and now charged the fallen victim with his axe. Rayvac roared a massive battle cry as he turned around and punched the charging old man with his bloody fist, loud cracking sounds erupted as Milo fell backwards, dropping his weapons and clutching his chest from loss of wind and broken bones. Tor roared at the sight and hit the Barbarian with his head in a full-on charge driving them both a few feet from the injured Milo.

Tor noticed the injury and blood of the Barbarian's severed fingers did not slow his atttacker as Rayvac grabbed Tor by his horns and with great strength, twisted, lifted up and slammed the Minotaur back upon the ground. Tor, as a Minotaur, was naturally strong but having used his Magesti abilities so much had left him still slightly winded, but he did not have the luxury to rest if he wanted to live. Rayvac was already upon him, bringing his long sword straight down. Tor swung his arm in a defensive blow that knocked the blade to the side, putting a slice in his arm instead of being staked in the chest.

Tor managed to get to his feet but Rayvac was already raising his sword again. Tor looked for his weapon but was afraid he would not find it in time. Rayvac let out a cry as he held his sword in his good hand and swung it at the Minotaur's head. Tor flinched as the arm holding the sword suddenly flew past his head. Confused, he looked up at the Barbarian who cupped the bleeding stump where his arm once was. Milo, barely able to stand, staggered as he smiled through the pain, holding an axe in one hand and the other held against his injured torso. Milo nodded as he collapsed in unison with Rayvac.

"Milo?" Tor called out as he started to move towards the old man when two things caught his attention. He saw Diamond and a few horses being chased by Tazarians heading right for them and a butterfly that had flown right up to him and seemed to deliver a message to him from Shirlynn.

"Your powers aren't magic, are they? I can feel a strange sensation coming from you," Tyson observed as he dodged another whip attack from the shadow warrior's shadowy ribbon like tentacles that streamed from her body.

"You can say, me and my gifts are quite ancient. I've been around a lot longer than any of you and have waged deadlier battles than this," Kae's strange voice said with a hissing laughter.

Tyson hated the fighting but realized his powers really had an effect on his foe. Not to wear himself out and using the help of his gloves he invented, he was able to send small powerful bursts of light that kept her and her attacks at bay. He managed to keep a low level glow around his body that seemed to lessen the impact of the shadow warriors connecting hits. It was a dance he was catching on to, but he would soon grow tired from using his Magesti and this shadow lady in front of him, he had no doubt she could out last him. He tried to come up with a plan when he heard a scream.

He looked over and saw Milo being punched in the chest and flying backwards, hitting the ground. His instinct was to run to him but the distraction cost him dearly. He was yanked to the ground as four ribbons made of darkness grabbed each of his arms and legs and dragged him towards Kae. The blow to his head from hitting the ground had made him loose his concentration and the glow of his Magesti faded away. Kae laughed as he was dragged closer to her. A strange butterfly suddenly flew next to his ear and, to his amazement, gave him a message with instructions causing him to glance over towards Shirlynn.

Owen, fully armored, the shield in one hand and his staff held tight in his other, he looked up at the winged creature hovering before him. Draelv may be a cloned version of a Huelgon, but he was a magical creature himself wearing magical armor and welding an Artifact of Power. As a Knight of Begonia, he was not afraid and resonated with bravery and the determination of victory. The opponent before him was not very bright as he kept sending attacks made of fire that just deflected off of the knight thanks to his armor and shield. Sir Owen knew he had to end this quickly so he could get to Shirlynn, the one he was sworn to protect.

Owen took his staff and thrust it forward, causing it to detach towards the top and fly forward, a small arrow point popping out from the tip and hitting Draelv and piercing his wing like a spear. Owen's end, still attached by a silver chain, held firm in his hand as he tried to yank it free but found his weapon stuck in the now torn wing. Draelv grabbed the chain and ripped it from Owen's hand with a firm tug before ripping the weapon from his wing and tossing the weapon aside as he reverted back to human form and dropping to the ground, his wing no longer visible but the pain still there.

"You think you won?" Draelv asked as he locked eyes with the knight. "That shield may prevent me from burning you but there are other ways around that since you have not truly mastered or become one with the Artifact you hold."

Owen held the shield up as he saw his opponent's eyes flicker red as his skin became a scaly red indicating he was calling on the power he possessed. The shield shimmered, ready to repel the fire that never came. Owen started to wonder what his foe was up to when he noticed where Draelv was looking. Owen glanced down at the small hole in his armor and he suddenly felt the burn and blisters underneath throbbing with pain and heating up. The shield protected him from being burnt alive but not from the heat. He looked back up at the Huelgon clone.

"Finally realized that I don't need to set you on fire. I can feel the heat of your burn and through the kink in your armor, I can connect with it and fuel it. You now have a choice to make, cook alive in your armor or retract it to allow you and your wound to breath while leaving you vulnerable to attacks," Draelv gloated pushing with his powers as Owen felt the blisters worsen and the heat becoming unbearable as the knight began to sway and feel light headed.

"You've lost this battle old friend," Docanesto said as he and Tracker walked towards the old cleric.

"We are not friends," Shirlynn spat as she held tight to the staff. She could sense her companions around her and it was not good for many of them. She had to find a way to make sure the staff did not fall into this evil Elf's hands and that the Order of the Cleric carried on, or Bergonia may lose the coming battle.

"Hand over the staff," Docanesto demanded as he prepared a spell.

"If you want it, then here!" Shirlynn screamed as she sent up a prayer and invoked the full power of the staff and swung it at the dreaded Fire Elf.

"Staff!" Taker declared as the charred being instantly reached out its hand and catching the staff before it could hit his master.

Shirlynn felt a strange sensation pass between her, the staff and Tracker. A very powerful and healing light burned upon Tracker causing him to scream so loud even Docanesto stepped back away from the two. Whatever was happening neither of them could let go of the staff. A sudden idea came over Shirlynn and she wished it into motion as two butterflies erupted from the staff and flew in opposite directions. As Shirlynn's attention was drawn back to the event unfolding before her, she saw that pieces of the charred man were beginning to crack and flake off. She looked at the staff, and the creature's hand that was touching it was now completely exposed and she could see the flesh healing and coming back to life. She then looked up and where the staff's light was burning brightest, she could see part of Tracker's chest starting to be exposed as well as one final chunk coming off revealing his face. "It can't be."

The light of the staff finally vanished as Tracker let go causing Shirlynn to fall back and land on her bottom. She looked up and saw only the very front of his face was exposed and not fully healed but it was enough for her to recognize the evil traitor she thought long dead. "Ferron, how?"

"Who Ferron? My name is Tracker," the now partially charred covered being said. Shirlynn looked and could feel that this was the Elf that had betrayed them so long ago as well as his brain was healing but very slowly. If he gained his memories, it might take some time.

"You were our spy. I can't believe you lived. A holder of one of the Artifacts and in my presence the whole time," Docanesto said as he moved closer to the half-charred Elf. "Where is the sling?"

"Sling? No, staff," Ferron said pointing to the object in Shirlynn's hand.

"It doesn't matter, I have the staff, soon the shield and the master of the sling. This battle is truly my victory," Docanesto gloated as he reached down and lifted Shirlynn up into the air by the throat with one hand.

"Not while I still live. Now!" Shirlynn managed a gagged scream pushing the last of her strength causing the staff to pulse twice, sending out two last butterflies and then turned enough to see Stephanie making her way towards her.

"Shirlynn?" Stephanie mouthed in horror.

"You are now the last. Protect the staff," Shirlynn said more from her eyes than her voice as she flung the staff through the air and right into Stephanie's hands.

"You witch," Docanesto swore as his hand ignited in flame and spread to consume Shirlynn's entire body moments after she sent up one final prayer.

Tyson could hear someone screaming but with the black tentacles from Kae completely wrapped around his body suffocating him and draining his light he could not see what was happening. He was about to give in to the darkness when he felt a butterfly land on his ear and then explode filling him with a command and a newfound healing energy. In that moment, he was instantly in touch with his Magesti and reached out, connecting with every particle of light in and around them all. Taking the boost in strength he had just received, he pushed his Magesti gift with everything he had causing the entire area around them all to explode in a brilliant burst of light that instantly dissolved his bondage of darkness. Tyson looked over and saw Kae's form flickering and right before he lost his vision in the blinding light of his Magesti, he had caught a glimpse of Kae's true form.

"What is happening?" Stephanie asked as the screaming finally stopped and she was engulphed within a blinding light. She gripped the staff tight as she kept her eyes closed from what she assumed was Tyson's doing. This must have been the rest of Shirlynn's plan. As she tried to figure out what that plan was, she felt a powerful gust of wind slam into her. She tried to ask the staff for help and call out to Shirlynn but just as she could almost see Shirlynn's form in her mind, burning and then thrown to the ground, a wind like she had never felt before, slammed her body from all sides and then lifted her up into the air. She tried to call out over the roaring wind but the image in her mind vanished as she felt one last blast of wind lift her higher and toss her with great speed before she gave in and blacked out.

****

Stephanie tried to open her eyes but the effects of the blinding light left her seeing spots. She thought she could still hear the roaring of the wind but realized the air was calm. As her sight returned she realized what she was hearing was the ocean crashing upon the shore of the beach she was sitting on. She looked down and saw she was still gripping the staff and then looked back out at the ocean as the light started to fade from the setting sun. Stephanie scratched her head and was amazed that Tor's gust of wind had carried her all the way to where Silversword met the Western Sea. As she stood she gasped in realization that she was facing the wrong way towards the water. There was no way she was on the shores of Silversword. Then she wondered, where was she?

She heard a sound and looked around to find that the only thing on this beach was her and an injured Drogan. Wondering where her friends were, she gripped the staff and carefully stepped back as the wounded creature tried to get to its feet. Stephanie tried to find the strength for another fight when a girl with long curly brown hair, barely wearing any clothes and carrying a wooden spear stepped past her and stood between her and the Drogan. The creature snarled but the girl, who looked to be about Stephanie's age, did not even flinch. She closed her eyes and raised her arms. Water began to form in mid-air and build as water from the ocean flowed up to join it. She then swung her arms down making the water shoot out in a powerful blast hitting the Drogan hard and slamming him into the sandy beach.

"You can do magic?" Stephanie asked as she then realized the magic alarms were nowhere to be heard and she was no loner glowing. She realized that she definitely wasn't in Silversword.

"Not magic. I don't know what it is. Just a gift I was blessed with and ever since this dream I had, I've started growing more powerful with it," the girl shrugged as she then looked over her shoulder to where the beach met a thick forest and then gave out a strange animal call.

Stephanie wondered if she was a Magesti like Tor and Tyson when something in the forest snatched her attention. With loud snarls, about a half dozen wolves of various shades darted out and ran with great speed at the waterlogged Drogan. The creature barley moved when the wolves attacked and tore it to shreds. "It's been a long time since anything has touched our land."

"Where am I?" Stephanie asked as she had to force herself to look away from the carnage.

"You are on the Forbidden Isles," the girl answered and then called out again as several men and woman, all wearing similar outfits, walked out of from the trees. None of them carried weapons.

"You're not going to kill me, are you?" Stephanie asked as the wolves finished and then carried the Drogan's carcass of into the forest.

"No, not yet," the girl said as a bird call made them both look up.

"Zain!" Stephanie called out, for the first time thankful to see the bird.

"It seems you do know Zain," the girl said with a strangeness in her voice. "It's because of him you and your friends are allowed to live for the moment."

Stephanie was taken by the interaction and familiarity between Zain and the girl but was more focused on the allowed to live comment. "Allowed to live?"

"Yes, until we get you to Xia where Mistress Zalena awaits your audience and passes her judgement," the girl said as she made another noise making the men suddenly shift and transform into wolves and bears before running off into the forest. The females shifted into falcons and panthers forming a scouting and protective barrier around Stephanie and the girl with the spear, who nudged the princess turned cleric to move forward towards the forest and beyond.

Chapter Thirty:
Lucian & The Chosen One

"The closer we get the worse the smell," Semaj commented as they approached the Gooblyn City. Coming from a farm, even he had never encountered such filth and odor as these creatures and their environment.

"I don't know, pretty close toss-up between them and the Ogres," Thom added trying to lighten the mood as they all were currently being escorted by Goblins and Hobgoblins right to their enemies and possible deaths.

"You still haven't told us what King Snoog or Docanesto wants with us?" Ard-Rich asked, with his strength returned his body had reverted back to his younger appearance. He saw the looks he had gotten from the group upon seeing him in his true more older form and knew from the glares he got from Essej, the truth would soon have to come out. He knew he should tell his old friend, but that would mean giving it all up.

"Silence, you do not get to know or question the great King Snoog's orders," the leader of the Goblins snapped back as a Hobgoblin growled, licking his lips wishing for a bite.

"Are you sure this is wise?" Semaj asked, stepping up behind the elders in the group.

"We must find and secure the safety of the Magestic. Things could be tragic, especially if the Magestic is in the hands of Drol Greb's forces," Essej said as he kept his eyes on their fast approaching destination.

"Since we are getting close, can you sense the Magestic?" Anna asked quietly as she moved closer to Semaj, careful not to get too close to Nat.

"I feel pulled forward, but," Semaj paused as he felt a throbbing in his head, closed his eyes, placed his fingers on his temple and pushed. He could feel something inside him trying to reach out and connect with a familiar energy source. He tried to focus, gain clarity but realized it all seemed effortless when he was dreaming. With that final thought, he felt something change inside him and felt Anna was there even before she placed her hand on his shoulder. He tried to scream as a power exploded from him the instant Anna's fingers made contact with his body, a wave of heat and fire erupted all around the group.

"Anna, what are you doing?" Thom screamed as Nat jumped backwards from the fire that suddenly erupted outwards from where Anna and Semaj were standing.

"I didn't," Semaj heard Anna start to plea as a dizziness and ringing in his ears drowned out the sound from all around him. The Magesti within Anna seemed to be engulfing him, not burning but merging. In panic, he willed it away causing another blast of fire to pulse out sending the fire and Anna away from him. He swayed as the ringing stopped and sound flooded back to his ears, sleep pulling at his body.

"Stand back, I must snuff out the flames," Essej's voice could be heard as wind began to touch Semaj's face. His air and consciousness leaving him, his body falling to the ground as the sight of fire and Goblins flickering before darkness consumed his vision.

"No, the Goblins!" Semaj jerked his eyes open and leapt onto his feet, drawing his sword realizing the fire would cause the fowl creatures and their Hobgoblin pals to think they had waged war on them. As he prepared to fight, he realized he no longer felt the heat of the fire or heard the sound of battle.

Keeping his sword ready, Semaj rotated in a circle as he saw that he was not only alone but stood on a large stone bridge, the wind hitting him from all sides. To the north and south of him, about five feet away was a stone ledge that came up high enough to help prevent stepping off. To the east and west, the bridge extended another ten feet or so before arching downward and out of sight. He moved to the southern ledge and discovered he was very high up in the sky. He looked down and saw a very feint battle raging below, several massive red spots of glowing fire slowly decreasing in size and number.

"How did I get up here?" Semaj asked out loud, to himself, as he looked left and right seeing the arched bridge leading down to the large mountains to the west and what must be the Gooblyn City on the other end. "Essej's wind vacuum must have sucked me up here, but where did this arched bridge come from?"

"We are in your dream vision place that your power creates," Anna said as she walked up from the west end of the bridge.

"I thought I had prevented myself from passing out," Semaj shrugged as he put his sword away. "What happened?"

"You started acting funny. When I touched you, it was like you ripped my power from me and sent it out in all directions. Then you did it again and our connection severed when I fell back from you. Then you got that look in your eyes and I felt the familiar pull and blacked out moments after I heard Essej scream at Thom. I woke up alone on the arched path and headed up when I sensed you," Anna responded as she gave her friend a calming smile.

"I was trying to use my power to track the Magestic but didn't mean for this to happen. We need to get back and help our friends but I can't seem to wake up," Semaj said as he had no luck connecting with the power within him.

"Usually these dreams are your power trying to tell you where you need to be or what comes next. Maybe we're stuck here till you figure it out?" Anna suggested as she really did not understand how any of this worked or even why any of this was really happening to all of them.

"We are above the battle and not a new location so we are on the right path," Semaj muttered as he tried to sort the dream vision out. "To the east I can strangely see the Gooblyn City with clarity with a small pull, so the Magestic we need to find is there, but, part of the city has a grey decaying section and another that has a gold haze as if it isn't really there, and, in the middle, some kind of familiar void that I can't figure out."

"Is it possible there are more than one Magestic in the city? I mean, we know the evil forces working against us are looking for the Chosen One and could have gotten their hands on some of the others like me," Anna said as she closed her eyes and felt more than one familiar power sources coming from the direction of the city as well as behind her.

"I sense it too. There's the mountains and the pull I feel must be Noraxa, but I also can see a body of water overlapping it, like an orange fog. Which doesn't make sense since the Magestic from under the Frosted Waters is already with us."

"I really hope Noraxa will be okay," Anna said thinking of the Dwarf that had sacrificed herself to save all of them.

"I'll be just fine," a voice huffed causing the two to look over to the western side to see a female Dwarf walking up and over the arch path towards them.

"Noraxa!" Anna screamed running to hug the Dwarf but was stopped in her tracks by a death glare.

"It's good to see you. How close behind us are you?" Semaj asked, never thinking he would see the Dwarf here in his dream vision.

"I believe I am still in the mountains with those annoying creatures. What's going on? Last thing I remember was using my Magesti to keep us all safe and from plunging to our deaths before blacking out. Then I recall opening my eyes, seeing the Gnomes and Lorax hovering over me inside a mountain cave, then a powerful sensation yanking me back into darkness.

"I woke up in mid toss as I was flying away from the mountains and to this bridge. I would have missed if I hadn't grabbed my axe and embedded it in the top side of the ledge. Before pulling myself up and over the side, I managed to notice some kind of battle far below. I felt a strong pull up a long path to the top and grumbled until the stones under my feet started to go up, over and down propelling me to the top here. When I saw you two, I realized I must be in one of your dreams again," Noraxa said as she shifted the battle axe in her hand as she moved passed Anna and towards Semaj.

"Your powers must be growing if you were able to pull her from that far away," Anna commented as Semaj nodded before filling Noraxa in on what had happened to them since the Gnomes took her to safety.

"Great, now I owe them one. If you could end this dream, I'll get us moving as fast as we can to help with the Goblin battle," Noraxa said as she thought of the battle happening down below them.

"I'm trying to figure that out."

"Then you better hurry. They are attacking in full force after you blasted them with fire," Thom said as he shimmered into existence right before them, arms in motion as if he had been fighting something.

"Thom, your crystal pulled you here with us. Did you bring the others? Semaj, who's defending our bodies?" Anna panicked as the realization came to her and she turned to the person responsible for where they were.

"I hadn't thought of that," Semaj added as he began looking around for Essej and the others in their group.

"Essej did the moment you started doing your thing. He sent words on the wind telling me to use my crystal to not pull people in with you, just to keep everyone out, especially him," Thom said, his body flinching before he continued.

"The words came into my mind and used all my power with the crystal to send a spell out to prevent me and anyone from being pulled into your dream world. As I released the spell I saw Anna drop, worried I was too late and focused the spell on Essej hitting him with a blast that severed the connection keeping him in the real world. I felt myself being pulled so I refocused the spell and moved it on me and spread it out to Nat and Ard-Rich. I think it was working when I felt something odd at the same time I saw the Goblins attacking, and the thought of being with you two entered my mind. Before I could do anything, I appeared here, but I keep seeing flashes of me fighting Goblins," Thom said as he appeared to flinch again at nothing.

"That's because you are in two places at once," a voice answered causing them to turn and see the Océan known as Ard-Rich standing on top of the bridge's ledge before hopping down next to them.

"How is that possible?" Anna asked looking back at Thom, who flinched again.

"I felt myself being pulled into a sleep when a magical blast came from Thom and hit Essej and then me. Essej was free but I was still on the verge between worlds. Then I thought I saw something, but a surge of power came from Thom and I felt myself giving into the pull to Semaj. Before I blacked out, I saw Thom split in two, one form vanished while the other, which looked more like a spirit wearing a very solid glowing crystal, began to battle the Goblins," Ard-Rich explained.

"Then what I am seeing is the crystal in the real world using a spirit form of me to help battle and protect your sleeping bodies while I'm here to be with you guys," Thom said as he flinched, saw a quick flash of him, Nat and Essej battling Goblins while protecting the three sleeping bodies in the middle of their protective formation. He then glanced down to see the crystal around his neck was very feint and translucent, as if it wasn't really there.

"Are you okay?" Semaj asked his friend.

"Feeling a bit dizzy," Thom said, flinching again.

"I imagine he can't keep this up for long, or any of them out there. You need to wake us up before any more forces advance on them," Noraxa said as Anna agreed thinking of her mistrust of Nat.

"Too late for that. As soon as I saw your group attack with fire I commanded an attack to go and retrieve you all. I would have joined them to make sure the Chosen One wasn't accidently killed, but something familiar came over me and I used my magic and connection to pull myself here with my new friend."

"It's you," Semaj said as he and his group turned to see, stepping up from the east side of the bridge, a male form along with a strange larger creature behind him. Ard-Rich quickly confirmed that the creature was an Orgite, but they all knew who the other figure was, the invading man from all the other dreams. He was quite a distance from them, but he was visually clearer than he was from the previous dreams.

He had about the same build as Semaj, but his age was hard to tell as his face was covered with an odd purple, rough and scarred looking markings. His attire told them that he was a strong leader of great importance. The man that had been chasing them in the real world and trying to reach them in these dreams had finally caught up to them. The man smiled "Greetings, I am Lucian Darkheart and this here is my new-found friend, King Oltar who has pledged his colony's forces and Magesti to me."

"Um," the Orgite started to mumble, but was still too confused about what was going on and where he was, to contemplate what Lucian had just announced.

"Lucian Darkheart, Docanesto and Drol Greb's forces will not prevail," Ard-Rich declared as he stepped forward placing himself between his group and Lucian.

"I think you are too old and weak to be who I'm looking for and I laugh at the Dwarf. So, which one of you three is the Chosen One?" Lucian asked as he looked at Thom, Anna and Semaj. He felt something from everyone in front of him so he was in the presence of the Chosen One and probably his group of Magestics. He glanced at Thom, a very different sensation come from him than did the others. He wondered, was he the Chosen One?

"I'll give you something to laugh at when I chop you off at the knees," Noraxa said as she raised her axe and moved up next to Ard-Rich.

"I think when my father returns to Bergonia, I'll declare the immediate extinction of all Dwarves, starting with you," Lucian laughed as he began to call on his magic to form dozens of arrows made of fire above the palms of his outstretched hands.

"I thought we were protecting all creatures of magic?" Oltar started to mumble when something caught his eye. He turned to see a creature scamper real fast back the other direction and down the pathway they had come up. He could not tell if it was a Goblin, Gooblyn or Hobgoblin as it was already gone from sight. He felt an odd connection, and not wanting to be a part of what was happening, he started to head back down and follow the creature.

"Incoming!" Rich-Ard screamed as the flaming arrows headed towards them.

"I can't get my crystal to respond," Thom panicked.

"Allow me," Anna said as she called on her Magesti, reaching out to the flaming arrows and willing the heat to cool and the fire to disperse. She put out every arrow but one, that managed to graze Thom's arm.

"Ouch!" Thom shouted as he placed his hand over the exposed, burnt and blistering patch of skin on his arm.

"You okay?" Semaj asked glancing at his friend.

"I'll be fine but it seems the crystal and all its magic is on the other side," Thom answered as not being able to call his magic to heal his burn confirmed his fears, he was powerless here.

"Semaj, we will hold him off but you need to work on waking up and getting us out of here. I don't think we can really be hurt here but we can't risk him finding out who the Chosen One is," Anna said as she focused on the area of bridge in front of Lucian and caused a wall of fire to shoot straight up separating him from them.

Semaj watched the flaming wall as he tried to will himself awake. In the past when Lucian had arrived, he had been able to snap out of it, but for some reason he was being held here and he did not know why. He kept trying, but something at the wall of fire pulled for his attention along with a high pitch laugh.

"You use fire when my primary magic is fire based?" Lucian laughed as he called on his magic to make the wall of fire part, allowing him to step in-between.

Semaj watched as there seemed to be a little friction between Anna's Magesti created fire and the magic Lucian was using on it, but both seemed to adapt with each other. Almost as if Lucian had a connection to the Magesti. Semaj could see the evil man's lips moving but did not need to hear anything to know another spell was being cast. Semaj gave a call of warning as Lucian released his spell, waved his arms up, over and down in an arch motion causing the two walls of fire to arch down, merge and flow upon the ground towards the group like a river of fire.

"Noraxa, the bridge!" Ard-Rich commanded as the female Dwarf closed her eyes and called on her Magesti.

Still feeling weak, it took her longer to connect and push her power towards the bridge floor. The stones began to shake, crack and break apart but she feared that she would not get it to crumble before the river of fire reached them. She looked up at Ard-Rich and saw his face age as he closed his eyes and tapped into his Magesti. His arms began to extend and then his hands shifted and took on the shape of large mallets. He ran forward and at the edge of where Noraxa was causing a quake, brought his mallet shaped hands down with all his enhanced Océan strength. It was enough force that the bridge crumbled and fell to the depths below taking the river of fire with it. She was about to release her power, when a boost of strength came from Semaj patting her back with gratitude, causing her to give one final push to make a quake so strong it took the rest of the bridge from where it collapsed to the end of the arch path down to the depths below, taking Lucian with it.

"We stopped him, here, but he'll be coming for us with his army out there," Ard-Rich said as he walked away from the edge that had collapsed.

"We need to get back to real world," Anna said turning to Semaj.

"I'm trying," Semaj said as he closed his eyes, feeling something help and attack his abilities all at the same time. He gave another push and he looked at Noraxa who gasped suddenly.

"I think I'm waking up," the female Dwarf said, as she appeared to be fading away.

"Looks like it worked," Lucian said as he suddenly flew up from the depths and hovered near the edge of the crumbled bridge in a glow laced with magic and fire. "This dreamscape lets you do more than you ever thought possible, like flying or casting a spell to send non-Chosen Ones away."

"Don't worry, I'll bring help as fast as I," Noraxa started to say before vanishing all together.

"We have to do something before he finds out the truth," Ard-Rich called out to the three young ones as he stood and faced their attacker.

"Be gone!" Lucian shouted as he released his spell again hitting the old man with a blast of fiery magic that caused him to fade away.

"So it wasn't me?" Semaj asked quietly to himself as he looked where Noraxa and Ard-Rich had been and then up at Lucian, feeling what he felt before coming from the man in front of him.

"We won't let you and your evil prevail," Anna declared as she grabbed her daggers and sent them flying through the air.

"Foolish girl," Lucian laughed as he brought himself down onto the edge of the bridge causing the magical glow around him to shift and deflect the daggers before extinguishing. "I know you're not the Chosen One. That leaves just you two, but which one?"

Semaj felt his opponent working up a spell again and he closed his eyes. Screaming internally at his powers, that if it would not send them all back, to at least show him what he needed to see. He started to feel something odd happening when Lucian released his spell. Semaj gulped as a strange sensation came over him and he suddenly vanished from sight.

"I figured the Chosen One was a coward but here is proof. Standing behind everyone for protection and letting them do all the fighting. I had a feeling it was you, even before my spell sent the other one away."

"I will stop you!" Thom shouted taking the que and, no matter what happened next, solidifying Lucian's belief that Thom was the one he was looking for to protect his friend, the true Chosen One.

"No, you won't. Not here or back out there. Now, I hate to be a party downer, but I need to get back to the real world." Lucian smiled and then cast one final spell that caused him to explode in a flash of fiery light obliterating the rest of the bridge with Anna and Thom on it.

****

Semaj opened his eyes and looked around. Was he dead? Back in the real world? As he stood up, he could sense he was still in the dreamscape caused by his abilities. Where was he? There was no sign of the bridge, Lucian or his friends. Did Lucian send him here? No, his gut told him that his powers had granted one of his demands, to take him to what he needed to see before leaving this place.

Semaj looked around and noticed he was standing in what looked like a dining area. There was plenty of food and scraps everywhere, but no sign of life of any kind. The room appeared to be completely empty. As he started to walk towards a door, he heard something sniffle. He turned to see something under the table.

"Hello?" Semaj knelt down and peaked under the table.

"Please don't hurt me," a voice answered back.

"You're the creature that was with Lucian and ran away," Semaj said recognizing the odd creature. "I won't hurt you if you promise the same."

Semaj stepped away from the table as the creature crawled out from under the table and stood up. Semaj fidgeted nervously as the creature moved closer, towering over him. Unlike most of the creatures he had come across on this quest of his, this one bore a slight smile and despite his appearance, gave off a friendly vibe. It was proving true, that the Magestics were made up of all manner of creatures and beings. Humans were not the only ones that possessed the power of the Magesti.

"What is this place?" The Magestic asked.

"I'm not really sure. It's almost like a dream world that the Magesti pulls those like us into." Semaj said, trying to be careful, as he did not know if this Magestic was a potential friend and ally or was loyal to Lucian.

"So, you are like me? Can do strange things?" The Magestic asked holding up his gloved hands and staring at them with fear.

"You could say that. I am Semaj." He was vague but figured there was no harm in giving up his name, just not *who* he really was.

"Oltar, King of the Orgites."

"Pleasure to make your acquaintance, your highness. What brings you away from your kingdom? Does Lucian have you prisoner?" Semaj asked carefully feeling out the creature before him.

"No, I am with him of my own free will," Oltar said but then trailed off and turned away.

"But?" Semaj pried.

"I discovered that I could do things, bad things and didn't know why. When I met Lucian, he explained I was special and that he could help me understand my power and help him to bring justice back to the world of Bergonia for the creatures of magic and stop the evil being known as the Chosen One. Thing is, the more I am with him and after seeing him in this strange place of dreams, I am not sure who is evil and who is not," Oltar said turning back to face Semaj.

Semaj stared at the Orgite and reached out with his ability and saw an aura come alive around Oltar. It was grey and images of sickness and decay flashed within the aura. "You bare the Magesti of Death."

"It appears that much is true. Lucian said it is a good thing, but how can causing death be good?"

"That is the only thing Lucian and I agree on. Your gift is meant for good, but not anything else Lucian has said or represents. Each Magestic has the ability to harness their own Magesti and with all the Magestics joining with the Chosen One we can protect all from the coming evil."

"My mind is fuzzy, but I do recall the dream with the Dragon and I feel that you were there. Which Magesti are you?"

"Then you must remember, the Chosen One is not the evil one. Lucian is leading the evil forces of Drol Greb. I agree, what the humans did to the creatures of magic was unacceptable, but what Drol Greb plans is worse. He plans to invade Bergonia and completely destroy and conquer it, using all manner of beings to achieve this. Each of the Magestics are descended from an original group that had stopped Drol Greb once before many, many years ago. The Magesti has awakened in each of the descendants now that this evil is trying to return. The Chosen One must now bring all the Magestics together and stop him. Only by doing this will Bergonia be saved and can move towards a more peaceful world for all, humans and creatures of magic," Semaj explained all that he had come to learn and accept since taking this journey from his home.

"It's a lot to take in," Oltar said as he wondered if his hunger to explore was more than he intended to bite off.

"I know how you feel. Until this, I was happily living on a farm where everything I've experienced and encountered were things of unmentioned stories. What I do know is that Lucian is on the wrong side and we must come together to stop him for the good of Bergonia," Semaj said convincing himself of his role for the first time.

"How do I know you are telling the truth and Lucian is really the evil one?"

"Because he is," a strange crackly voice answered from behind them.

Semaj turned to see a small strange looking shape stepping out from behind the large chair at the head of the dining table. He could tell it had to be a Goblin, but something was keeping its features and appearance blurred. Reaching out, Semaj tried to see past the masquerade, but only saw a gold aura surround the Goblin-like figure with a brain and other images he could not quite make out. Something within and from without, assured him he was looking at the second mysterious Magestic.

"Who are you?" Oltar asked.

"I am like you and from what I've gathered from the human's mind, he is telling the truth. I was at the dream with the Dragon and now with clarity I know I possess the Magesti of the Mind," the creature answered.

"Why can't we see your face?" Semaj asked worried that his identity had been exposed to something he didn't know was friend or foe.

"Unlike Oltar, I am a prisoner of the Gooblyn King. Forced to help him. He doesn't know what I am. He thinks I am a Goblin wizard of sorts and forces me to aid him. If my identity was exposed or others knew I existed and King Snoog wasn't the one with the powers, I would be killed. In the real world, I am not as smart and only get impressions and minor telepathy, but here I seem to be capable of more. Let me show you."

Semaj could feel the familiar tug when a Magesti was being used. As he started to reach out he instantly felt like he was slammed into a wall. The impact on his mind was so hard that he actually fell back onto his bottom. He looked over at Oltar but his vision shifted and he started seeing images, select ones from his own memory playing out for the Orgite King to see. After a few seconds, the images vanished and despite a small headache, he was fine. Oltar was rubbing his head as well as their Goblin friend who looked weakened and almost losing control over his coverup.

Don't worry, I only showed him what he needed to know. Your identity as the Chosen One will be kept safe.

"What?" Semaj asked as the words still echoed in his mind.

I'm in your mind. Only you can hear me. Just think it and I can hear you.

How do I know I can trust you and you won't reveal me to Lucian or Snoog?

I am not like the other Goblins. I want a better life. A life of freedom. One where we all live free and I believe the Chosen One can do that, not Lucian, I believe in you.

I can sense something else. What do you want? Why keep my secret?

Revealing your identity could lead to more focus on you and stopping you. In return for helping you and joining you, you must help me. Free me and protect me from Snoog.

"We are headed to the Gooblyn City now. Some of my friends are fighting the Goblins now in the real world. We thought we were coming for one but we will come for both Magestics, if you join us," Semaj said out load, looking towards Oltar.

"I don't know what that was, but memories can't lie. If I can join you and help you in any way, I will," *but not at the cost of my colony's safety and peace*, Oltar finished to himself.

"You can't side with Lucian. All of our colonies can still live in peace if we all side with the Chosen One," the Goblin snarled at the Orgite.

"Stay out of my mind!"

"You really shouldn't use your gifts like that, especially on friends and allies," Semaj said as he realized he would see if Essej knew any tricks to protect his mind from invasion. He did not fear the new Magestic but he was still cautious.

"Sorry, like I said before, here I can do more than in the real world."

"You know both of us, why not tell us who you are?" Oltar asked the featureless Goblin.

"Not yet, until my freedom is secured."

"Then how will we find you?" Semaj asked.

"When you get to the Gooblyn City, I will find you."

"Semaj, you seem to be fading," Oltar said as Semaj looked down at his translucent hands.

"I must have seen what I was meant to see. Don't worry, I will be coming for both of you. Oltar, you will see, no good will come of you and your people succumbing to Lucian's will," Semaj said as he closed his eyes and willed himself awake and pushing the same for the rest of his friends. He opened his eyes and saw the two Magestics were gone just as he felt his body jerk awake.

Chapter Thirty-One:
Goblins Everywhere

"Semaj, no!" Essej screamed but was too late.
Something had triggered a spark between Anna and the boy and now a wave of fire had blasted outwards. He saw Semaj fall to the ground as the Goblins roared in outrage at the unintentional attack. Essej began to call on his powers over the wind when he felt a familiar tugging. Semaj was pulling at and calling to the Mejesti. Essej redirected his powers and sent instructions onto the wind with great speed to Thom, whose crystal seemed to be already reacting to his best friend's gifts.

"Essej?"Ard-Rich asked his old friend in alarm.

"Semaj caused a reaction with Anna's Magesti and is now pulling everyone into his power's dreamscape," Essej said making sure his words only fell on Ard-Rich's ears. He then shifted to see Thom burst in magical light as he and his crystal worked their magic.

"Anna's down," Nat said, holding back a smile, as the girl fell down next to Semaj moments before a magical light left Thom and then engulfed the entire area in a quick blinding explosive pulse. "There's too much magic and energy going on around us for me to tell what happened to them. Is there a magic user attacking us?"

Seeing the Elf searching frantically Essej had to ease her mind by giving her a partial truth. "There is no magic user attacking. They are asleep and Thom's magic is both preventing and causing the rest of us from joining them."

"Send word to King Snoog. Goblins, Hobgoblins, attack!" Essej heard one of the fowl creatures scream while a small figure raced off towards the Gooblyn City.

Essej knew he had to stop the Goblin from getting help. He began to focus on the Goblin, wings forming and starting to rise into the air when he started to feel sleep overcome him. He glanced at Thom, urging more effort. If he was pulled in, they would be defenseless and at the mercy of the Goblins and Drol Greb's forces would find victory. Essej almost felt defeated when a blast of magical energy hit him, severing the connection and giving him a newfound strength. Thom had succeeded. He had full control over his body and mind.

"The boy's succeeding. Nat is fine and I feel the connection severing," Ard-Rich said while Essej, seeing the Goblin gone, took flight.

Essej was high in the air and willed his eyes to focus. Heading towards the Gooblyn City, he saw the running shape of the Goblin. Essej, reaching out with his powers, commanded the wind to lift a small tree branch and thrust it forward with great speed and strength. Essej cheered to himself when he saw the Goblin jerk, drop and lay still. He may be ancient, but he still had it. No time for celebrations. Essej refocused his pull on the winds back to snuffing out the fires and pushing the Goblin forces away from his group.

"I'll make sure nothing gets close to Semaj," Nat said as wrist blades extended and she took a defensive stance by Semaj's sleeping body. She still did not understand what was causing this but she hoped Thom would end it soon. In the meantime, she had to focus on the battle and keep Semaj safe.

"Good, I'll, I'll," Ard-Rich started to say when he felt something weird come over him. It was not from Thom's crystal or Semaj's pull into the dreamscape, but his Magesti itself. His vision blurred and he suddenly saw a girl, with a tail, as if she were being drawn into a sleep. No! He could not allow her to be pulled in. Reaching out with his Magesti to connect with the girl's Magesti, he tried to counteract with Thom and Semaj's powers. A powerful sensation passed between him, Thom and the girl and in a flash, the girl snapped back to where she was and Ard-Rich accepted the trade and gave into the sleep.

"Sorry, it had to be done," Ard-Rich whispered, glancing around to see everyone battling before resting his eyes on Thom. Right before he blacked out, he saw the boy split in two.

"We lost Ard-Rich," Nat said as she saw the Océan collapse and then freeze in her steps as she glanced over to Thom, who appeared to be the one causing all this magic.

In a display of magical lights, she watched Thom literally split in two. In panic that he had been attacked by an unseen foe, she looked around and saw nothing. She then looked back to Thom to see him vanish from sight leaving his second form behind, translucent and wearing a very solid and brightly glowing crystal.

"Natureza, the Goblins are breaking through," Essej called out as he sent a strong gust of wind to lift Ard-Rich up and toss him next to the other two sleeping bodies.

"It's just the two of us now," Nat grumbled as she saw the Hobgoblins pushing past the wind and charging towards her.

Nat leapt through the air, coming down between the sleeping and the attacking hoard. With quick speed and accuracy, she used her wrist blades to slice and stab any that got close to Semaj and the other bodies. Nat could not believe where she had ended up in her journey. Setting off she had been fully committed to Lucian and had every intent on finding the Chosen One for him. In reality, she should be assisting the Goblins in this battle, not killing them. Somehow, things had changed for her the moment she had met Semaj.

He was different from anyone she had ever met. Simple, polite and very good looking. He had no powers and there was nothing special about him. He had got mixed up with his friends and ended up joining them on their mission to protect the Chosen One, find the Magestics and stop Drol Greb, which meant coming to odds with Lucian and stopping him as well. She never thought she would go against her longtime friend or fall for another man, but here she was defending Semaj with her life.

Not only did she like Semaj, but the longer she traveled with the group, she grew less concerned with finding out who the Chosen One was and more about truly wanting to help them, help Semaj. She was no fool and not one to be blinded or tricked by anyone. She had come to see that Lucian was on the wrong side. The Chosen One was not evil. Drol Greb and Docanesto were the ones with ill intent against Bergonia and the races that inhabited her. She still did not think Lucian was the evil one. Just maybe his fathers had misled him. If she could talk to him, she knew she could convince him that he should be helping them and not trying to kill them.

She heard a hungry growl and turned to see a pack of Hobgoblins move from behind and advance towards Semaj. Nat turned to meet them, but was attacked by two Hobgoblins from the other side. She swore, knowing she had let herself get distracted by her thoughts. This mistake could cost her or Semaj their lives. As she wrestled with the two Hobgoblins, a strange force of energy hit them and propelled them up and away from her. She quickly leapt to her feet to find the source of the blast.

Standing off to the side was the figure of Thom. He was translucent and almost spirit like. The crystal around his neck was glowing very bright and appeared to be very solid. Looking at his eyes, he seemed to be in a hypnotized state. His lips moving, calling on spells but it was as if the crystal or something else was controlling him. Another magical spell was let loose, hitting the Hobgoblins that were about to attack Semaj and the other sleeping bodies, blasting them to pieces. Thom, without pausing, shifted and sent more magical blasts at the attacking hoard of Hobgoblins and Goblins.

"Thom, are you with us?" Nat asked, taking out two more fowl creatures while stepping through the burning ground, her abilities allowing her to not be affected by the heat of the fires still burning.

"It appears he has managed to split himself in two. His body going into where the other's minds are while his crystal animates his spirit and magic to help fight out here," Essej said more to himself in amazement than actually explaining anything to the female Elf.

"At least the sensation to sleep is gone," Nat added as she took another glance at the crystal around Thom's ghost-like form. She felt something more from Thom and his magic now. If she had any doubts before, they were now gone after this. There was no other explanation than Thom was the Chosen One. Just like Semaj, she had grown a fondness for the young magic user and, Chosen One or not, she would stand by him.

Essej glanced at the Wild Elf, still not knowing what game she was playing or what she was truly up to, and nodded. Semaj trusted her and so far, her actions showed no ill towards them or Semaj. If she had started out as a spy for Drol Greb, it appeared that was no longer the case. Something or someone had moved her to their side, unless she was really committed to her deception. Either way, she would prove useful in this fight and they needed her. For now, he would keep an eye on her and be ready to strike the moment she stopped being an ally.

A sharp pain brought his mind and eyes back from the Wild Elf and down to his leg. His scaly skin and distance in the air had prevented the poorly thrown Goblin spear from impaling him, but his age and growing tired body did allow the very sharp tip to graze him with a cut. It was nothing serious, but the shock of it caused him to lose concentration and drop to the ground, wings vanishing and skin reverting back allowing the cut to throb and seep a little more blood. With a cheer of victory, the Goblins charged right at him to finish the job.

In his younger days, he would have finished them off with no problems, but his body and powers were not what they used to be. He could feel the toll it was taking on him. If he spent all his energy now, he feared he might not have anything left for the battle yet to come when they faced Docanesto's forces at the Gooblyn City. Essej Slowly got to his feet, making eye contact with the hoard of creatures charging him, weapons ready, and reached out to the wind in hopes he had enough left in him. He could hear Nat calling out from behind him. "Essej, we are completely surrounded!"

Essej tried to concentrate, tuning out the Wild Elf. Just as he felt his connection with the air, something very hard hit him in the chest knocking him off his feet and taking the very breath and hold on his power away from him. Cupping his chest in pain, he saw a large rock lying next to him. He heard a cheer and saw the vicious creature raise another rock and smile as dozens of its brethren ran past trying to be the first to take their wounded prey. Essej, unable to catch his breath or strength, waited for the final blow from his enemy. He saw the rock and several spears headed right at him and pushed himself to fight back. Angry screams rose as all weapons and Goblins suddenly were met by a strong force and deflected backwards. Essej was confused for a moment, as he knew he had not been the one that had caused this.

The old Huelgon managed to get to his feet as he watched the space in front of him begin to glow with a strange white-blue energy. The cries of the enemy grew as Essej looked up and around to see that a magical shield had formed all around them, a dome of white-blue light that easily kept the Goblins, Hobgoblins and their weapons from breaking through. Essej knew who was responsible before he turned and saw it with his own eyes. Standing in the middle, next to their sleeping companions, was Thom's spirit form, arms raised as magical energy flowed from them and his crystal to the top of the shield he had created.

"How long do you think he can hold this?" Nat asked, while she shifted her attention from Thom to the massive hoard of creatures piling up and around the entire magical dome and finally resting upon Essej.

"I do not know, but the moment he stops, we will be overwhelmed," Essej said as he wrapped a piece of torn cloth around his already slowly healing cut.

"Thom, can you hear me? We need you to fly us all out of here or something," Nat pleaded as she moved away from Essej and closer to the magic user.

"The state he is in, there are limits to his magic. We should count our blessing he has managed to help us thus far," Essej said, the growing number of Goblins attacking and piling up against the magical barrier making him nervous.

"You can't use your power over the wind to blow them all away?"

"Even in my younger days, a feat like that against so many in such a solid, congested mass would take power and strength I fear I am lacking at this time." Nat could hear the truth in the rasp of the ancient being's voice.

Nat knew she had to do something. She had come too far to die at the hands of these petty low-level creatures and she could not save herself if it meant abandoning Semaj to a terrible fate. Nat swore at her newly welcomed weakness as she stared at the sleeping body and then knelt down, touched her fingers to the ground and closed her eyes. There had to be some animal out in this awful land that she could connect to and urge to help them against the Goblins. There was nothing within range. She was ready to give up when something nibbled at the edge of her senses. Eyes widening, she pushed with one final plea. "Hope this works."

"What did you do?" Essej asked as he felt something from the Wild Elf and then, with his heightened senses, heard a strange call that he had not heard in many lifetimes as moisture began to seep up from the ground, murky, muddy water slowly coating the ground.

"Saving our lives," Nat declared, sounding exhausted as she moved to prop the sleeping bodies up so they would not drown. Thom's magical shield would protect them from what was about to come but it would not hold back all the water seeping from the ground.

The creatures stopped and turned as many of them started sliding down from the edges of the shield in result of the rising muddy water from the ground that now started to tremble. Essej went to one knee as he eyed the now thin-coated land outside the shield and then fell back as something erupted from the ground followed by a hoarse, gurgling call. A pale white, circular creature, about three feet wide and completely featureless except for a large mouth housing rotating sharp teeth and small, hair-like tentacles covering its ten-foot long body.

"An Earthern Parasite," Essej whispered as the large worm-like creature slammed onto the ground, crushing and smacking back the Goblins and Hobgoblins with its body as it moved in a slithering motion as it finished emerging from the hole. Once its tail end was fully out, a rush of water gushed out like a geyser, the hole closing up behind causing the water to land upon the ground and start flooding the area outside the shield. The Earthern Parasite whipped around on swampy land, giving off more calls before it tilted its gaping mouth back down upon the ground and slowly worked its way back down into the ground.

"I was surprised how many were located deep down under Ogra. It took everything in me to push and convince them to shoot straight to the surface and then return back from where they came," Nat said as the ground shook, followed by the same call, a few dozen of the Earthern Parasites erupted near them and throughout the area around the battlefield as well as slightly down to the more southern area. It did not take long before the creatures were back into the ground leaving the surrounding area an instant swampland, water knee high outside of the magical shield and luckily only ankle high inside.

"Why would you risk unleashing those things unchecked back upon the surface world just to flood our enemy? The water will soon flow and recede out across the land and we'll be back to where we are but only fighting in the mud," Essej scolded as he saw the drowning enemy starting to gain their footing as the water slowly began to go down.

Nat smiled. The Earthen Parasites were one of the very few creatures that only the older, more advanced races remembered. They used to roam across Bergonia, causing destruction and instigating mayhem until they were forced to migrate deeper into Bergonia's earth. Far enough down that they never came near the surface again, content in burrowing deep within the earth, their ability to draw moisture to them to drink, and moisten the dirt to burrow through with ease and speed. Their tentacles were used to help them move but also move the dirt around them to reseal the holes and tunnels they made instantly. With them gone, earthquakes and sinkholes, among other things vanished.

"Don't worry, they are long gone and headed back down deep below. I pushed enough that they will forget they were up here or ever want to venture back up to the surface. I just needed them to get our real back up," Nat said as two different sounds rose into the air, but only one that made Essej's eyes widen with realization.

The first sound was that of the Goblins and Hobgoblins screaming in terror as those that had survived the flash flood and crushing of the parasite now faced a new threat. Essej realized the flash flood was only meant to make it easier and faster for the Snakzards to reach them and feast upon the Goblins. The half snake, half lizard creatures leapt from the water to expand and swallow whole any of their prey that had been tossed in to the air. For those thinking they were lucky enough to move to dryer, less watered areas still were attacked by the Snakzards that sprouted legs and hunted on land and into the trees.

The Second was the call Essej had thought he heard and hoped he was wrong when he first scolded Nat. Unfortunately, it was as he feared, the one thing that desired and fed upon the Earthern Parasite and the main reason the parasites had to be driven deep down away from the surface world of Bergoina – The Swarm. The Swarm were thousands of tiny insects that congregated and moved together as one when the scent and sound of the Earthen Parasite ignited their hunger and they attacked to feed. No one knew why the Swarm only feeds on the Earthern Parasites, but any race or being in their path was still at danger. If provoked, angered or simply in the way, the Swarm would attack. Their razor sharp stingers could cut through or penetrate almost any flesh resulting in certain death to any victim engulfed by the Swarm.

"What have you brought back upon our world?" Essej asked as he looked up into the sky at the large massive black moving cloud approaching them.

"We needed help and when I felt the presence of the Earthen Parasite I figured our only option was using them to bring the Snakzards closer to us. Then the Swarm would take care of and drive them away along with the Goblins when they realized their desired feast was no longer here," Nat said, knowing her plan was not completely thought out.

"What about the Swarm? It took years after the Earthen Parasites left for them to finally die off and vanish," Essej said as the sky immediately around their shield went dark with the buzzing of the Swarm and their victim's cries and screams.

"If you use your control over the wind and I push for them to leave, I'm sure that should do the trick." Nat knew she did not sound very confident with her statement.

"Not sure what I've missed but looks like your shield is about to go." A voice interrupted the argument, causing Nat and Essej to look behind them and see Ard-Rich getting to his feet. They both quickly glanced from a swaying Thom to a slowly flickering shield of magic.

"You're awake!" Essej screamed in excitement as he looked down to see Anna and Semaj still asleep and then taking in the disappointment at no signs of them waking.

"Looks like things aren't any better in the outside world," Ard-Rich trailed off as he saw the Swarm and Snakzards attacking each other and the Goblins.

"What happened? Where's Semaj?" Nat asked as she knelt down and gave the boy a gentle shake.

"Lucian attacked us and sent me back here. Thom, Anna and Semaj must still be fighting him," Ard-Rich answered as he tried to touch the crystal and ghost form of Thom but drew his hand back from the instant shock.

"Lucian has been trying to get at the Chosen One this way for a long time now. Looks like he finally succeeded," Essej mumbled as he looked at his old friend.

"He knew it wasn't me," Ard-Rich started to say when a loud scream interrupted him.

They all turned to see Thom, screaming as his body became solid as his crystal and shield flickered out seconds before he went silent and collapsed into Ard-Rich's arms. Nat took as protective stance over Semaj as the two older men moved closer to her and away from the Swarm that was now free to reach them. Nat saw Essej trying to call on his gifts when a sudden flash of light, heat and smell of burnt insect drew her attention. There was now walls of fire helping separate them from the deadly insects.

"Anna, my child, glad to have you back," Essej smiled with relief.

"Why isn't Semaj awake?" Nat demanded, holding his body up out of the muddy water that had now rushed in and slowly receded.

"He's not? I was hoping that's what happened to him." Anna was now worried trying not to let this news take her focus away from the fire that was keeping back the strange insects. The ground was wet, so she had to really push herself to make the ground ignite in flames and then shoot as far up as she could to make the walls tall enough to keep out the Swarm. She was working on a boost from Semaj, Thom and the dream world and did not know how long she could manage this great feat of fire.

"Anna, what happened after I left?" Ard-Rich asked, gently placing Thom next to Semaj, glancing upwards in relief to see the Swarm was moving away from the fire and focusing their attention on the Goblins and Snakzards instead of the opening clear above the walls of fire.

"Semaj vanished right before Lucian launched an attack on me and Thom. I assumed he came back here," Anna swallowed hard before continuing, "Lucian will be coming and he has declared his sights on Thom."

"Lucian now knows what I've discovered," Nat whispered to herself as she looked at Thom and then over to Semaj and shouted with relief.

"Semaj, thank Venēăh you are okay," Essej praised as he moved towards the boy, who was rubbing his eyes as he quickly stood up.

"Where did you go?" Anna demanded.

"Thom?" Semaj panicked looking down at his friend.

"He'll be okay once he recovers from overdoing his magic," Essej responded, urging Semaj back on track.

"I was pulled to a different place within the dream place. I met the two Magestics that are being held in the Gooblyn City."

"Who are they?" Ard-Rich asked.

"One is the Orgite King and the other is a Goblin. The king is there by choice but the other is being held prisoner by King Snoog. The Goblin will help us if we free him but Oltar, he is on the fence on who to trust, us or Lucian. I promised them both we would come for them."

"Then we go and free them while protecting the Chosen One," Essej said as he saw Nat look down at Thom, who was starting to wake. For now, it seemed wise to let the Wild Elf and Lucian believe what they thought they knew.

"We have to be careful, whether Oltar is there on his own or not, the queen may not take too kindly to him being away from the Orgite Colony," Nat added as she saw the light from the fire dimming.

"Sorry, I don't think I can hold this much longer," Anna Sparks said as her strength started to fade with her fire.

Semaj, for the first time, took a look at what was transpiring outside the walls of fire. There were swarms of small insects flying everywhere attacking snake-like creatures that fed on some with satisfying hunger for more while others died from the insects that managed to cut their way out from their heads. Despite all the commotion of the two battling creatures, there were still Goblins everywhere, trying not to get caught in the middle. "What are those things?"

"According to my books, they are the Swarm and should be extinct due to…"

"The Earthern Parasites, which are back as well thanks to her," Ard-Rich interrupted Thom with a glare at Nat.

"It was the only option to save us."

"We can all see how that's working out," Anna spat back at the Elf as she started to feel feint.

"In fairness, the Goblin's focus on us has drifted," Semaj added and then went silent from a return death glare.

"But the Snakzards are showing no fear from the Swarm. It's actually drawing them," Ard-Rich said as he and the group watched the battle raging outside the slowly fading wall of fire.

"How are you feeling?" Essej asked as he made his way towards Thom.

"That whole being split between the real and dream worlds has left me spent. I barely have the strength to stand." Thom said as he even felt his connection to the crystal's ability to trigger his memory of everything he has read in his books to weaken. Thom glanced down, still amazed how his books managed to have stayed with him during this journey. *Magic.* Thom chuckled to himself as he tapped the bag and then looked at his companions.

"That's what I was afraid of. I need you to gather your strength and get us to where we need to be," Essej said as Nat turned to the crystal wearer and smiled, "You have been chosen, you can do it. Get us to the Gooblyn City just like you had sent Semaj in the dream world."

Thom nodded at Nat as Essej continued to bark orders. "Wild Elf, you too must give all you got. I need you to push at both the Swarm and the Snakzards to urge them to return from where they came. While you do that I will use my gifts with the wind to help propel the Swarm up and away and Anna will redirect her fire to the ground and make a moving wall driving the Snakzards and any Goblins and Hobgoblins away."

"With you two doing that, combined with Nat urging them to leave should do the trick. Semaj and I will do what we can to fend off anything that might venture through," Ard-Rich said as he concentrated and his face seemed to age as his arms and hands shifted into sharp blade-like weapons.

"I don't," Anna began to say when words upon the air landed quietly upon her and Semaj's ears made her stop and nod at Essej.

"Now!" Essej commanded as Anna reached out and brought the walls of fire down to ankle height. Nat then closed her eyes touched the ground with one hand and reached toward the air with the other. Once she felt the connection with the Swarm and Snakzards she urged them to leave and go back from which they came. Once the creatures paused Essej nodded at Semaj and Anna before he gave everything he had to command the wind to swoop in and push the Swarm upwards with all its might.

With Nat distracted, Semaj reached deep within himself and then placed his hand upon Anna's back. A powerful force of energy passed between him and his friend. Anna felt the Magesti within her suddenly get a power boost, a new-found strength and energy coursed through her body. Semaj removed his hand and stepped back as Anna used her infused power to ignite the fire around them. The fire flared and then started moving outwards and away from Anna and her group, making the Snakzards and Goblins move away to avoid being burned. Anna kept pushing, urging the fire to keep going as far as it could to drive their enemies away.

"It's working," Semaj cheered as he saw the Swarm heading straight up and out of sight.

"Not entirely," Ard-Rich said as a couple Hobgoblins leapt through the fire and started running towards them.

The Océan met the two and managed to take them down with his bladed arms. He was about to move back towards his group when two more leapt through. As he fought them and drove his blades through their necks he saw dozens more, encouraged by the Goblins, ready to leap past the fire. The fire was getting farther away but the Goblins had no intention of leaving like the Swarm or Snakzards had. Ard-Rich ran back to the group, "Thom, do what you're going to do. Were about to be attacked again."

Thom looked up as Semaj touched his shoulder with encouragement. He continued to concentrate on his crystal, trying to find the strength and power to get them out of this situation. Whispers, followed by words swirled within his mind as the crystal began to glow again. Thom gave in to the crystal and the magic, letting the words in his mind travel to his lips. "Keta Su Omfr Rehe!"

Semaj jumped back as light erupted from the crystal and six balls of white-blue light shot out from Thom's out stretched hand. Semaj drew his sword as the balls of magic swarmed around above their heads while hoards of Goblins and Hobgoblins made their way past the fire and moved towards them. They were coming from all around them. Semaj knew there was no way they could fight and survive against so many in their tired state. A group of Hobgoblins leapt upon Ard-Rich seconds before a ball of light hit where the Océan had stood.

"Semaj, the boost still has the fire moving for now, but I don't think I have anything left in me," Anna swayed as she brought her daggers to her hands ready for a battle she was not sure he had the strength to fight.

"You must all fight. I can't let up until I am confident the Swarm is pushed far enough up into the air that they take Nat's nudge to return from where they came," Essej said as he continued to propel the wind upwards with great force.

"Humans," Nat laughed at Anna, and drawing her weapons, she charged head on into a group of Goblins while Anna huffed and charged another group coming from another direction.

Semaj turned to Thom and saw he had dropped to one knee. Using the crystal and magic had really drained him. Whatever spell he had unleashed not only appeared to be doing nothing but make balls of light dance around but had sapped the last of his friend's energy. Semaj glanced around and could no longer see any of his friends and companions as they were consumed in battle. There were Goblins everywhere he turned. He glanced up and saw a ball of light floating above him. Semaj closed his eyes as he felt the ball hit him followed by the sound and force of Goblins grabbing him from all over. He tried to fight but a strange sensation overtook his body and he gave into the light and faded into the dark.

"Semaj, wake up!" He finally heard a voice and opened his eyes to find Essej standing over him.

"I'm alive?" Semaj asked as he looked down and padded his body. No stab wounds or blood. He then looked around, getting to his feet and sighed with relief. Standing all around him was his entire party, exhausted and alive.

"Thom saved us, barely," Nat said as she pushed past Anna and extended her hand to help Semaj up.

"Where are we?" Semaj asked as he could hear the commotion off in the distance and then saw they were not far away from what he had to guess was the Gooblyn City.

"The end of your journey," a woman said as a shadow casted over them and they all looked up to see a woman atop a large bat-like creature.

Chapter Thirty-Two:
The Rescue

"Drocana!" Nat shouted as the large Tazarian descended and landed between the group and the Gooblyn City.

"Natureza, we meet again. This time I will kill you," Drocana declared as she stood high upon her Tazarian, raising a large spear, ready to strike.

"There will be no killing, yet," a voice commanded as everyone turned to see a man riding a large black hound out of the front gates of the Gooblyn City surrounded and followed by six more hounds with riders as well as more Goblins and Hobgoblins gathering near and around the area.

"Great, more of those creatures," Thom said as he looked at Anna, trying to guess which of them looked more tired.

"You must be Lucian," Essej said identifying the young man leading the opposing force.

"I see you escaped my greeting party. I would have met you sooner but I was held up by an unexpected dream, Chosen One," Lucian smirked as he looked right at Thom.

"You're evil will end here," Thom shouted back.

"Nat, my dear, would you be so kind as to bring him to me?" Lucian motioned with his hand causing everyone, including Semaj to look right at the Wild Elf.

"I told you she was not to be trusted," Anna said, raising her weapons.

"Lucian, she isn't loyal. She tried to kill me when I tried to expose her and the Chosen One," Drocana said, spear aimed right at the Wild Elf.

"Nat would never betray us or Lucian," a voice came from a man upon a Fire Hound behind Lucian.

"Aksurh, main rule of a Barbarian, never trust anyone, especially those you call friend," Fylla grunted as she moved her hound up next to Aksurh.

"I guess we will see where her loyalty falls," Sev whispered as the Fire Fairy landed on Lucian's shoulder. "Notice her color tone?"

"Who is this?" Gabrielle asked as she looked at Nat, tapping her eye patch. "Another lover?" The pirate felt glares from both Nat and the Fire Fairy.

"I have every faith in you, Nat. For anyone to question her, means she did her job infiltrating the enemy and finding the Chosen One for me. Unlike my father's failed attempt at a spy," Lucian said locking eyes with Drocana, daughter of Docanesto.

"Is that true?" Semaj asked looking at Nat, his gut still telling him she was not bad, at least not anymore.

"Bring him!" Drocana commanded as the two creatures stepped forward, wings spreading.

"Drogans!" Anna exclaimed, looking at Thom, who was eyeing the creatures that had killed his boyfriend, Lars.

"No, you do not command this army," Lucian declared as a ball of fire left his hand and hit the Fire Elf off her Tazarian. "She will bring him to me, now!" Nat shivered at the tone and eye contact from her oldest friend and one-time companion. She was torn between what her mind and her heart were telling her to do.

"Lucian, I think maybe if we all sat down and talked," Nat started to say when Lucian leapt up so he was standing on the back of Frrr and screamed back at her.

"If you want to keep your head you will not defy me!"

"Don't talk to her that way," Semaj started to say when a strange feeling hit him when he made eye contact with the man. He was still far enough away from them but it was like he was seeing right into him.

Lucian hesitated for a second, shook off the feeling and redirected it towards his anger. How dare she question him in front of his army and side with someone other than him. She was supposed to be his. Raising up his hands he called forth his fire magic, creating a spear made of pure fire and launching it at the man who had dare talk back to him and seemed to have taken his girl's loyalty from him. The spear would have hit the mark if Nat had not pushed him aside and took the spear to her backside, confirming his suspicions as he did not intend to kill him but see how Nat felt.

"Nat!" Thom gasped as she lay on the ground, her back exposed and smoking from where the spear of fire had hit.

"I'll be fine," Nat said as her nature protected her from the fire being a true threat. She would just be a bit sore.

"You took a hit for me," Semaj said as he glanced at Anna causing her to blush and turn away and then look back at Nat and jerk back in surprise.

"Her ture form revealed," Drocana gloated as Lucian gave her a warning look.

"As well as her loyalties," Lucian growled to himself.

Semaj, look, I was right," Anna said now stepping between Semaj and whatever was in front of them, daggers ready.

"Semaj, Thom," Nat whispered as she looked at both boys as she looked at her hands and became speechless. That magic filled spear Lucian sent had forced her skin to shift back to its grey color and her hair to the color of night. She saw Semaj stare at her and then at Drocana. They looked the same, except her eyes were not red nor did she have red body markings or red streaks in her hair. Those she usually had created to fool those in Docanesto's army, letting them and Lucian thinks she had fully taken the fire.

"Nat, are you a Fire Elf? Are you really like Drocana?" Semaj asked as he still saw the good in her eyes.

"No, I never fully commited. You have to believe," was all Nat got out when Lucian's voice belted across the distance.

"You can have her. She is as dead to me as will anyone else that defies me or my fathers," Lucian decalred trying to hide the hurt from the betrayal of one of his friends.

"Lucian, I will not allow Drol Greb to destroy Bergonia. I stopped him once and I will do it again," Essej proclaimed as he moved front and center of the group, Ard-Rich joining him. They would have to worry about the Elf later.

"The sworn enemies of our fathers. Essej and the Chosen One must be brought down in the name of Drol Greb!" Drocana screamed as she mounted her Tazarian and this time, Lucian noted that those around him took notice of her words.

"Kill them all, except, I want the Chosen One unharmed, for now. Bring him to me alive!" Lucian commanded as the Goblins and Hobgoblins charged the group, followed soon after by the rest of his party leaving him, Sev and Gabrielle to hold back and observe.

"There's no way we can survive this," Semaj said as the enemy began to close in, taking his attention away from Nat, as she just sat there with pleading eyes and Anna standing near her with daggers ready.

"No, just the Chosen One has to," Essej said as he quickly commanded the wind to send a strong gust outwards to blow the enemy back and then dive back, down and around to create a cyclone of mud, water and dirt around them. "It won't keep them back for long but it will give a moment of privacy to make our next move."

"To do what? I don't think I have enough strength to teleport all of us again, maybe a few but not very far," Thom panicked as he suddenly felt the whispers that encouraged him to reach deep into himself and the crystal, looking for a spell or something to help them.

"The Chosen One needs to get into Gooblyn City, find the two Magestics and get out," Ard-Rich answered as he looked over at his old friend.

"How are we to do that?" Anna asked as she could hear the enemy getting closer as the windstorm started to weaken.

"Thom, you will teleport yourself, Semaj and Anna into the city or as close as you can and sneak in while the battle here distracts their attention," Essej said as he swallowed hard at the decision that he and his old friend had made.

"We can't leave you here to fight all them," Semaj said as he looked to Nat, who now stood up and composed herself.

"The three of us are the best equipped to fight here. I know trust in me has been tainted, but I will prove myself here fighting for you and your friends," Nat said as she took Semaj by the hand and then looked over to Thom. "Essej is right, as the Chosen One you are too important and until things get straightened out it is best that you three focus on your mission."

"We can't trust her," Anna said looking at Semaj and Essej.

"I can stay and fight."

"Not as well as the rest of us and we can focus better without worrying about you here," Nat said as she took the courage and kissed Semaj. She did not know if it was her, him or the awkwardness of the move, but she managed to miss and connect her lips on his chin. She stepped back quickly as Semaj slightly blushed but with a slight smile.

Anna all but screamed as she turned and faced the elders of the group. "Even if Thom manages to get us away from you, the second they see us gone," Anna objected as she tried not to look at what the traitor had just tried to do. Why was Semaj so blind?

"That is where I come in," Ard-Rich said as he stepped over, put his arm around Thom and Semaj and pulling them towards him in a quick hug. The contact with Semaj was just enough to trigger a boost to his Magesti before he let go, turned and now with two strange glowing hands, planted them on Thom's shoulders.

Ard-Rich stared into the young mage's eyes and called on his Magesti. With the boost he had received, he had the strength to wrap his power around himself and then extend it upon Thom. After a few seconds, the Océan stepped away, placed one hand on his chest and the other on his waist and closed his eyes. Keeping the image of Thom in his mind, he let the Magesti do the rest. It was not long before his body and very clothes shifted, twisted and reshaped themselves into something new.

"I don't believe it," Semaj said rubbing his shocked eyes as he stepped back and looked at two identical version of Thom. The only difference between Ard-Rich and Thom was that only one of them was wearing a glowing crystal around their neck.

"That will definitely make them think the Chosen One is still with us, until they notice the missing crystal and you two," Nat said, hating to be blunt and ruin the moment.

"Not necessarily. I am getting better with my magic, but most of what I do still comes from the crystal guiding me and putting images and spells into my head. The minute they started talking about their plan, I was guided and instructed," Thom interjected with excitement as the crystal began to glow brighter and Thom knelt down.

With a trance like state falling over his face, Thom picked up a rock about the size of his crystal. With his other hand, he grabbed his crystal and then touched it to the rock and pressed, muttering a bunch of words. Casting his spell, a white-blue light engulfed both hands and then faded. When he pulled his hands apart, his crystal fell back upon his chest while in his other hand the rock was now a glowing crystal just like the one around his neck. He handed the crystal to Ard-Rich, whose neck shifted as parts of it took shape to form a string that latched onto the glowing crystal and hold it against his chest making him look identical to Thom and his crystal.

"You can duplicate your crystal?" Anna asked in amazement.

"I wish. It is a spell of illusion. The rock only looks like my crystal but there is enough magic in the spell placed on it to give the wearer a little control over it," Thom said as Ard-Rich nodded, touched the crystal on his neck and concentrated.

The crystal on the Océan's neck flashed a light upon Anna and Semaj before it dimmed a little. Anna gasped as she saw a figure that looked just like her and Semaj appear right next to them. Thom laughed as Anna reached out and put her finger right through her twin. "Both are also illusion that Ard-Rich can control. I don't know how long the spell will last but this should help fool them long enough for us to do what we need to do."

"Go, now!" Essej commanded as he felt his control over the wind weakening.

Thom grabbed both his friend's hands, closed his eyes, found the words and then looked right at the Gooblyn City, "Keta Su Ideins!" In a blinding flash of light, the three were gone.

"Here they come," Nat said as one of the first Goblins ran through only to be stabbed by her wrist blades.

Ard-Rich killed two more Goblins as they found the mages fingers were now very sharp blades that sliced right across their throats. He pushed a few thoughts and hoped the illusions would work. Fake Anna put out her hands and created walls of fire that made the Goblins stop from advancing while fake Semaj ran around dodging and confusing the Hobgoblins, as they grew angry on why they could not get their claws on the human. With the fire illusion assisting, Essej was able to focus and choose more immediate threats to hit with gusts of wind.

"We may be fooling these unintelligent creatures but I think our cover is about to be blown," Nat said as she saw Lucian's forces and her friends now upon them.

****

"Wait, Nat," Semaj heard his voice fade out and come back along with his vision.

"Why are you worried about her? How can you trust her, now, after seeing her true form and yet another lie?"

"Anna, I can't explaine it, but I trust her," Semaj said thinking back to the almost kiss and trying not to blush.

"That's because of,"

"Anna, for the record, I trust her too."

"Fine, we can talk about this later," Anna said in a huff causing Semaj to look away and at their surroundings.

He did not need his sight to know they were no longer with their group. The smell alone told him Thom had succeeded. They were at the Gooblyn City, and from the look of things, he knew they were actually within the city walls. Semaj wrinkled his nose as he moved next to Thom.

"Wow, I've never smelt anything so bad, and I've been to your place," Thom coughed, trying to change the subject while dodging a glare from his best friend, but then got dizzy and stumbled.

"Are you okay? I know you've been practicing with Nat, but you've been pushing yourself too far with this magic of yours," Semaj asked as Anna frowned at the name but kept her eyes on their surroundings. Despite the battle going on with their friends outside, the Gooblyns inside the city carried on clueless with their lives.

"It won't be my magic that kills me," Thom laughed as he held his nose and looked around. "I was worried about us sneaking through this place but we've yet to be noticed."

"I think we might be getting some help," Semaj said as he could feel the tug of a Magestic using their abilities and when he concentrated, he could see a faint gold aura connected to the Magesti of the Mind. Semaj squinted his eyes and he thought loudly a note of thanks.

I am using a combination of my abilities to push them to not notice or pay attention to you and your friends. I am not that advanced in using my Magesti but the Gooblyns and my fellow Goblins have very simple minds. It also seems that with you near, I can easily speak fully with you with our minds.

Where are you? We will come free you.

Not yet. After the Orgite King fled the dream and before Lucian raced off to battle, Oltar was placed in a cell until Lucian got back. You must rescue him first.

Where are the dungeons?

I will help guide you.

"Semaj, are you okay?" Anna asked as she and Thom moved their absentminded friend back behind some boxes.

"One of the Magestics was talking to me," Semaj said as he blinked his eyes, shook his head and slightly rubbed his temples.

"Where is he?" Thom asked, looking around and questioning his friend's sanity.

"I don't see anyone but us," Anna added with a shrug towards Thom.

"He has the Magesti of the Mind. I could hear him in my head," Semaj snapped a little as he tapped his forehead.

"What did he say?" Thom asked while keeping an eye on all the disgusting creatures moving about all around them.

"He is helping keep us from being noticed. He said we need to find King Oltar first as he is being held prisoner." Semaj closed his eyes and while listening to the Magestic in his head, he reached out with his powers and felt a tug. "This way."

The three slowly moved, trying to stay in the shadows. Semaj trusted the voice in his head, but Anna did not want to press their luck and rely on the Magestic hiding them from view. Soon Semaj had led them to an area that was blocked by two Gooblyn guards. Semaj was sure the cells were past the guards as he felt a pull and the voice in his head confirmed it as well. Now they had to figure out how to get past the guards. The Magestic had indicated he could not hide them with a full on confrontation. "Any ideas?"

"I can probably knock them out," Thom suggested as he moved his fingers to his crystal.

"No, the glow of the crystal might give us away and you need to preserve your strength in case we need a fast getaway," Anna said and then smiled. "I got this."

Anna closed her eyes, connected with her Magesti, and then reached out until she came in touch with the area around the Gooblyn guard's heads. She knew attacking or killing them would not be the right option if they wanted to sneak in without detection. She willed the area around their heads to heat up and get hotter and hotter. She could see the beads of sweat forming on their faces. She was being careful to only heat the area and not cause it to burst into flame. She was beginning to think her plan would not work when the two guards passed out from the heat and conked their heads together propping each other up.

"You did it!" Semaj cheered as he looked at the guards who appeared to be asleep and upright.

Go!

"I'm told for us to move now," Semaj said as the three friends moved quickly across the room, past the guards and into the dungeon, unnoticed.

"Smells even worse in here," Thom gagged as he looked down the long room with cells on each side and only a few torches that barely lit the room.

There are never any guards inside. Only time a guard comes in is to provide food and water, if they remember. Most that are placed in there are forgotten about, until a guard remembers to dispose of their bodies. I will let you know if trouble comes your way.

"We are safe for now," Semaj said as he reached out and followed the pull, leading his friends down the rows of cells.

Semaj looked back and forth, as they passed the cells. Most were empty but many were filled with real sick looking creatures while others had bodies or bones of those that had died in their cells. It made him sad. No manor of creature, good, bad, human or magical deserved to be treated this way. It only reaffirmed his mission and what could happen if Drol Greb and his forces were to invade and take over Bergonia. His sadness paused when he felt a strong pull to his right followed by a message in his head. *In there.*

Semaj turned and moved closer to the cell and peered in. The lighting was poor but he could make out a fairly large figure. He did not need a description or an introduction to know that this was the Orgite and Magestic he had come to find. The Orgite looked up and smiled. "The voice said you were here for me."

"You can hear things too?" Thom asked as he and Anna stepped up next to Semaj.

"Not until now. Before, it was impressions and feelings that help was coming. Once you three stepped into the dungeon, the voice became clear and told me you were here to free me. Wait, I recognize all of you, from that strange dream I had before I woke up and Lucian threw me in here. I am Oltar." The Orgite King got to his feet and walked a few paces before the chain around his ankle stopped him.

"I am Semaj, this is Thom and Anna here is just like you," Semaj introduced.

"You are?"

"Yes, I'm a Magestic," Anna said as she held her hand up and caused a small flame to appear in her palm that helped light up their area.

"What can you do?" Thom asked as he found himself in awe of seeing another creature that he had only read from his books that he touched from within the pouch that seemed to magically keep them with him.

"I'm cursed. My touch can cause bad luck and death," Oltar said with fear as he held up his gloved hands causing Thom to take a nervous step back.

"Your powers are a gift not a curse," Anna assured the Orgite King as she looked at his gloved hands and then gave him a smile.

"That's what Lucian told me. That my gifts were special and I could do great things with them," Oltar said as he gave a doubtful stare to the three on the other side of his cell.

"This will probably be the only time I will admit that he is right. Your gift, the Magesti is very special and very important. In time you will learn to use and control them. I, with the help of my friends will train and be there for you. All the Magestics, including you, are Bergonia's champions to stop Drol

Greb," Semaj said in a voice even he noticed was growing more confident as he started to really accept his new role in life as the Chosen One.

"Semaj is right. Lucian is the evil one, not us," Anna added.

"I know what you say is true, now," Oltar agreed as he looked at his chain and then the bars of his cell that Lucian had placed him in.

"Then why are you with him?" Thom asked as he continued to look around for a way to open the cell.

"I always had the desire to explore, leave the safe walls of the Orgite Colony. Lucian came along, said the right things, promised to help me with my curse and I threw caution to the wind and snuck away with him. I was excited until the longer I was with him the more I saw he was not the good person I was fooled to believe," Oltar confessed.

"It's okay, what matters is we are here to get you out of here and join us," Semaj said as he shook the cell's bars.

"I can probably get it open," Thom said as he swayed a little, trying to find the spell and strength to cast it.

"There has to be another way. You need to reserve your strength," Anna said as she worried about the toll the magic use was taking on her friend.

"Allow me," Oltar said as he pulled his gloves off, grabbed the chain, closed his eyes and began to pull. Semaj instantly felt the tingling sensation of a Magesti being called upon. He watched as after a few pulls, the chain against the wall seemed to weaken and then break away from the wall. Feeling the drain from using his gift, Oltar stumbled over to the bars, gripping them with both hands to catch his balance. Semaj looked at the king as Thom interjected. "You could have freed yourself this whole time?"

"There is no way I could get past all of them out there. Even with my gifts I am not strong enough to take them all on, even if I was able to free myself." Oltar looked at the three as he moved his hands up and down the bars.

"You can do it, let me help you," Semaj said as he placed his hand on the Orgite's arm, causing the Orgite to jerk, not from the touch but from the power boost that passed between them.

Oltar could feel his Magesti flourish and flow though his entire body. With the touch from the boy he had added strength and seemed to gather an instinctive intuition on what he needed to do next. He pushed his power out of his body, through his hands and into the bars. He then reached out, felt the ends of the bars that touched all around the walls, floor and ceiling and commanded his Magesti to move to each of those points and weaken them. He felt the bars weakening as he pulled and soon fell back as the bars ripped away and crashed off to the side, freeing the Orgite King.

"That's one way of doing it," Thom joked as they all helped the Orgite to his feet.

"I can't believe what I…wait, you are…" Oltar began to say when a sharp pain in his head stopped him.

No, do not say it out loud. The identity of the Chosen One can not be risked of exposure. Now hurry, the guards out front woke but the noise from the cell breaking alerted them and they are on their way.

"We have incoming," Semaj said as Oltar realized the voice in his head had spoken to the human as well.

The two outside Gooblyn guards were entering quickly where the group had entered from. Anna stepped forward, ready to attack when Oltar stepped in front of them all. "I still got some power to work off."

Oltar reached out his arm and pointed at the two guards. Taking hold of the remaining boosted Magesti within him, he reached out and felt the area around the Gooblyns, and sent the entire left-over energy directly at them. The incoming guards suddenly tripped over each other, falling to the ground while accidently impaling each other with their spears. "I didn't mean to kill them."

"It's not your fault, you were working with boosted power. In time you will learn to better control your Magesti," Semaj assured the Magestic of Death.

"We better get moving," Anna said as they all felt a push in their heads for a sense of urgency.

"Wait, let me take care of this," Thom said as he closed his eyes, crystal glowing and then snapped his fingers. "Klesshac Easerel!" Oltar hopped grabbing his leg, more from shock than pain, as a blast of white-blue light zapped the shackle around his ankle causing it to open and fall away from the Orgite.

"That will make it easier to walk," Oltar said as he rubbed his ankle and then, turned, moved forward to follow after the three humans that were now traveling down the opposite end.

"Hurry, the Magestic in my mind told me there is a passage down at the far end that will lead us to where he is being held," Semaj said, rubbing his temple.

The four moved quickly down the length of cells until they came to a dead end. *There.* Semaj heard the voice and looked to the ground and saw what looked like a loose panel. Oltar walked over and pulled it aside to reveal a dark passageway. The three easily crawled into it while the Orgite King barely fit. Semaj was worried that the Orgite King was going to get stuck but managed to squeeze through. As they moved through the darkness, guided only by the sensations sent to them, they finally reached the end of the passage way and back out into the open.

"Where are we?" Anna asked as she stood up, looking around while Thom and Semaj helped pull Oltar through the passageway's exit.

"In throne room of King Snoog, Gooblyn City ruler," a quiet, hoarse voice came drawing their attention towards a large structure resembling a throne.

Semaj and Anna ran up to the throne and soon discovered a cloth covered box behind it. Anna pulled the cover off to reveal an average sized crate underneath. Both of them managed to pull the lip up to reveal a smaller figure inside. Semaj felt the pull, knowing this creature was the Magestic they were looking for. Anna used her Magesti to create a small flame in the palm of her hand to give them some light. Inside, the figure jerked back covering its eyes from the light causing Anna to gasp.

Semaj felt the impression in his mind and quickly motioned for Anna to move her flame back so its light would not hurt the creature's eyes from a source it had been deprived of for so long. The creature lowered its arm and stood up, peering right at Semaj. The creature came up barely above his waist, slightly hunched from being in the crate. His green skin had a slight pale color as well as its eyes were all white, large and glazed over from being devoid of light for so long. He only wore a piece of cloth around his waist section. Despite the Goblin's pale, scrawny and wobbly appearance, Semaj could see and feel the intelligence within its mind. The Goblin smiled. "Help out?"

Semaj and Anna carefully lifted the Goblin out of the crate he had been imprisoned in. "Who did this to you?" Anna asked already knowing the answer.

"Snoog," the Goblin choked out and then stared up with his weird large eyes. *I already know who all of you are. I am called Gort. Hope you all don't mind. With the Chosen One right here I can use my telepathy easier with all of you. Allows me to communicate better and saves on my voice.*

"It's very quiet?" Thom asked as he looked around the empty room.

I am using my Magesti to influence the other Goblins and Gooblyns to not come in here, which isn't that hard since no one ever wants to be in Snoog's throne room.

"How did you come to be his prisoner," Semaj asked glancing at the box that had served as the Magestic's cell and home. Semaj gave the Goblin a small boost and suddenly words and images flooded their heads telling a story in a matter of moments.

What I tell you, I only know from being in his mind. Snoog is actually a hybrid, father was an Ogre and mother an Orgite which resulted in Snoog. An abomination by both race's standards, the baby was left to die in the marshes. Fortunately, an Elf traveling stumbled upon him and gave him to a female Goblin to care for and raise. When Snoog got older, it was clear he didn't quite look like other Goblins and was made fun of and picked on but his Goblin mother cared for and protected him as her own and kept him isolated.

Well, until the day the Elf, Docanesto returned and made Snoog a deal, swear allegiance to Drol Greb and follow his will unconditionally and in return he would make him a king. Snoog did and Docanesto had the current king killed and declared to all that Snoog was a Gooblyn and only looked different because he was the marked chosen one of Drol Greb. With that and a magical staff, Docanesto had made Snoog King of the Gooblyns.

King Snoog ruled with a mean and iron fist but it was becoming more and more obvious something was different about him and it was not the claim he was chosen. He started making enemies and fear that he might be removed from the throne caused him to panic until not long ago when he stumbled upon a special Goblin, me.

I had always felt different and smarter than most Goblins. For that reason, I kept trying to become a higher class Gooblyn with failed and punishable rejection after rejection. Suddenly, I discovered I could read or give off impressions so I used it and got myself accepted into the city and walk around without being questioned. I may not have been officially made a Gooblyn but this was good enough for me to start a better social status.

Then one day, being too overconfident, I forgot to use my Magesti and several Gooblyn Guards saw me as a Goblin and called me out. They started beating me and preparing to take me to the dungeons when I accidently sent off a strange sensation from my mind and it hit Snoog as he was parading by. He turned and looked right at me and not being new to magical things, knew I had done something. He immediately had me brought to his throne room.

I feared it was the end but had an idea. Knowing I couldn't lie and that this might be my way in for real, I told Snoog that I had strange magical abilities. I didn't know what I was or what my powers were until the night of the dream with the Dragon, but I knew I was special and it would secure safety for me and my mom. He gleamed in the fact of what I could do and what it would do for him and his status as the true king. He offered me a deal that if I agreed to keep my abilities secret and serve him unconditionally, he would promise me safety and protection for me and my mom.

I agreed immediately, even though I should have used my gifts as what I thought the deal meant was different from what Snoog intended. He grabbed me and placed me in that crate. I protested but he insisted that he was keeping his word of letting me live and the crate would prove complete security and protection for me. He gave me two choices, get in the crate and serve him as agreed upon or accept a death sentence where I would have to watch my mom tortured and killed before my eyes first before dying myself.

So, I jumped into the crate and that is where I have been, using my gifts to make Snoog appear to be a more powerful king and squash any notions for anyone to question or challenge him. The only hope I had, was after the dream, the Chosen One would one day come and free me. Here you are.

"That is just awful," Anna cried as the thought of what Snoog did made her anger flare as hot as her Fire Magesti.

"Where is Snoog right now?" Semaj asked.

He left when war was declared and Lucian took command of his army to attack all of you outside the Gooblyn City.

"That is where you are wrong you traitorous rodent!" A loud roar came form behind them.

"Snoog," Gort managed to say as they all turned to see a large figure stomp before them, a dozen Gooblyn Guards with spears ready to defend their king at his side.

Oltar noticed that with Gort not helping the king he did not come off as big and scary as when he first met the Gooblyn King. Before any of them could respond to the grotesque king, Gort screamed both out load and in their minds as the Gooblyn King threw an image into the Majestic's mind that reflected out into the rest of theirs via the Magestic, Gort's dead mother.

"I told you I would kill her. I was going to make you watch but when I learned of your betrayal I accidently killed her when I grabbed her," Snoog growled with a hideous laugh. "Now come kneel before your king and beg for forgiveness."

"He is not going." Was all Semaj got out before a powerful blast of magical light hit him, transforming him into stone.

"Semaj!" Thom and Anna both screamed in unison as they stared at the motionless stone statue that had once been their best friend. Anna not only felt her heart break but her body, all the way down to her Magesti, jolt from the sudden disconnection from Semaj.

"That will be enough out of you, Chosen One."

"How did he know?" Thom looked at Anna and then at the two possible traitors, Oltar and Gort.

"Impossible," Gort whispered as he nearly fell to his knees.

"You really think that all this time using your gift and connecting to my mind that I would not benefit. Not only did it improve my intelligence, but I could listen in on your thoughts and impressions when you used your abilities while blocking you from mine. That's right, I know who all of you are and have been watching and waiting for this very moment. Now with the Chosen One as a bargaining chip and all you Magestics serving me, I can finally get out from under Docanesto's rule and focus on becoming the Emperor of all Ogra," Snoog belted out a loud and evil laugh as he commanded his guards to capture them all.

Anna, fueled with anger did not hesitate as two daggers were in her hands and flying outwards causing two of the guards to fall when they connected with their faces. Just as three more moved closer to her she called on her Magestic causing their front chest piece to burst into flame. As they scrambled in shock and pain, they managed to collide with a bunch of their other fellow guards. Anna looked over and saw that Oltar was starting to sway from lack of use and experience with his Magesti but he was holding his own.

"We can't leave without finding away to save Semaj, so no need to reserve my energy. "Mesfla Upter!" Thom screamed as his crystal lit up and he waved his arms upwards.

Magical light flashed as the Gooblyn guards that had been on fire exploded in flame seconds before the fire erupted on their bodies and spread to several guards nearby and right towards Snoog. Snoog swung his staff in front of him in a defensive motion, light searing off of it as it turned the wall of fire to stone before it reached him. Snoog kicked the stone fire to the side and sent a blast right at Thom. Anna could not even scream as she saw her other friend turn to stone and Oltar quickly following after that.

"Might as well surrender, you can't beat me," King Snoog laughed as Anna looked at the three statues and then at

Gort, who was on the ground quivering from weakness and all the use of bright lights.

"Never," Anna said as she brought two more daggers into her hands and searched for the energy to tap into her Magesti.

"You are nothing compared to the power of my staff," Snoog said as he stood tall, face scowling with all his menace, bringing his glowing staff out in front of him.

"That includes you," Thom said as he leapt forward, the stone appearing to melt and fade away revealing his perfectly fine form.

Thom grabbed the staff and his crystal lit up, pulsing in rhythm to the light of Snoog's staff. With two choice words the staff and his crystal flashed as the beam of light from the staff backfired turning Snoog to stone. Thom cheered as he stepped back, breaking off Snoog's fingers as he held firm to the staff and taking ownership of it. He then turned and faced the Gooblyn Guards, his crystal making it very easy to use the staff, turned every one of them, dead and alive into stone. "Once again, the secret of the Chosen One is secured."

"Great job you two," Anna said as she saw Oltar drop to one knee, completely stone free. Anna rushed over to help Gort up, as he was truly spent from pushing his powers so hard to make Snoog think he had turned Thom and Oltar to stone while blocking the Gooblyn King from their minds as they plotted their attack. As the Goblin pushed his Magesti, Oltar used his to give Snoog enough bad luck to actually miss them with his staff and help allow the staff to backfire upon him when Thom made his surprise attack.

"This staff is something. I don't know if it's me or my crystal, but I can feel the magic flowing through this thing."

"Can you help Semaj?"

"Staff, reverses."

"I'll give it a shot," Thom nodded to both Anna and Gort as he raised the staff and pointed it at the statue of Semaj. The crystal around his neck began to glow with the staff. He was not sure if it was his crystal, the staff or both guiding him on how to use the staff to set his friend free. It did not matter, Thom embraced the magic and released the magic of the staff causing

Semaj to be swallowed up by the staff's magical light. Thom smiled as he heard Anna scream in relief as the stone shifted to flesh, bringing Semaj back to life.

"Semaj, are you okay?"

"Yes, just a little stiff." Semaj smirked as his friend hugged him in hysterical laughter.

"What was it like?" Thom asked.

"I could see and hear everything going on. I just couldn't move or feel anything," Semaj said as they all looked over at Snoog, knowing he was probably aware of everything, gave them chills.

"Thank you, my new friends," Semaj said to both his newly found Magestics.

"Where do we go from here?" Oltar asked as he looked at the group of humans.

"We were instructed to free you and then get as far away from the Gooblyn City as possible," Thom said thinking about Essej's very serious instructions to him.

"We can't leave our friends though," Semaj said as he knew deep down that his and the Magestics wellbeing was priority.

"Losing battle. Saw. Snoog mind. Friends. Will die." Gort had to really force himself to speak. He closed his largely odd eyes and then opened them fast. "Battle. Alerted. Incoming."

"We have to go," Thom said as he urged everyone to get close together while casting a magical spell to place a barrier on the doors that should keep them sealed long enough for them to escape.

"We can't just abandon them," Anna pleaded.

Semaj thought of Nat and the otehrs and swallowed hard. "Sorry, Thom you know what you have to do."

Thom nodded as his crystal came to life and he shouted the command that caused a massive orb of magical light to make them all vanish instantly from sight.

Chapter Thirty-Three:
The Final Fight

"We are not going to survive this one, old friend," Ard-Rich's voice came from Thom's mouth.

"All that matters is that Semaj gets the Magestics to safety. I made sure Thom would follow those orders," Essej said as the cyclone of mud had died out and he used everything he had to try to send hurricane level winds at the oncoming forces.

"If I can only get to my friends and convince them, we won't have to die today," Nat declared as she sliced through a few more Goblins to get a better view of the group coming towards them, which included her long-time friends, with Lucian hanging back and watching the battle unfold.

"That is as likely as these creatures continuing to think I am a magic user," Ard-Rich said as his finger blades shot out stabbing two more Goblins while the magic illusion made it appear as if Thom had sent a magical blast at the creatures. He glanced back and saw the two illusions of Anna and Semaj flicker a little. The illusions were still fooling the Goblins and Hobgoblins, but he was having trouble maintaining them while concentrating on the battle all around him.

"He didn't say you had to be brought to him alive," Drocana said as she dove her Tazarian right at the traitor.

Nat ran with all her speed, bouncing off the head of an approaching Goblin, she propelled herself upwards, wrist blades extended. The Tazarian swayed in reaction to the figure heading straight for it allowing Nat to grab the reigns with one hand and with the other, plunge her blade right into the beast's eye. The Tazarian roared in pain, shaking its head and body. Using the moment, Nat flipped up onto the back, lunged herself at Drocana, hitting the beast's rider and pulling her off her mount, but not before she swung her arm and sliced through the Tazarian's wing. Nat and Drocana fell to the ground below as the beast flew off in pain and injury.

"You will," was all Drocana got out before the impact of the ground knocked the wind out of her. Nat, using her enemy's body to take the brunt of the fall, propelled herself up at the last moment to somersault up into the air and land on her feet, blades ready, facing her enemy and waiting for Drocana to get up.

"You get the Chosen One, I will gut the Huelgon," Fylla commanded as she raised her weapon high and urged her Fire Hound towards Essej while the other hound carrying a Fire Elf along with the two Drogans in the air raced after the disguised Ard-Rich.

"I'll handle the other two," Aksurh said as he commanded his hound to lead a group of Hobgoblins at the images of Anna and Semaj.

"Lots of traitors to deal with," Sev said into Lucian's ear as they looked at both Nat and Drocana.

"I will deal with both of them, well whomever may still be alive after their battle," Lucian growled as he felt more anger towards his friend than the daughter of one of his fathers.

"Shall we join the fight?" Gabrielle asked as Lucian shook his head.

"No, as you can see, with Snoog's forces combined with mine, this will be over soon. No point in dirtying your pretty hand," Lucian said with a smile that caused Sev's blood to boil.

"Barbarian," Essej nodded as the female warrior charged towards him.

"A label forced upon my people that I now proudly accept."

"Only because you chose to turn your backs on your fellow humans and those of the races that fight for good to side with the evils of Drol Greb."

"You are the traitor to all the races you mixed blood. You help those that have harmed those of magic. We have the honor to fight with those that wish to take back Bergonia so all the races can live as one, non-human and human."

"You really think that is what Drol will do? If he succeeds, all who will oppose him he will destroy or enslave, no matter the race, including humans. You think you will be treated equally? All humans, including you Barbarians, will be treated as fodder and will be enslaved or killed without a second thought from Drol. You mean nothing to him."

"Liar!" Fylla screamed as she raised her broadsword in one hand and battle-axe in the other and leapt off her hound, landed on the ground, kicking a rock right at the Huelgon before continuing her charge.

Essej gasped as the wind and strength was knocked out of him from the impact of the rock hitting him in the stomach. As he took pause to regain his composure, his control over the winds ended and started to die. He knew he may not survive this battle but that was okay. He just had to last long enough to ensure Semaj and the others made their escape. Until then, he would find the strength to fight on. With a push, his wings extended and he shot straight up as the female Barbarian's blade missed him, barely.

"You think you have the advantage?" Fylla made a sharp whistle noise from her lips that caused Essej to turn in surprise as the Fire Hound, with great strength, had leapt into the air, bit into his leg and flung him back to the ground. Essej grunted in pain as the hound landed upon him, pinning him, teeth snarling inches from his throat waiting for the command as Fylla walked towards them, weapons ready and laughing.

"Chosen One, surrender now," the Fire Elf demanded as he and the Drogans were now upon Ard-Rich.

Ard-Rich knew he would have one shot at this and began pulling on his Magesti. He then brought his hands together allowing them to fuse and shift together forming a single spear shaped weapon. Thanks to the illusionary magic, it appeared to look like he was casting a spell which only made the over confident Fire Elf mock him. With all his strength, he forced his body spear to shoot outwards with great strength. The Fire Elf's confident smile to deflect the spell turned into pure shock as the spear impaled him right through his head. Ard-Rich then jerked upwards making the Fire Elf fly across the area, the now lifeless body hitting the ground as Ard-Rich's arms turned back to normal.

Lucian inched forward as he saw the Chosen One use a magical blast to hit, kill and fling the body of his last Fire Elf effortlessly with his magic. He was almost impressed but the Drogans suddenly diverted his attention. "No!" Lucian screamed as both Drogans opened their mouths and each sent a blast of fire, hitting and consuming the Chosen One in flames.

Aksurh and his forces reached the girl and boy, who he thought had an odd appearance. He could have sworn there was something off about them. He motioned for the Hobgoblins to charge ahead and attack. He brought his hound to a stop and watched as the Hobgoblins were having difficulty laying a claw on them. He squinted his eyes and could have sworn he saw the girl, flicker? "They're not real," Aksurh muttered as he urged his hound to go right for the girl. There was no way she could evade a hound if she was real.

The hound was nearly upon Anna when a flash caused the hound to jerk back, almost dismounting its rider. Aksurh got his hound under control to see the Hobgoblins retreating from a girl who now stood next to the boy, the Chosen One and two figures behind him that he could not make out. This gave him greater pause as the girl raised her arms and pointed past him. He felt a wave of heat and heard a voice call out. He turned to see the Chosen One about to be hit with two fire blasts, but the flames diverted and went over the Chosen One in an arc, sparing him from being burned alive.

"Wait a minute," Aksurh suddenly said as he realized there were now two Chosen Ones as he looked back and forth with confusion.

"Nice save, Anna," Semaj said as his friend continued to concentrate and draw away the heat making the flames slowly vanish.

"Thanks for the minor boost or I wouldn't have been able to divert it in time."

"What are you doing here?" Ard-Rich asked in frustration as he reverted to his own form upon seeing Thom.

"We couldn't leave you all to die," Thom said as he waved his hand causing his illusion spell to fade away along with the duplicates of his two best friends.

"We had your escape covered," Ard-Rich said as he turned to face the two Drogans.

"Sure you did," Anna said as she looked over and saw the hound on Essej and a large muscular woman moving towards them. She nodded to Thom who used what little energy he had to send two magic blasts, each hitting the hound and Barbarian to knock them away from Essej.

"You fools," Essej swore as he sent a blast of wind to at the two Drogans and unmounted hound near Ard-Rich before a sharp pain made him cuff his leg. Thanks to his scaly skin at the time, it had prevented the hound bite from causing more damage than it had.

"I know you wanted us to go, but I convinced Thom to ignore your commands and bring us back. We have the Magestics with us, we can retreat back into the mountains," Semaj said as he drew his sword and fended off a Goblin as he made his way to find Nat. He was surprised to find himself getting more confident with his sword. Then again, he had felt the pull of Oltar's Magesti, giving the attacking creatures around them some back luck.

"It didn't take much convincing. We all need to stick together," Thom added as he held up the staff he took from Snoog and cast an illusion spell to make it invisible. He had received the impression from their new Magestic, that it might not be a good idea to reveal Snoog's condition.

"I'll deal with all of you later, but first we need to get Semaj and the Magestics to safety," Essej said as he tried to find his strength despite the pain in his leg and the exhaustion of his age setting in.

"You are not going anywhere," Aksurh said as he touched his amulet and revoked the magic, instantly growing in size.

"Great Venéăh, a Giant," Anna exclaimed as Thom's eyes went wide.

"I thought they were extinct," Thom added as he tried to recall his ancestral grandfather's books.

"They all but were, except the rumors that some had survived by going into deep exile," Ard-Rich said as he glanced from his old friend to the large creature in front of them that caused even the Goblins to pause and stare up at it.

"Boy, are there more of you?" Essej asked as the group moved closer together behind him.

"That's none of your concern," Fylla said as she raised her weapon high and moved towards the Giant along with the two Drogans and three hounds. The Goblins and Hobgoblins circling around the two sides, waiting for the command to attack while staring up at the Giant.

"We don't stand a chance against a Giant," Oltar whispered as he and Gort kept close behind Anna and Thom.

"Thom?" Anna placed a hopeful hand on her friend's shoulder who was touching his crystal and chanting quietly, "Ndse, Lphe! Ndse, Lphe! Ndse, Lphe!"

"Look, little glowing bugs will save them," Fylla laughed as she saw a handful of little glowing insects fly from around the Chosen One and then zip off towards the west. "Crush them!"

Aksurh nodded as he lifted his giant foot and stepped towards the group in front of him, the Goblins and Hobgoblins charging in as well.

****

"Nat!" Semaj screamed as he made it to the Elf, Wild or Fire he did not know or care at the moment. .

"Semaj, what are you doing here? You should be long gone by now," Nat said in panic as Drocana was now on her feet.

"Is this the one that turned you traitor?" Drocana asked with a smirk as she formed a bow made of fire and released two flaming arrows right at the boy running at them.

Semaj came to a halt, raising his sword to deflect the two arrows of fire when he tripped and fell forward, hitting the ground allowing the arrows to fly over and hit two Goblins in the distance. Semaj looked towards the arrow's marks and then glanced further to see Oltar glancing his way as the pull of his Magesti was being pushed as much as the king could at the enemies.

"I never miss," Drocana swore as she moved towards the boy.

"You stay away from him," Nat commanded as she had both her wrist blades ready, stepping between the two.

"I thought I had to be wrong, but you are in love? With a human? You betray Lucian and our race. I will enjoy making you watch his painful death when I present both of you to my father and Drol Greb," Drocana said as she realized that there was something more between this simple human boy and Lucian's female pet.

"I betray nothing. We are on the wrong side," Nat said as she leapt into the air in a twirling motion, wrist blades extended out.

"Bergonia belongs to us," Drocana countered, blades of fire igniting in her hands as she leapt up to meet her attacker, deflecting and kicking Nat to the side.

"Bergonia belongs to everyone. That is what I see now," Nat said as she flipped back onto her feet and charged her enemy.

"You will answer for your betrayal."

Drocana leapt up, summersaulting over Nat and landing behind her. Nat turned but not before the Fire Elf managed to slam the side of her flaming sword into her back. Nat fell forward. Her ability to withstand the elements protected her from the actual fire, but the impact still hit her like a hammer, sending her falling forward. She was not sure she could survive a direct attack from even a sword only made of pure fire. She tried to get up but felt the tip right at the edge of her back.

"You are in your true form, so why don't you use the fire against me? You may not have sworn fully to it but it still resides in you. Or are you afraid of it consuming you and letting your human lover see what you truly are, a Fire Elf of Drol Greb?"

"Go to Le.." Nat began to spit when Drocana shoved her face down with a kick of her foot.

"Surrender!"

"Never!"

"Then you leave me no choice," Drocana said as she raised the weapon in her other hand when a rock hit her wrist causing her to flinch in pain and turn her attention away from Nat.

"Stand away from her," Semaj said as he gripped his sword.

"You humans think you are so tough."

"I won't let you hurt Nat or anyone in Bergonia."

"You still defend her after her lies to you? Foolish human," Drocana laughed as she turned toward the boy, kicking Nat in the head to knock her out. She then, with pure rage and hate, screamed at Semaj, "You think that you are entitled to this land? Force us away like we are nothing?"

"I didn't do it, and I'm not saying my human ancestors weren't wrong, but how is it any different if you attack doing the same thing. We can all live together, forge a new Bergonia."

"I will not let your lies and corrupt words affect me like it did her," Drocana said as she raised her flaming swords and ran at the boy, wondering if she should just kill him now. No point in letting a simple human live. She would still get joy in watching her father torture the traitor Elf.

Allow me. A voice came from inside Semaj's mind just before it seemed to channel through him and expel outwards. A massive scream that caused the evil female Fire Elf to dropped to her knees, swords extinguishing while gripping her head and matching the scream with her own voice.

"Get out of my head!" Drocana screamed as she bent forward, placing her gripped head between her legs.

"Sorry," Semaj instinctively murmured as he felt Gort and his Magesti leave his mind while he tried to keep his balance from the surprising display of power that had passed through him and to the Fire Elf before him.

"You did this." Drocana spat, blood dripping from her ears, eyes and nose.

Semaj did not realize how powerful that mental blast had been, but as the Chosen One he tends to be able to boost the abilities of the Magestics. He stared at the Fire Elf and hesitated with his raised sword. He had fought the Goblins, but killing a defenseless Elf seemed as wrong as killing a person. He knew times have changed and Bergonia was on the line, but how much did he really have to change? Semaj contemplated and realized he could just knock her out when a strong blow hit him in the chests knocking the wind out of him as his back and head hit the ground hard.

"Humans, always weak, then again, you aren't human, are you? Well not fully human," Drocana hissed as she unclintched her fist, stepped forward and placed the top of her foot on his chest, pressing hard, while putting the tip of a flaming blade near his neck.

Semaj could still see drips of blood as she wiped them away with her other hand, staring hard at him. He wanted to speak but he could not find the energy or his voice. He realized that his moment of hesitation had cost him and now maybe Nat and the rest of the world their lives. He had dropped his sword when had been hit and realized he was truly defenseless.

"The question is, if you are not fully human, then what are you?" Drocana asked as she leaned forward and sniffed the air around him. Semaj could feel his eyes watering. He had failed. Then the Fire Elf jerked up and stepped back away from him.

"Wait a minute. It can't be. Did we have it wrong? You are the," Drocana started to reveal when her voice was cut off and replaced by a gurgling sound.

Semaj sat up and saw blood running out of her mouth and the front of her throat where the tip of a blade poked through. Nat was standing behind Drocana, left wrist blade piercing her neck while raising her other arm high above her head. Semaj gasped as Nat plunged her other wrist blade deep into the top of the Fire Elf's head. With a wild scream, Nat jerked her blades out letting Drocana's lifeless body fall to the ground. She then stumbled and dropped near him and tried to smile.

"You stopped her from."

"Killing you, yes, you're welcome."

"I don't know what to say." Semaj looked at her beautiful grey skin and into her eyes. He moved his hand towards her face and leaned in when she caught his arm and stopped him, with a gentle smile.

"We don't have time. Grab your sword. Your friends still need us."

Semaj looked away from Nat and saw the battle waging with his friends and what appeared to be a Giant.

"Move!" Essej shouted as the foot came down sending shockwaves across the ground, making it hard for anyone to keep their footing.

"Thom, do something," Anna commanded.

"I can't, that last spell took a lot out of me, and for some reason I can feel the magic still sucking the energy out of me," Thom said.

"Then all is lost," Oltar said as he was feeling drained as well and did not know how much more bad luck he could dish out.

"It is over. Goblins, kill them all and bring the Chosen One to me," Fylla said as she moved forward and then stopped when something passed right by her causing a sharp sting and small cut to appear upon her right arm.

"Rescue Gnomes, save our new friends," a small voice shouted from above.

"Well, now I've seen it all," Ard-Rich laughed as he looked up to the sky above them.

Coming down were a few dozen Rockflies. Ard-Rich had never seen them travel so far from the mountains. These hand sized insects were the color of rocks, had four large wings to give them flight and a sharp pointed nose to allow them to tap into the mountains for food. Sitting on top of them is what really had his attention. Each Rockfly was mounted by a Mountain Gnome holding on for dear life with Nalyd and Avon leading the charge. The Gnomes were using the Rockflies to fly at the Goblins and Hobgoblins, stabbing them with their pointed noses.

"Gnomes? Aksurh, squash them already." Fylla was now annoyed as the Gnomes and Rockflies were distracting the Goblins and Hobgoblins from the task and fight at hand.

The Giant nodded and raised his foot when the ground began to shake so badly that he lost his footing and fell to the ground, squashing and knocking Goblins away that had been under and near him when he hit face first upon the earth below. Fylla swore but turned when she heard more rumbling and looked to the west to see a small group heading towards them. She shook her head as it appeared to be two Dwarves sitting upon Frostites leading a force of a few other Frostites and ten very large brown mountain Earthites, mountain cousins of the Frostites, but were larger and had claws and teeth sharp enough to dig and climb upon mountains made of solid rock.

"Noraxa!" Anna cheered as the cavalry had arrived.

"As soon as I woke, with the help of Nalyd, we got as many Gnomes to help and made our way here," Noraxa said as her forces were now upon the Hobgoblins and Goblins standing between them and her friends.

"How did you get here so fast?" Thom asked forcefully as he was still short of breath.

"These glowing orbs appeared, pulsing. Some of them vanished when the Rockflies and Earthites suddenly appeared. The Gnomes mounted the rockflies and we all started to move out of the mountains when two orbs continued on west and the others, one by one exploded into nothingness. I discovered with each explosion, we were propelled closer to you. When the last one exploded we were within site of this battle," Noraxa said as she closed her eyes.

"Thom, that's probably why you are feeling like this. Your spell worked and kept pulling from you as it kept bringing us help." Anna said as she saw the large Orgite King take a seat upon the ground, exhausted from the over use of his gift. She wanted to head into battle but knew she must stay here and protect her fellow Magestics and Thom. As Oltar's Magesti faded, she felt another go active near her.

Noraxa's Magesti pulsed within her body as she connected with it and reached out. She could feel the ground toward the north and south and pushed with her Magesti. The earth began to shake as she pushed even harder. Soon the ground began to quake as the earth ripped on each side creating a large crack in the ground on the north and south sides causing many creatures to fall in while separating the surviving Goblins and Hobgoblins from them. "There, we are no longer surrounded," Noraxa said, feeling drained.

"That will give us a better chance, thank you," Essej nodded to the Dwarven Magestic.

The hound that had been with the Giant howled in anger and charged at the Dwarves. It bared its teeth as it leapt into the air at Noraxa. With surprising courage, Lorax pushed his Frostite to jump in front of his true love and he raised his axe. The axe shimmered as the blade hit the hound and just like hitting paper, the axe's blade sliced the creature in half with ease and no resistance. He turned to smile but was met with a scowl under a blood covered face and decided to urge his Frostite to keep fighting onward.

"What is this? I thought it but a story of legends. The most coveted weapon of all warriors. The Axe Artifact of Power. Drogans, bring me that axe at all costs," Fylla demanded as she urged her hound to charge at the male Dwarf.

Anna reached out and caused the air in front of the Drogans to burst into flame. She knew it would not hurt them but it did cause them to reel backwards and pause their advance upon Lorax. Noraxa, whispered a command to her Frostite, Freezia, who raised up and roared. This caused the other three riderless Frostites to nod and charge head on at Fylla and her hound. Fylla, weapon raised, leapt off her hound and landed upon the back of one of the Frostites while the other two engaged her hound. Noraxa and Freezia both screamed in agony as they saw Fylla make short work of the Frostite she had landed on. The death of one of their own caused the other two Frostites to glance over, allowing the hound to rip out the throat of one of them. The hound would have gotten the second, but two Earthites managed to pounce upon the hound, exacting lethal revenge upon it.

"Nothing will stop me from getting that axe," Fylla said as the Frostite and two Earthites moved towards her only to be batted away by a large hand.

"We need to pull back," Aksurh said as he tried to get to his feet after saving his friend.

"Never," Fylla said when she was picked up into the air. "Put me down!"

"We need to retreat," the Giant said as Fylla looked down upon the battlefield from high above to see they were now losing. Essej and Ard-Rich moving to take on the Drogans while their remaining forces handled what Goblins and Hobgoblins had not been blocked by the two earthquake cracks in the ground. She hated defeat and refused to give up. She was about to scream when a loud voice boomed over the battlefield.

"I have sat back long enough," Lucian said, his voice being amplified by a devise Gabrielle had given him. "You think you have this battle won?"

"Be ready everyone," Essej said as he used his powers to cause a gust of wind to hit the approaching Nat and Semaj to lift and propel them over the crack in the ground so they could join the rest of them.

"Noraxa, glad to see you," Semaj said as he and Nat ran up and turned to see that both sides were pausing and looking towards Lucian, waiting for the next move.

"We need to retreat back into the mountains," Ard-Rich said addressing the only path they had, unless they charged head on at the enemy in front of them.

"You will not be going anywhere," Lucian laughed as Semaj and his forces saw a small Fairy fly past and head towards Lucian and Gabrielle. A large roar caused them all to turn back to the mountains.

"Ogres, want revenge, declared open season on us. Ogres wait at base of mountain," a Gnome reported as it flew up to them on a Rockfly, following shortly after the Fairy.

"It is done, the Ogres have agreed to join your army if you promise to feed them all the Gnomes and the Dwarves as well has giving them part rulership of the mountains and surrounding Ogra land," Sev said landing upon Lucian's shoulder.

"Good, we can deal with the actual details later," Lucian smirked as he held the device back up to his mouth. "You have nowhere to go, surrender the Chosen One to me now."

"You will never have him," Essej said using his powers to carry his voice back upon the wind while Ard-Rich had everyone gather together and Noraxa had all the Earthites and remaining Frostite surround them in protection. Nalyd and all the Fockfly riding Gnomes flew around above keeping watch and waiting instructions.

"We are ready," Gabrielle whispered to Lucian after a Gooblyn had ran up to her.

"On my command," Lucian said as he looked over his shoulder and saw hundreds of Goblins, Hobgoblins and Gooblyns gathering behind him.

"Noraxa, if you received a boost could you take them all out?" Semaj asked quietly to the Dwarf.

"No, we can't risk upsetting this land and those that live below any more than she has already," Essej said looking at the two large cracks and knowing that even in desperate times they had to be carful of using untrained powers upon the land around them and what consequences it could unleash.

"He's right," Ard-Rich said thinking of what Nat had let loose and may not be far enough below to risk bringing them back up.

"He's referring to the creatures Nat unleashed earlier," Sev said as they were able to hear the group below thanks to another devise Gabrielle had produced to amplify hearing.

"We don't want those below but that gives me an idea from above," Lucian smirked as he used his magic and yanked up something from the ground and coated it in fire. "Take this and go as high and as fast as you can and then release it into the air above." Sev took the ball of fire and darted skyward.

"What is that about?" Gabrielle asked.

"If it works, a wonderful surprise for our friends," Lucian laughed and then shouted through the device in his hand. "Charge!"

Gabrielle, following Lucian, rode their hounds forward as their forces of Goblins, Hobgoblins and Gooblyns advanced forward with great speed. The Giant, Barbarian and two Drogans returned to the battle knowing the reinforcements would soon be joining them in the fight. This would be the end of the Chosen One and his evil forces. Lucian would bring the victory for his fathers and Drol Greb would have his victory over Bergonia.

"Thom, you have to get us out of here," Anna pleaded as she began heating up the ground under the Giant's feet.

"I just don't have the energy to get us all out of here," Thom said in exhaustion as something was still draining him.

"What about," Essej began when Semaj interrupted him.

"No, we all stand together."

"Heads up!" Noraxa shouted as the enemy forces were now upon them.

With a quick command, the Gnomes upon Rockflies and the Earthites charged forward to engage the enemy. Essej sprouted his wings and took to the sky, the wind coming to his command to cause interference with the two flying Drogans while Ard-Rich and the Dwarves took to the ground forces. Nat darted into battle while Semaj and Anna stood near Thom, Oltar and Gort, who did his best to hide his identity, to protect them from harm as they were the most defenseless at the moment.

"Nat, you traitor," Fylla spat as she was now on the ground and crossed the path of her former friend. "I guess you are as fake as those red markings you wore."

Nat glanced at her grey skin, void of the marking those who fully take the fire displayed upon their bodies, then looked up at her friends. "Fylla, Aksurh, you both have to believe me. Lucian, all of us, have it wrong. The Chosen One isn't the enemy. They are working to bring us all together for the better of Bergonia," Nat tried to explaine when she was cut off by having to dodge her friend's weapon that had almost took off her head.

"We all swore a friendship to Lucian and you betrayed us all. For that you will die," Fylla said as she swung again.

Nat tried to roll but a loud clank and snap caused her to stop and look up. Lorax, sitting upon his Frostite, was right next to her. His Axe placed in front of her as Fylla jerked back from her weapon splitting in two upon impact with the Artifact of Magic. With growling anger, the Barbarian reached behind her and pulled a secondary sword from her back and charged at the Dwarf. "I will have that axe."

"Back off, he's mine," Noraxa declared as she tried something new.

She focused her Magesti around Freezia's paw, causing a vibrational tremor around it just as her animal friend lifted up on her hind legs and swatted at the female Barbarian. The blow from the tremor laced paw sent a surprised Fylla up and into the air, flying at a great speed and force. A visible claw mark across her body started to drip with blood as she flew away from them. Fylla's hound roared in anger and leapt to attack in revenge but was quickly blown backwards by strong blast of wind.

"The next wave of Goblins are almost upon us," Essej said as a large grunt made him look forward, making eye contact with the Giant. After a brief pause, Aksurh turned and took large strides away from them so he could reach and catch his friend before she fell to her death.

"Die!" A growling voice screamed as the two Drogans flew towards Essej, both opening their mouths to launch a blast of fire at him.

Anna looked at the two and called forth her Magesti. Once she was in touch, she reached out and felt the heat within the two creatures. She knew she could not stop their blasts of fire but had another idea. Pushing with her Magesti, she poured everything she had to heat up and pump as much fuel into their fire. Anna let out a cry as the fire exploded with intensity, the fire coming out of and engulfing both Drogan's heads. Anna released and swayed as her power stopped and she saw both creatures drop to the ground. She doubted they were dead but at least it would stop them for now.

A large growl made Anna turn her attention as she saw Fylla's hound darting back into action, but not before Lorax, with great luck, swung his axe and severed the head clean off the beast. "I think I'm getting the hang of this."

"Only because the axe is enchanted," Nat murmured as she got to her feet, paused and looked upwards.

"That's as close of a thank you as you'll get," Noraxa spat as she moved up next to Lorax.

I am doing the best to hide me and the large Orgite King from their attention but Lucian's mind is screaming. He and his forces are about to reach us and he will clearly notice me if I'm not carful.

Semaj nodded at the Goblin Magestic but it was Nat's voice that sent him in panic. "I felt it and I was right. Lucian somehow brought the Swarm back!" Semaj and the others looked up to a large dark cloud of insects descending from the sky above.

"We will try but we are falling fast," Nalyd said as he and Avon flew next to them, several of their Gnomes having already flown to meet the Swarm, unknowingly headed to their immediate demise.

"No, Nalyd, tell your people to pull back and stay clear," Semaj said with dread and fear at the approaching enemy from above and ahead of them.

"We won't survive this," Ard-Rich said as something tugged at the back of his senses.

"Ahh!" Thom screamed.

"Are you injured?" Anna asked turning toward her friend.

"No, I felt a sudden surge of energy. As if what ever was draining me has stopped. I think I can save us or at least buy us time to retreat."

"Thom, you don't have the energy."

"No, but enough to do the trick."

"What's that?"

"Steal a trick from an old fat king," Thom said as he moved his hand forward, Snoog's staff reappearing as he cupped both hands firmly around it. Letting his magic supplement that of the staff, he let it take over and invoked the staff's power as he wished all those that intend to harm him and his friends be stopped. A powerful blast of energy shot out and away from Thom in a massive pulse.

Semaj watched in awe as the energy pulse moved quickly upwards and outwards. All of the Swarm instantly turned to stone as the pulse passed through them, causing them to rain down like stone pellets. It was clear that the spell was having no effect on the Gnomes or any one of his friends and allies. He saw Lucian come to a screeching halt as the forces of Goblins and Hobgoblins in the lead were touched and turned to stone.

"The Chosen One is more powerful than I thought," Lucian said as he reached for all the power and magic from within as he could and unleashed a wall of fire in front of him like he had never done before.

Gabrielle squinted from the heat as Lucian poured his might and magic building a large thick wall of fire between them and the stone turning magic. The pulse hit the wall of fire but did not stop. The fire began to turn to stone but it was holding and slowing the pulse. Lucian kept pushing, feeling himself getting weak, as he kept replacing the fire as quick as it turned to stone. After what seemed like eternity, the pulse faded and Lucian was able to stop. Frrr shifted to keep his friend and master from falling off of him while Gabrielle moved her hound to his side to place a hand on him to help hold him up.

"No!" Lucian swore as he looked at the massive thick wall that now stood between him and the Chosen One.

"Hey, you saved us," Gabrielle praised as she glanced at the creatures behind them that had escaped the fate of their fellow races who had been on the other side of the stone wall.

"I don't care about that. Now the Chosen One will escape. Get that wall down now!" Lucian screamed, feeling drained from the great feat of magic he had just performed. The Goblins, Hobgoblins and Gooblyns stormed the wall, some banging on it while others piled on top of each other to try and climb over.

"Hurry fowl creatures, before they escape and you face the wrath of your lord and master, Lucian!" Sev shouted as he came down and hovered between Lucian and Gabrielle after he was sure it had been safe to return.

"It's working!" Anna praised as the Swarm and Goblins started turning to stone.

"Almost," Semaj said as he saw the wall of fire go up between Lucian and the oncoming pulse and then turn to stone and holding.

"Now's our chance to go," Essej said as he glanced over and saw the Giant catch Fylla and drop into the chasm Noraxa had made, just as the pulse touched him.

"They are starting to climb over. We won't make it far," Nat said as she and the others gathered together. She noticed fingers almost reaching the top of the wall and they could feel something hitting the wall, slowly causing cracks.

"We, the Tremendous Twelve will stand by our new friends," Nalyd's little voice declared as Avon and ten other Mountain Gnomes cheered from the ground below, their Rockflies nowhere to be seen.

"The remaining Earthites will guard the wall but they will not allow anyone to ever ride them," Noraxa said as the five remaining beasts charged the wall and made quick work of the very few Goblins that had made it over the wall.

"Thom,"

"I can't, Semaj. I am literally spent," Thom said as he even looked pale enough to make Anna give a slight gasp.

"I can't carry all of you and we only have the two Frostites," Essej said as he too was feeling his age.

"Then we will do what you cannot," a voice said causing them to turn to face the west to see ten horse-like creatures, each baring a rider. The horses were all shimmery and reflected all the colors of the rainbow. Their manes and tails almost looked like mist and their hooves looked like clear bubbles. When Semaj looked at the woman on the lead horse, he recognized her from when he had fallen under the water.

"Mi-Ta, what are you doing here?" Ard-Rich asked with a very upset and scolding tone.

"I had a strange dream, it was as if you were in trouble but was forced awake before I could determine the extent of it. I wasn't sure but, in my tail, I knew you needed me. So, I rounded up a few soldiers and snuck upon land to search for you. As we approached the mountains, searching for you, these glowing orbs showed up and in a strange explosion we found ourselves deep in the mountains. We followed the orbs, and when each one exploded we moved closer here until the final one dropped us right behind you, grandfather. What is going on?" Mi-Ta asked as she kept her eyes on Semaj.

"I am so sorry. There is so much I need to tell you and that I've kept from you," Ard-Rich muttered, not sure what to say or where to begin.

"Dear child, we don't have much time. The fate of all Bergonia falls on us getting the Chosen One and the Magestics here to safety before Lucian and his hoard of Goblins and Hobgoblins over take us," Essej said as the girl broke eye contact and looked to the wall where more and more creatures were falling over.

"I recognize this one from before. Out of curiosity and kinship to my grandfather, I will help you all to safety until we can sit and all can be explained and figured out," Mi-Ta said as she glanced at Semaj and then glared at Ard-Rich.

"Where did you find such beautiful horses?" Anna asked as Semaj nodded, wondering the same thing as he had not seen any sign of horses on this land.

"They are Sea-Horses. Like us they can turn their tails to legs. They should get us out of here as their hooves can draw moisture and run faster than most as it's like they are gliding upon water," Ard-Rich added as he and Essej urged everyone to get onto a Sea-Horse.

Everyone started to move when a large explosion caused the wall to break away in the center and dozens of Hobgoblins to pour through, some getting past the startled and injured Earthites. Semaj was already on the back of a Sea-Horse and Lorax was now on one as they were trying to get the large Orgite onto the back of his Frostite. No matter how fast they claim the creatures could run, she knew they would not all make it in time. Reaching within, she then pushed out with her Magesti. The ground ignited and with her might, she created a wall of fire that stretched from one chasm to the next and miles high. "That should hold them back."

"You wish," Lucian growled as his hand burst through the wall of fire, grabbed Anna and yanked her back out of site.

"Anna!" Thom shouted as he moved toward the wall but was blown back by a blast of fire that also caused the fire wall to part in the middle and slowly fizzle away.

"Chosen One, surrender or the girl and your friends will die," Lucian said as he moved forward upon his hound, hands spread out causing the fire wall to fade, his hoard waiting his command to attack.

"Thom, we have to go," Ard-Rich said as Thom and Essej were the only ones not on a Sea-Horse or Frostite ready to dash away.

"We can't leave Anna," Semaj pleaded as Nat knew Ard-Rich was right and urged the Océan rider to start moving as she locked eyes with Lucian.

"Ard-Rich is right, Semaj. As long as you are free he won't hurt her. We can rescue her later. Our priority is to get you to safety," Essej said as he moved towards Thom and Ard-Rich gave the command to retreat to the mountains.

"No!" Thom and Semaj both screamed as the Sea-Horses and Frostites raced off with great speed and Essej sprouted wings, grabbed Thom and threw him onto a Sea-Horse and called forth a strong wind to distract Lucian and his forces to allow him to turn and fly off after the retreating group.

Do not worry. I will stay behind and keep an eye on Anna. I can sneak back in without notice and keep up the persona that Snoog is still alive.

The voice was projected to both Thom and Semaj and they knew it was too late to protest or try and get the Goblin Magestic. Thom sniffeled, wiped a tear and then threw the staff at the Goblin. *You will need this then.*

Thank you. Semaj thought back as the Goblin was already nowhere to be seen.

"Stop them!" They all heard Lucian scream in the distance as they gained ground between them and their enemy.

"She will be safe. If I know Lucian, he will not harm her. He will keep her and use her until he has y... the Chosen One, Thom, in his hands," Nat said as her steed moved along side Semaj's.

"We will get them back, friend Semaj," Nalyd said causing Semaj to look down, not realizing the Gnome had been sitting between him and the Océan rider.

"Yes, we will," Semaj said wiping tears from his eyes, fearing he had just lost another friend. He could see it in Thom's eyes too, he was thinking of Lars.

"If we make it to the mountains, how will we get past the Ogres?" Noraxa started to ask when right on que a voice boomed off in the distance ahead of them.

"I will eat every one of you," Retep, the alpha Ogre of the Western Mountains said as they saw the large forms of Ogres heading their way.

"How is it they are moving this far away from the mountains?" Ard-Rich asked in surprise.

"Grandfather, we should head north or south," Mi-Ta said as they all came to a stop, knowing they only had moments to make a decision before Retep or Lucian caught up to them.

"We can't," Essej said, trying to think looking to the west and east at their fast-approaching enemies.

"We go back for Anna," Semaj cried as he leapt off of the Sea-Horse.

"We will get her back," Nat said coming up behind him and flinched when he shrugged off her touch.

"We only have one option," Ard-Rich said as he gave a sad nod to his old friend.

"Semaj, can you give him a boost?" Essej asked, eyes watering ever so slightly.

Semaj reluctantly paused and laid his hand upon the elder Océan and felt a surge of power pass between them. Ard-Rich screamed as he placed his hands upon the ground and forced his Magesti to do what it had never done before thanks to Semaj. The ground shifted and soon a large tunnel formed beneath his hands leading down and beneath the earth. He then used his other ability to commandthe water to come them with great speed. "That should take you all directly under the mountains and to," Ard-Rich started to explain when he swayed, looking much older than he had moments before.

"Grandfather, I can feel the ocean's water moving into the tunnel. What did you do?" Mi-Ta asked as she leapt off her steed and clasped her grandfather's hands.

"What I should have done a long time ago. I kept something that belonged to you, but no more. I am so sorry," Ard-Rich said as he moved his hands and slapped them to the side of her face and reached for every ounce of Magesti in his body and forced it all directly into his granddaughter.

"What is going on, grandfather?" Mi-Ta's question becoming a scream as she felt a strange burning power flow into and spread throughout her whole body, merging with and increasing something that had been already within her.

"You are the Magestic of Body and now the only and rightful descendent of that Magesti. Promise me you will save everyone here and no matter what, protect the Chosen One at all costs. I love you my sweet, sweet child," Ard-Rich said as he whispered one last apology and fell backwards, lifeless upon the ground.

"Grandfather!" Mi-Ta cried out in agony as the rapidly aging body of her grandfather now lay in front of her, looking as if he had been dead for ages.

"Child, your grandfather was one of my oldest friends and I share your loss, but you must hurry. Honor his wishes and get us to safety," Essej said as he pushed for all of them to get closer to the tunnel Ard-Rich had made before sacrificing himself.

"I," Mi-Ta started to speak and then looked to her fellow Océans.

"I will eat you and crush you," Retep said as Nat looked over to see the Ogres were now a dozen feet from them.

"Hurry!" Nat shouted as she turned to see Lucian, fire forming in his hands, was about to swarm them with his army.

"For Grandfather," Mi-Ta said as she commanded her fellow Océans to work with her and to grab hold of the rushing water and accept it back into their bodies. Shifting form and gaining control over the water itself.

"You have no where to run," Lucian laughed as he charged right towards Semaj.

Semaj drew his sword and prepared to exact revenge for Anna. He could hear the rumbling of the Ogre army but he did not care. He wanted Lucian and that was all that mattered. He charged at the evil man upon the hound, sword raised high. "You will not get in the way of me reaching the Chosen One," Lucian laughed as he shifted his hound to the side and swung his arm to back hand the annoying boy.

Semaj swung his sword to block the hit and the back of his hand hit that of Lucian's hand. Semaj felt the wind knock right out of him as their contact triggered a strange explosion of light that sent Lucian, his hound and nearby forces flying backwards while Semaj flew just has hard in the other direction. He waited for the hard impact of the ground but instead felt the sharp splash of water as it engulfed his body. The cold shock causing him to black out. He could feel his body moving fast as he went in and out of consciousness until he finally opened his eyes and saw he was surrounded by water and chocked as he opened his mouth and water rushed in.

"Don't worry, for now, I will honor my grandfather's final wish," Mi-Ta whispered in his ear as the water swirled around him and he fell back into darkness.

Epilogue
It Ends

Semaj opened his eyes and despite his memory of water, found he was quite dry and breathing air. He appeared to be laying on a bed of soft seaweed. He sat up and noticed he was in a small room, the walls were smooth and curved as if he was in a giant bubble. Sitting cross-legged on the floor was an old familiar face that now looked very aged with grief, worry and tiredness. "Essej?"

"Good, you are finally with us," Essej said as he motioned the boy to sit down next to him.

"Us?" Semaj asked as he looked around and saw no one else in the room before taking a seat upon the ground.

"Sorry, I'm still a little weak and having trouble keeping myself from fading back to reality," Thom said as he appeared next to Semaj.

"Wait, this is one of my dreams? Where are the others?" Semaj asked starting to panic, the feeling of what he had lost already and not wanting to add more loss, overtaking his emotions.

"All our bodies are safe along with the others. Mi-Ta kept Ard-Rich's wishes and brought all of us to the safety of her castle, deep among her people's underwater city," Essej said, the sound of sadness in his voice at the mention of his old friend they had just lost.

"They are holding a ceremony to celebrate the life of Ard-Rich. We are not allowed to participate. They created a large room with air for all of us to stay in until they are done and are ready to deal with us," Thom said as he started to fade and then come back.

"Did we all make it?" Semaj asked looking between the two.

"Nat, Lorax, Noraxa, Freezia and Oltar are all in the room with us. Unfortunately, Mi-Ta and her warriors were only able to grab us eight and seven of the Gnomes before sealing the tunnel up behind them to escape Lucian and the Ogres. I do believe Nalyd and Avon were the only Gomes I recognized,"

Thom answered as Semaj's face calmed knowing the rest of them had all made it.

"We escaped but not with all the Magestics," Essej said, his face vacant and lost in deep thought.

"We have to go after Anna," Semaj demanded as he thought about their good friend in the hands of their enemy.

"We will and Lucian will pay if he so much as harms her in any way," Thom promised an oath.

"I just wish I knew if she was safe," Semaj added, his anger turning to fear and concern.

"That's why we are here," Thom said as he looked over at Essej.

"In my dream?"

"Semaj, you have the ability to track and find the Magestics because of your special connection to their Magesti. Just like that time in my father's cave, we will reach out to all the Magestics. Except this time, with the help from Thom and I, we will only view in on them. This, by not pulling any in, we can keep Lucian out," Essej explained as he encouraged the boys to form a circle with him on the floor holding hands. "Now close your eyes and concentrate."

Semaj could hear Essej talking, something about him, Magestics and their Magesti but he could not really hear the words clearly as his mind started to shift and focus as he thought of Anna and the other Magestics. He opened his eyes and found himself, alone, in his bedroom back home on the farm. He almost cheered thinking it had all been a horrible dream until he heard the screams and went and looked out his bedroom window to see everything in flames, people running from Drogans. Then he realized he was now in a dream within his dream.

With a heavy heart, he turned and walked out his is front door to find himself standing in the palm of Dwin's large claw. He was back in the cave but this time Dwin was just a stone statue and the cave was very dark, the only light seemed to be radiating from himself. Being in the cave made him think of the last time he had been here and had brought forth all the Magestics in one place. With a small smile he turned to face the cave balconies only to find he was now standing on top of the Frosted Waters. To the left was Bergonia, with swarms of

Drogans flying everywhere and to his right was the land of Ogra where for the first time he saw the races of that land coming together. Then there was the large fire burning bright to the South where the Unknown Lands reside and where Drol Greb and his forces were building as intensely as the fire itself. But, a small beacon of light drew his attention to the ice he was standing on.

In the ice he saw his reflection, glowing brightly. As he watched himself he thought of where he had started and the journey that brought him to where he was now. He was becoming the Chosen One as he searched for his Magestics, who in turn were becoming one with their Magesti. The more he thought about this the more his reflection glowed and shifted. He peered closer as his reflection had now become a map of all of Bergonia and its surrounding lands. In certain spots, the ice melted allowing thirteen bubbles, all different colors to rise up out of the water and rest upon the map. Some were far apart and others where right next to each other.

He knew right away that each bubble represented one of the Magestics and their location. He accepted this and willed to see each one and the bubbles started to shake and one by one move up and towards him. In the background he could faintly hear Essej's speech but his words coming clear when Semaj's attention was brought to a bubble that moved from the map, to his face, hovered and then popped as it vanished with the image within, starting with those closest to where he was standing. Some he knew, others just vague memories from the time in the cave with Dwin.

The Frosted Waters. The bubbles rose from the location on the glowing map on the ice. The first one flew up, glowed brown showing Noraxa sleeping in a large room next to Lorax and Freezia. *Magestic of the Earth.* The bubble popped as the next one came up and showing the same room but of Oltar sleeping, glowing grey. *Magestic of Death.* Semaj shuddered as the next bubble, glowing Orange showed him the image of Mi-Ta with her family and people, honoring the late Ard-Rich. *Magestic of the Body.* The bubble popped as the next set began to rise into the air.

Ogra. Semaj already knew who these were before the bubbles even reached him. Tears formed in his eyes when he saw Anna in a dungeon cell. *Magestic of Fire.* The red glowing bubble vanished as the second bubble, glowing gold, showed Gort sitting on the statue of Snoog holding a staff before vanishing as well. *Magestic of the Mind.*

Drol Death Desert. Two bubbles moved off the eastern edge of the Desert, near Argoth. Semaj wiped away the tears as he focused on the next set of bubbles. The first bubble glowed black and showed two, what appeared to be brothers, visiting in a small dark room. *The Magestic of Dark.* The second bubble glowed purple and showed a man, in the same room but sitting by himself. *The Magestic of the Soul.* He could not make out his face before the bubble vanished but he saw what he thought was Marcus holding a girl off to the side. His heart raced at seeing his other two friends alive.

Movement caught his eye and he realized the next set were coming. His attention was then drawn to an area of the map he had never heard of before as three bubbles rose into the air together. He leaned forward and saw an island off the western coast of Bergonia. Semaj's begain to wonder what it was when he heard Essej's voice as the first of the bubbles reached him.

The Forbidden Isles. Semaj looked into the one glowing white and saw what looked like a strange half man half bull creature running through a forest before it vanished. *The Magestic of Wind.* The next bubble, glowing yellow, caught this eye as he saw a struggle within and then a man being thrown into a cage with several other bodies. The bubble popped before he could get a closer look inside the cage. *The Magestic of Light.* The last bubble glowed with a pretty blue color as Semaj saw two women within. One, with blond hair and looked battle worn, was being escorted forward by another woman with a spear. He had no idea which one was…*The Magestic of Water.*

Forest of Spirits. Semaj jumped and turned as he knew this location on the map. It was where all the beings of magic were said to have been exiled to. He never believed the stories that Thom had always told him. Here it was with two bubbles coming from it. One bubble was green while the other was pink. They vanished quickly and he barely caught site of what looked like a small creature with pointed ears, similar to Nat, minus the grey skin, and the other was a girl who appeared to have the body of a horse. *The Magestic of Life. The Magestic of Heart.* That was the last of them. Even though he had not physically found them all, he was glad to see they were slowly coming together. Semaj started to turn from the map when he saw one final bubble, floating in the air well above the map.

Semaj paused as he realized there was thirteen bubbles but he only remembered twelve balconies back in the cave. Semaj stared at the final bubble as it glowed silver and then flew towards him. Instead of acting like the other bubbles, it slammed right into him as he heard Essej's voice. *The Magestic of Everything.* Silver mixed with all of the other twelve colors swirling around him with great intensity.

"Wait a minute," Semaj said out loud as the light and colors were gone and he now found himself standing back in the room, Thom right next to him while Essej stood in front of them, both arms stretched out, one pointing towards them and the other at, "Lucian? How did he get here?"

"I find it funny you think you could keep me out. I have realized my connection to the Chosen One is more than I thought," Lucian said, rubbing his wrist while looking past Essej at the two boys behind the Huelgan.

"You better not have hurt Anna. We will come for her," Thom shouted.

"I hope you do. As long as the Chosen One surrenders, I will allow a reunion with your girl," Lucian smirked as he held open his palm and let a ball of fire form. "I may not be able to find you, but I know where to find the Magestics and when I hunt them down, I will finally put an end to the Chosen One and his Magestics, starting with the girl with fire."

Semaj saw the ball of fire expand and shift into the shape of a map with little balls of fire indicating the general vicinity of where he had just seen the locations of the Magestics on his map moments before. Anger towards Lucian and the thought of him hurting Anna and the others erupted his very being. He opened his mouth, but before he could say anything and charge, Essej's voice and powers stopped him cold.

"The Chosen One will be under my protection for as long as I live," Essej declared as two powerful blasts of wind shot forth from his arms. One hitting Lucian and sending him backwards, fading away. The other slamming into Semaj and Thom causing him to jerk upwards.

"I'm awake," Semaj gasped, out of breath as he looked around and saw everyone safe and sleeping, except Thom and Essej who were just now sitting up as well. Semaj got to his feet and took in a deep breath. His old life was over and it was time to completely embrace his destiny. He was the Chosen One, the Magestic over all Magesti. He would gather the others and put an end to Drol Greb once and for all.

****

"Sev, I've sent word to the Queen of the Orgites. Once we unify the races on Ogra into one unified army we can plan the hunt for the Magestics," Lucian said walking into the room with the map he had made from his dream, only to stop suddenly in his tracks.

"Lucian, my love," Sev said as he turned around quickly, hiding the globe, whose glow and the image within went dark.

"Am I interrupting something?" Lucian asked, a frown and smile fighting each other for dominance upon his face.

"Oh, no. I was just."

"Reporting to my father?"

"What are you talking about?"

"Oh, dear sweet Sev. How I love when you squirm. You think you could hide reporting my every move to my father, to Docanesto?"

"You know?"

"I've always known. You think I would believe that you could summon a group and get us out of the Unknown Lands without getting caught? I just allowed it, part of me using it for help to get where I wanted to go, and the other, hoping with all my heart that it could not be true. Not another betrayal. Not from someone I loved so dearly," Lucian said as he let the smile prevail and slowly walk towards his lover.

"Lucian, I meant no harm. I was making sure you were protected. I did it for love," Sev pleaded.

"Sev, I loved you, almost more than anyone I have ever loved, but even with that, you know I can't tolerate disloyalty and betrayal, especially from a lover," Lucian growled as he grabbed Sev by both arms, hands heating up with his fiery magic.

"Lucian! Don't!" Sev screamed as he shrunk down to his Fairy form to escape Lucian's grasp. He turned to dash off to safety, but was not fast enough, as Lucian's hands erupted in fire and slammed together upon him.

"Sev," Lucian whispered with sadness as the screams were replaced with the smell of charged flesh.

"Lucian, everything okay in here?" Gabrielle asked as she came running into the room, and slightly jerked back from burning smell.

"Never better. Just making room for only you," Lucian said, turning and shaking the ashes off his hands as he grabbed the female pirate and pulled her into a big embrace.

****

It had been a long journey but Docanesto had made it back to the Unknown Lands and was now walking into the room where the witches brought forth the image of Drol Greb's face. He moved forward and then bowed, dropping to one knee. "Master."

"Rise, my old friend. It has been too long. What transpires?" Drol Greb asked.

Docanestso was afraid to mention his failure to get the staff but was surprised when Drol listened and smiled with satisfaction at what he did get and discover, along with the burning of Silver to further the fall of Erikson. "What of our boy?"

"It seems Lucian has located the Chosen One," Docanesto said as he filled in his master on all he knew, including the fall of his own daughter. "Before I could pry more out of Sev, I heard Lucian walk in."

"Then it appears both our spies have met their end," Drol Greb said with no emotion at all while Docanesto held back his grief for his daughter.

"I can send more up to Ogra or go and take control myself of the situation and the captured Magestic."

"No, let our boy handle Ogra for now. We have much more that acquires our attention. Gather the forces and prepare for war. Bergonia and the Age of Humans has come to an end."

About The Author

James Berg lives in Nebraska with his loving husband and three wonderful dogs. This is his first published novel, but has been creating and writing stories ever since he was little and first put pencil to paper. He is currently working on the next of what he hopes to be many stories in the Books of Bergonia series.

Made in the USA
Middletown, DE
22 August 2022

71180290R00376